SANITY & TALLULAH
SHORTCUTS

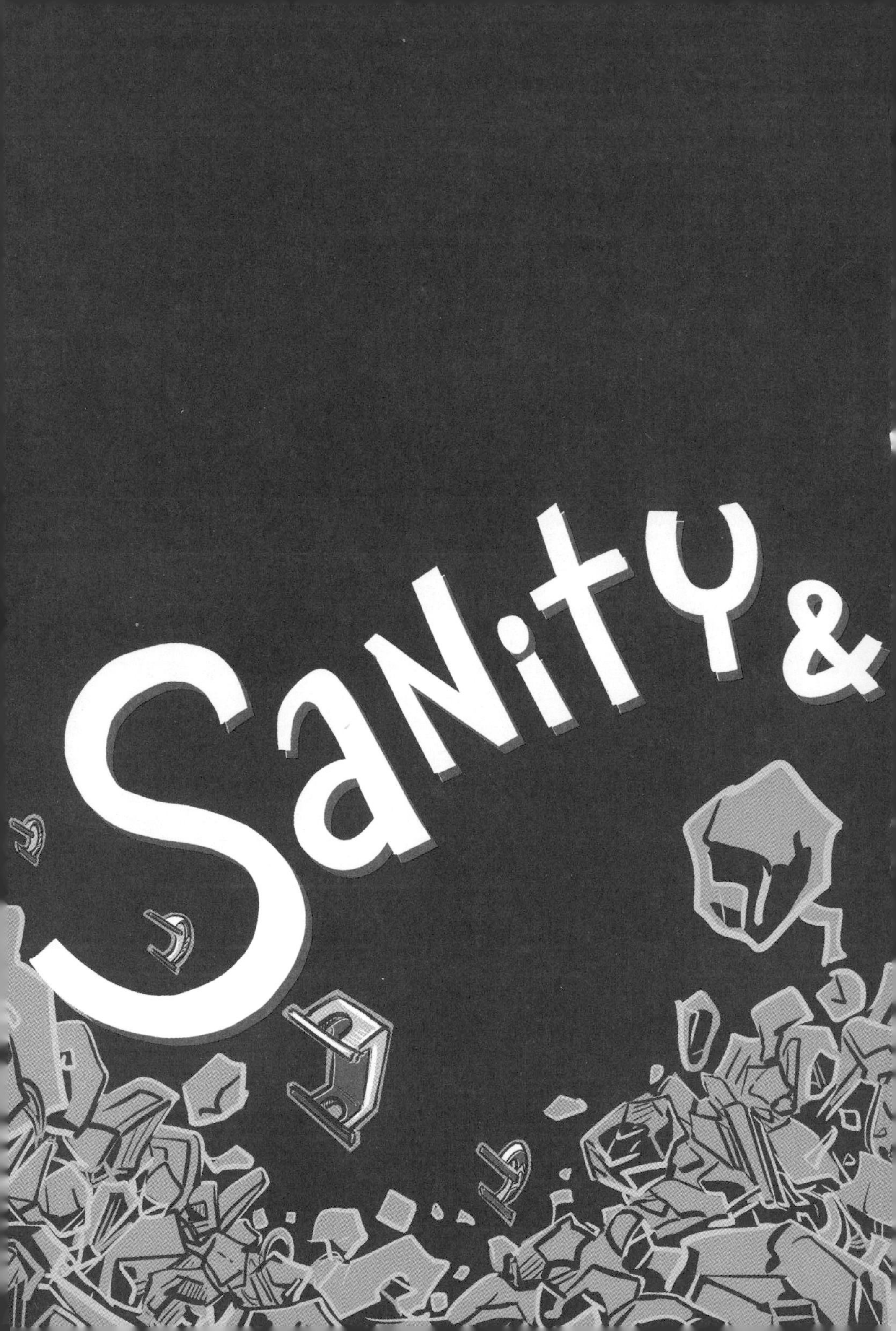
SaNitY &

TALLULAH

SHORTCUTS

MOLLY BROOKS

Little, Brown and Company

NEW YORK   BOSTON

About This Book

The illustrations for this book were drawn on 96 lb. recycled bristol with Deleter G-Pen nibs dipped in Koh-I-Noor Rapidograph ink. This book was edited in succession by Rotem Moscovitch, Tracey Keevan, and Andrea Colvin and designed by Ching N. Chan. The production was supervised by Bernadette Flinn, and the production editor was Jake Regier. The text was set in Gargle, and the display type is hand lettered.

Little, Brown and Company
Hachette Book Group
1290 Avenue of the Americas, New York, NY 10104
Visit us at LBYR.com

First Edition: April 2021

Little, Brown and Company is a division of Hachette Book Group, Inc.
The Little, Brown name and logo are trademarks of Hachette Book Group, Inc.

The publisher is not responsible for websites (or their content) that are not owned by the publisher.

Library of Congress Cataloging-in-Publication Data

Names: Brooks, Molly (Molly Grayson), author, illustrator.

Title: Shortcuts / Molly Brooks

Description: First edition. | New York : Little, Brown and Company, 2021. | Series: Sanity & Tallulah | Audience: Ages 8–12. | Summary: When most of the adults on space station Wilnick come down with the flu, Sanity and Tallulah are tasked with delivering turbopumps to another station, but when they take a shortcut, they accidentally end up on the other side of the blockade.

Identifiers: LCCN 2020042076 | ISBN 9780759555532 (hardcover) | ISBN 9780759555525 (trade paperback) | ISBN 9780759555884 (ebook) | ISBN 9780316628488 (ebook other)

Subjects: LCSH: Graphic novels. | CYAC: Graphic novels. | Space stations—Fiction. | Science fiction.

Classification: LCC PZ7.7.B765 Sh 2021 | DDC 741.5/973—dc23

LC record available at https://lccn.loc.gov/2020042076

ISBNs: 978-0-7595-5553-2 (hardcover), 978-0-7595-5552-5 (pbk.), 978-0-7595-5588-4 (ebook), 978-0-316-59231-4 (ebook), 978-0-316-62849-5 (ebook)

Printed in the United States of America

LSC-C

Printing 1, 2021

For Amy,
the mother of my cat-children

SANITY & TALLULAH SHORTCUTS

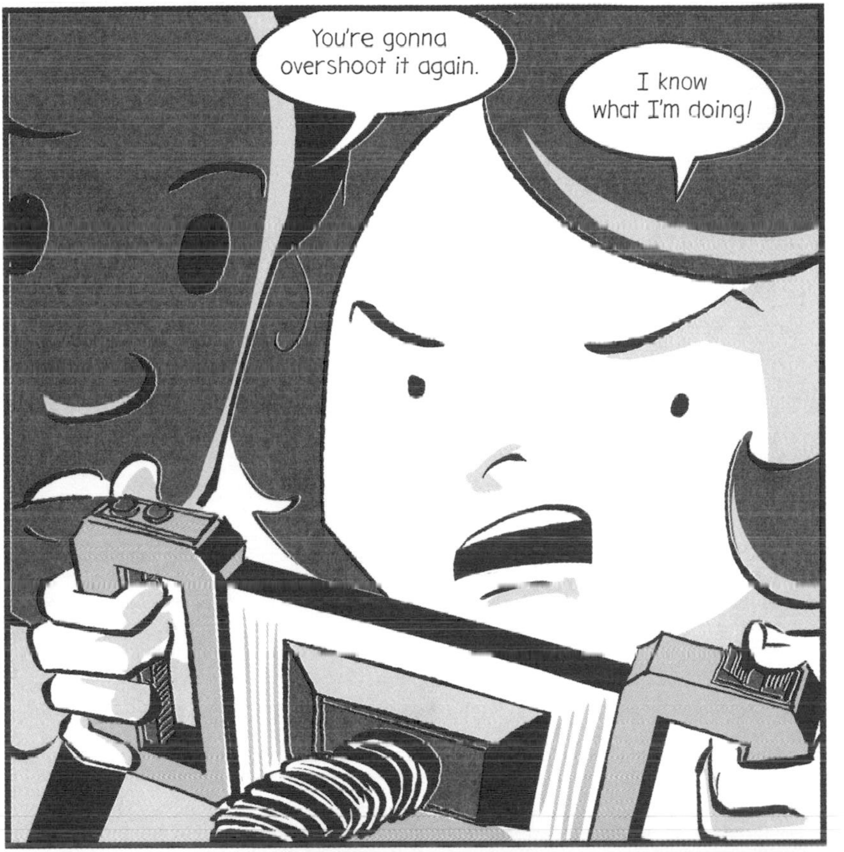
You're gonna overshoot it again.
I know what I'm doing!

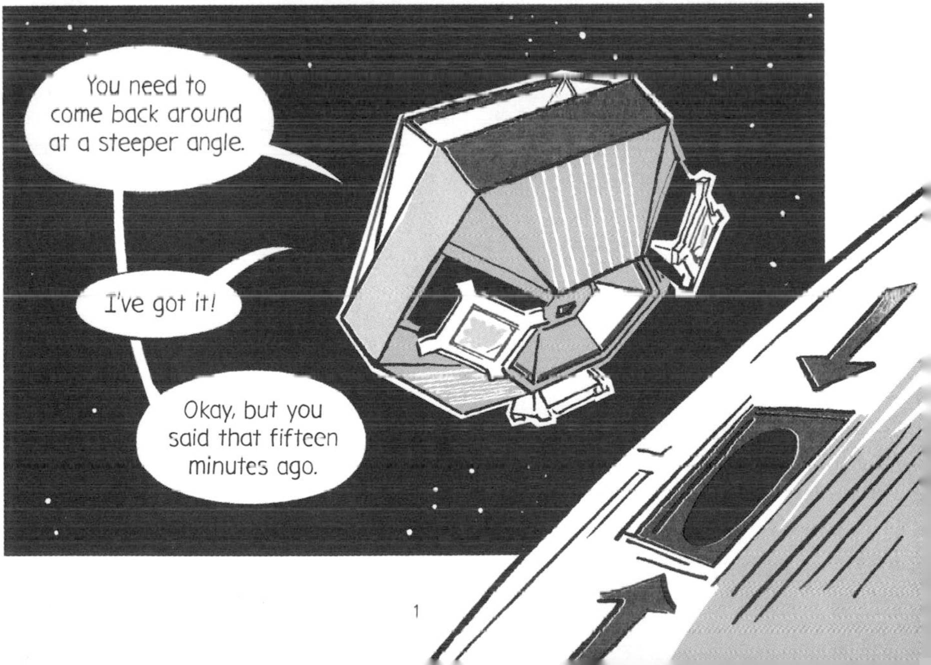
You need to come back around at a steeper angle.
I've got it!
Okay, but you said that fifteen minutes ago.

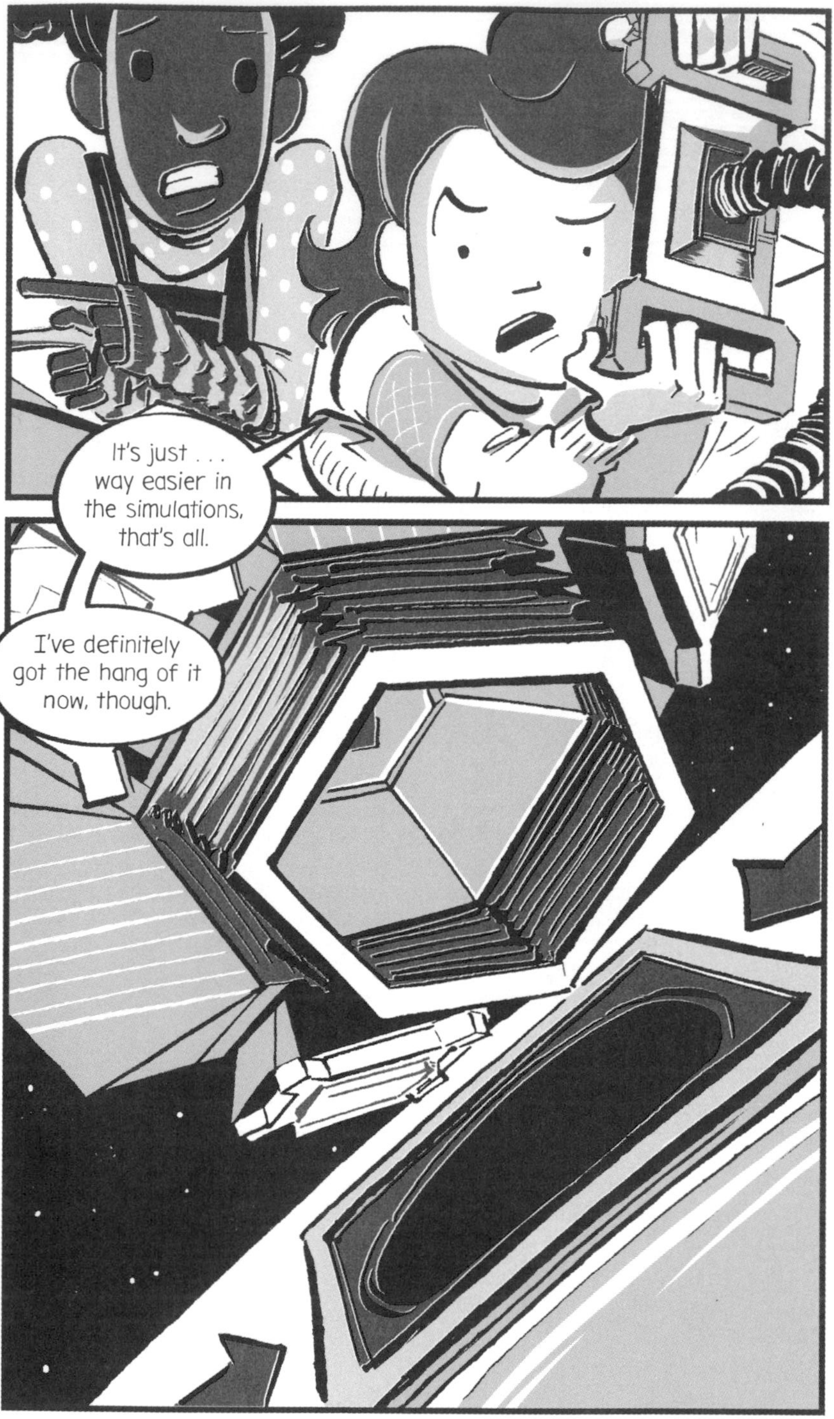
It's just . . . way easier in the simulations, that's all.
I've definitely got the hang of it now, though.

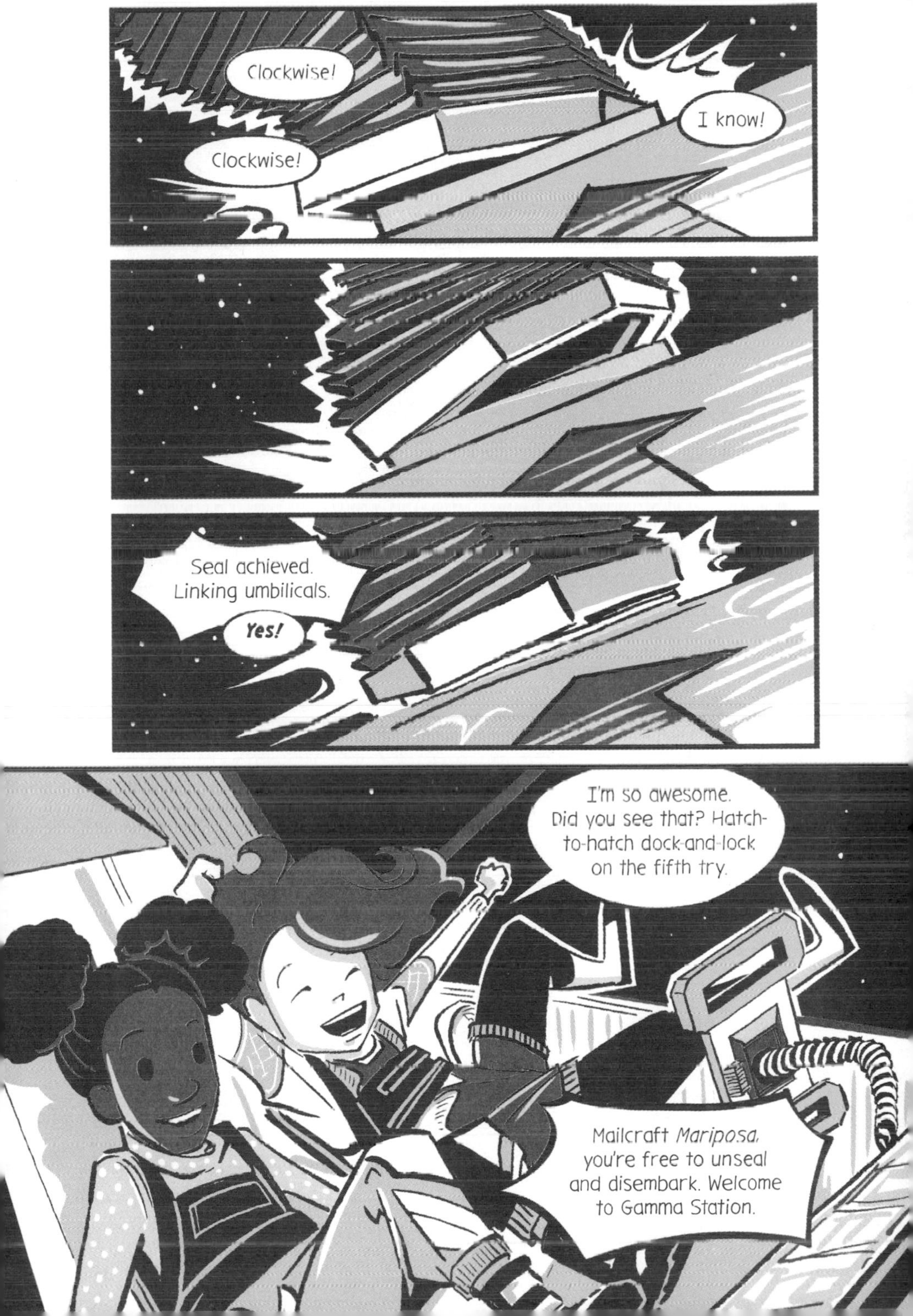
Clockwise!
Clockwise!
I know!
Seal achieved. Linking umbilicals.
Yes!
I'm so awesome. Did you see that? Hatch-to-hatch dock-and-lock on the fifth try.
Mailcraft *Mariposa*, you're free to unseal and disembark. Welcome to Gamma Station.

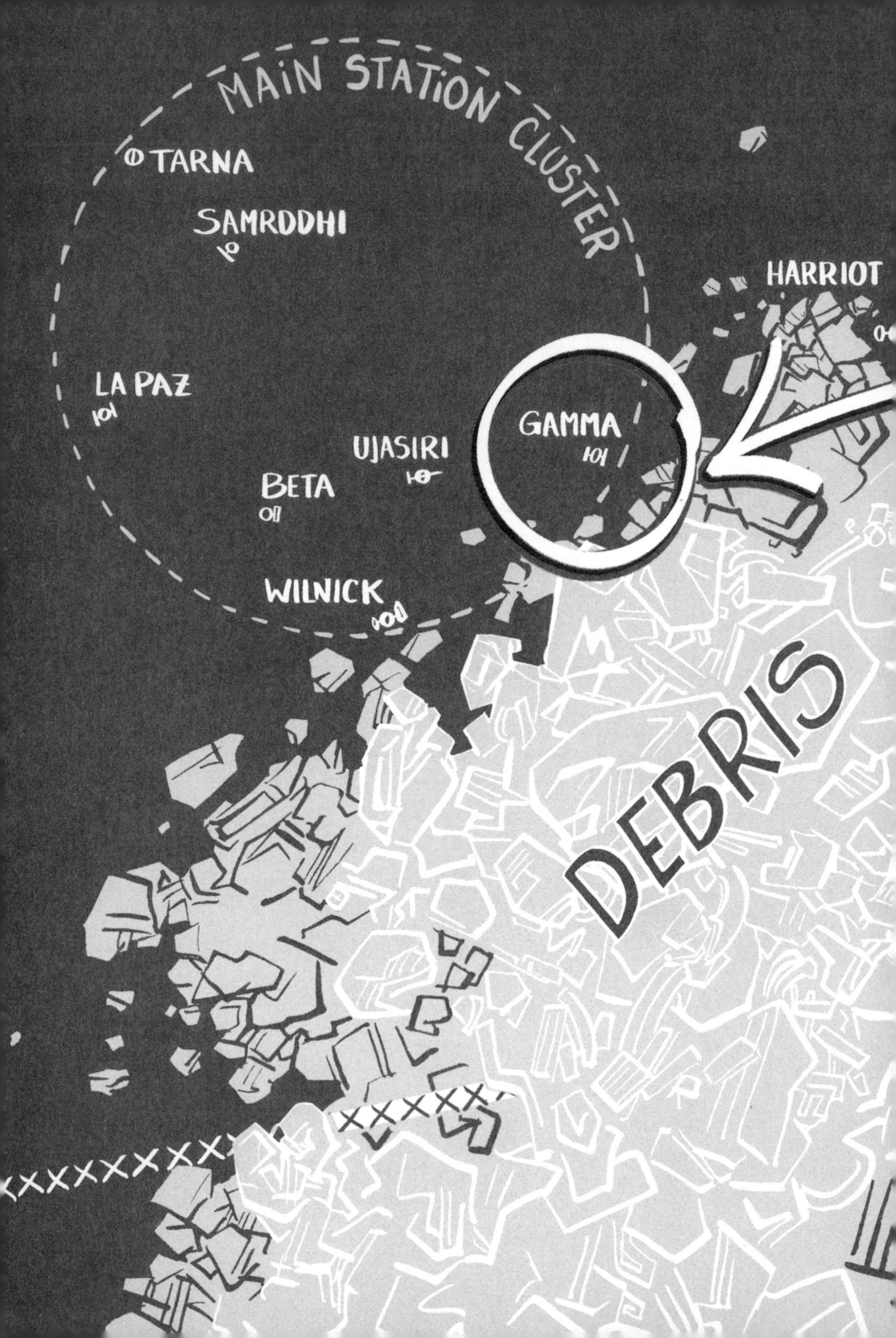
MAIN STATION CLUSTER
TARNA
SAMRDDHI
HARRIOT
LA PAZ
GAMMA
UJASIRI
BETA
WILNICK
DEBRIS

Captain's Log: we are here! yay!!
CLOUD
EPSILON
01
TORTUGA
01
BREAKER SPACE
UNITED TERRITORIES
BLOCKADE XXXXXX

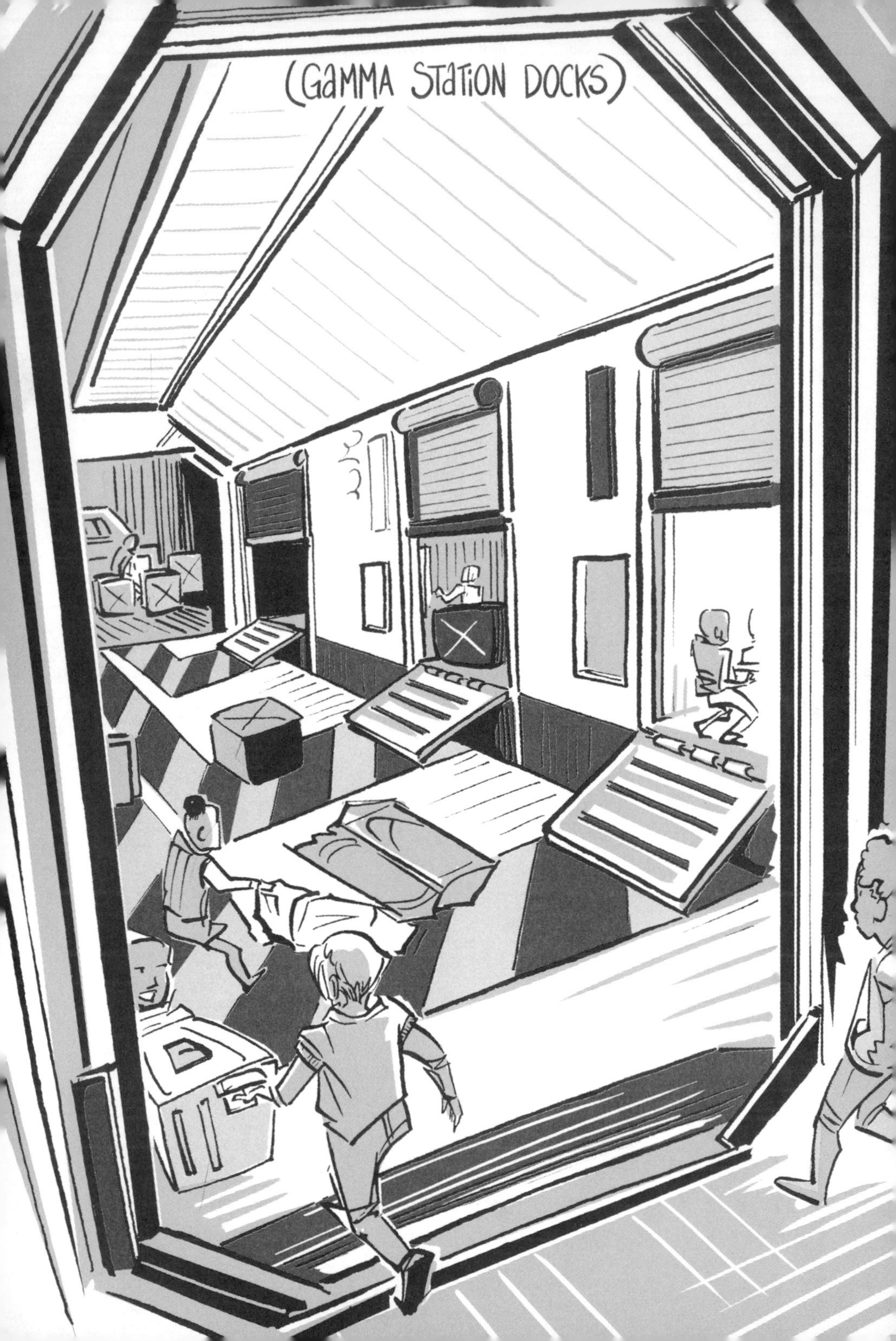
(GAMMA STATION DOCKS)

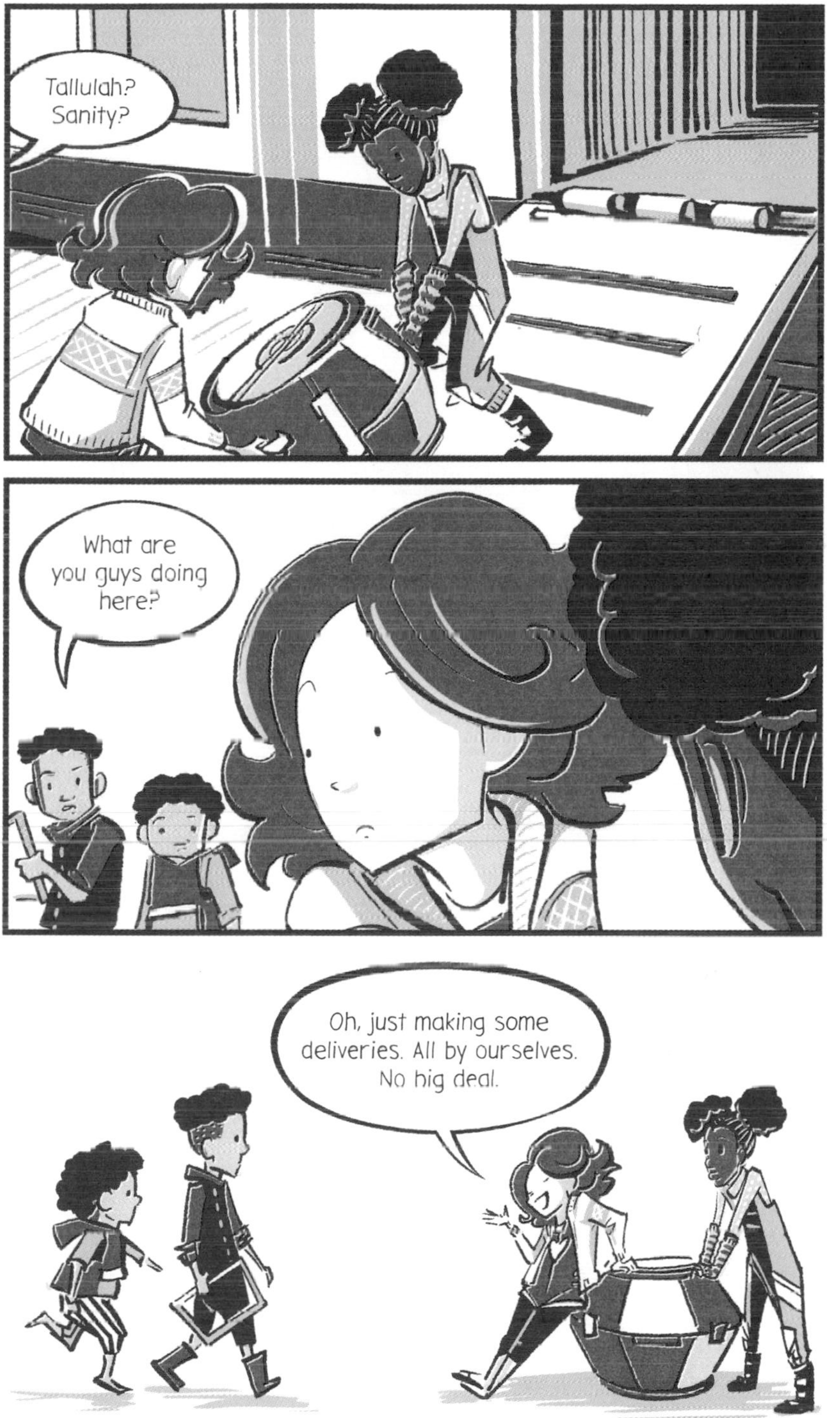
Tallulah? Sanity?
What are you guys doing here?
Oh, just making some deliveries. All by ourselves. No big deal.

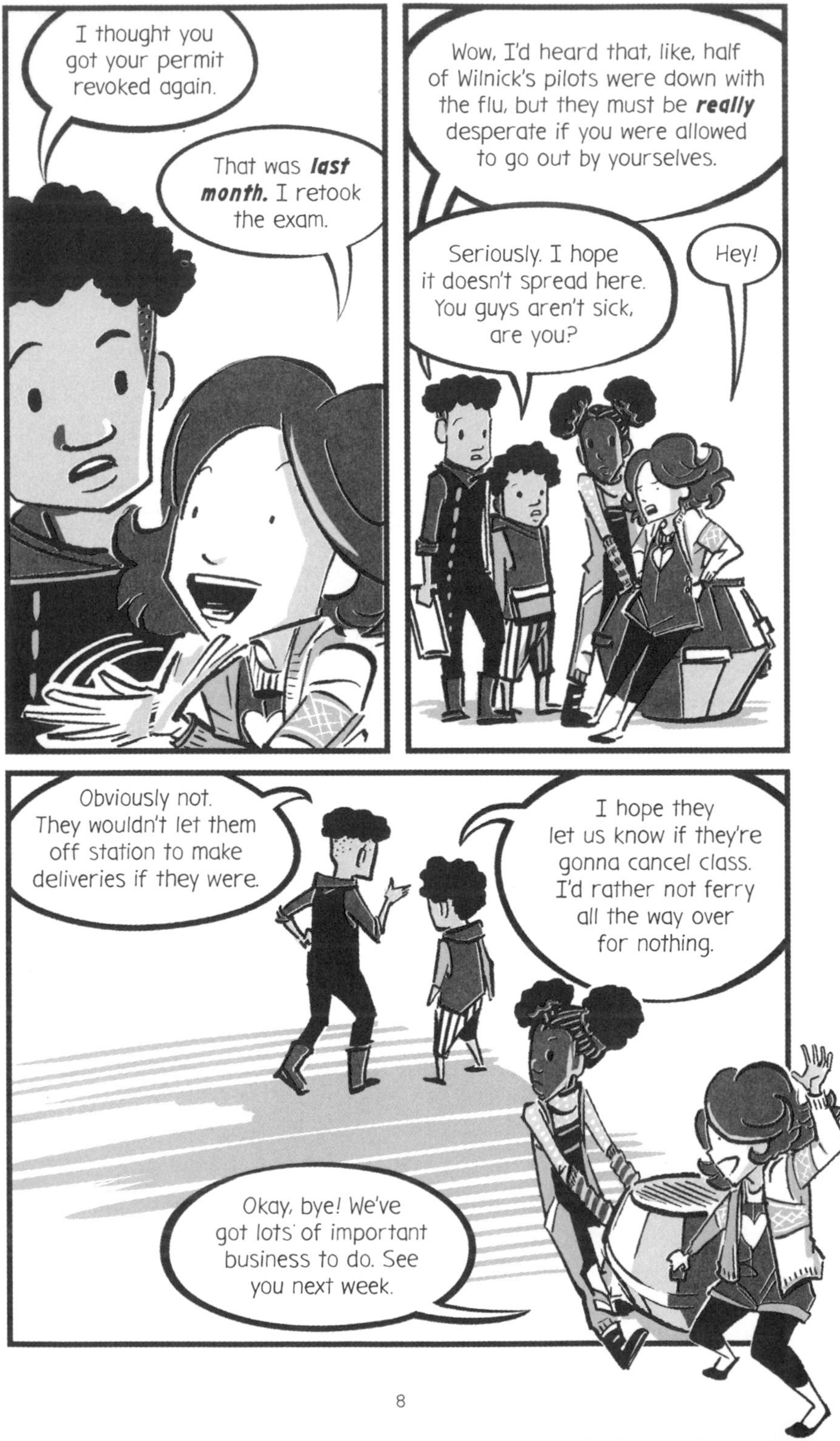
I thought you got your permit revoked again.
That was **last month.** I retook the exam.
Wow, I'd heard that, like, half of Wilnick's pilots were down with the flu, but they must be ***really*** desperate if you were allowed to go out by yourselves.
Seriously. I hope it doesn't spread here. You guys aren't sick, are you?
Hey!
Obviously not. They wouldn't let them off station to make deliveries if they were.
I hope they let us know if they're gonna cancel class. I'd rather not ferry all the way over for nothing.
Okay, bye! We've got lots of important business to do. See you next week.

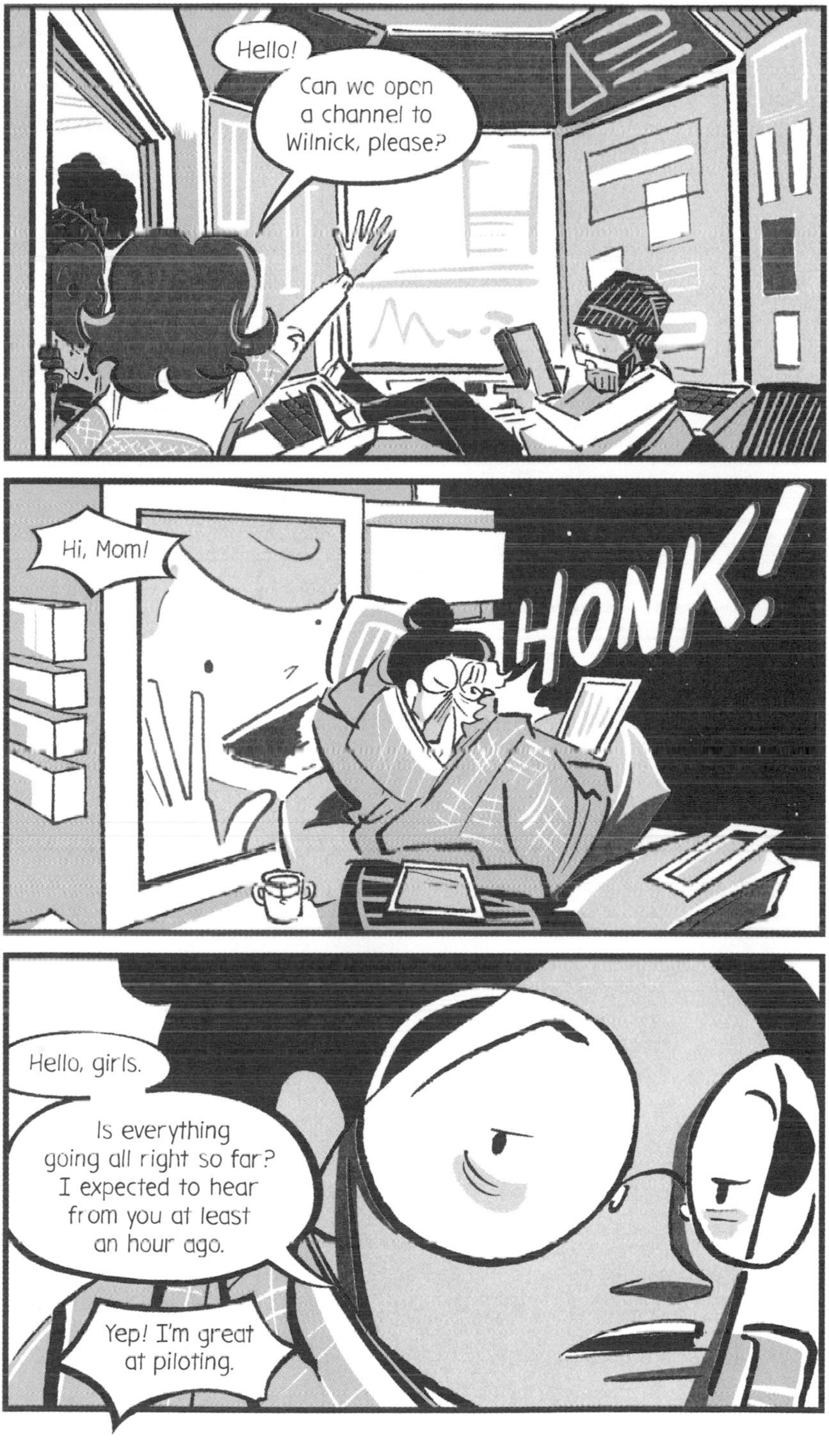
Hello!
Can we open a channel to Wilnick, please?
Hi, Mom!
HONK!
Hello, girls.
Is everything going all right so far? I expected to hear from you at least an hour ago.
Yep! I'm great at piloting.

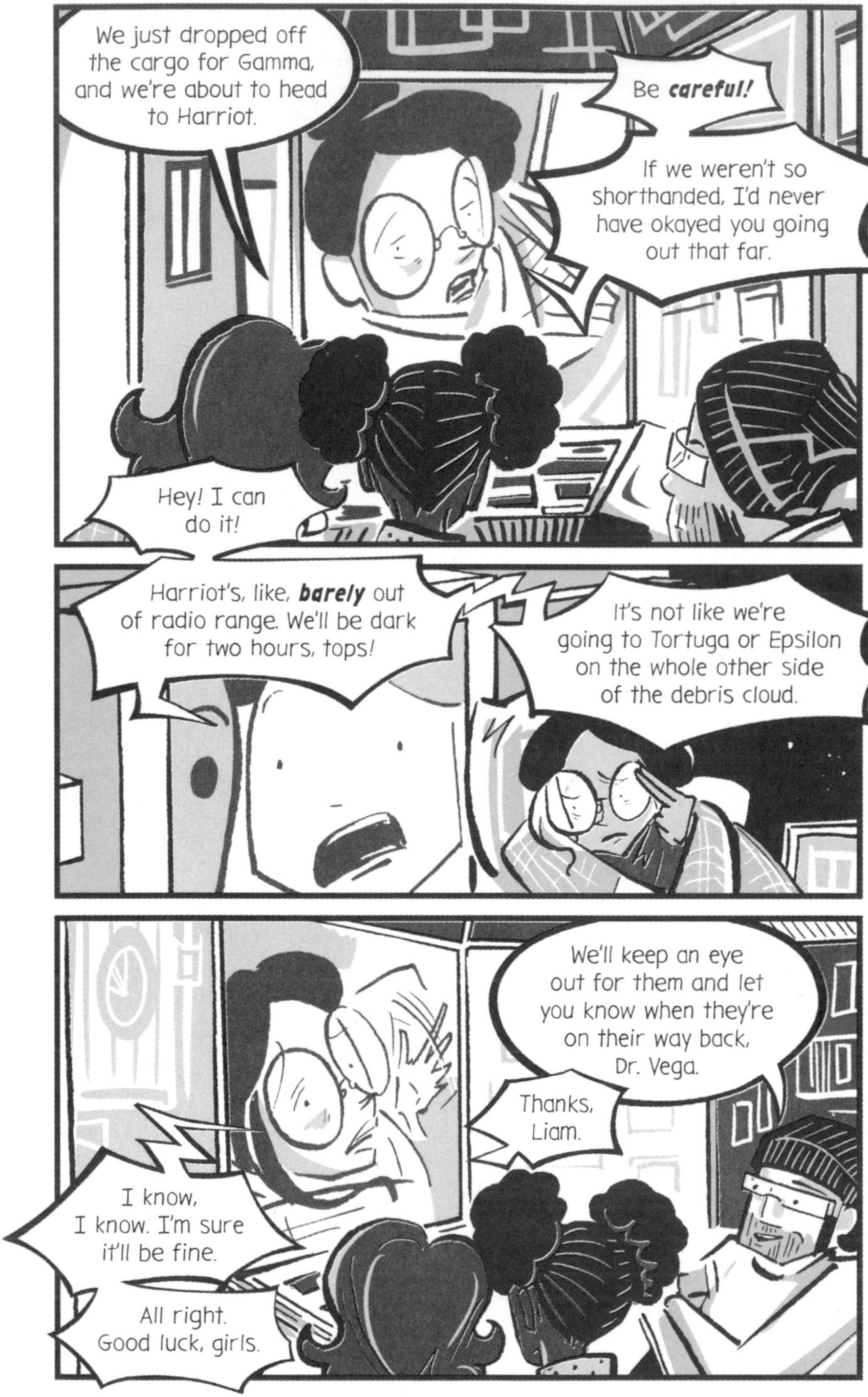
We just dropped off the cargo for Gamma, and we're about to head to Harriot.
Be **careful!**
If we weren't so shorthanded, I'd never have okayed you going out that far.
Hey! I can do it!
Harriot's, like, **barely** out of radio range. We'll be dark for two hours, tops!
It's not like we're going to Tortuga or Epsilon on the whole other side of the debris cloud.
We'll keep an eye out for them and let you know when they're on their way back, Dr. Vega.
Thanks, Liam.
I know, I know. I'm sure it'll be fine.
All right. Good luck, girls.

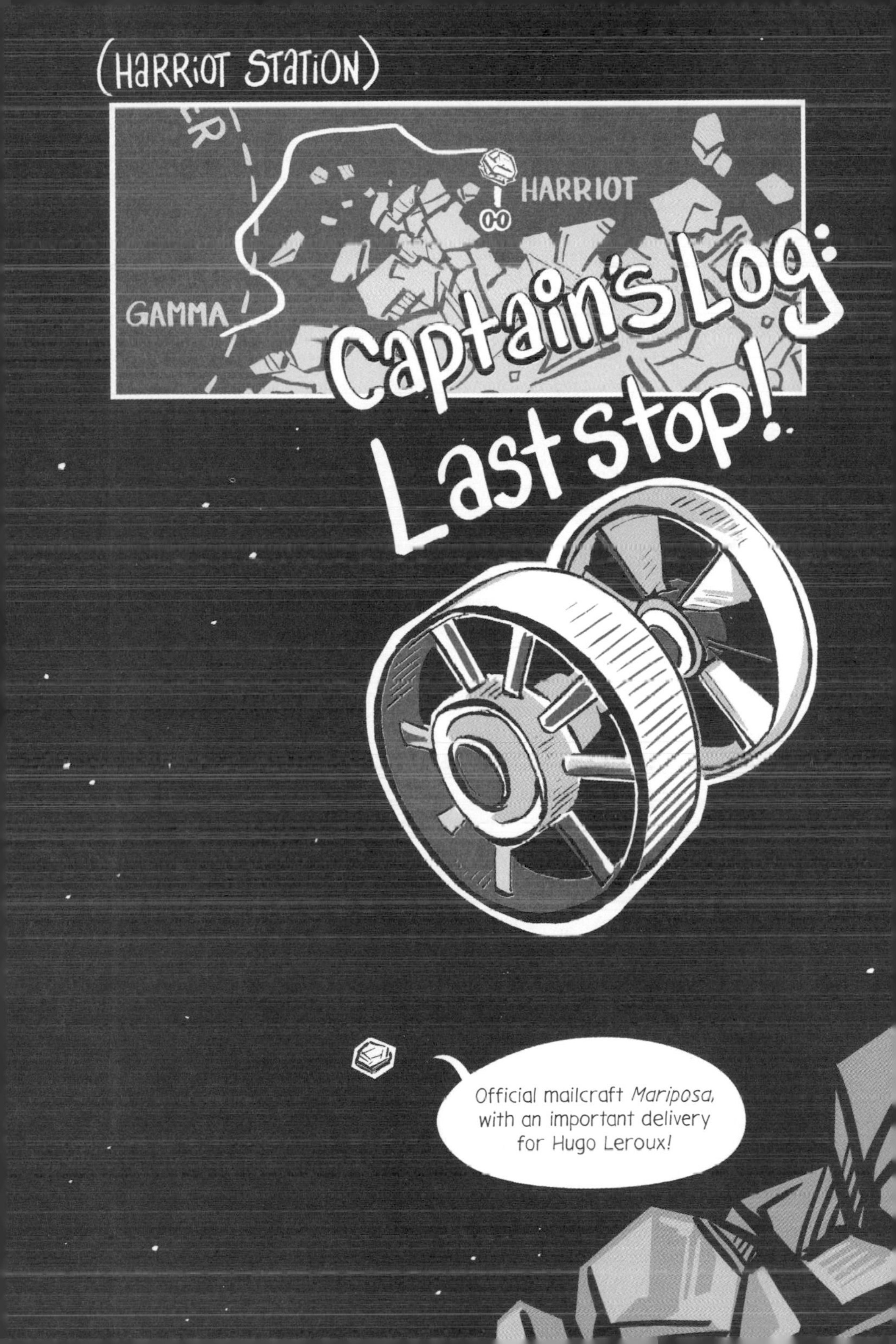
(HARRIOT STATION)
HARRIOT
GAMMA
Captain's Log:
Last Stop!
Official mailcraft *Mariposa*, with an important delivery for Hugo Leroux!

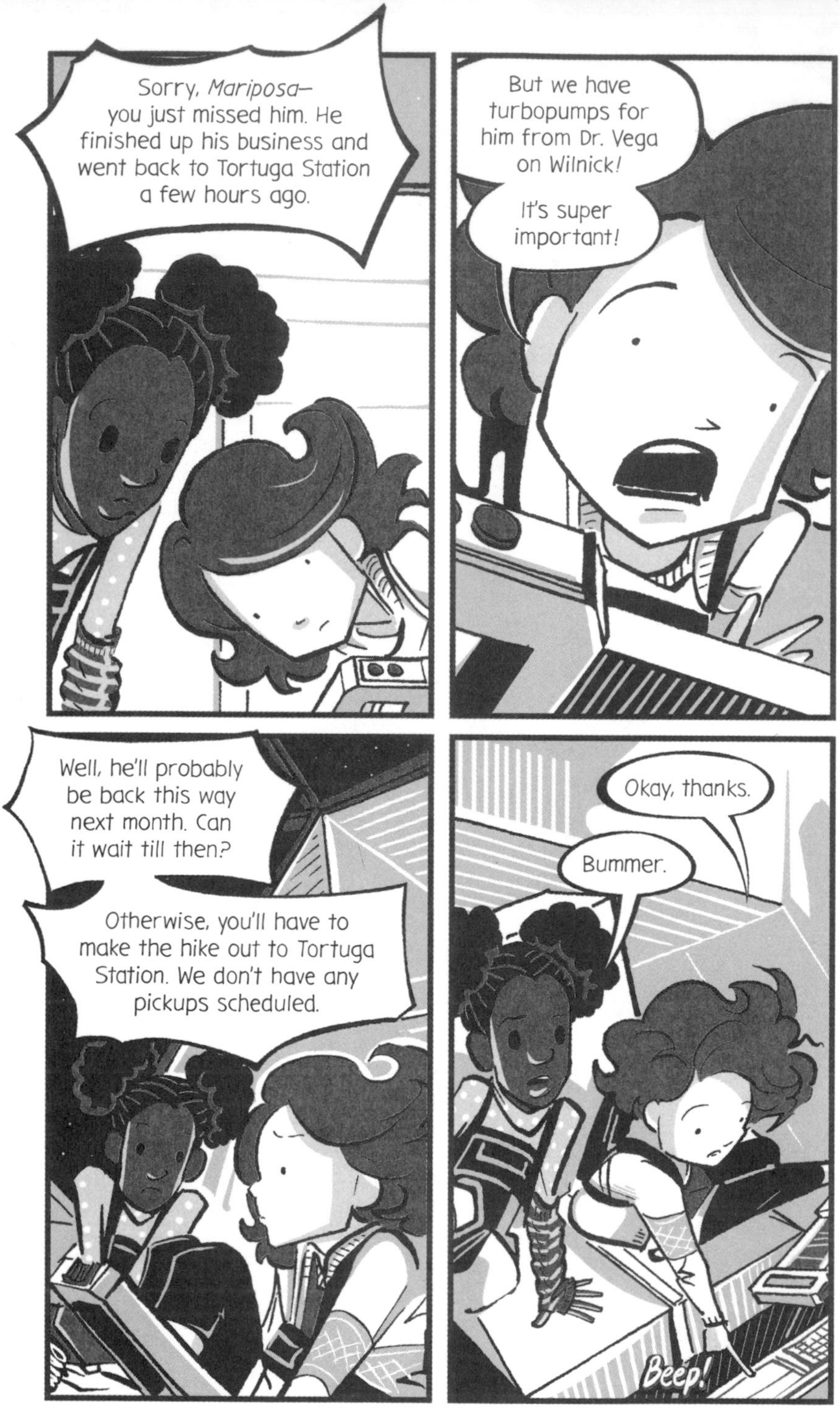
Sorry, *Mariposa*— you just missed him. He finished up his business and went back to Tortuga Station a few hours ago.
But we have turbopumps for him from Dr. Vega on Wilnick!
It's super important!
Well, he'll probably be back this way next month. Can it wait till then?
Otherwise, you'll have to make the hike out to Tortuga Station. We don't have any pickups scheduled.
Okay, thanks.
Bummer.
Beep!

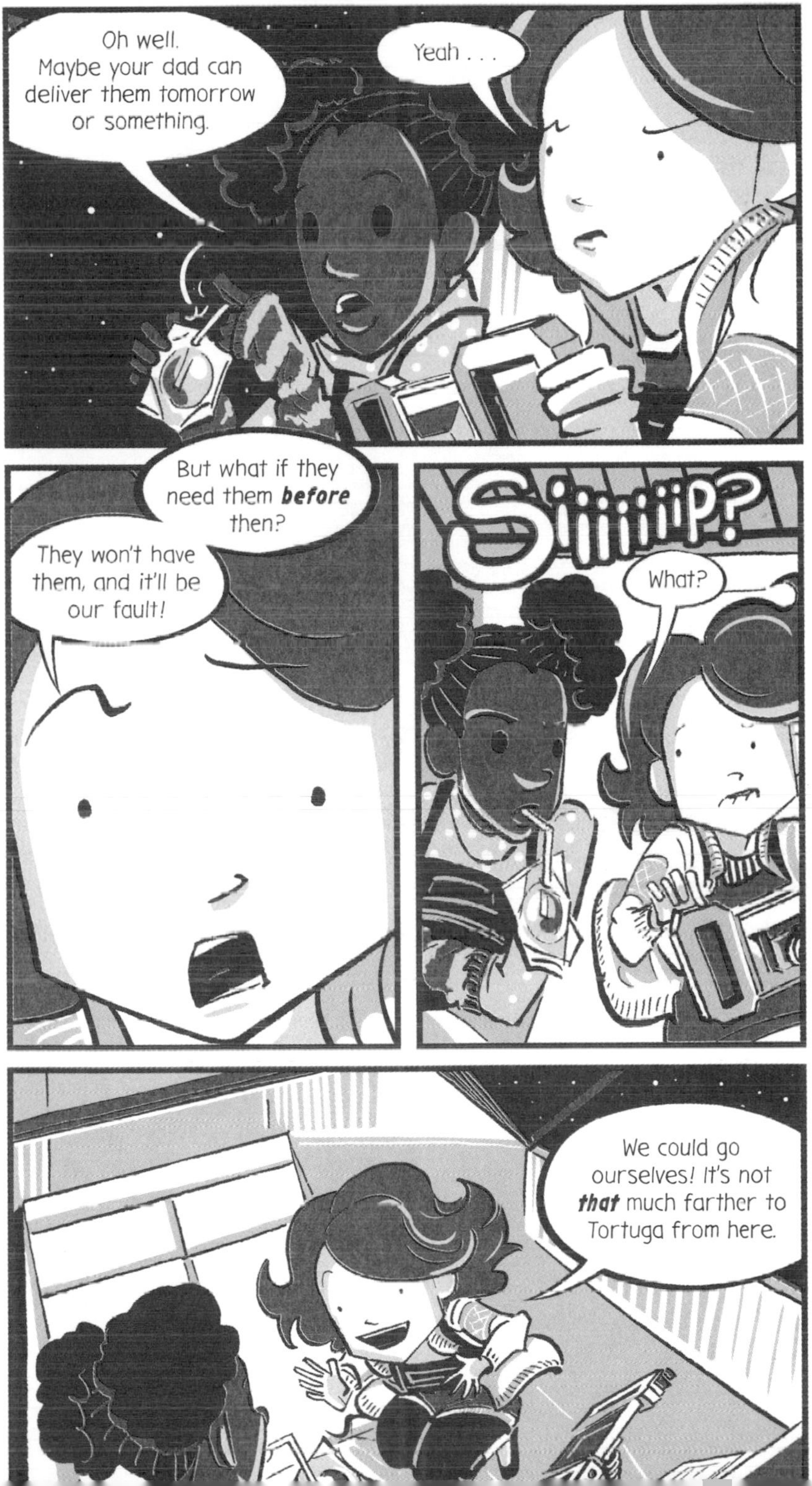
Oh well. Maybe your dad can deliver them tomorrow or something.
Yeah . . .
But what if they need them **before** then?
They won't have them, and it'll be our fault!
Siiiiiip?
What?
We could go ourselves! It's not **that** much farther to Tortuga from here.

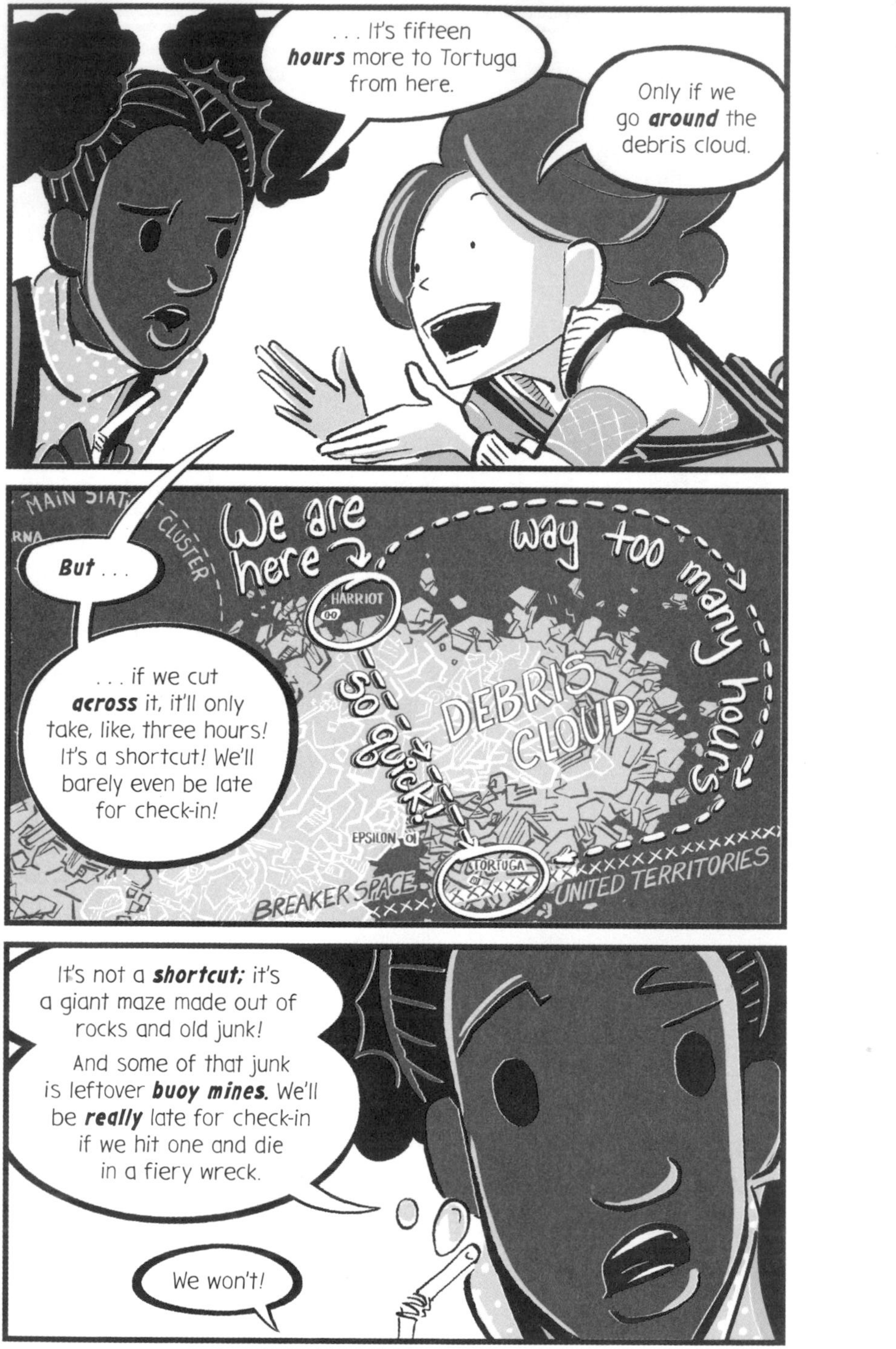

. . . It's fifteen **hours** more to Tortuga from here.
Only if we go **around** the debris cloud.
But . . .
We are here
way too many hours
HARRIOT
CLUSTER
. . . if we cut **across** it, it'll only take, like, three hours! It's a shortcut! We'll barely even be late for check-in!
so quick!
DEBRIS CLOUD
EPSILON-01
TORTUGA
BREAKER SPACE
UNITED TERRITORIES
It's not a ***shortcut;*** it's a giant maze made out of rocks and old junk!
And some of that junk is leftover **buoy mines.** We'll be ***really*** late for check-in if we hit one and die in a fiery wreck.
We won't!

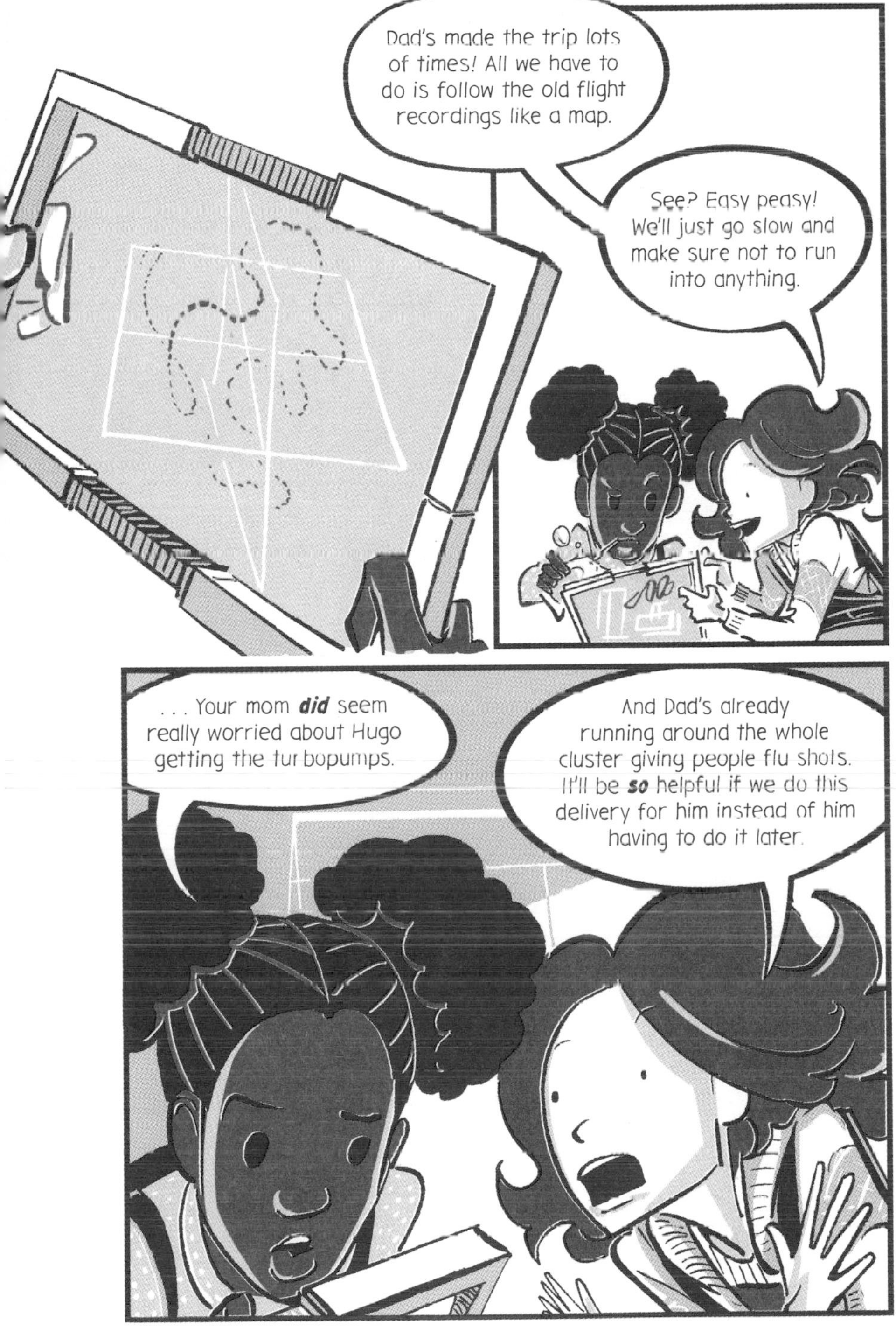
Dad's made the trip lots of times! All we have to do is follow the old flight recordings like a map.
See? Easy peasy! We'll just go slow and make sure not to run into anything.
. . . Your mom ***did*** seem really worried about Hugo getting the turbopumps.
And Dad's already running around the whole cluster giving people flu shots. It'll be ***so*** helpful if we do this delivery for him instead of him having to do it later.

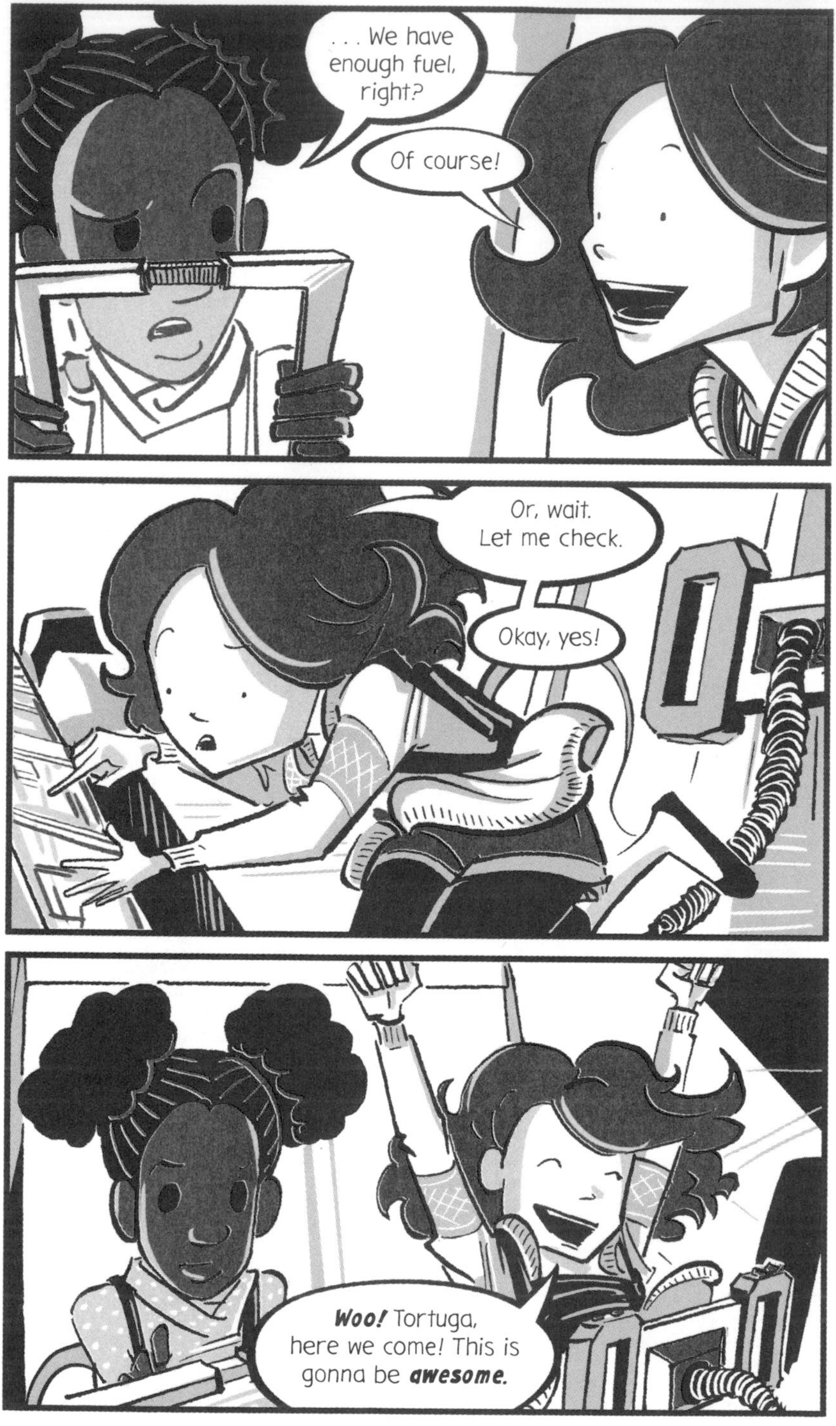
. . . We have enough fuel, right?
Of course!
Or, wait. Let me check.
Okay, yes!
Woo! Tortuga, here we come! This is gonna be ***awesome.***

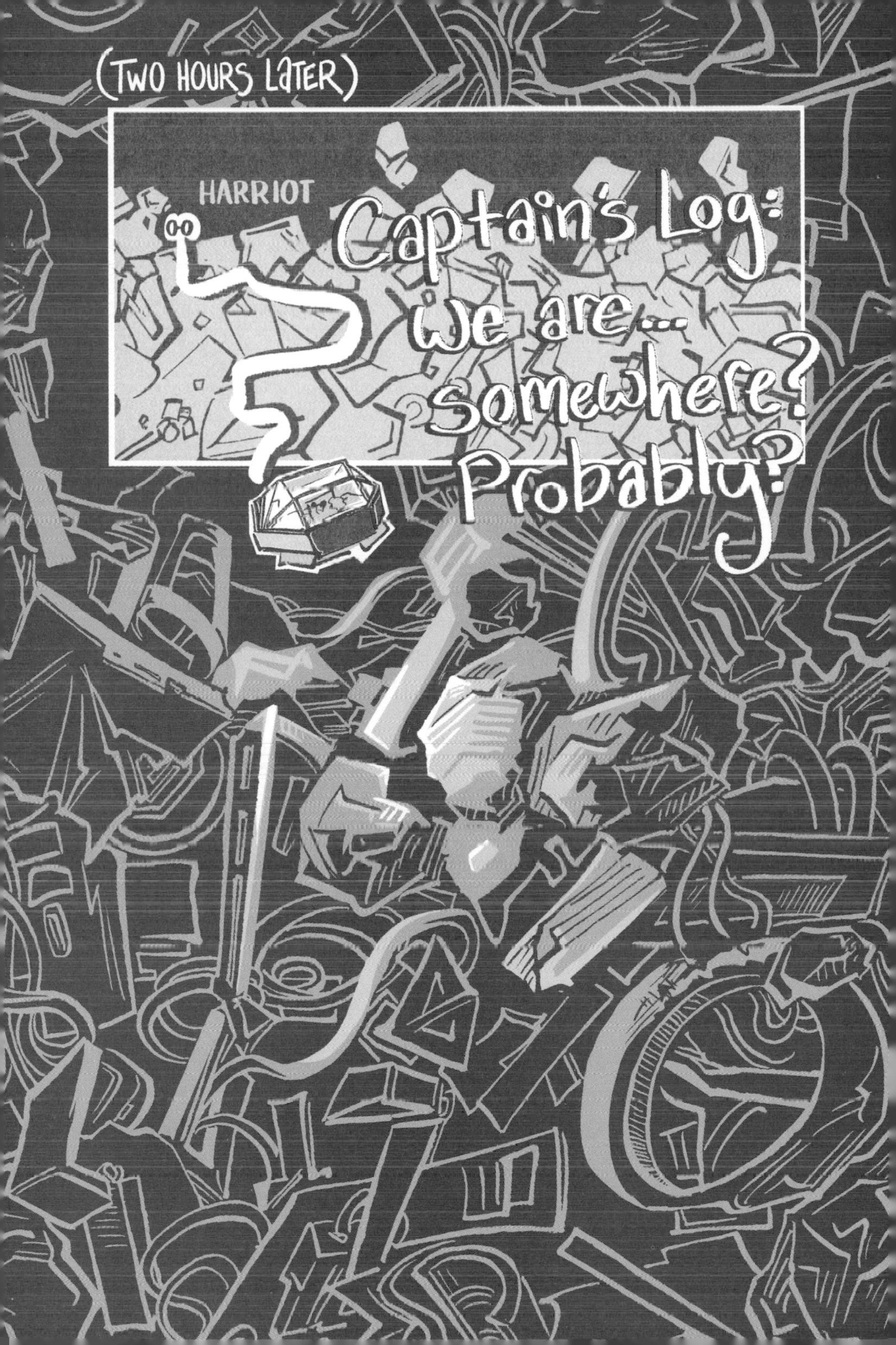
(TWO HOURS LATER)
HARRIOT
Captain's Log: we are... somewhere? Probably?

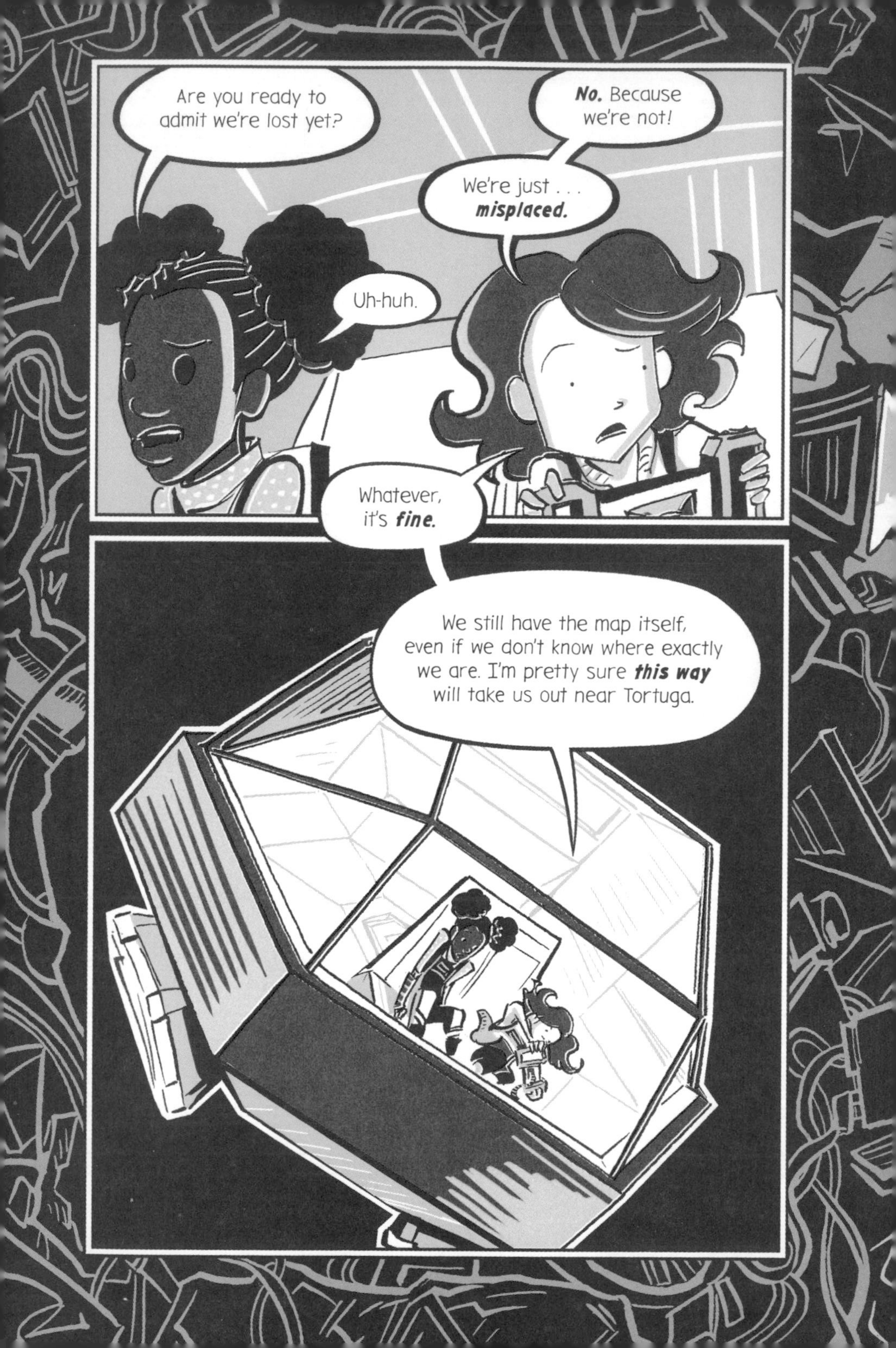
Are you ready to admit we're lost yet?
No. Because we're not!
We're just . . . ***misplaced.***
Uh-huh.
Whatever, it's ***fine.***
We still have the map itself, even if we don't know where exactly we are. I'm pretty sure ***this way*** will take us out near Tortuga.

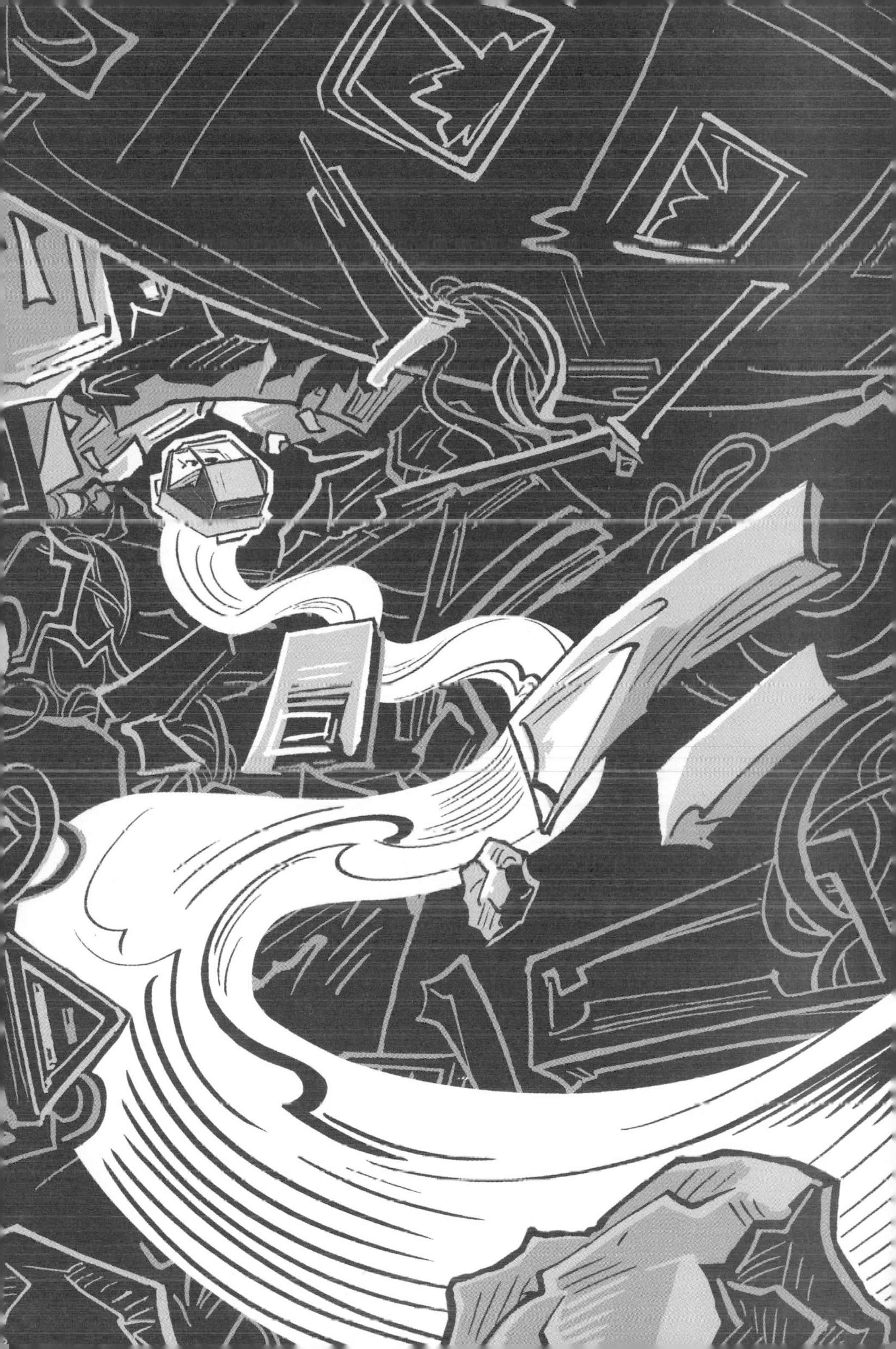

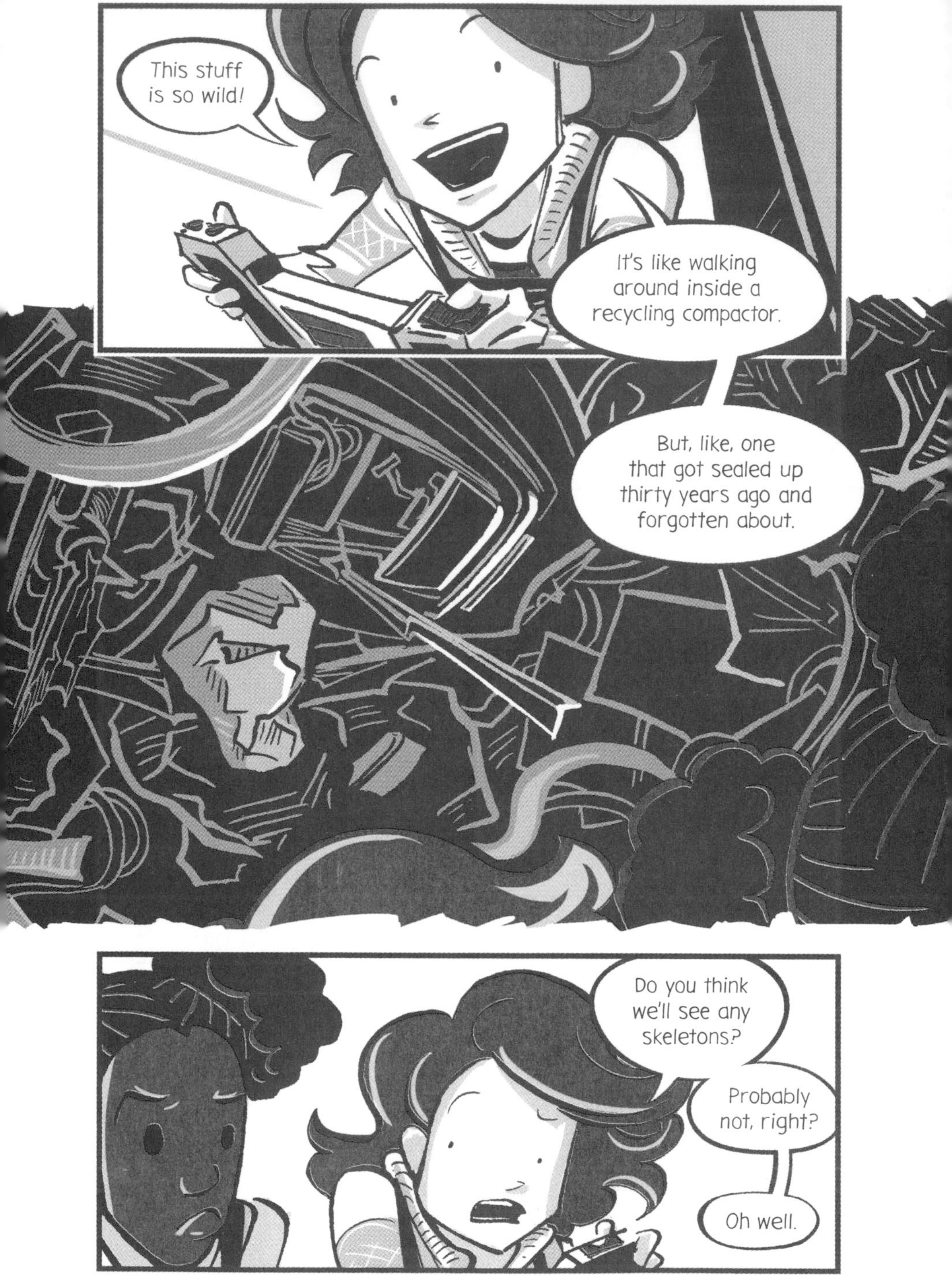
This stuff is so wild!
It's like walking around inside a recycling compactor.
But, like, one that got sealed up thirty years ago and forgotten about.
Do you think we'll see any skeletons?
Probably not, right?
Oh well.

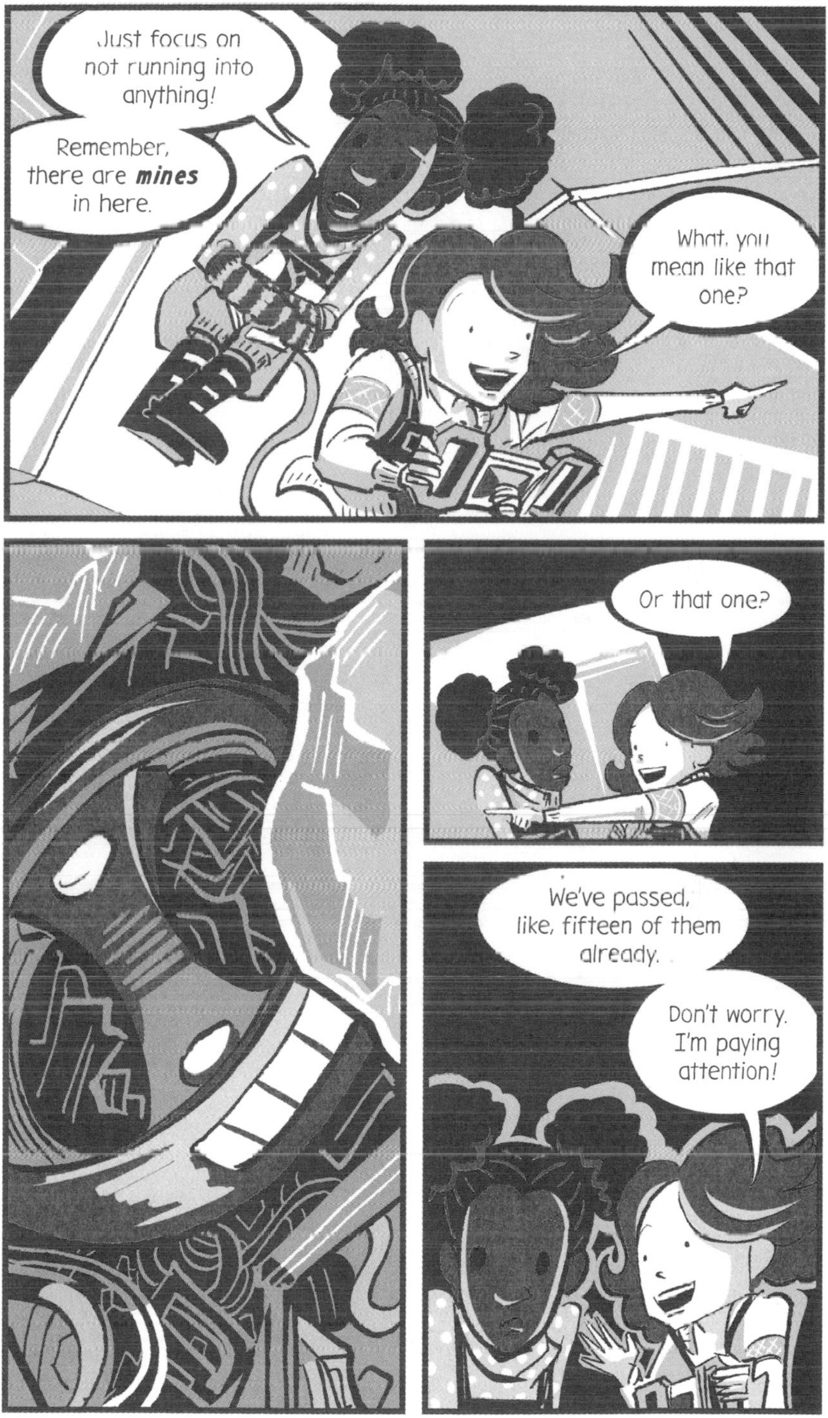
Just focus on not running into anything!
Remember, there are *mines* in here.
What, you mean like that one?
Or that one?
We've passed, like, fifteen of them already.
Don't worry. I'm paying attention!

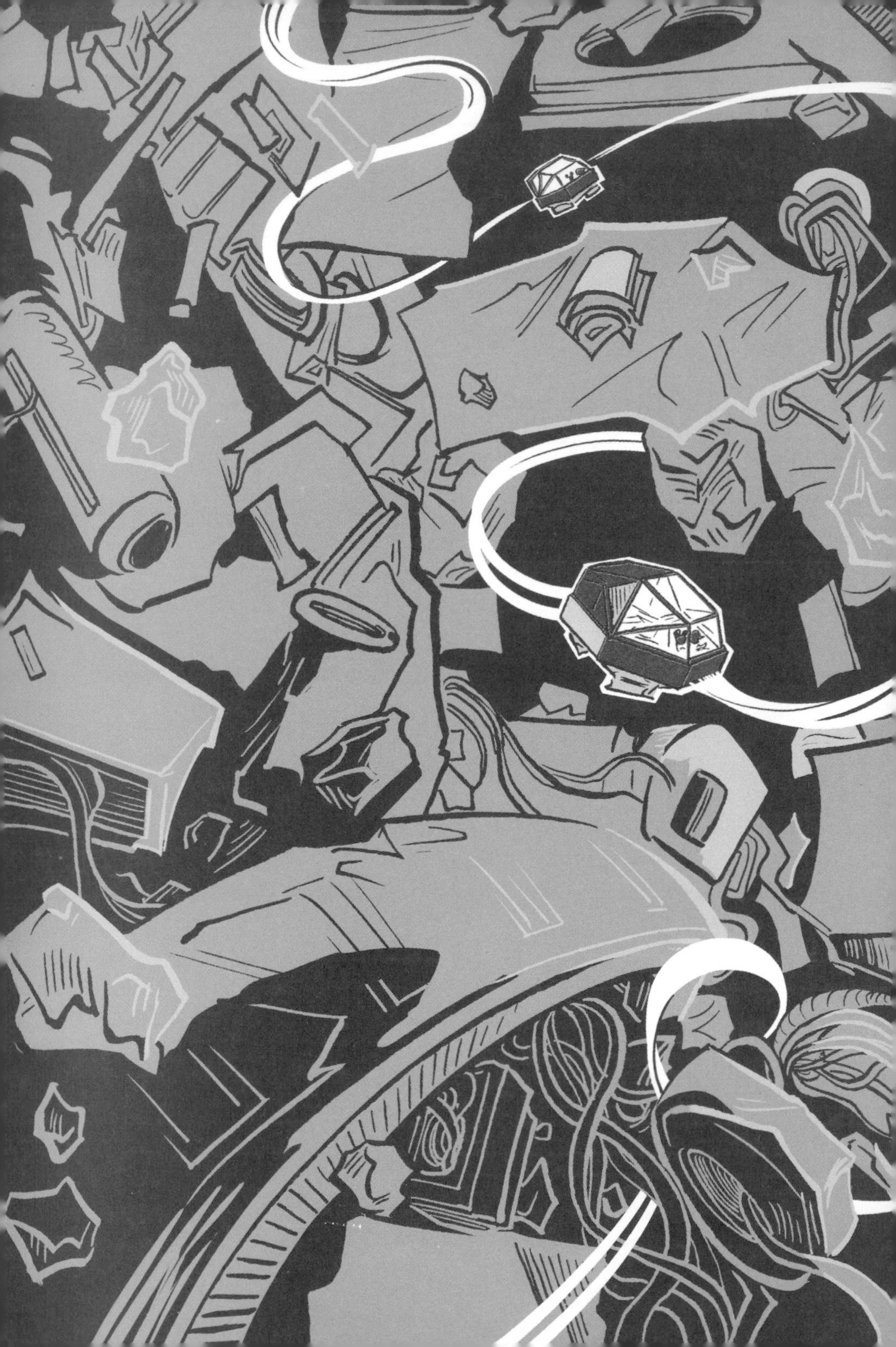

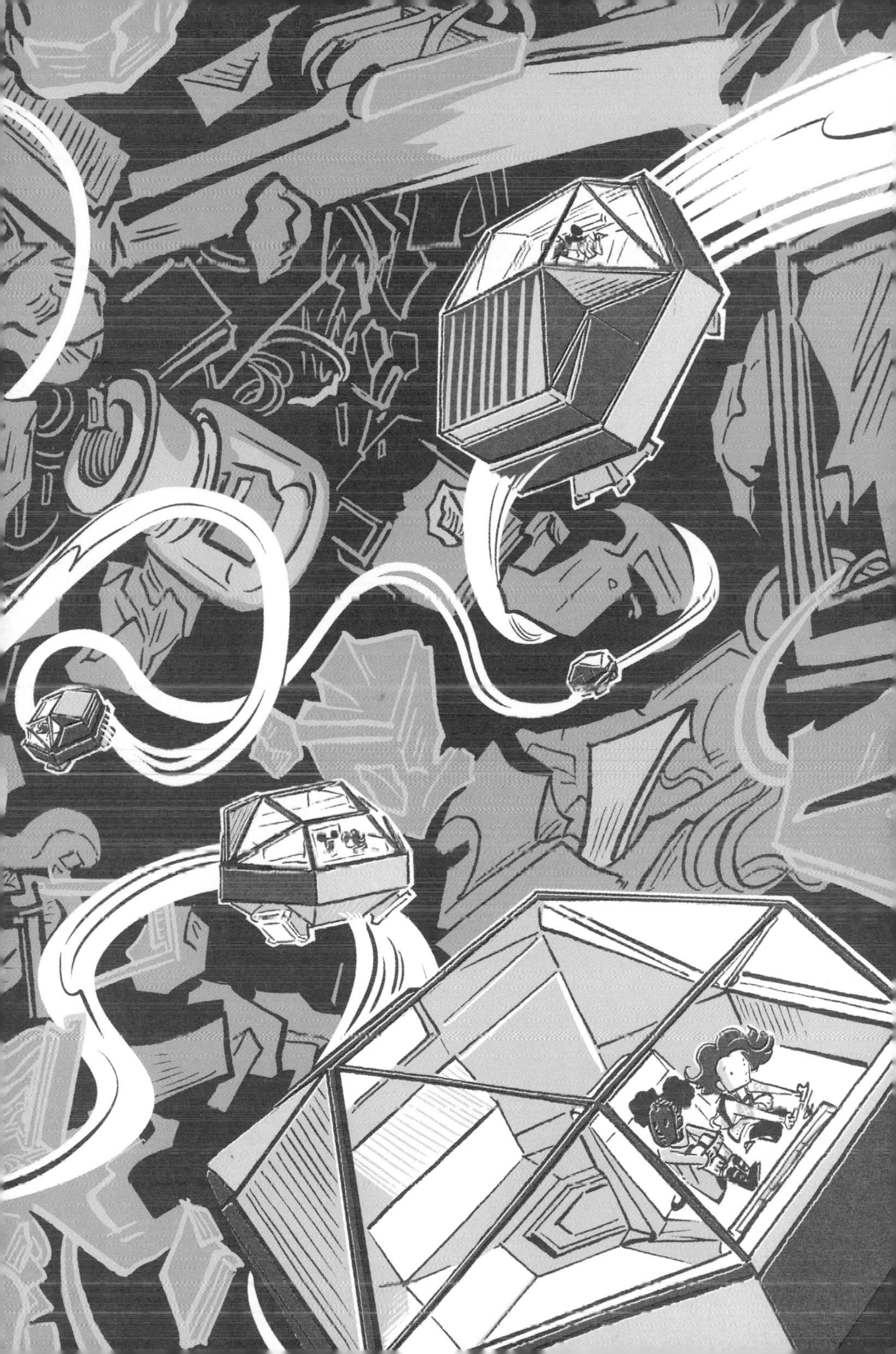

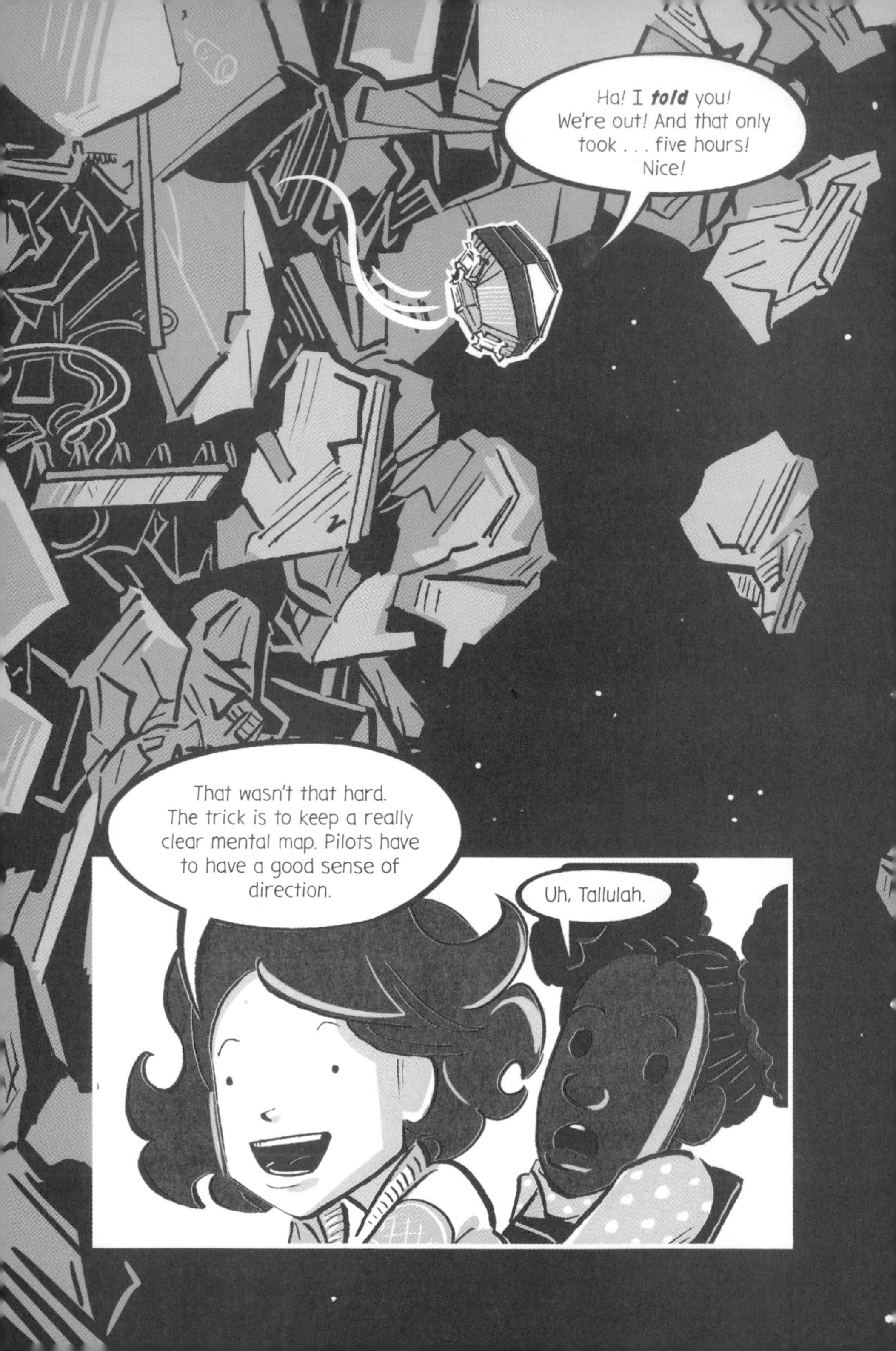
Ha! I **told** you! We're out! And that only took . . . five hours! Nice!
That wasn't that hard. The trick is to keep a really clear mental map. Pilots have to have a good sense of direction.
Uh, Tallulah.

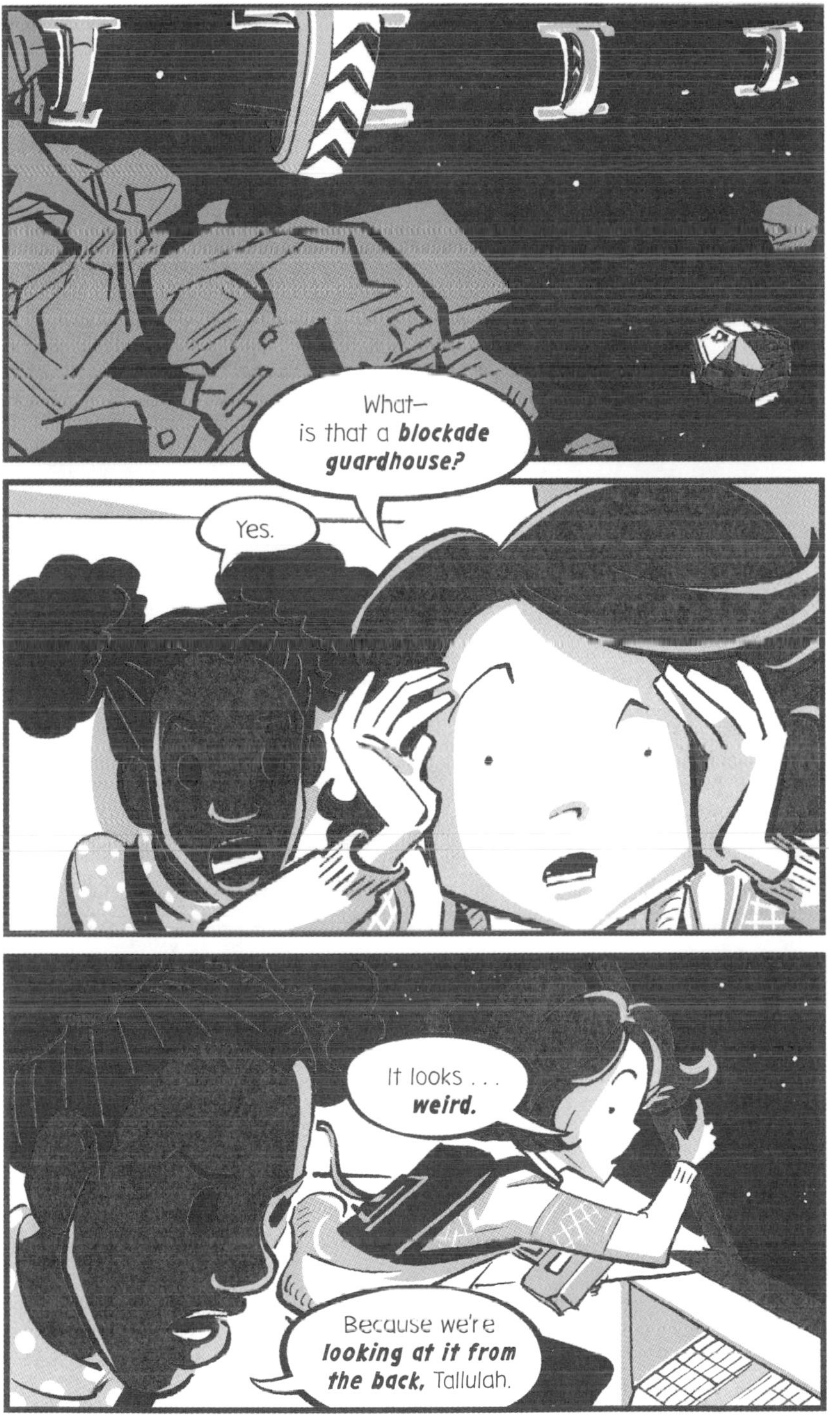
What— is that a **blockade guardhouse?**
Yes.
It looks . . . **weird.**
Because we're ***looking at it from the back,*** Tallulah.

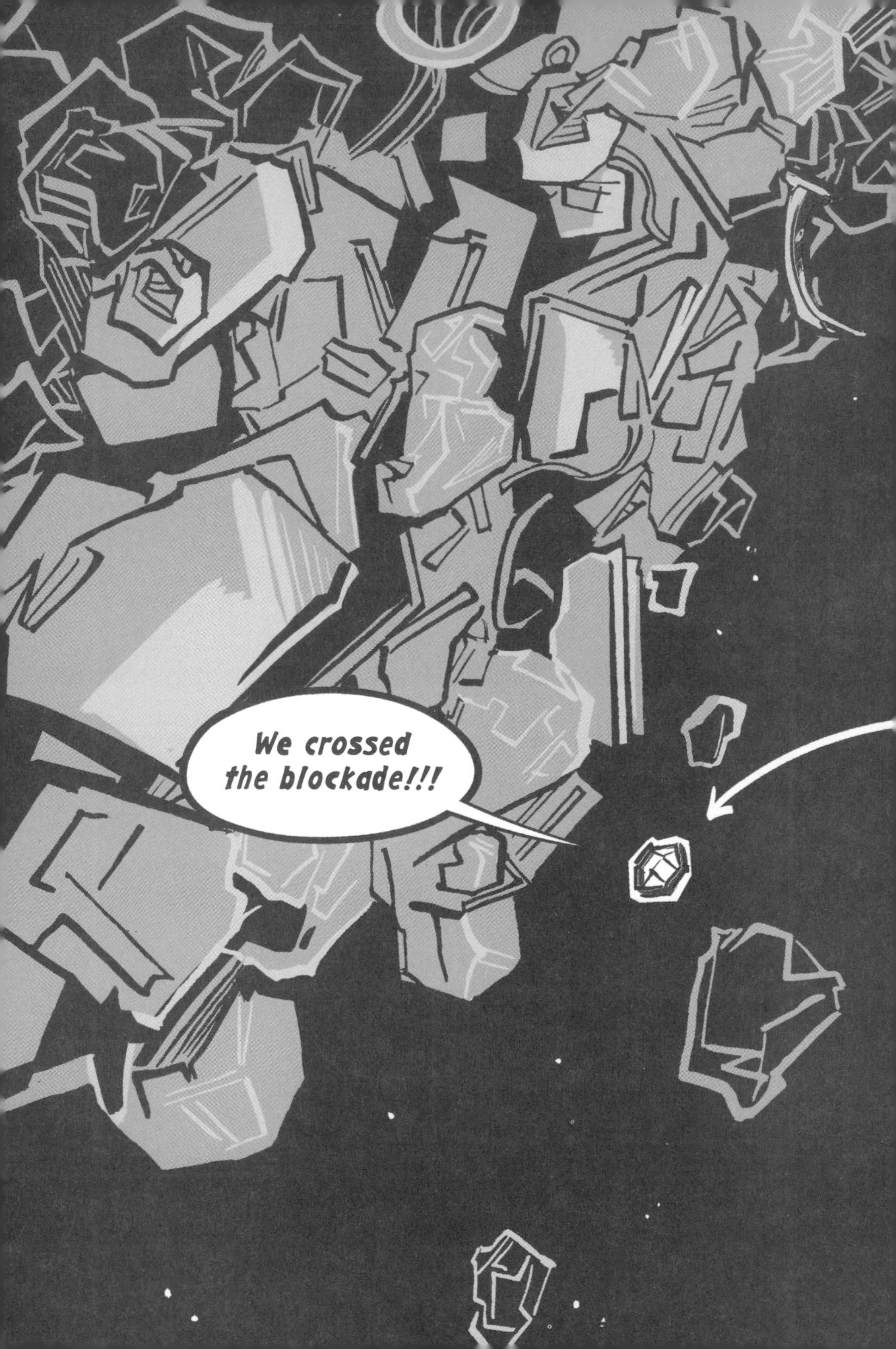
We crossed the blockade!!!

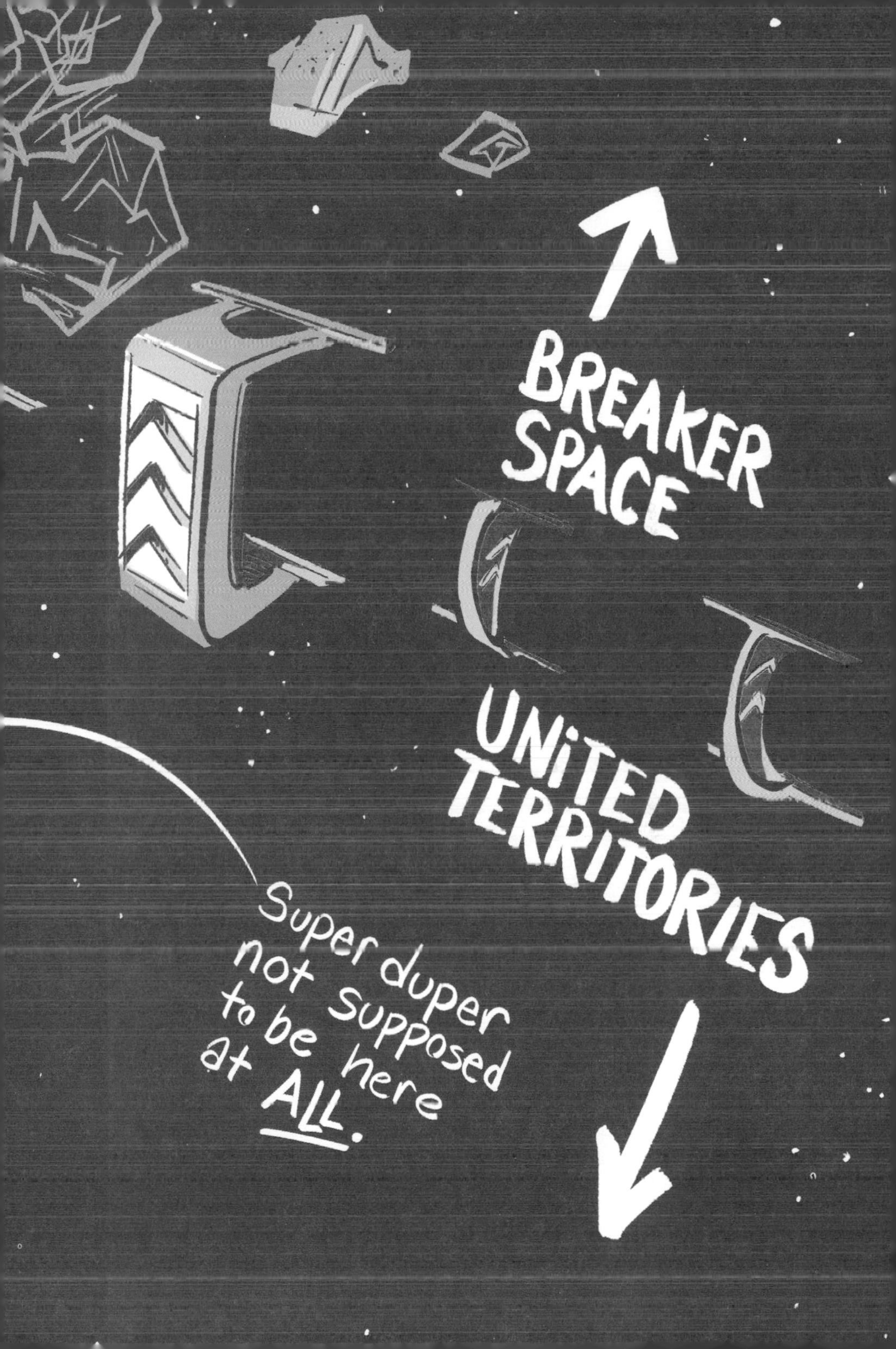
BREAKER SPACE
UNITED TERRITORIES
Super duper not supposed to be here at ALL.

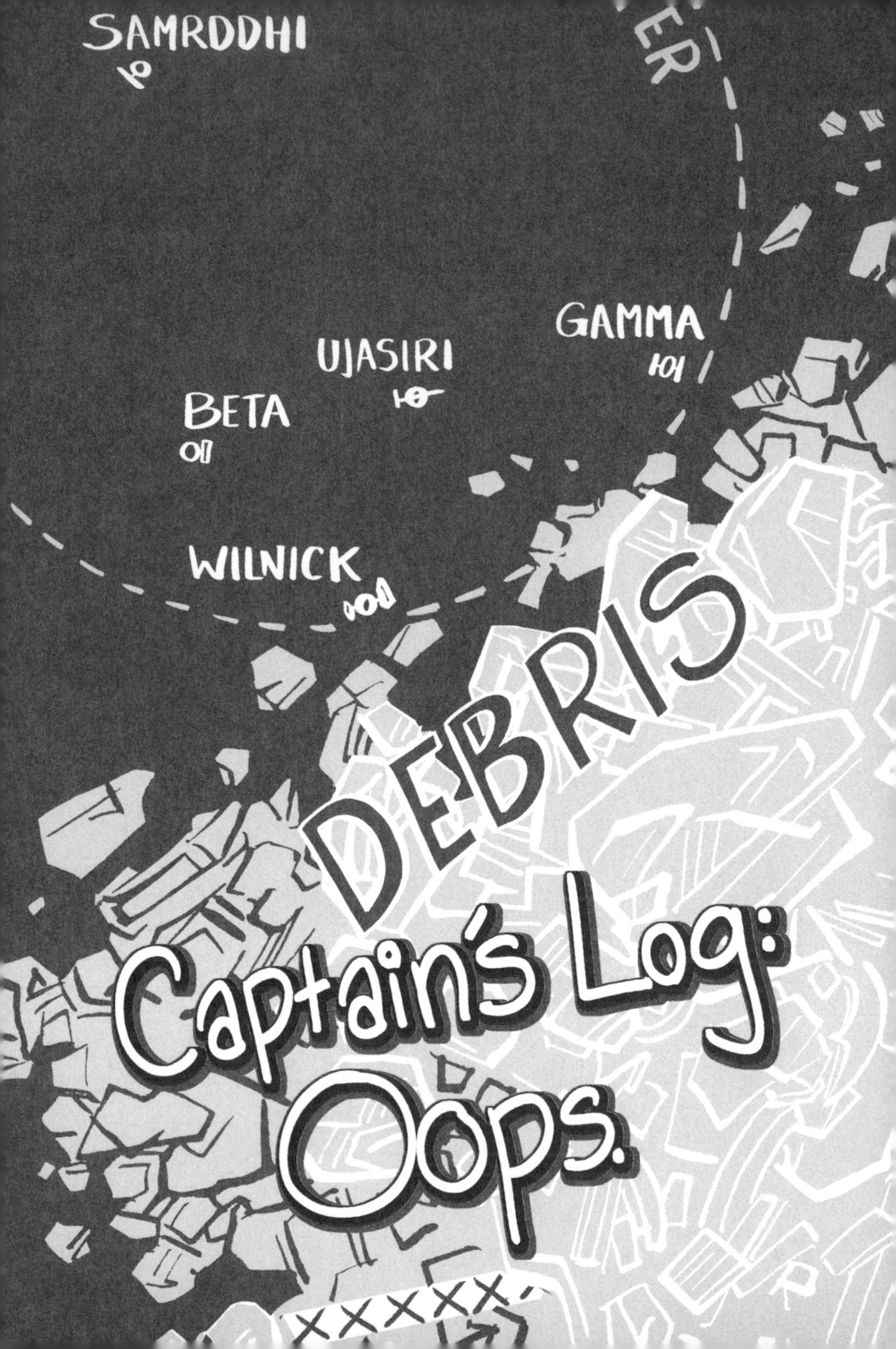
SAMRDDHI
ER
GAMMA
UJASIRI
BETA
WILNICK
DEBRIS
Captain's Log:
Oops.

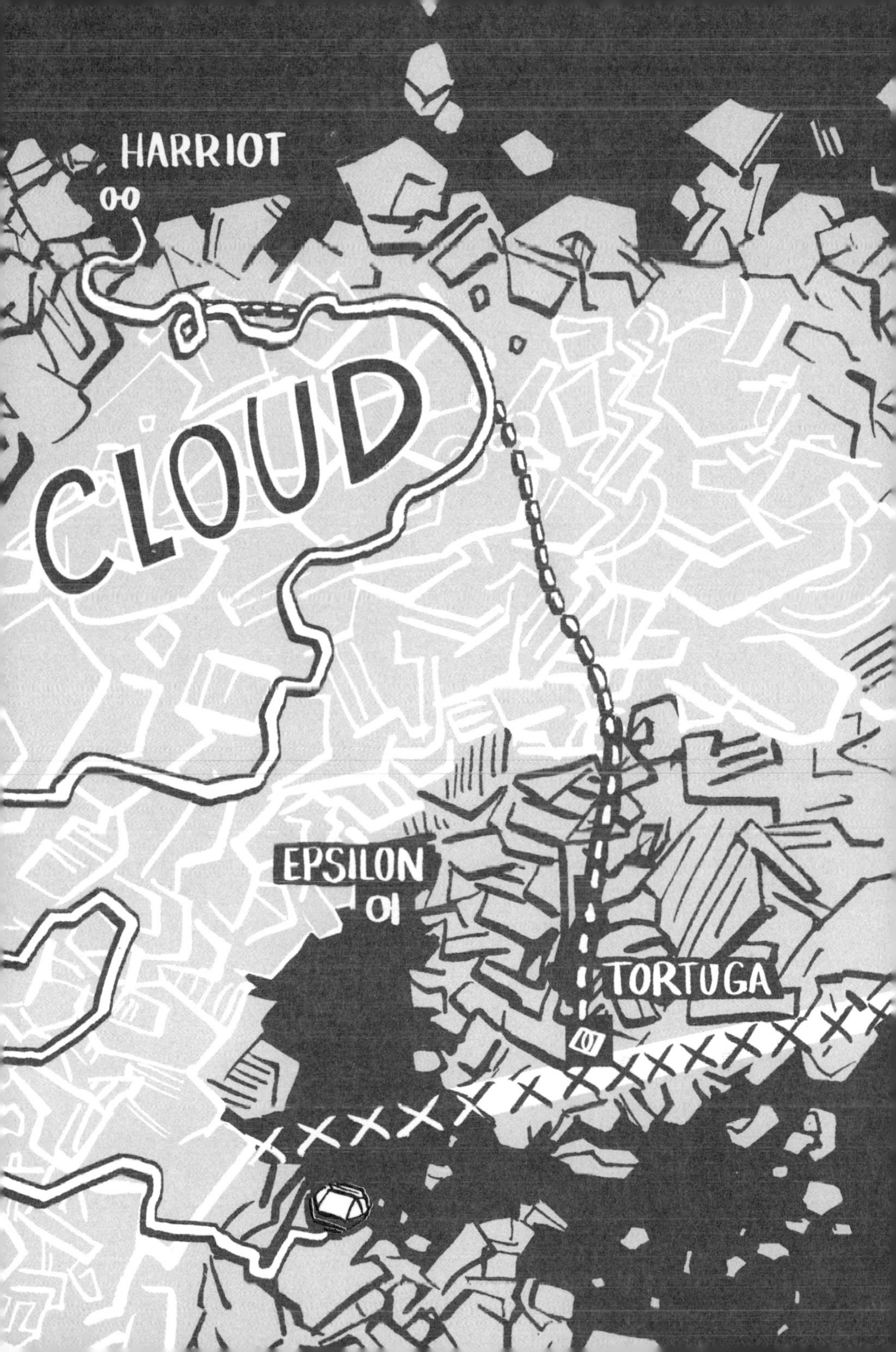
HARRIOT
00
CLOUD
EPSILON
01
TORTUGA
01

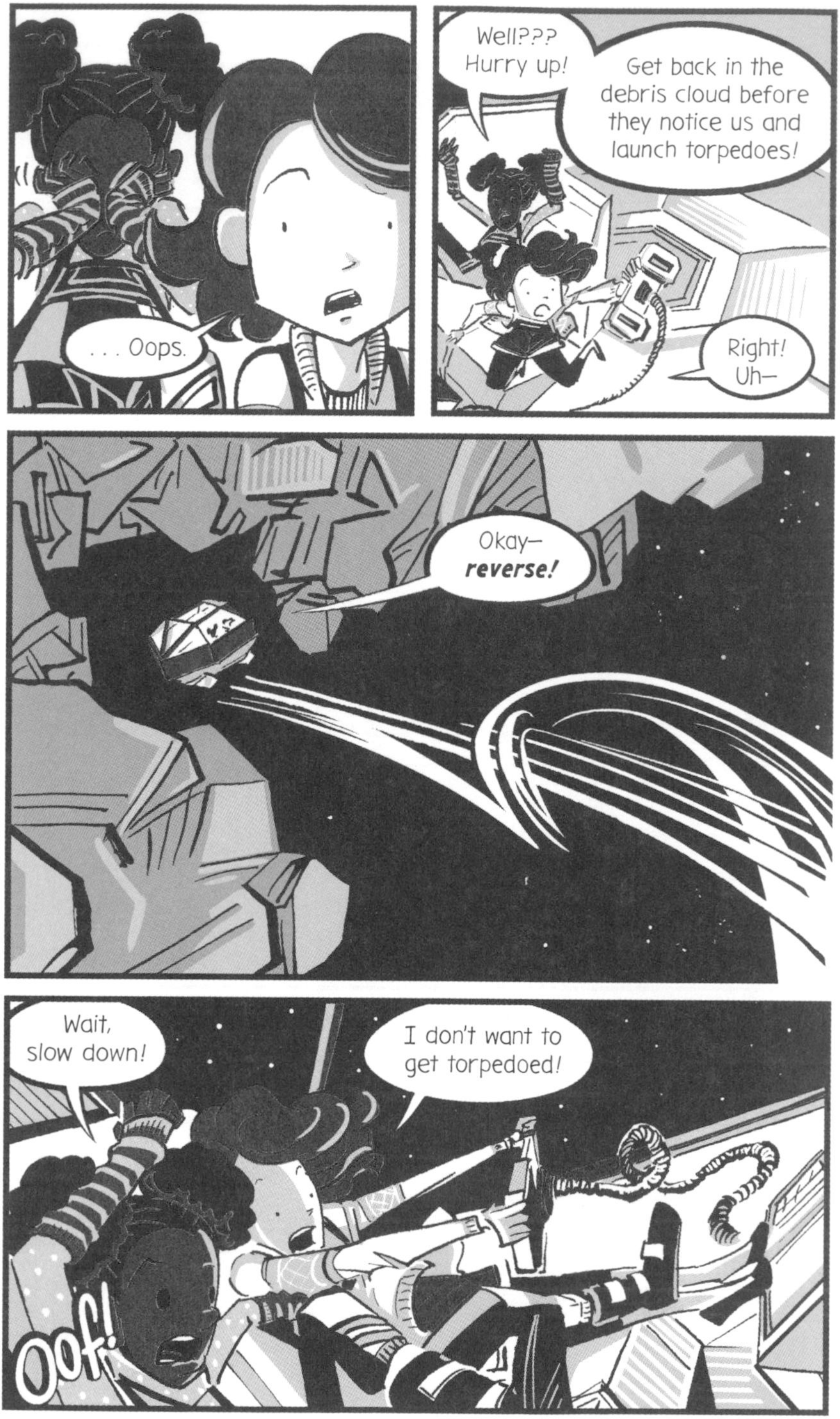

. . . Oops.
Well???
Hurry up!
Get back in the debris cloud before they notice us and launch torpedoes!
Right!
Uh–
Okay–
reverse!
Wait, slow down!
I don't want to get torpedoed!
Oof!

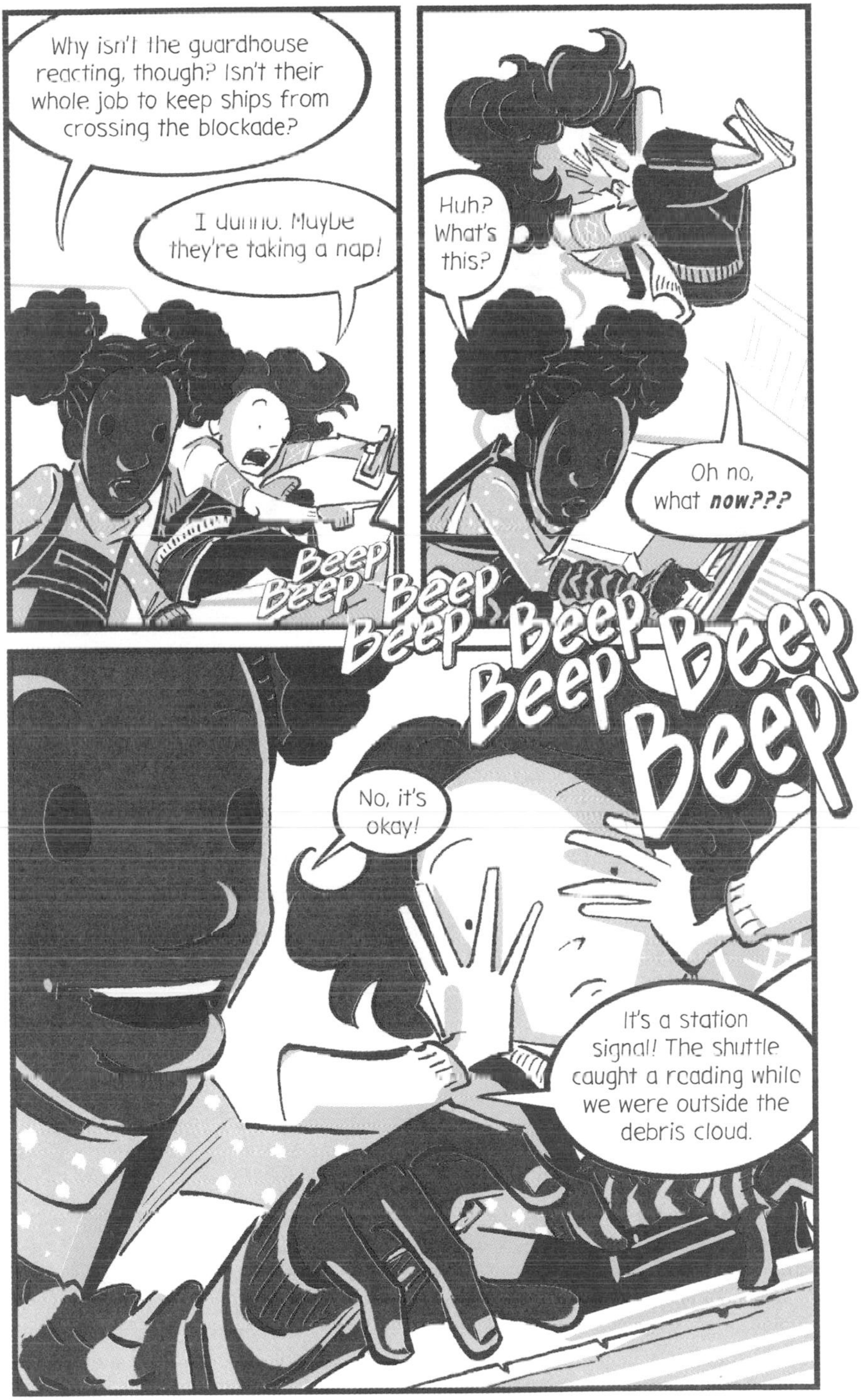
Why isn't the guardhouse reacting, though? Isn't their whole job to keep ships from crossing the blockade?
I dunno. Maybe they're taking a nap!
Beep Beep
Huh? What's this?
Oh no, what now???
Beep Beep Beep Beep Beep Beep Beep
No, it's okay!
It's a station signal! The shuttle caught a reading while we were outside the debris cloud.

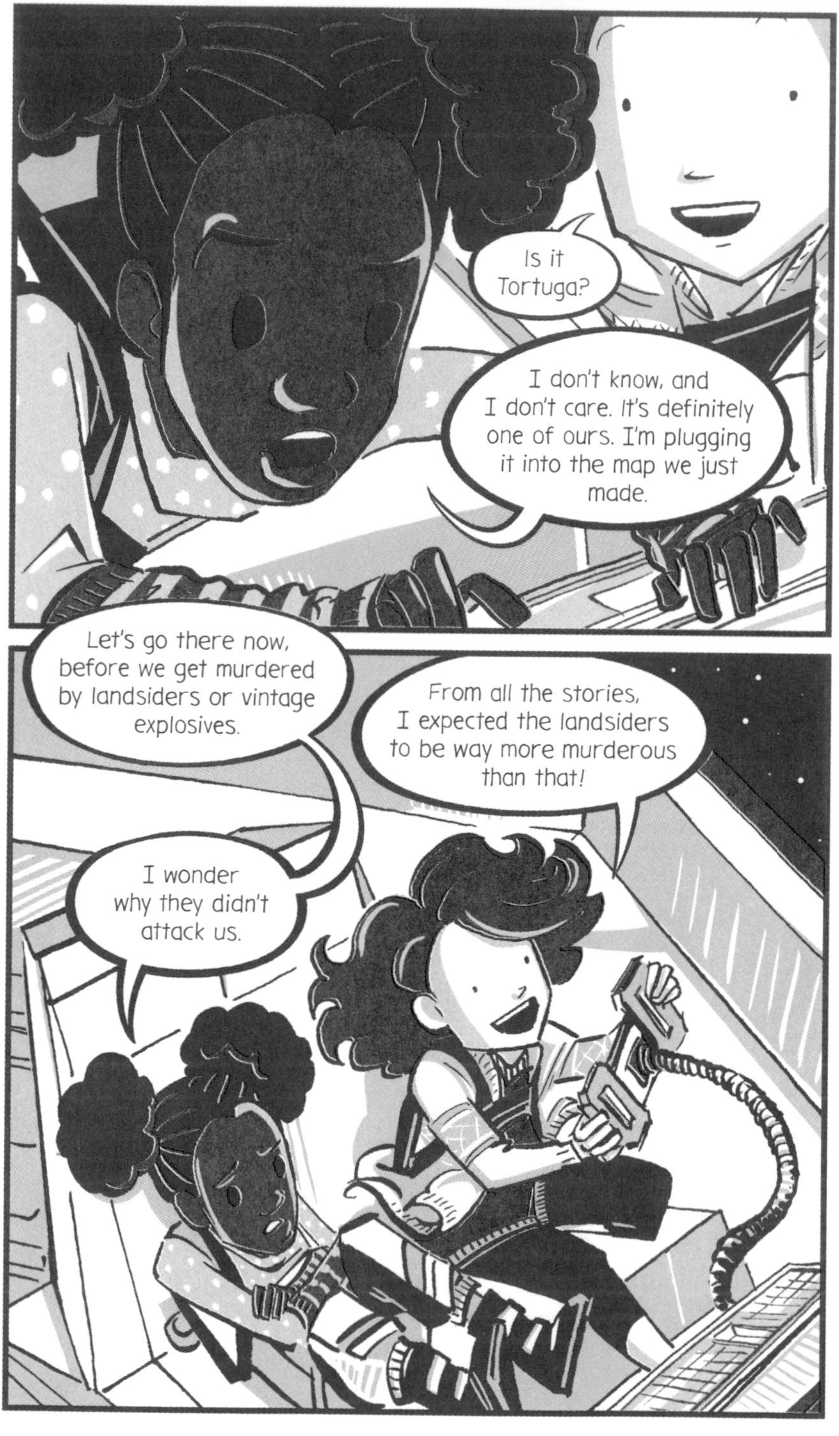
Is it Tortuga?
I don't know, and I don't care. It's definitely one of ours. I'm plugging it into the map we just made.
Let's go there now, before we get murdered by landsiders or vintage explosives.
From all the stories, I expected the landsiders to be way more murderous than that!
I wonder why they didn't attack us.

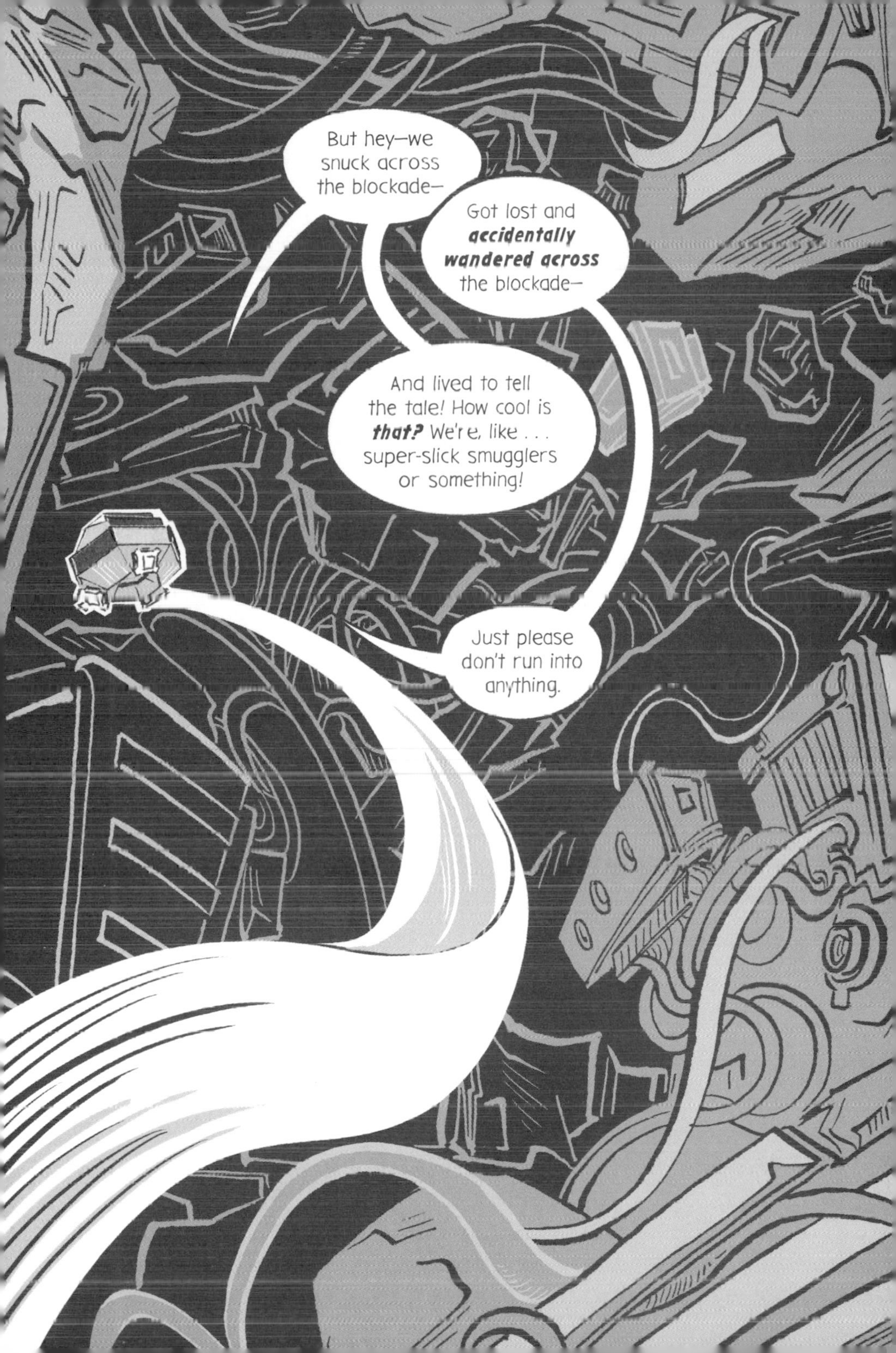
But hey—we snuck across the blockade—
Got lost and **accidentally wandered across** the blockade—
And lived to tell the tale! How cool is ***that?*** We're, like . . . super-slick smugglers or something!
Just please don't run into anything.

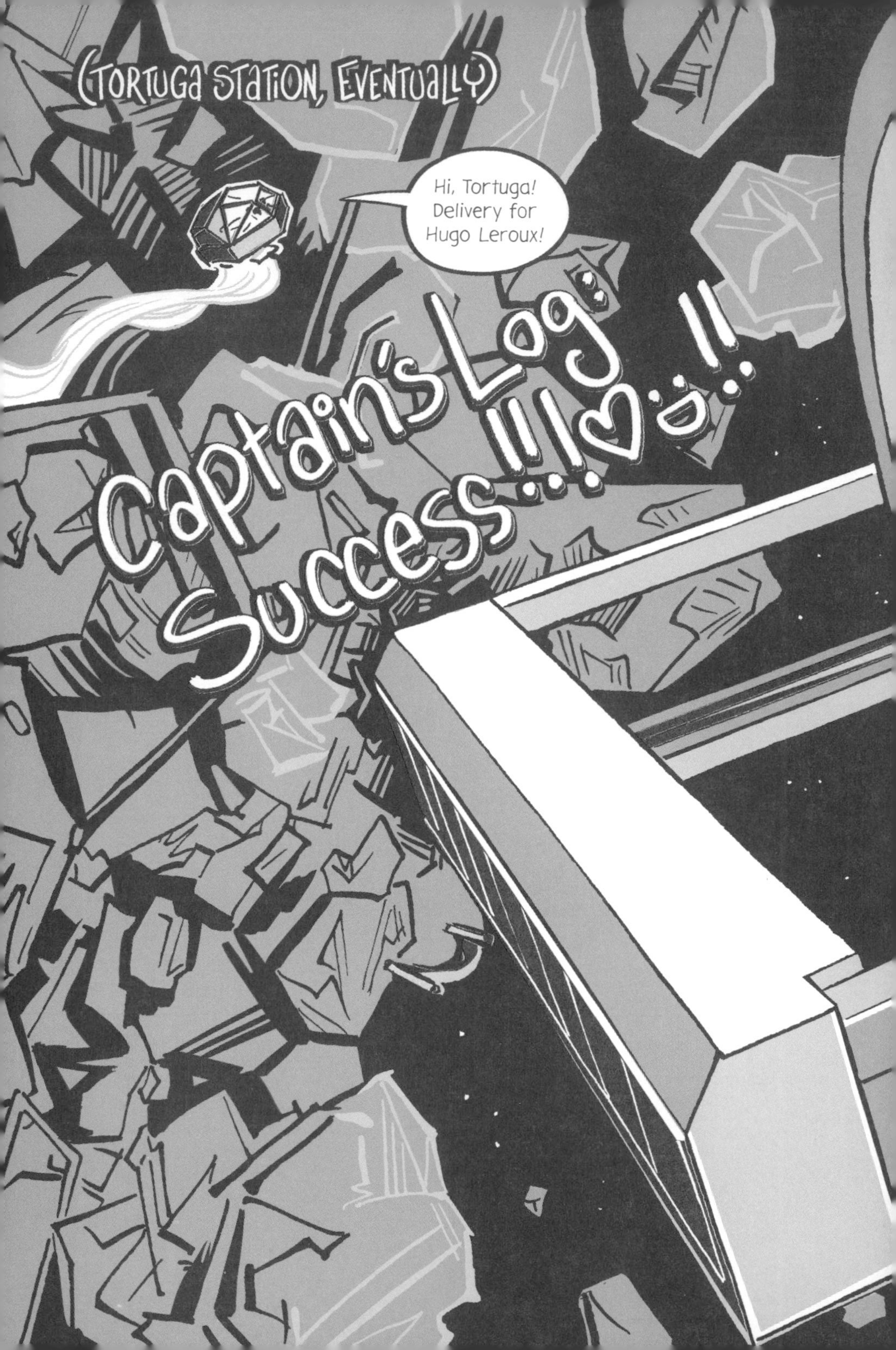
(Tortuga Station, Eventually)
Hi, Tortuga! Delivery for Hugo Leroux!
Captain's Log: Success!!!!♡:D!!

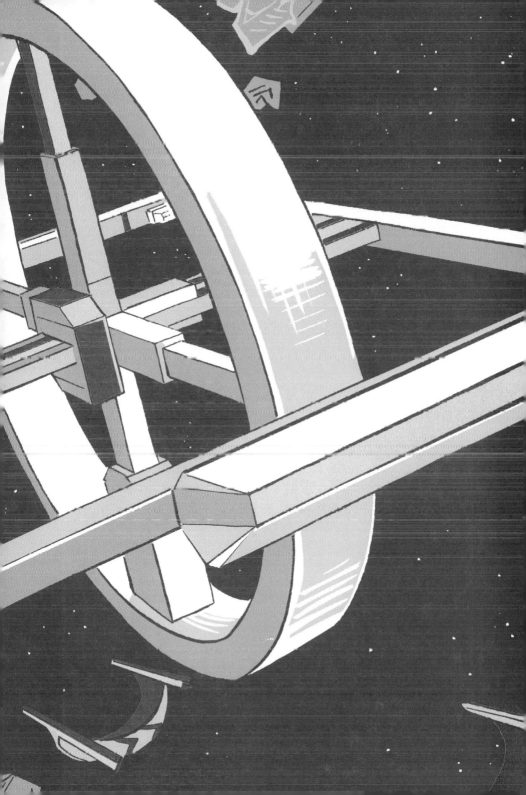

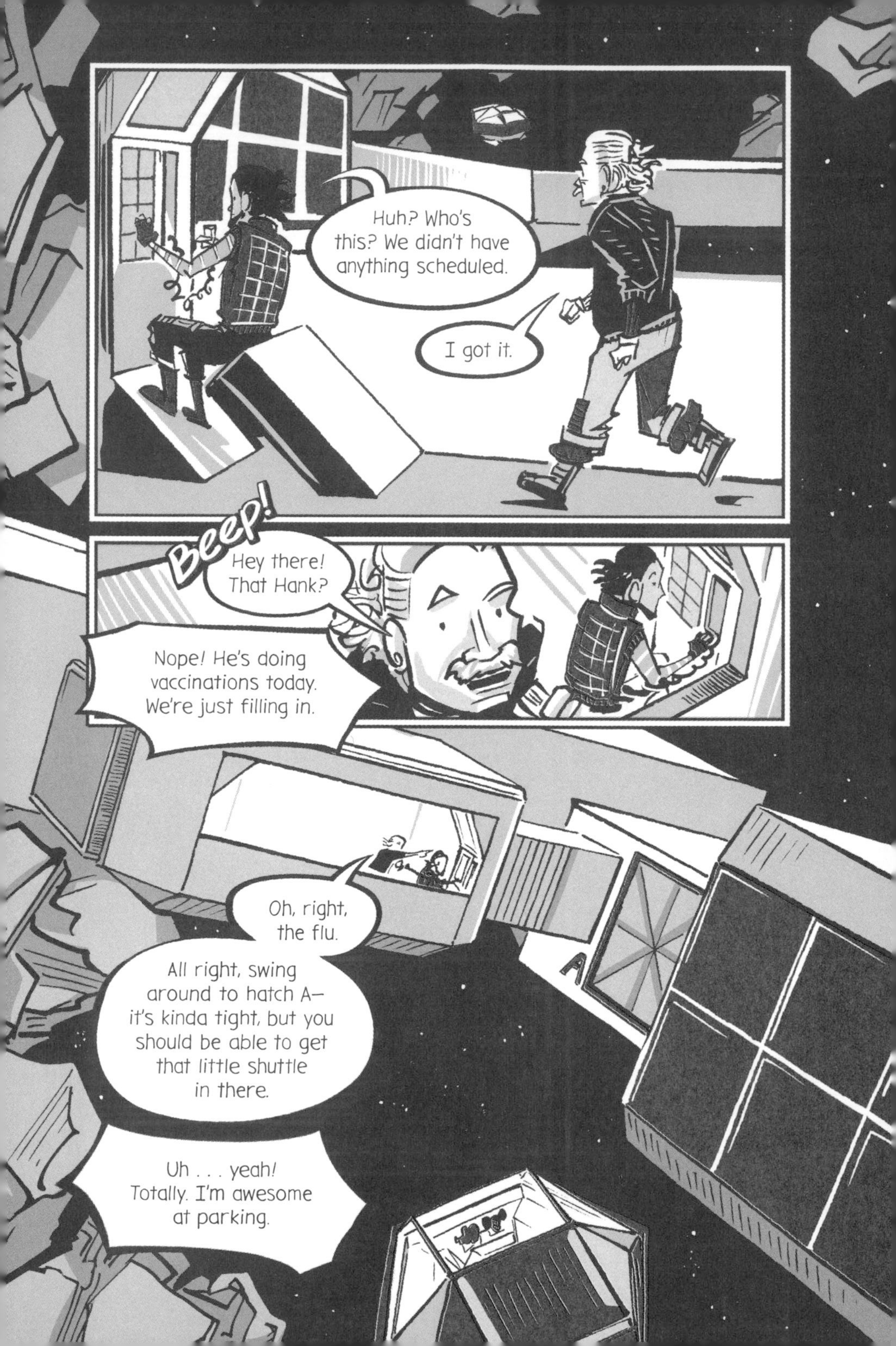
Huh? Who's this? We didn't have anything scheduled.
I got it.
Beep!
Hey there! That Hank?
Nope! He's doing vaccinations today. We're just filling in.
Oh, right, the flu.
All right, swing around to hatch A— it's kinda tight, but you should be able to get that little shuttle in there.
A
Uh . . . yeah! Totally. I'm awesome at parking.

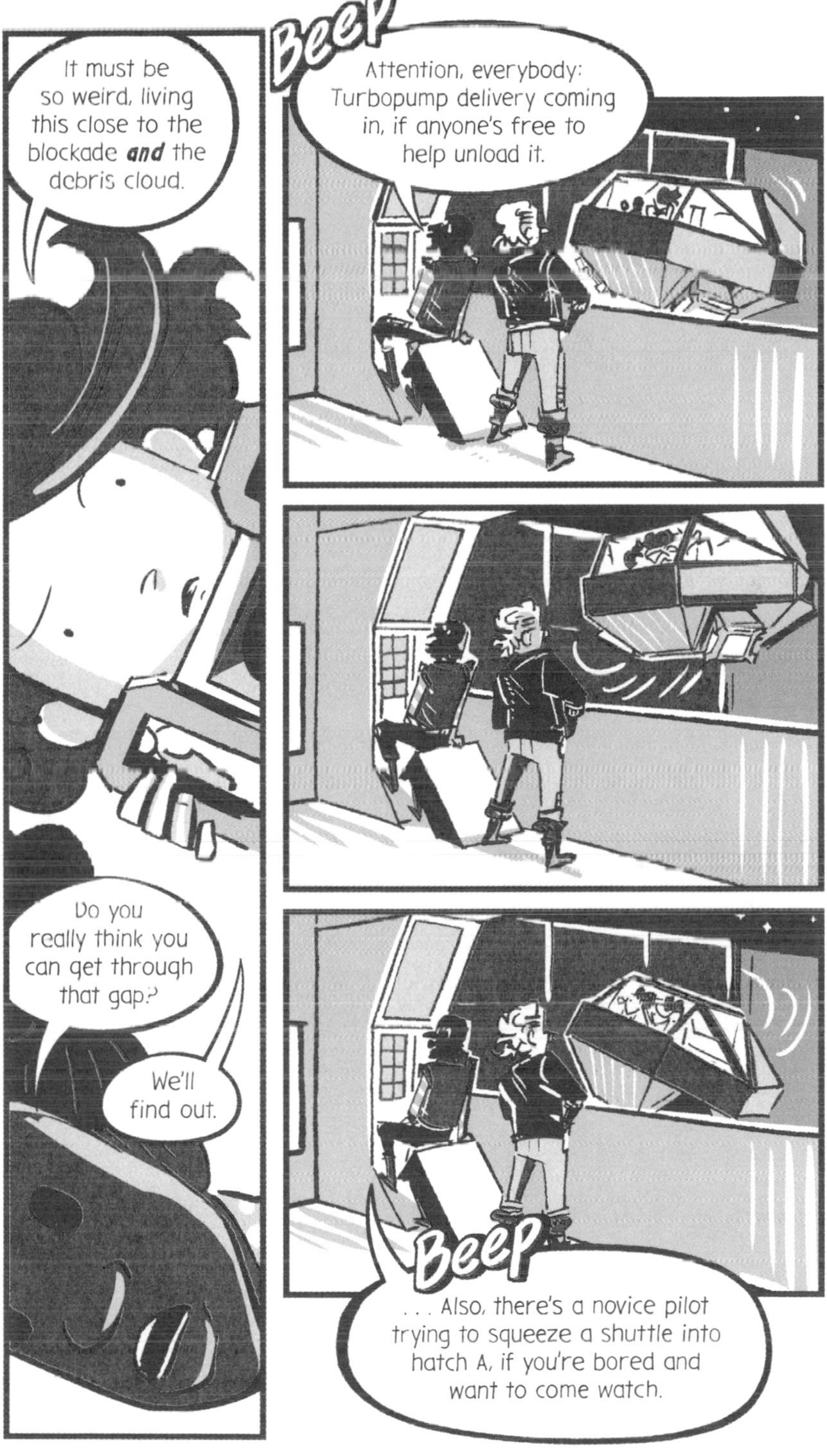
It must be so weird, living this close to the blockade **and** the debris cloud.
Beep
Attention, everybody: Turbopump delivery coming in, if anyone's free to help unload it.
Do you really think you can get through that gap?
We'll find out.
Beep
. . . Also, there's a novice pilot trying to squeeze a shuttle into hatch A, if you're bored and want to come watch.

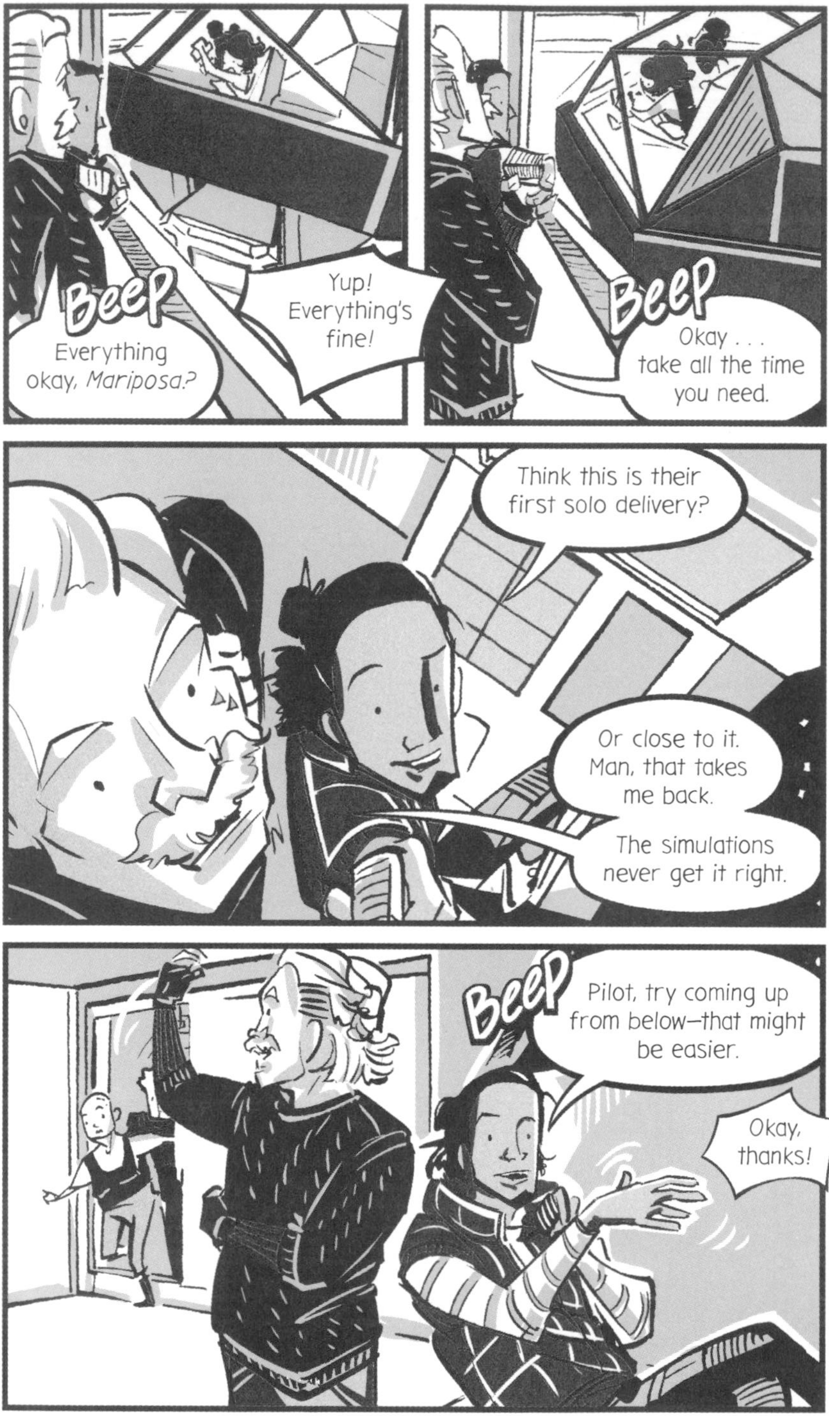
Beep
Everything okay, *Mariposa?*
Yup! Everything's fine!
Beep
Okay . . . take all the time you need.
Think this is their first solo delivery?
Or close to it. Man, that takes me back.
The simulations never get it right.
Beep
Pilot, try coming up from below—that might be easier.
Okay, thanks!

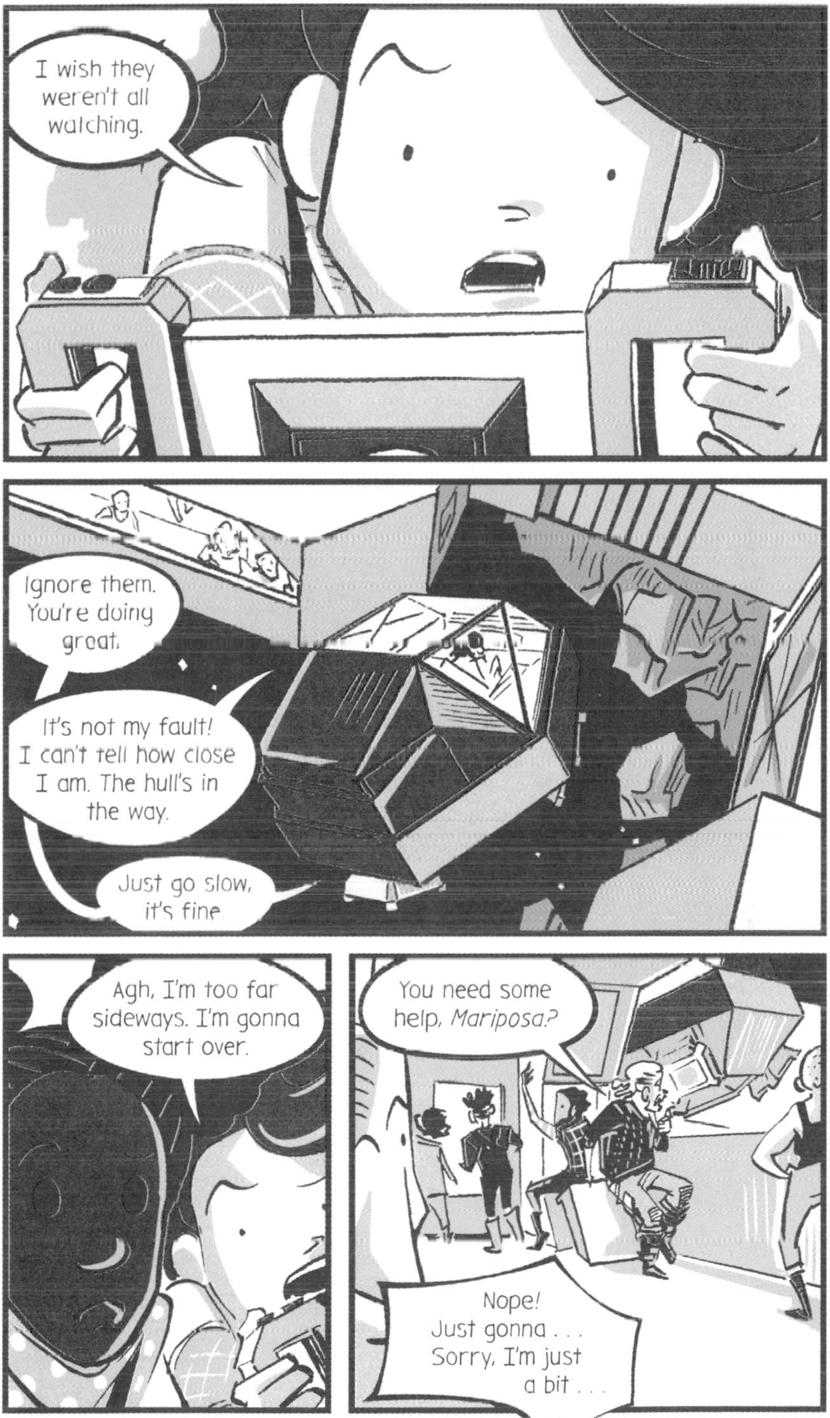
I wish they weren't all watching.
Ignore them. You're doing great.
It's not my fault! I can't tell how close I am. The hull's in the way.
Just go slow, it's fine.
Agh, I'm too far sideways. I'm gonna start over.
You need some help, *Mariposa?*
Nope! Just gonna . . . Sorry, I'm just a bit . . .

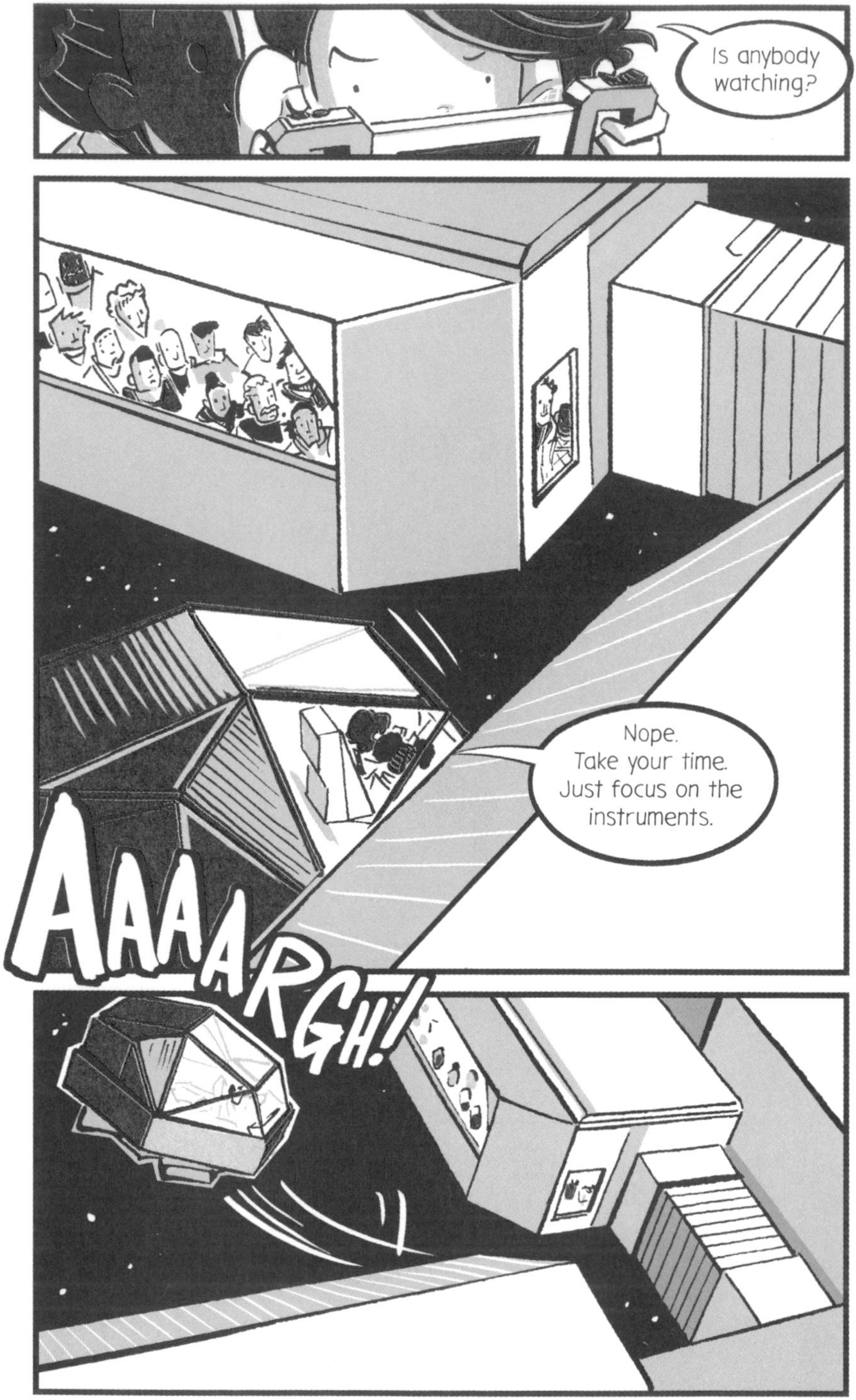
Is anybody watching?
Nope. Take your time. Just focus on the instruments.
AAAARGH!!

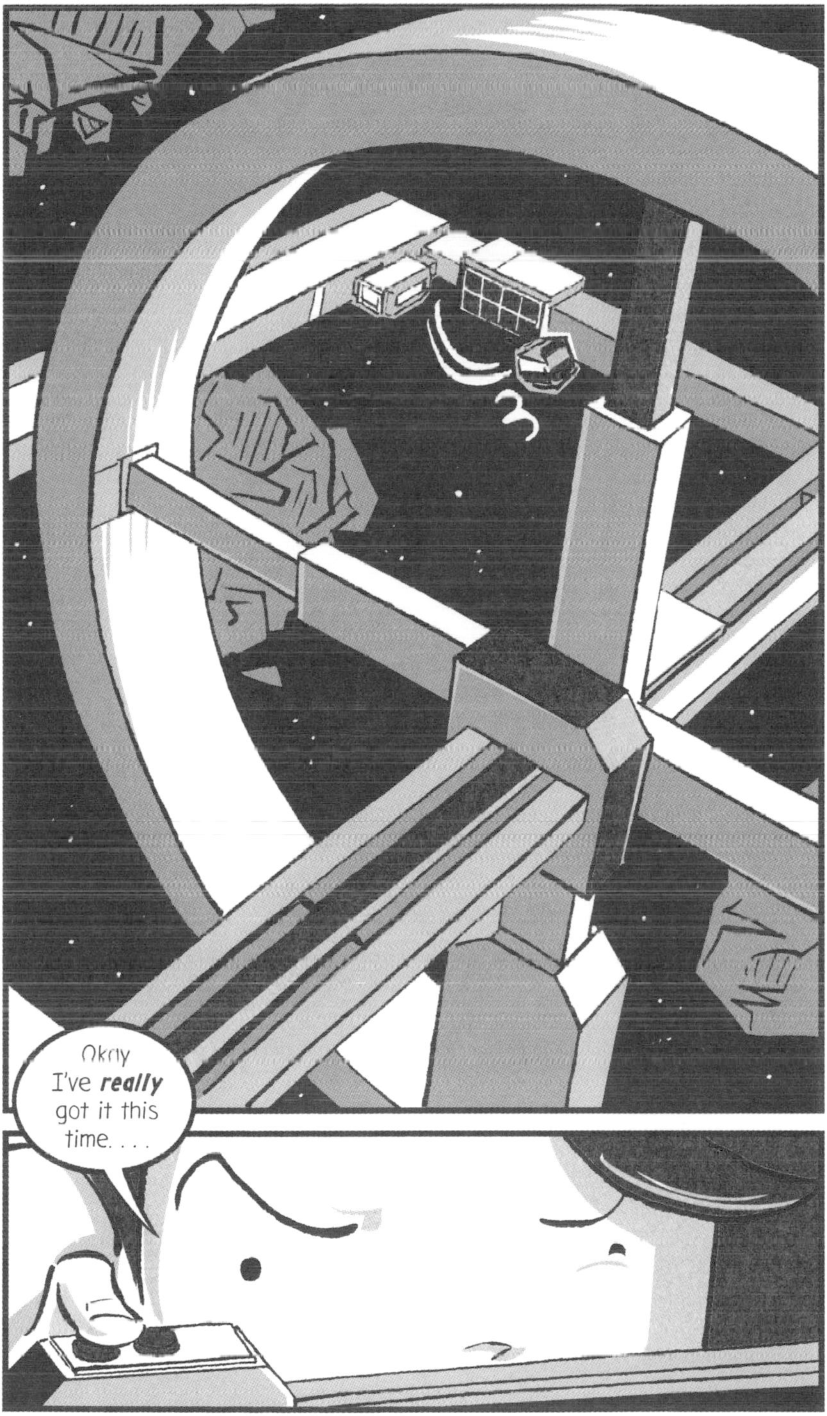
Okay
I've ***really*** got it this time. . . .

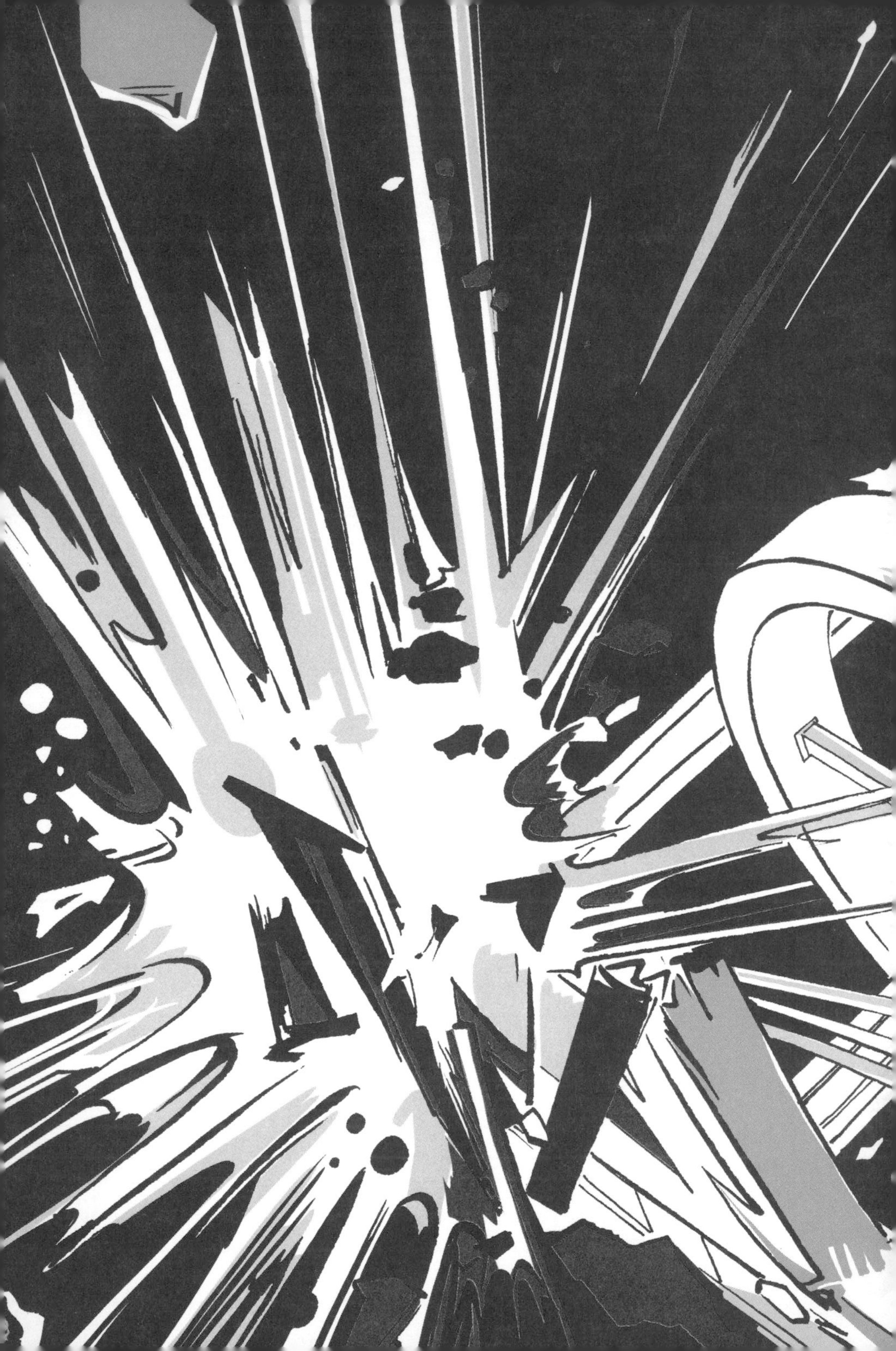

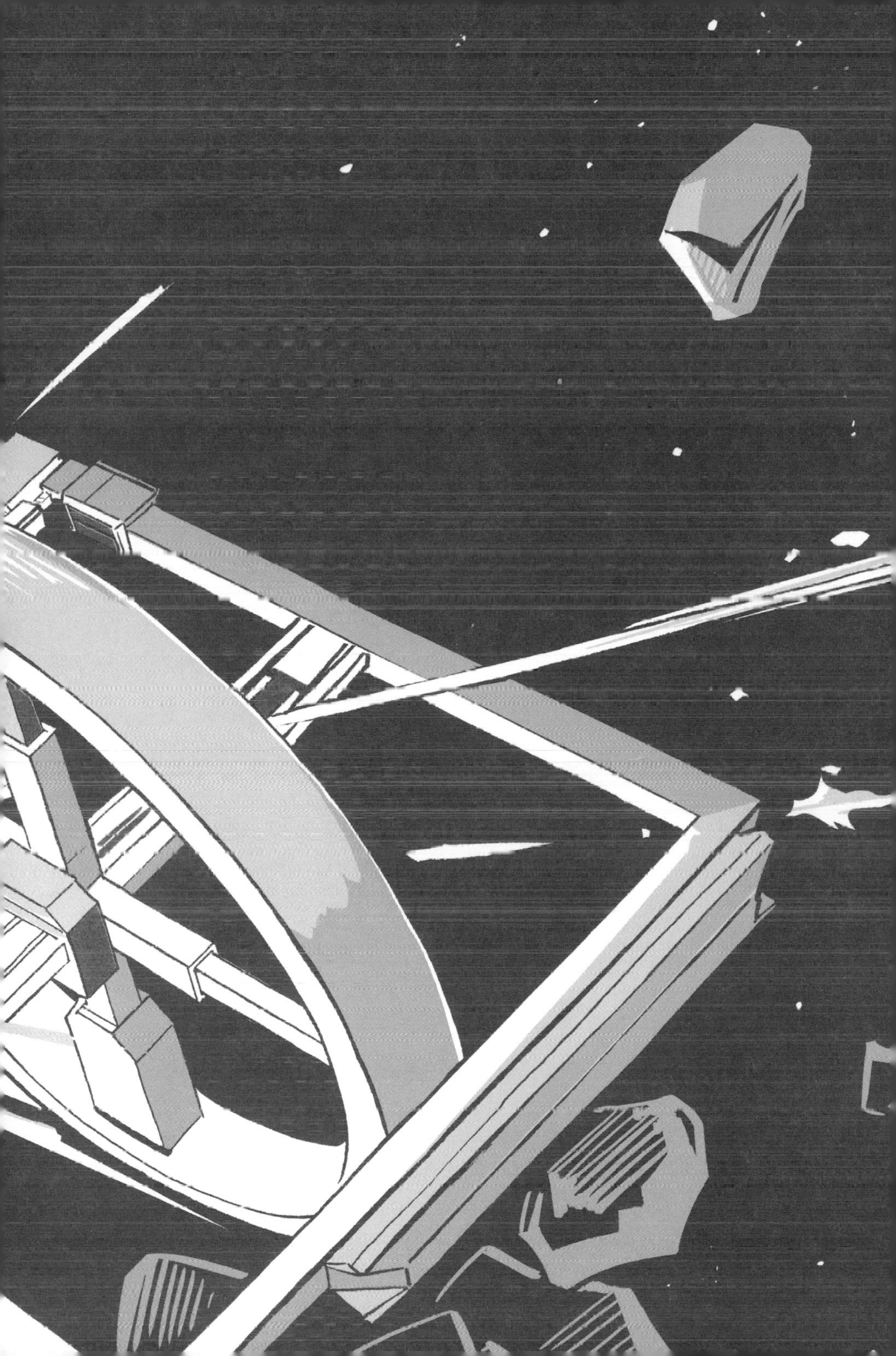

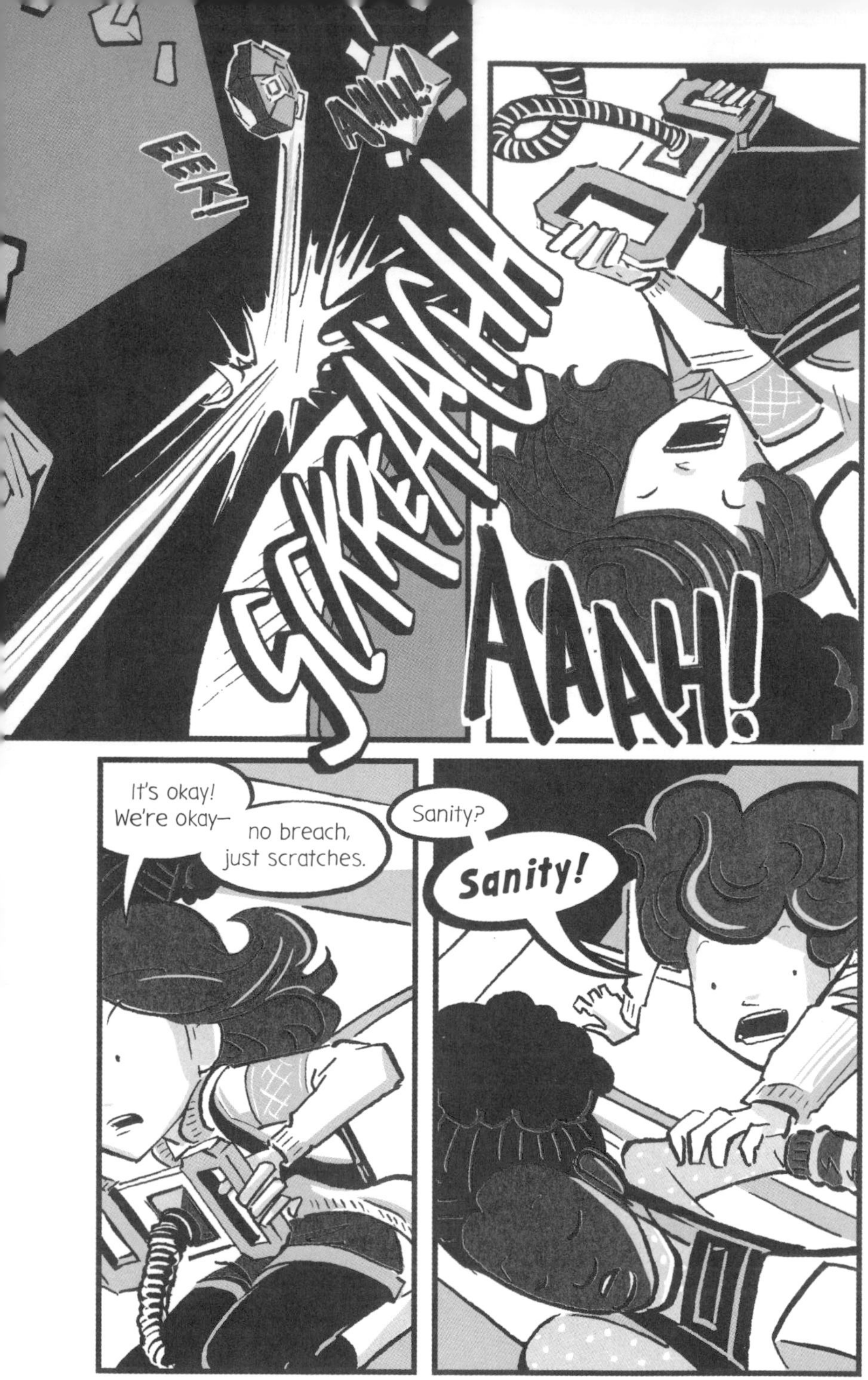
EEK!
AHH!
SKREACH!
AAAH!
It's okay! We're okay—
no breach, just scratches.
Sanity?
Sanity!

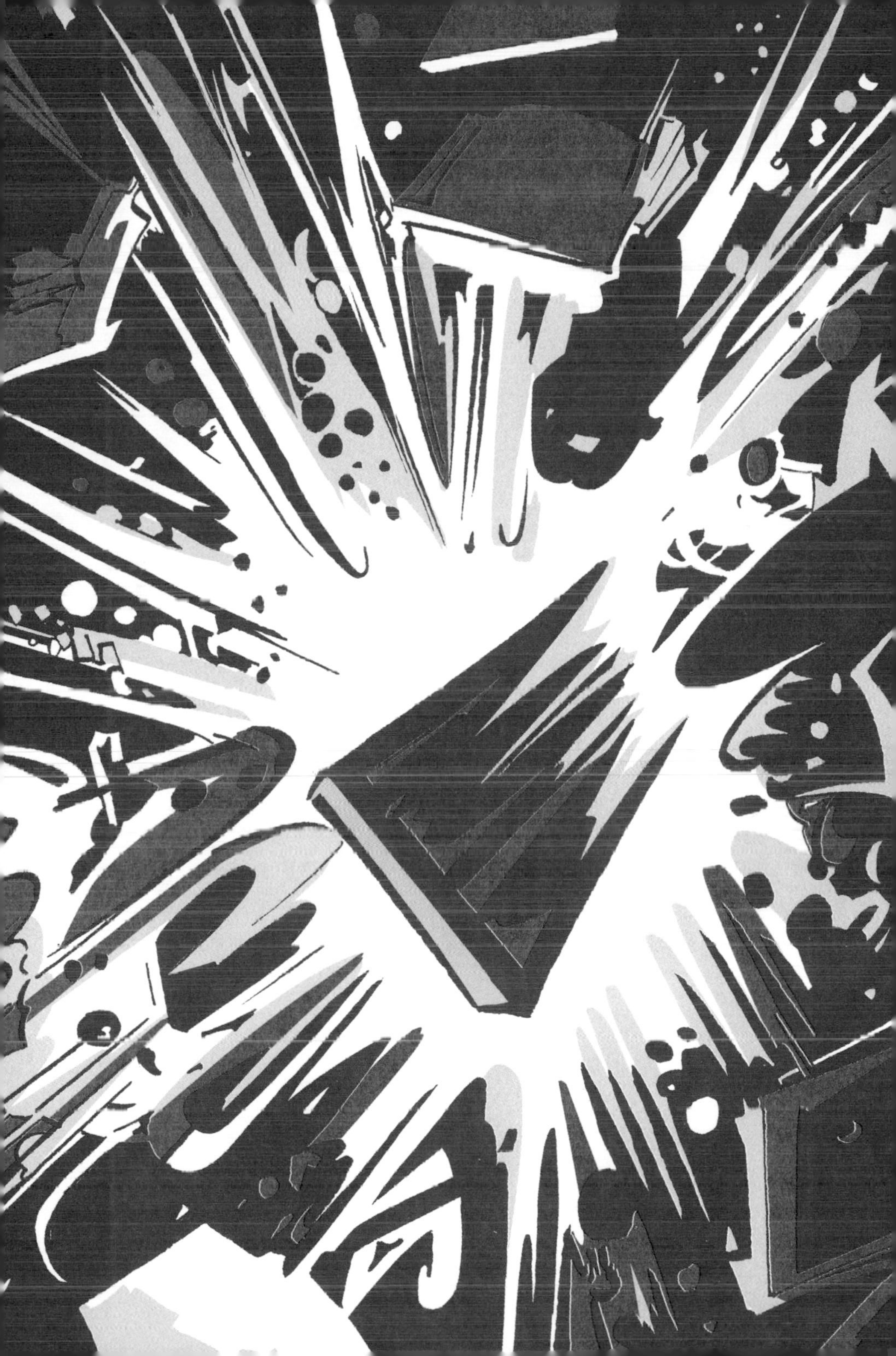

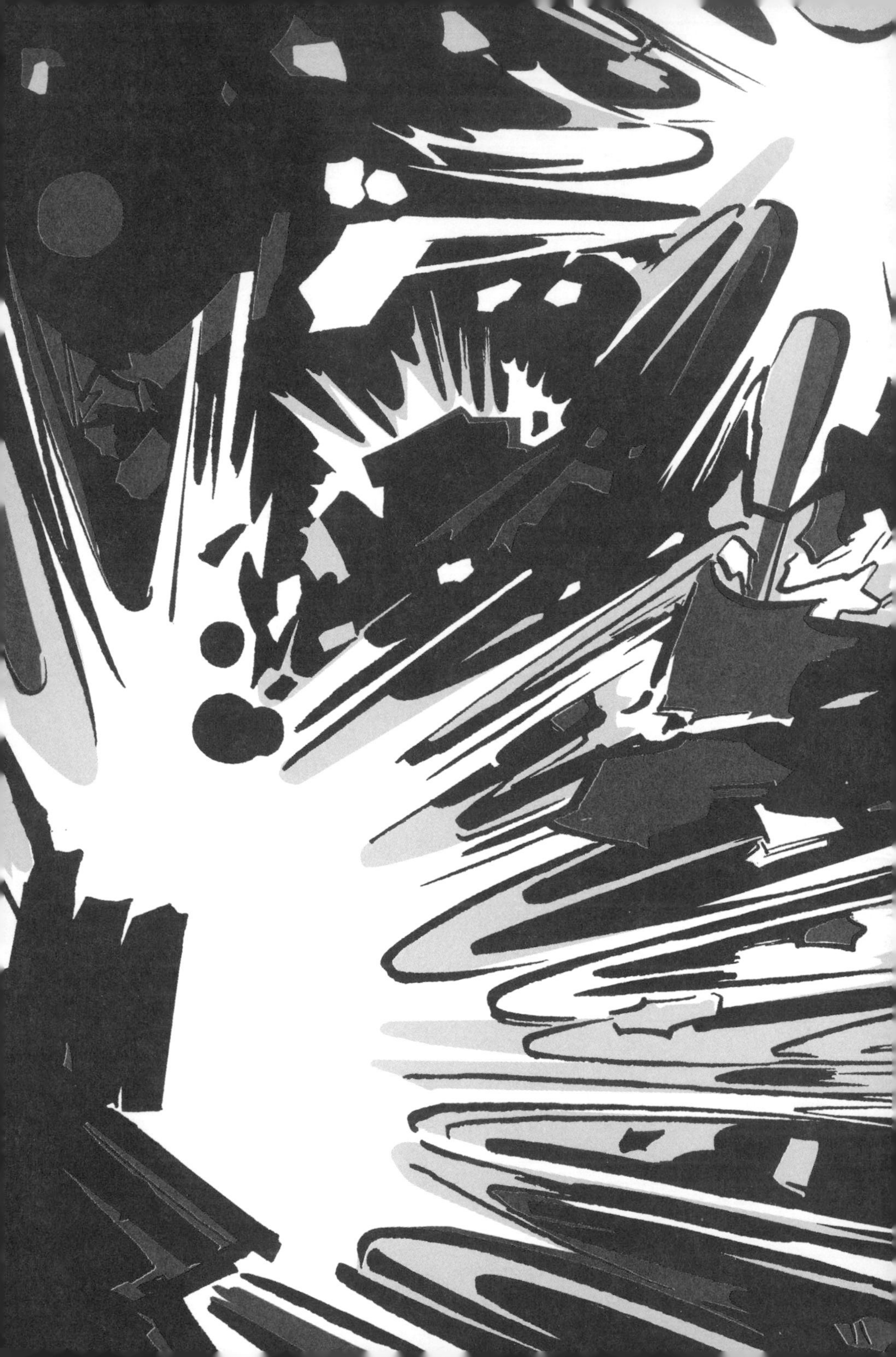

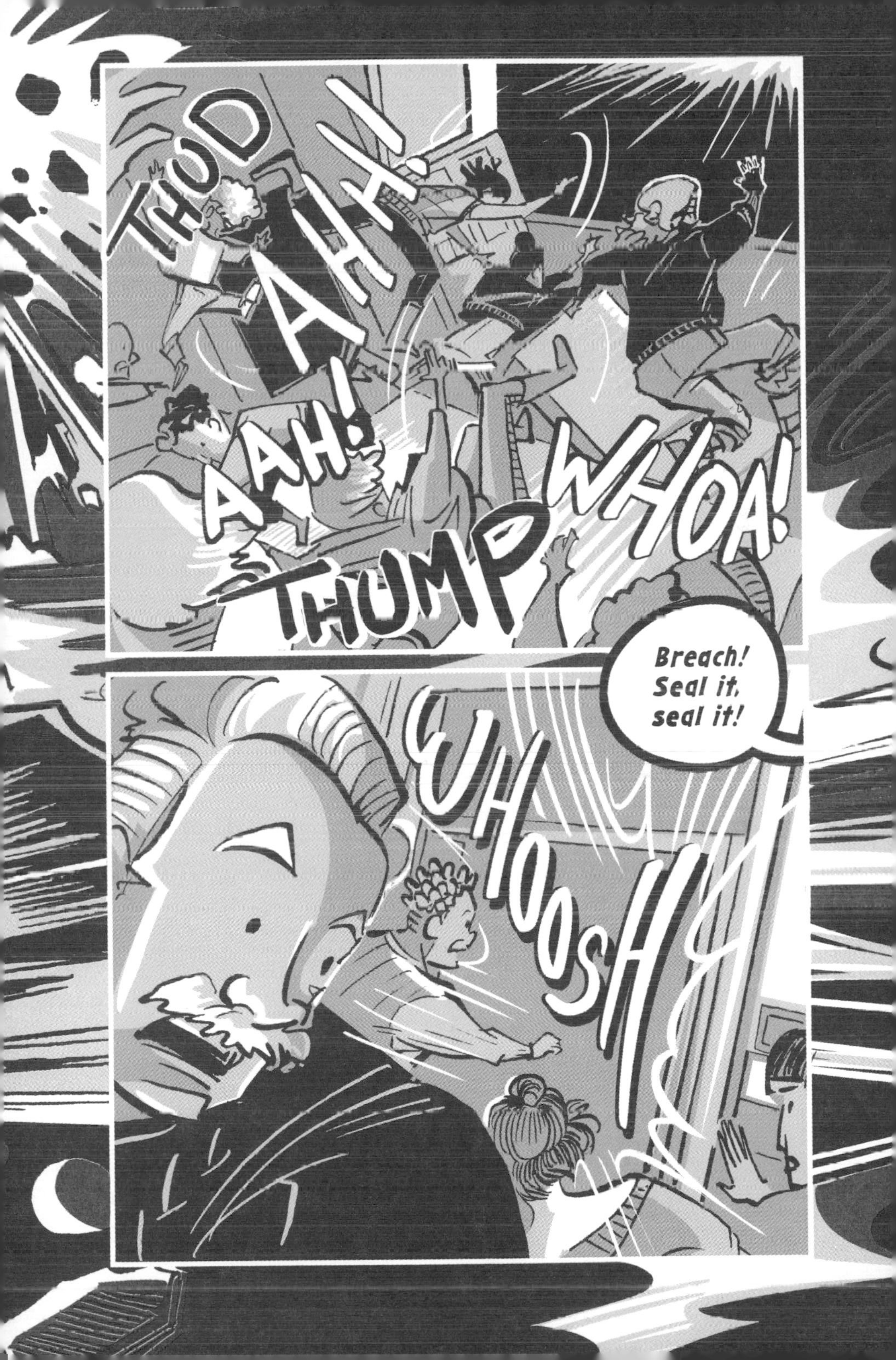
THUD
AHH!
AAH!
WHOA!
THUMP
Breach! Seal it, seal it!
WHOOSH

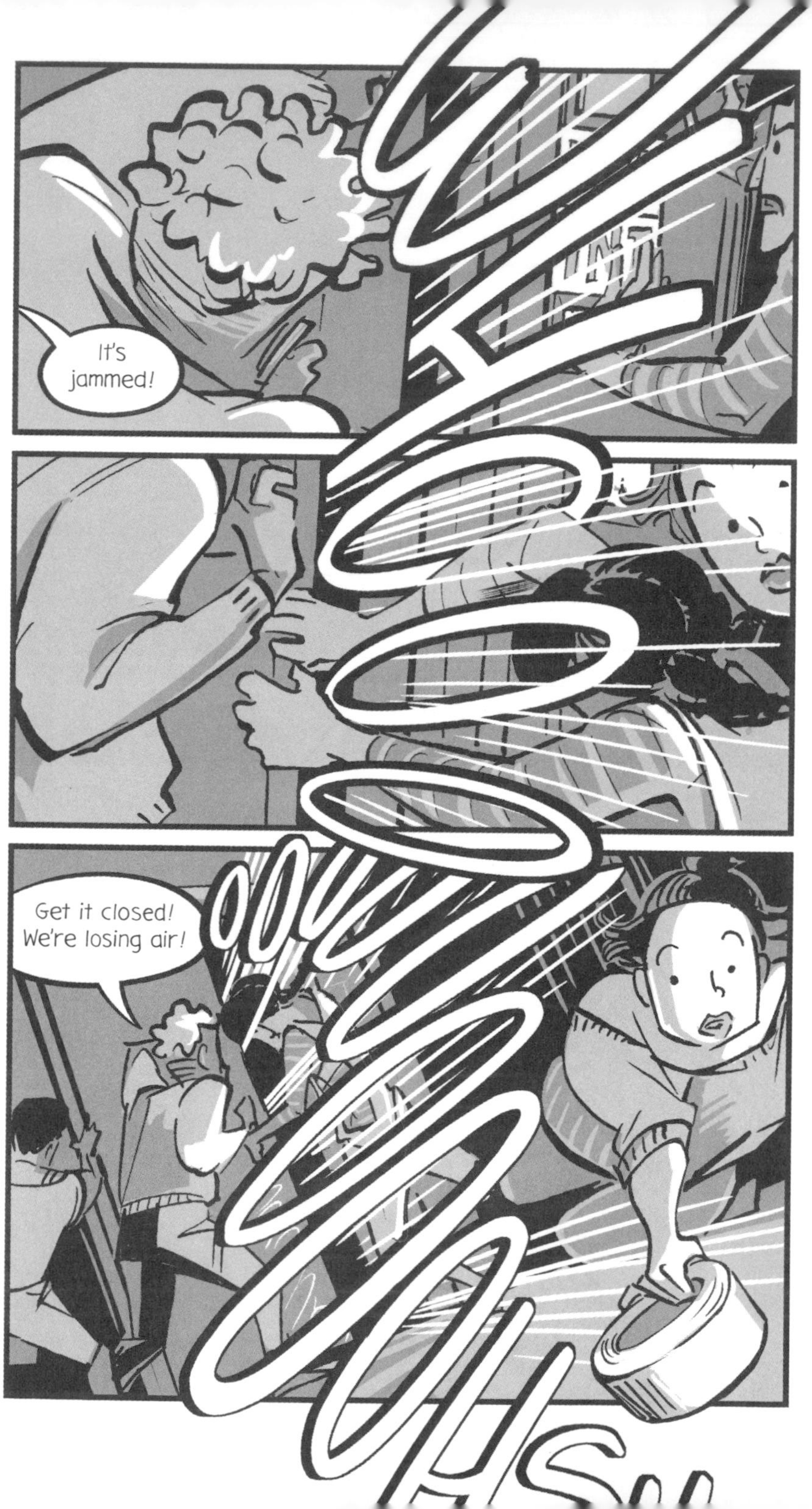
It's jammed!
Get it closed! We're losing air!

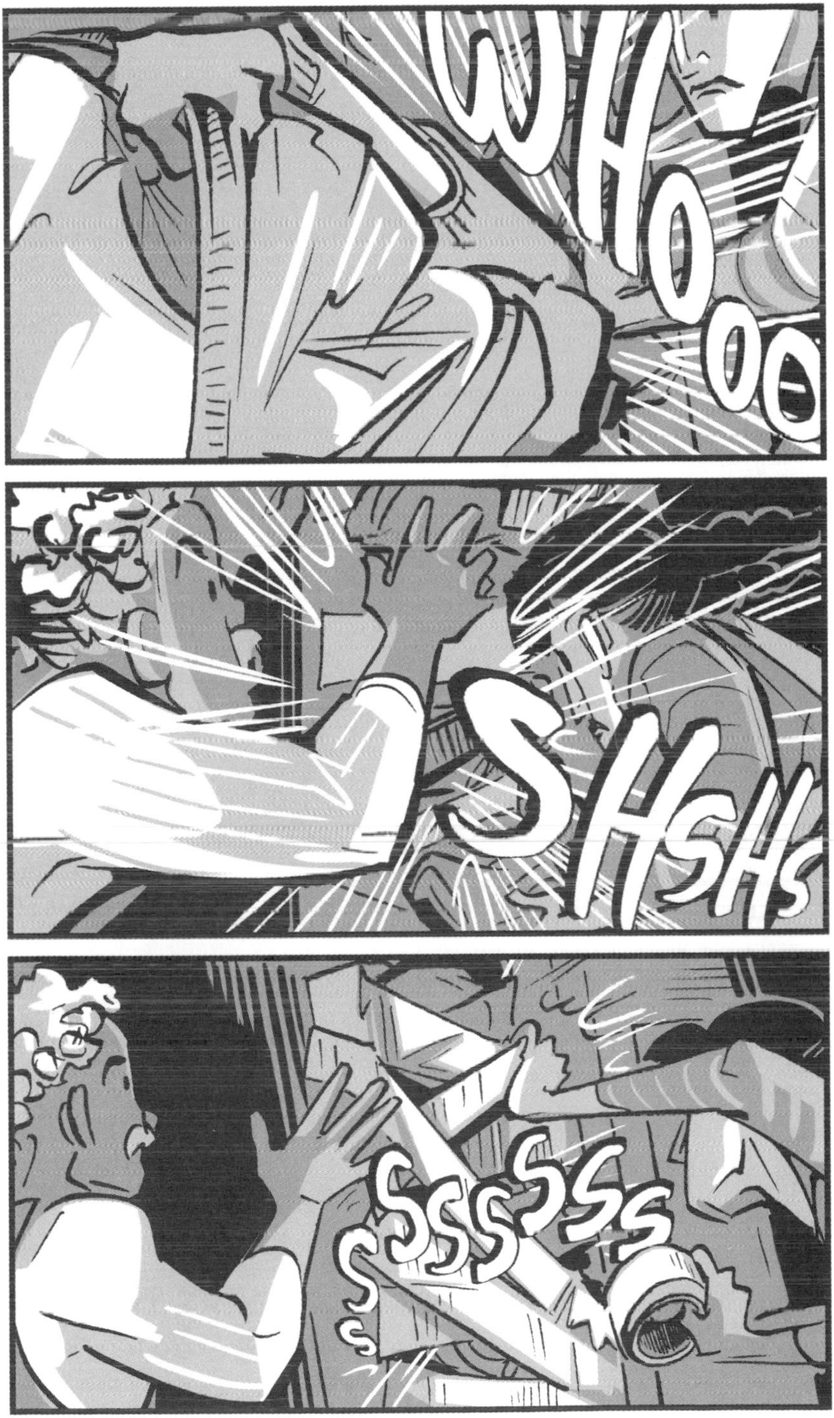
WHOOOO
SHSHs
SSSSSSSs

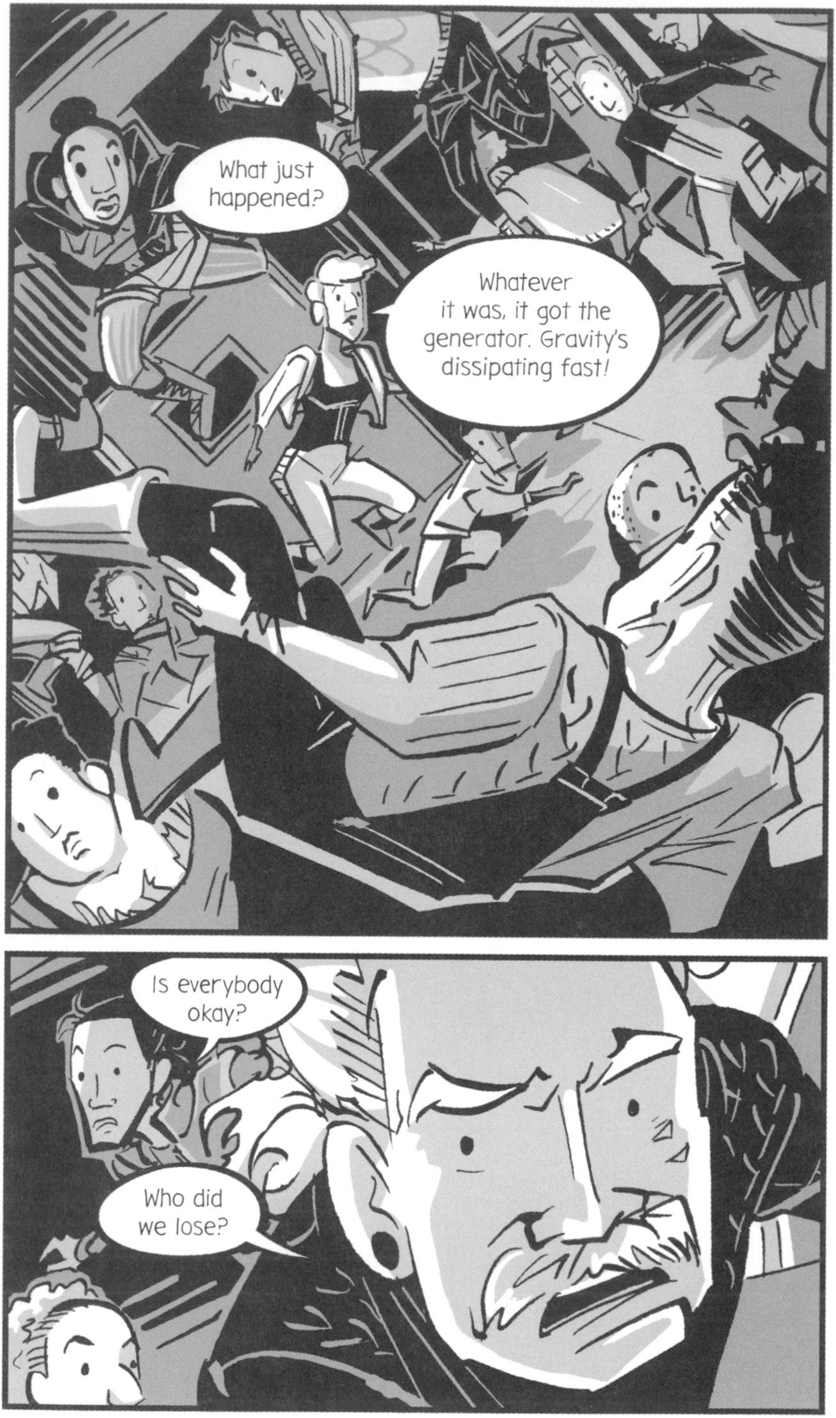
What just happened?
Whatever it was, it got the generator. Gravity's dissipating fast!
Is everybody okay?
Who did we lose?

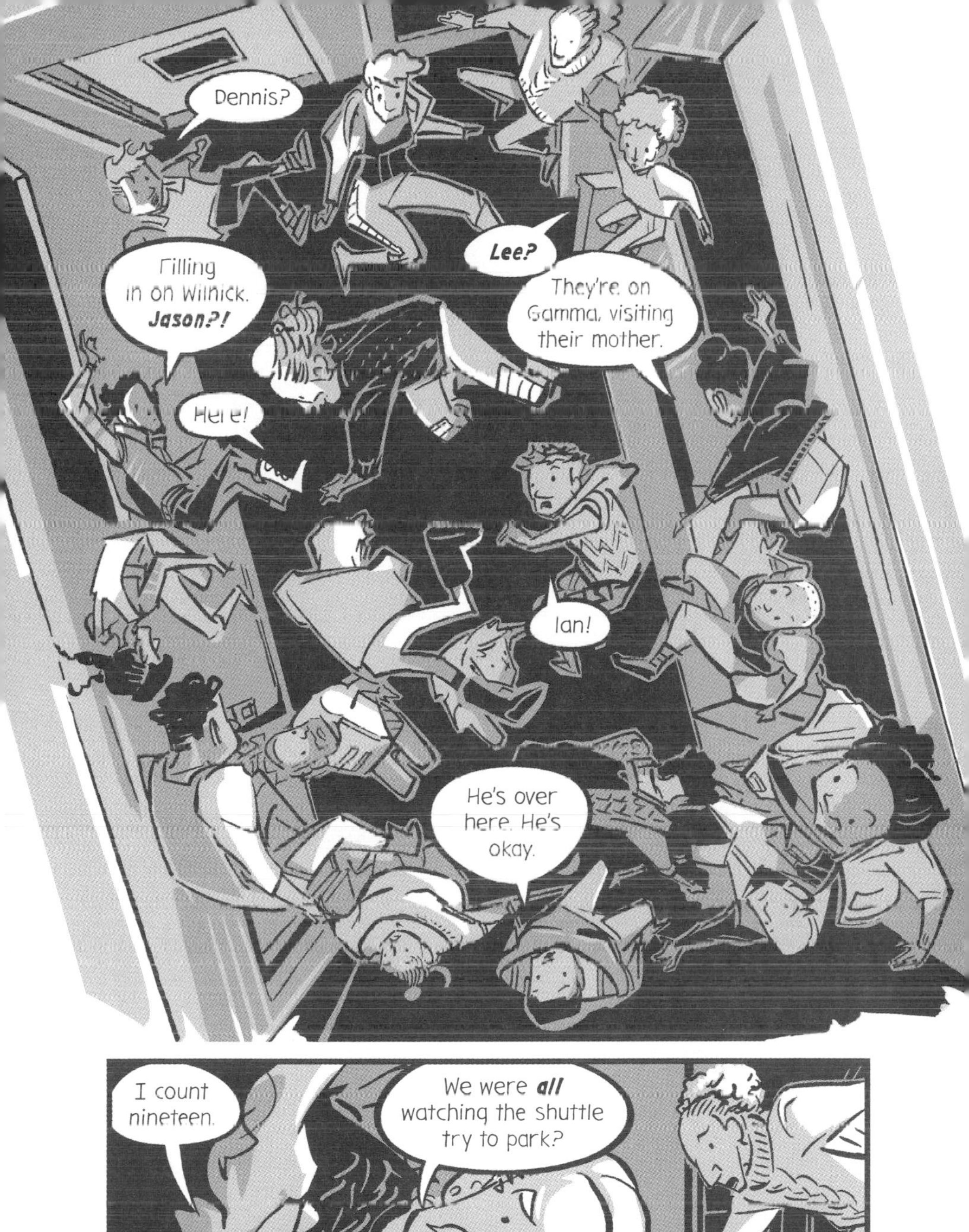
Dennis?
Lee?
Filling in on Wilnick. ***Jason?!***
They're on Gamma, visiting their mother.
Here!
Ian!
He's over here. He's okay.

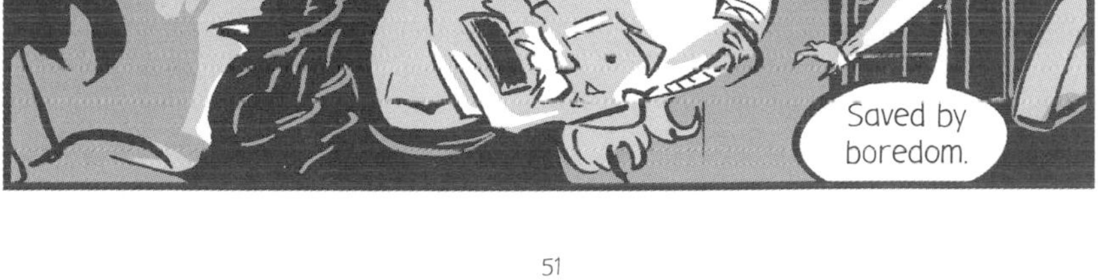
I count nineteen.
We were ***all*** watching the shuttle try to park?
Saved by boredom.

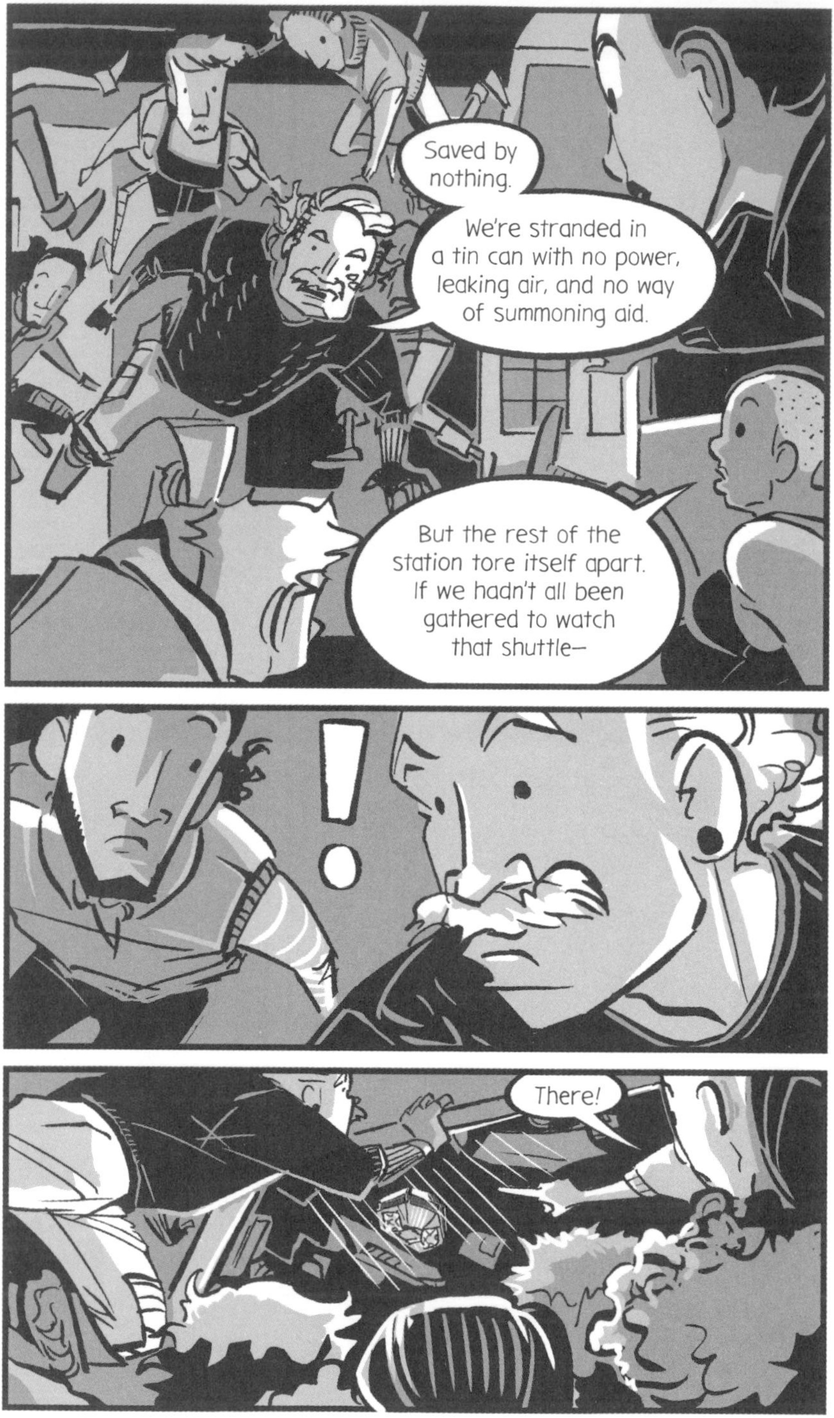
Saved by nothing.
We're stranded in a tin can with no power, leaking air, and no way of summoning aid.
But the rest of the station tore itself apart. If we hadn't all been gathered to watch that shuttle–
!
There!

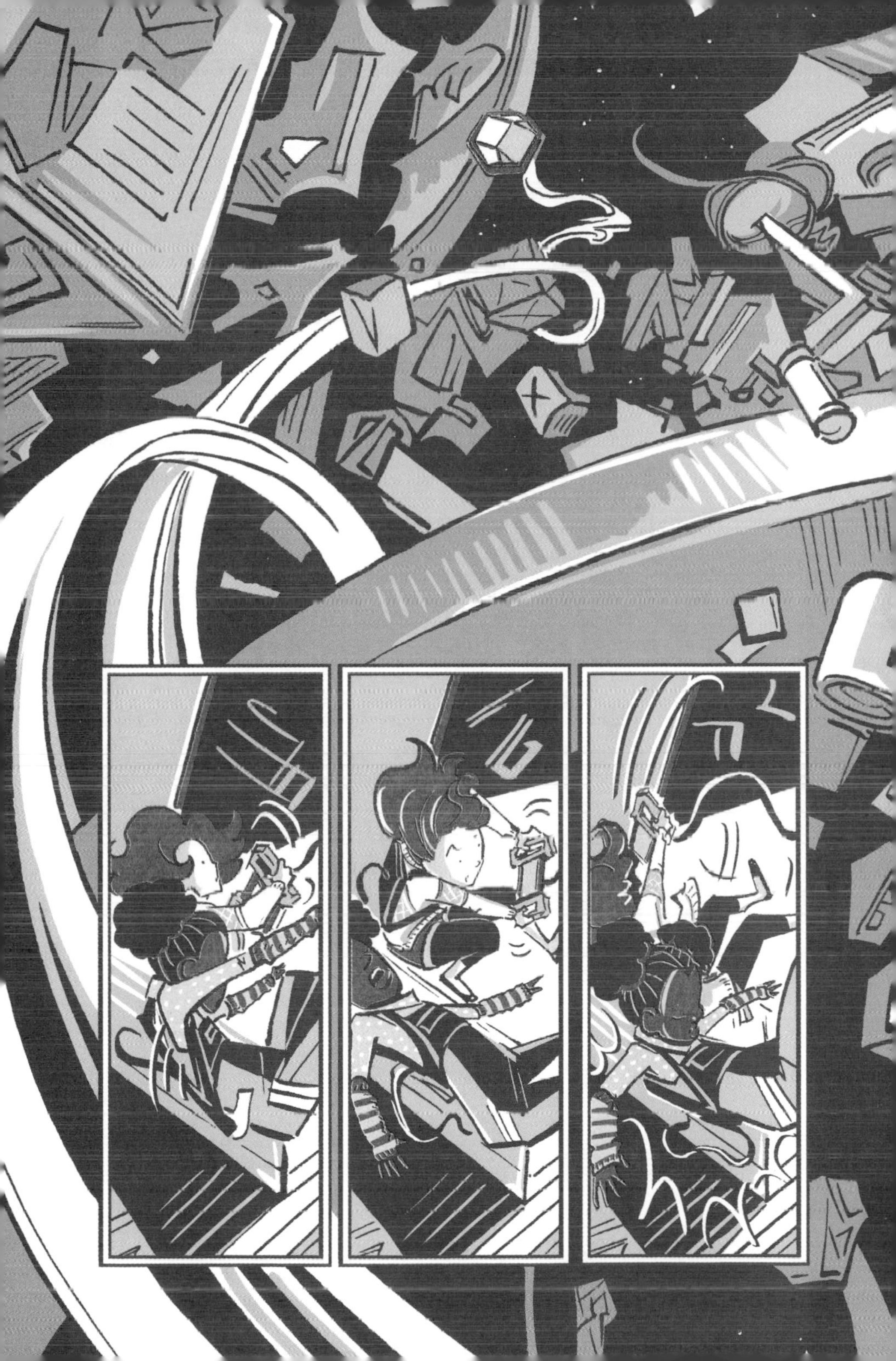

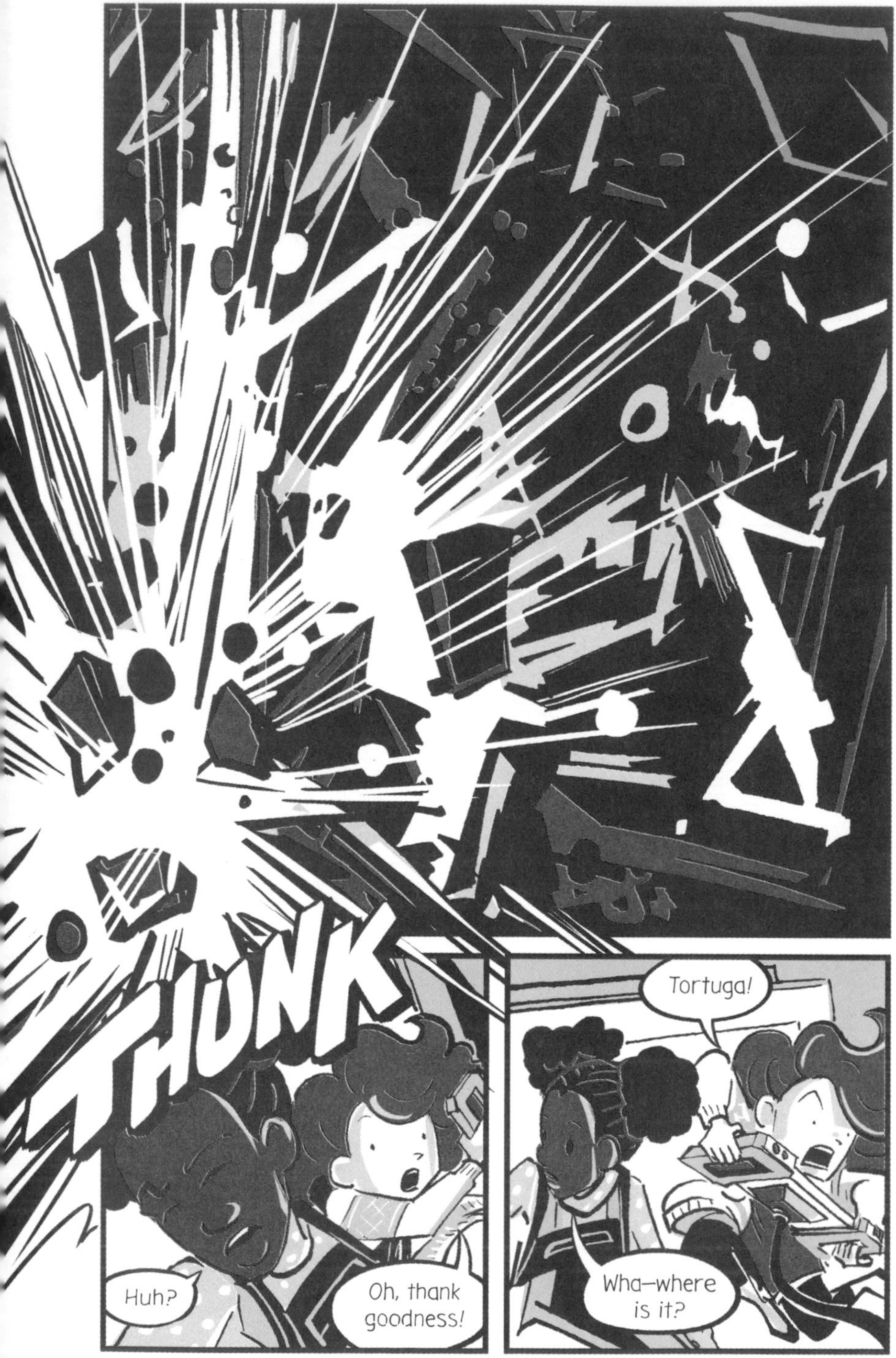
THUNK
Huh?
Oh, thank goodness!
Tortuga!
Wha—where is it?

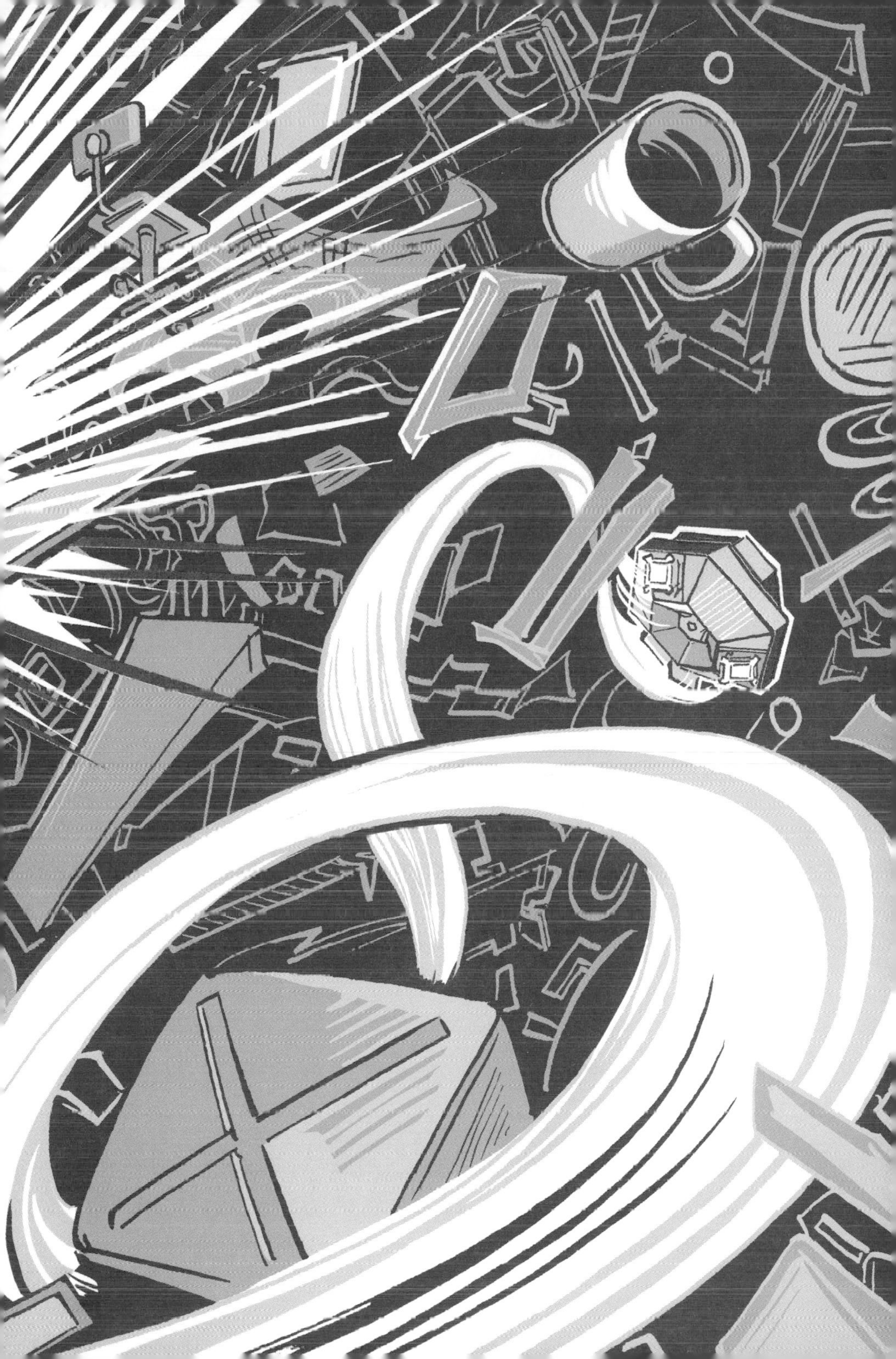

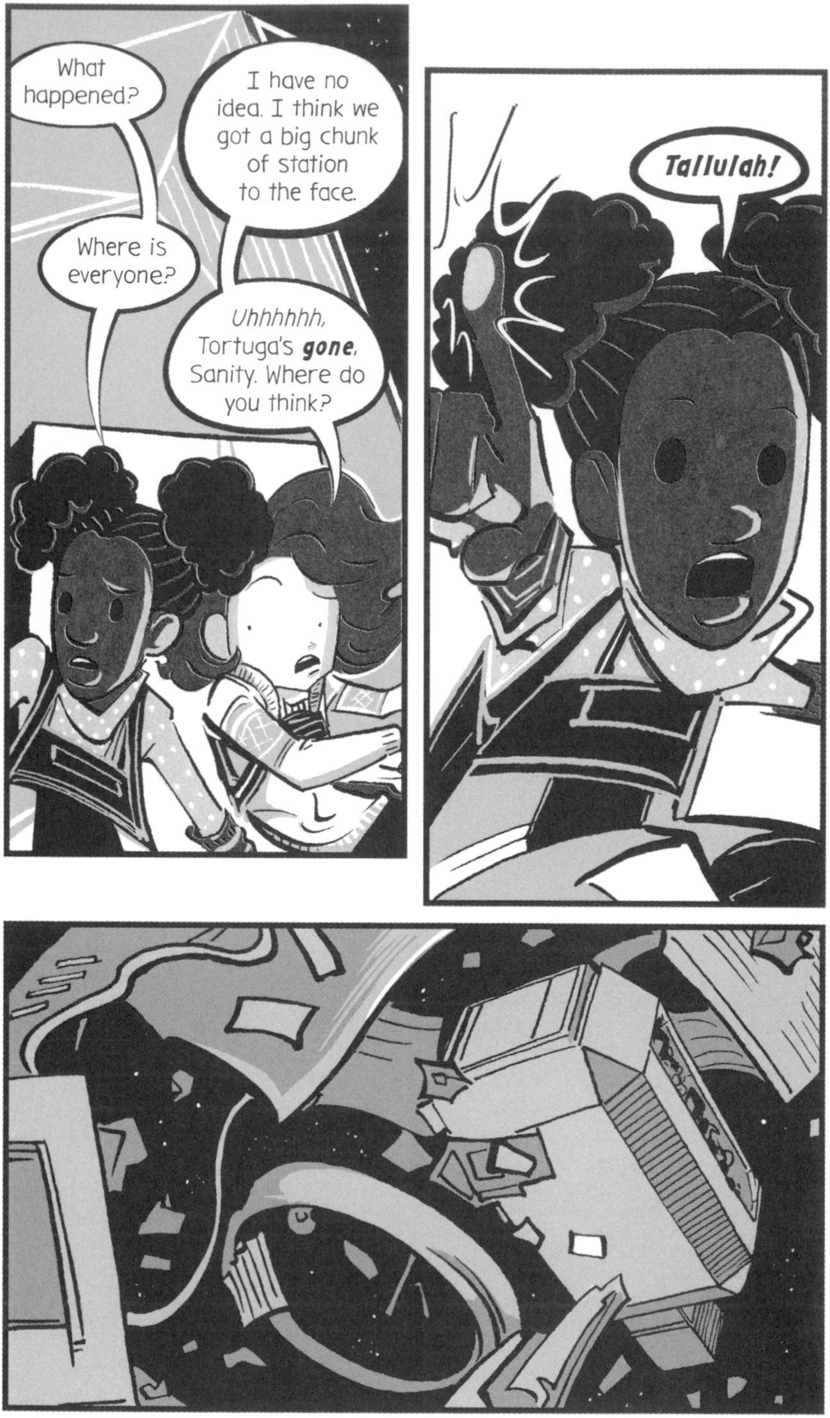
What happened?
I have no idea. I think we got a big chunk of station to the face.
Where is everyone?
Uhhhhhh, Tortuga's **gone**, Sanity. Where do you think?
Tallulah!

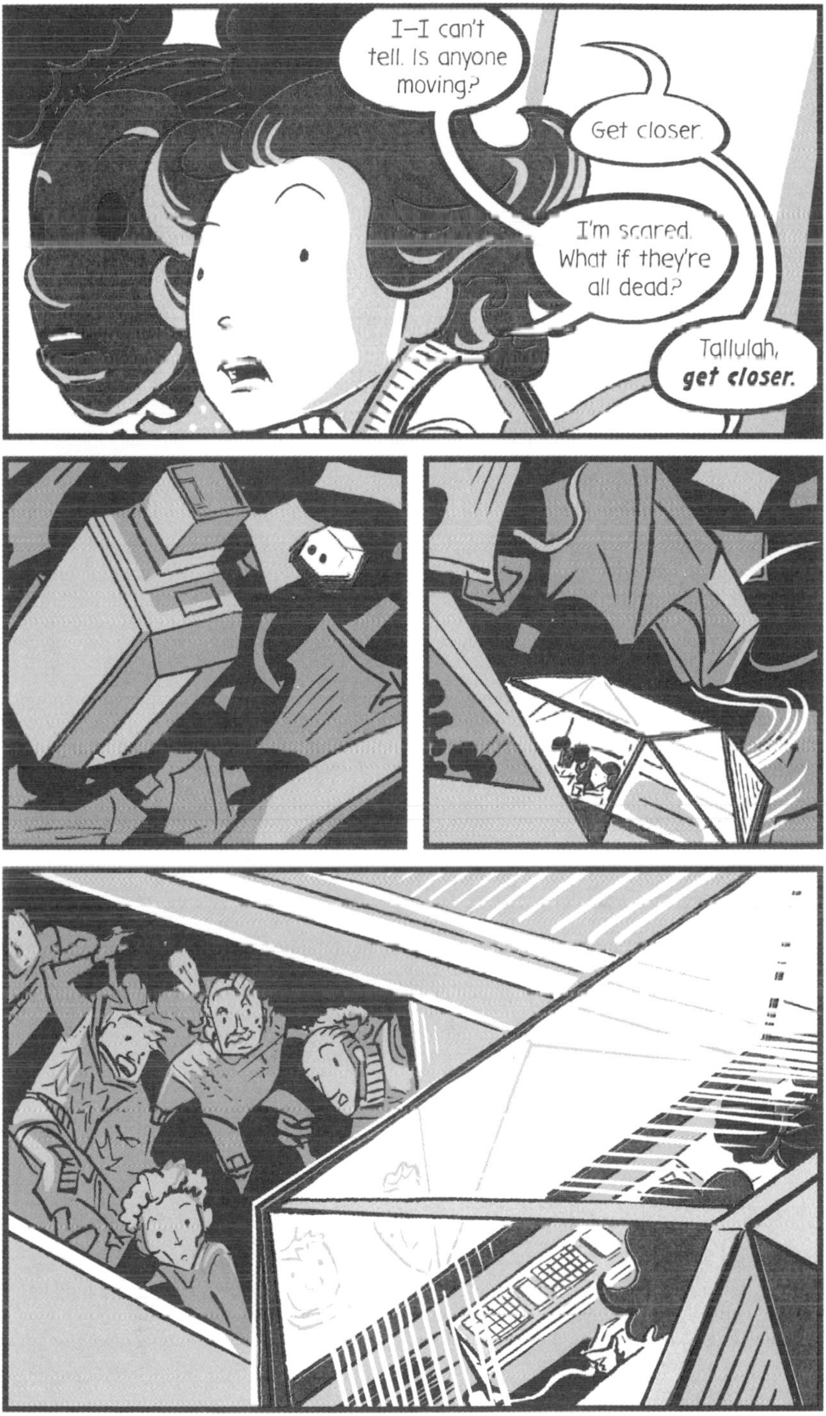
I–I can't tell. Is anyone moving?
Get closer.
I'm scared. What if they're all dead?
Tallulah, **get closer.**

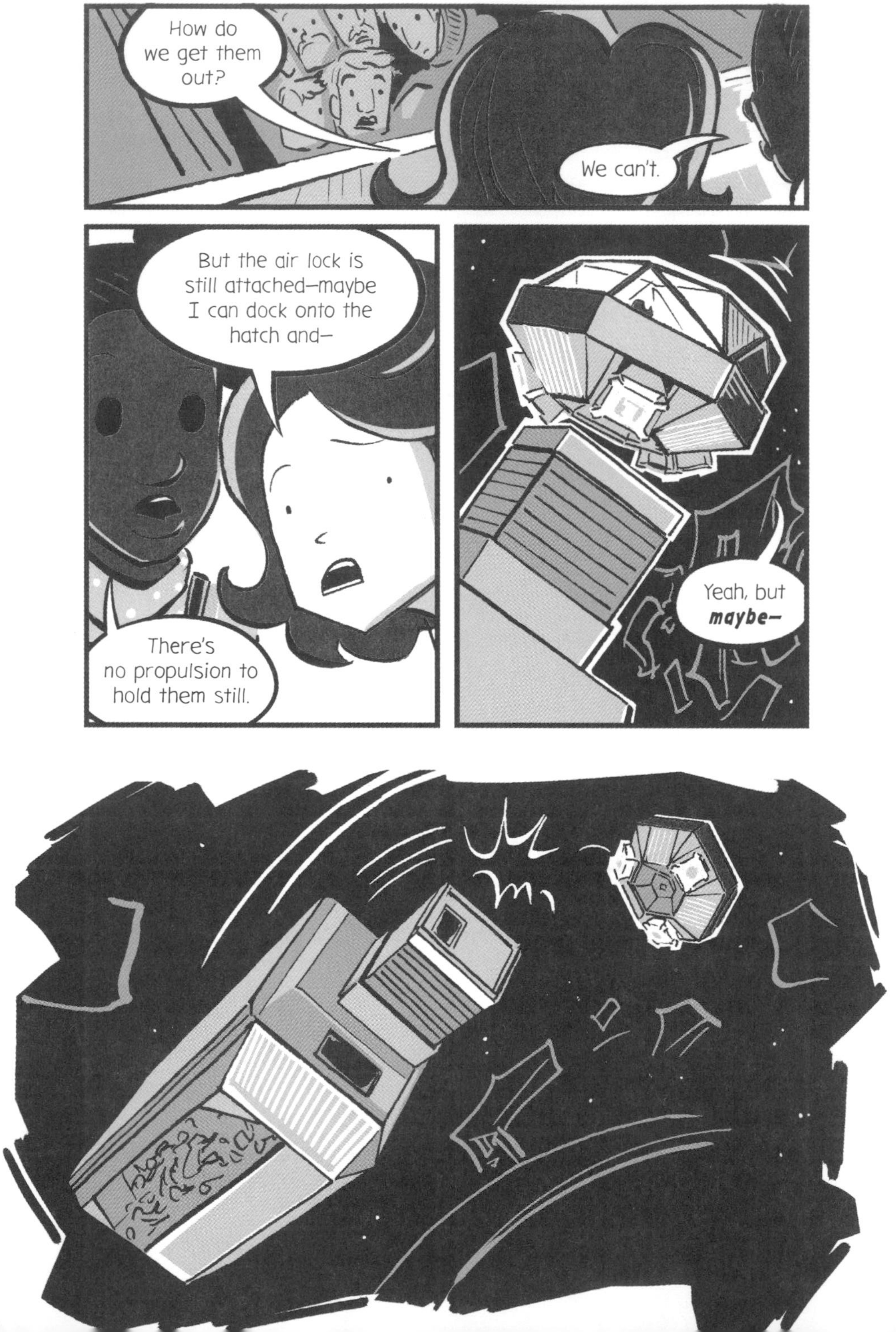
How do we get them out?
We can't.
But the air lock is still attached—maybe I can dock onto the hatch and—
There's no propulsion to hold them still.
Yeah, but **maybe—**

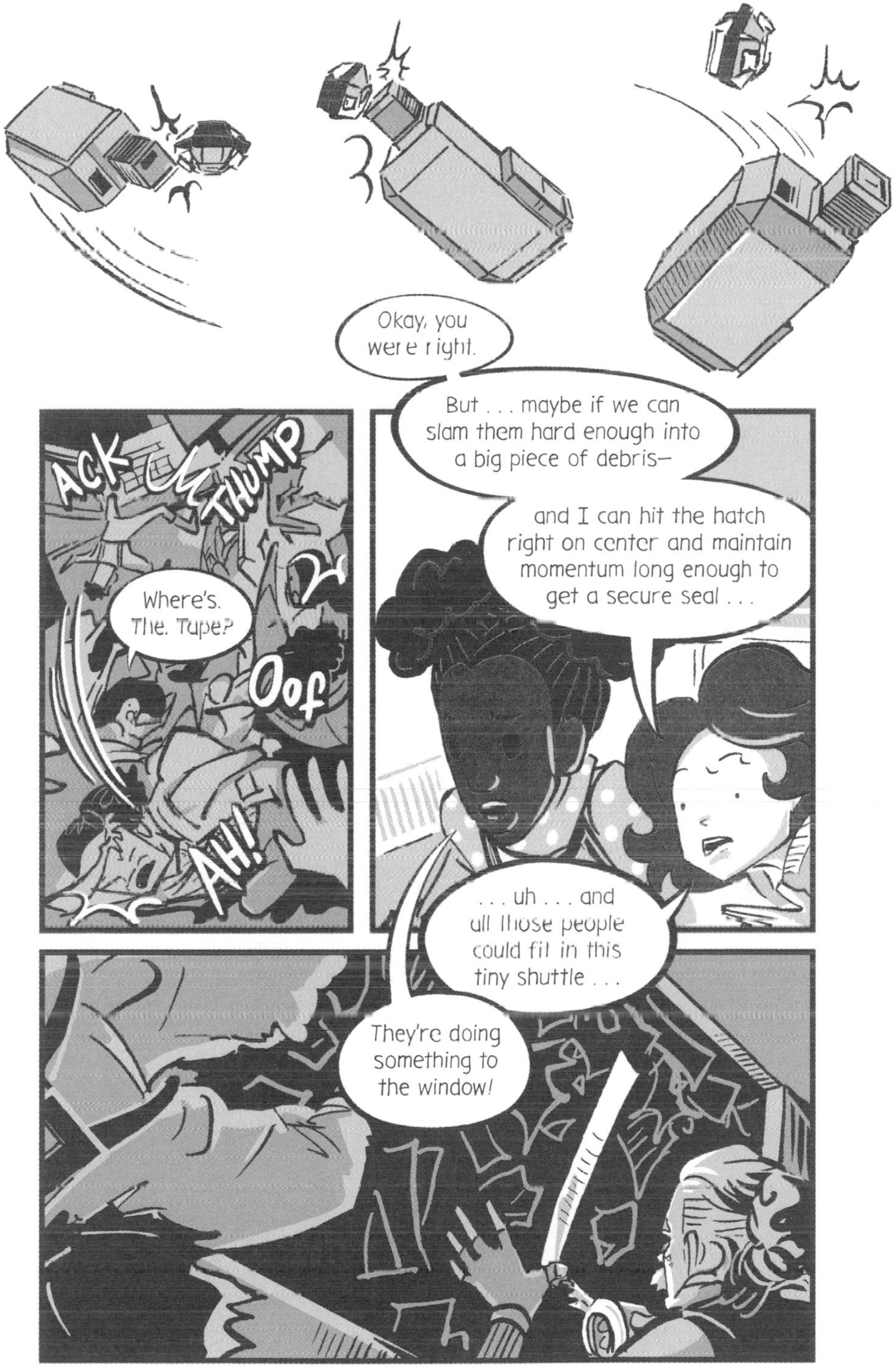
Okay, you were right.
But . . . maybe if we can slam them hard enough into a big piece of debris—
ACK
THUMP
Where's. The. Tape?
Oof
AH!
and I can hit the hatch right on center and maintain momentum long enough to get a secure seal . . .
. . . uh . . . and all those people could fit in this tiny shuttle . . .
They're doing something to the window!

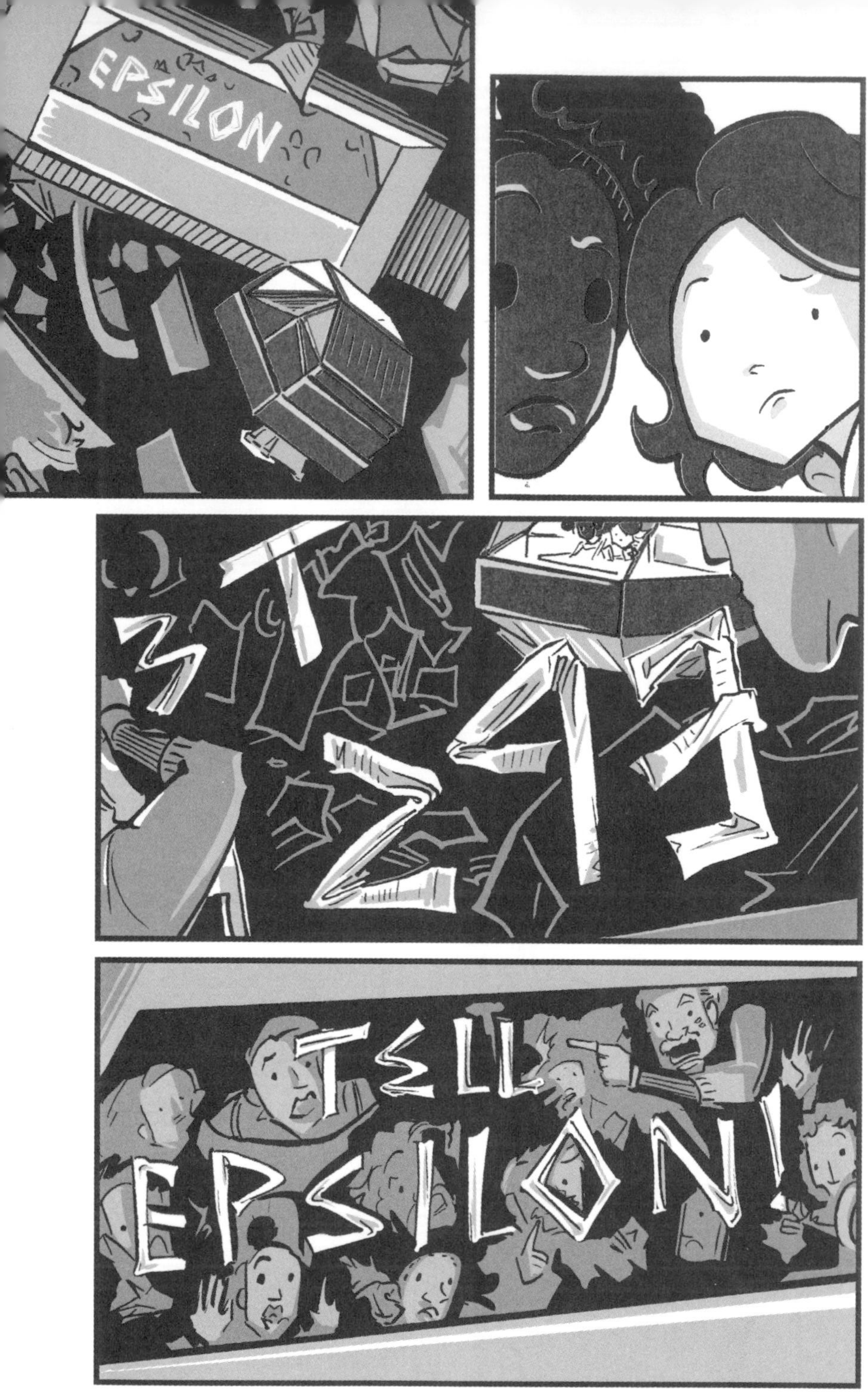
EPSILON
TELL EPSILON!

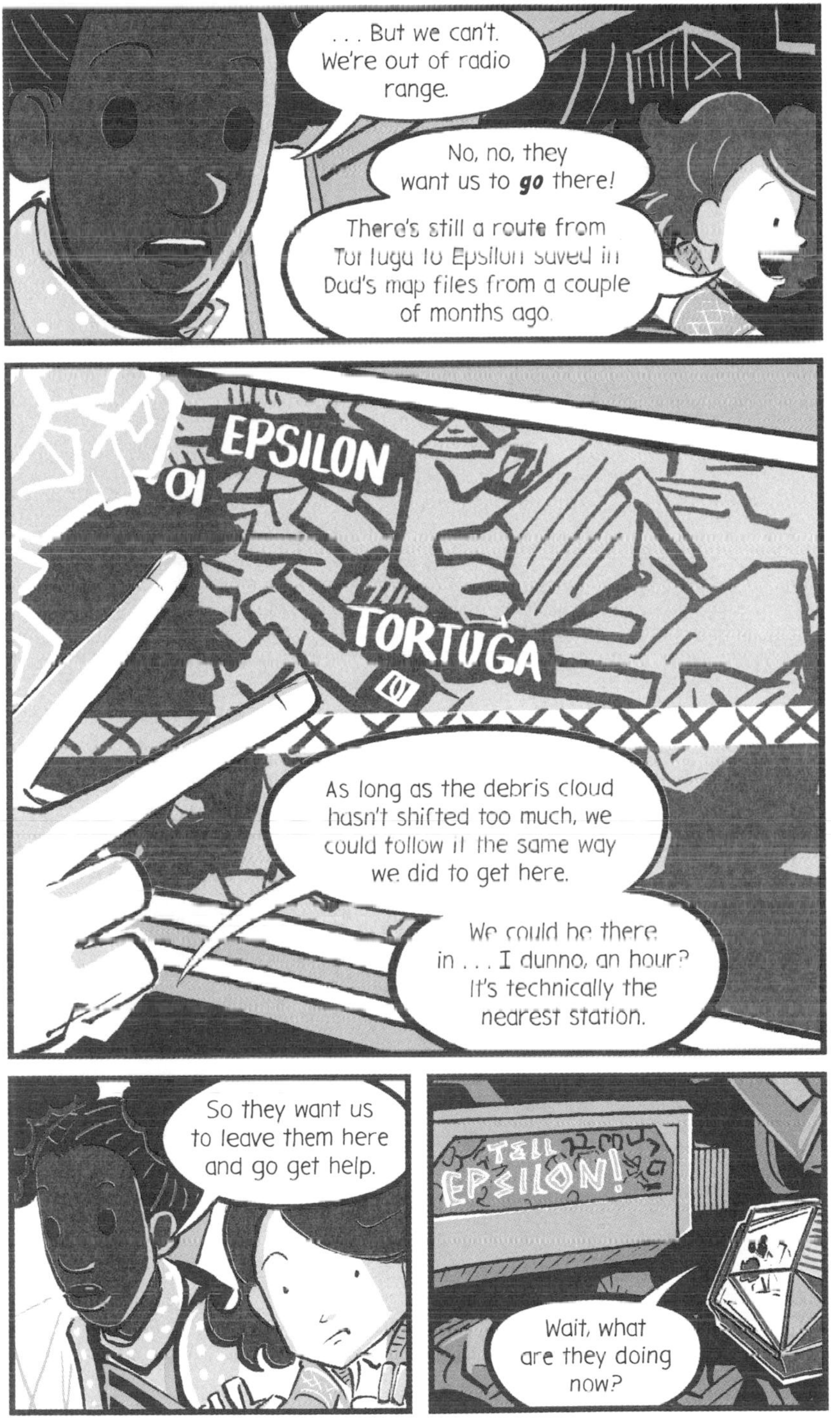

. . . But we can't. We're out of radio range.
No, no, they want us to **go** there!
There's still a route from Tortuga to Epsilon saved in Dad's map files from a couple of months ago.
EPSILON
01
TORTUGA
01
As long as the debris cloud hasn't shifted too much, we could follow it the same way we did to get here.
We could be there in . . . I dunno, an hour? It's technically the nearest station.
So they want us to leave them here and go get help.
TELL EPSILON!
Wait, what are they doing now?

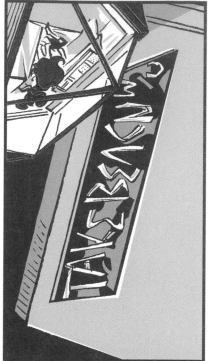

"Take beacon woo"?

Oh! Where's the frequency control?

We need to switch to the emergency channel and scan the immediate area with the directional antenna. There should be . . .

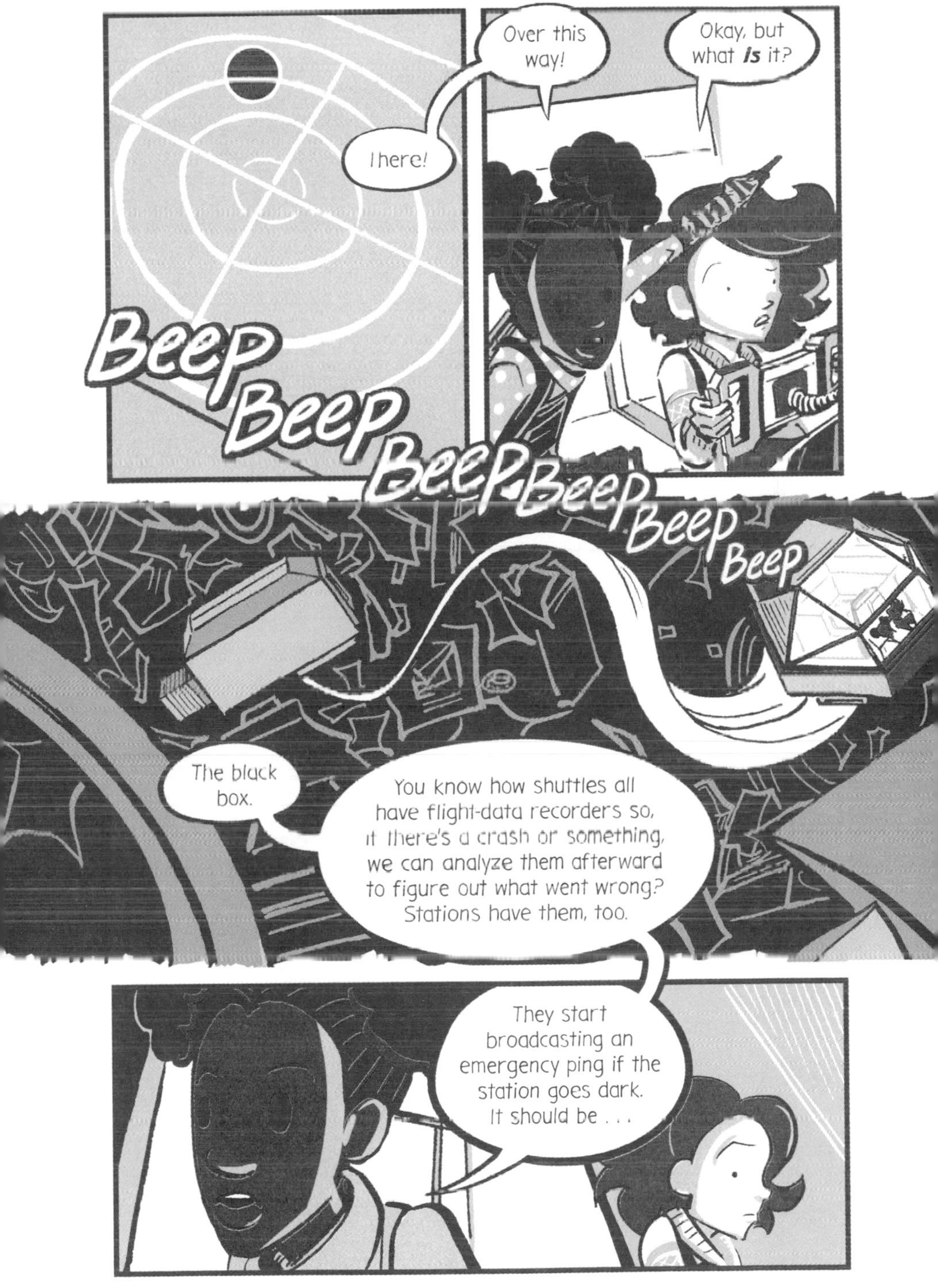
There!
Over this way!
Okay, but what **is** it?
Beep Beep Beep Beep Beep Beep
The black box.
You know how shuttles all have flight-data recorders so, if there's a crash or something, we can analyze them afterward to figure out what went wrong? Stations have them, too.
They start broadcasting an emergency ping if the station goes dark. It should be . . .

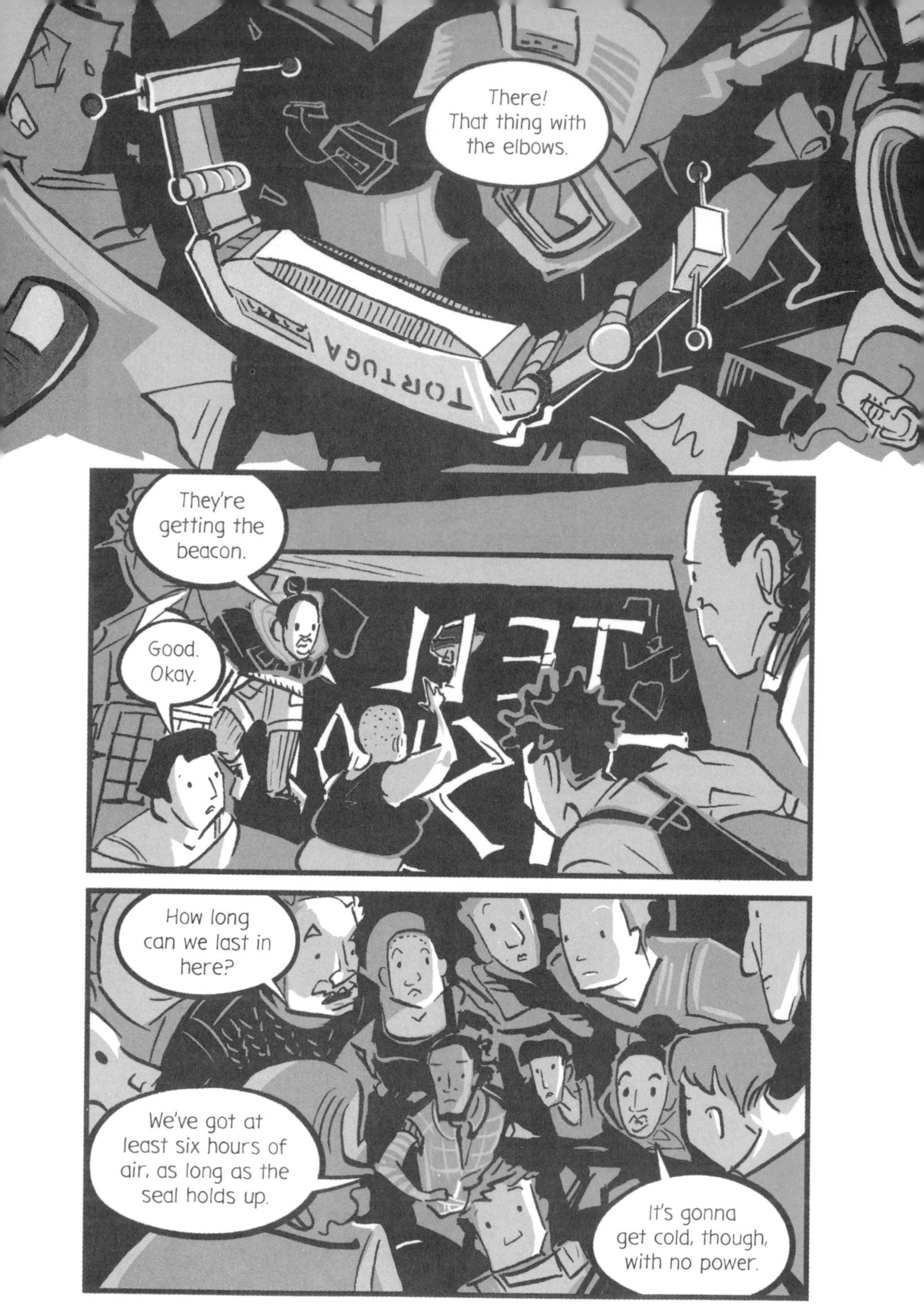
There! That thing with the elbows.
TORTUGA
They're getting the beacon.
Good. Okay.
How long can we last in here?
We've got at least six hours of air, as long as the seal holds up.
It's gonna get cold, though, with no power.

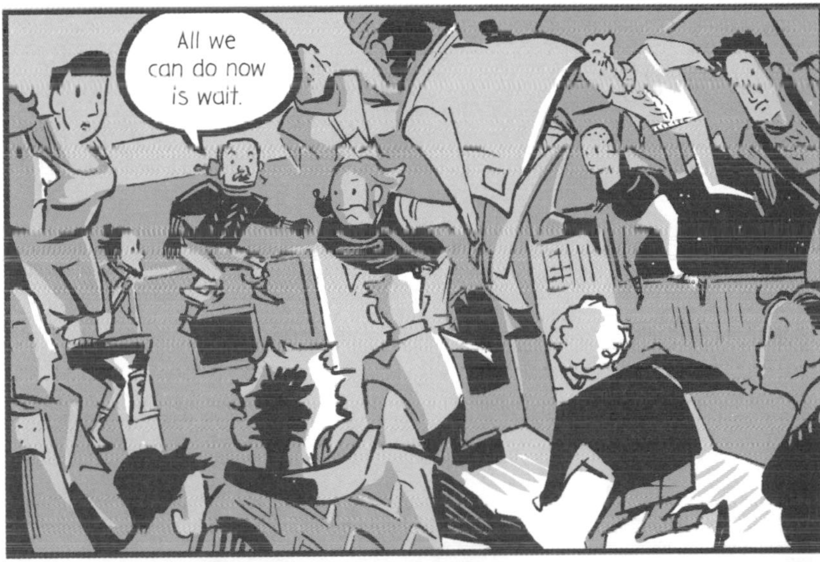
All we can do now is wait.

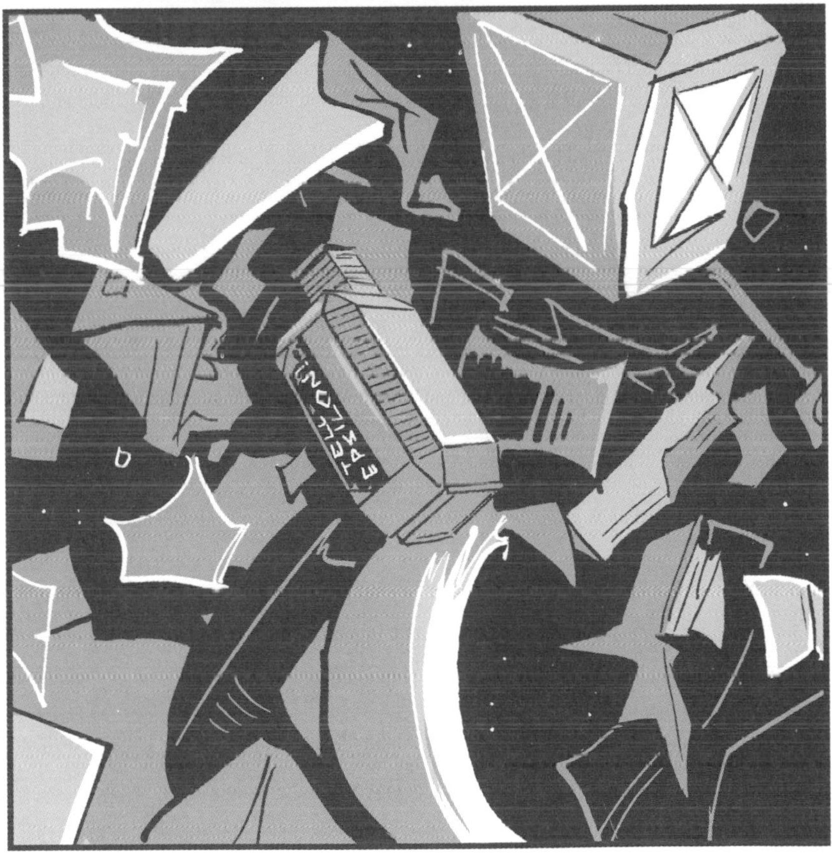

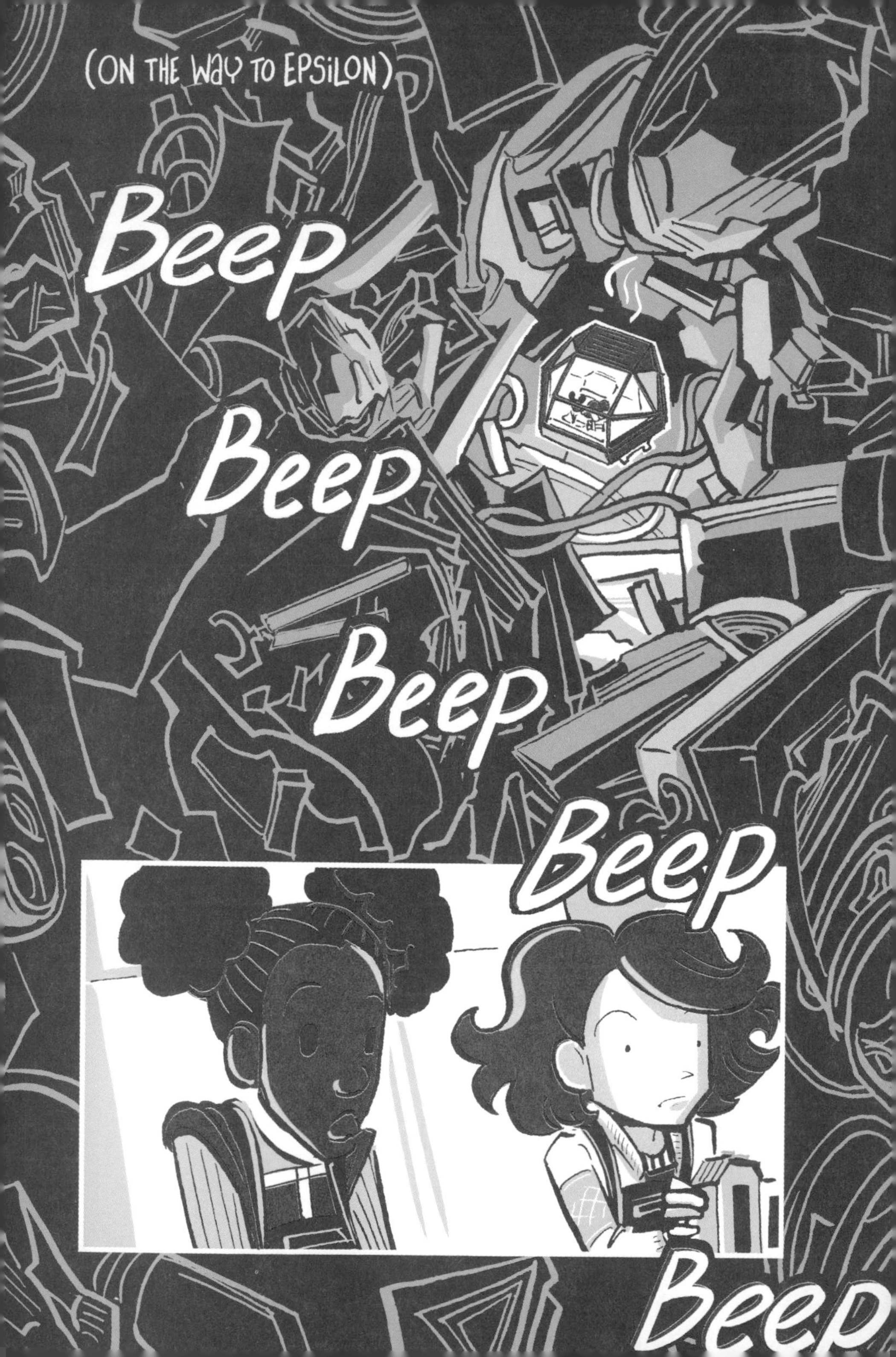
(ON THE WAY TO EPSILON)
Beep
Beep
Beep
Beep
Beep

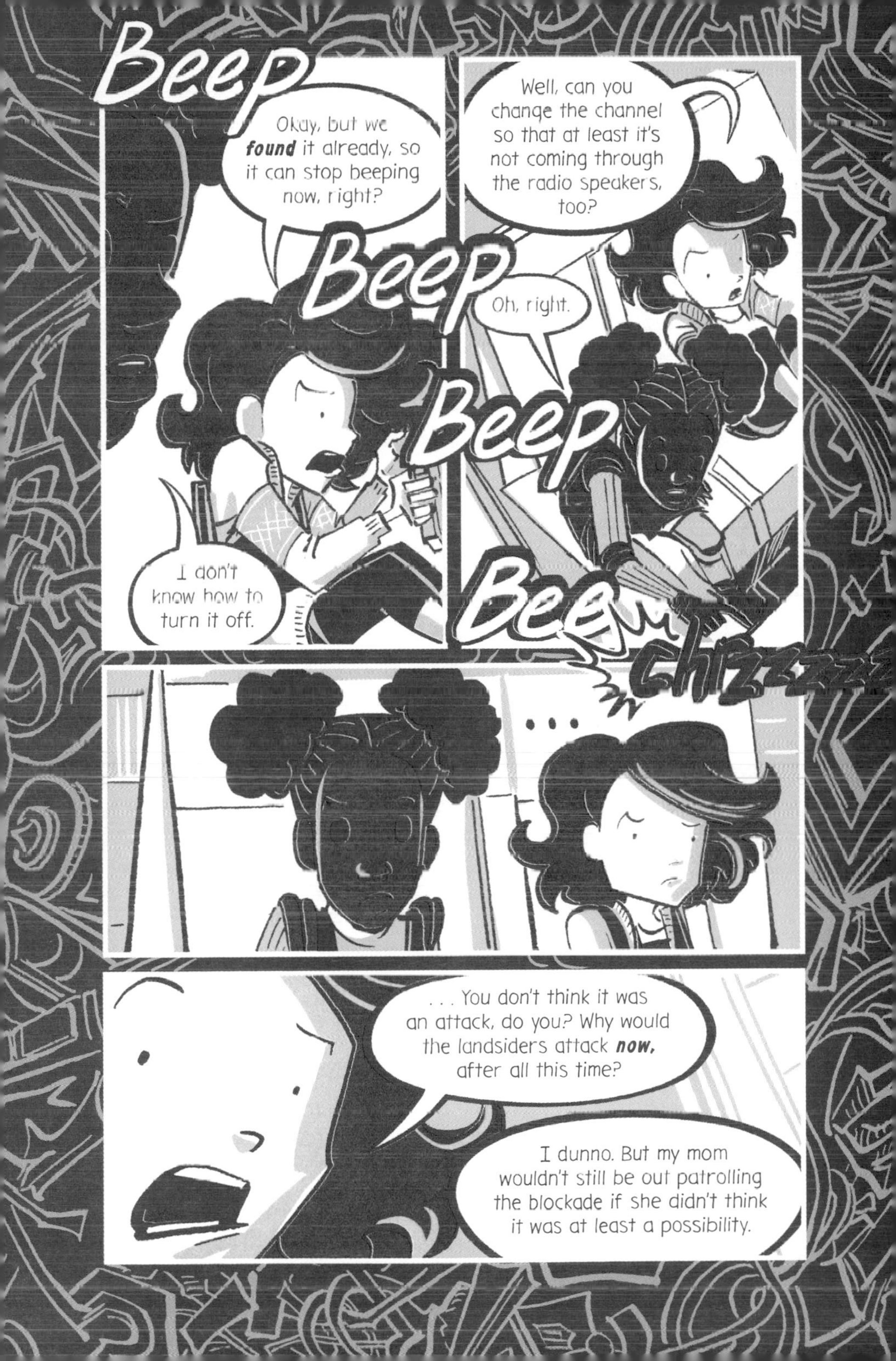
Beep
Okay, but we **found** it already, so it can stop beeping now, right?
I don't know how to turn it off.
Beep
Well, can you change the channel so that at least it's not coming through the radio speakers, too?
Oh, right.
Beep
Bee
chzzzzz
...
. . . You don't think it was an attack, do you? Why would the landsiders attack **now,** after all this time?
I dunno. But my mom wouldn't still be out patrolling the blockade if she didn't think it was at least a possibility.

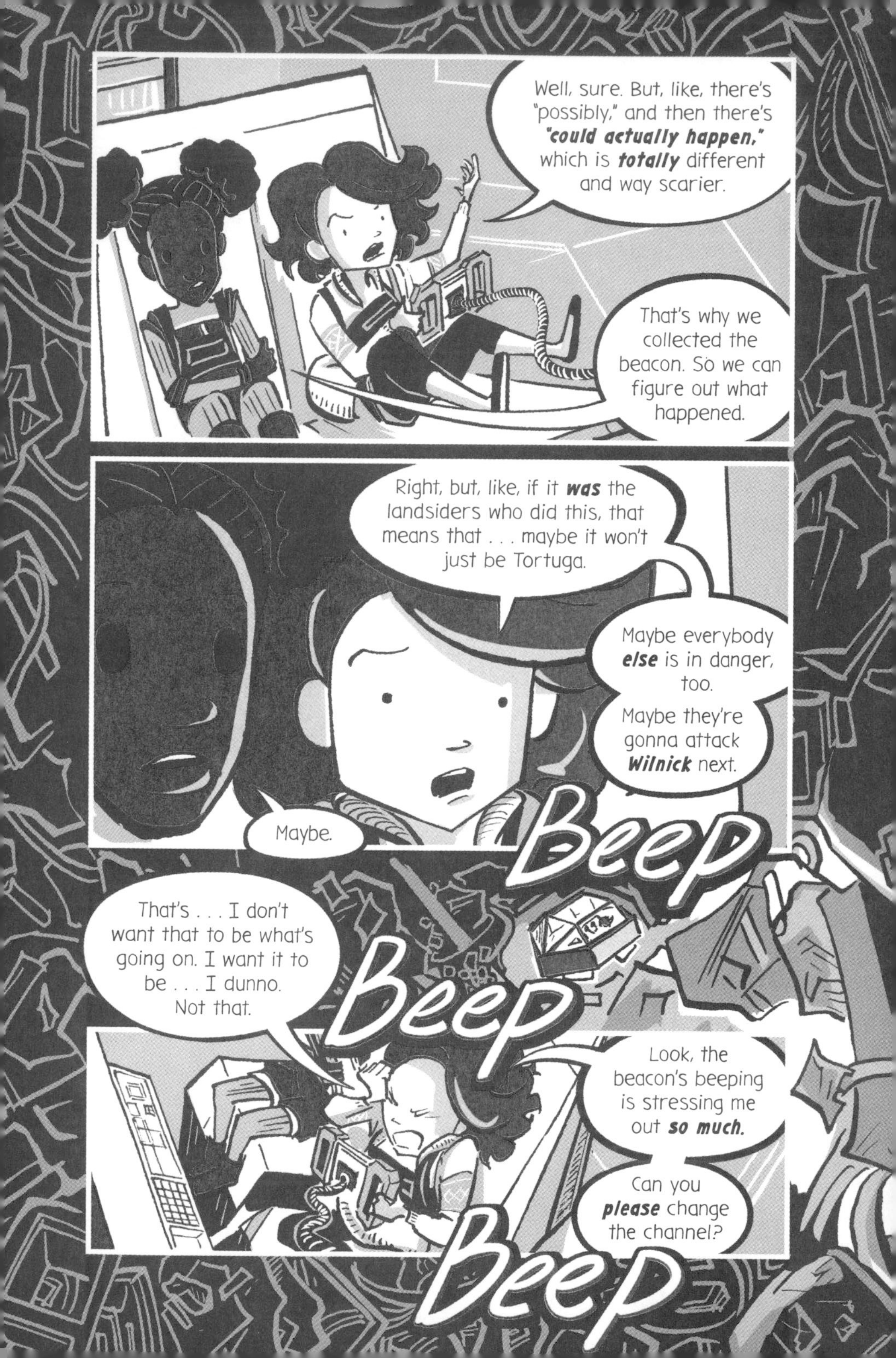
Well, sure. But, like, there's "possibly," and then there's ***"could actually happen,"*** which is ***totally*** different and way scarier.
That's why we collected the beacon. So we can figure out what happened.
Right, but, like, if it ***was*** the landsiders who did this, that means that . . . maybe it won't just be Tortuga.
Maybe everybody ***else*** is in danger, too.
Maybe they're gonna attack ***Wilnick*** next.
Maybe.
Beep
That's . . . I don't want that to be what's going on. I want it to be . . . I dunno. Not that.
Beep
Look, the beacon's beeping is stressing me out ***so much.***
Can you ***please*** change the channel?
Beep

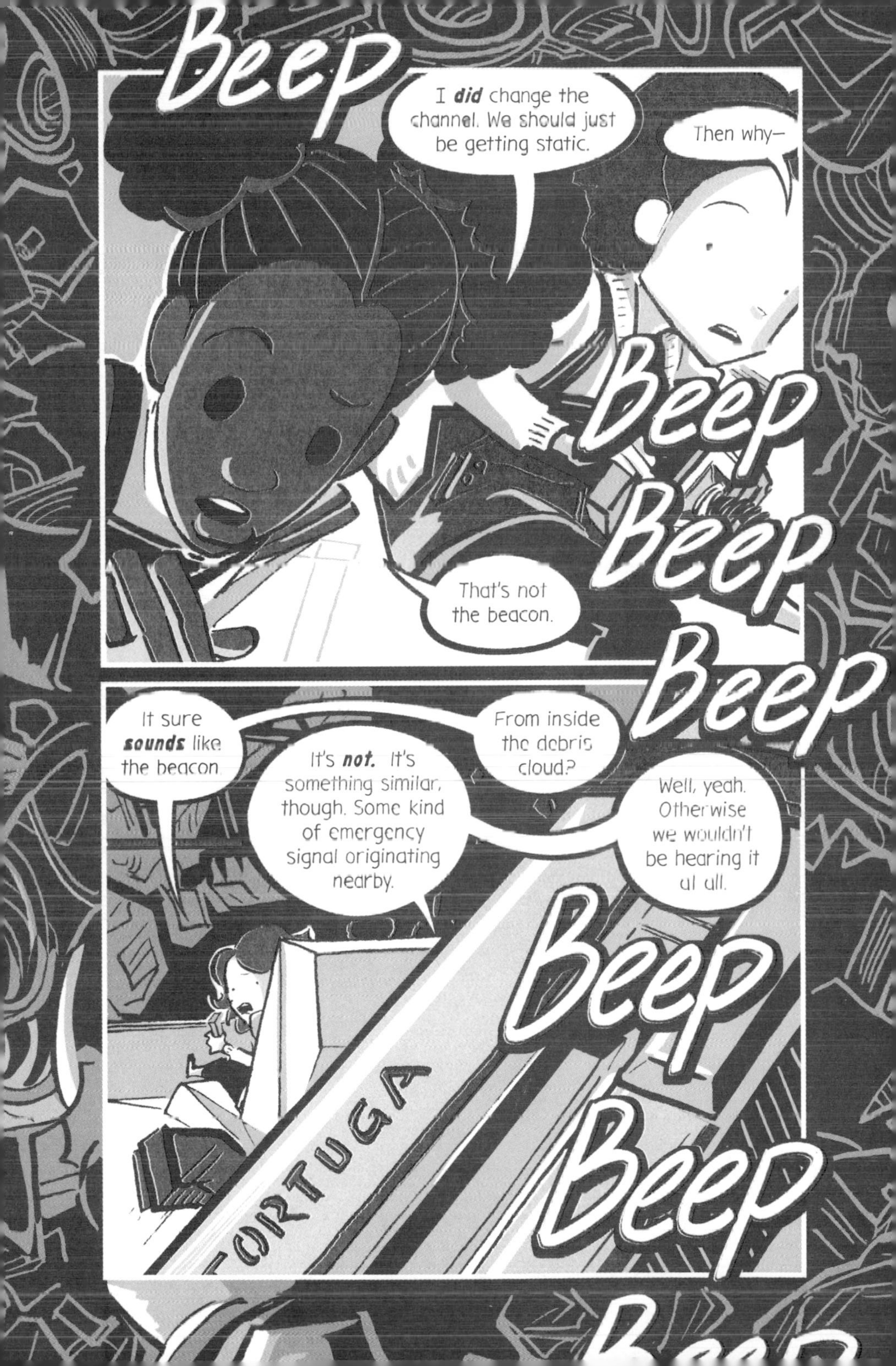
Beep
I did change the channel. We should just be getting static.
Then why—
Beep
Beep
That's not the beacon.
Beep
It sure sounds like the beacon.
It's not. It's something similar, though. Some kind of emergency signal originating nearby.
From inside the debris cloud?
Well, yeah. Otherwise we wouldn't be hearing it at all.
Beep
TORTUGA
Beep

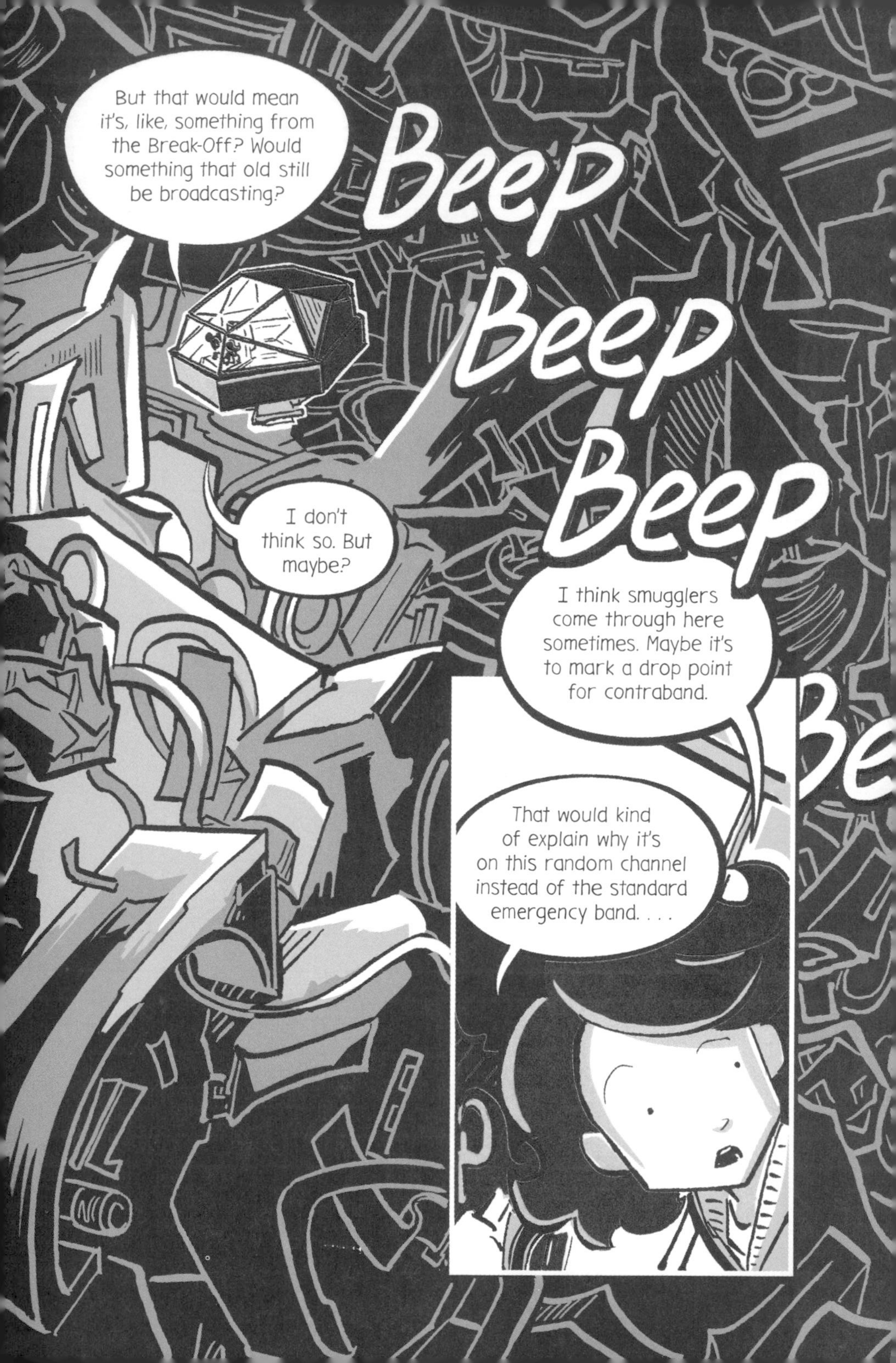
But that would mean it's, like, something from the Break-Off? Would something that old still be broadcasting?
Beep
Beep
Beep
I don't think so. But maybe?
I think smugglers come through here sometimes. Maybe it's to mark a drop point for contraband.
That would kind of explain why it's on this random channel instead of the standard emergency band. . . .

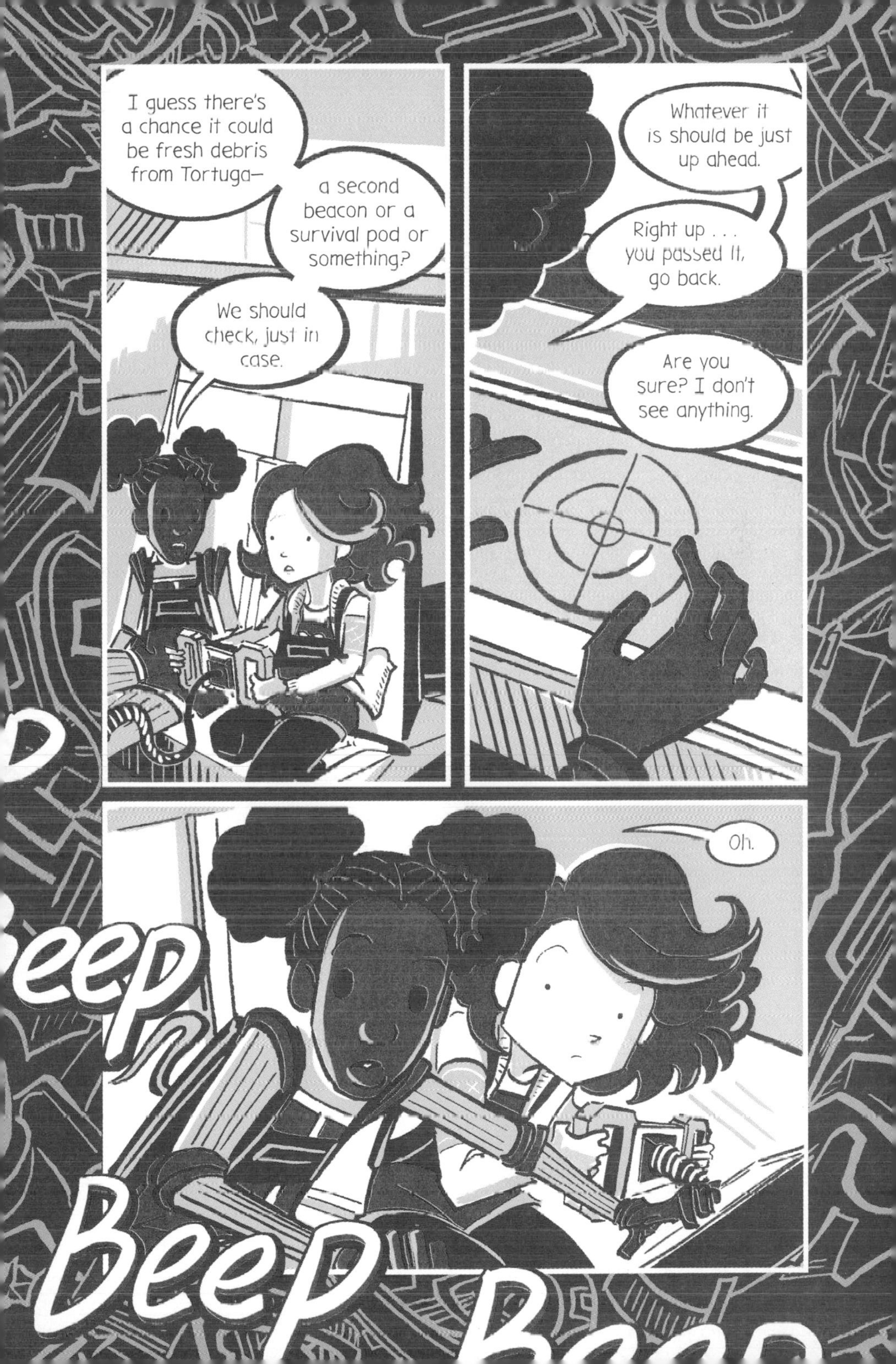
I guess there's a chance it could be fresh debris from Tortuga—
a second beacon or a survival pod or something?
We should check, just in case.
Whatever it is should be just up ahead.
Right up . . . you passed it, go back.
Are you sure? I don't see anything.
Oh.
Beep
Beep

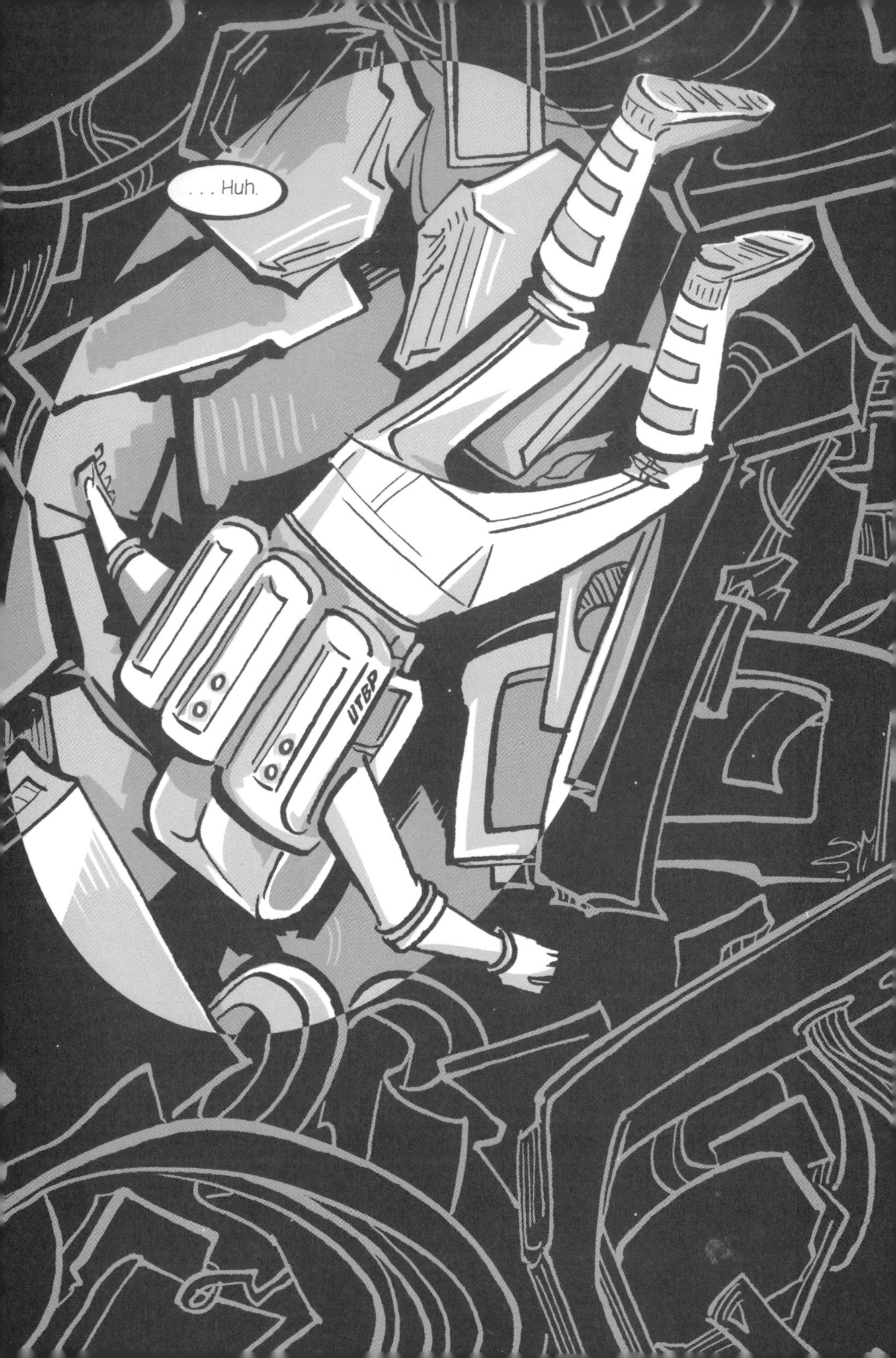
. . . Huh.
UTBP

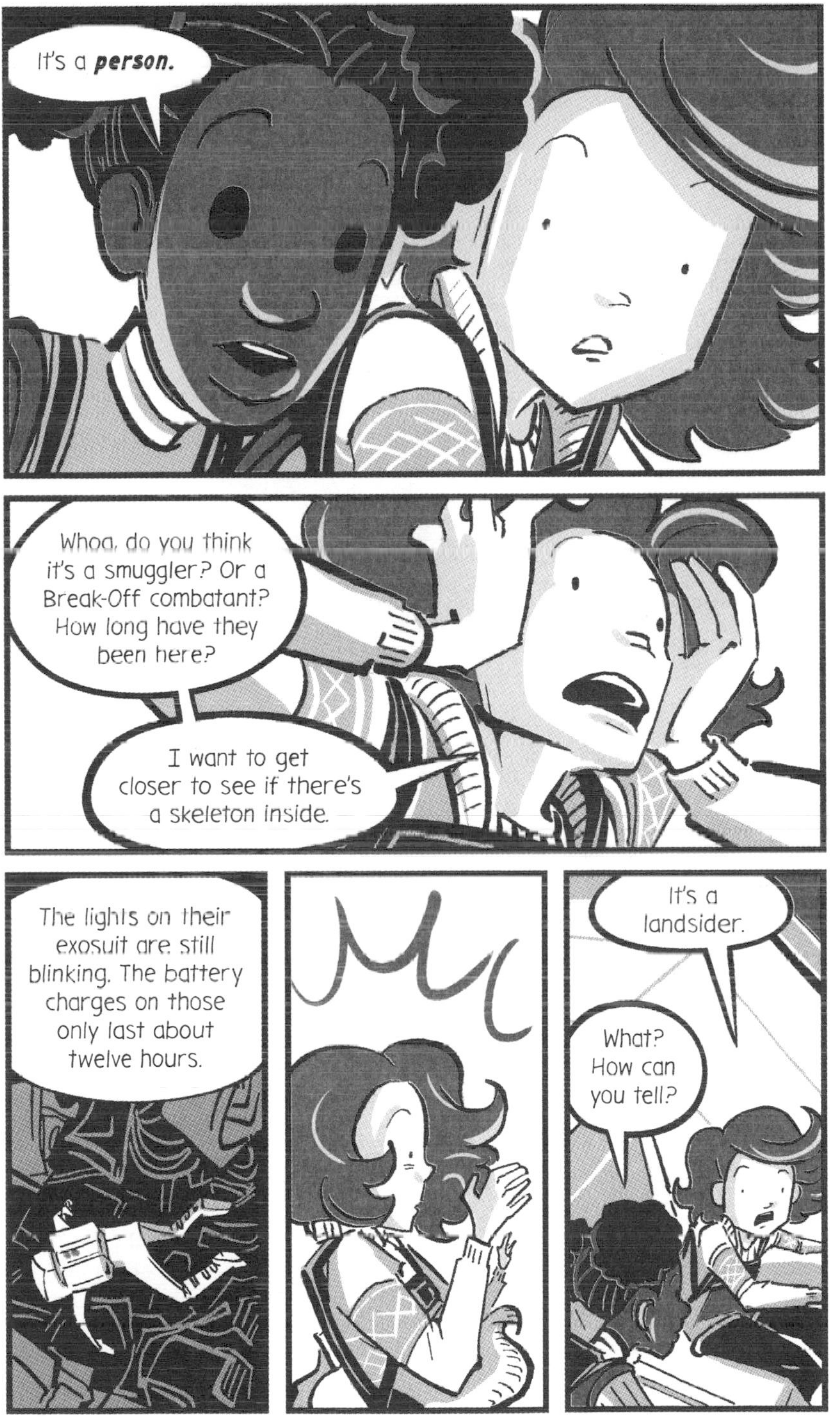
It's a **person.**
Whoa, do you think it's a smuggler? Or a Break-Off combatant? How long have they been here?
I want to get closer to see if there's a skeleton inside.
The lights on their exosuit are still blinking. The battery charges on those only last about twelve hours.
It's a landsider.
What? How can you tell?

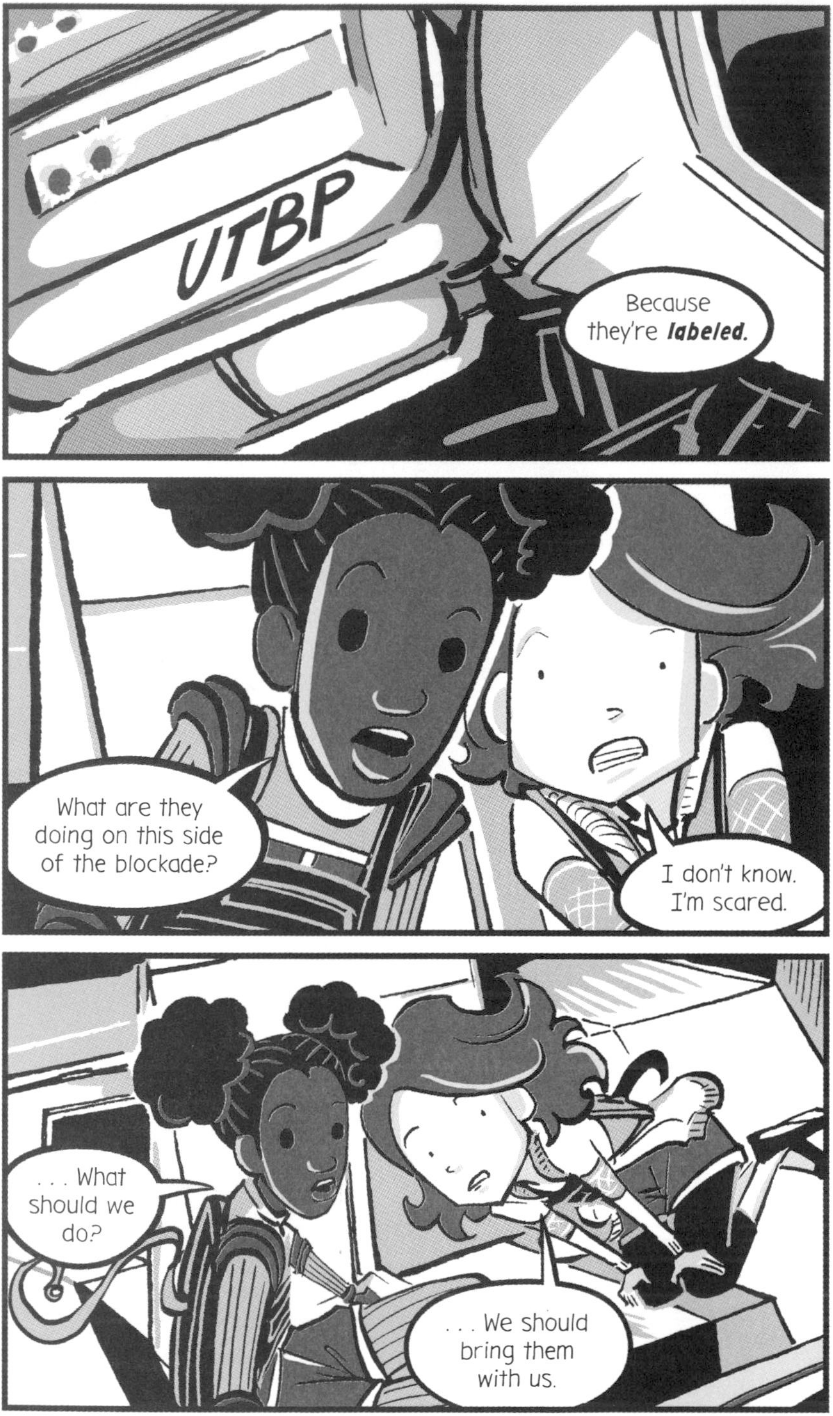
UTBP
Because they're ***labeled.***
What are they doing on this side of the blockade?
I don't know. I'm scared.
. . . What should we do?
. . . We should bring them with us.

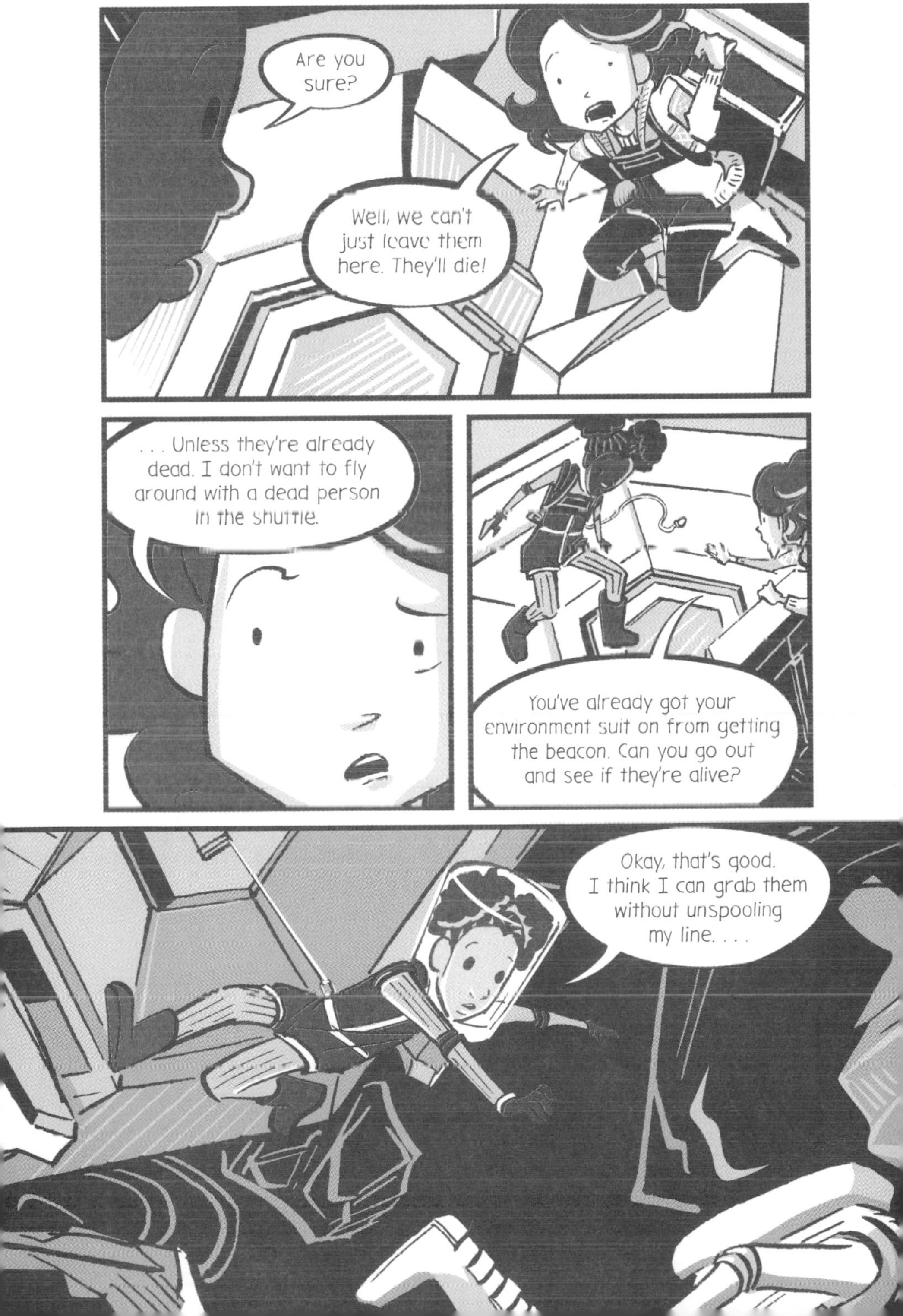
Are you sure?
Well, we can't just leave them here. They'll die!
. . . Unless they're already dead. I don't want to fly around with a dead person in the shuttle.
You've already got your environment suit on from getting the beacon. Can you go out and see if they're alive?
Okay, that's good. I think I can grab them without unspooling my line. . . .

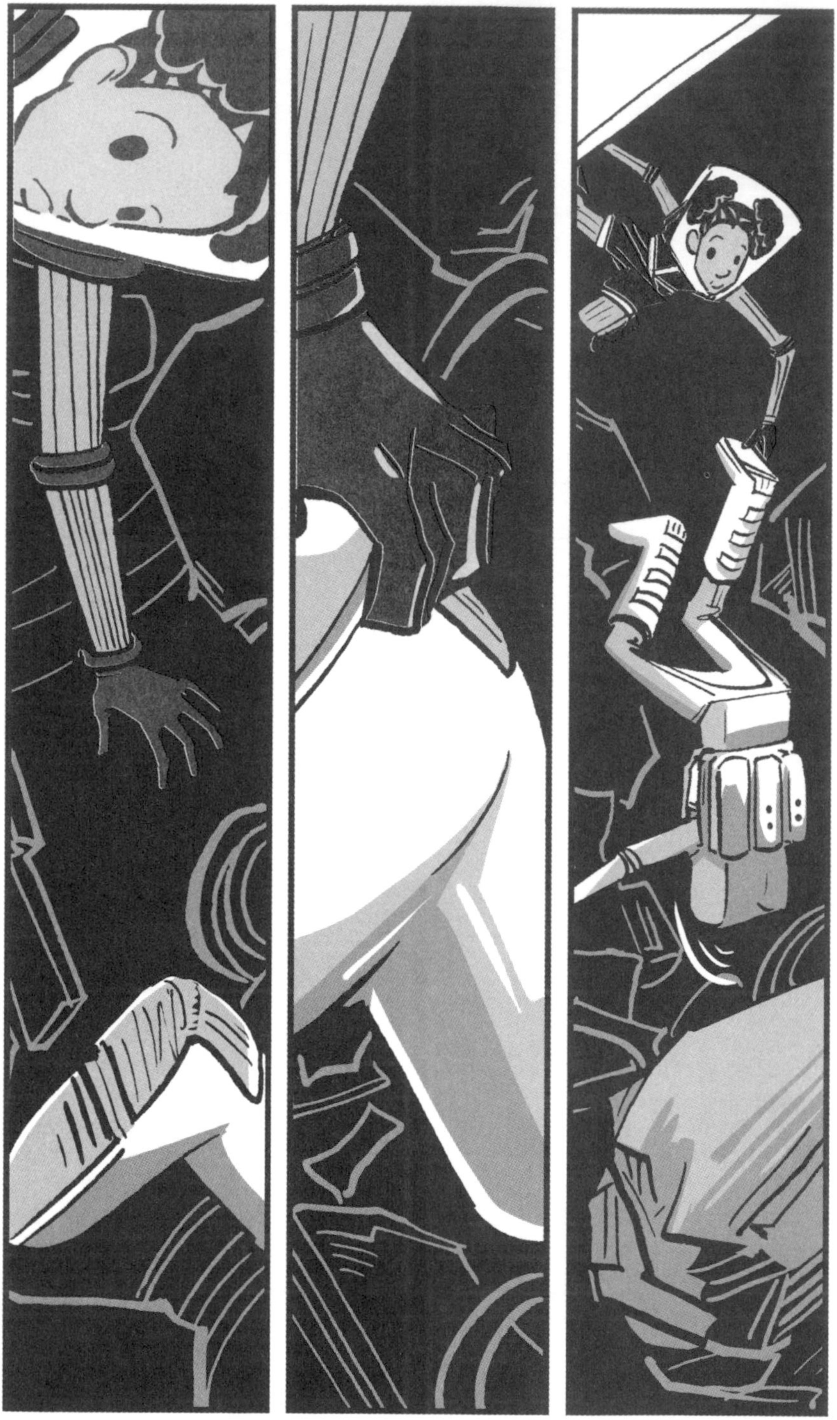

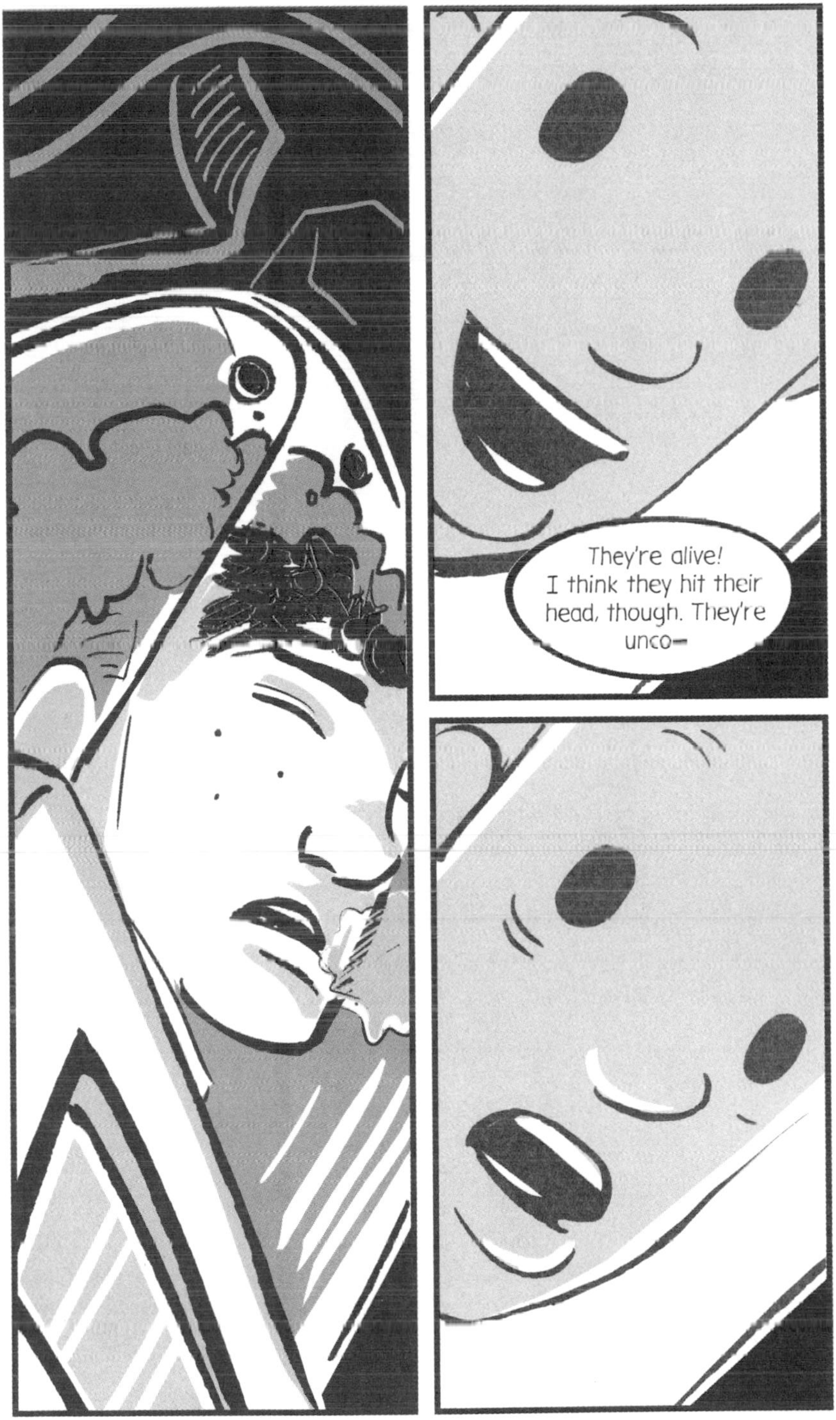
They're alive! I think they hit their head, though. They're unco—

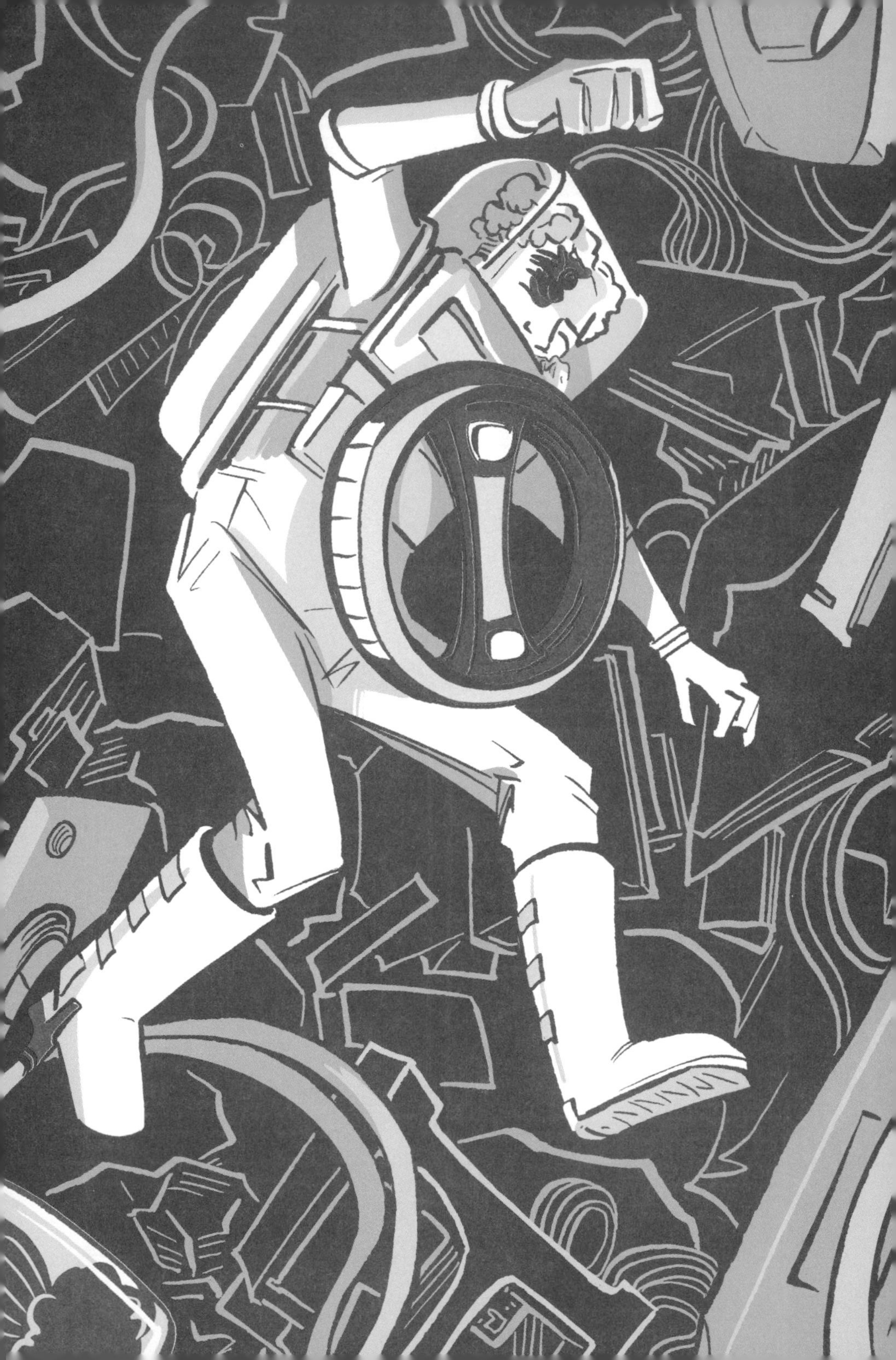

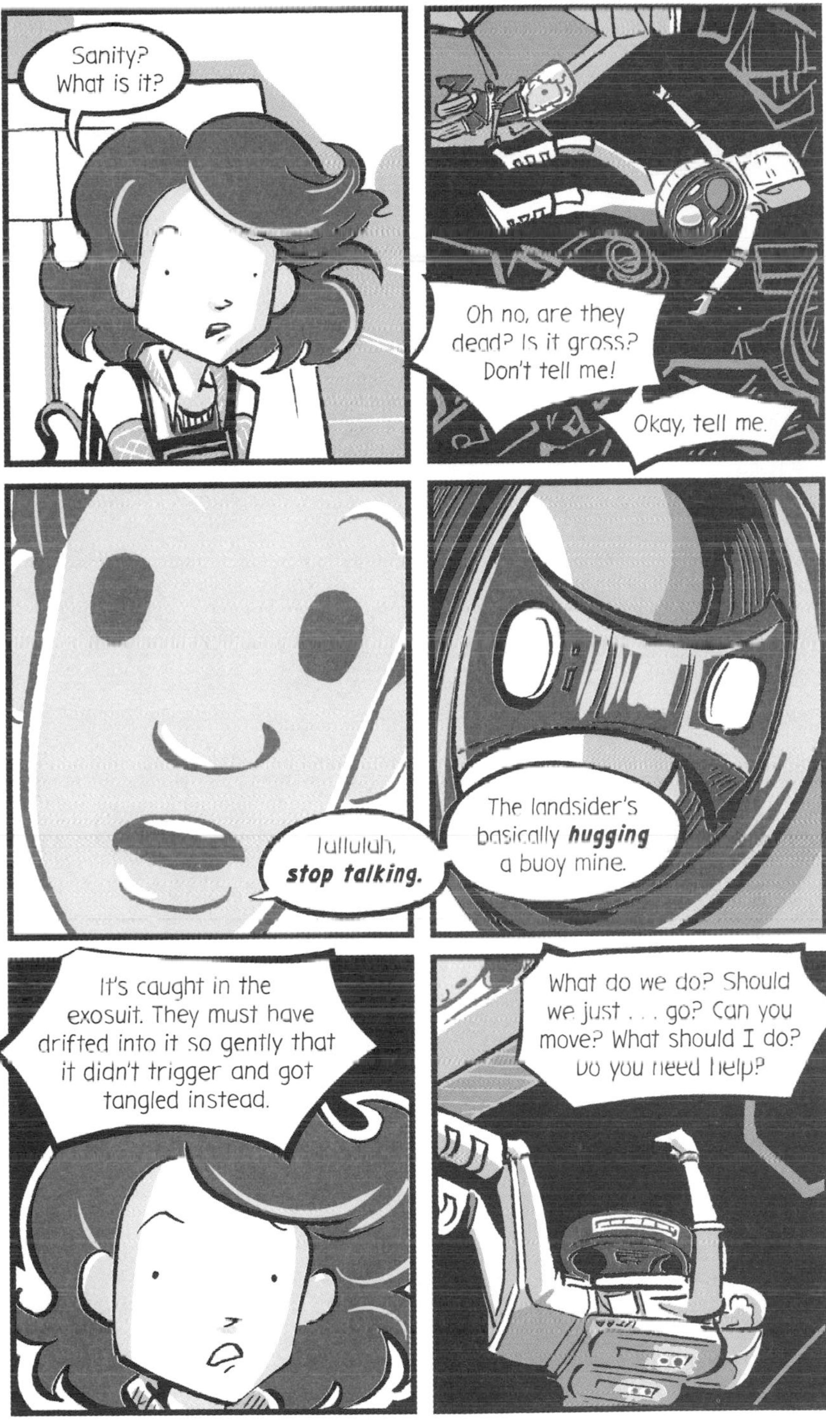
Sanity? What is it?
Oh no, are they dead? Is it gross? Don't tell me!
Okay, tell me.
Tallulah, **stop talking.**
The landsider's basically ***hugging*** a buoy mine.
It's caught in the exosuit. They must have drifted into it so gently that it didn't trigger and got tangled instead.
What do we do? Should we just . . . go? Can you move? What should I do? Do you need help?

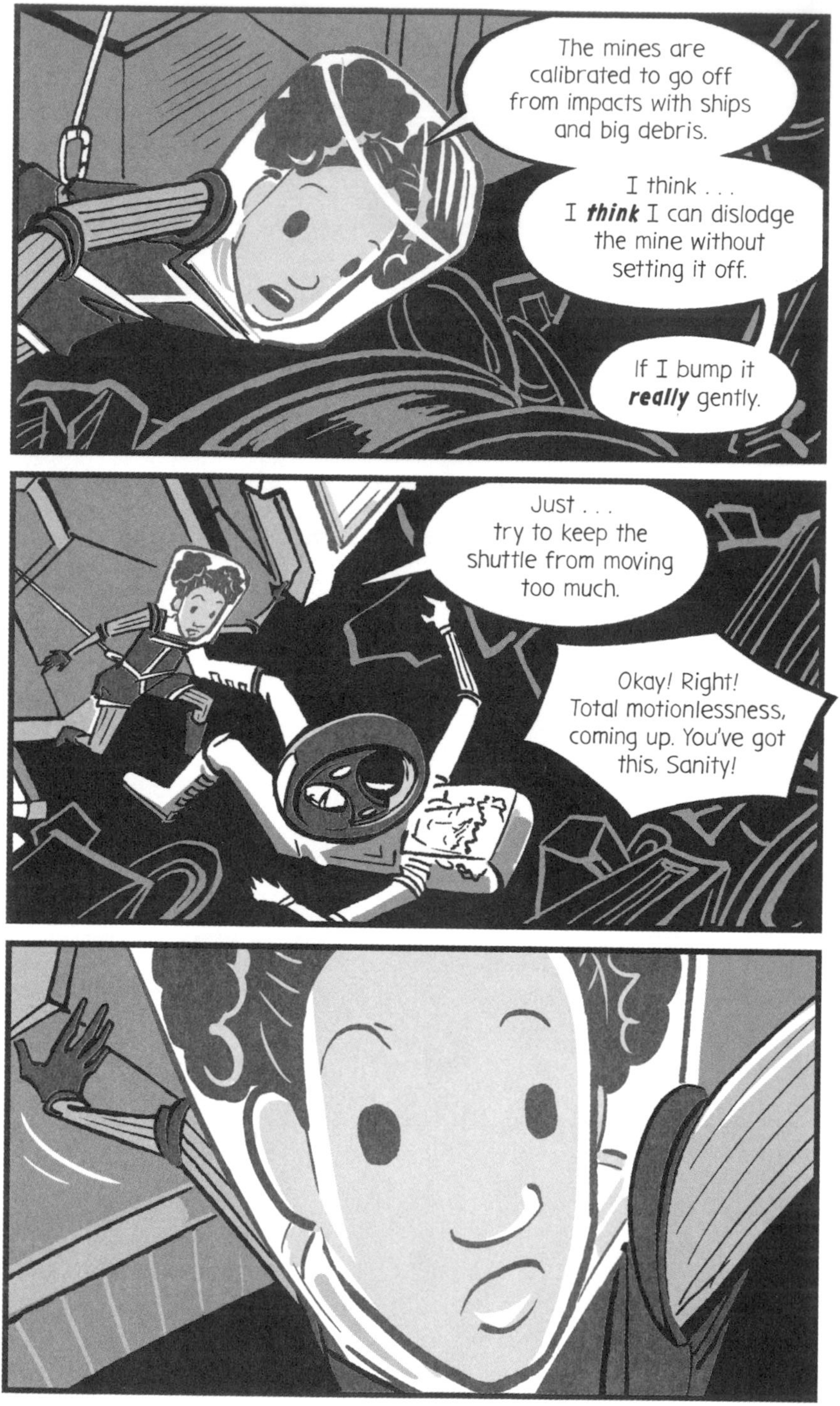
The mines are calibrated to go off from impacts with ships and big debris.
I think . . . I **think** I can dislodge the mine without setting it off.
If I bump it **really** gently.
Just . . . try to keep the shuttle from moving too much.
Okay! Right! Total motionlessness, coming up. You've got this, Sanity!

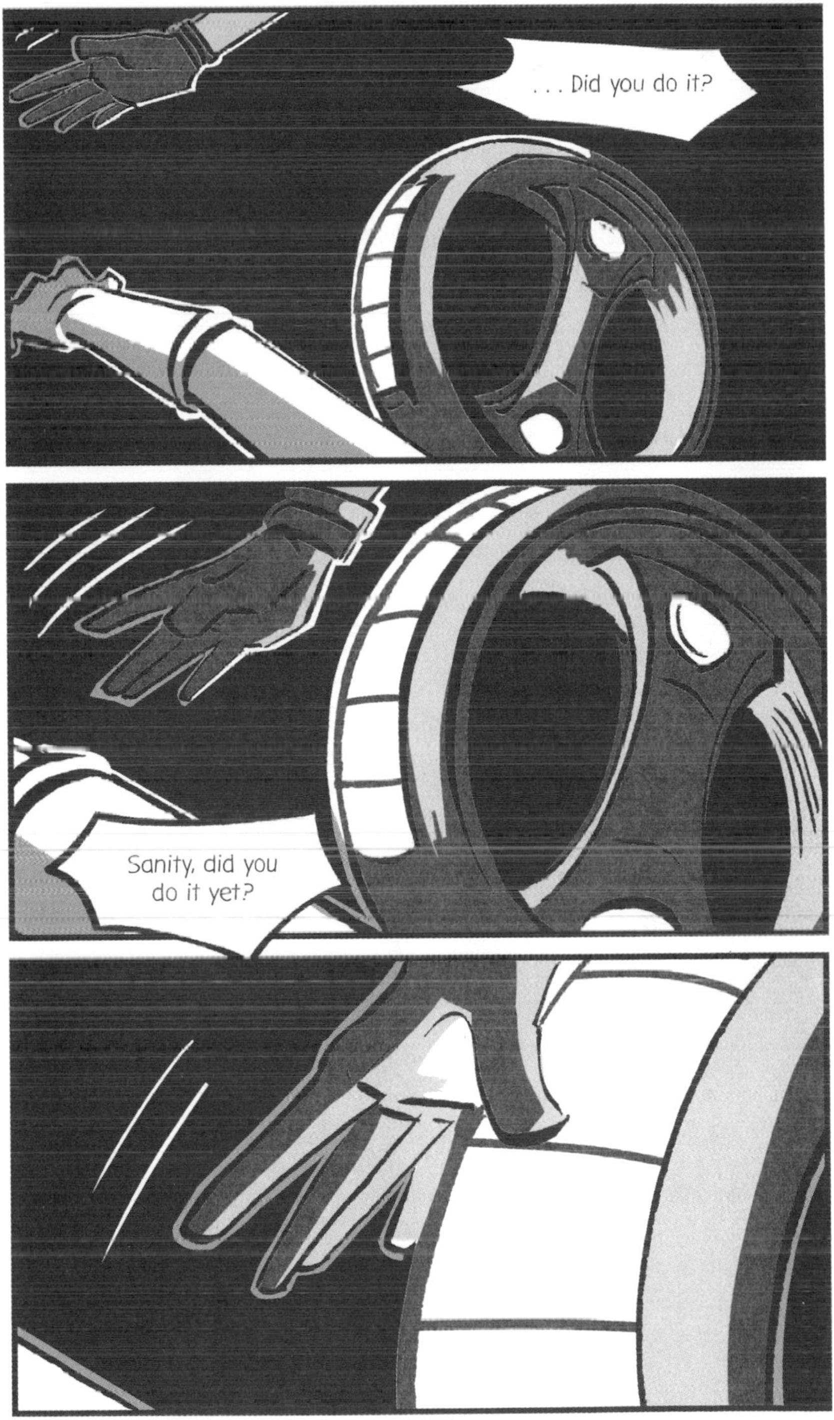
. . . Did you do it?
Sanity, did you do it yet?

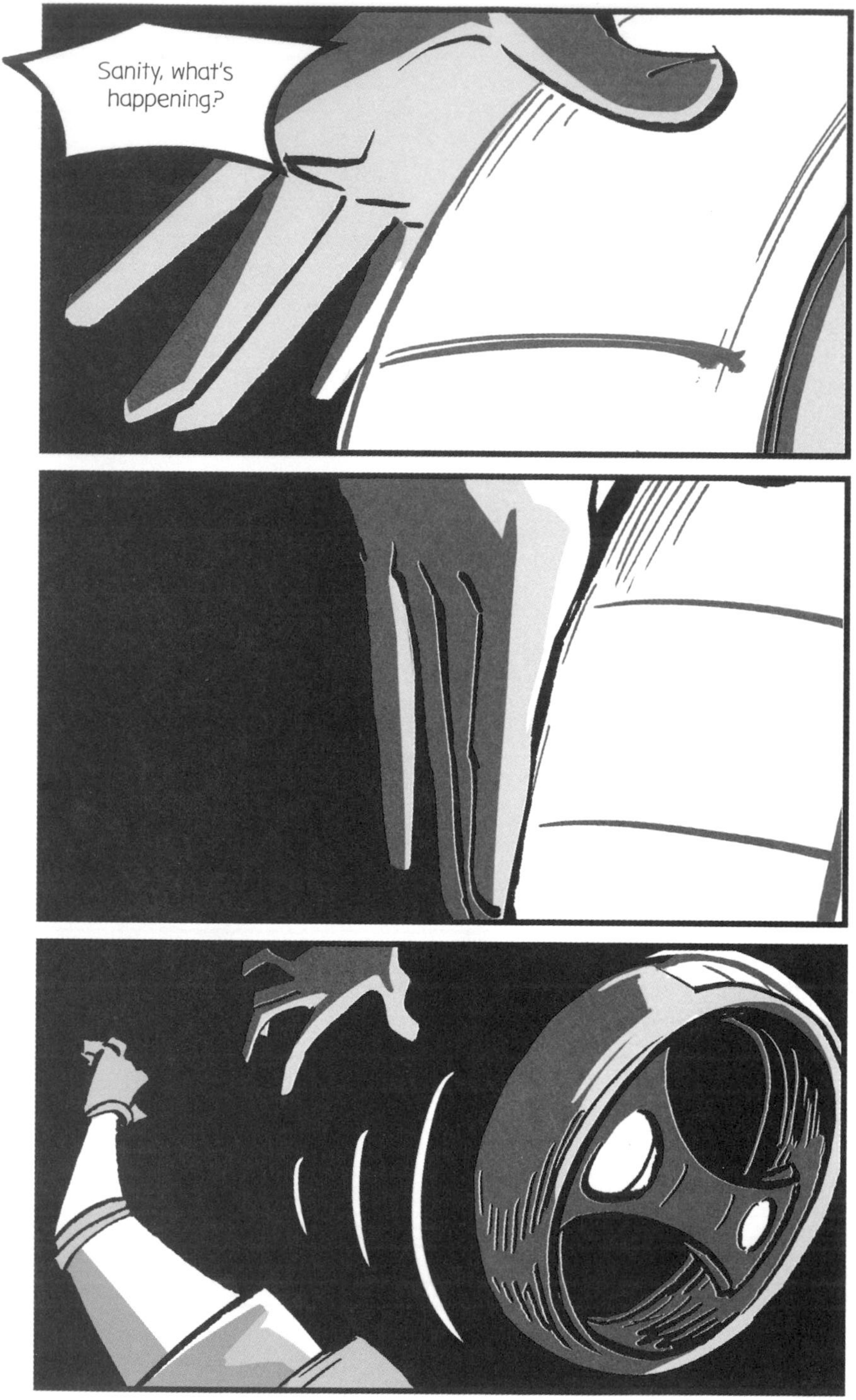
Sanity, what's happening?

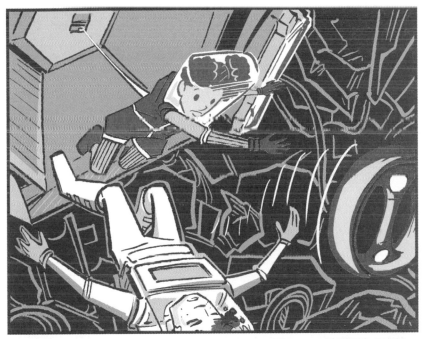

. . . Sanity?

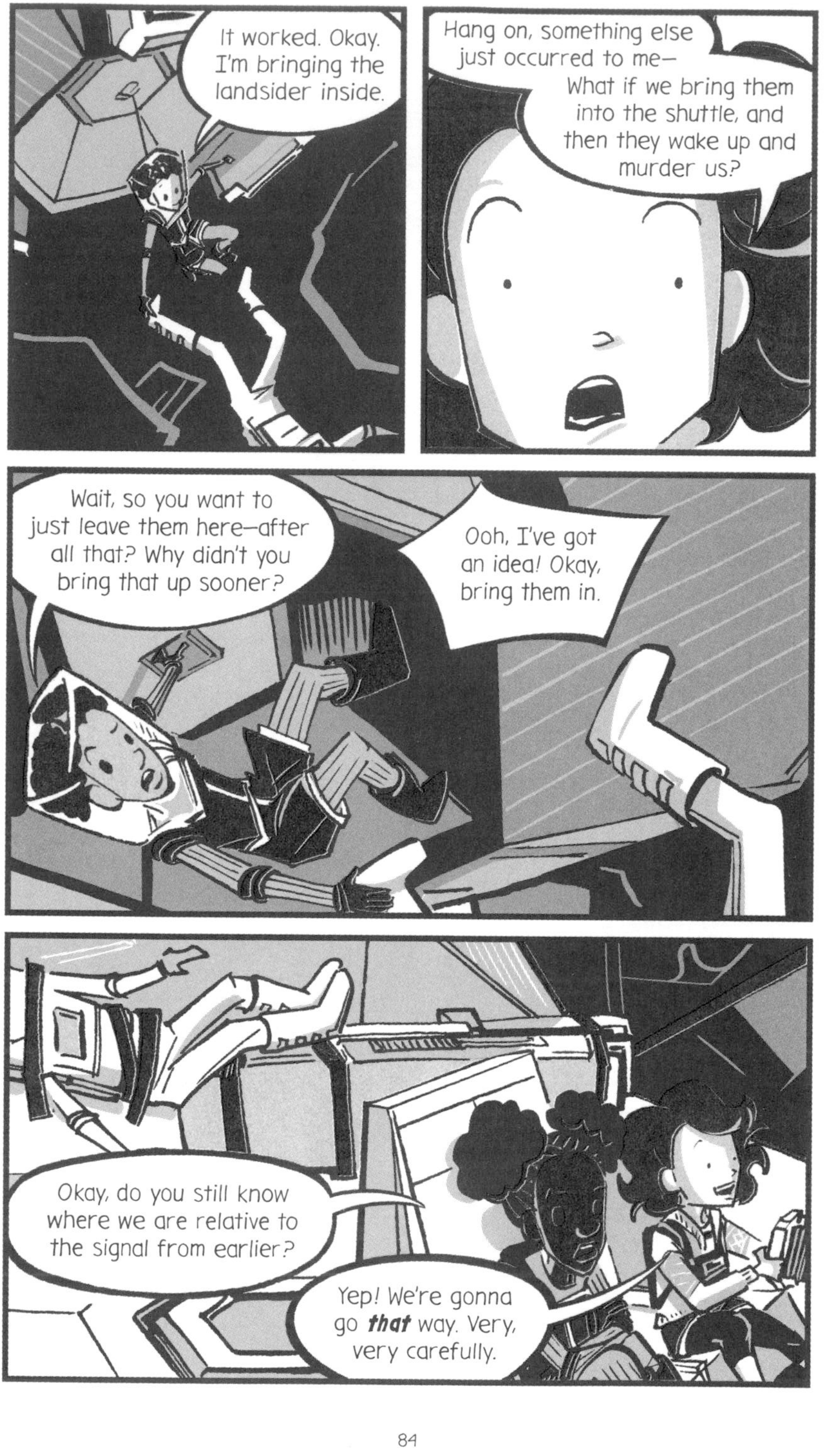
It worked. Okay. I'm bringing the landsider inside.
Hang on, something else just occurred to me—
What if we bring them into the shuttle, and then they wake up and murder us?
Wait, so you want to just leave them here—after all that? Why didn't you bring that up sooner?
Ooh, I've got an idea! Okay, bring them in.
Okay, do you still know where we are relative to the signal from earlier?
Yep! We're gonna go ***that*** way. Very, very carefully.

(STILL WAITING)

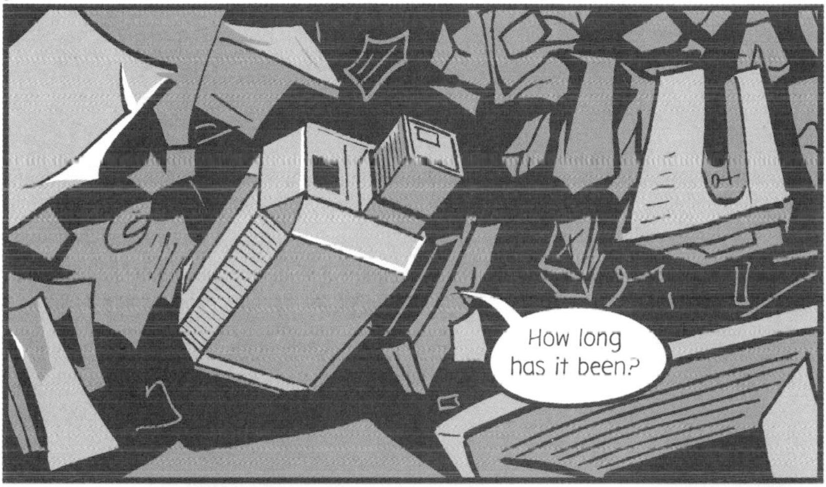
How long has it been?

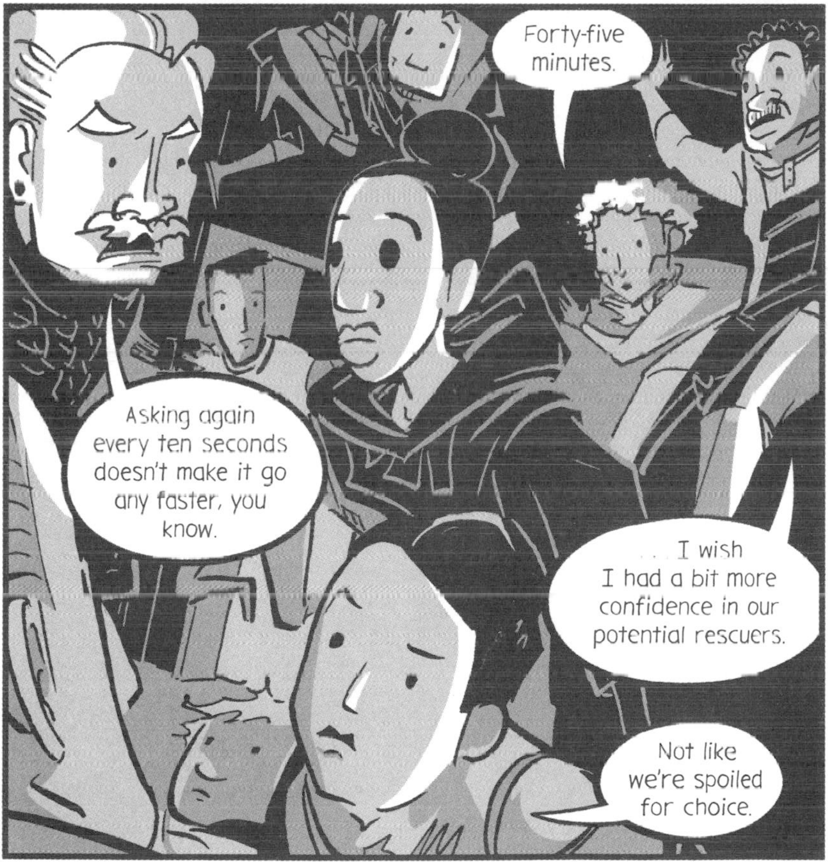
Forty-five minutes.
Asking again every ten seconds doesn't make it go any faster, you know.
. . . I wish I had a bit more confidence in our potential rescuers.
Not like we're spoiled for choice.

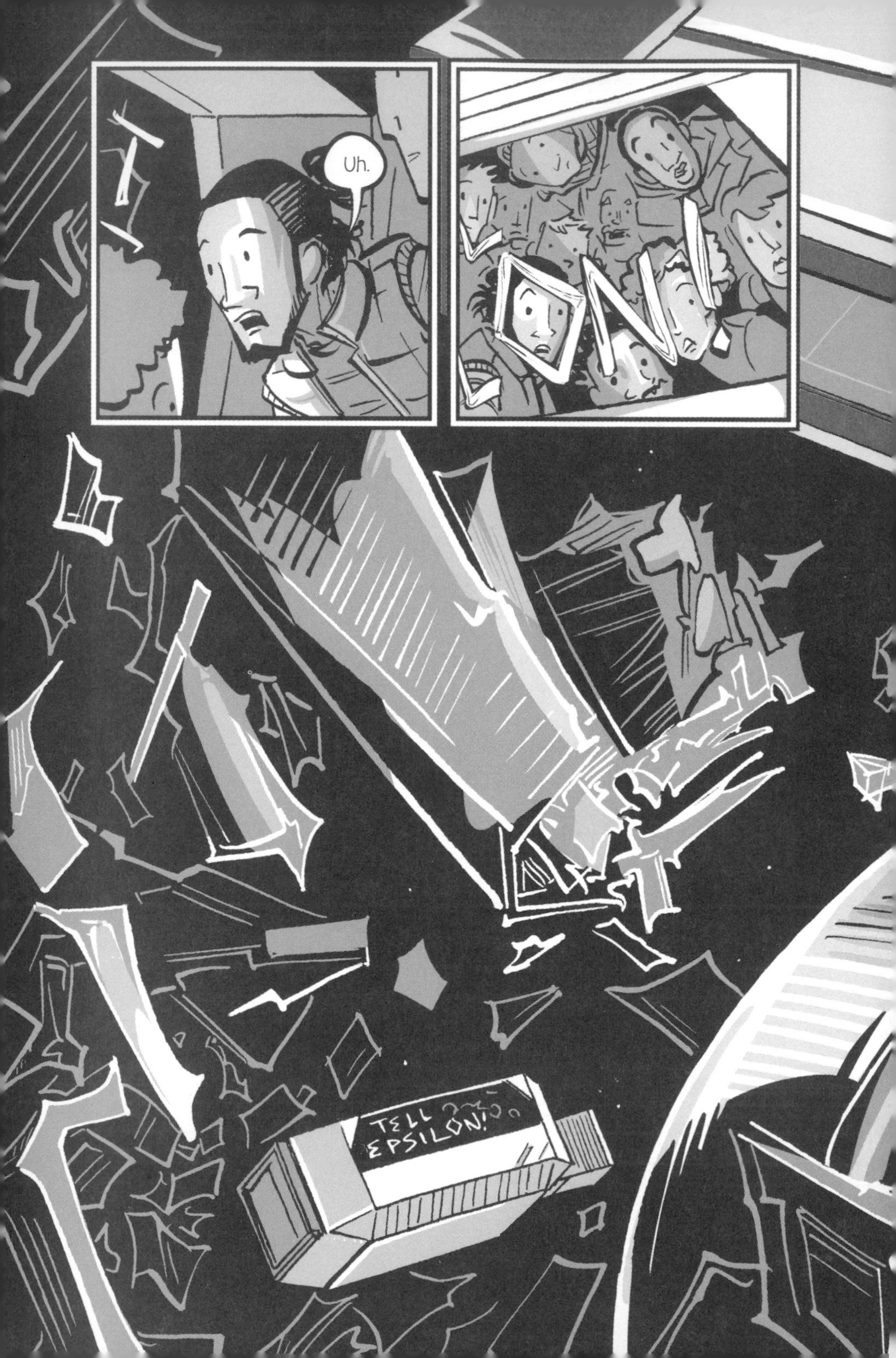
Uh.
TELL EPSILON!

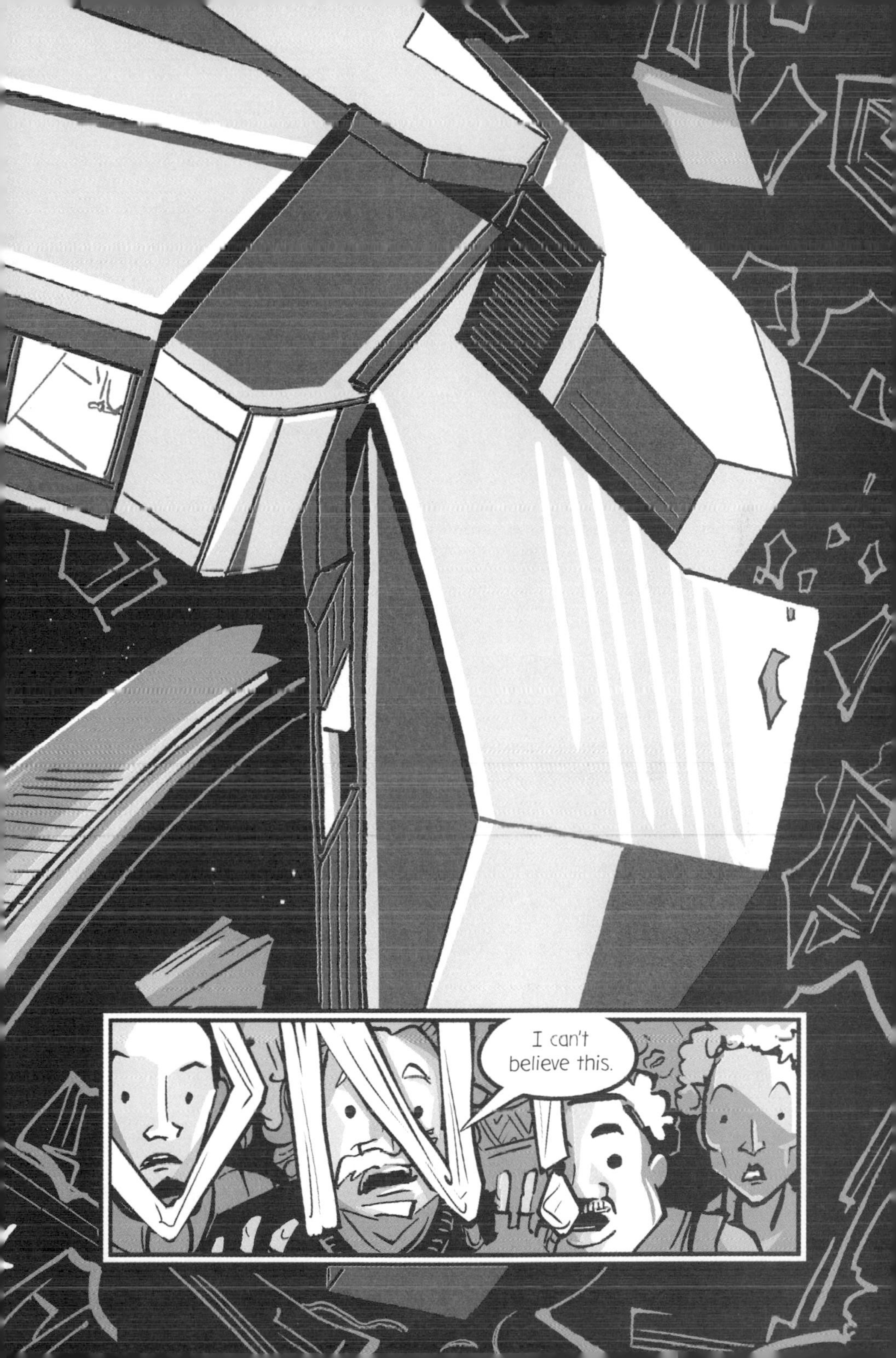
I can't
believe this.

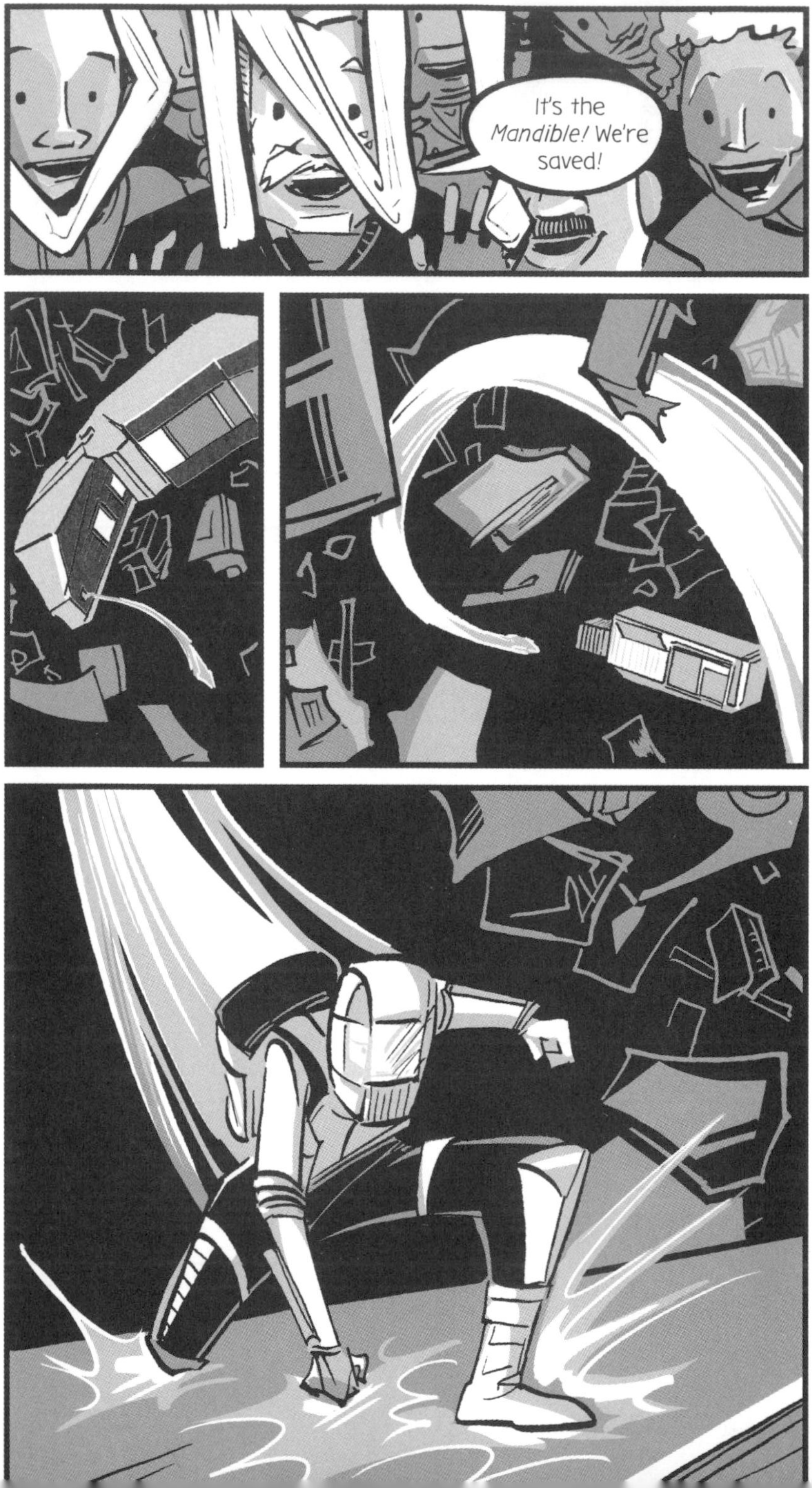
It's the *Mandible!* We're saved!

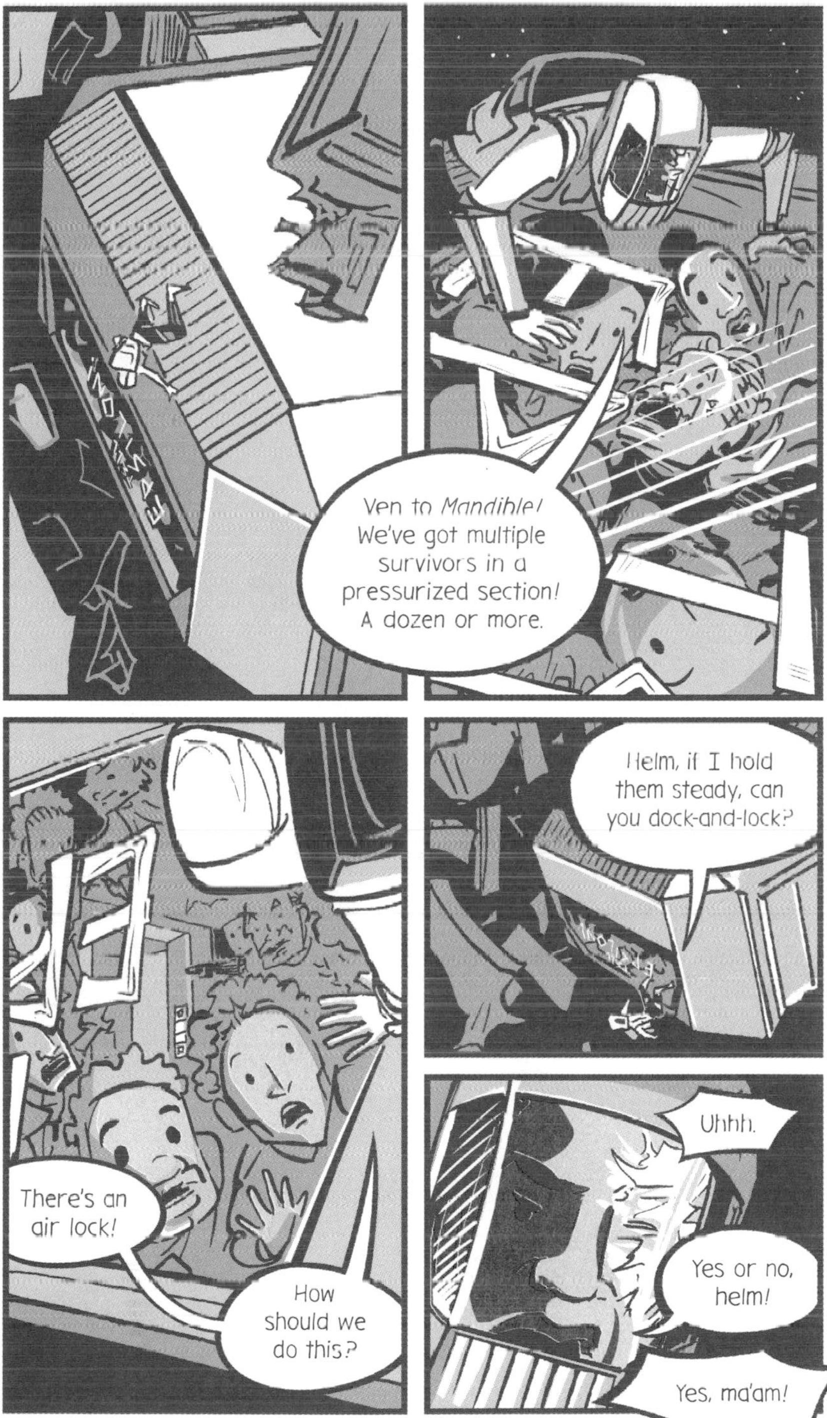
Ven to *Mandible!* We've got multiple survivors in a pressurized section! A dozen or more.
There's an air lock!
How should we do this?
Helm, if I hold them steady, can you dock-and-lock?
Uhhh.
Yes or no, helm!
Yes, ma'am!

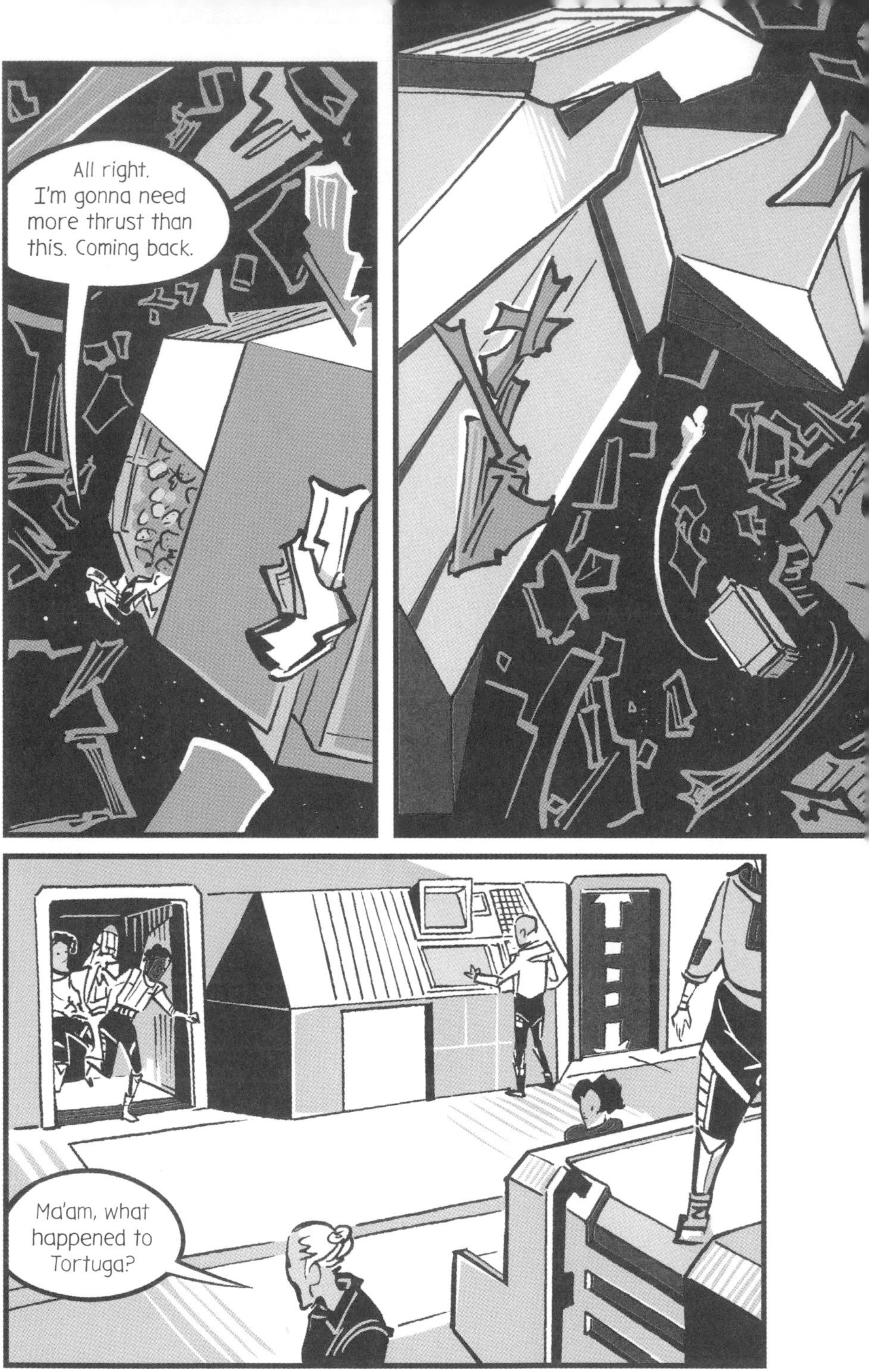
All right. I'm gonna need more thrust than this. Coming back.
Ma'am, what happened to Tortuga?

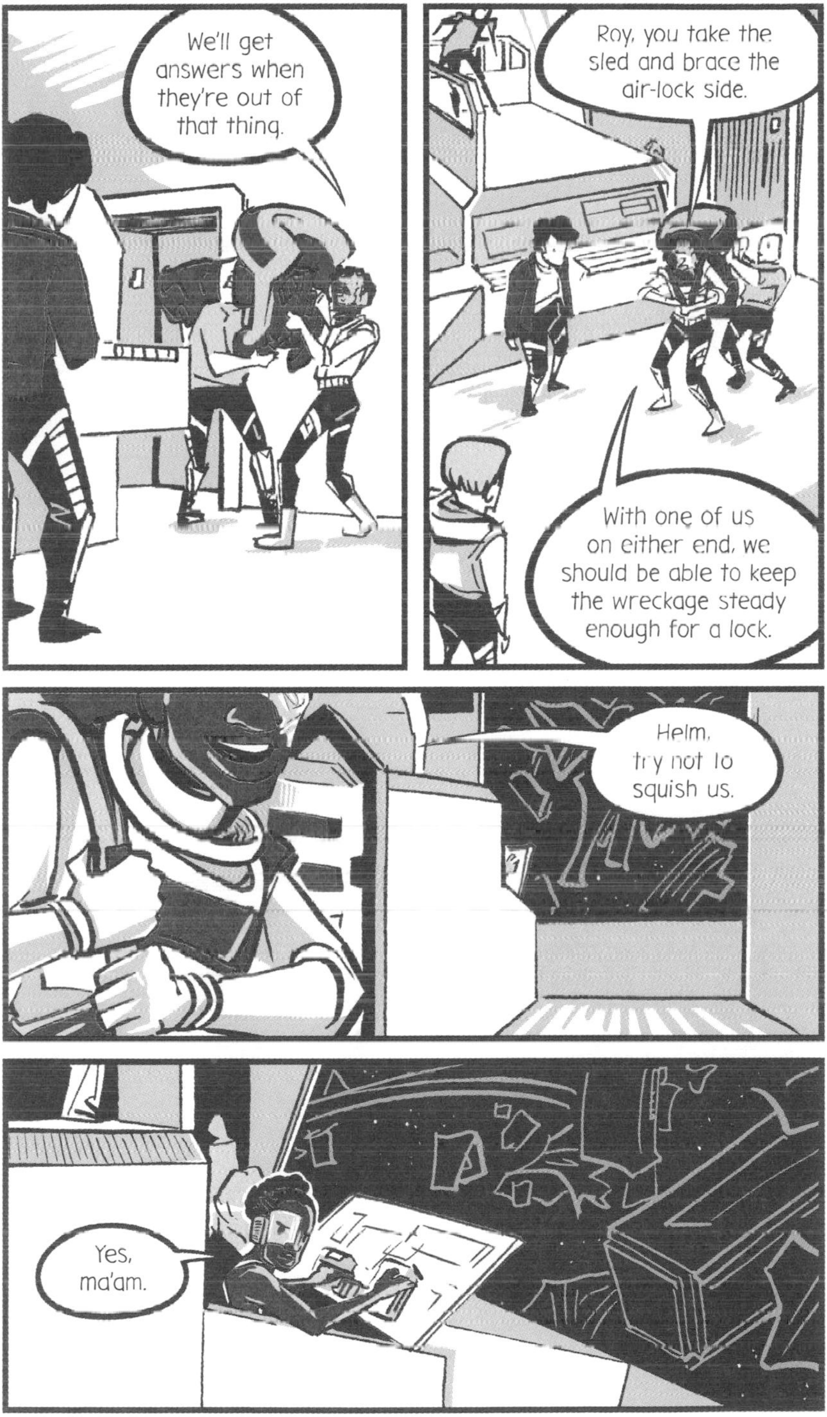
We'll get answers when they're out of that thing.
Roy, you take the sled and brace the air-lock side.
With one of us on either end, we should be able to keep the wreckage steady enough for a lock.
Helm, try not to squish us.
Yes, ma'am.

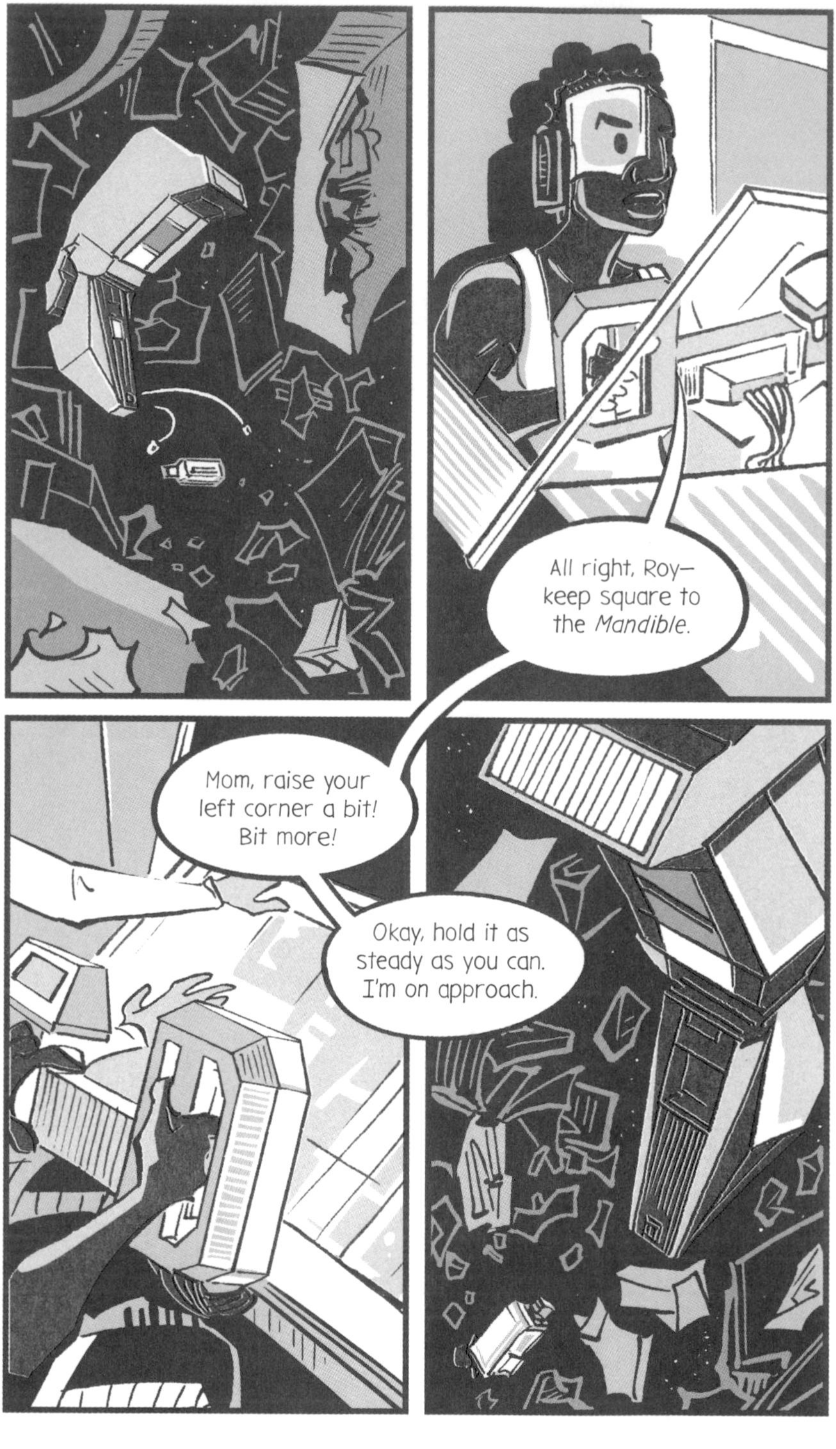
All right, Roy— keep square to the *Mandible*.
Mom, raise your left corner a bit! Bit more!
Okay, hold it as steady as you can. I'm on approach.

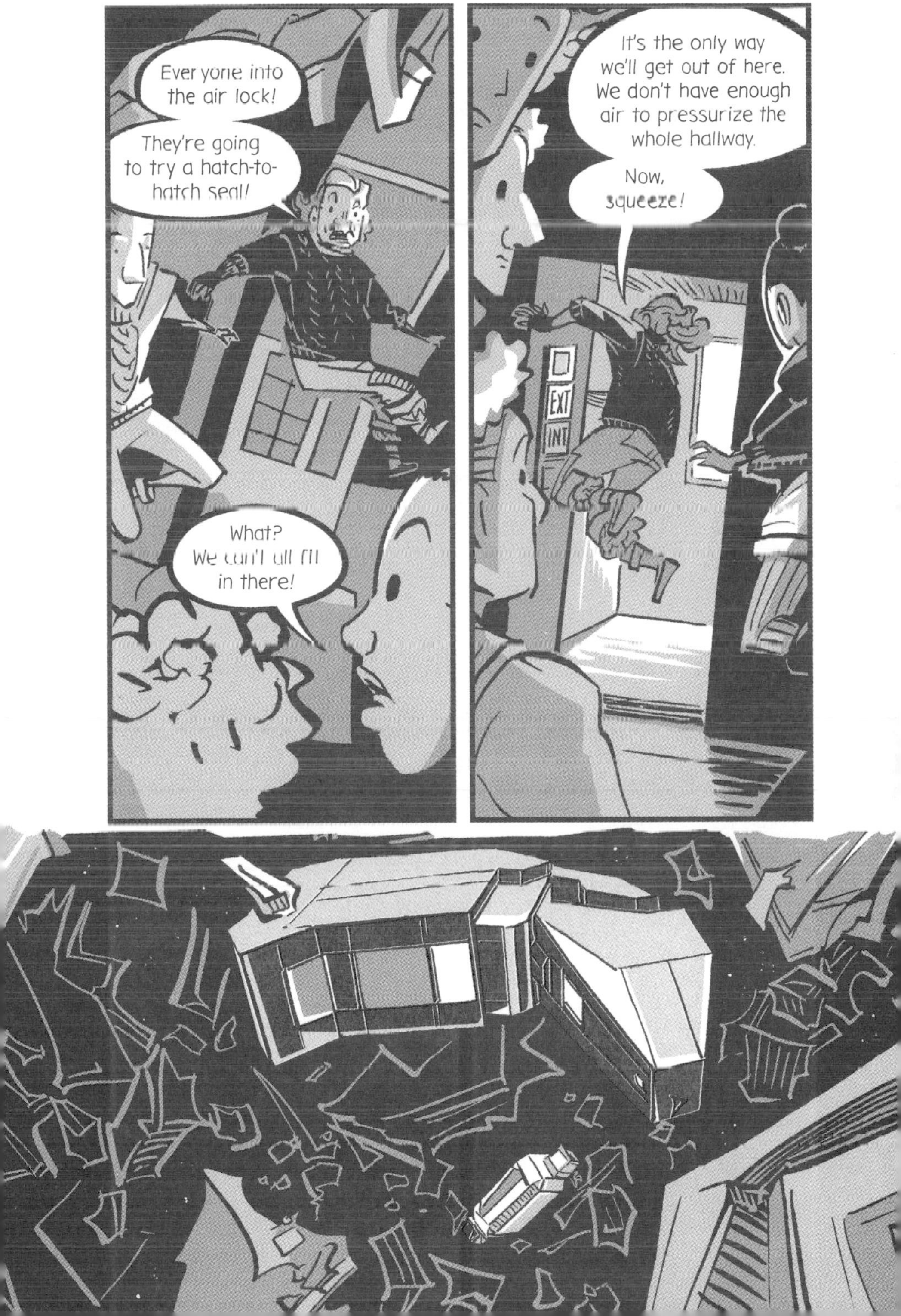
Everyone into the air lock!
They're going to try a hatch-to-hatch seal!
What? We can't all fit in there!
It's the only way we'll get out of here. We don't have enough air to pressurize the whole hallway.
Now, squeeze!
EXT
INT

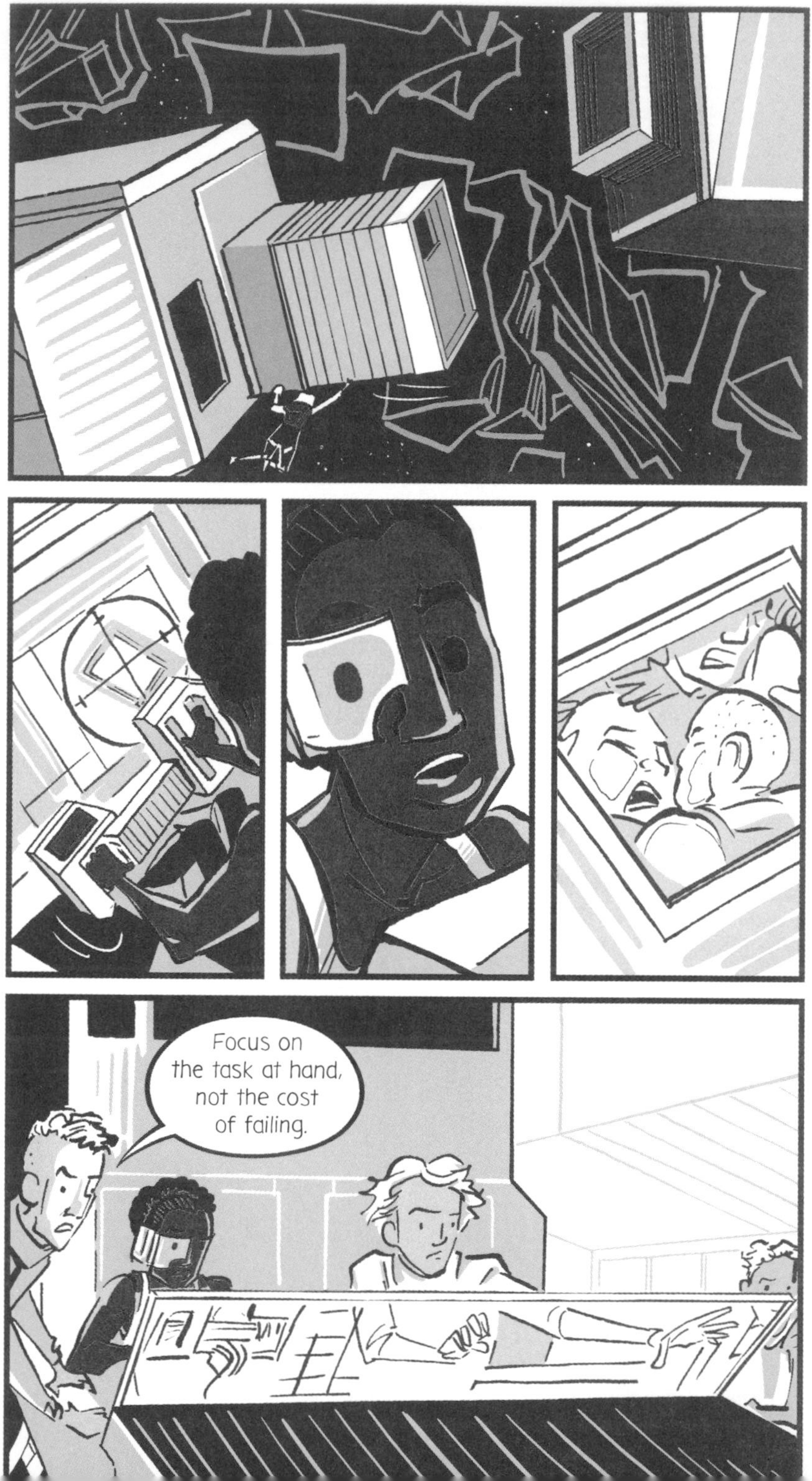
Focus on the task at hand, not the cost of failing.

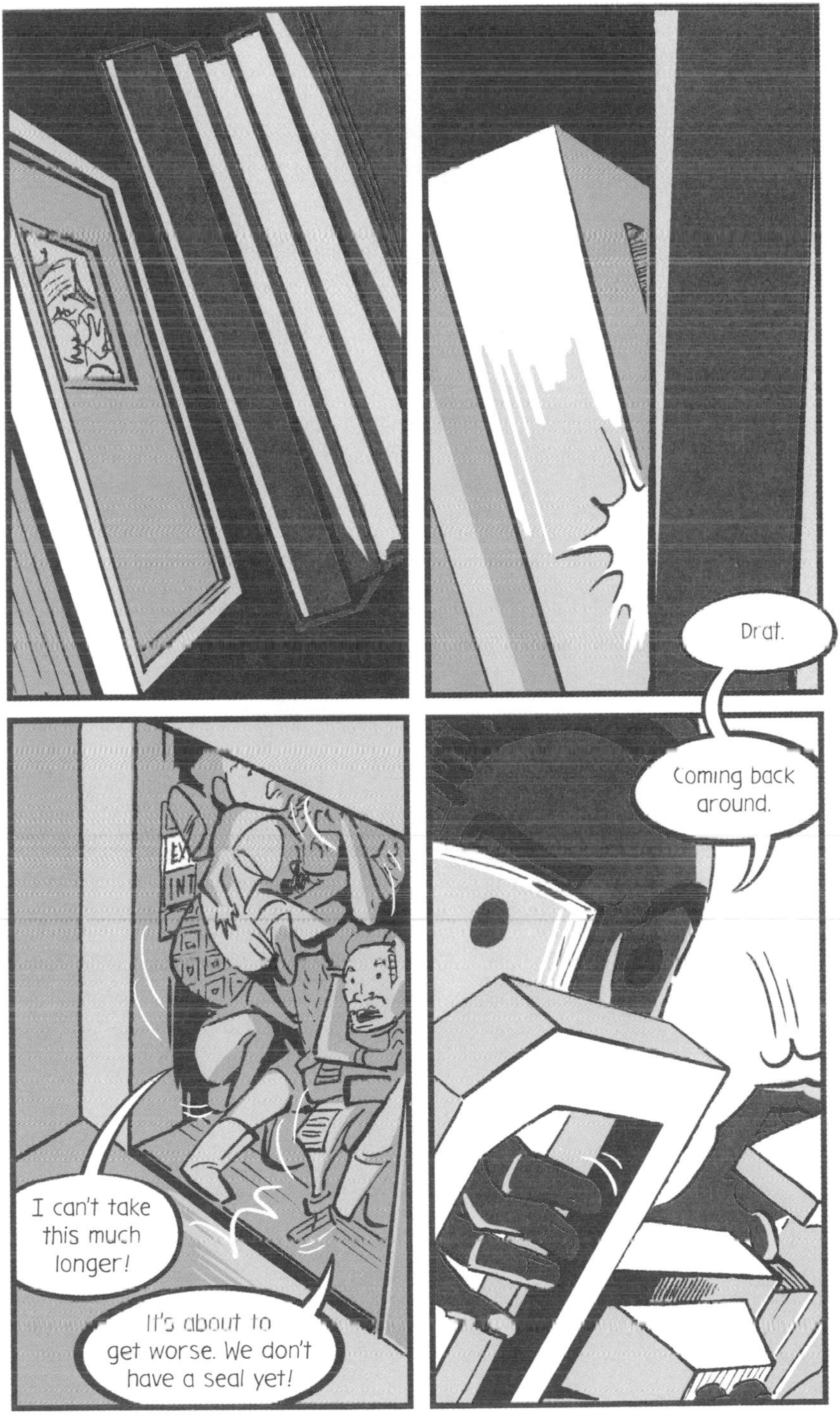
Drat.
Coming back around.
I can't take this much longer!
It's about to get worse. We don't have a seal yet!

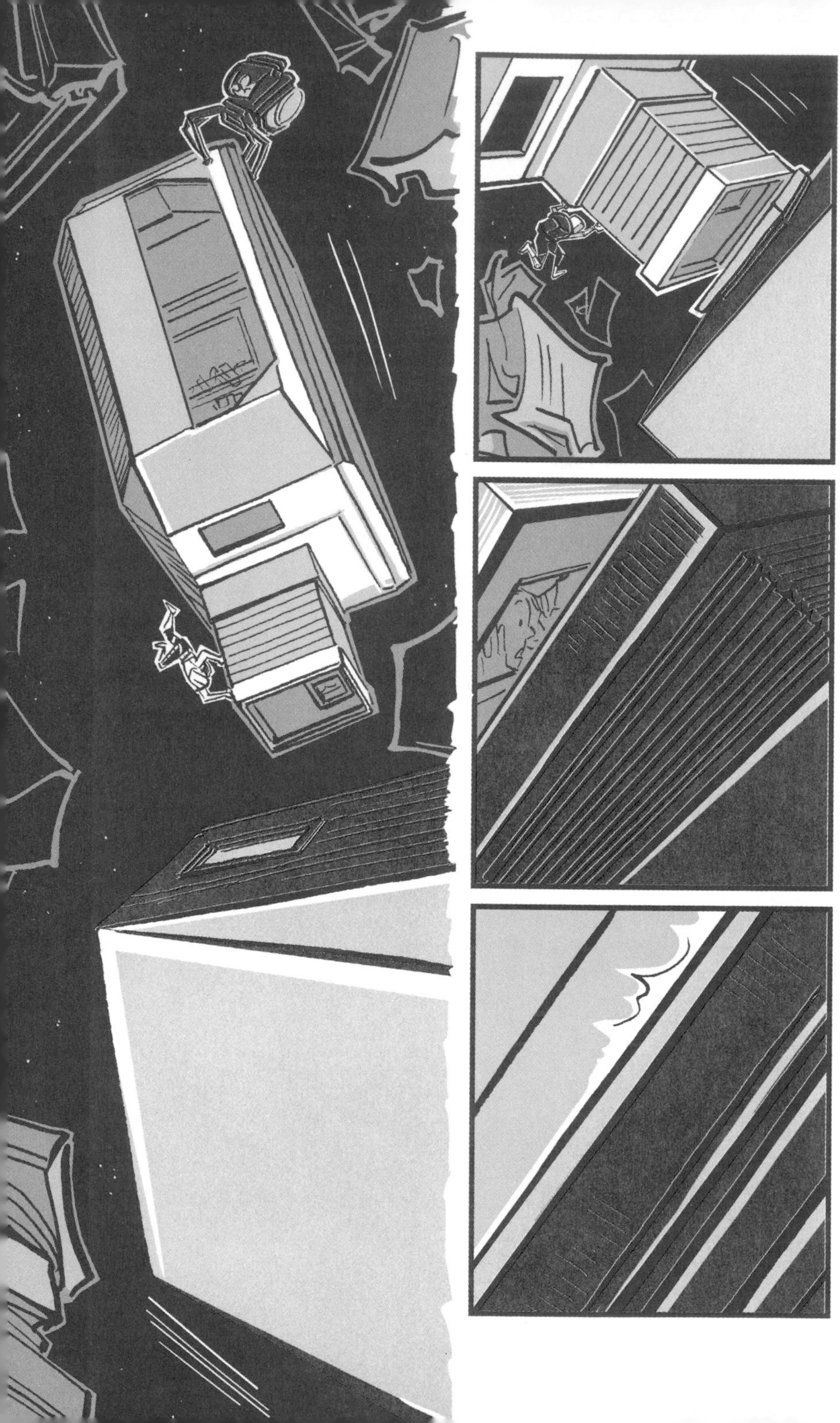

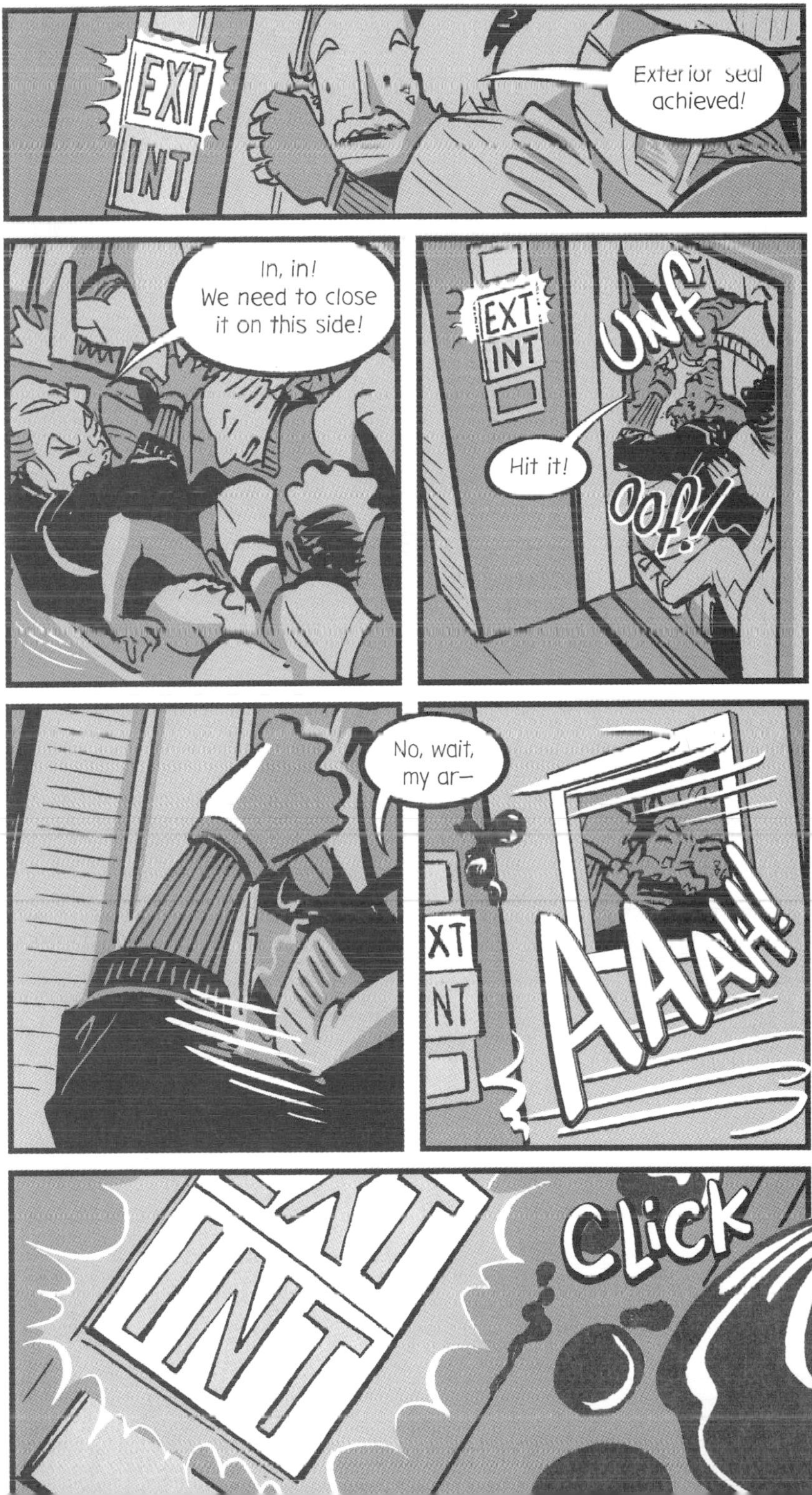
EXT
INT
Exterior seal achieved!
In, in! We need to close it on this side!
EXT
INT
UNF
Hit it!
OOF!
No, wait, my ar—
XT
NT
AAAH!
INT
CLICK

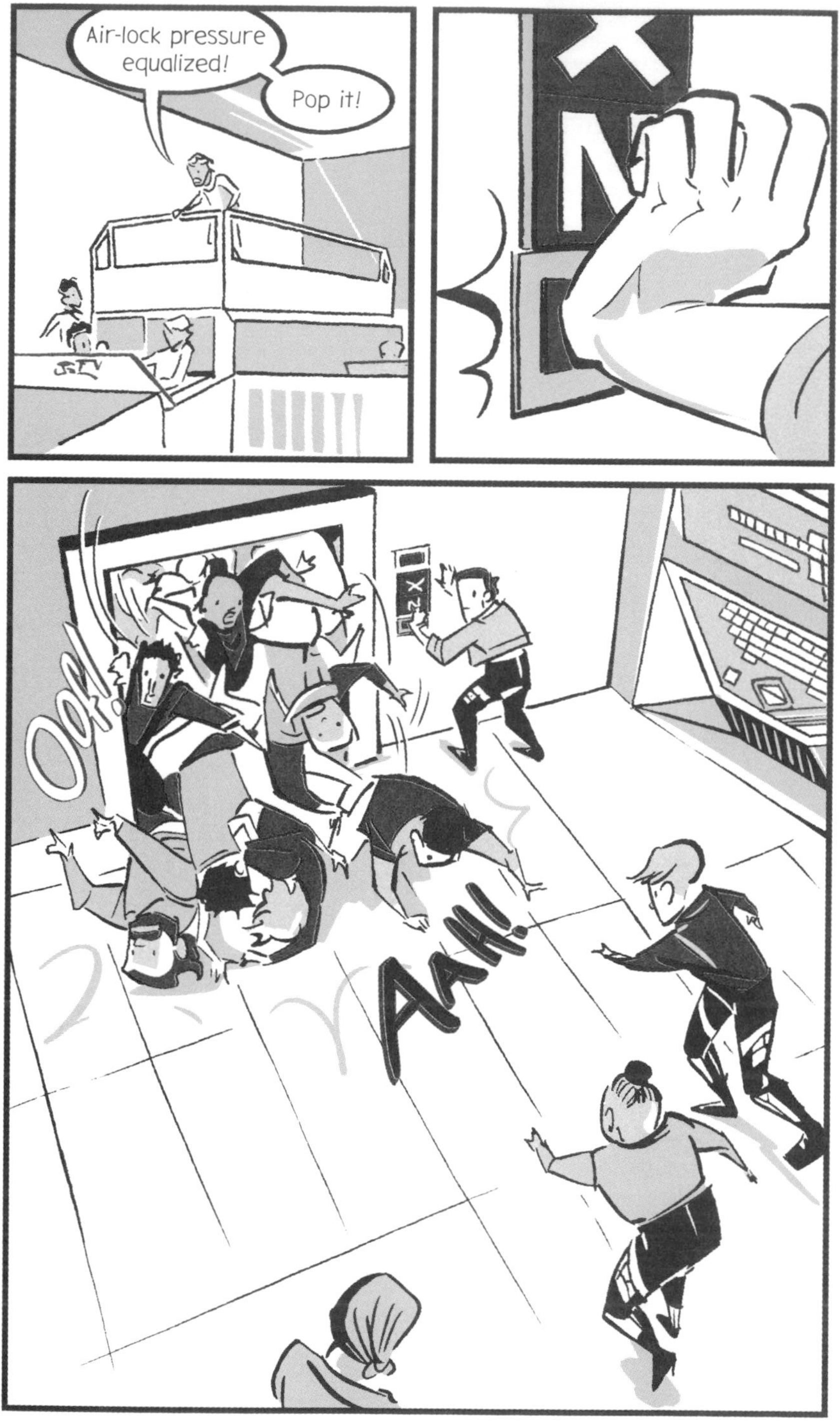
Air-lock pressure equalized!
Pop it!
OOF!
AAH!

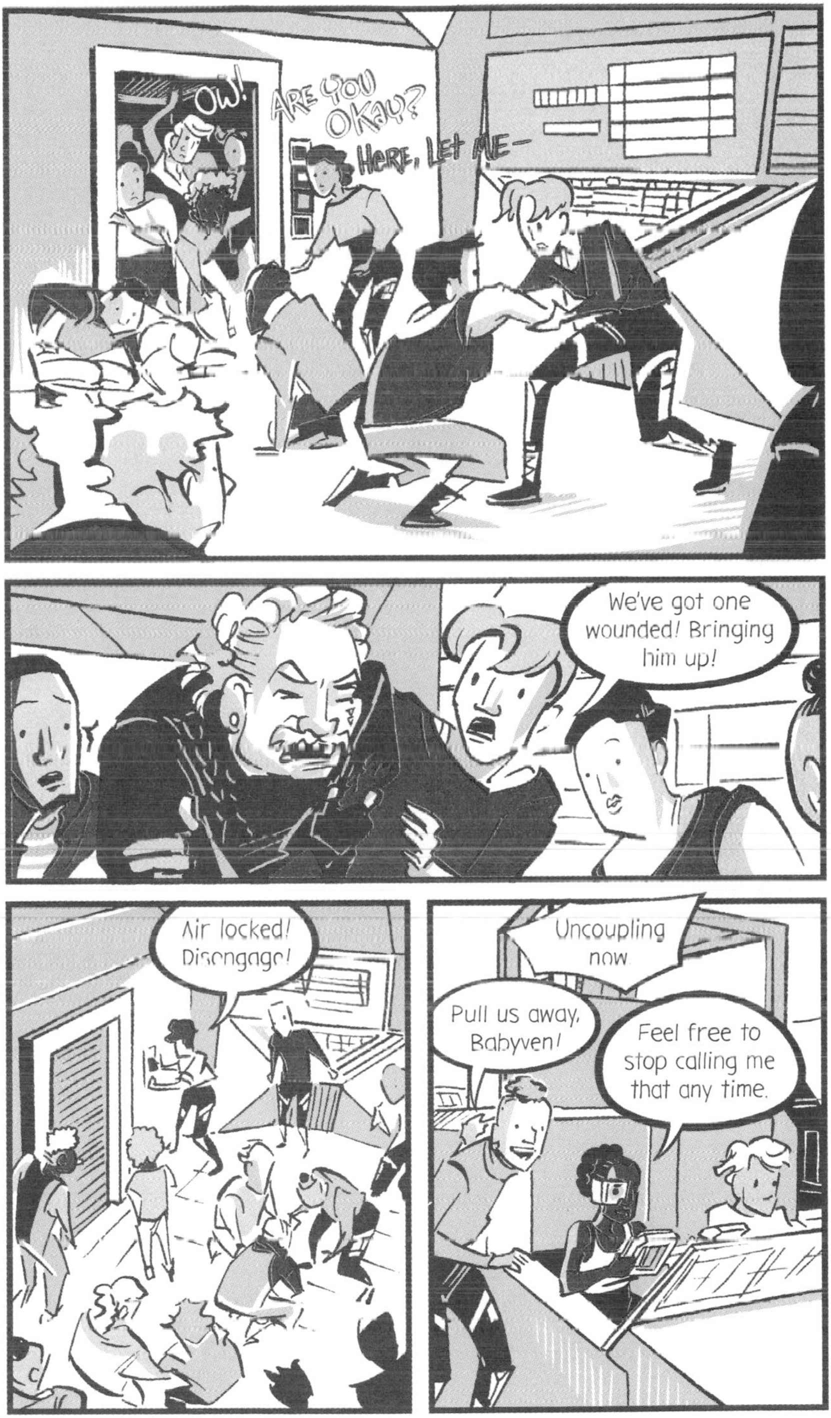
OW!
ARE YOU OKAY?
HERE, LET ME—
We've got one wounded! Bringing him up!
Air locked! Disengage!
Uncoupling now.
Pull us away, Babyven!
Feel free to stop calling me that any time.

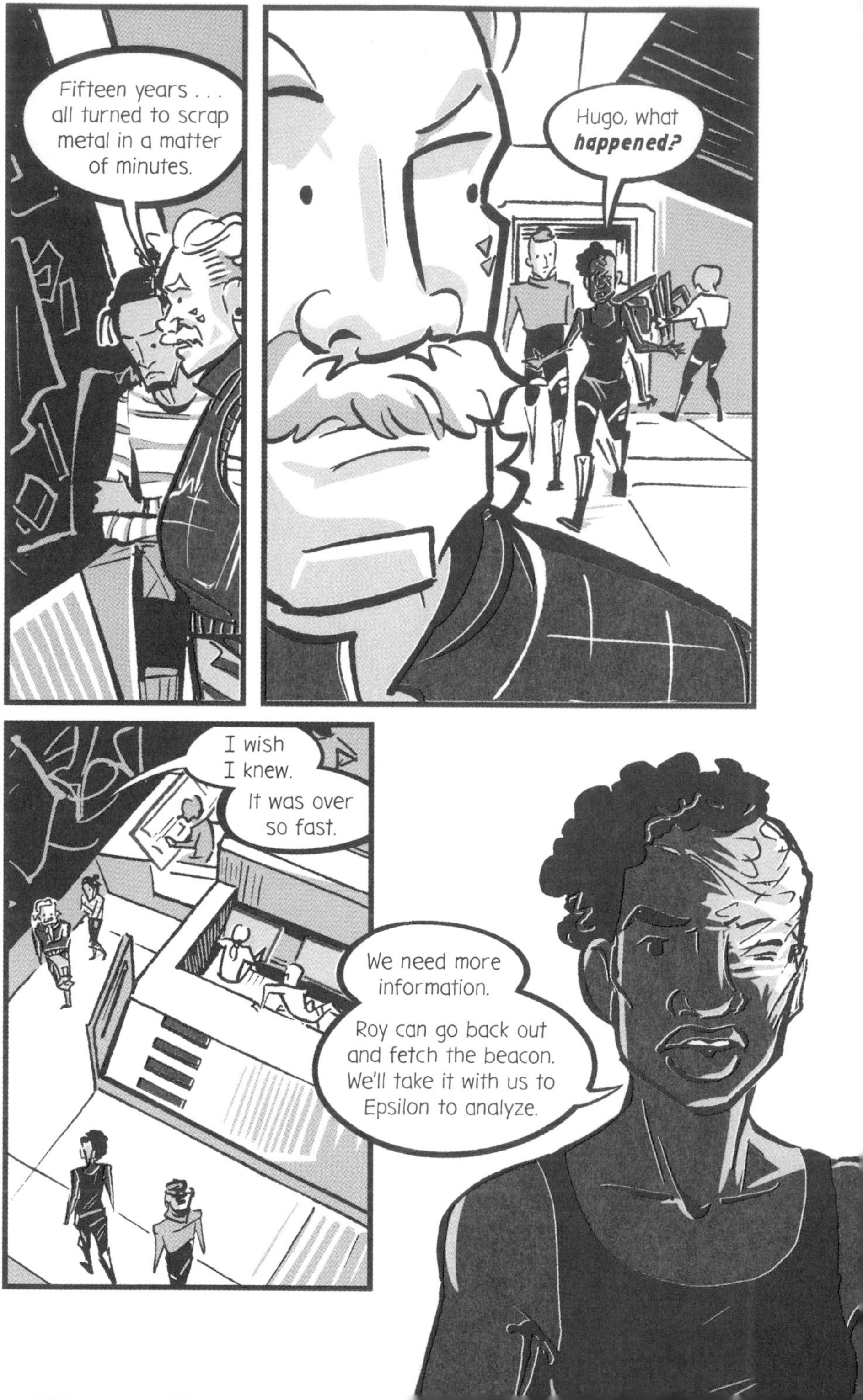
Fifteen years . . . all turned to scrap metal in a matter of minutes.
Hugo, what ***happened?***
I wish I knew.
It was over so fast.
We need more information.
Roy can go back out and fetch the beacon. We'll take it with us to Epsilon to analyze.

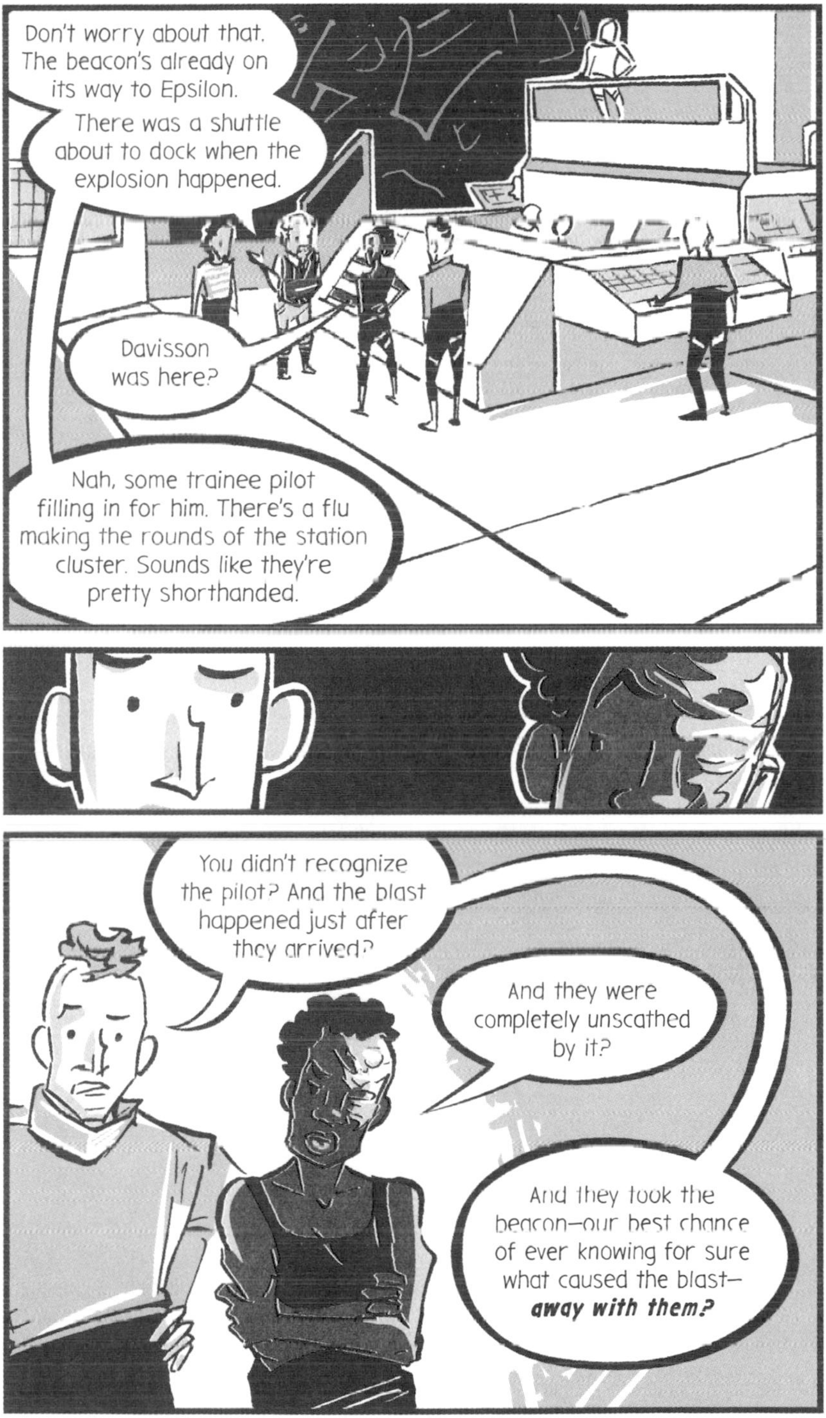
Don't worry about that. The beacon's already on its way to Epsilon.
There was a shuttle about to dock when the explosion happened.
Davisson was here?
Nah, some trainee pilot filling in for him. There's a flu making the rounds of the station cluster. Sounds like they're pretty shorthanded.
You didn't recognize the pilot? And the blast happened just after they arrived?
And they were completely unscathed by it?
And they took the beacon—our best chance of ever knowing for sure what caused the blast—**away with them?**

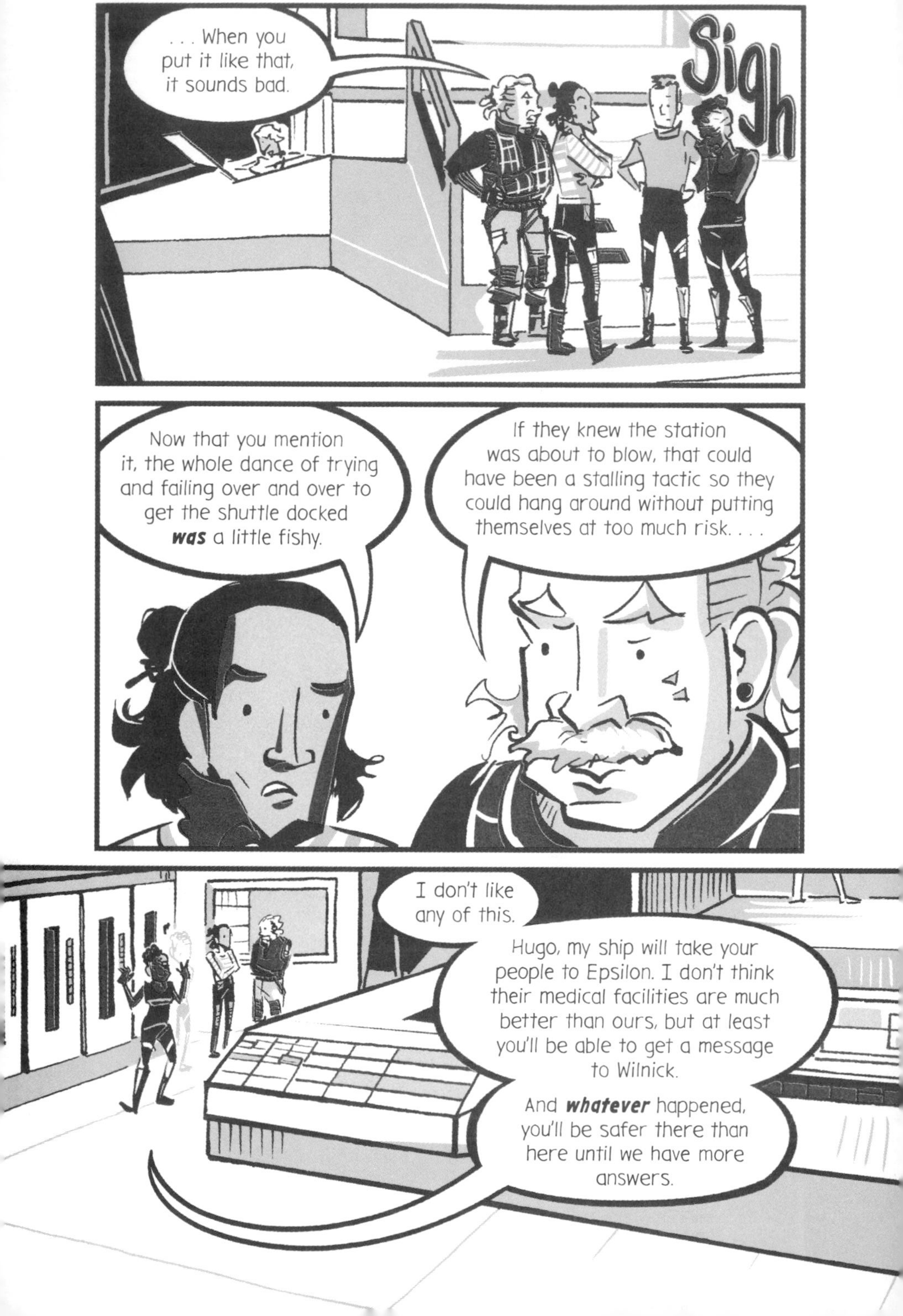

. . . When you put it like that, it sounds bad.
Sigh
Now that you mention it, the whole dance of trying and failing over and over to get the shuttle docked ***was*** a little fishy.
If they knew the station was about to blow, that could have been a stalling tactic so they could hang around without putting themselves at too much risk. . . .
I don't like any of this.
Hugo, my ship will take your people to Epsilon. I don't think their medical facilities are much better than ours, but at least you'll be able to get a message to Wilnick.
And ***whatever*** happened, you'll be safer there than here until we have more answers.

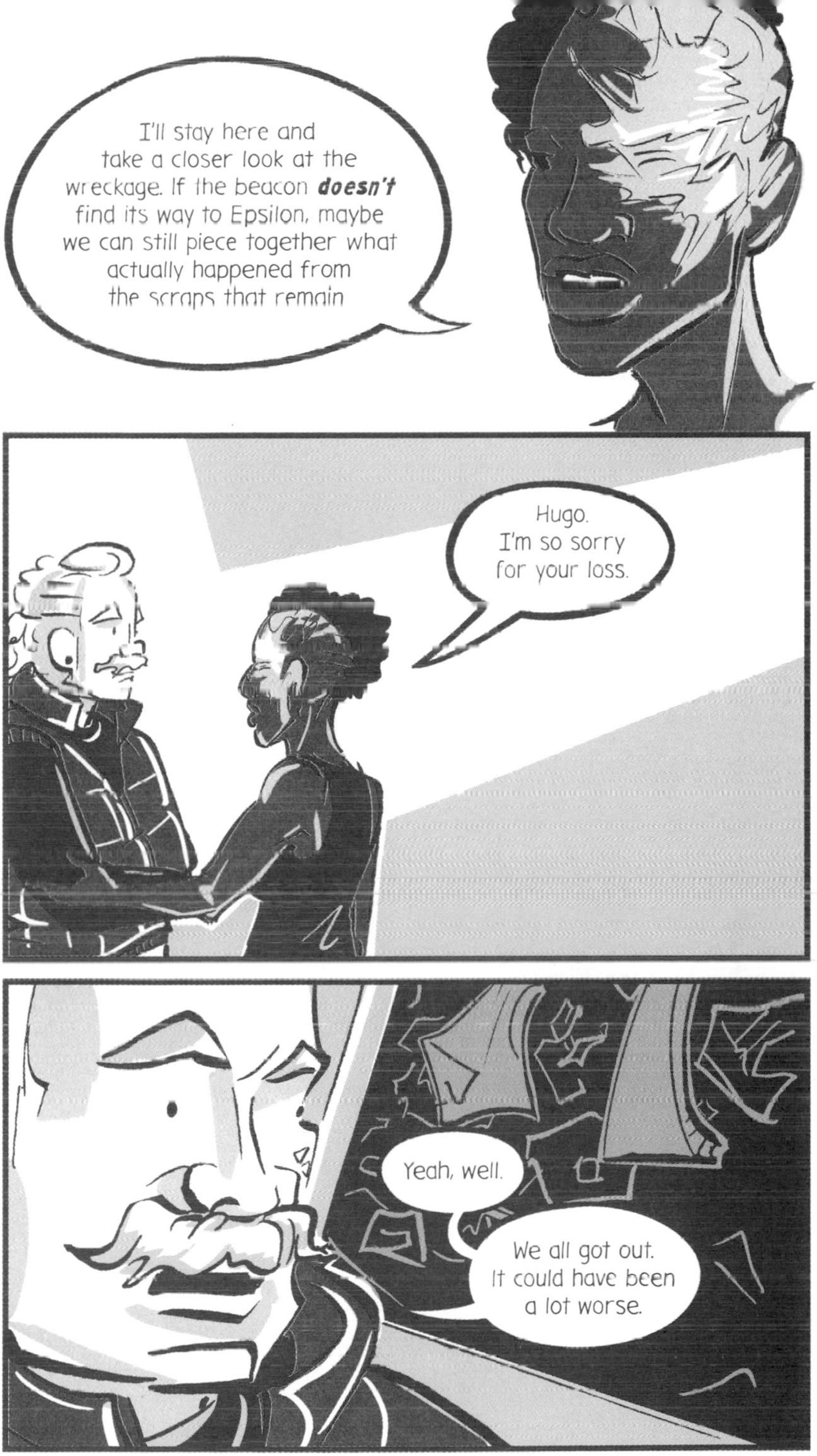
I'll stay here and take a closer look at the wreckage. If the beacon **doesn't** find its way to Epsilon, maybe we can still piece together what actually happened from the scraps that remain.
Hugo. I'm so sorry for your loss.
Yeah, well.
We all got out. It could have been a lot worse.

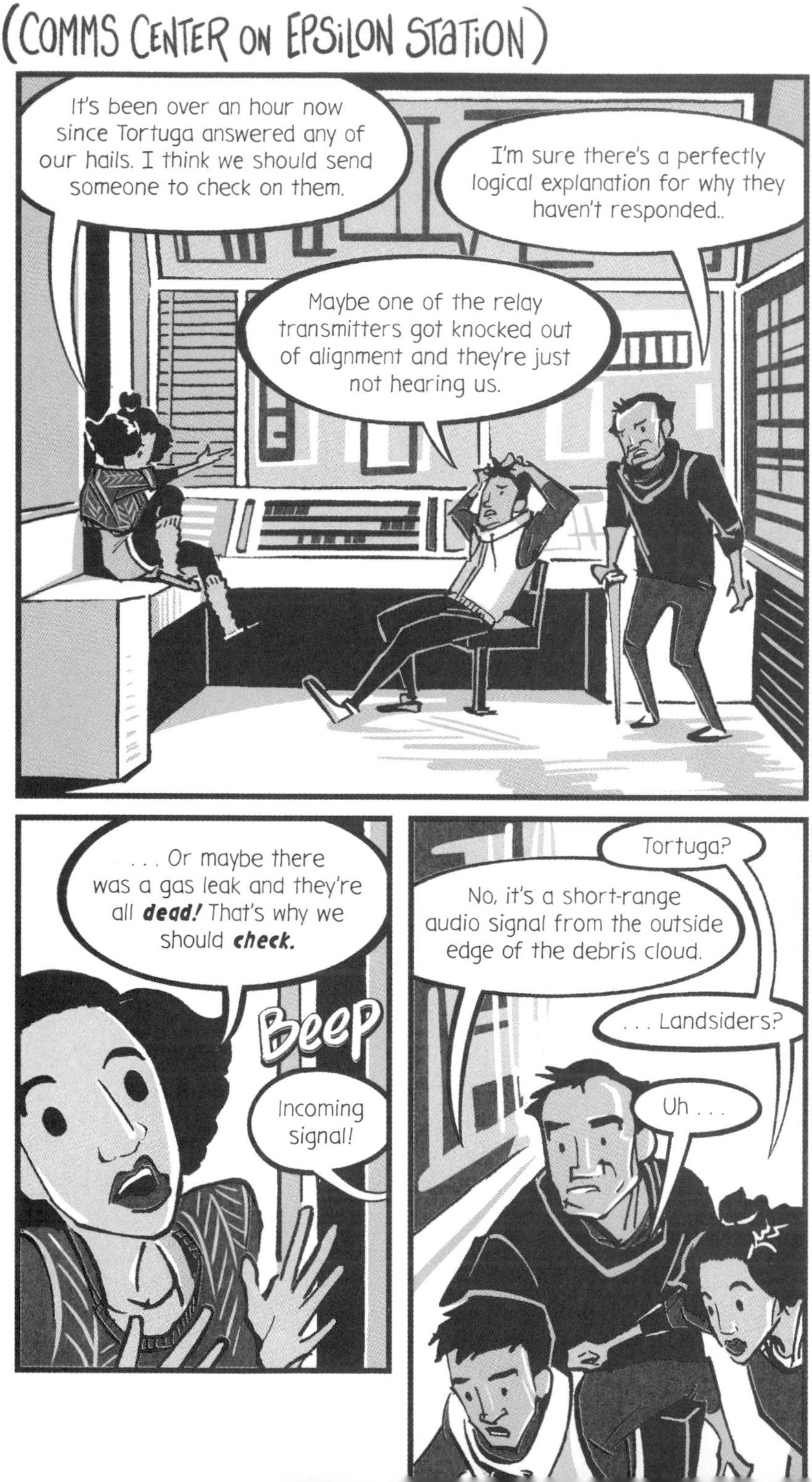
(COMMS CENTER ON EPSILON STATION)
It's been over an hour now since Tortuga answered any of our hails. I think we should send someone to check on them.
I'm sure there's a perfectly logical explanation for why they haven't responded..
Maybe one of the relay transmitters got knocked out of alignment and they're just not hearing us.
. . . Or maybe there was a gas leak and they're all **dead!** That's why we should **check.**
Beep
Incoming signal!
Tortuga?
No, it's a short-range audio signal from the outside edge of the debris cloud.
. . . Landsiders?
Uh . . .

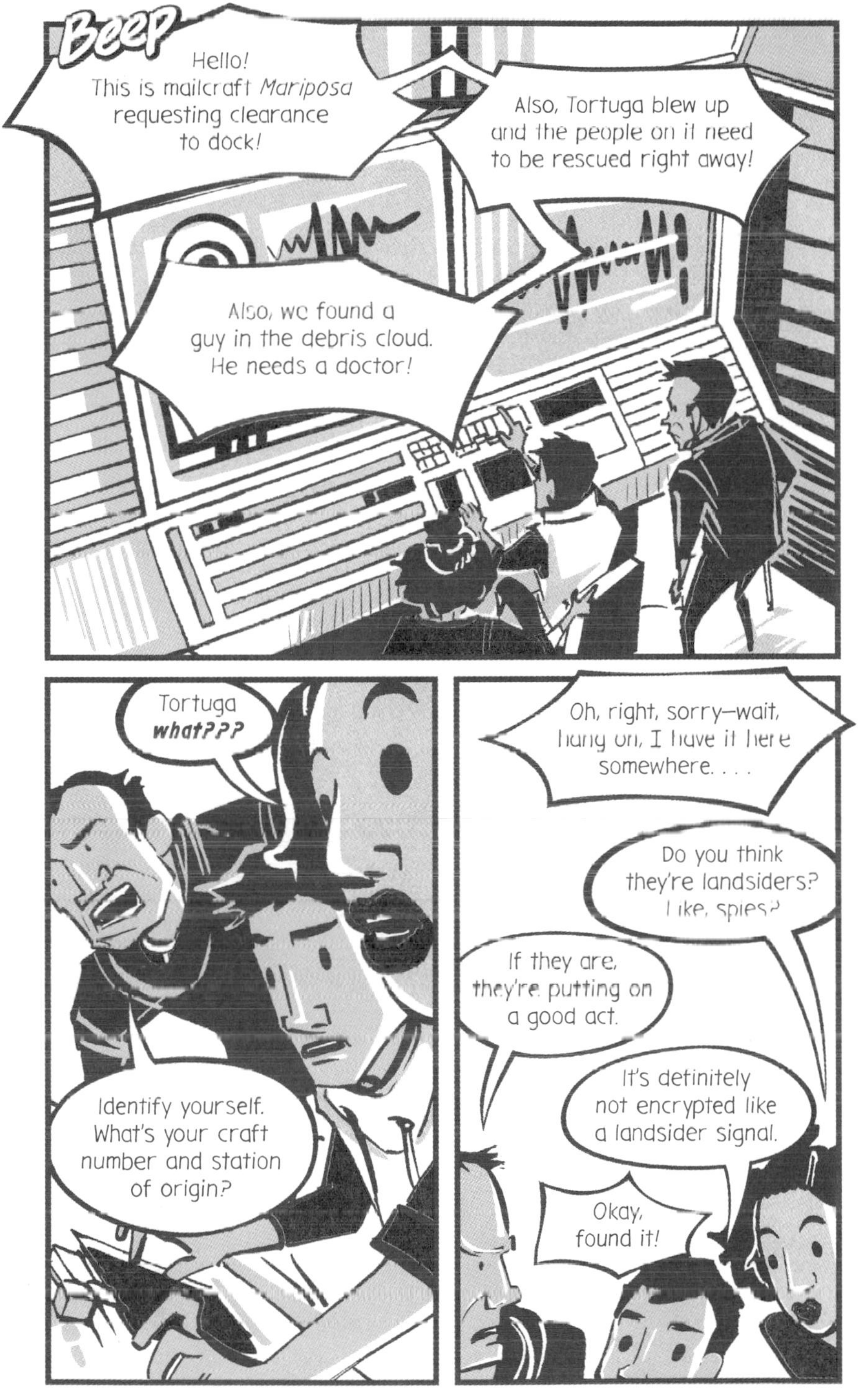
Beep
Hello! This is mailcraft *Mariposa* requesting clearance to dock!
Also, Tortuga blew up and the people on it need to be rescued right away!
Also, we found a guy in the debris cloud. He needs a doctor!
Tortuga *what???*
Identify yourself. What's your craft number and station of origin?
Oh, right, sorry—wait, hang on, I have it here somewhere. . . .
Do you think they're landsiders? Like, spies?
If they are, they're putting on a good act.
It's definitely not encrypted like a landsider signal.
Okay, found it!

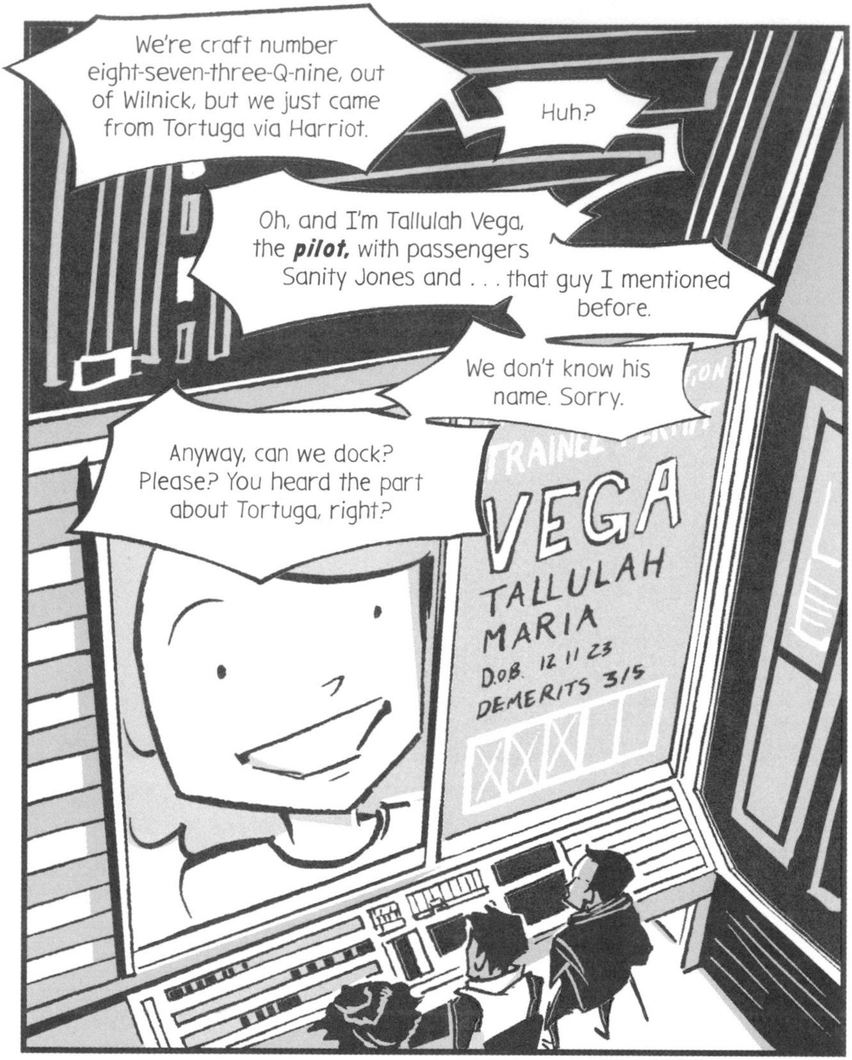
We're craft number eight-seven-three-Q-nine, out of Wilnick, but we just came from Tortuga via Harriot.
Huh?
Oh, and I'm Tallulah Vega, the **pilot,** with passengers Sanity Jones and . . . that guy I mentioned before.
We don't know his name. Sorry.
Anyway, can we dock? Please? You heard the part about Tortuga, right?
VEGA
TALLULAH
MARIA
D.O.B. 12 11 23
DEMERITS 3/5

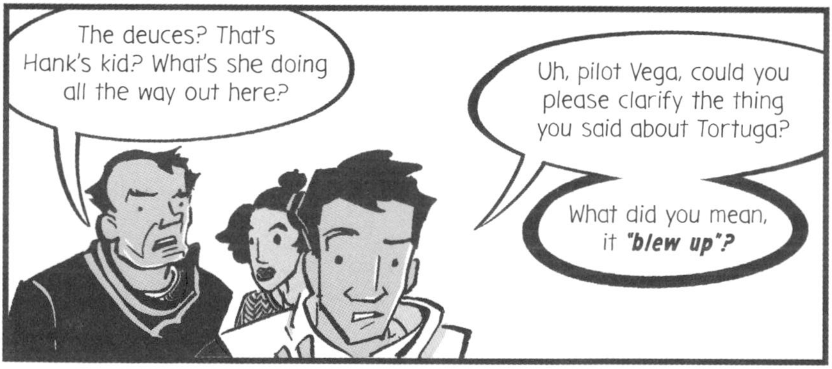
The deuces? That's Hank's kid? What's she doing all the way out here?
Uh, pilot Vega, could you please clarify the thing you said about Tortuga?
What did you mean, it ***"blew up"?***

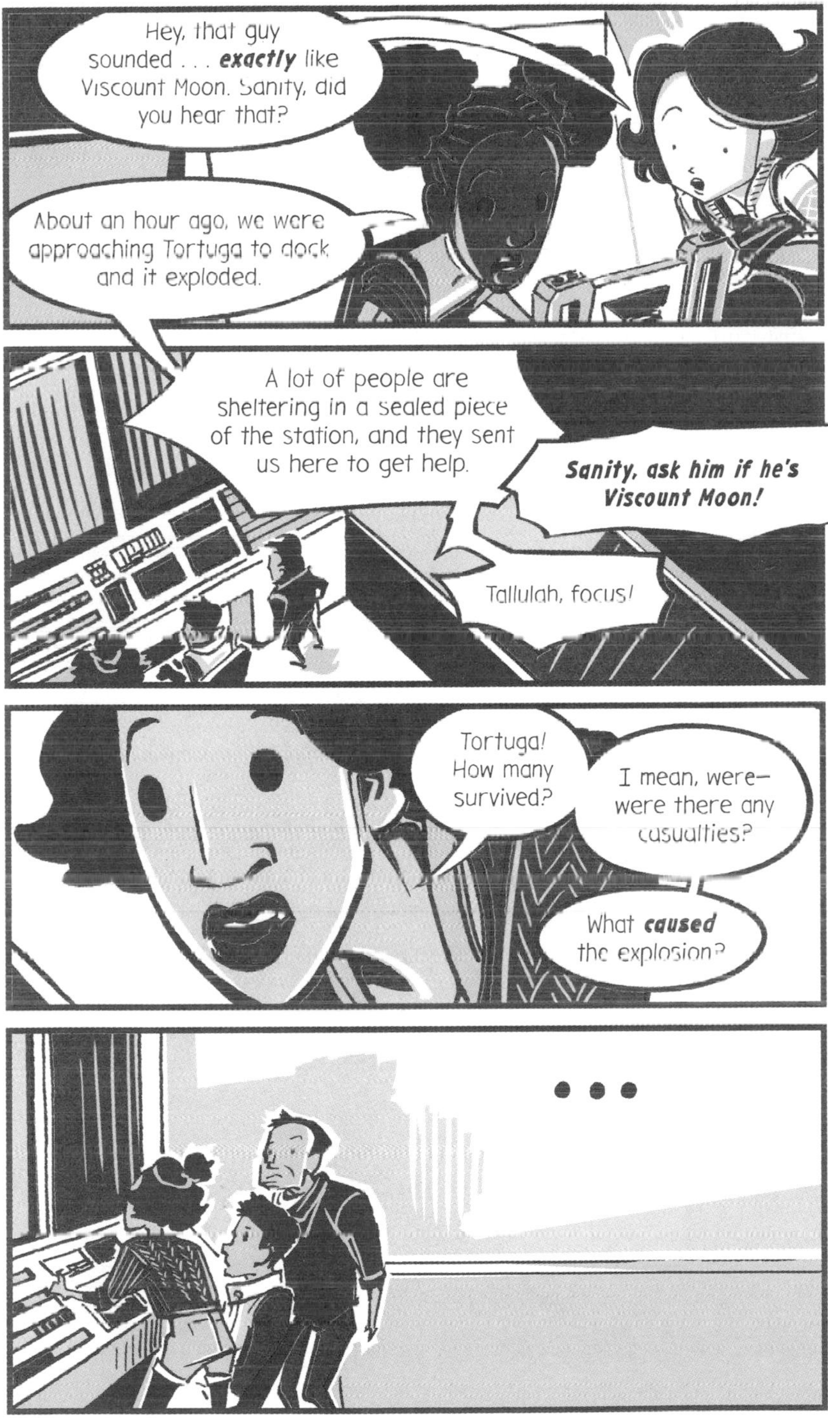
Hey, that guy sounded . . . **exactly** like Viscount Moon. Sanity, did you hear that?
About an hour ago, we were approaching Tortuga to dock and it exploded.
A lot of people are sheltering in a sealed piece of the station, and they sent us here to get help.
Sanity, ask him if he's Viscount Moon!
Tallulah, focus!
Tortuga! How many survived?
I mean, were—were there any casualties?
What **caused** the explosion?
. . .

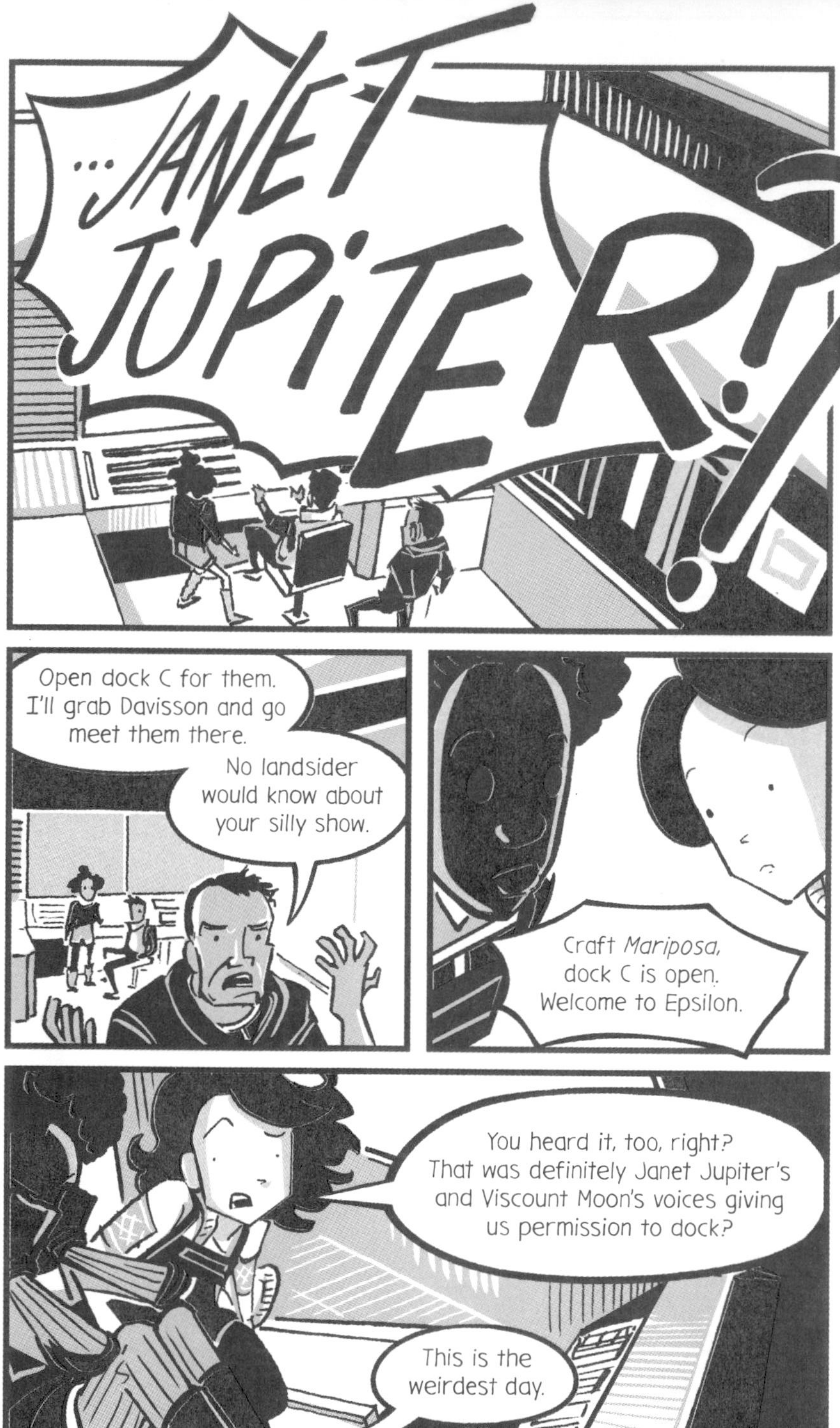
...JANET JUPITER?!
Open dock C for them. I'll grab Davisson and go meet them there.
No landsider would know about your silly show.
Craft *Mariposa*, dock C is open. Welcome to Epsilon.
You heard it, too, right? That was definitely Janet Jupiter's and Viscount Moon's voices giving us permission to dock?
This is the weirdest day.

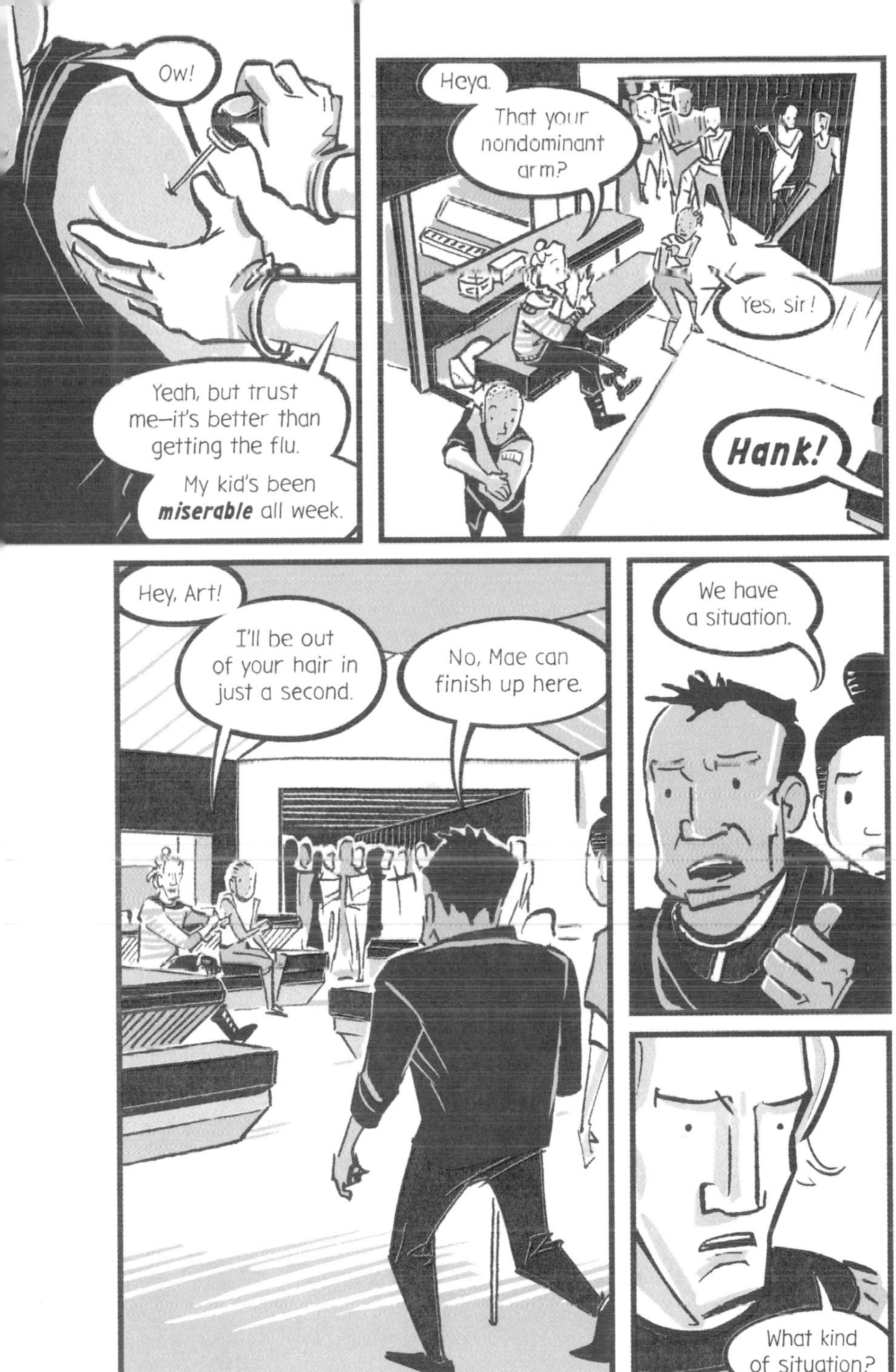
Ow!
Yeah, but trust me—it's better than getting the flu.
My kid's been **miserable** all week.
Heya.
That your nondominant arm?
Yes, sir!
Hank!
Hey, Art!
I'll be out of your hair in just a second.
No, Mae can finish up here.
We have a situation.
What kind of situation?

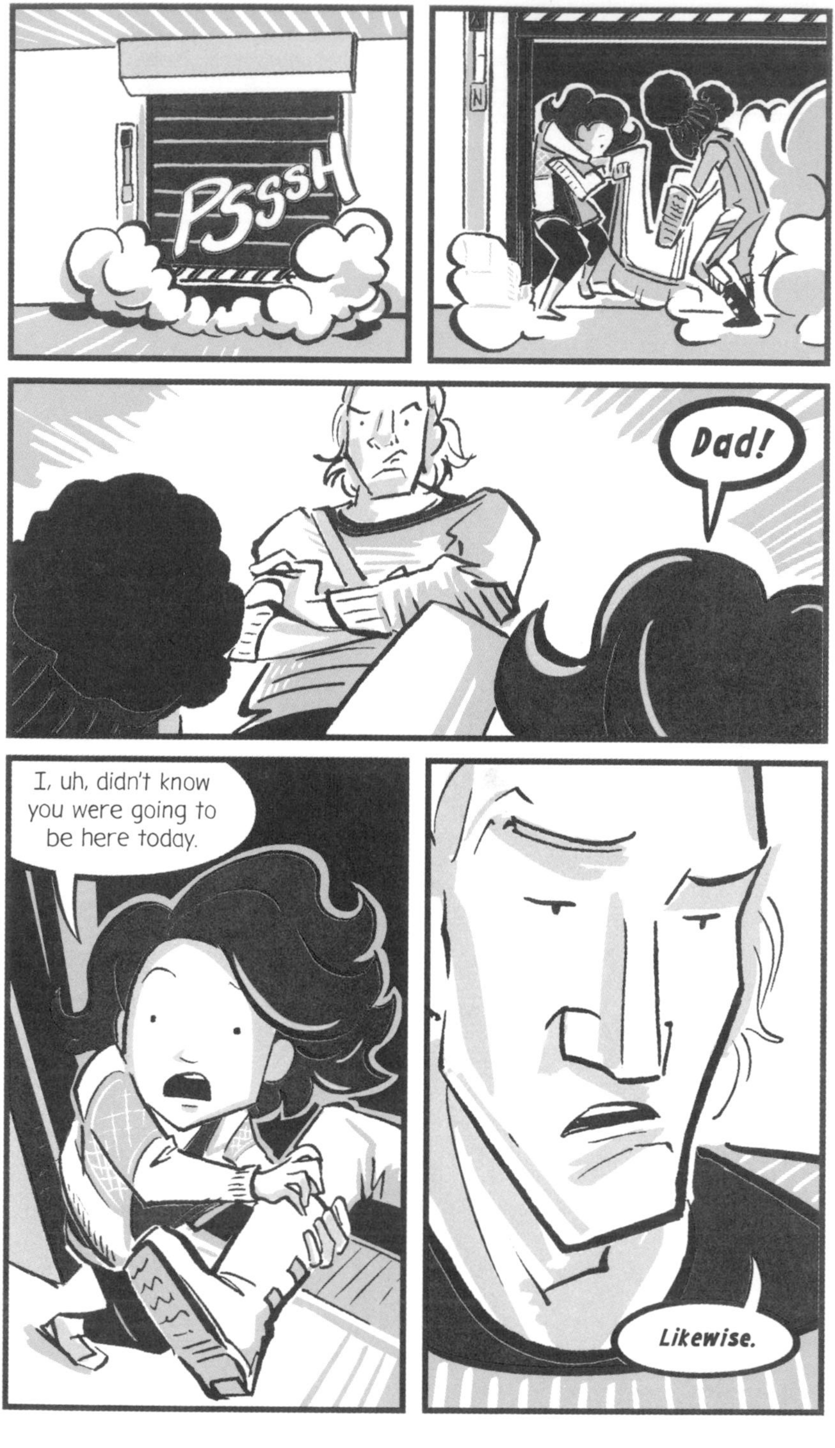
PSSSH
Dad!
I, uh, didn't know you were going to be here today.
Likewise.

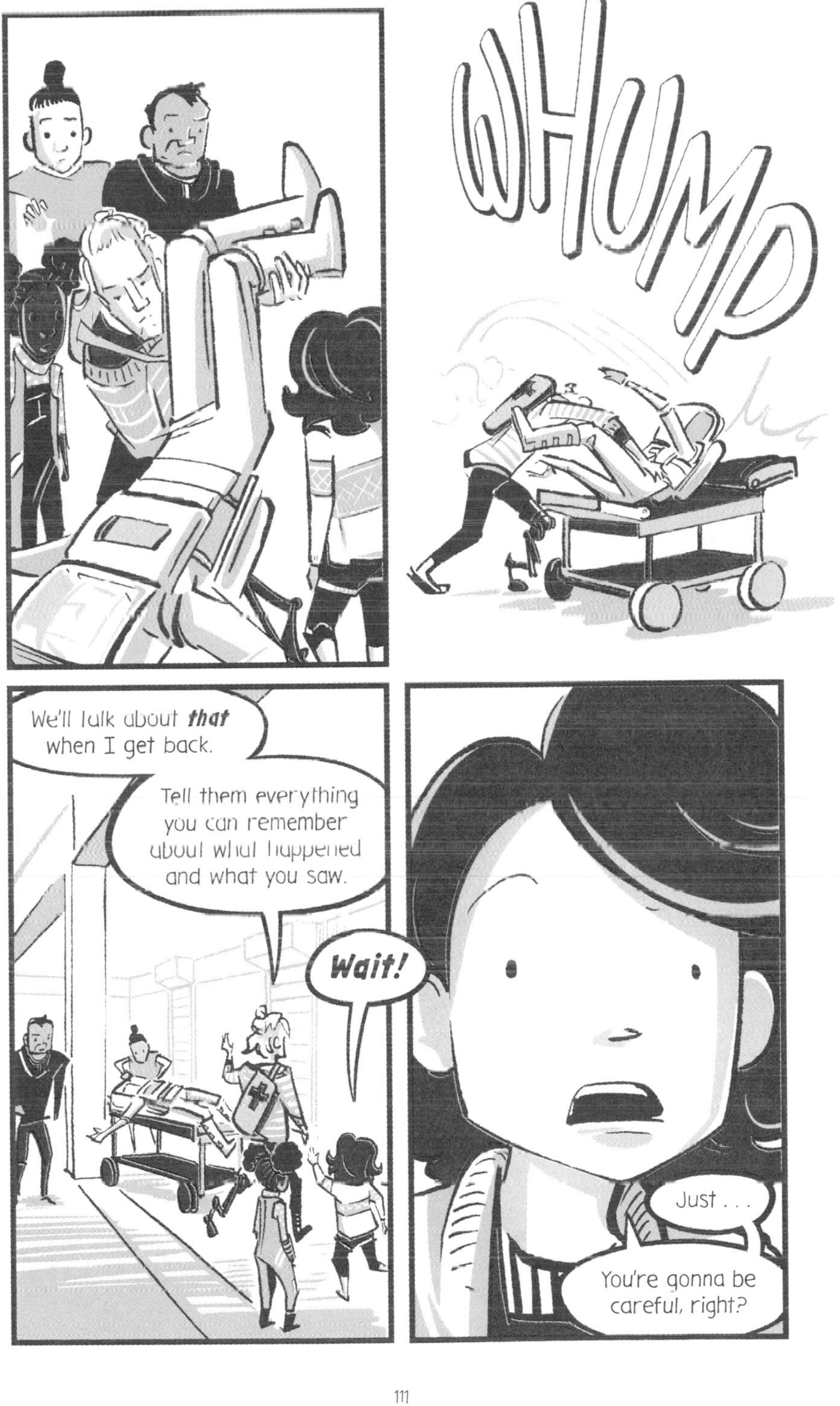
WHUMP
We'll talk about ***that*** when I get back.
Tell them everything you can remember about what happened and what you saw.
Wait!
Just . . .
You're gonna be careful, right?

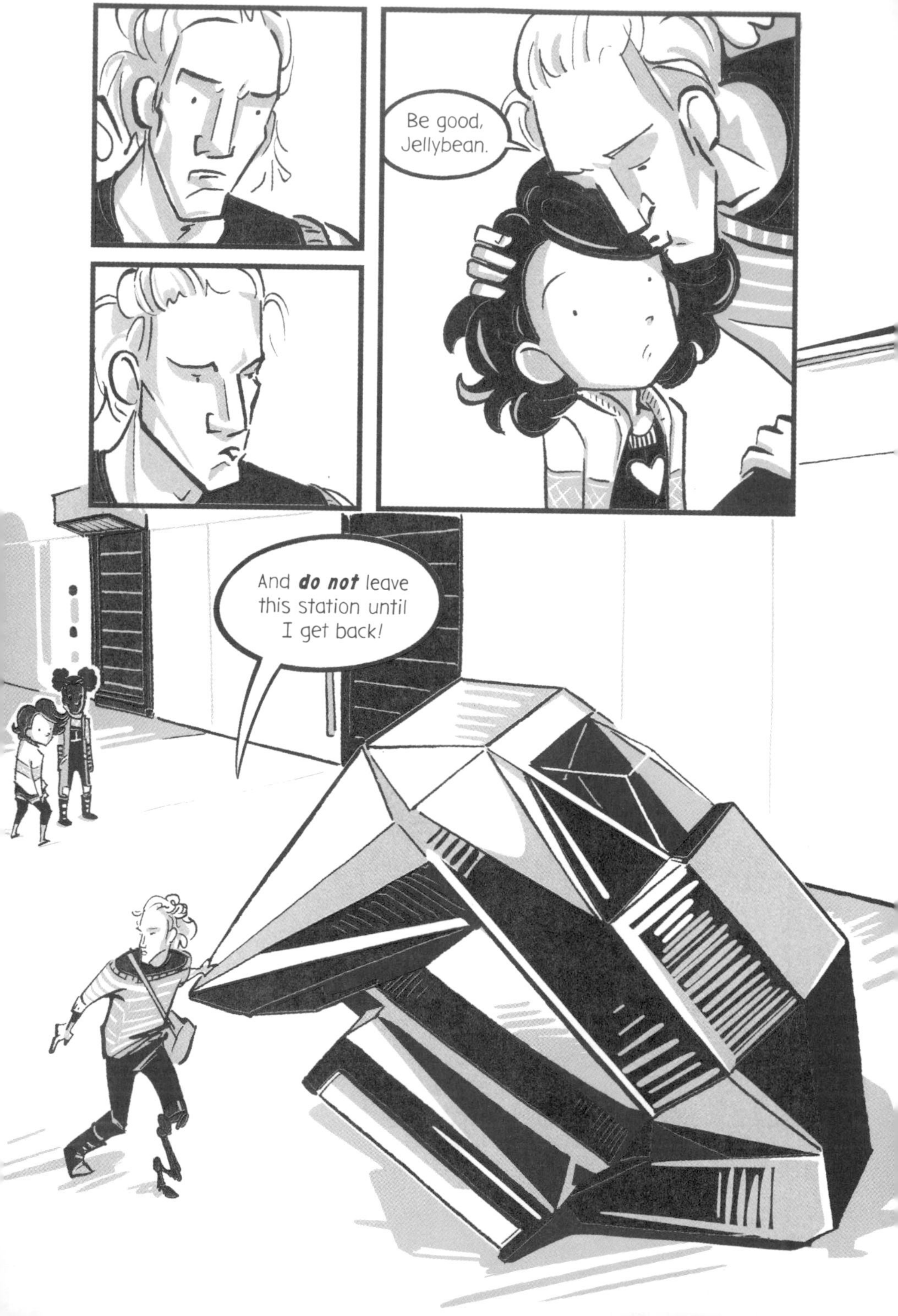
Be good, Jellybean.
And **do not** leave this station until I get back!

(MEANWHILE, ON WILNICK)

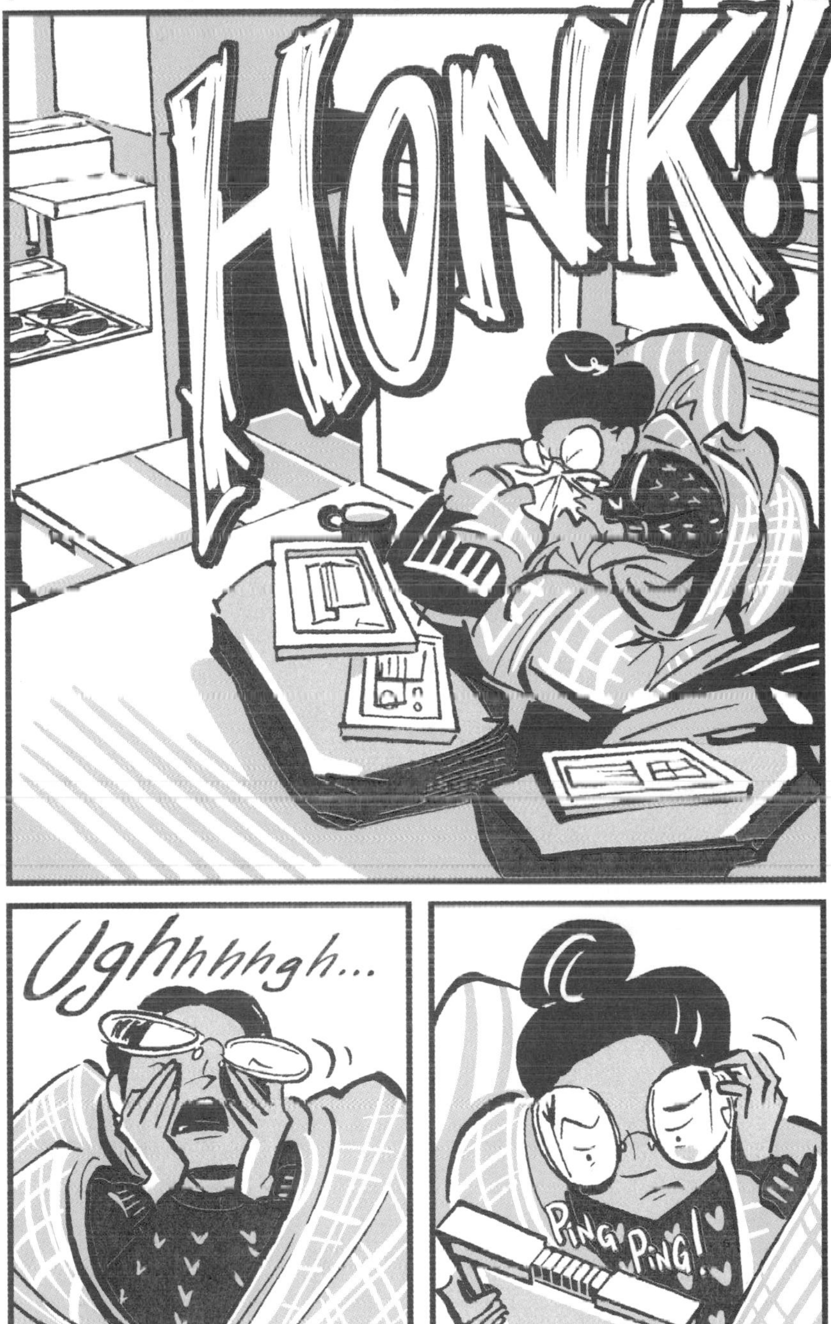
HONK!
Ughhhhgh...
PING PING!

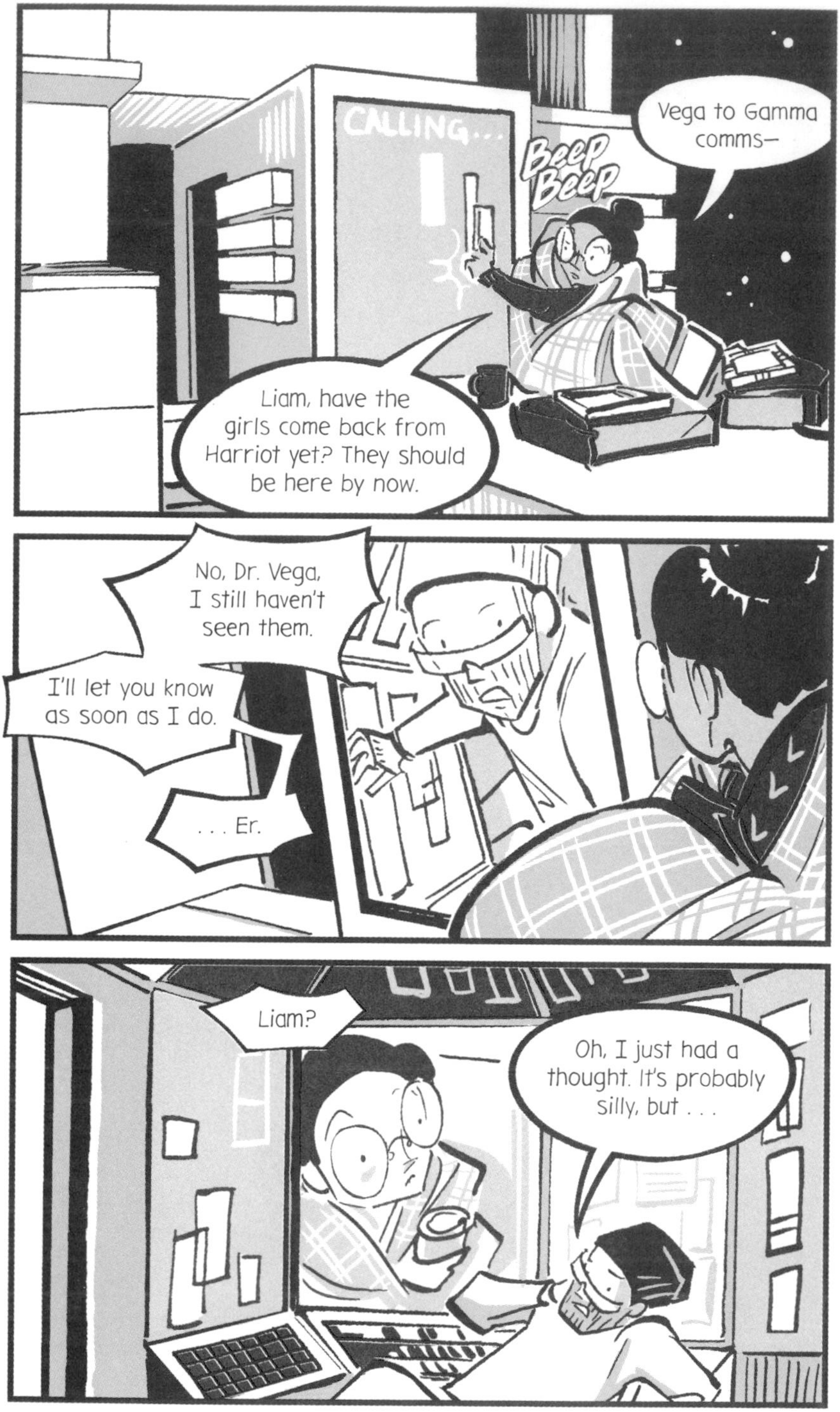
CALLING...
Beep Beep
Vega to Gamma comms—
Liam, have the girls come back from Harriot yet? They should be here by now.
No, Dr. Vega, I still haven't seen them.
I'll let you know as soon as I do.
. . . Er.
Liam?
Oh, I just had a thought. It's probably silly, but . . .

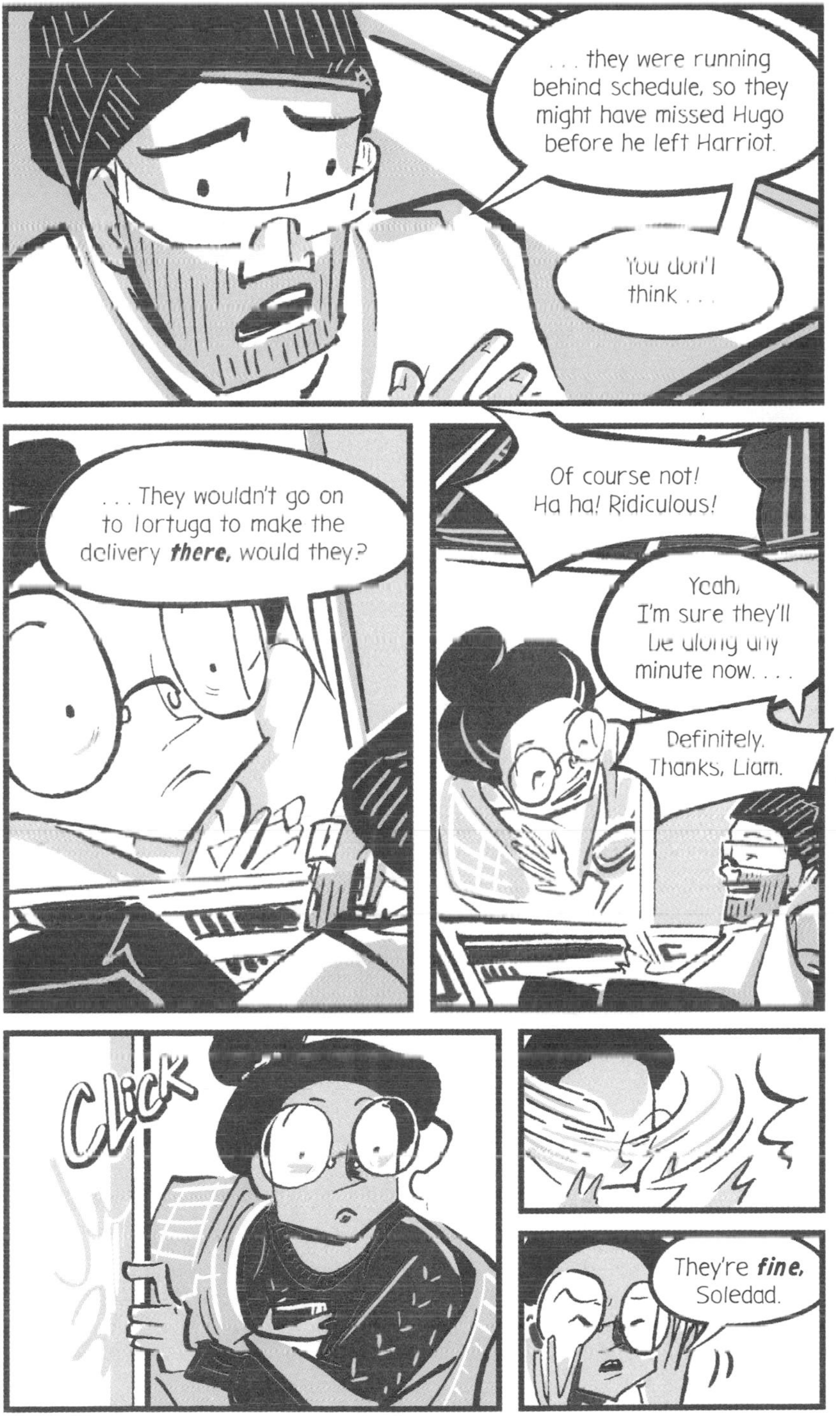
. . . they were running behind schedule, so they might have missed Hugo before he left Harriot.
You don't think . . .
. . . They wouldn't go on to Tortuga to make the delivery **there,** would they?
Of course not! Ha ha! Ridiculous!
Yeah, I'm sure they'll be along any minute now. . . .
Definitely. Thanks, Liam.
CLICK
They're **fine,** Soledad.

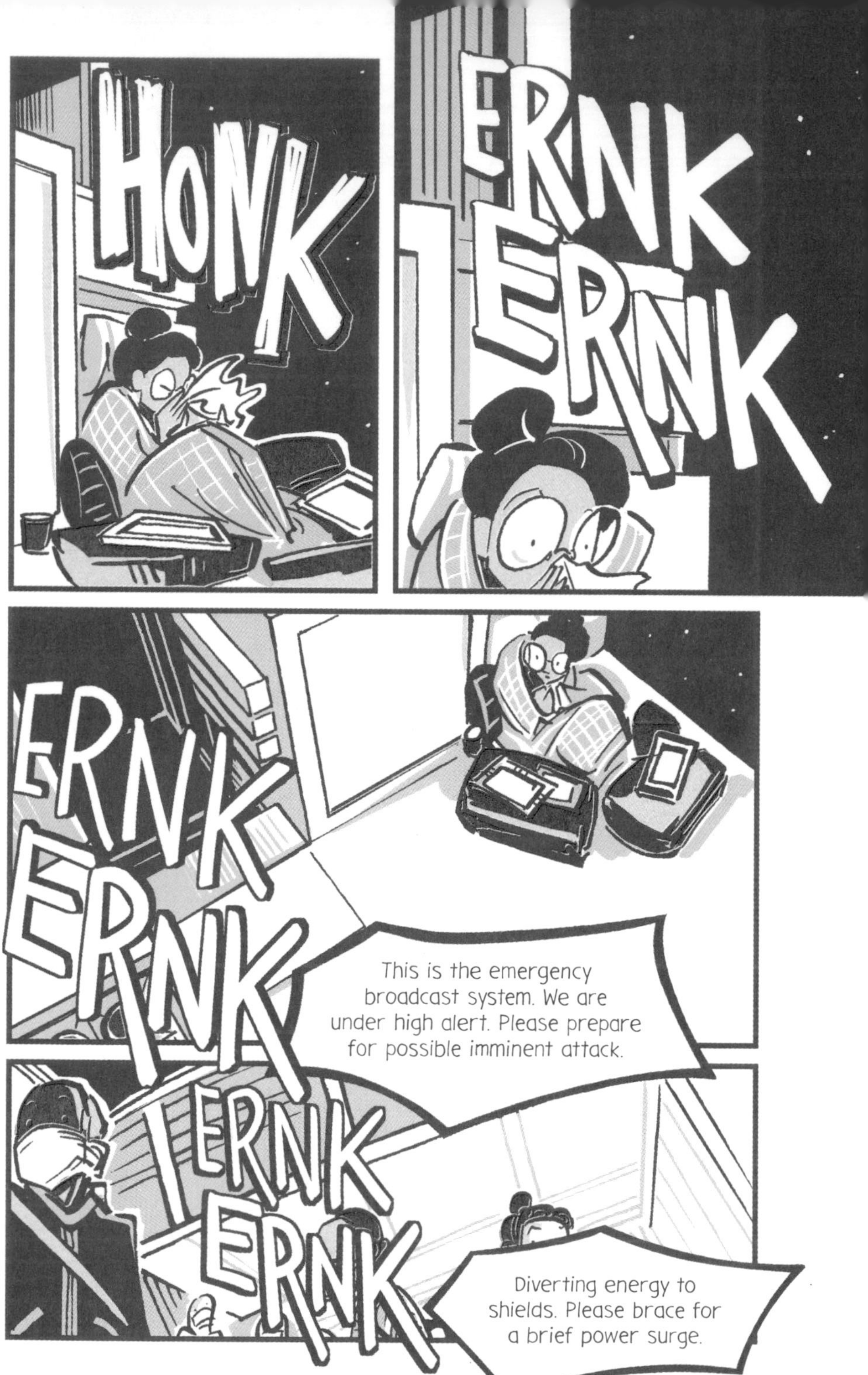
HONK
ERNK ERNK
ERNK ERNK
This is the emergency broadcast system. We are under high alert. Please prepare for possible imminent attack.
ERNK ERNK
Diverting energy to shields. Please brace for a brief power surge.

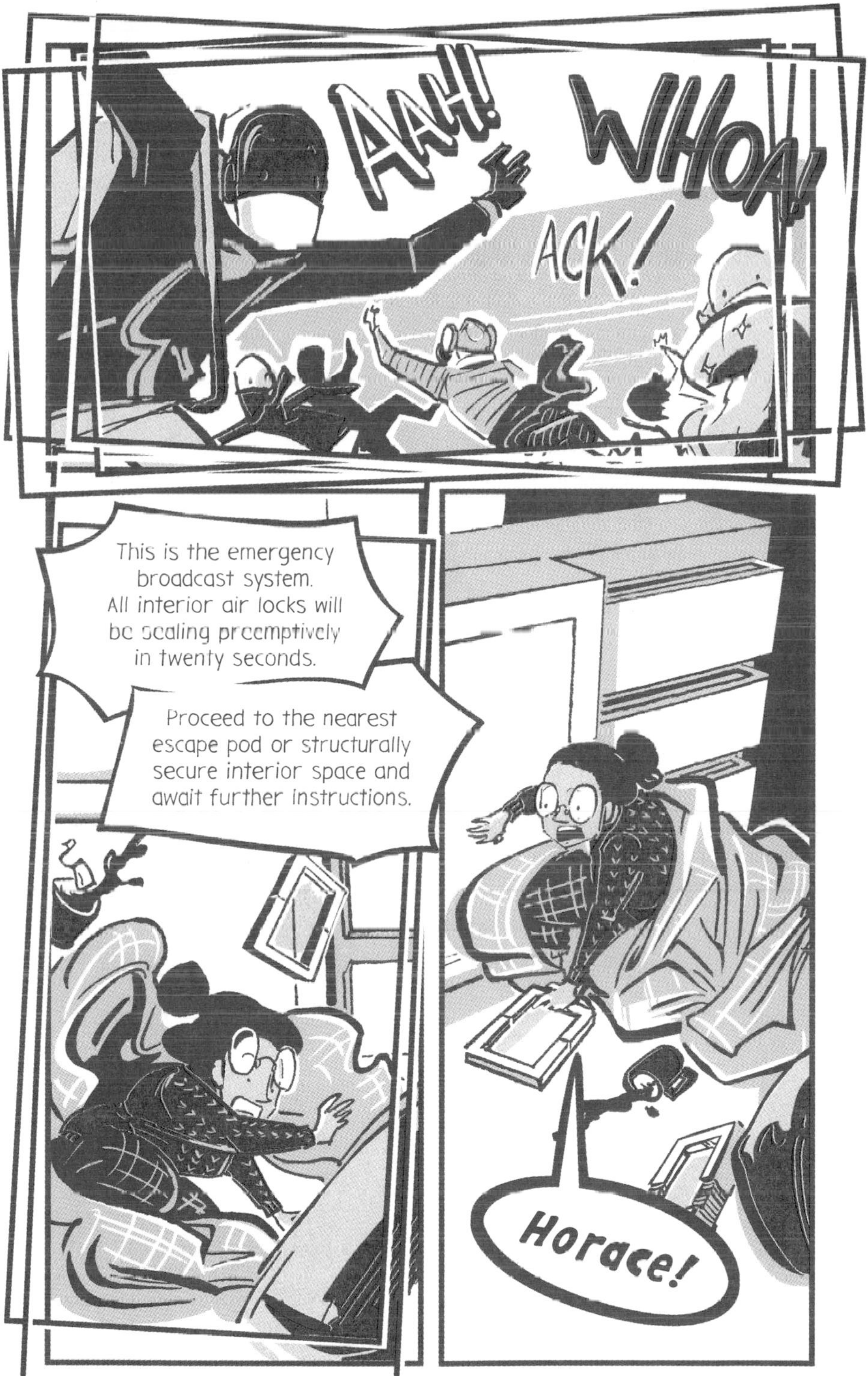
AAH!
WHOA!
ACK!
This is the emergency broadcast system. All interior air locks will be sealing preemptively in twenty seconds.
Proceed to the nearest escape pod or structurally secure interior space and await further instructions.
Horace!

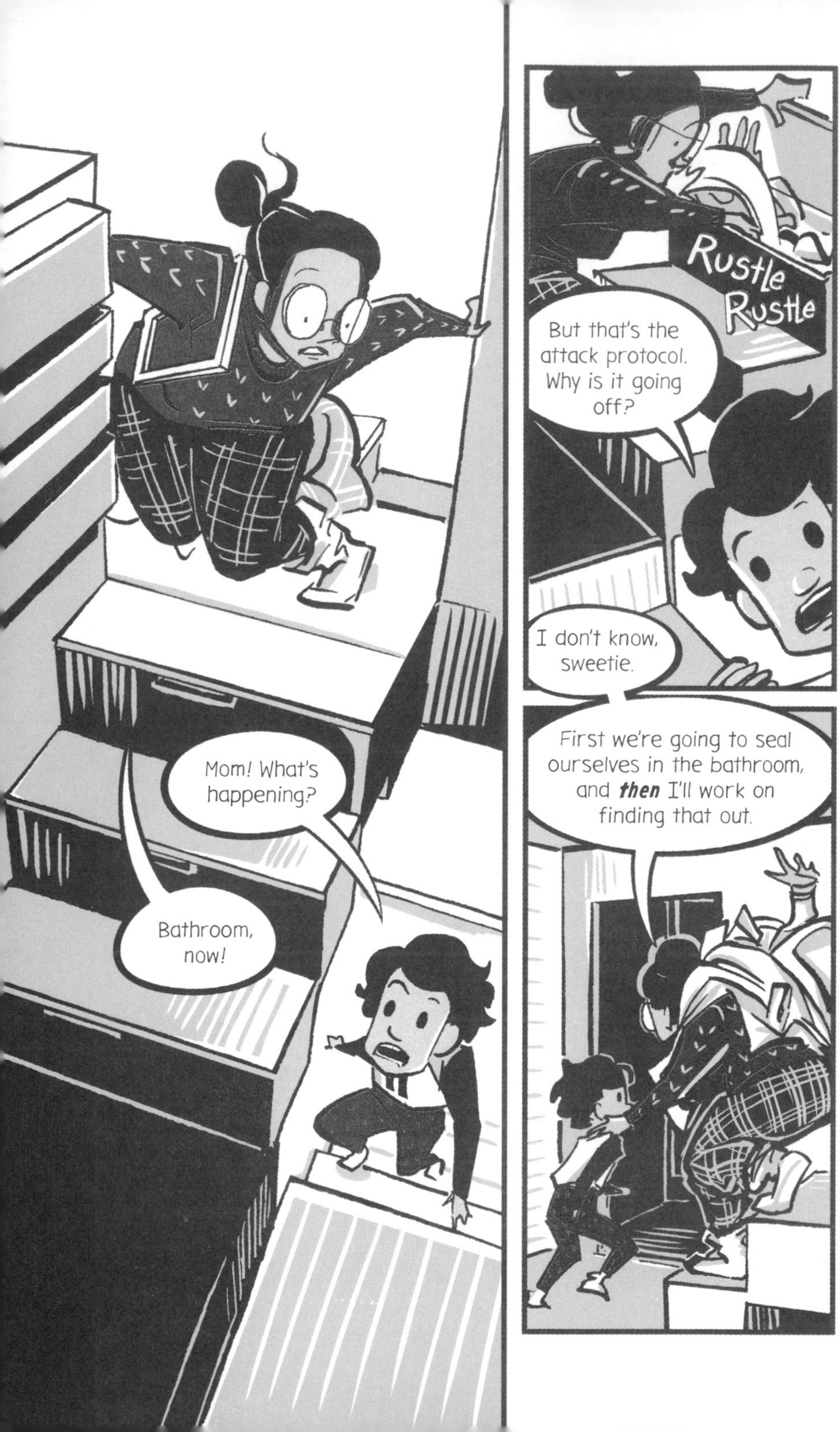
Mom! What's happening?
Bathroom, now!
Rustle Rustle
But that's the attack protocol. Why is it going off?
I don't know, sweetie.
First we're going to seal ourselves in the bathroom, and **then** I'll work on finding that out.

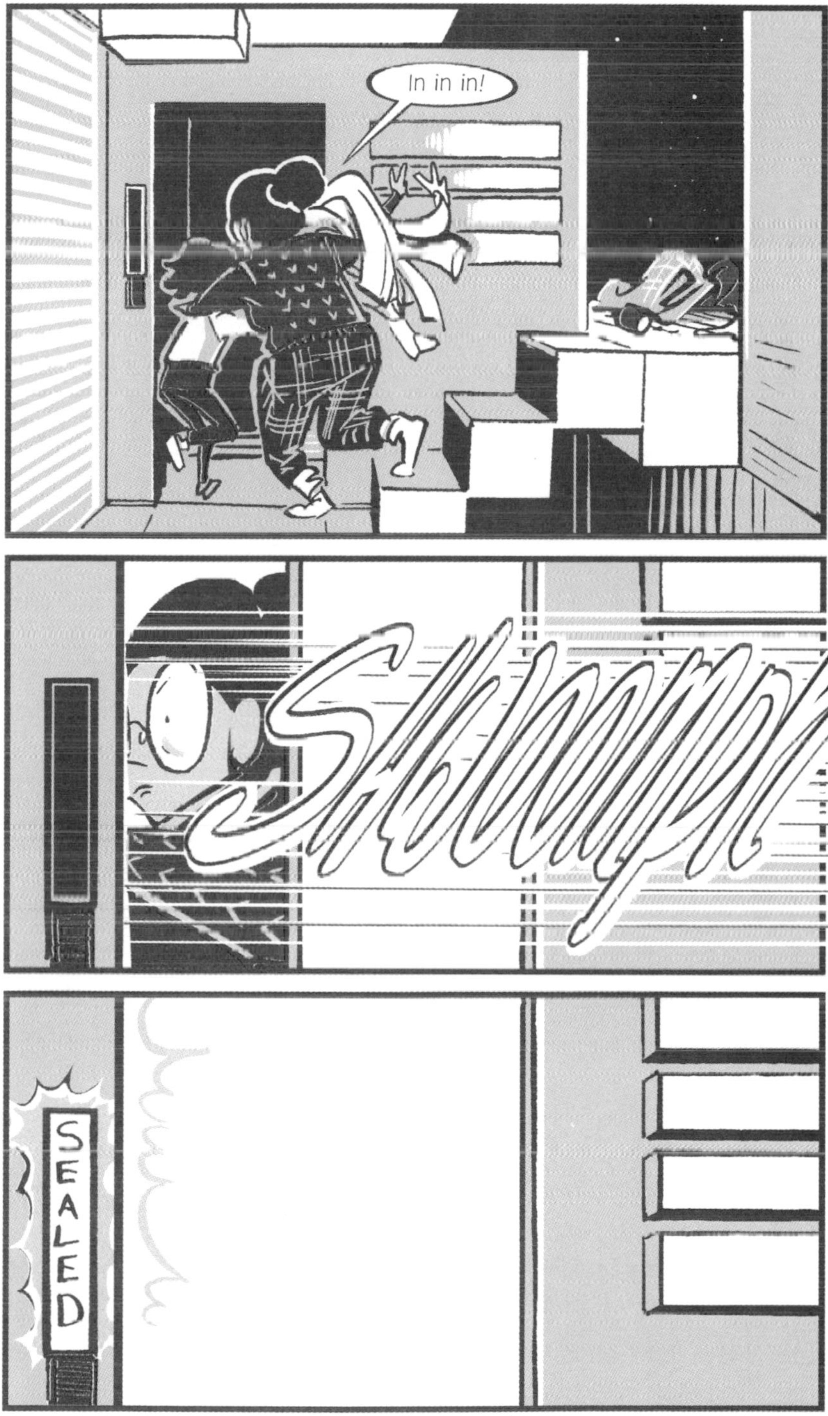
In in in!
SHUMPH
SEALED

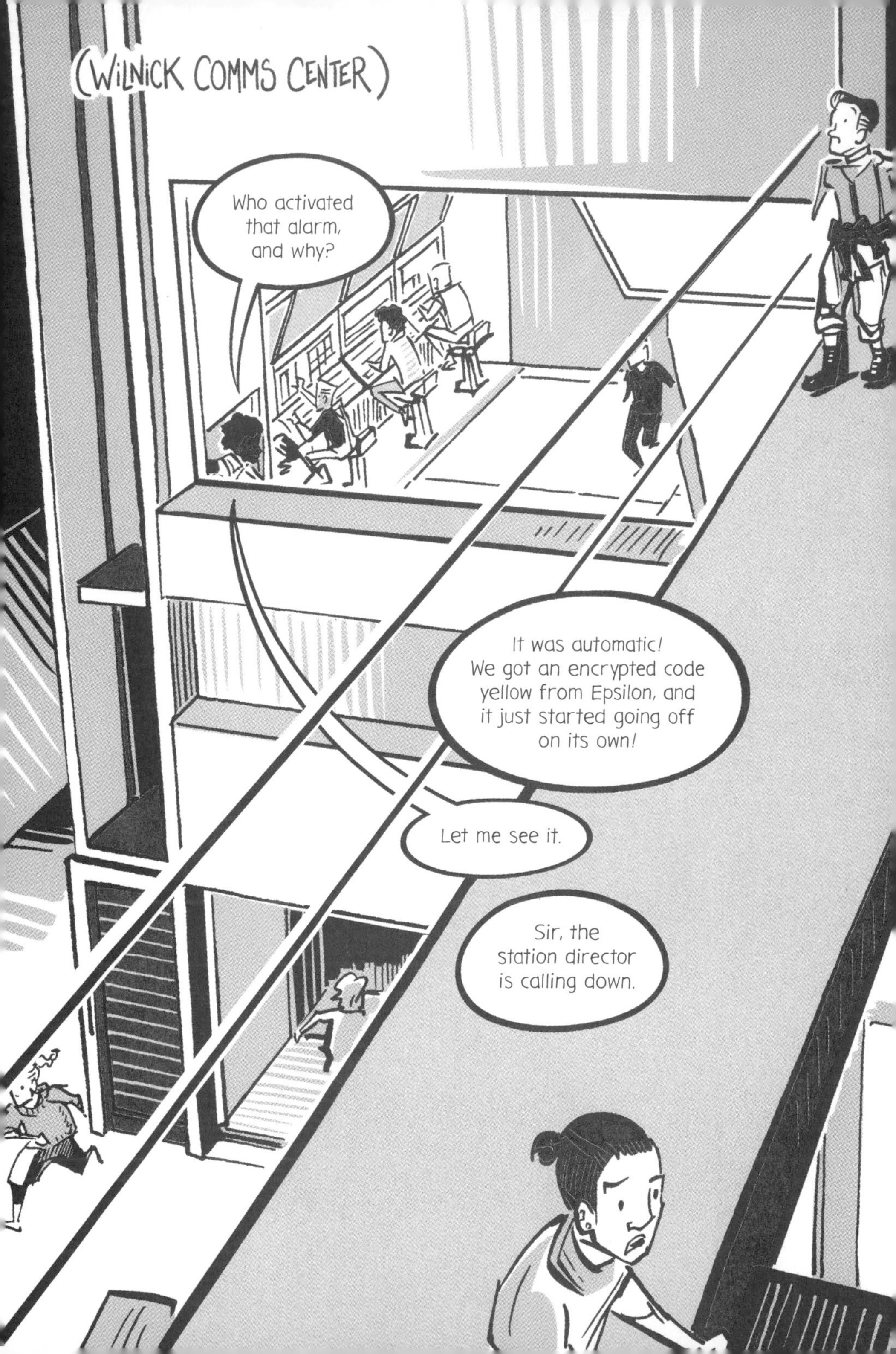
(WILNICK COMMS CENTER)
Who activated that alarm, and why?
It was automatic! We got an encrypted code yellow from Epsilon, and it just started going off on its own!
Let me see it.
Sir, the station director is calling down.

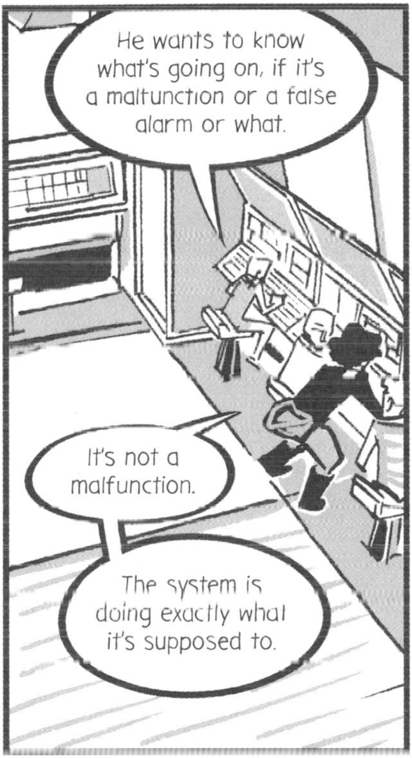
He wants to know what's going on, if it's a malfunction or a false alarm or what.
It's not a malfunction.
The system is doing exactly what it's supposed to.

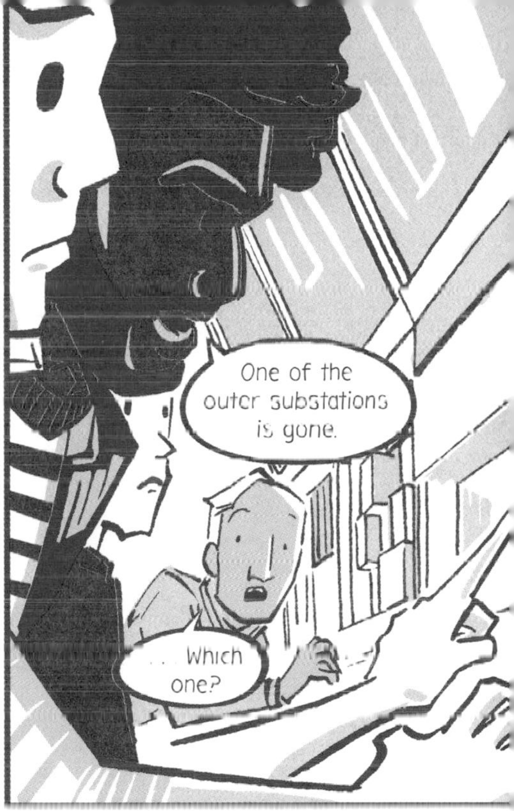
One of the outer substations is gone.
... Which one?

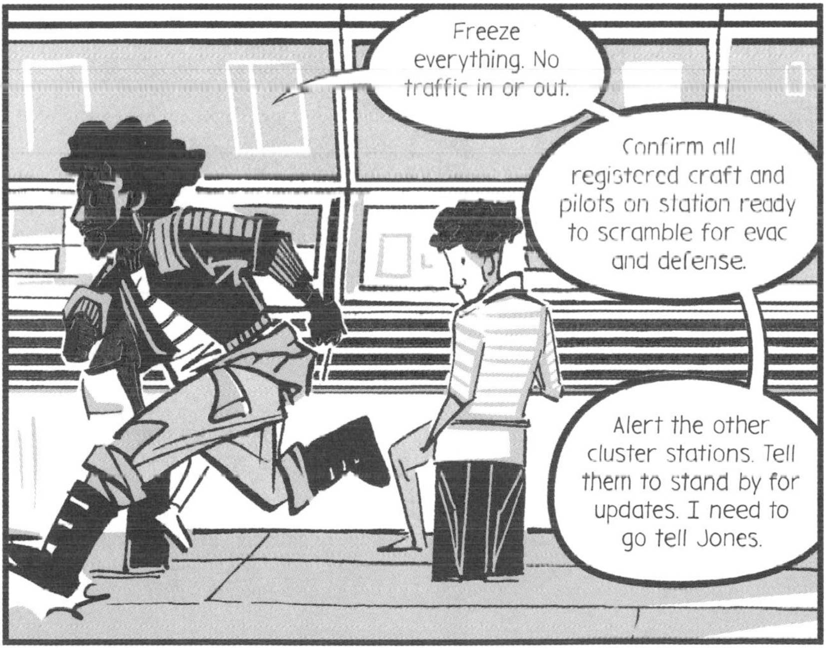
Freeze everything. No traffic in or out.
Confirm all registered craft and pilots on station ready to scramble for evac and defense.
Alert the other cluster stations. Tell them to stand by for updates. I need to go tell Jones.

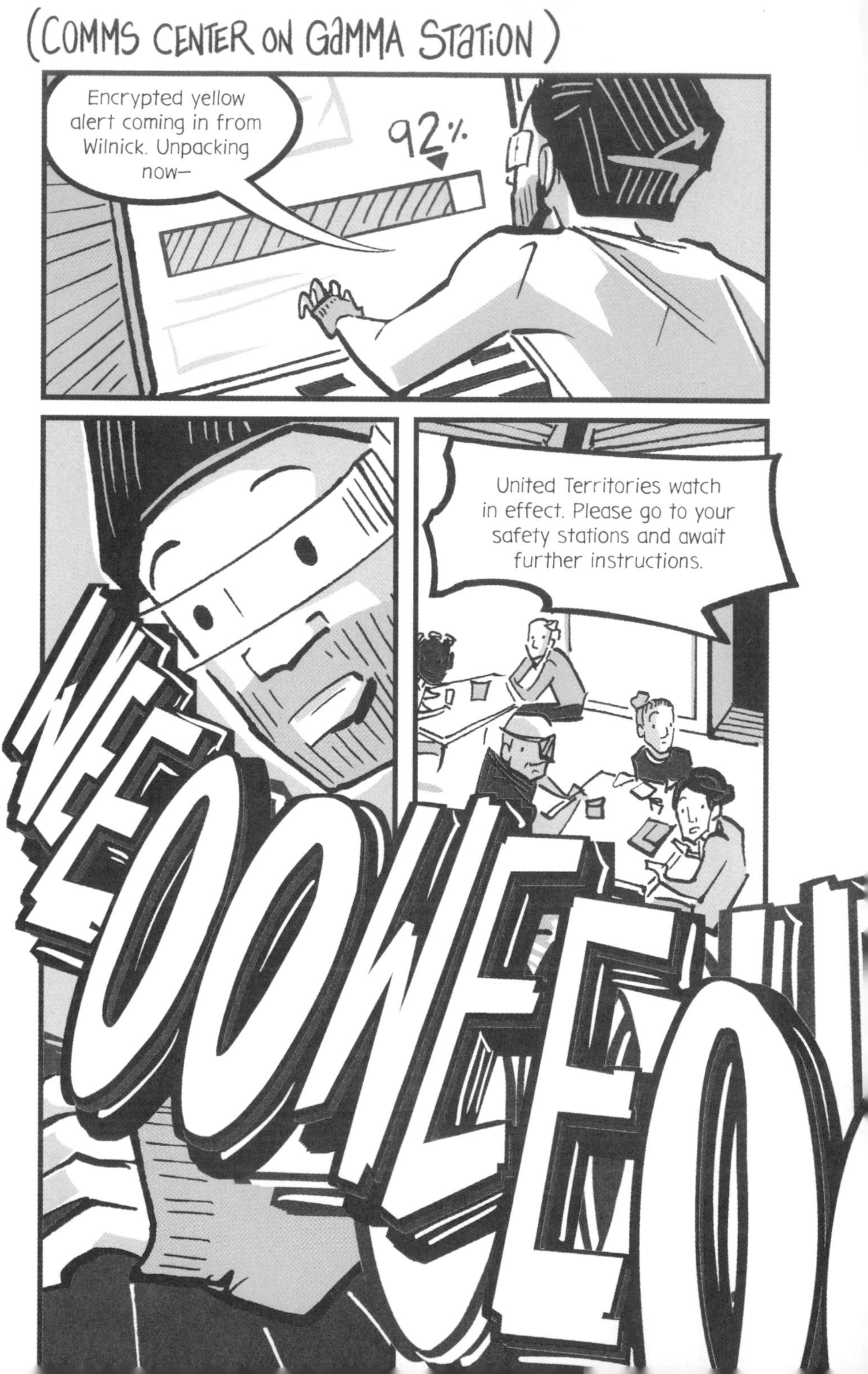
(COMMS CENTER ON GAMMA STATION)
Encrypted yellow alert coming in from Wilnick. Unpacking now—
92%
United Territories watch in effect. Please go to your safety stations and await further instructions.

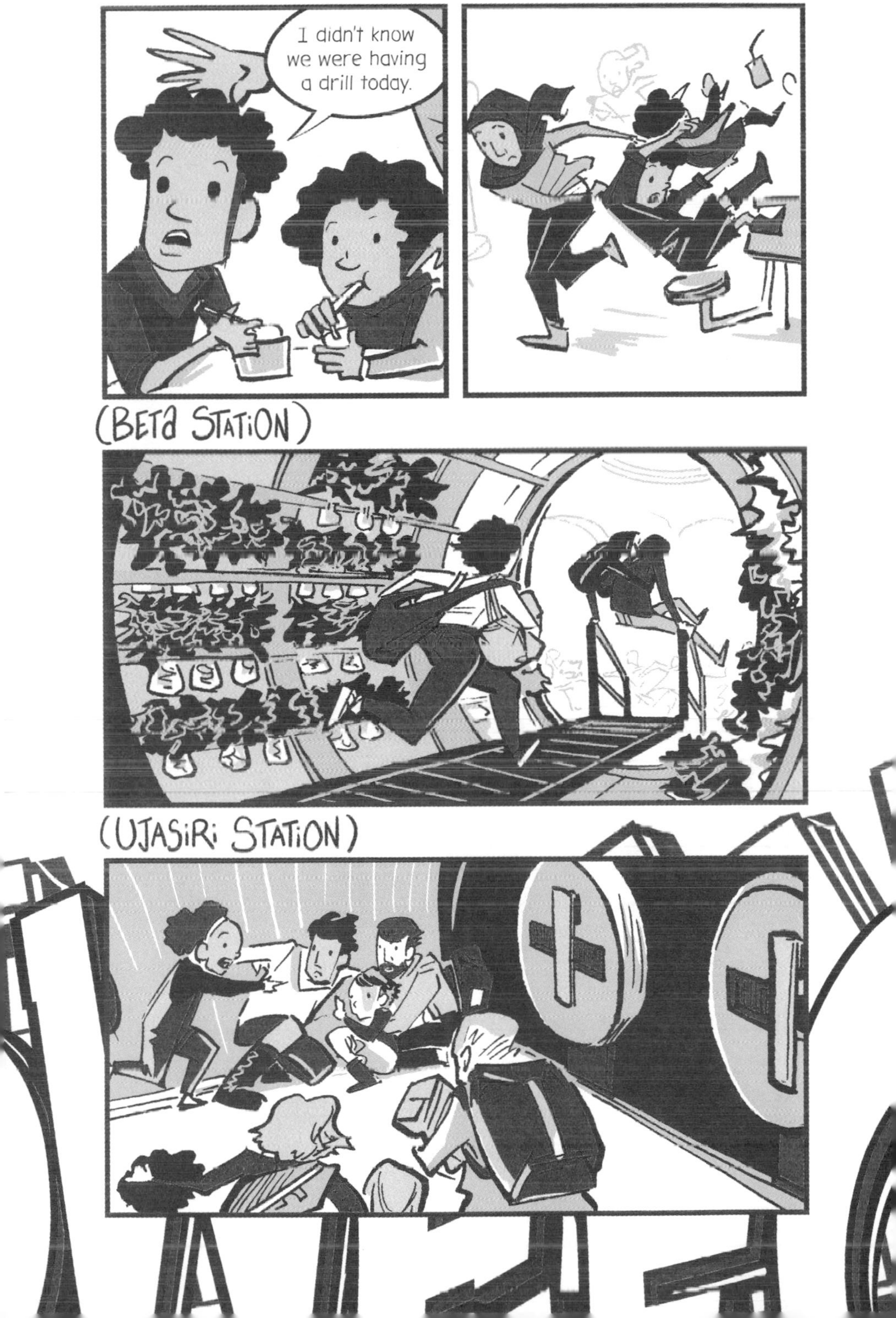
I didn't know we were having a drill today.
(BETA STATION)
(UJASIRI STATION)

(SAMRDDHI STATION)

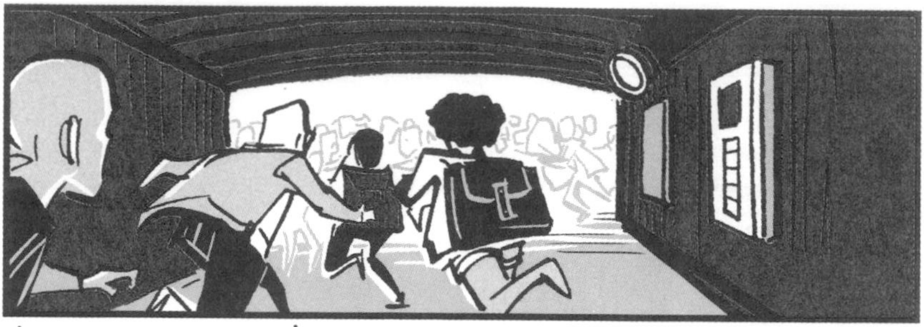

(LA PAZ STATION)

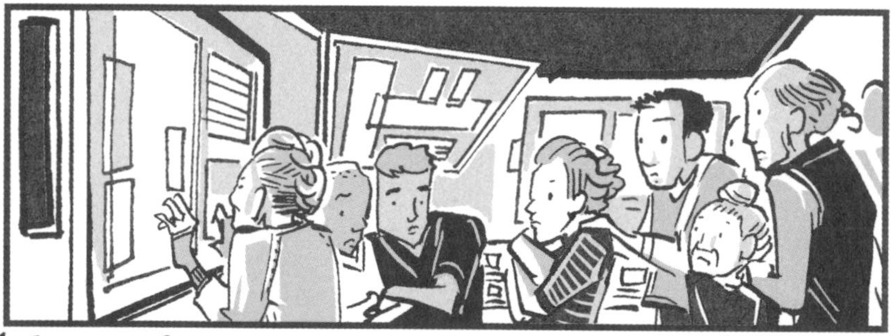

(TARNA STATION)

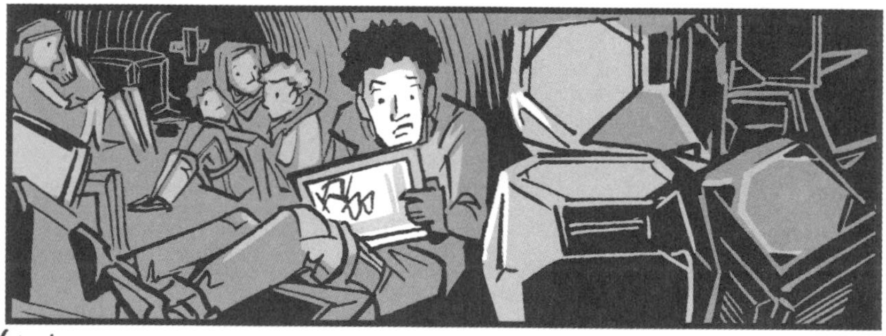

(WILNICK STATION)

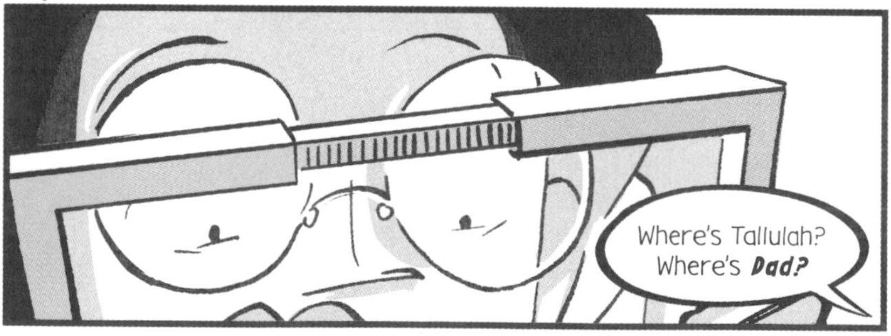
Where's Tallulah? Where's **Dad?**

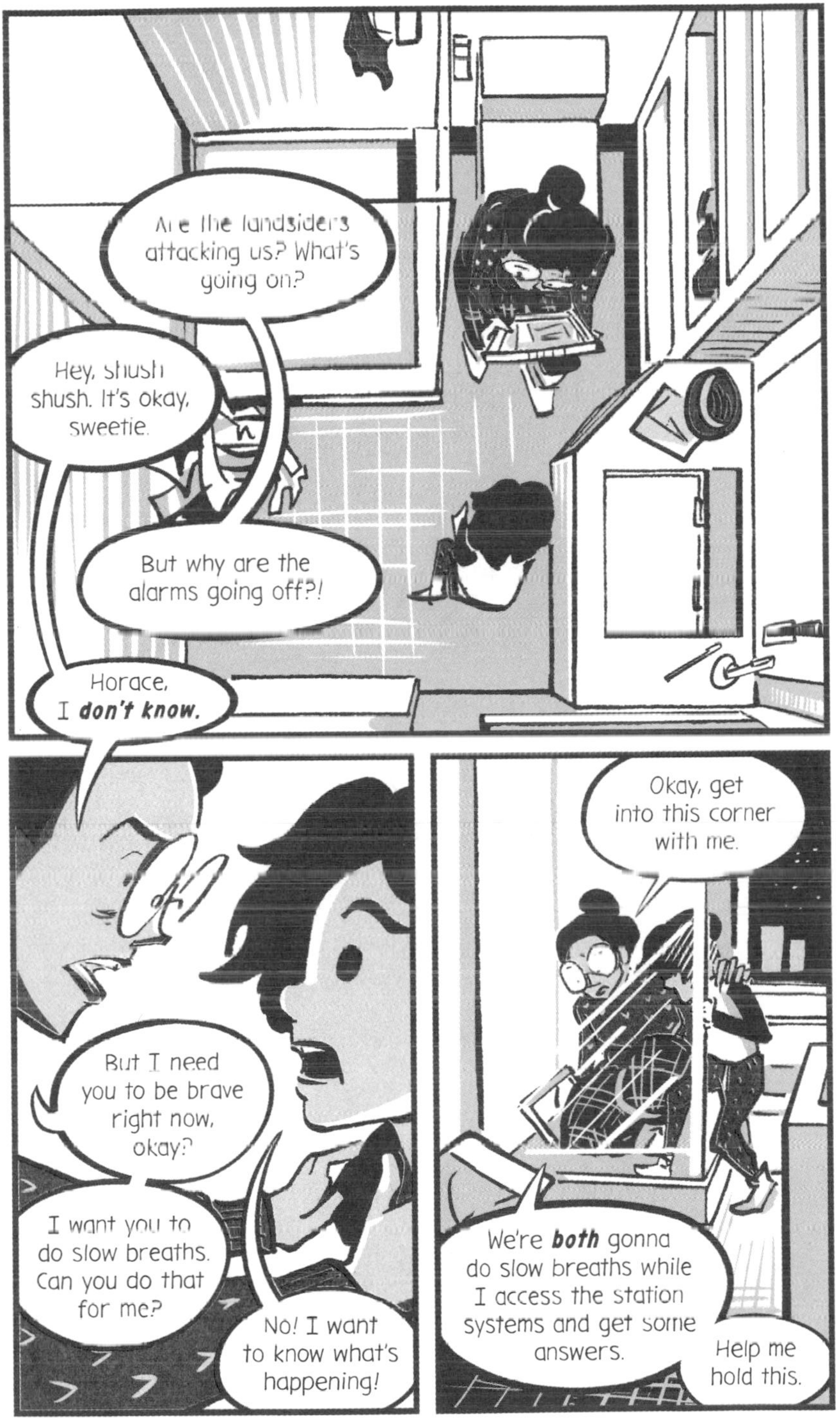

Are the landsiders attacking us? What's going on?
Hey, shush shush. It's okay, sweetie.
But why are the alarms going off?!
Horace, I **don't know.**
But I need you to be brave right now, okay?
I want you to do slow breaths. Can you do that for me?
No! I want to know what's happening!
Okay, get into this corner with me.
We're **both** gonna do slow breaths while I access the station systems and get some answers.
Help me hold this.

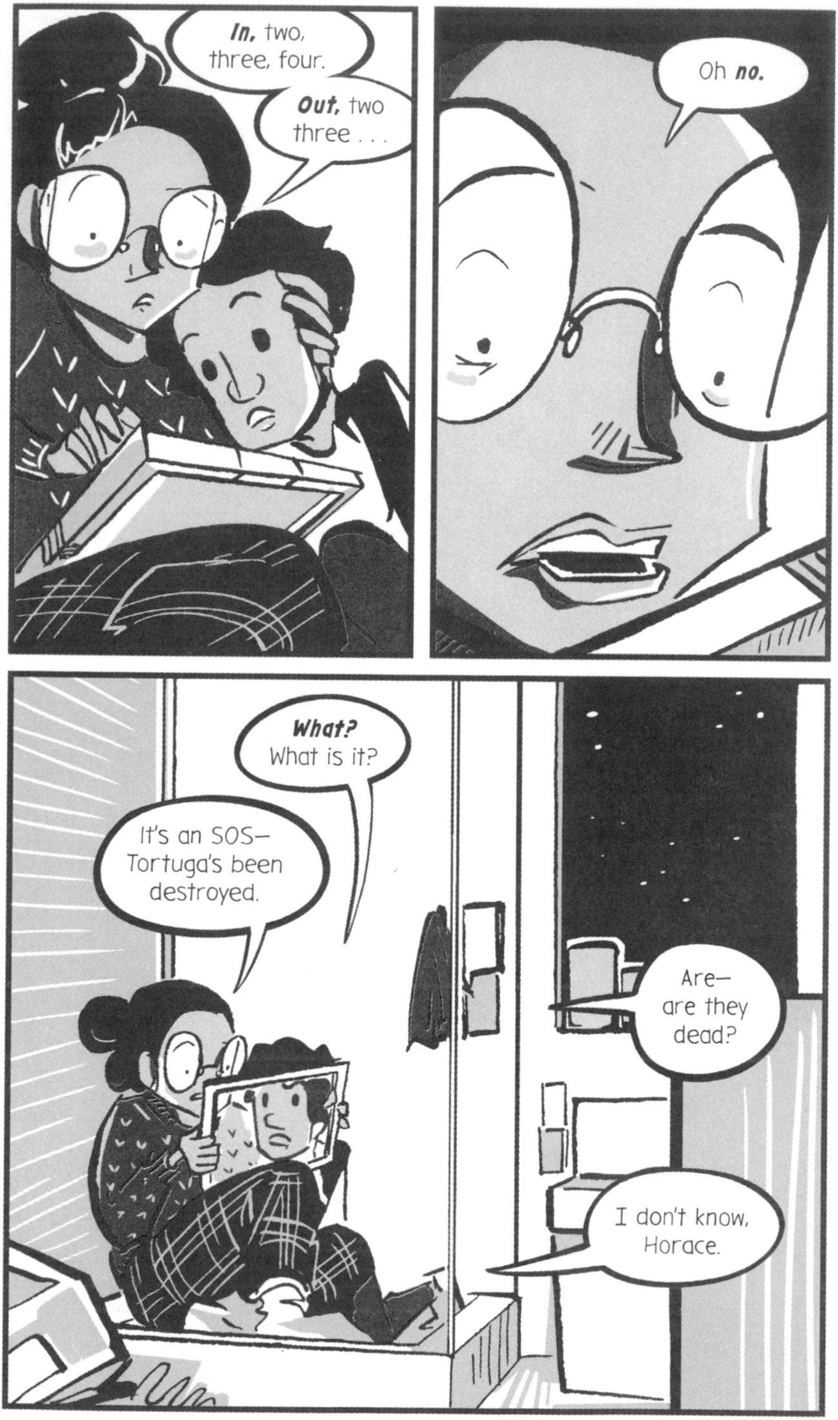

In, two, three, four.
Out, two three . . .
Oh **no.**
What? What is it?
It's an SOS— Tortuga's been destroyed.
Are— are they dead?
I don't know, Horace.

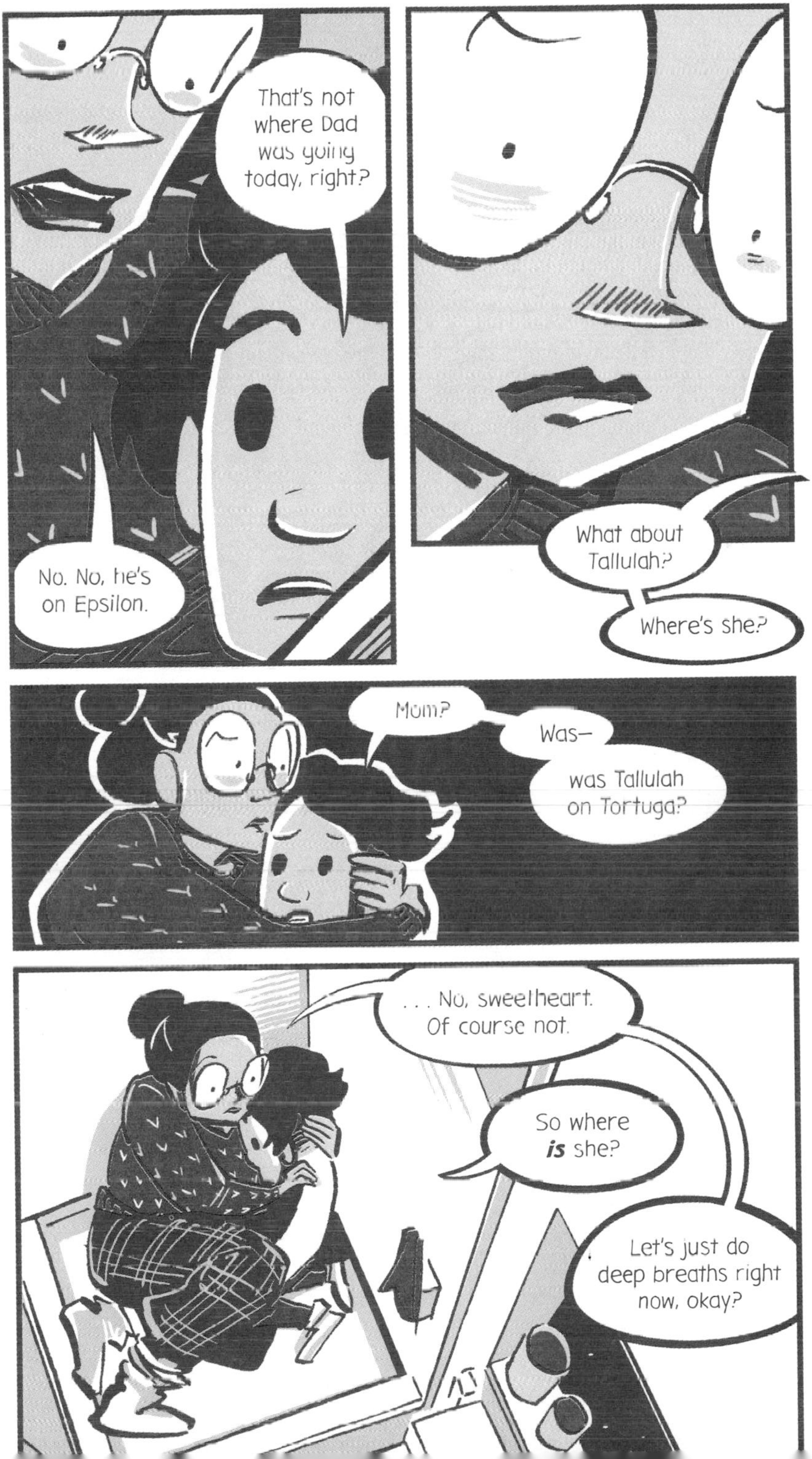

That's not where Dad was going today, right?
No. No, he's on Epsilon.
What about Tallulah?
Where's she?
Mom?
Was—
was Tallulah on Tortuga?
. . . No, sweetheart. Of course not.
So where ***is*** she?
Let's just do deep breaths right now, okay?

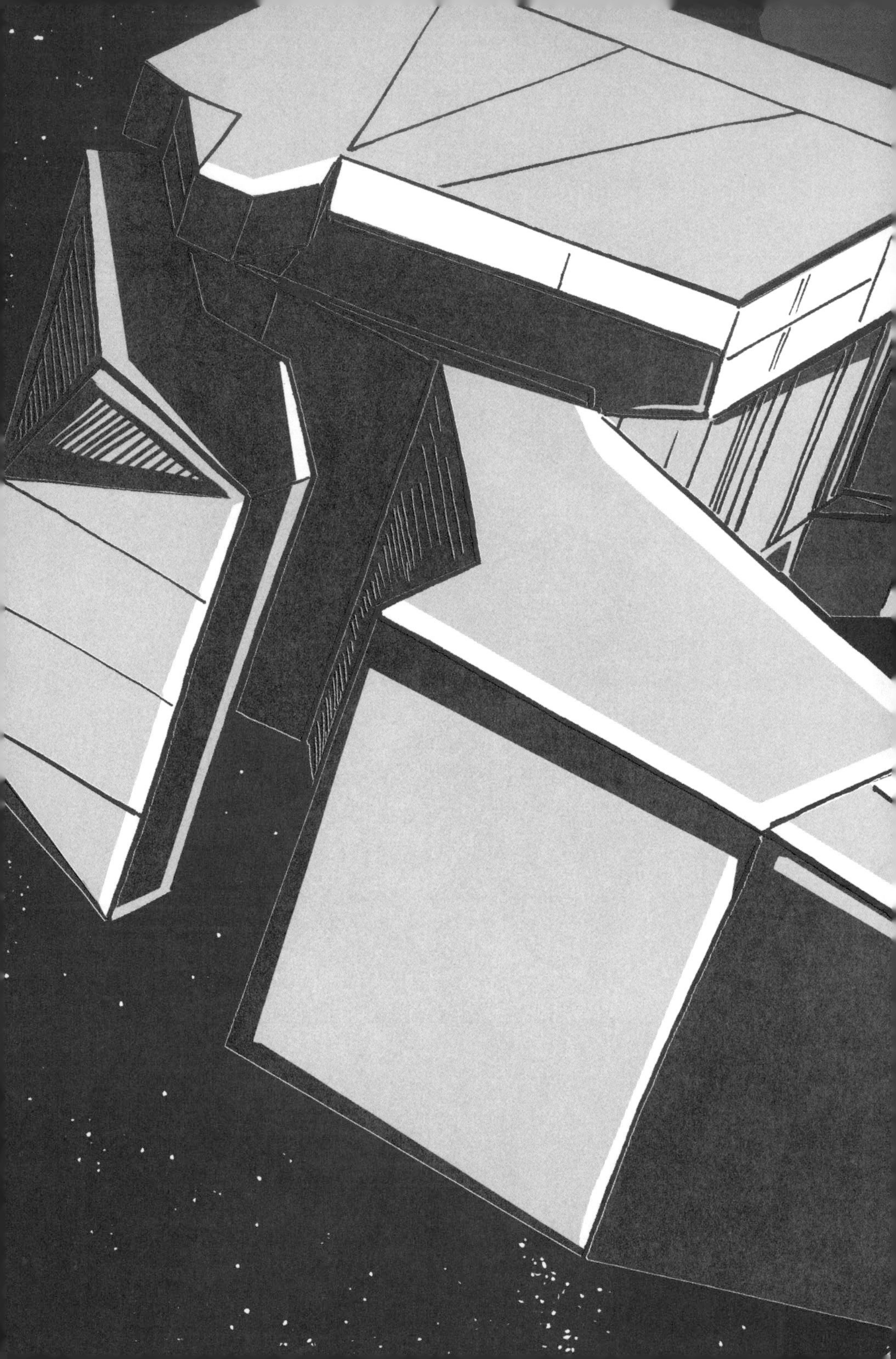

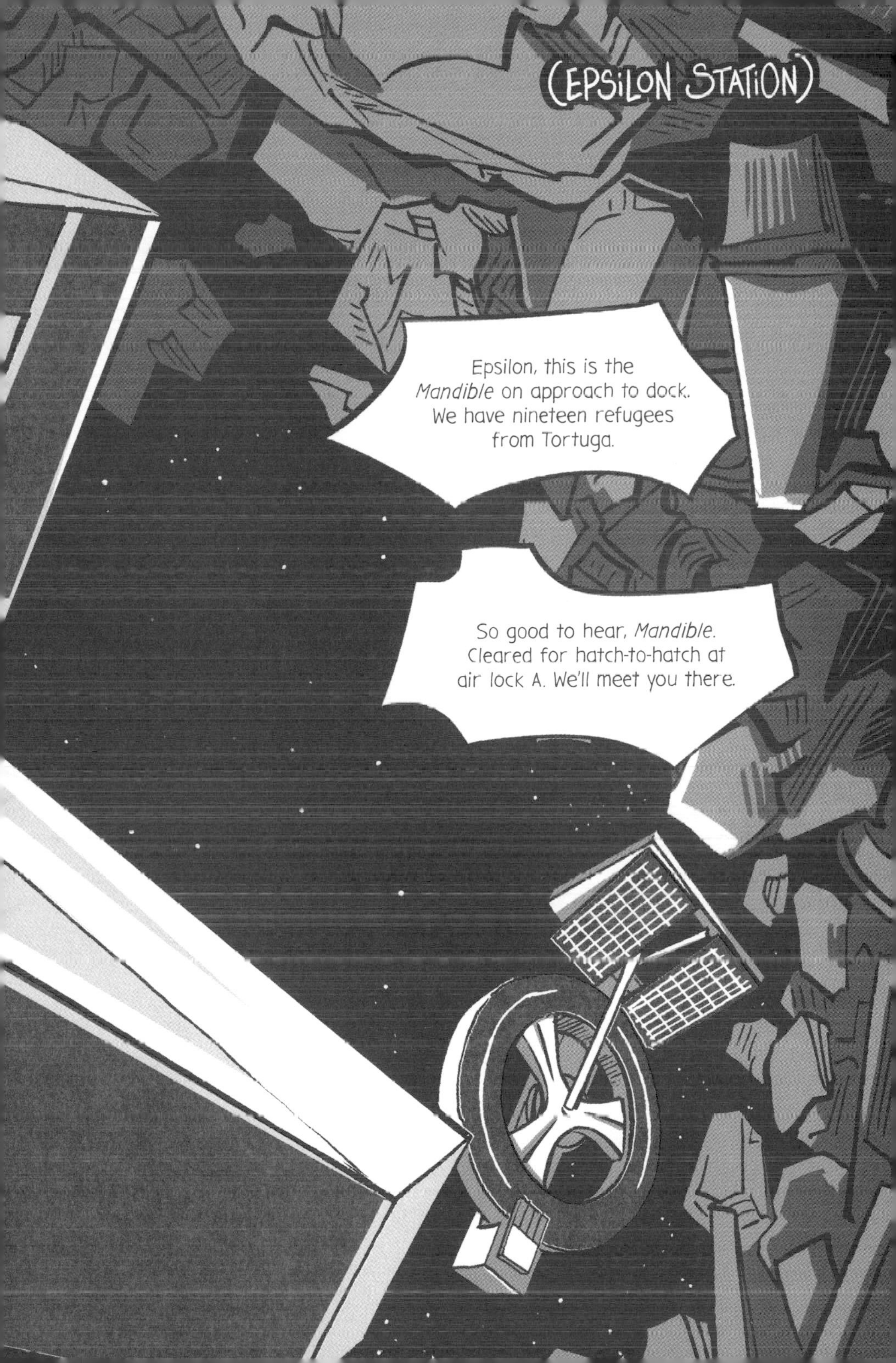
(EPSILON STATION)
Epsilon, this is the *Mandible* on approach to dock. We have nineteen refugees from Tortuga.
So good to hear, *Mandible*. Cleared for hatch-to-hatch at air lock A. We'll meet you there.

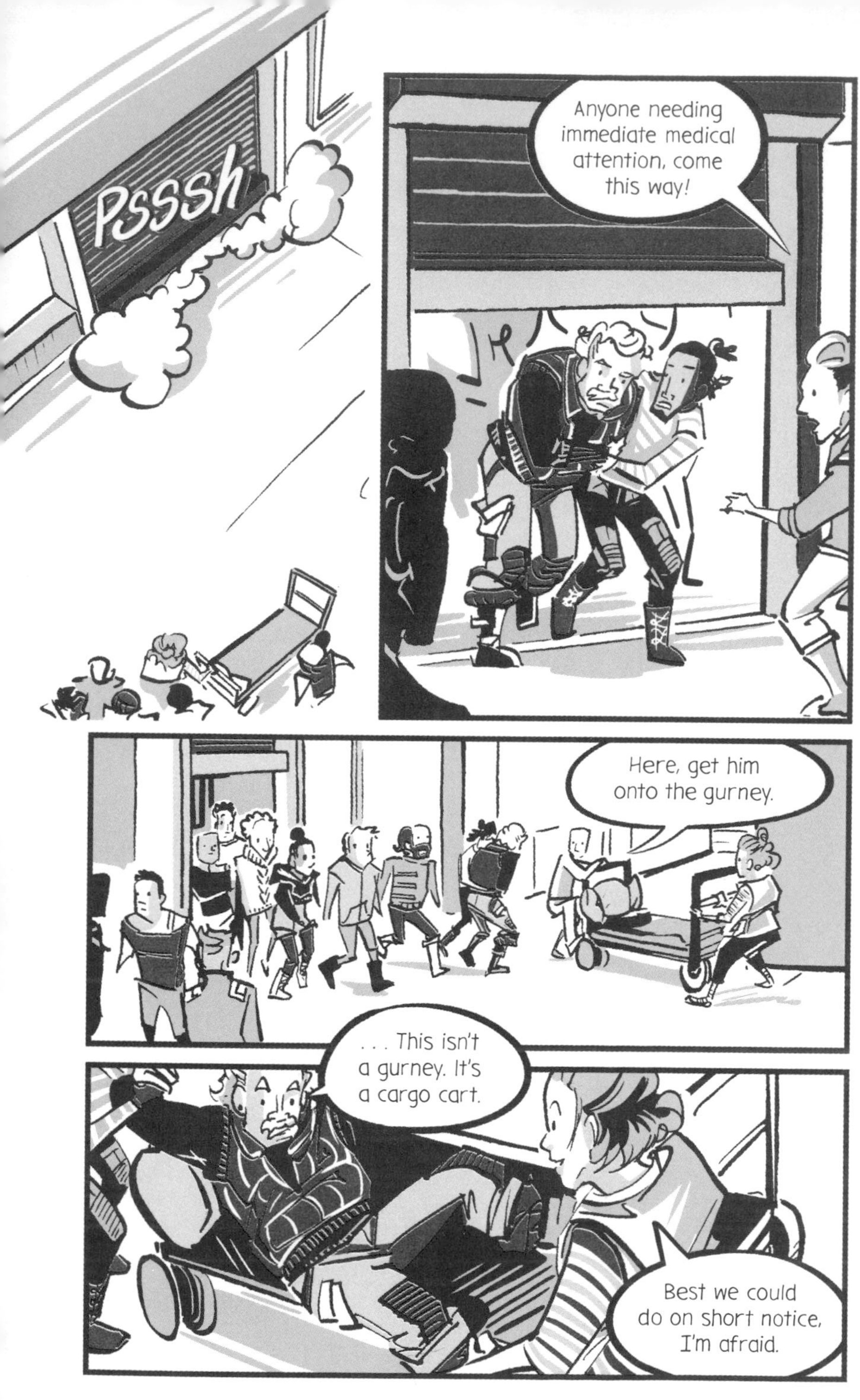
Psssh
Anyone needing immediate medical attention, come this way!
Here, get him onto the gurney.
. . . This isn't a gurney. It's a cargo cart.
Best we could do on short notice, I'm afraid.

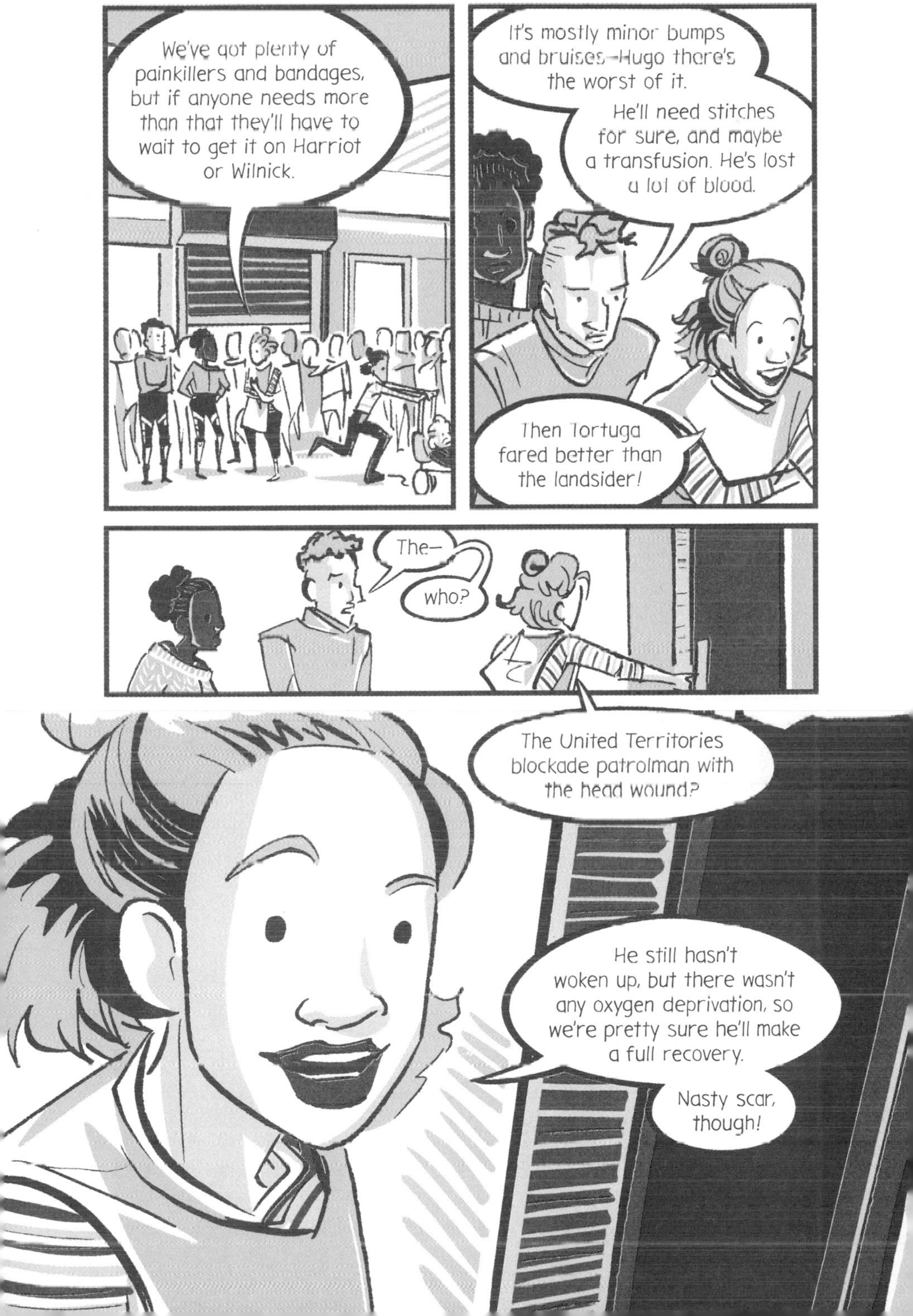
We've got plenty of painkillers and bandages, but if anyone needs more than that they'll have to wait to get it on Harriot or Wilnick.
It's mostly minor bumps and bruises—Hugo there's the worst of it.
He'll need stitches for sure, and maybe a transfusion. He's lost a lot of blood.
Then Tortuga fared better than the landsider!
The—
who?
The United Territories blockade patrolman with the head wound?
He still hasn't woken up, but there wasn't any oxygen deprivation, so we're pretty sure he'll make a full recovery.
Nasty scar, though!

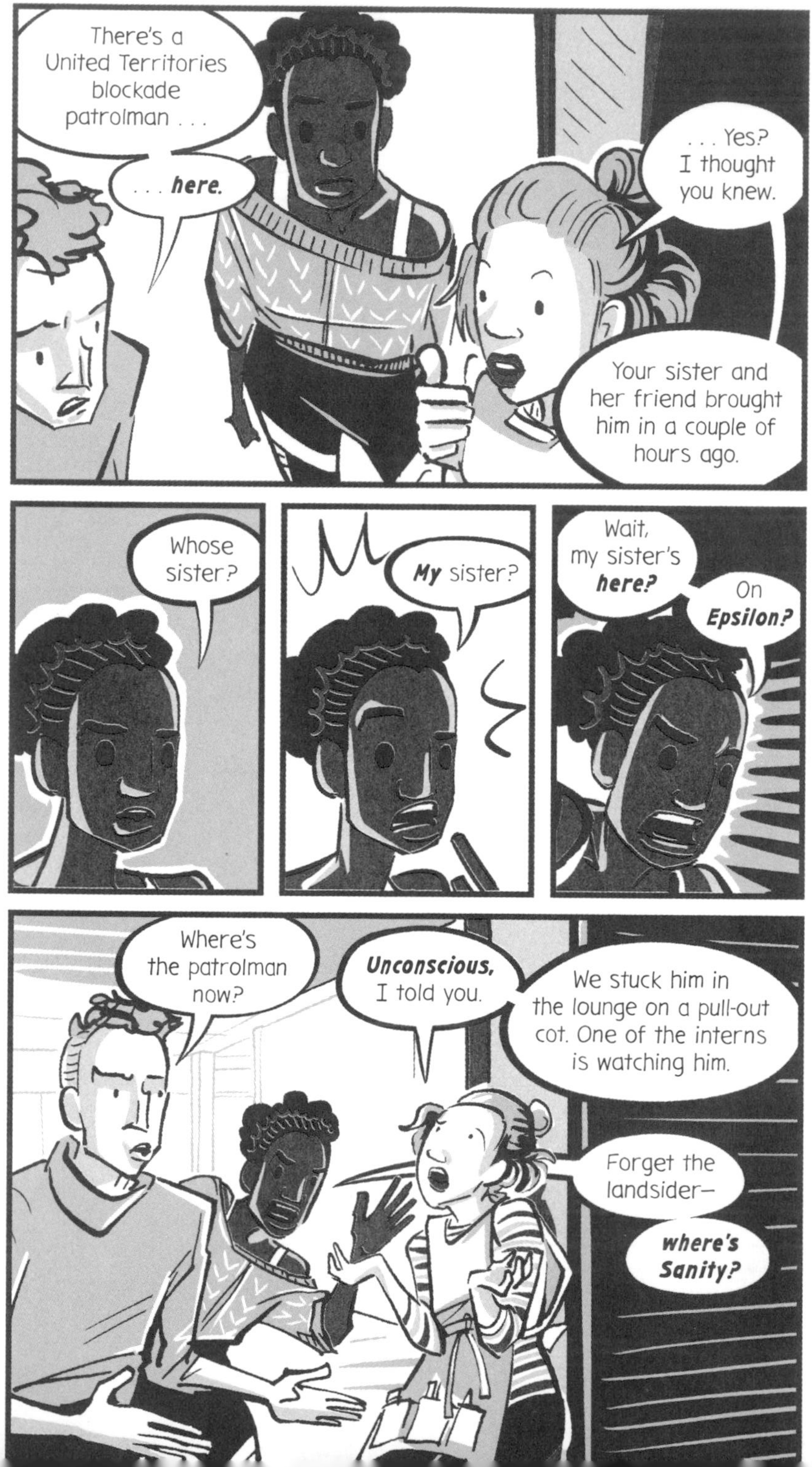
There's a United Territories blockade patrolman . . .
. . . **here.**
. . . Yes? I thought you knew.
Your sister and her friend brought him in a couple of hours ago.
Whose sister?
My sister?
Wait, my sister's **here?**
On **Epsilon?**
Where's the patrolman now?
Unconscious, I told you.
We stuck him in the lounge on a pull-out cot. One of the interns is watching him.
Forget the landsider—
where's Sanity?

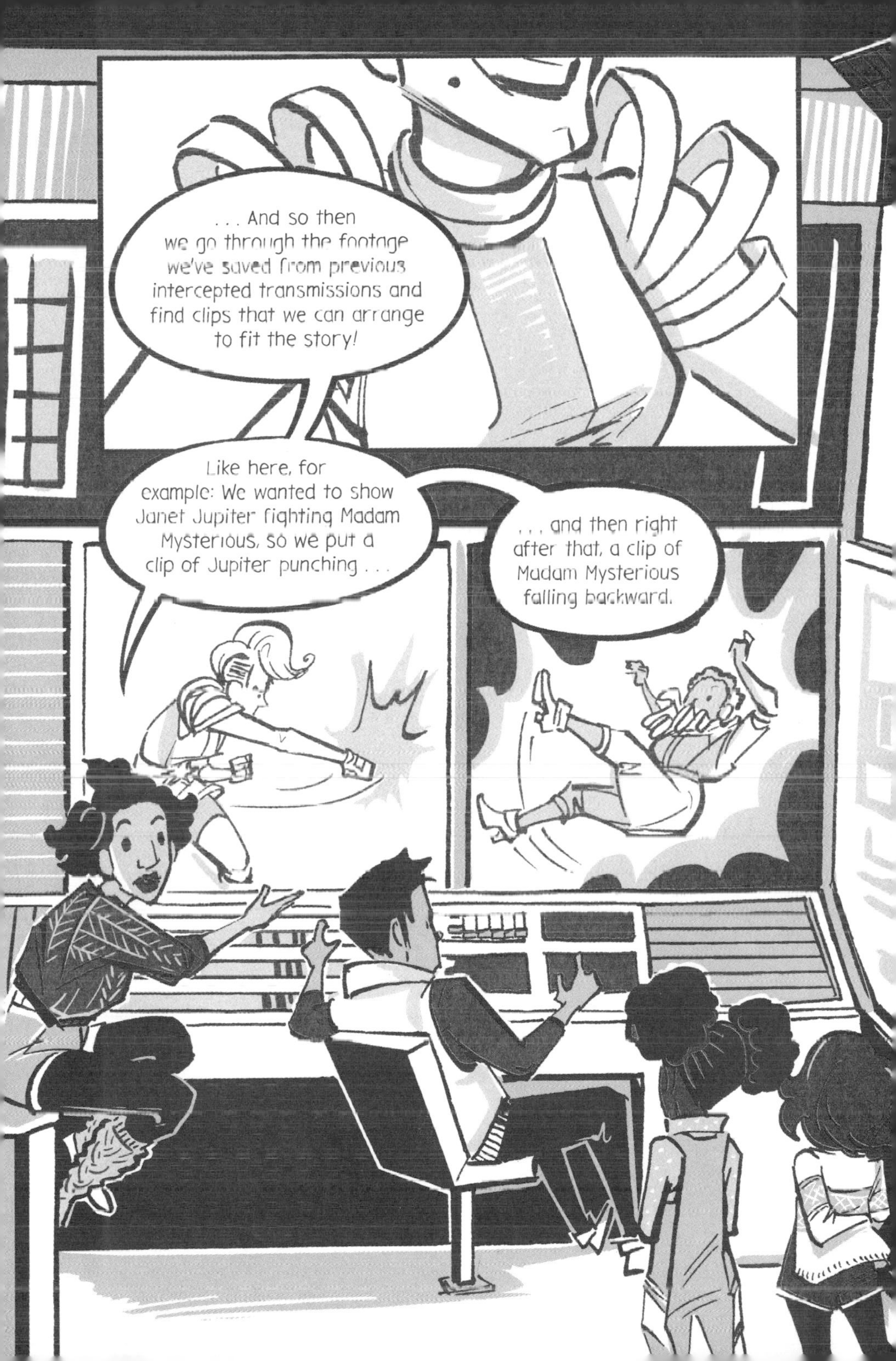
. . . And so then we go through the footage we've saved from previous intercepted transmissions and find clips that we can arrange to fit the story!
Like here, for example: We wanted to show Janet Jupiter fighting Madam Mysterious, so we put a clip of Jupiter punching . . .
. . . and then right after that, a clip of Madam Mysterious falling backward.

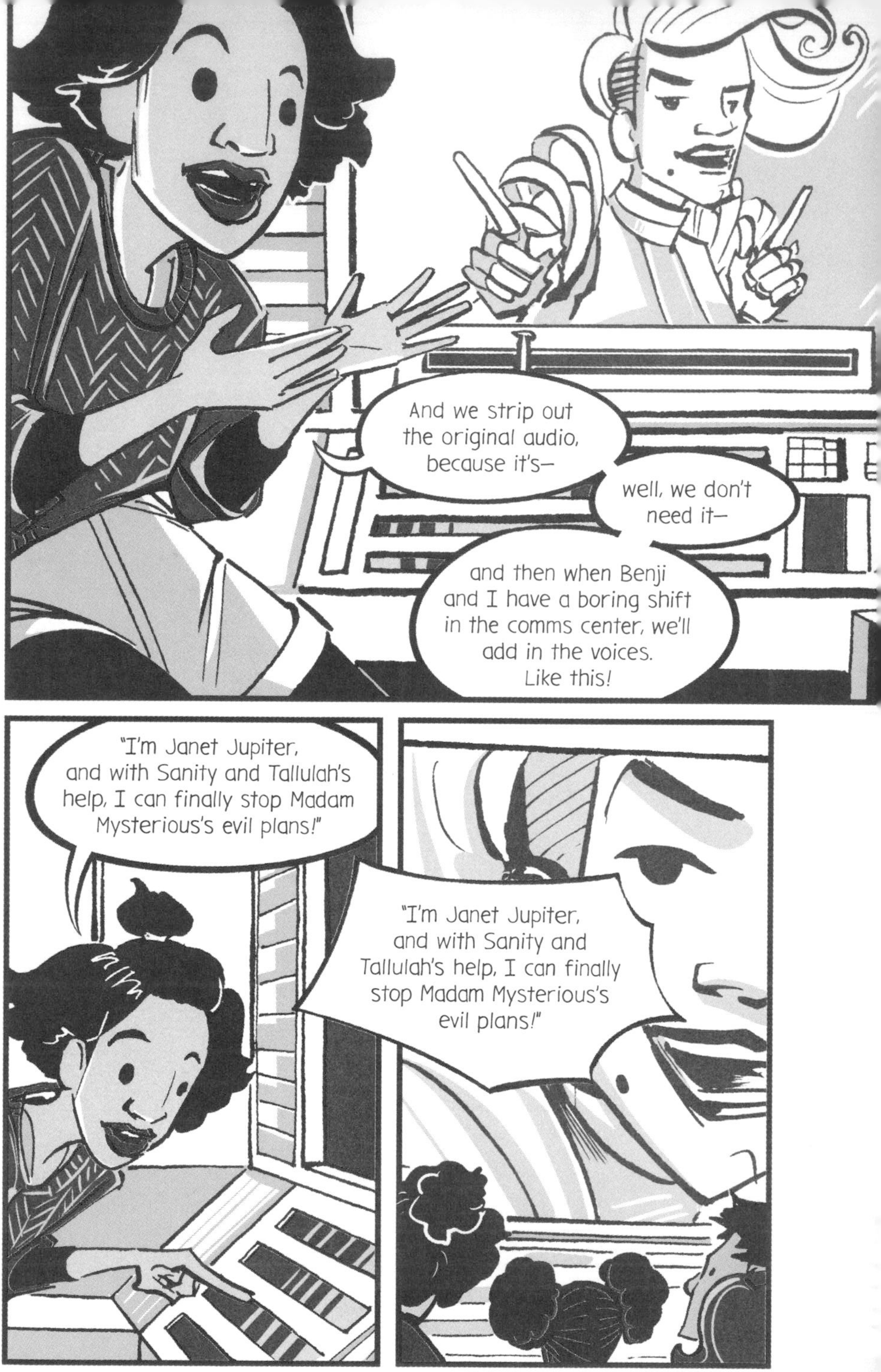
And we strip out the original audio, because it's—
well, we don't need it—
and then when Benji and I have a boring shift in the comms center, we'll add in the voices. Like this!
"I'm Janet Jupiter, and with Sanity and Tallulah's help, I can finally stop Madam Mysterious's evil plans!"
"I'm Janet Jupiter, and with Sanity and Tallulah's help, I can finally stop Madam Mysterious's evil plans!"

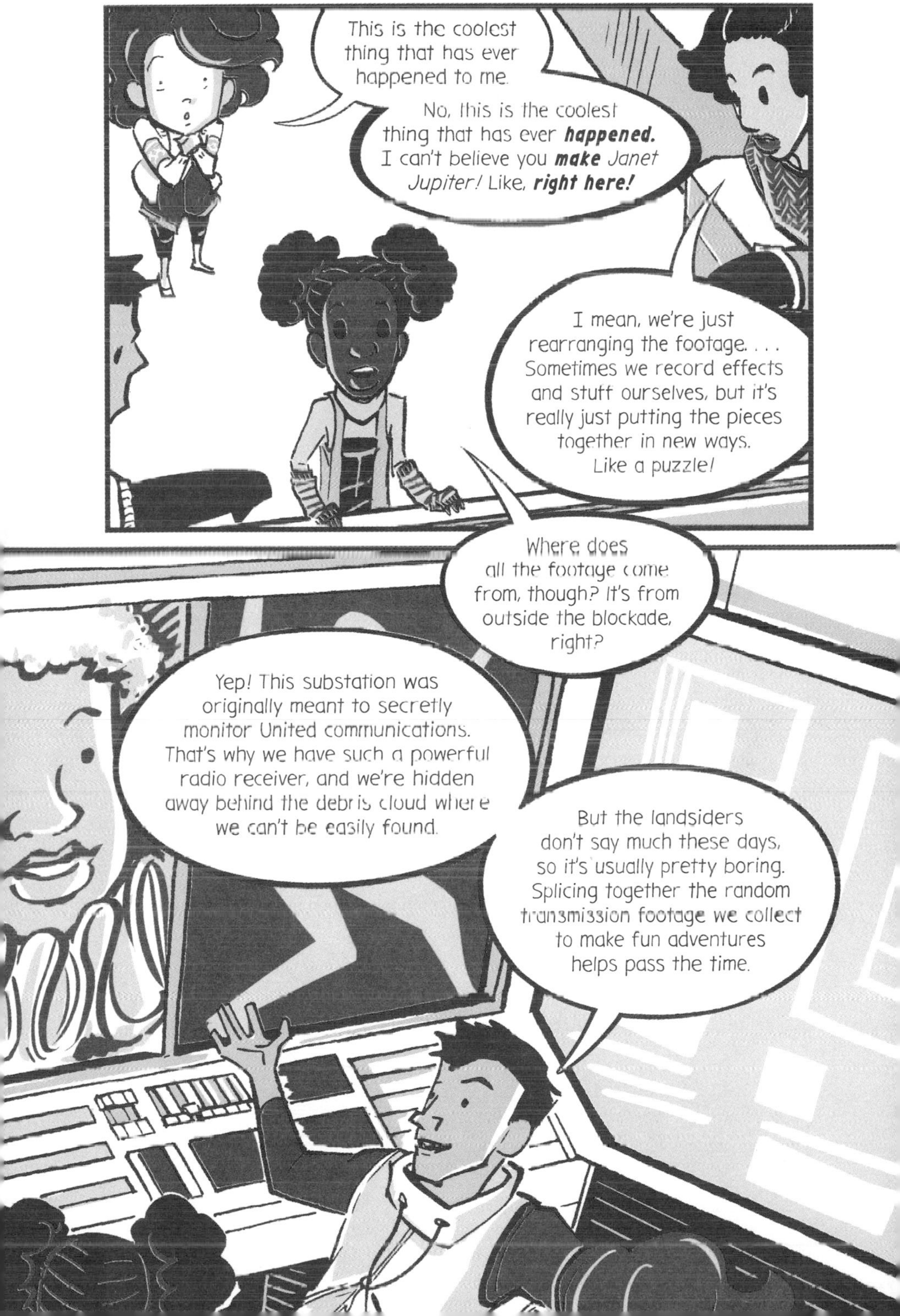
This is the coolest thing that has ever happened to me.
No, this is the coolest thing that has ever **happened.** I can't believe you **make** *Janet Jupiter!* Like, **right here!**
I mean, we're just rearranging the footage. . . . Sometimes we record effects and stuff ourselves, but it's really just putting the pieces together in new ways. Like a puzzle!
Where does all the footage come from, though? It's from outside the blockade, right?
Yep! This substation was originally meant to secretly monitor United communications. That's why we have such a powerful radio receiver, and we're hidden away behind the debris cloud where we can't be easily found.
But the landsiders don't say much these days, so it's usually pretty boring. Splicing together the random transmission footage we collect to make fun adventures helps pass the time.

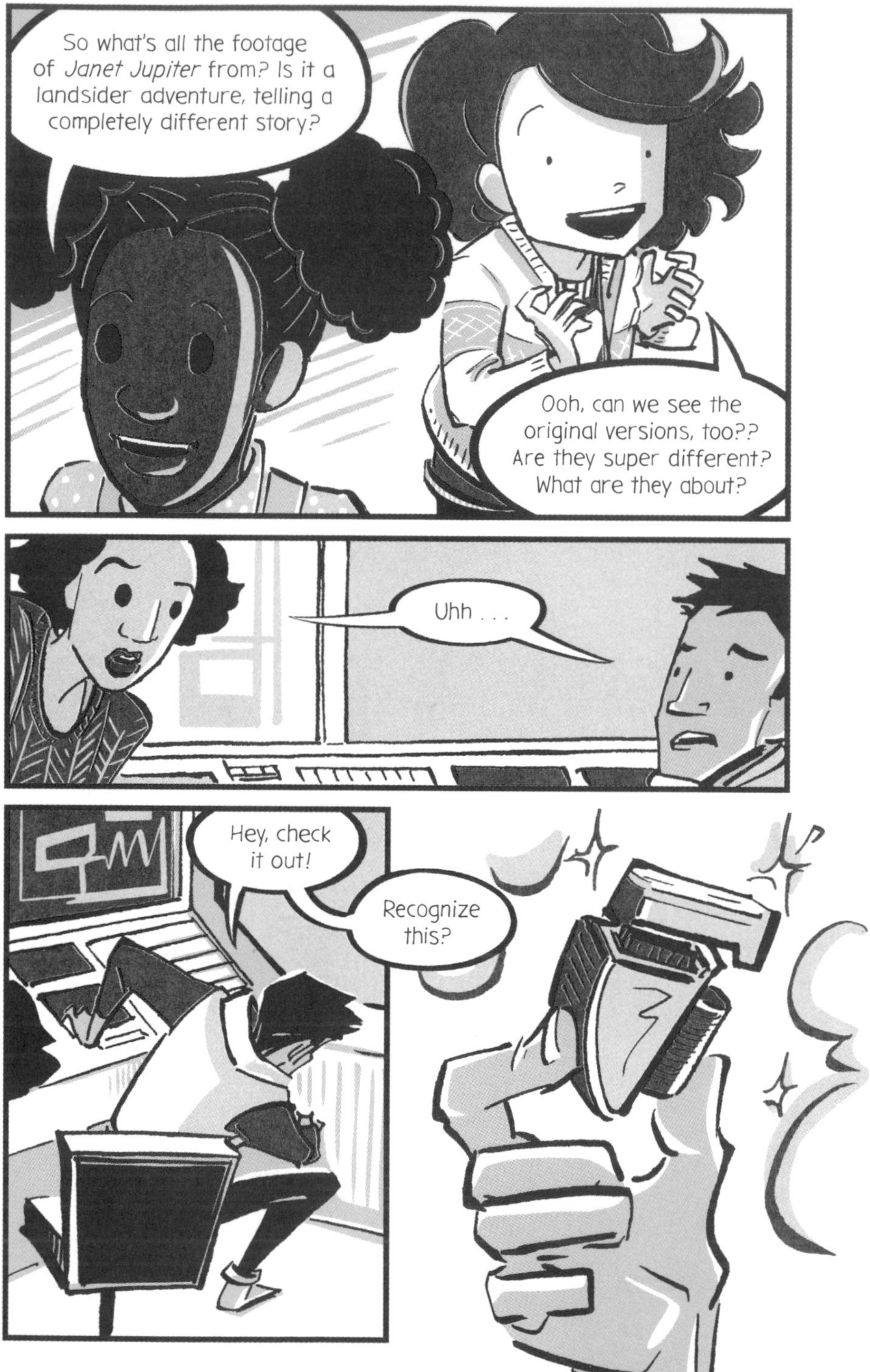
So what's all the footage of *Janet Jupiter* from? Is it a landsider adventure, telling a completely different story?
Ooh, can we see the original versions, too?? Are they super different? What are they about?
Uhh . . .
Hey, check it out!
Recognize this?

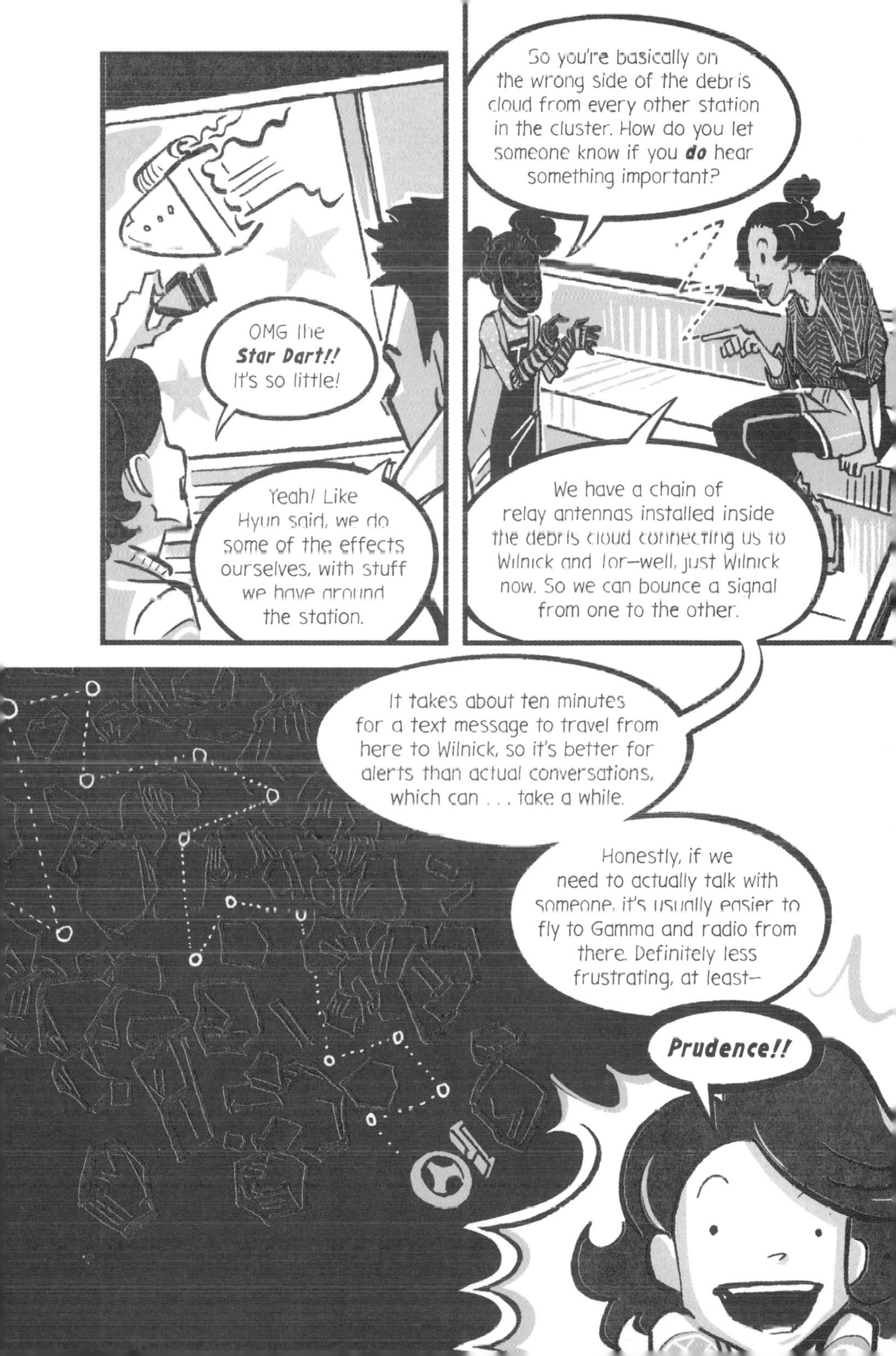
OMG the **Star Dart!!** It's so little!
Yeah! Like Hyun said, we do some of the effects ourselves, with stuff we have around the station.
So you're basically on the wrong side of the debris cloud from every other station in the cluster. How do you let someone know if you ***do*** hear something important?
We have a chain of relay antennas installed inside the debris cloud connecting us to Wilnick and Ior—well, just Wilnick now. So we can bounce a signal from one to the other.
It takes about ten minutes for a text message to travel from here to Wilnick, so it's better for alerts than actual conversations, which can . . . take a while.
Honestly, if we need to actually talk with someone, it's usually easier to fly to Gamma and radio from there. Definitely less frustrating, at least—
Prudence!!

Sanity. Constance. Jones.

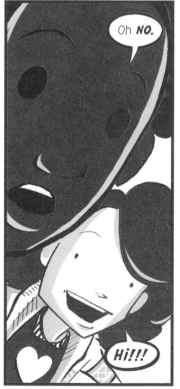

Oh **NO.**

Hi!!!

You're supposed to be on **Wilnick!** What are you doing out **here?**

You know, just hanging out! What about you? So wild, meeting up like this, right?

I mean, what are the odds???

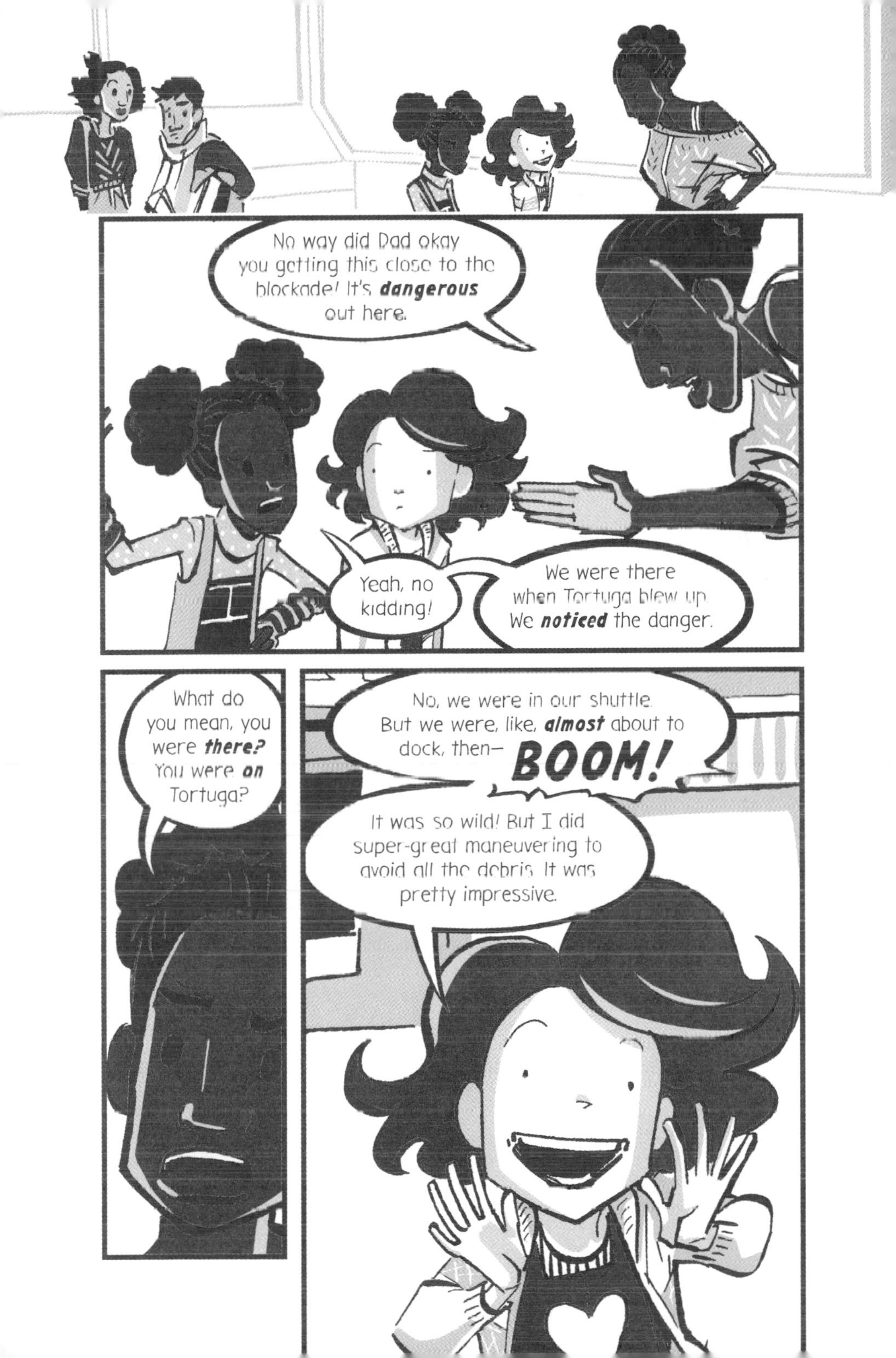
No way did Dad okay you getting this close to the blockade! It's **dangerous** out here.
Yeah, no kidding!
We were there when Tortuga blew up. We **noticed** the danger.
What do you mean, you were **there?** You were **on** Tortuga?
No, we were in our shuttle. But we were, like, **almost** about to dock, then—
BOOM!
It was so wild! But I did super-great maneuvering to avoid all the debris. It was pretty impressive.

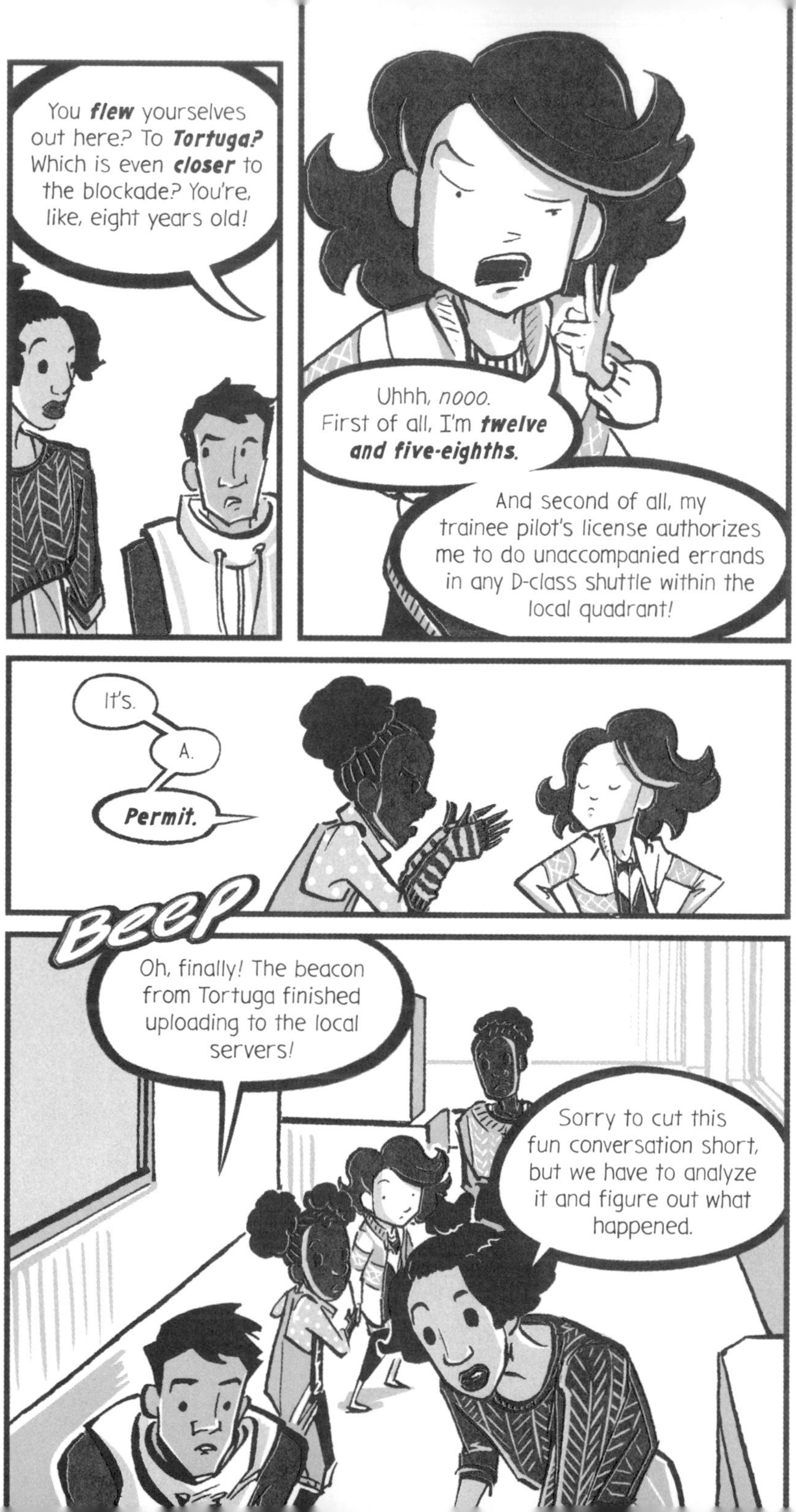
You *flew* yourselves out here? To *Tortuga?* Which is even *closer* to the blockade? You're, like, eight years old!
Uhhh, *nooo.* First of all, I'm *twelve and five-eighths.*
And second of all, my trainee pilot's license authorizes me to do unaccompanied errands in any D-class shuttle within the local quadrant!
It's.
A.
Permit.
Beep
Oh, finally! The beacon from Tortuga finished uploading to the local servers!
Sorry to cut this fun conversation short, but we have to analyze it and figure out what happened.

(TEN MINUTES LATER, ON WILNICK)

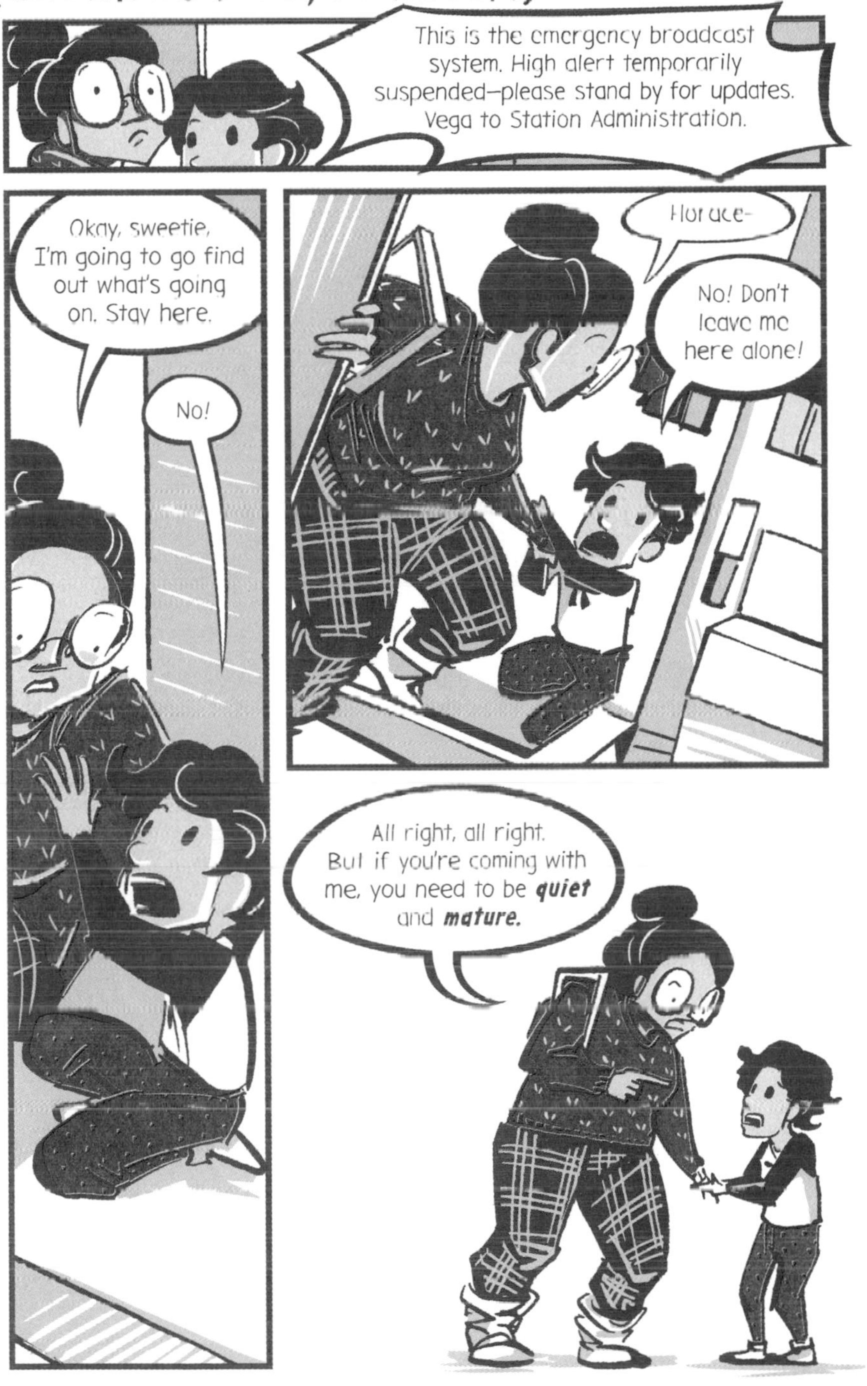

This is the emergency broadcast system. High alert temporarily suspended—please stand by for updates. Vega to Station Administration.
Okay, sweetie, I'm going to go find out what's going on. Stay here.
No!
Horace-
No! Don't leave me here alone!
All right, all right. But if you're coming with me, you need to be ***quiet*** and ***mature.***

(EPSILON COMMS CENTER)

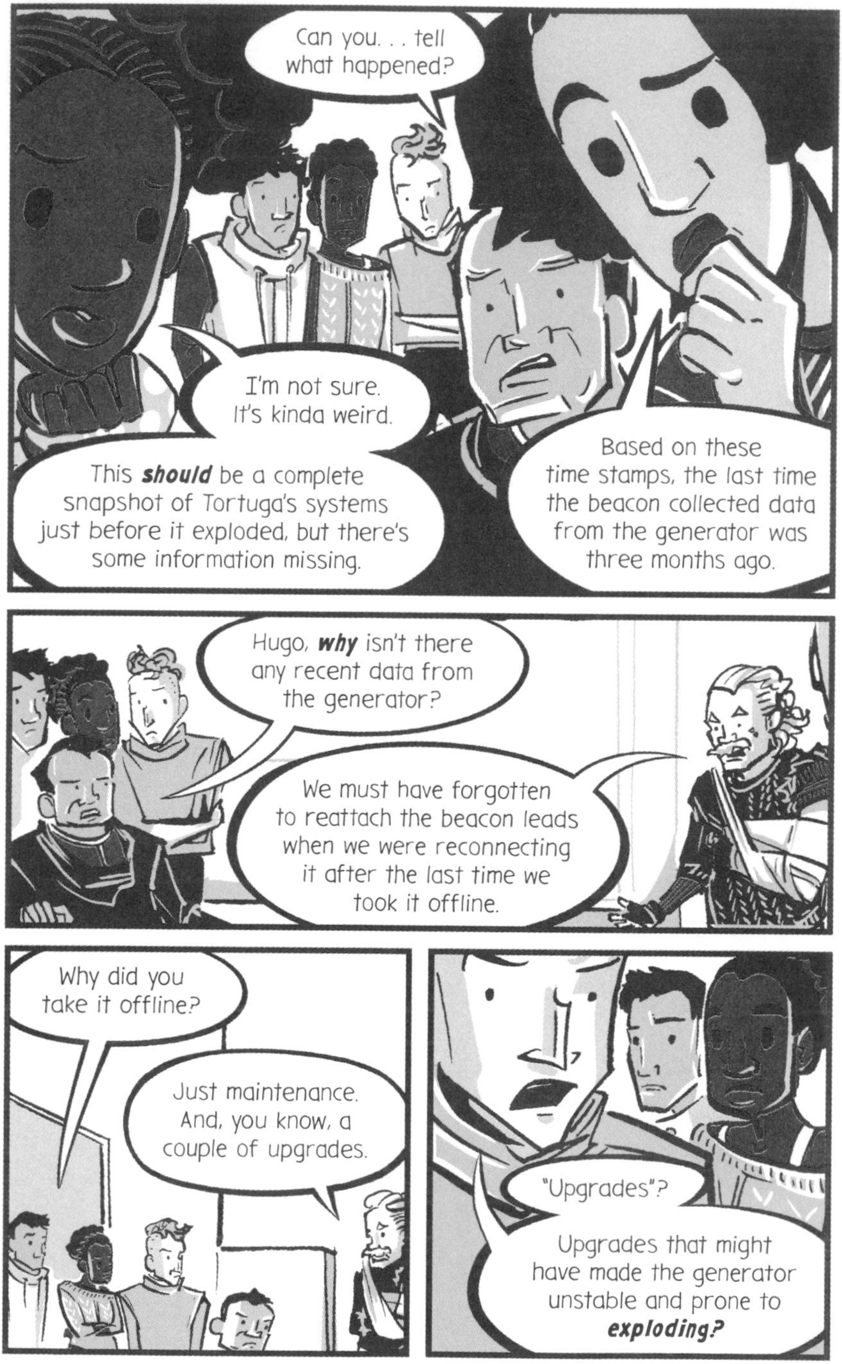
Can you. . . tell what happened?
I'm not sure. It's kinda weird.
This **should** be a complete snapshot of Tortuga's systems just before it exploded, but there's some information missing.
Based on these time stamps, the last time the beacon collected data from the generator was three months ago.
Hugo, **why** isn't there any recent data from the generator?
We must have forgotten to reattach the beacon leads when we were reconnecting it after the last time we took it offline.
Why did you take it offline?
Just maintenance. And, you know, a couple of upgrades.
"Upgrades"?
Upgrades that might have made the generator unstable and prone to **exploding?**

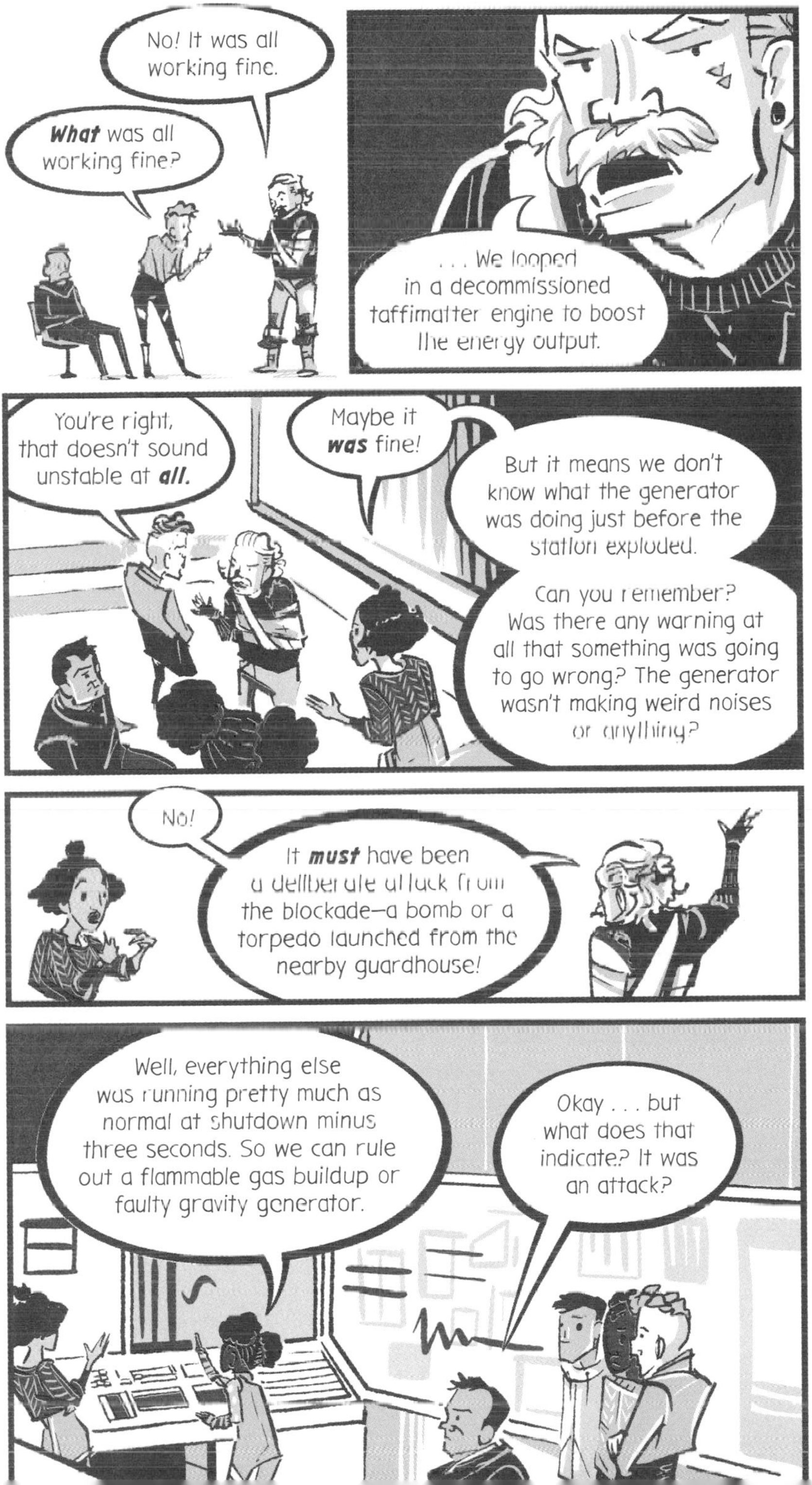
No! It was all working fine.
What was all working fine?
. . . We looped in a decommissioned taffimatter engine to boost the energy output.
You're right, that doesn't sound unstable at ***all.***
Maybe it ***was*** fine!
But it means we don't know what the generator was doing just before the station exploded.
Can you remember? Was there any warning at all that something was going to go wrong? The generator wasn't making weird noises or anything?
No!
It ***must*** have been a deliberate attack from the blockade—a bomb or a torpedo launched from the nearby guardhouse!
Well, everything else was running pretty much as normal at shutdown minus three seconds. So we can rule out a flammable gas buildup or faulty gravity generator.
Okay . . . but what does that indicate? It was an attack?

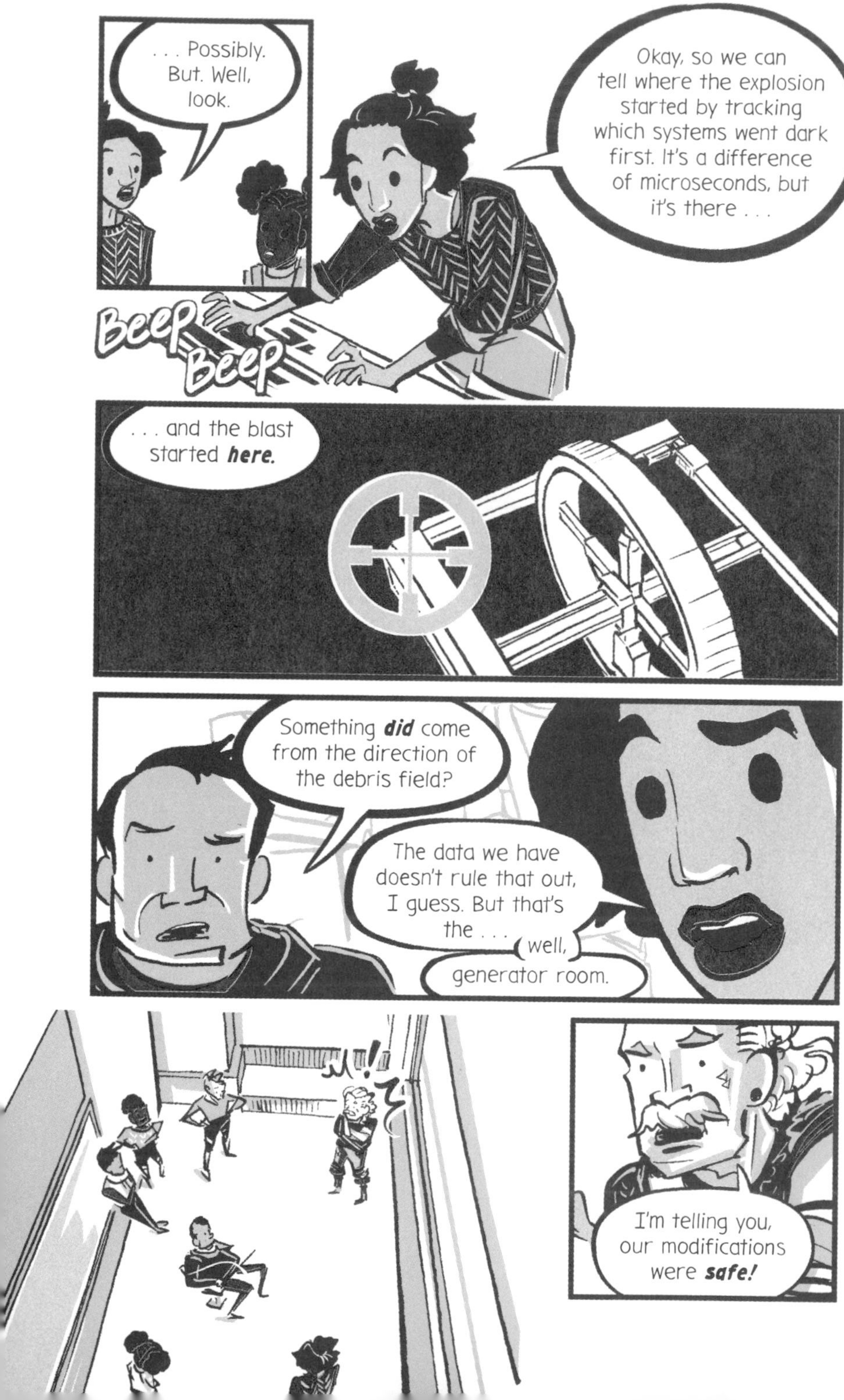

. . . Possibly. But. Well, look.
Okay, so we can tell where the explosion started by tracking which systems went dark first. It's a difference of microseconds, but it's there . . .
Beep Beep
. . . and the blast started **here.**
Something **did** come from the direction of the debris field?
The data we have doesn't rule that out, I guess. But that's the . . .
well,
generator room.
I'm telling you, our modifications were **safe!**

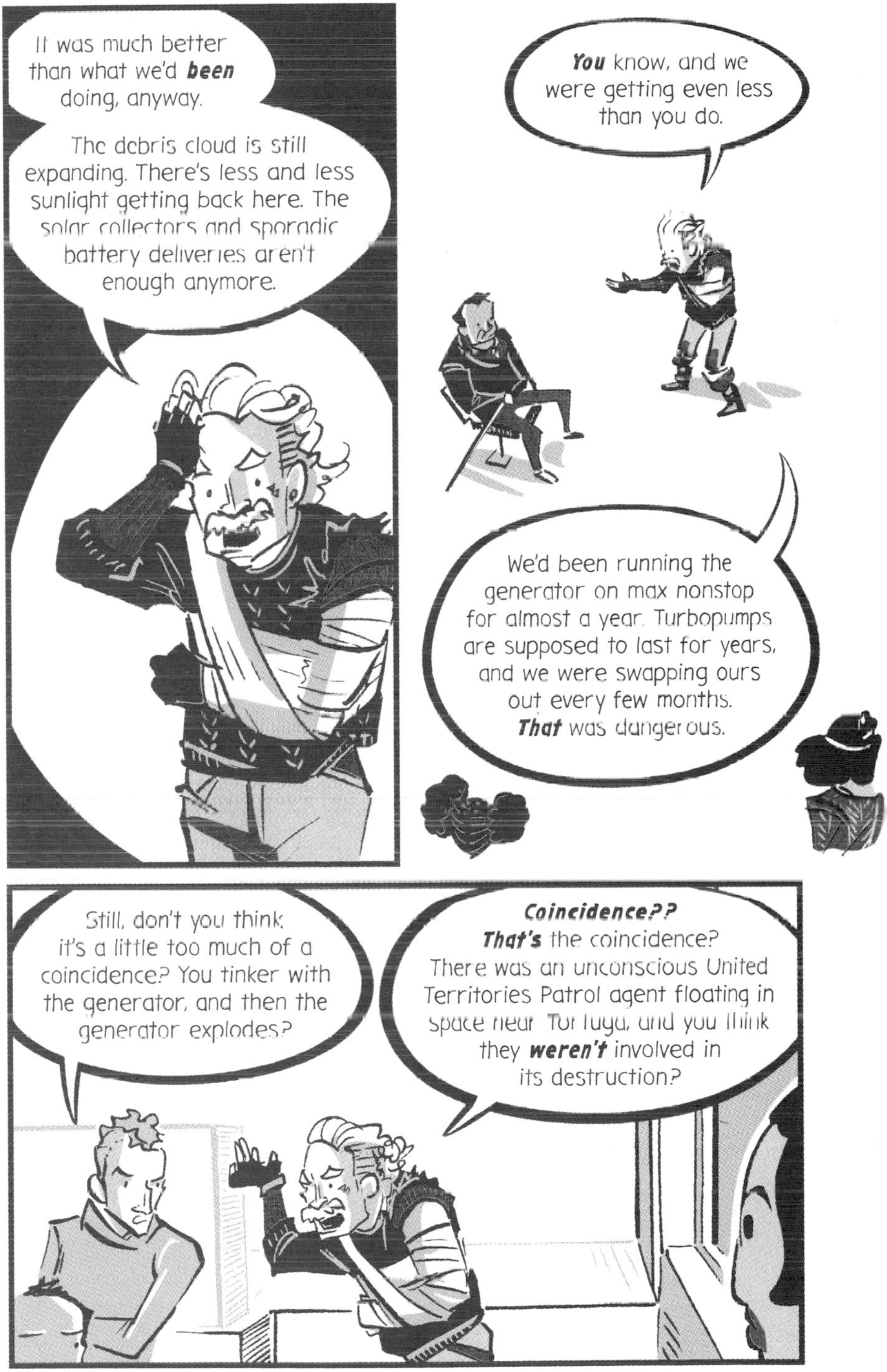
It was much better than what we'd **been** doing, anyway.
The debris cloud is still expanding. There's less and less sunlight getting back here. The solar collectors and sporadic battery deliveries aren't enough anymore.
You know, and we were getting even less than you do.
We'd been running the generator on max nonstop for almost a year. Turbopumps are supposed to last for years, and we were swapping ours out every few months. **That** was dangerous.
Still, don't you think it's a little too much of a coincidence? You tinker with the generator, and then the generator explodes?
Coincidence??
That's the coincidence? There was an unconscious United Territories Patrol agent floating in space near Tortuga, and you think they **weren't** involved in its destruction?

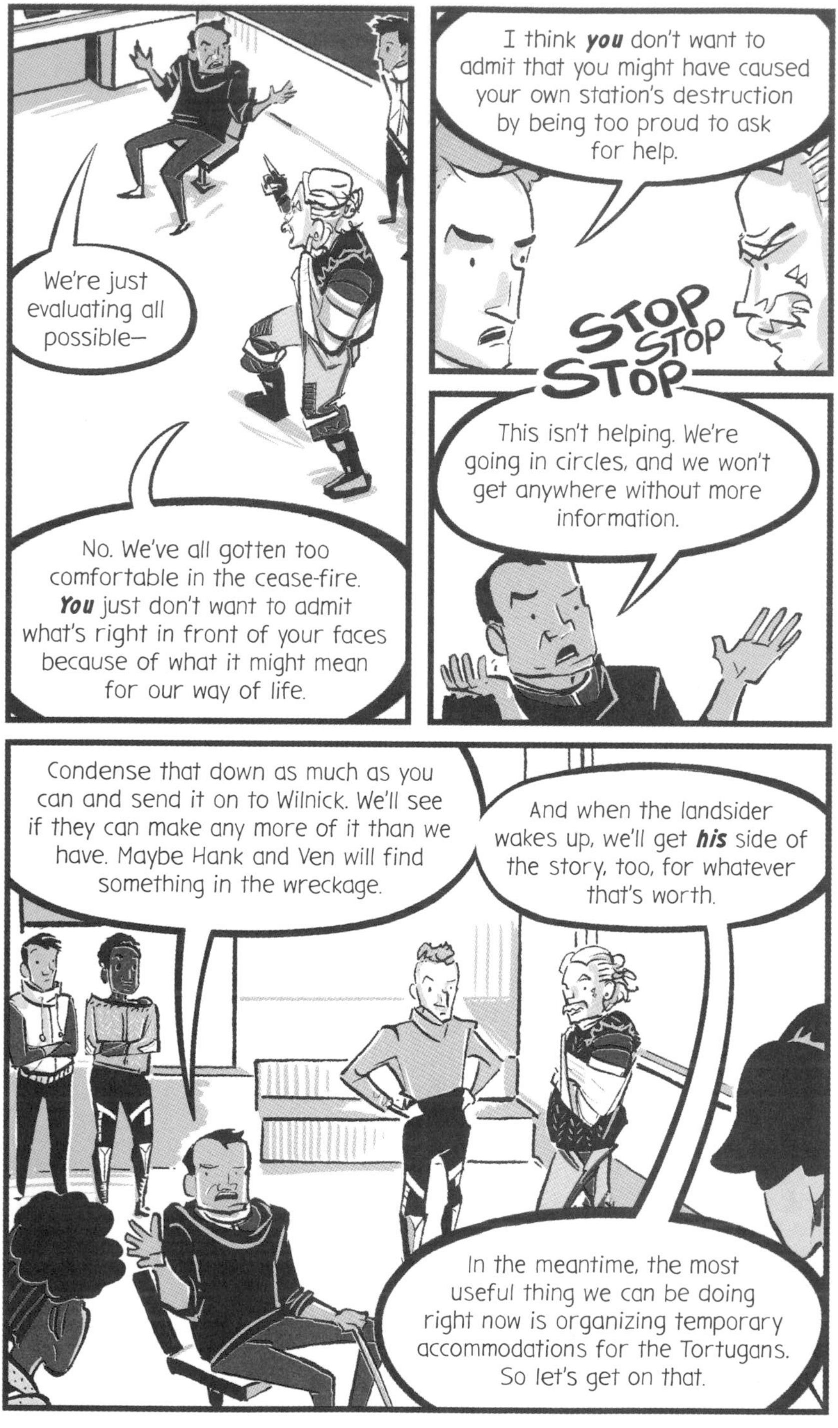
We're just evaluating all possible—
No. We've all gotten too comfortable in the cease-fire. ***You*** just don't want to admit what's right in front of your faces because of what it might mean for our way of life.
I think ***you*** don't want to admit that you might have caused your own station's destruction by being too proud to ask for help.
STOP STOP STOP
This isn't helping. We're going in circles, and we won't get anywhere without more information.
Condense that down as much as you can and send it on to Wilnick. We'll see if they can make any more of it than we have. Maybe Hank and Ven will find something in the wreckage.
And when the landsider wakes up, we'll get ***his*** side of the story, too, for whatever that's worth.
In the meantime, the most useful thing we can be doing right now is organizing temporary accommodations for the Tortugans. So let's get on that.

(MEANWHILE, ELSEWHERE ON EPSILON)

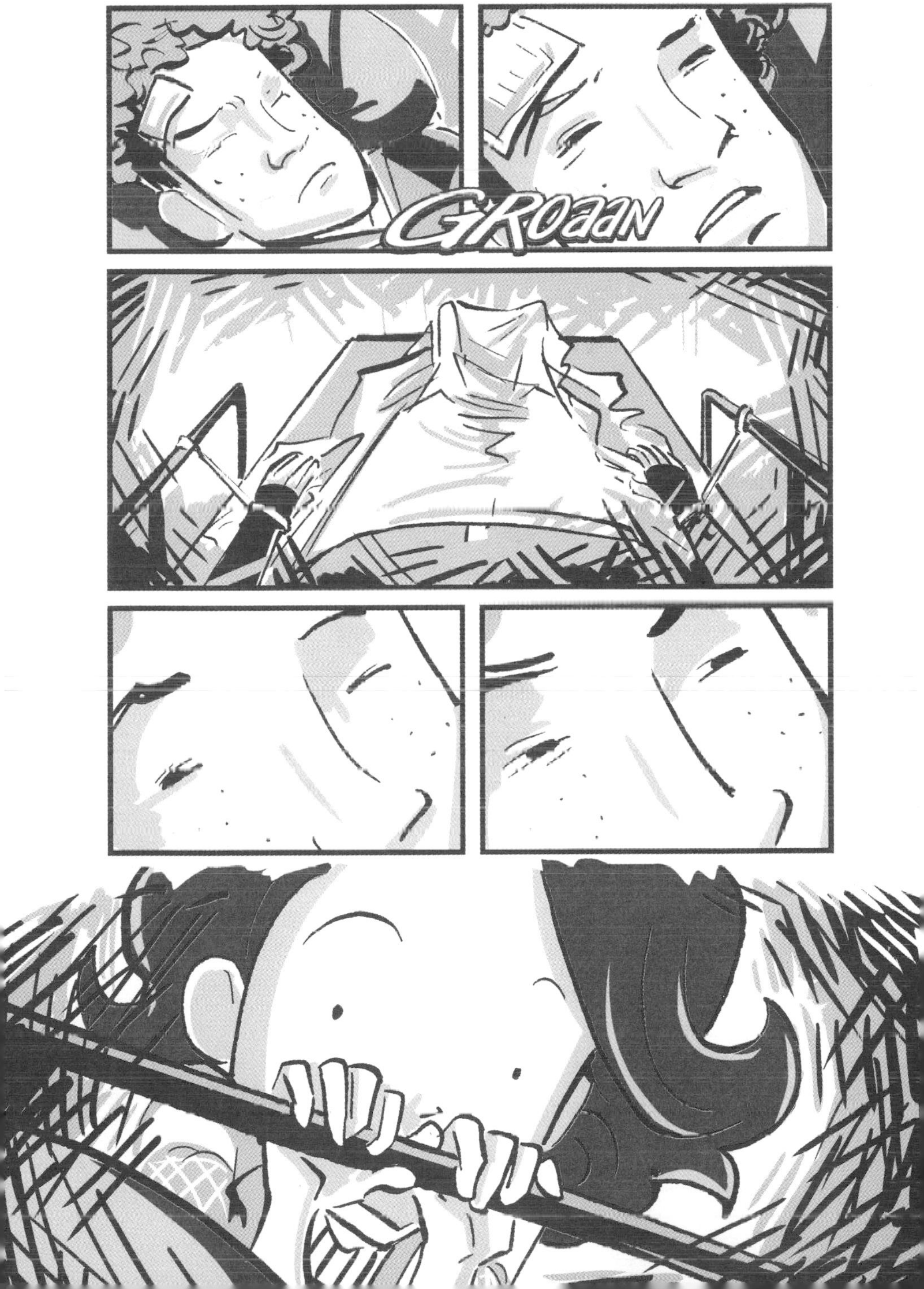
GROAAN

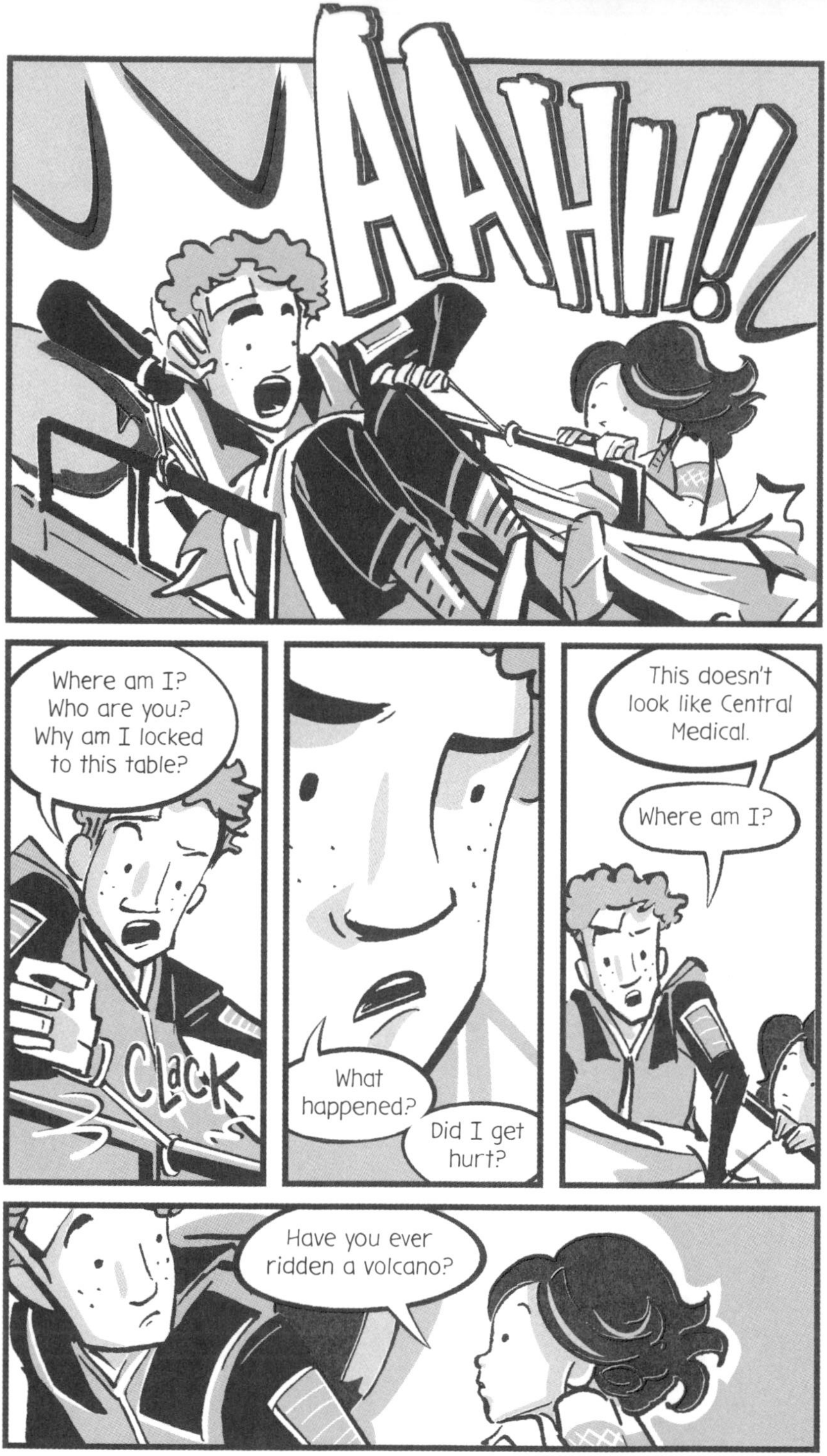
AAHH!!
Where am I? Who are you? Why am I locked to this table?
CLACK
What happened?
Did I get hurt?
This doesn't look like Central Medical.
Where am I?
Have you ever ridden a volcano?

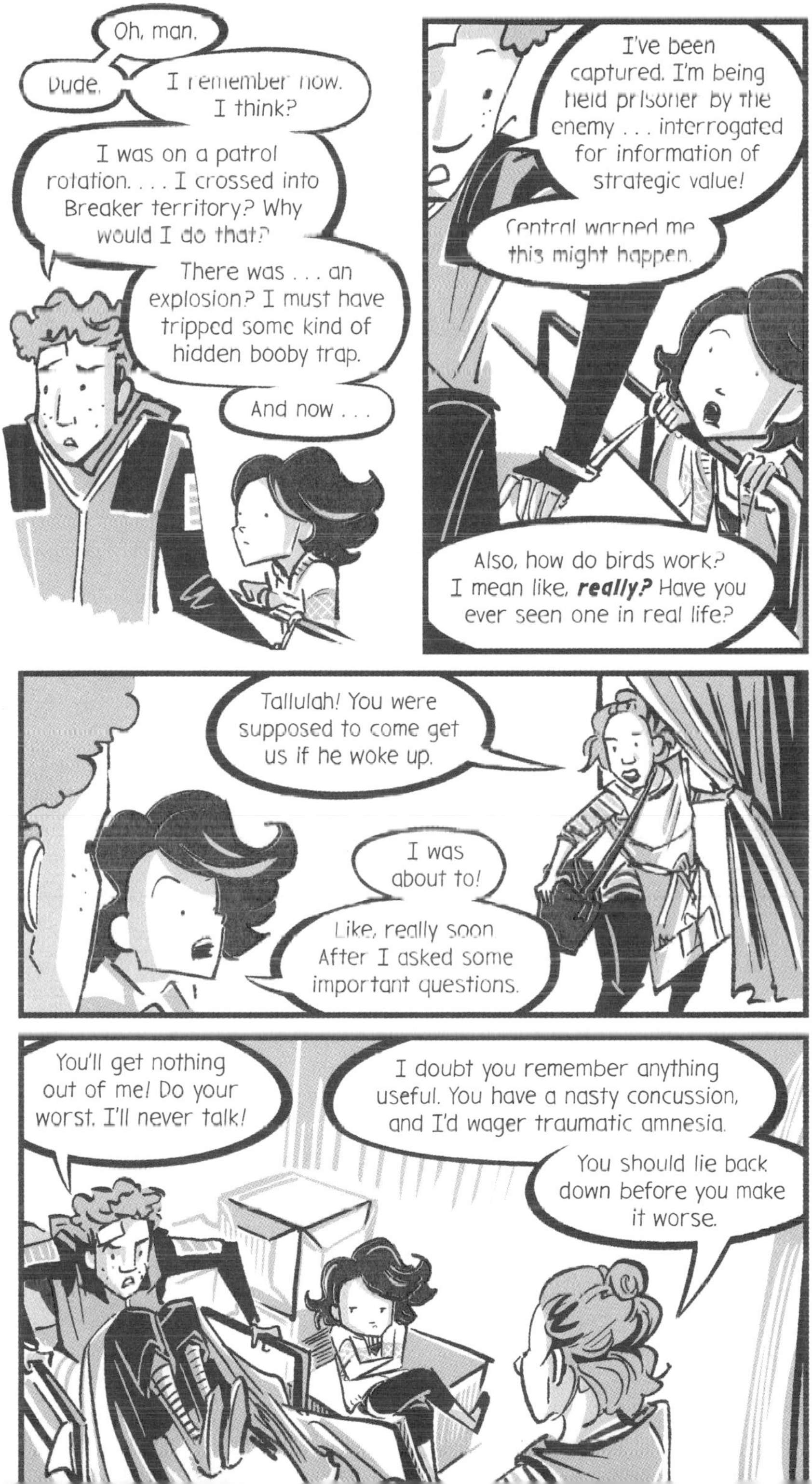
Oh, man.
Dude.
I remember now. I think?
I was on a patrol rotation. . . . I crossed into Breaker territory? Why would I do that?
There was . . . an explosion? I must have tripped some kind of hidden booby trap.
And now . . .
I've been captured. I'm being held prisoner by the enemy . . . interrogated for information of strategic value!
Central warned me this might happen.
Also, how do birds work? I mean like, ***really?*** Have you ever seen one in real life?
Tallulah! You were supposed to come get us if he woke up.
I was about to!
Like, really soon. After I asked some important questions.
You'll get nothing out of me! Do your worst. I'll never talk!
I doubt you remember anything useful. You have a nasty concussion, and I'd wager traumatic amnesia.
You should lie back down before you make it worse.

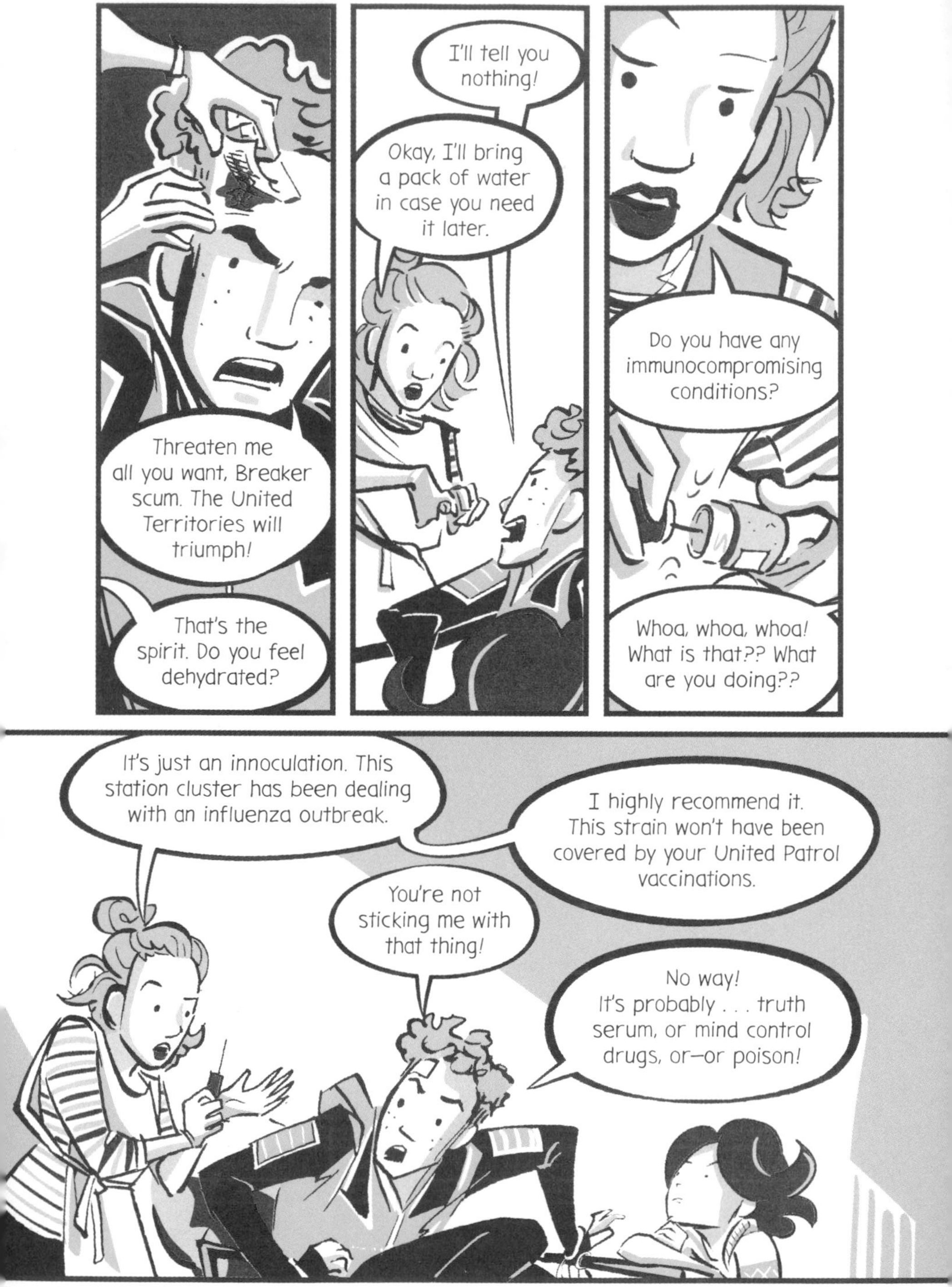
Threaten me all you want, Breaker scum. The United Territories will triumph!
That's the spirit. Do you feel dehydrated?
I'll tell you nothing!
Okay, I'll bring a pack of water in case you need it later.
Do you have any immunocompromising conditions?
Whoa, whoa, whoa! What is that?? What are you doing??
It's just an innoculation. This station cluster has been dealing with an influenza outbreak.
I highly recommend it. This strain won't have been covered by your United Patrol vaccinations.
You're not sticking me with that thing!
No way! It's probably . . . truth serum, or mind control drugs, or—or poison!

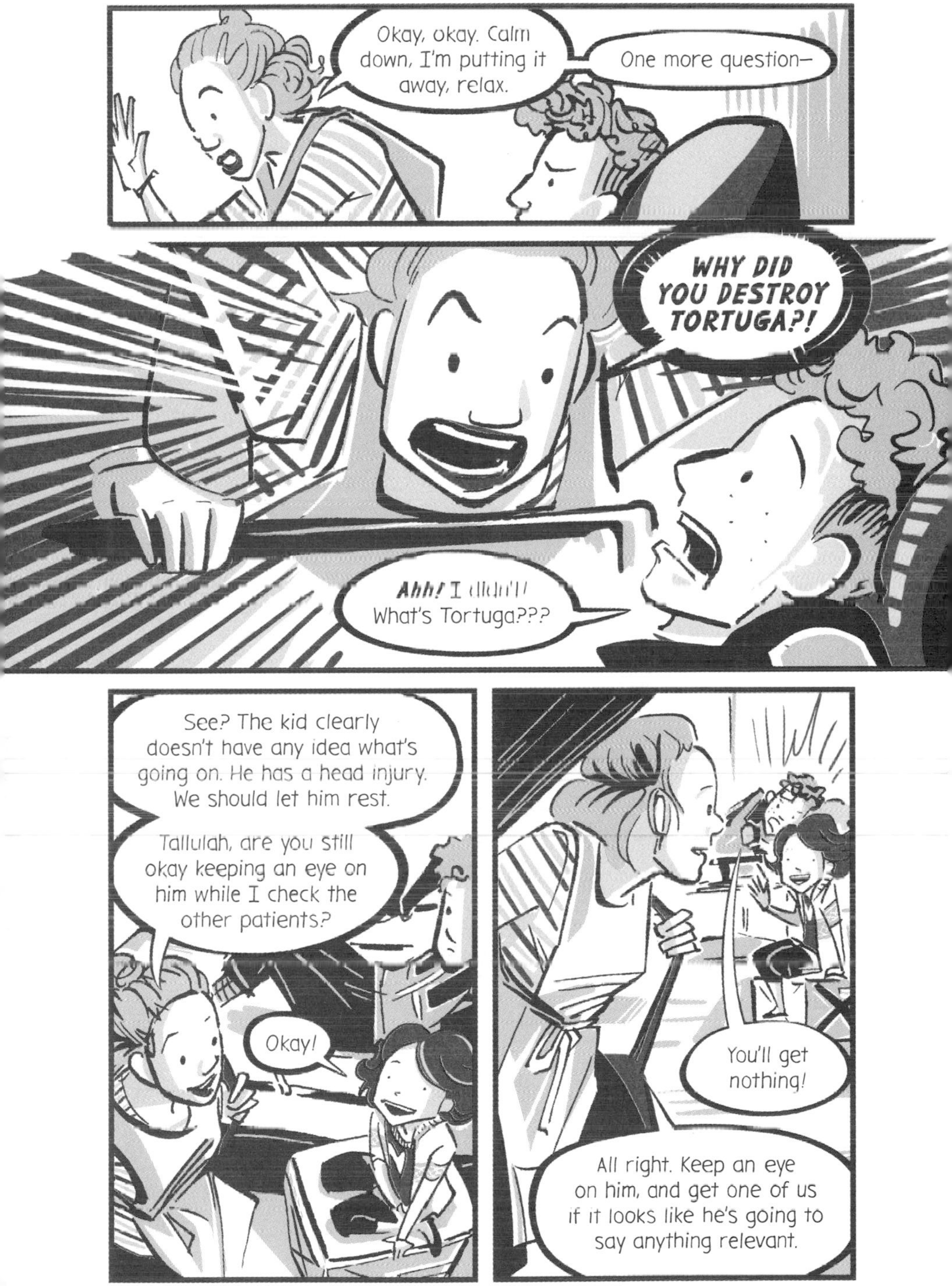
Okay, okay. Calm down, I'm putting it away, relax.
One more question—
WHY DID YOU DESTROY TORTUGA?!
Ahh! I didn't! What's Tortuga???
See? The kid clearly doesn't have any idea what's going on. He has a head injury. We should let him rest.
Tallulah, are you still okay keeping an eye on him while I check the other patients?
Okay!
You'll get nothing!
All right. Keep an eye on him, and get one of us if it looks like he's going to say anything relevant.

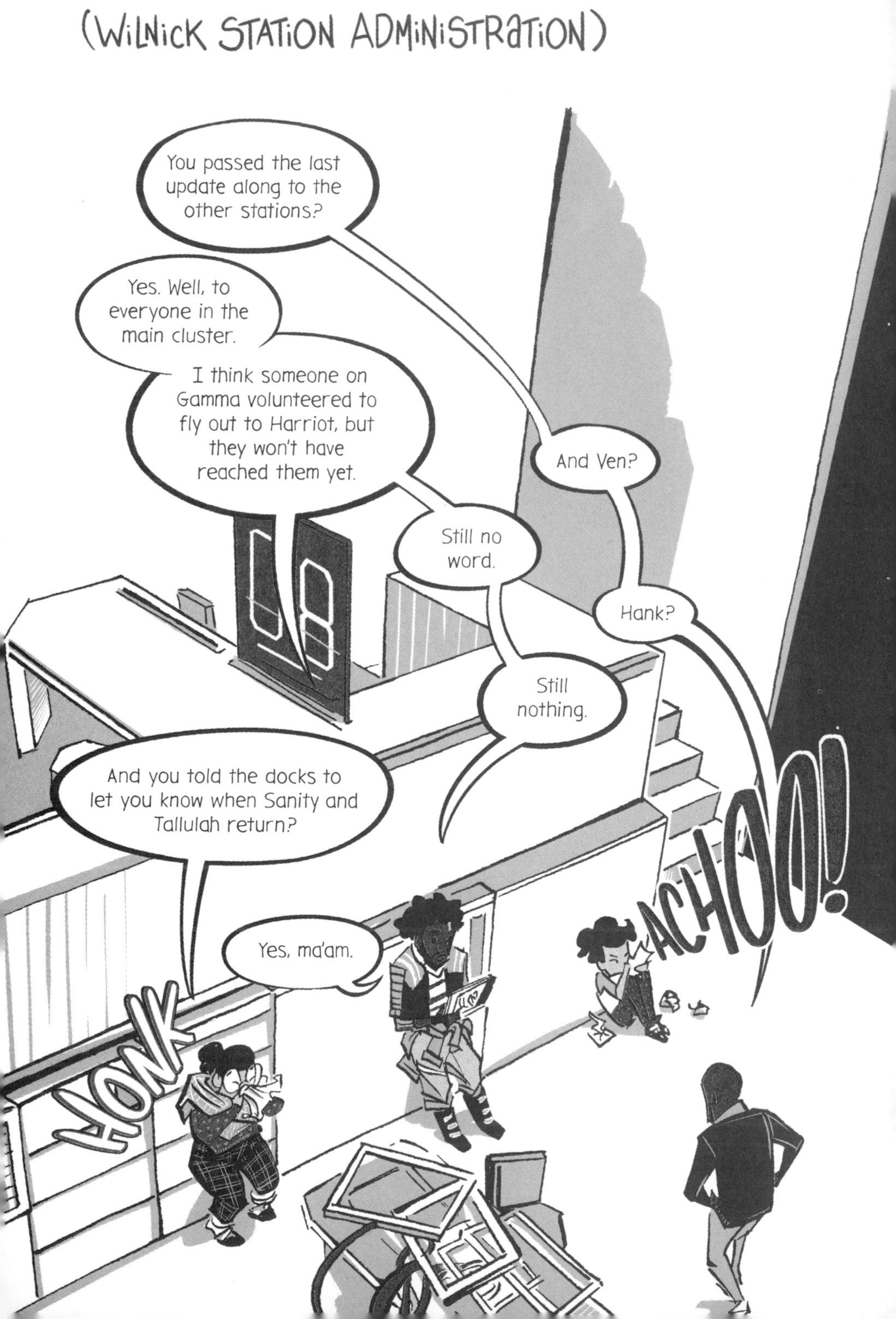
(WILNICK STATION ADMINISTRATION)
You passed the last update along to the other stations?
Yes. Well, to everyone in the main cluster.
I think someone on Gamma volunteered to fly out to Harriot, but they won't have reached them yet.
And Ven?
Still no word.
Hank?
Still nothing.
And you told the docks to let you know when Sanity and Tallulah return?
Yes, ma'am.
HONK
ACHOO!

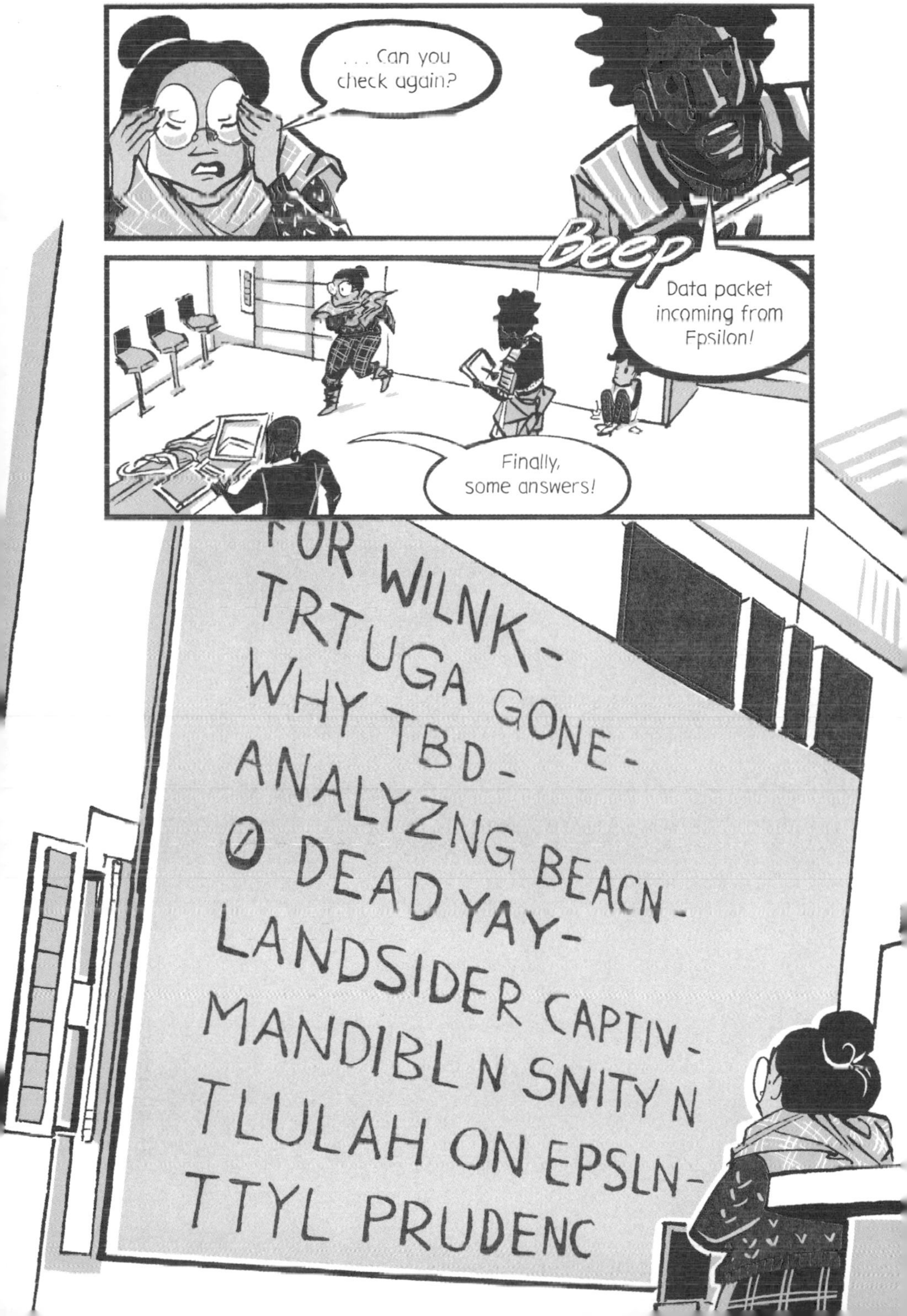

. . . Can you check again?
Beep
Data packet incoming from Epsilon!
Finally, some answers!
FOR WILNK-
TRTUGA GONE-
WHY TBD-
ANALYZNG BEACN-
0 DEAD YAY-
LANDSIDER CAPTIV-
MANDIBL N SNITY N
TLULAH ON EPSLN-
TTYL PRUDENC

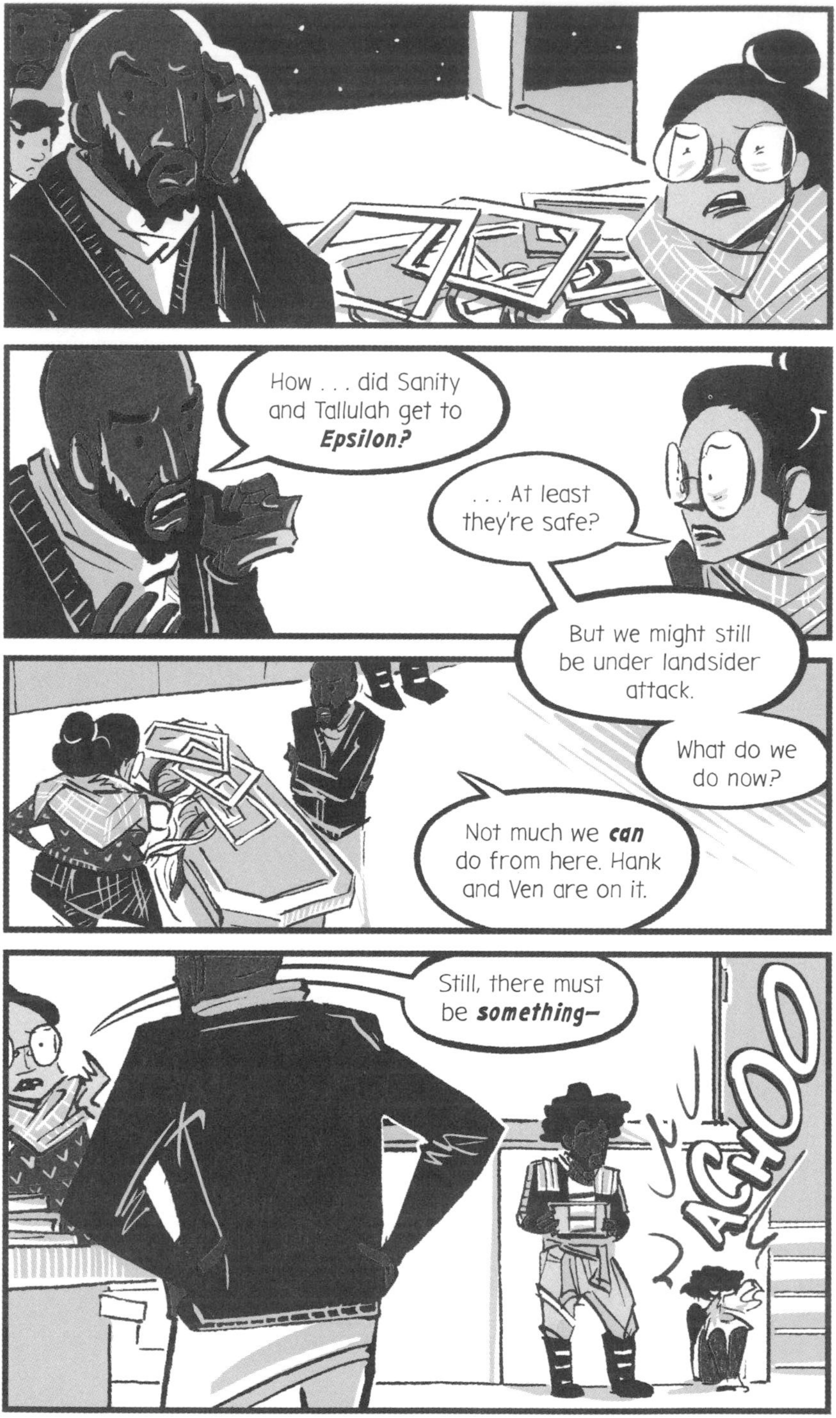

How . . . did Sanity and Tallulah get to **Epsilon?**
. . . At least they're safe?
But we might still be under landsider attack.
What do we do now?
Not much we **can** do from here. Hank and Ven are on it.
Still, there must be **something**–
ACHOO

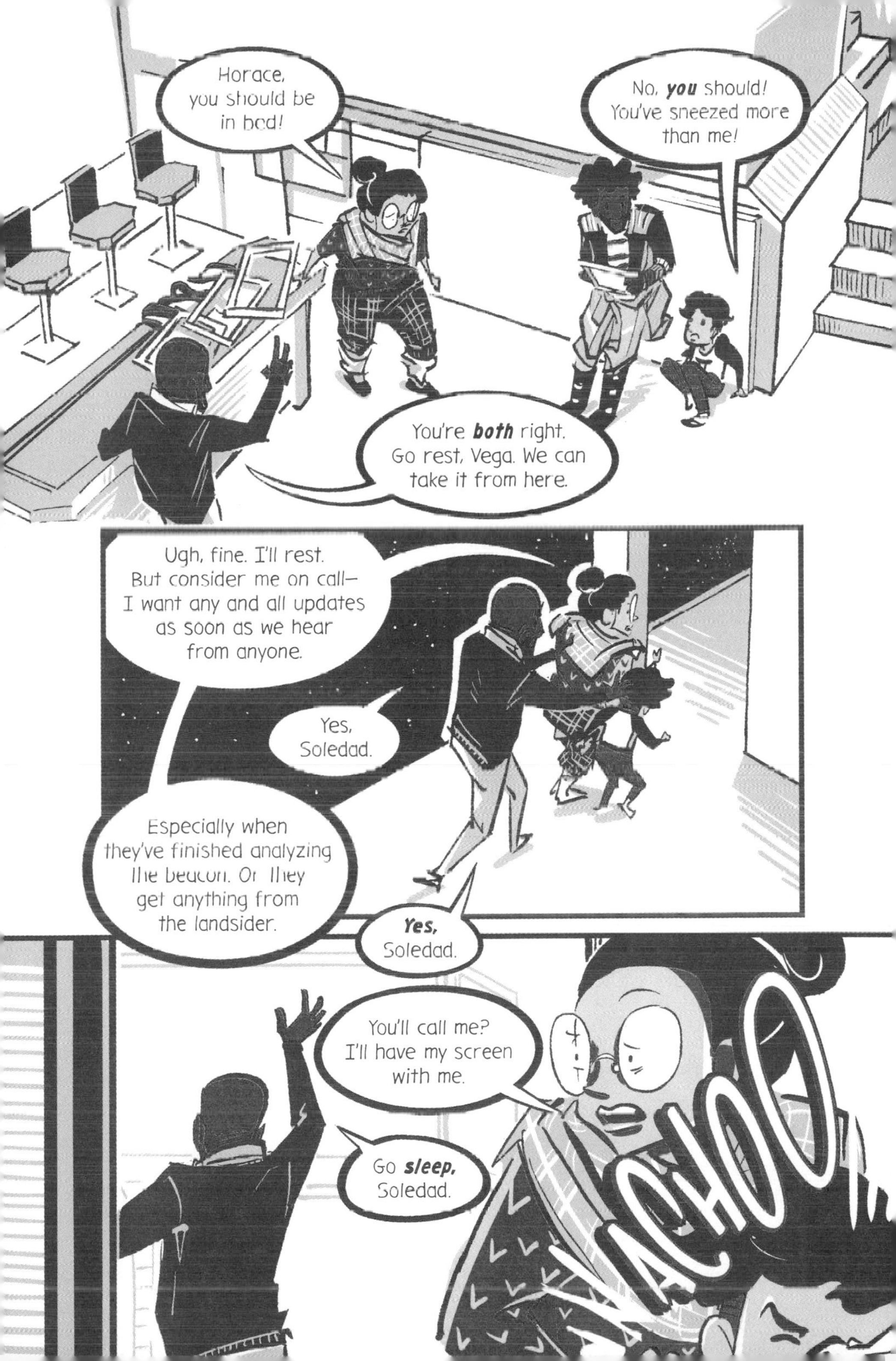

Horace, you should be in bed!
No, *you* should! You've sneezed more than me!
You're **both** right. Go rest, Vega. We can take it from here.
Ugh, fine. I'll rest. But consider me on call— I want any and all updates as soon as we hear from anyone.
Yes, Soledad.
Especially when they've finished analyzing the beacon. Or they get anything from the landsider.
Yes, Soledad.
You'll call me? I'll have my screen with me.
Go ***sleep,*** Soledad.
AACHOO

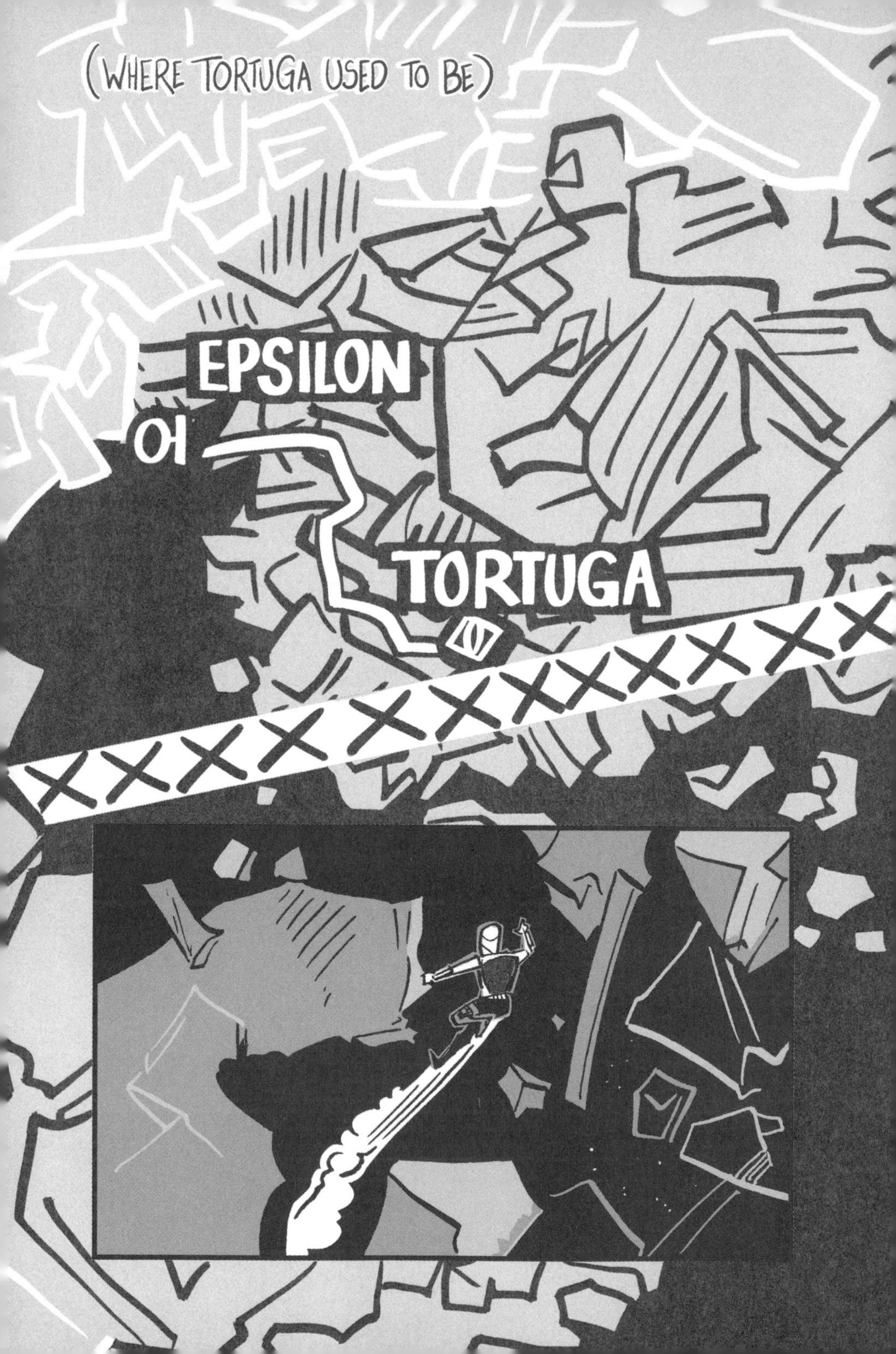
(WHERE TORTUGA USED TO BE)
EPSILON
01
TORTUGA

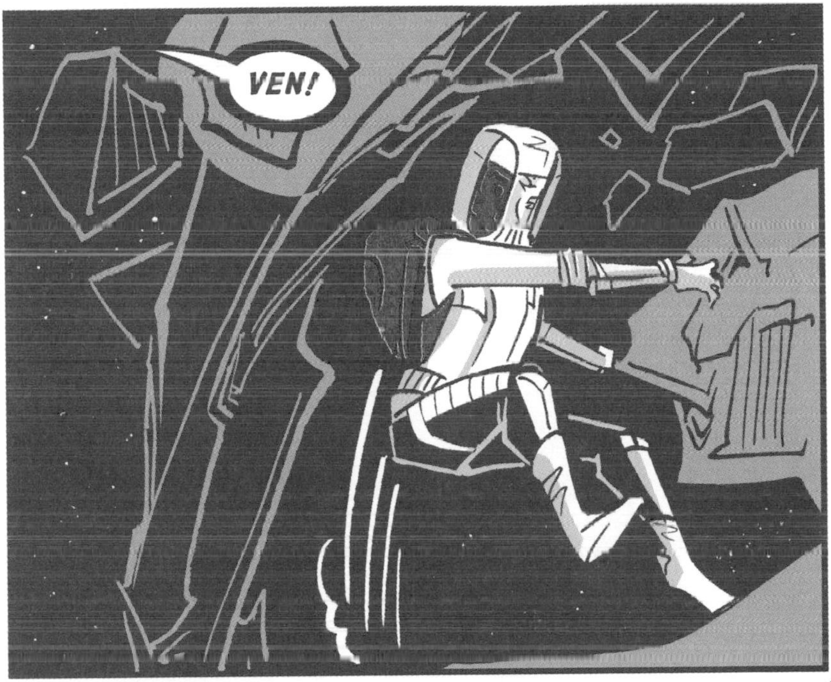
VEN!

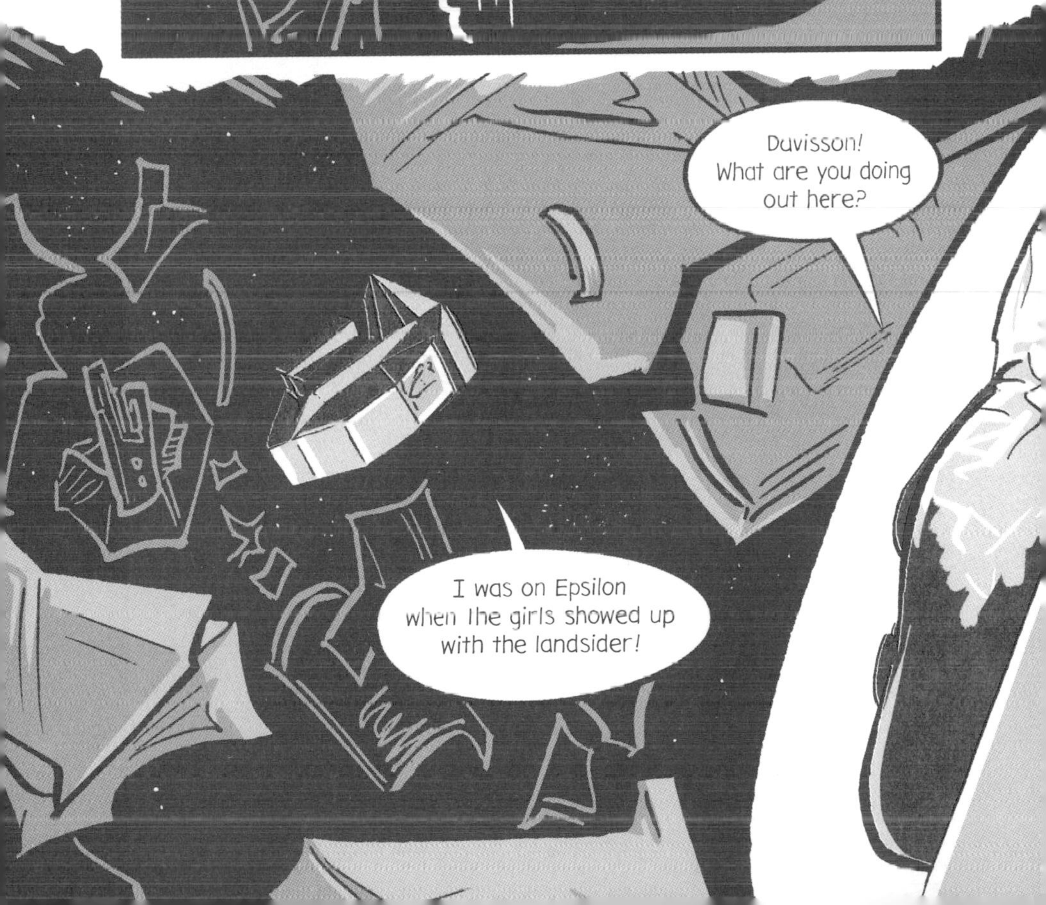
Davisson! What are you doing out here?
I was on Epsilon when the girls showed up with the landsider!

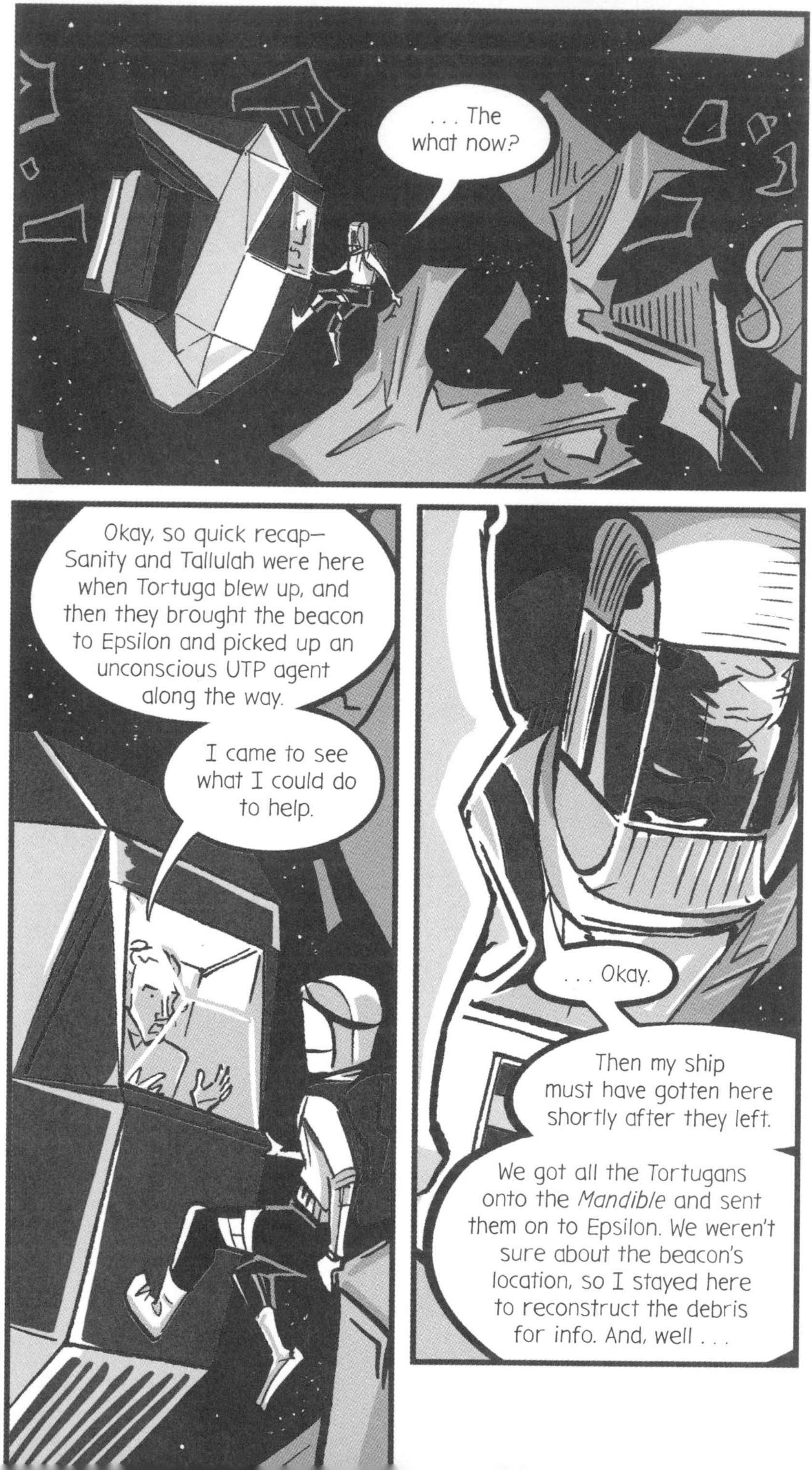
. . . The what now?
Okay, so quick recap— Sanity and Tallulah were here when Tortuga blew up, and then they brought the beacon to Epsilon and picked up an unconscious UTP agent along the way.
I came to see what I could do to help.
. . . Okay.
Then my ship must have gotten here shortly after they left.
We got all the Tortugans onto the *Mandible* and sent them on to Epsilon. We weren't sure about the beacon's location, so I stayed here to reconstruct the debris for info. And, well . . .

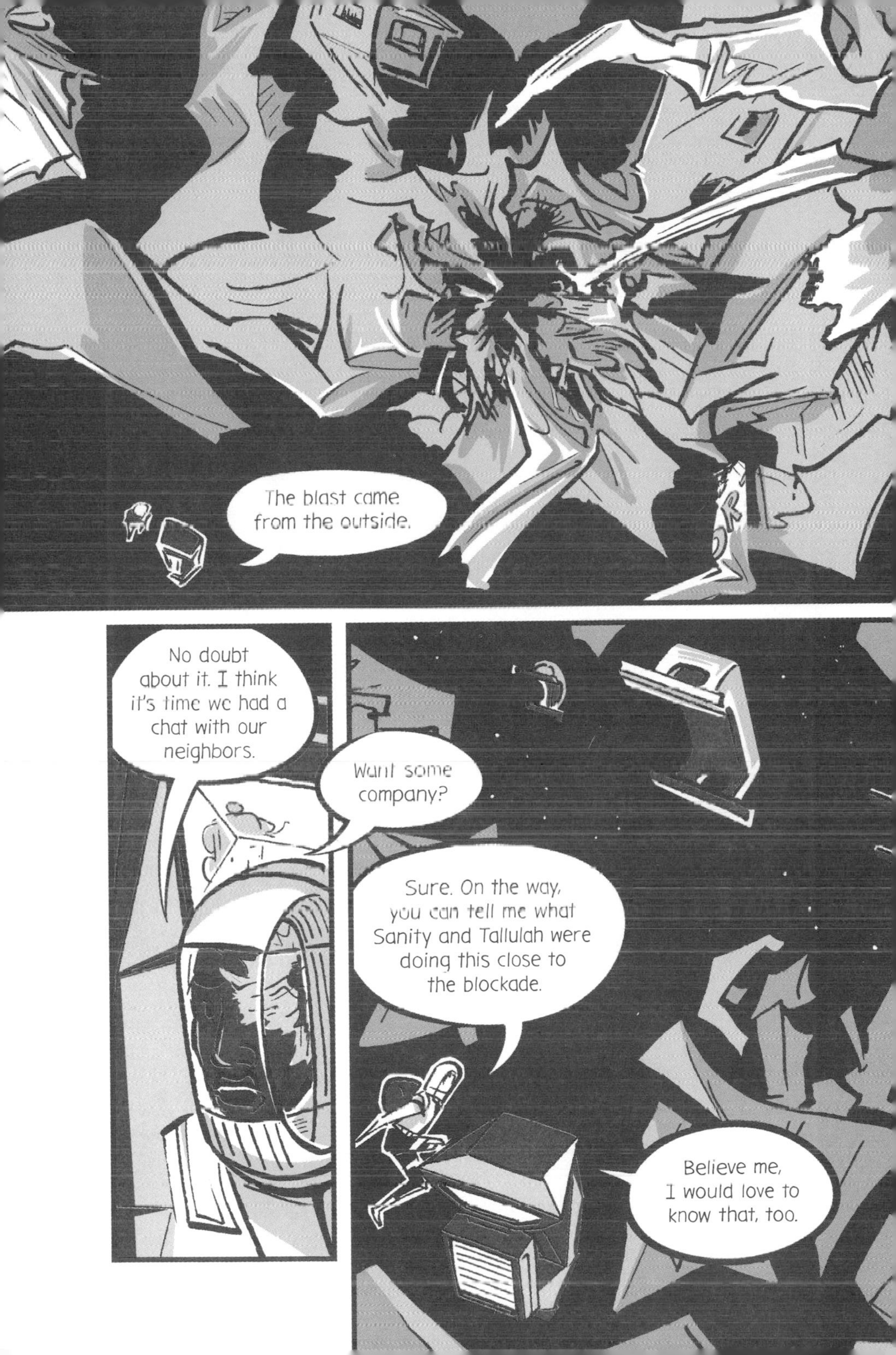

The blast came from the outside.
No doubt about it. I think it's time we had a chat with our neighbors.
Want some company?
Sure. On the way, you can tell me what Sanity and Tallulah were doing this close to the blockade.
Believe me, I would love to know that, too.

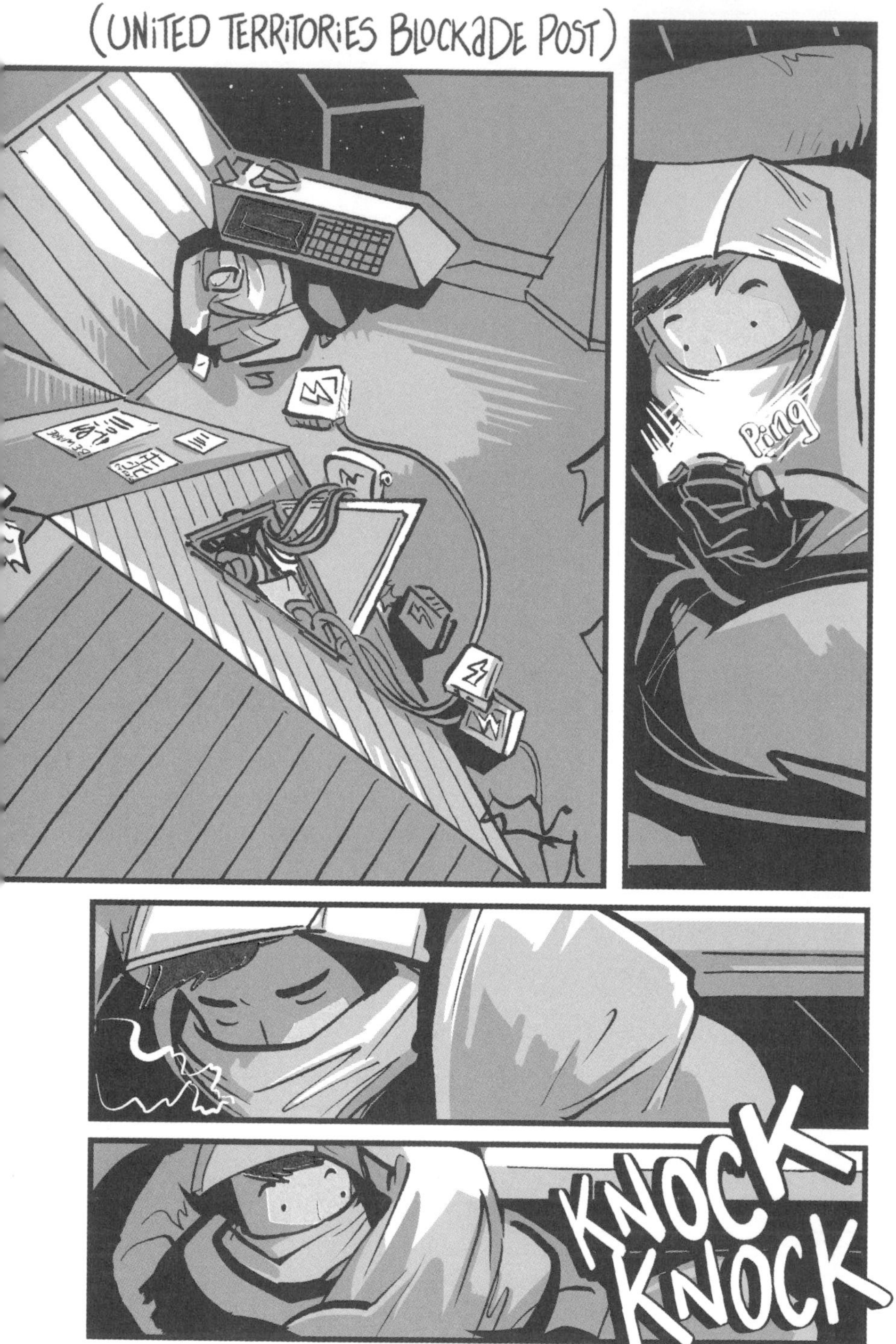
(UNITED TERRITORIES BLOCKADE POST)
Ping
KNOCK KNOCK

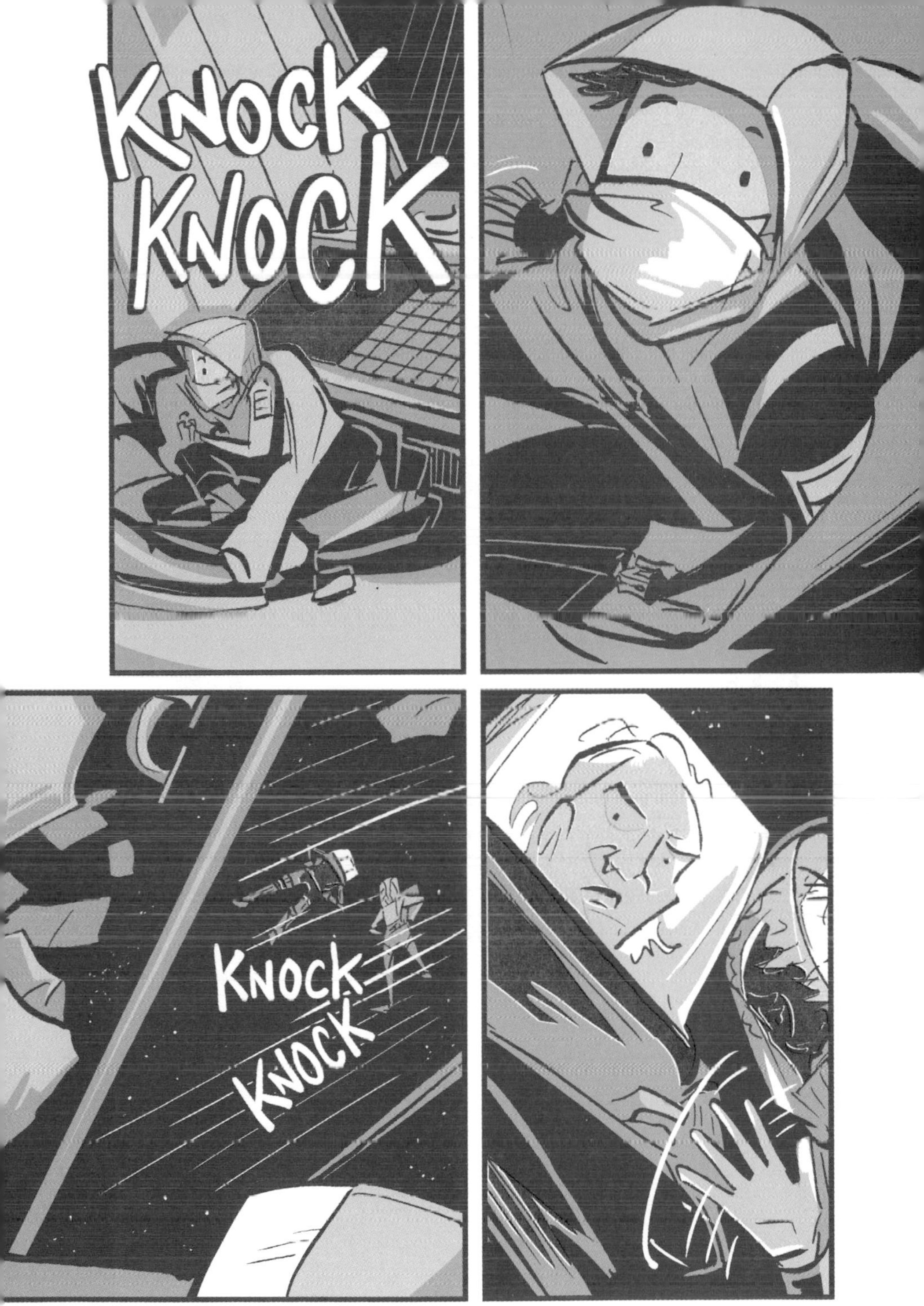
KNOCK
KNOCK
KNOCK
KNOCK

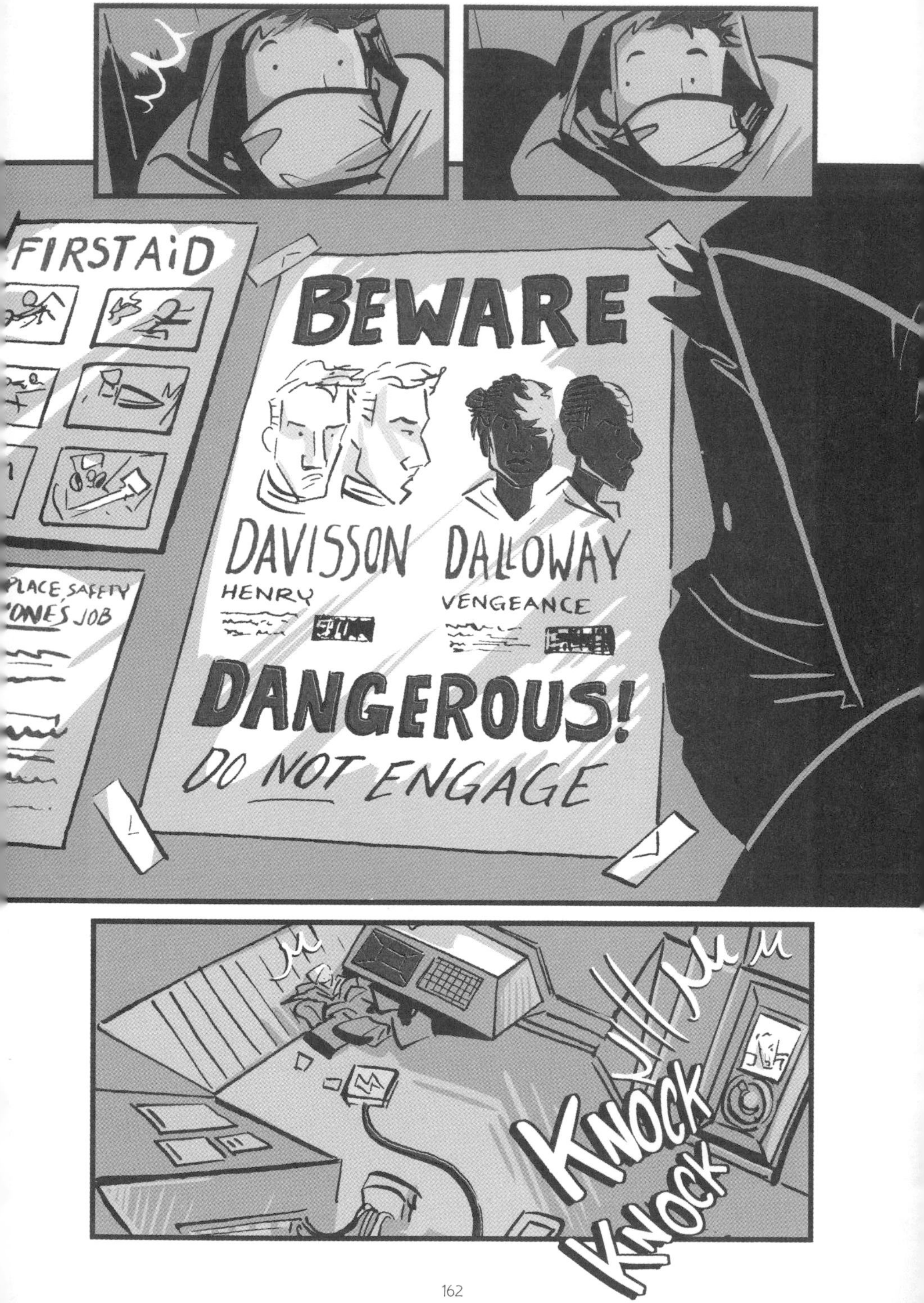
FIRSTAID
BEWARE
DAVISSON
HENRY
DALLOWAY
VENGEANCE
DANGEROUS!
DO NOT ENGAGE
PLACE, SAFETY
ONE'S JOB
KNOCK
KNOCK

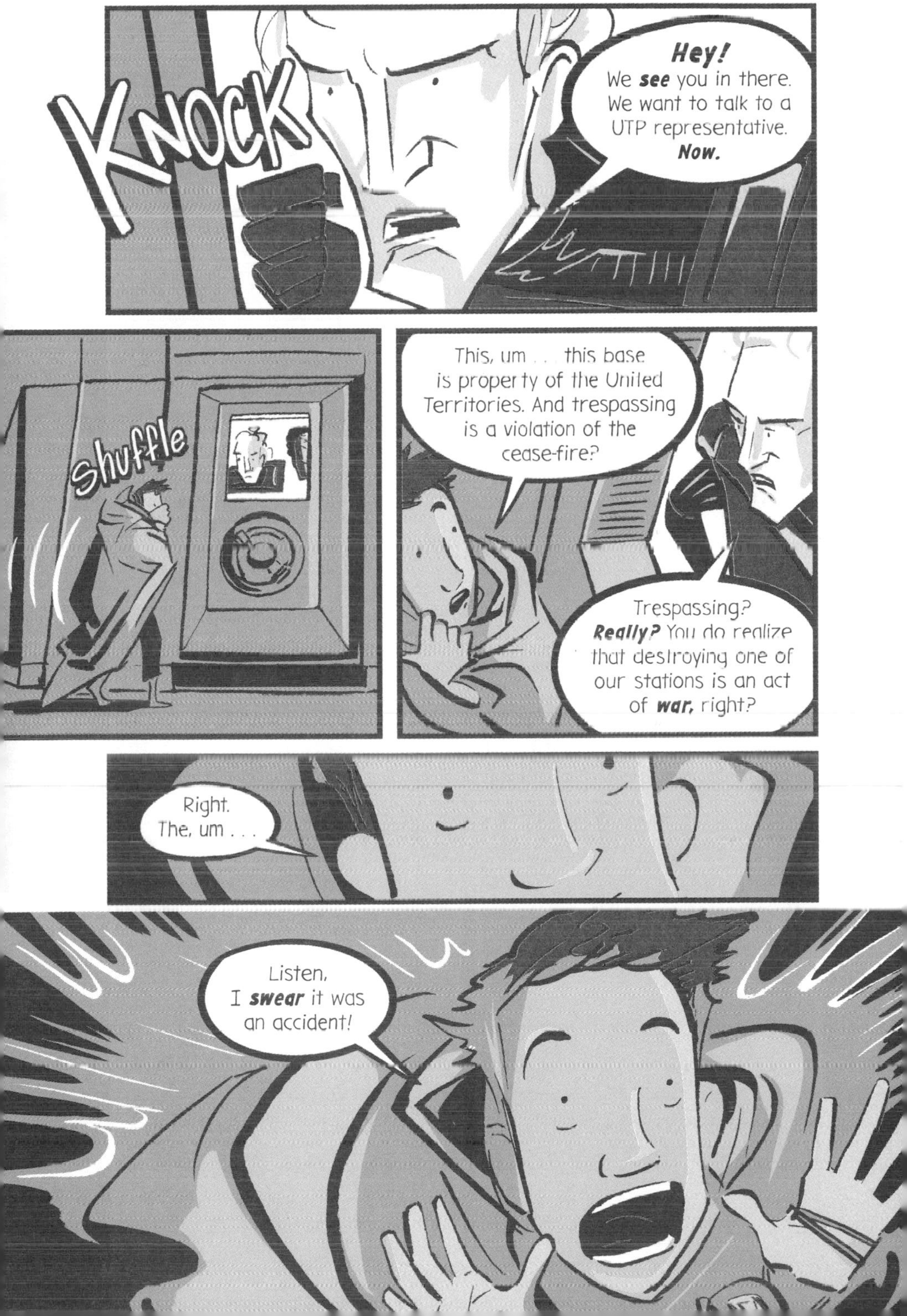
KNOCK
Hey! We see you in there. We want to talk to a UTP representative. Now.
Shuffle
This, um . . . this base is property of the United Territories. And trespassing is a violation of the cease-fire?
Trespassing? Really? You do realize that destroying one of our stations is an act of war, right?
Right. The, um . . .
Listen, I swear it was an accident!

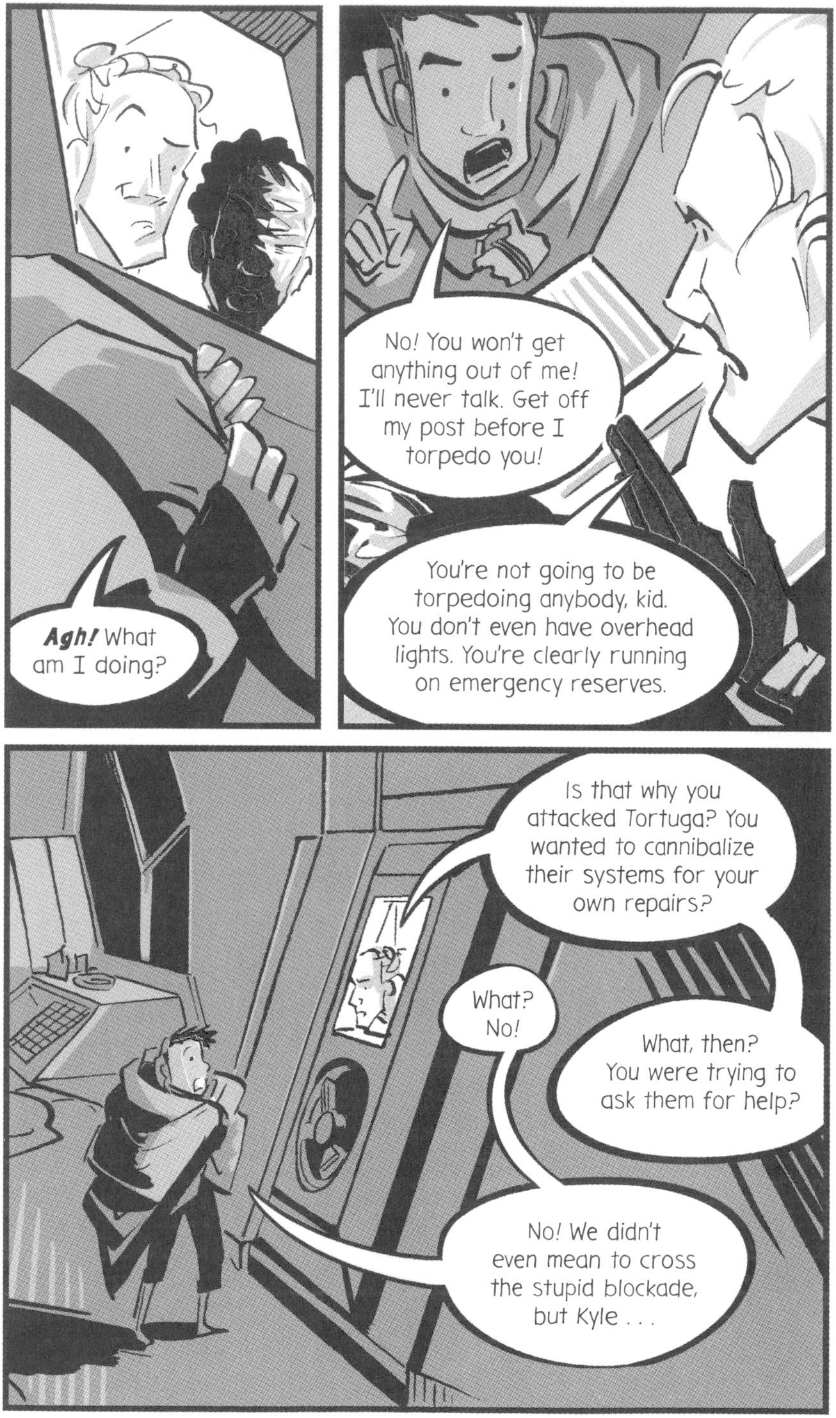
No! You won't get anything out of me! I'll never talk. Get off my post before I torpedo you!
Agh! What am I doing?
You're not going to be torpedoing anybody, kid. You don't even have overhead lights. You're clearly running on emergency reserves.
Is that why you attacked Tortuga? You wanted to cannibalize their systems for your own repairs?
What? No!
What, then? You were trying to ask them for help?
No! We didn't even mean to cross the stupid blockade, but Kyle . . .

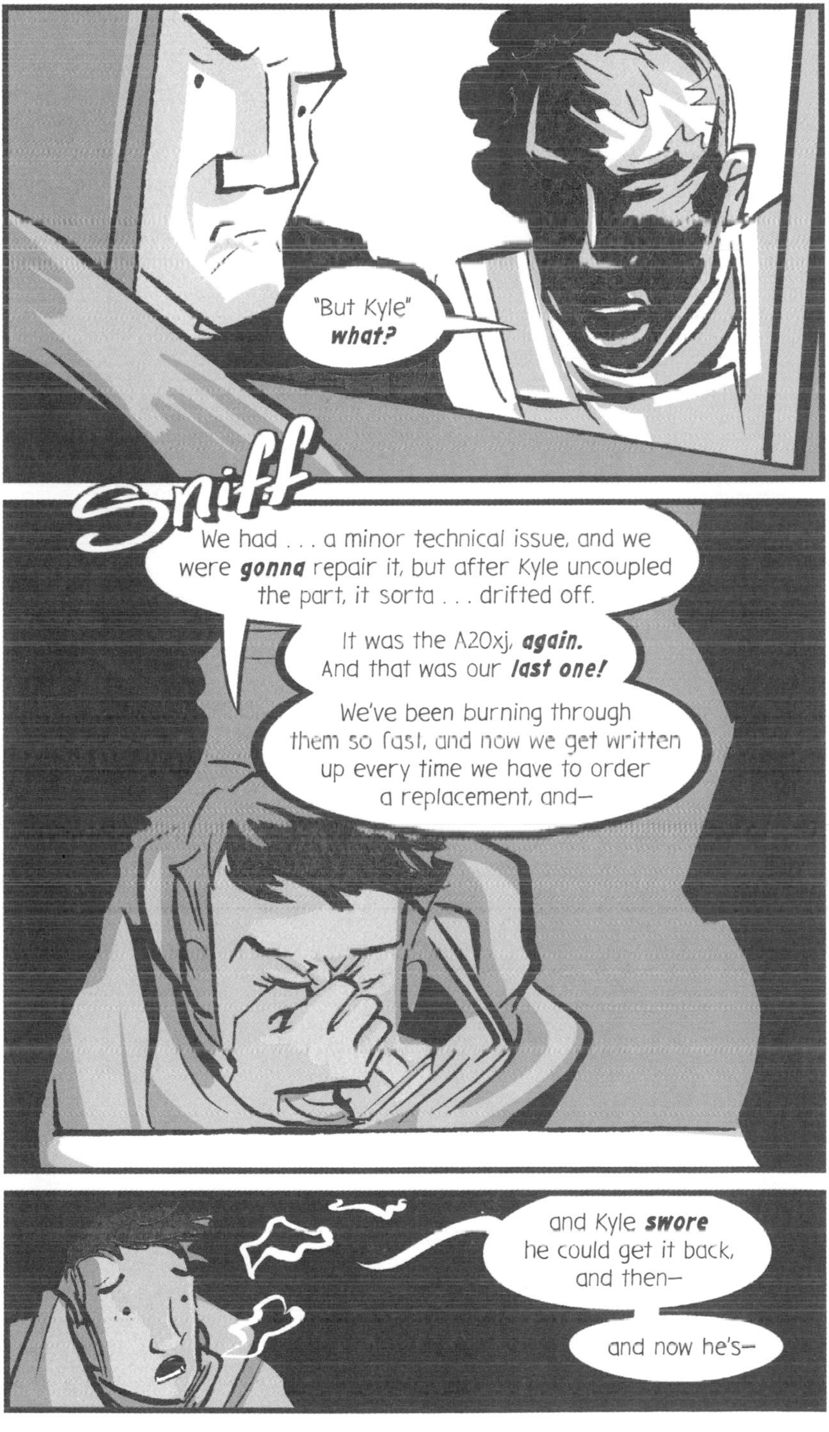
"But Kyle" **what?**
Sniff
We had . . . a minor technical issue, and we were **gonna** repair it, but after Kyle uncoupled the part, it sorta . . . drifted off.
It was the A20xj, **again.** And that was our **last one!**
We've been burning through them so fast, and now we get written up every time we have to order a replacement, and—
and Kyle **swore** he could get it back, and then—
and now he's—

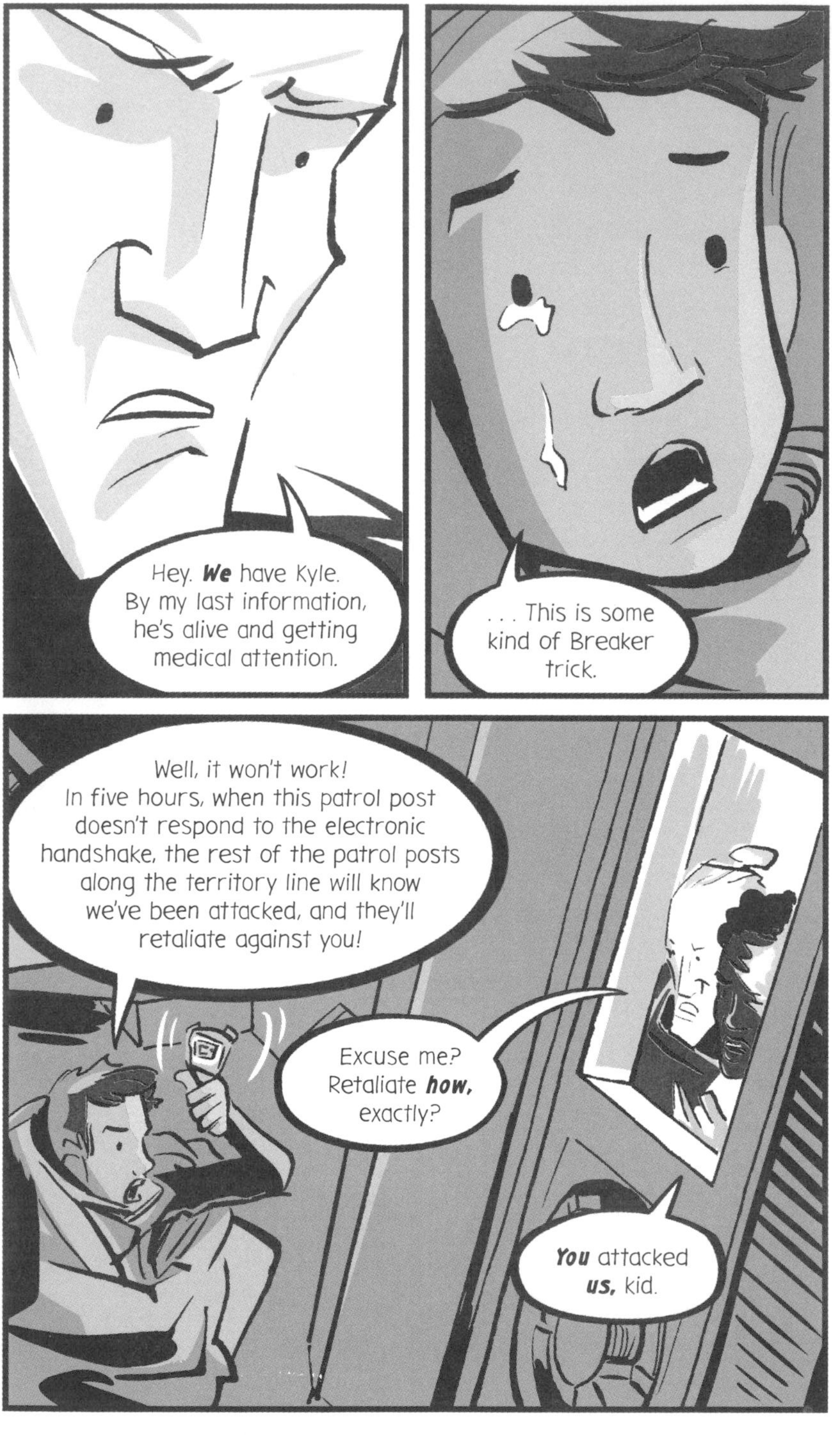
Hey. We have Kyle. By my last information, he's alive and getting medical attention.
. . . This is some kind of Breaker trick.
Well, it won't work! In five hours, when this patrol post doesn't respond to the electronic handshake, the rest of the patrol posts along the territory line will know we've been attacked, and they'll retaliate against you!
Excuse me? Retaliate how, exactly?
You attacked us, kid.

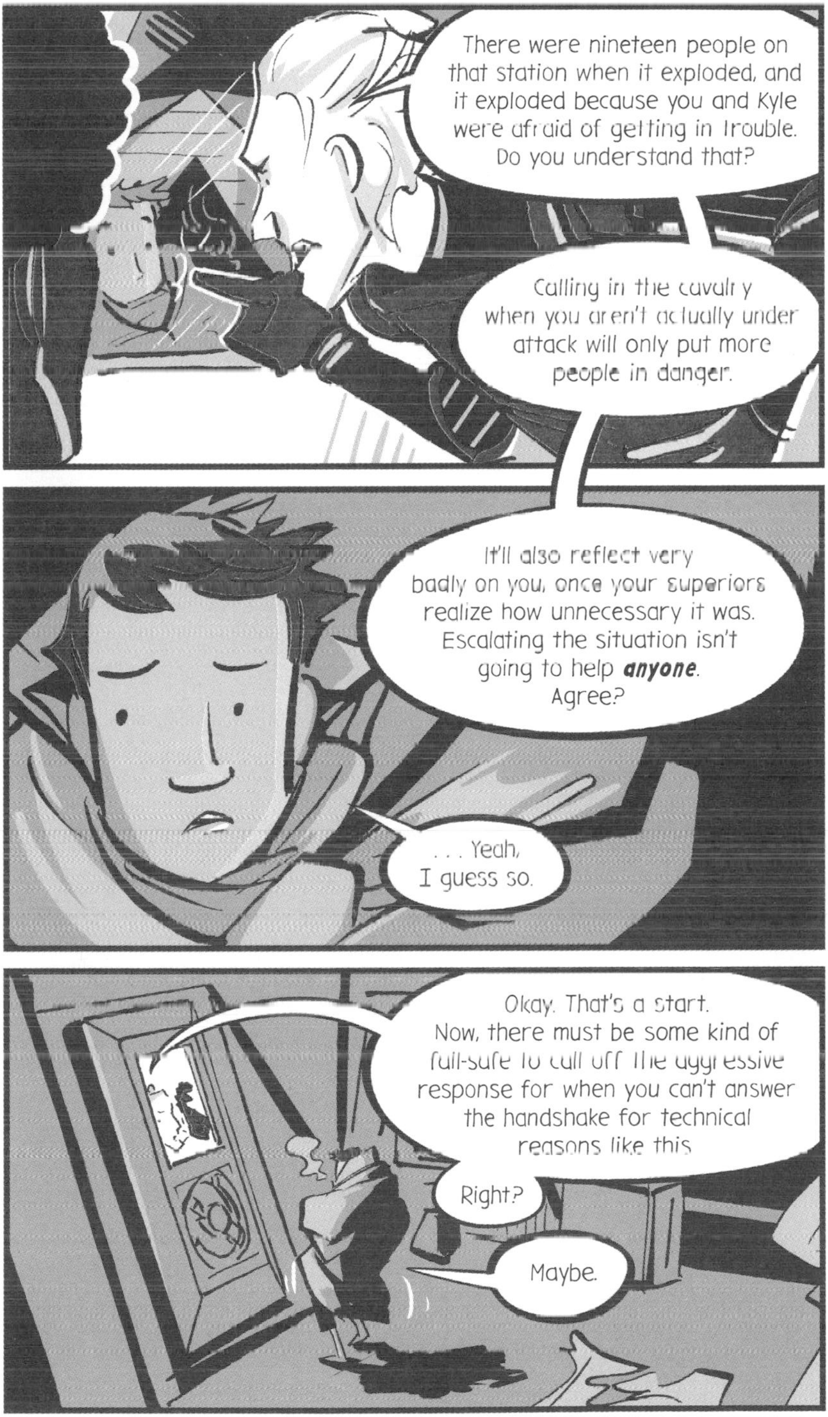
There were nineteen people on that station when it exploded, and it exploded because you and Kyle were afraid of getting in trouble. Do you understand that?
Calling in the cavalry when you aren't actually under attack will only put more people in danger.
It'll also reflect very badly on you, once your superiors realize how unnecessary it was. Escalating the situation isn't going to help **anyone**. Agree?
. . . Yeah, I guess so.
Okay. That's a start. Now, there must be some kind of fail-safe to call off the aggressive response for when you can't answer the handshake for technical reasons like this.
Right?
Maybe.

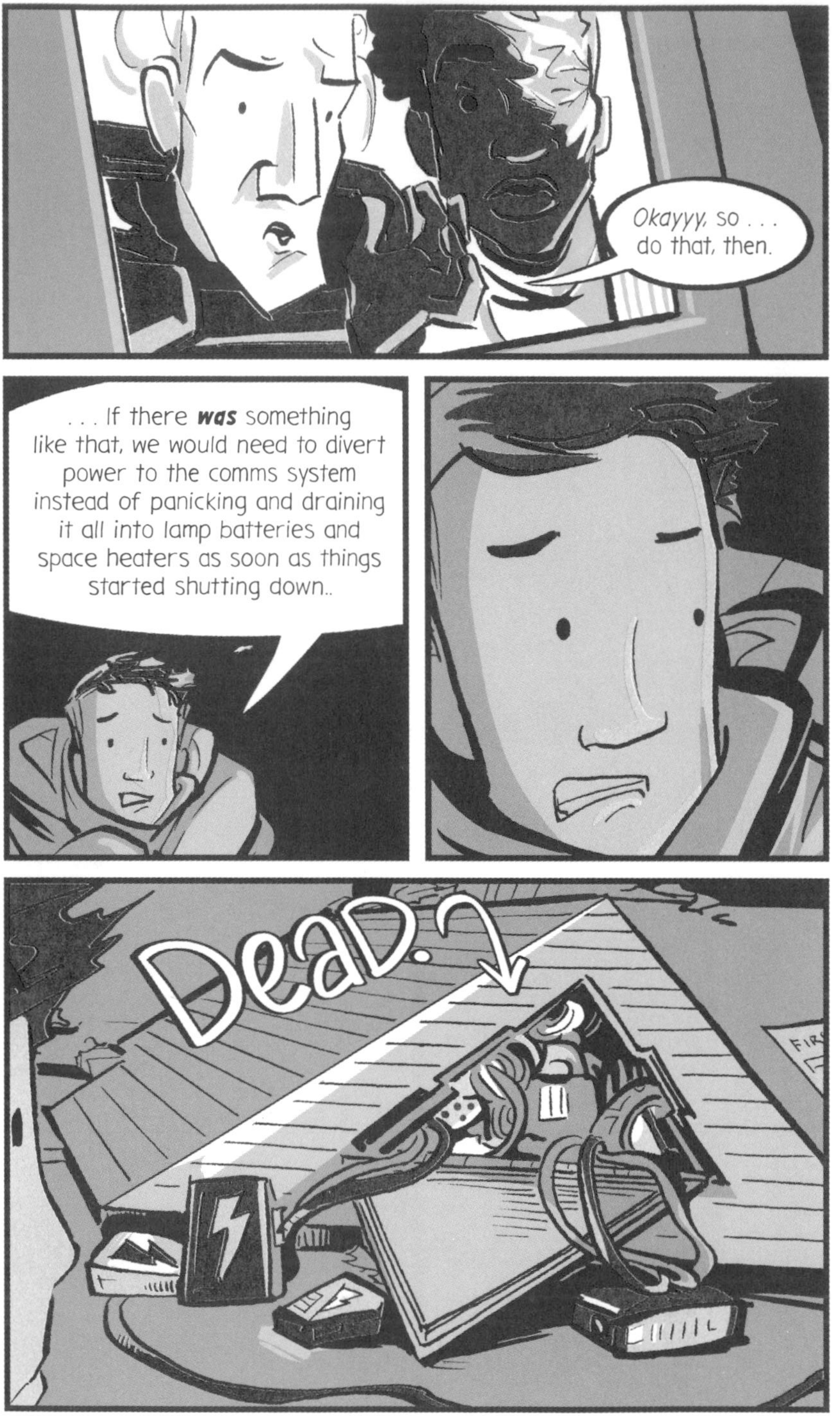
Okayyy, so . . . do that, then.
. . . If there **was** something like that, we would need to divert power to the comms system instead of panicking and draining it all into lamp batteries and space heaters as soon as things started shutting down..
DEAD.

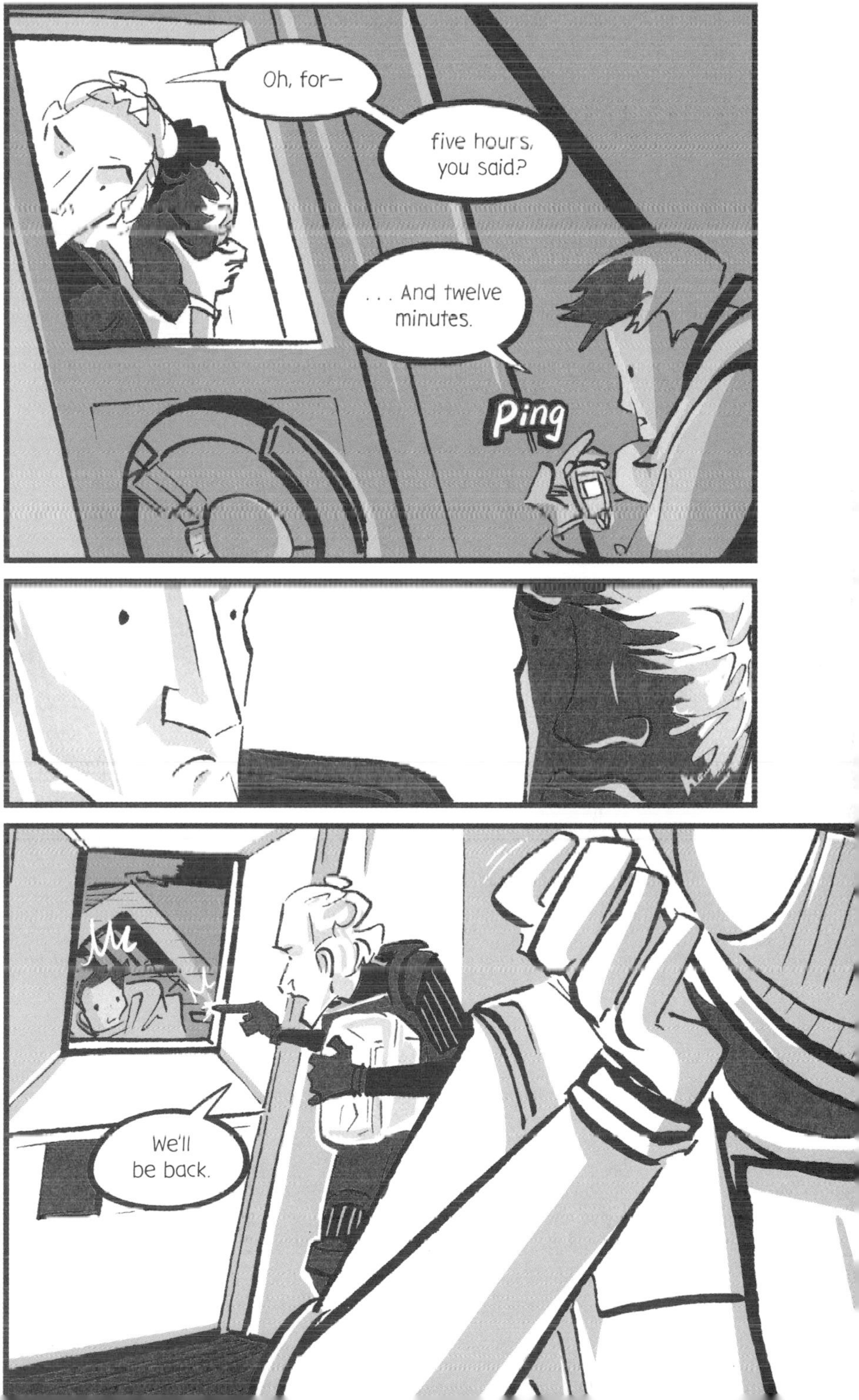
Oh, for—
five hours, you said?
. . . And twelve minutes.
Ping
We'll be back.

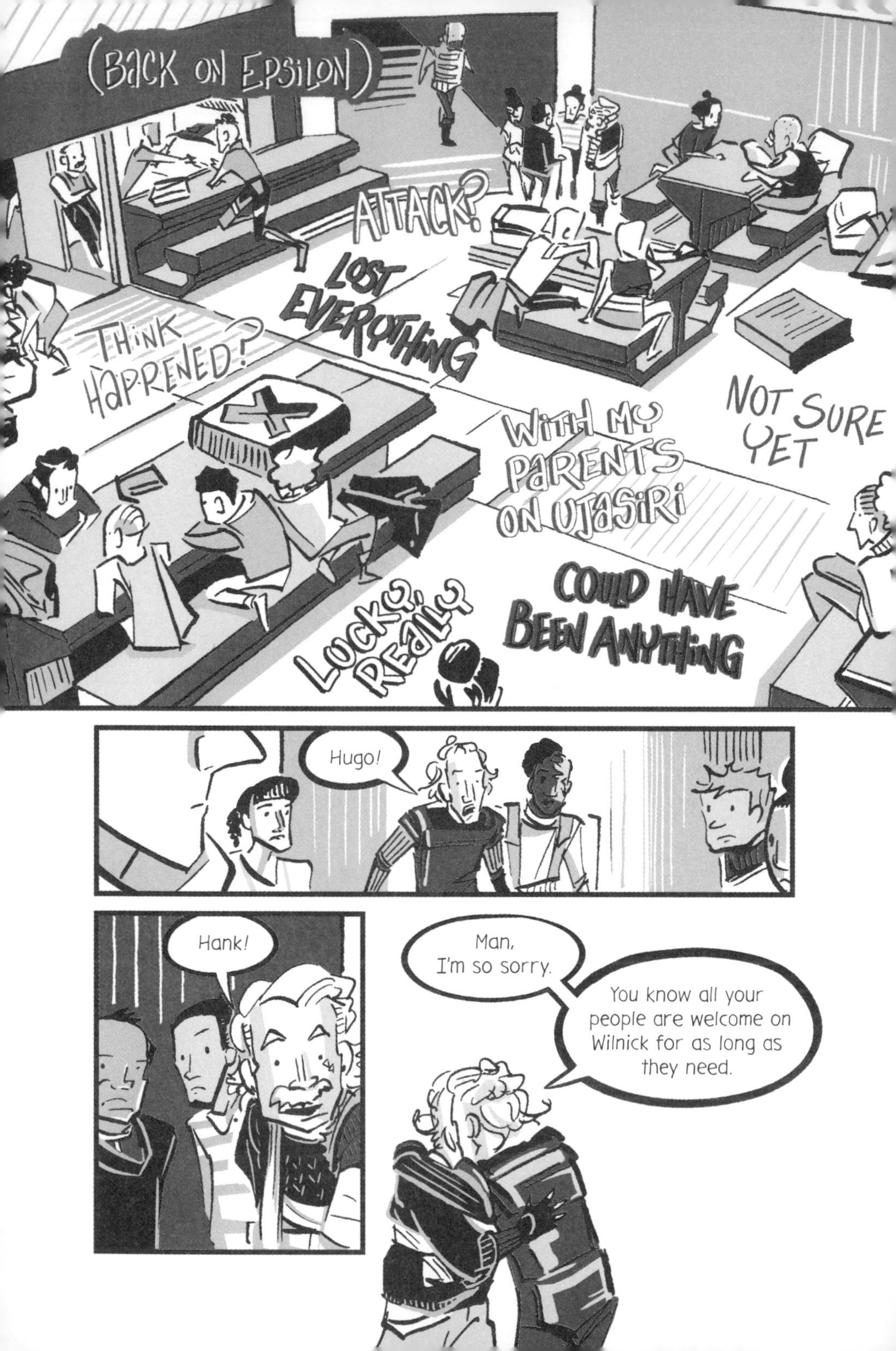
(BACK ON EPSILON)
ATTACK?
LOST EVERYTHING
THINK HAPPENED?
WITH MY PARENTS ON UJASIRI
NOT SURE YET
LUCKY? REALLY?
COULD HAVE BEEN ANYTHING
Hugo!
Hank!
Man, I'm so sorry.
You know all your people are welcome on Wilnick for as long as they need.

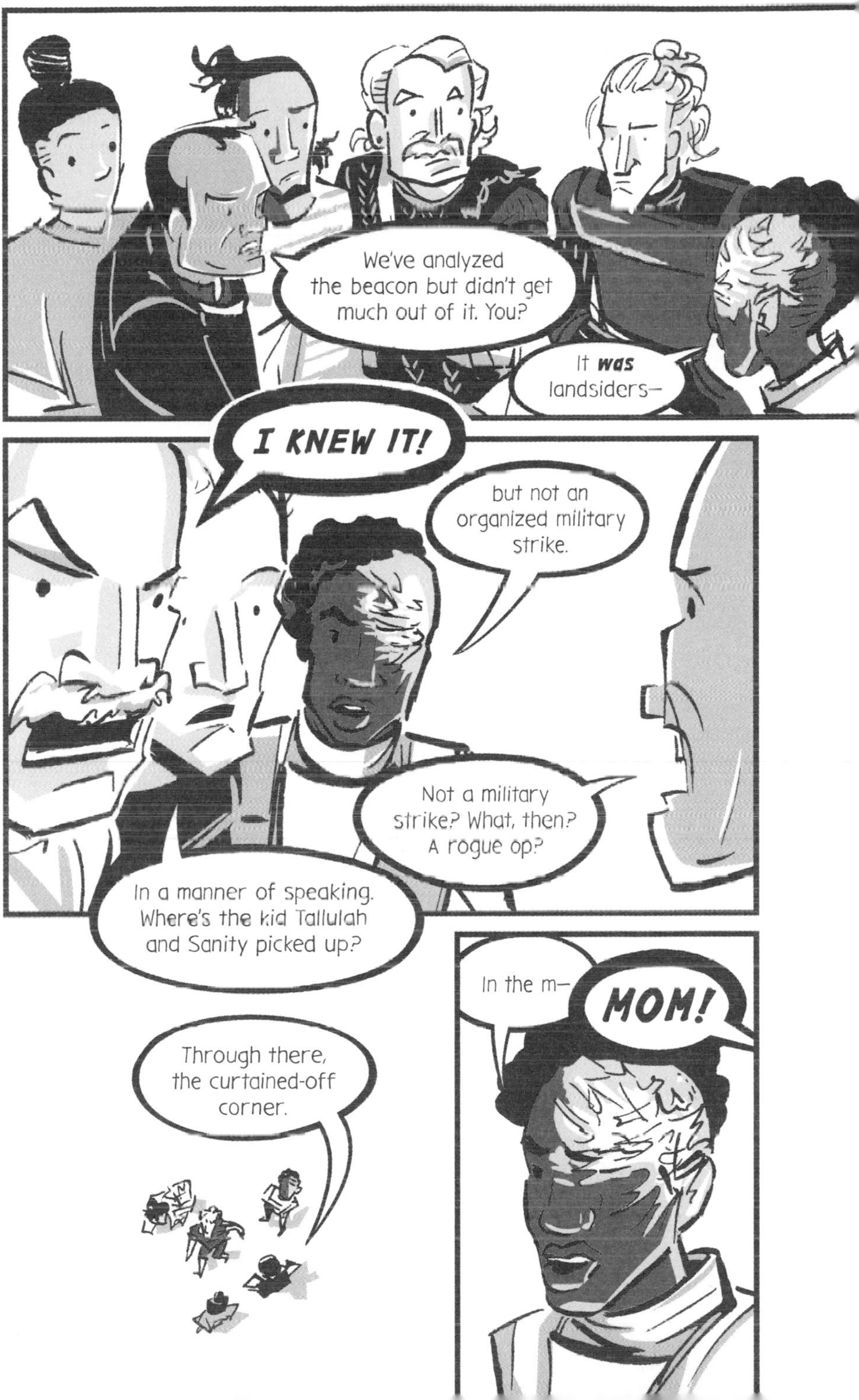
We've analyzed the beacon but didn't get much out of it. You?
It **was** landsiders—
I KNEW IT!
but not an organized military strike.
Not a military strike? What, then? A rogue op?
In a manner of speaking. Where's the kid Tallulah and Sanity picked up?
Through there, the curtained-off corner.
In the m—
MOM!

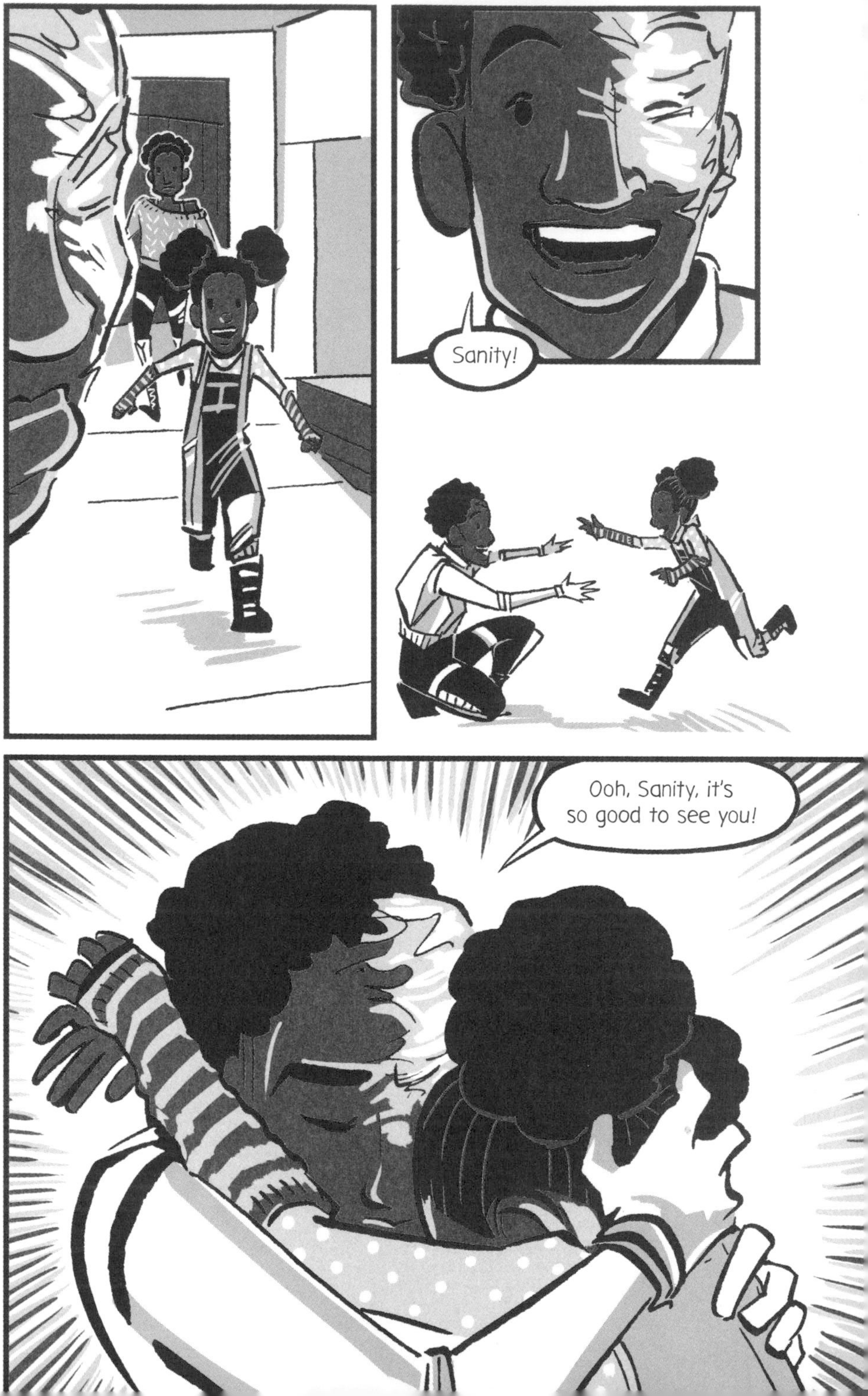
Sanity!
Ooh, Sanity, it's so good to see you!

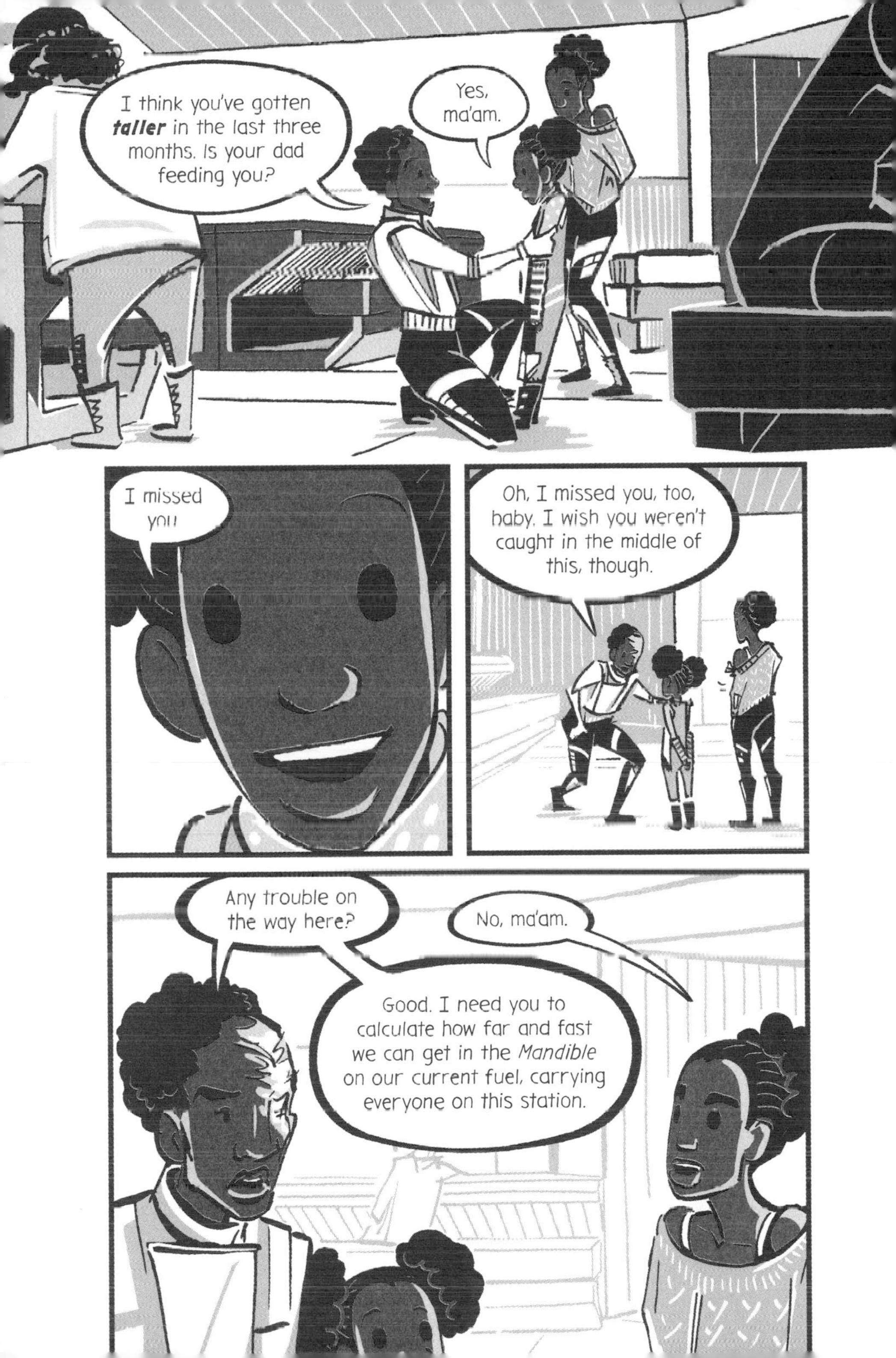

I think you've gotten **taller** in the last three months. Is your dad feeding you?
Yes, ma'am.
I missed you.
Oh, I missed you, too, baby. I wish you weren't caught *in* the middle of this, though.
Any trouble on the way here?
No, ma'am.
Good. I need you to calculate how far and fast we can get in the *Mandible* on our current fuel, carrying everyone on this station.

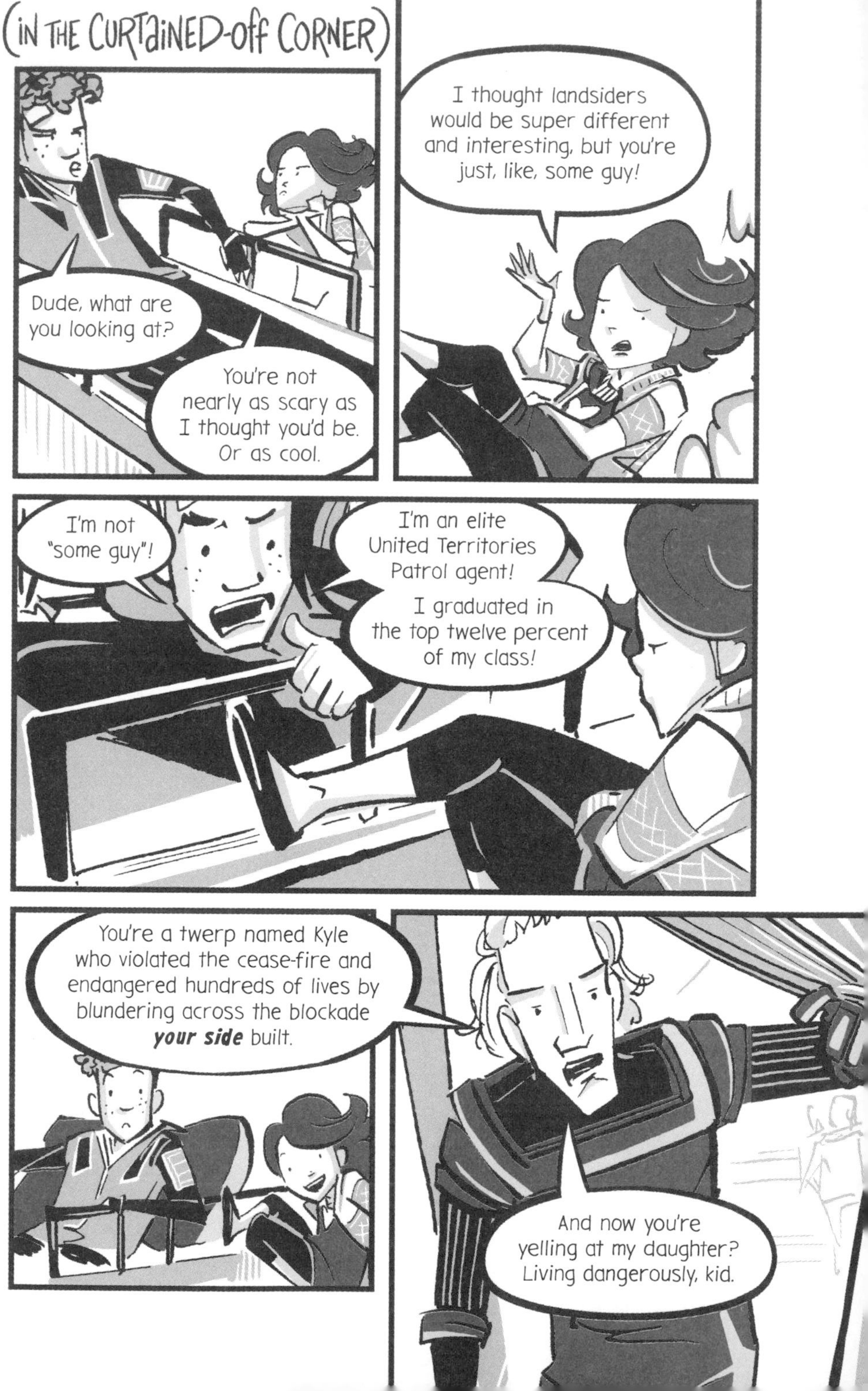
(IN THE CURTAINED-OFF CORNER)
Dude, what are you looking at?
You're not nearly as scary as I thought you'd be. Or as cool.
I thought landsiders would be super different and interesting, but you're just, like, some guy!
I'm not "some guy"!
I'm an elite United Territories Patrol agent!
I graduated in the top twelve percent of my class!
You're a twerp named Kyle who violated the cease-fire and endangered hundreds of lives by blundering across the blockade **your side** built.
And now you're yelling at my daughter? Living dangerously, kid.

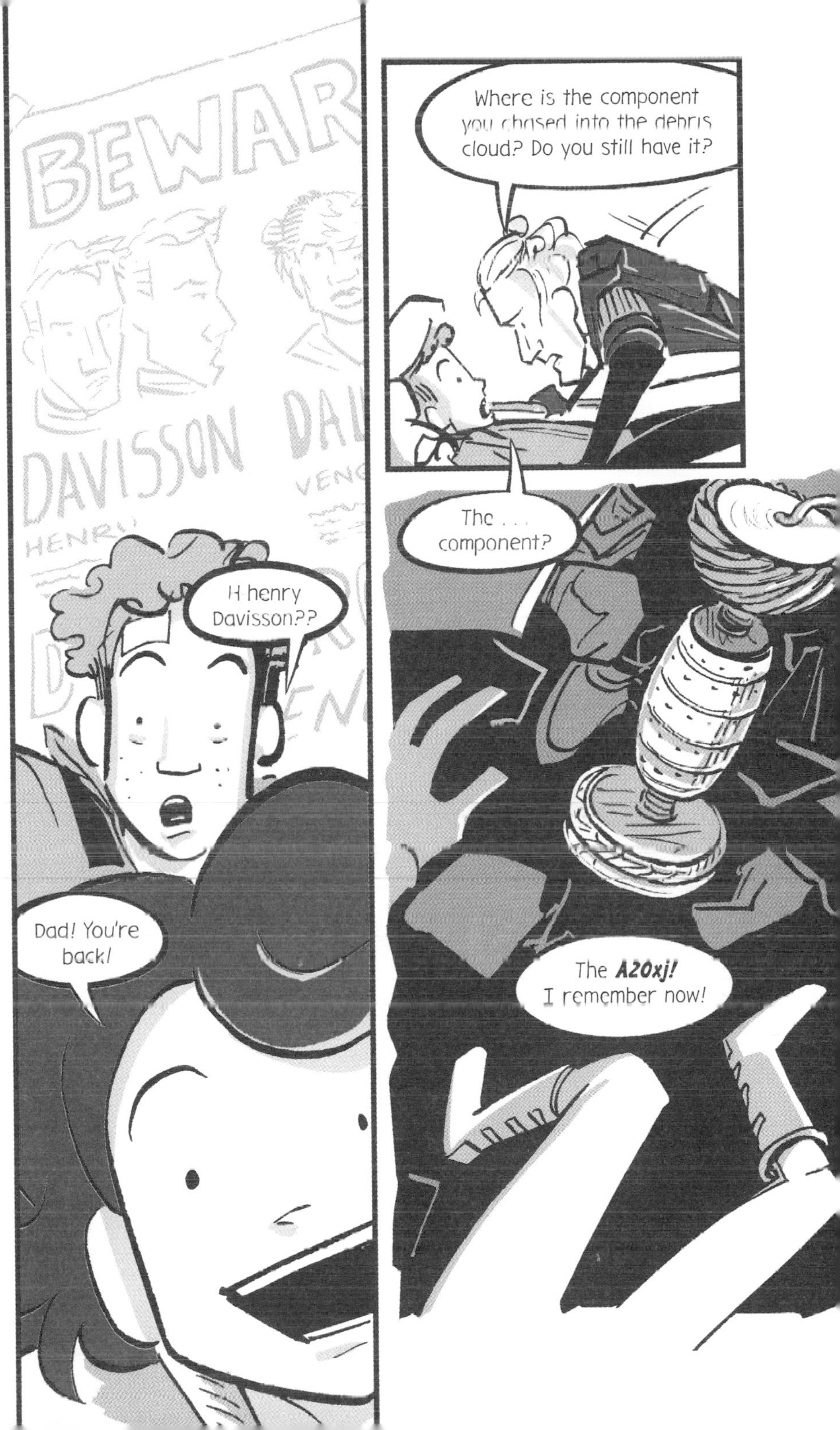

BEWAR
DAVISSON
HENRY
VENG
H-henry Davisson??
Dad! You're back!
Where is the component you chased into the debris cloud? Do you still have it?
The . . . component?
The **A20xj!** I remember now!

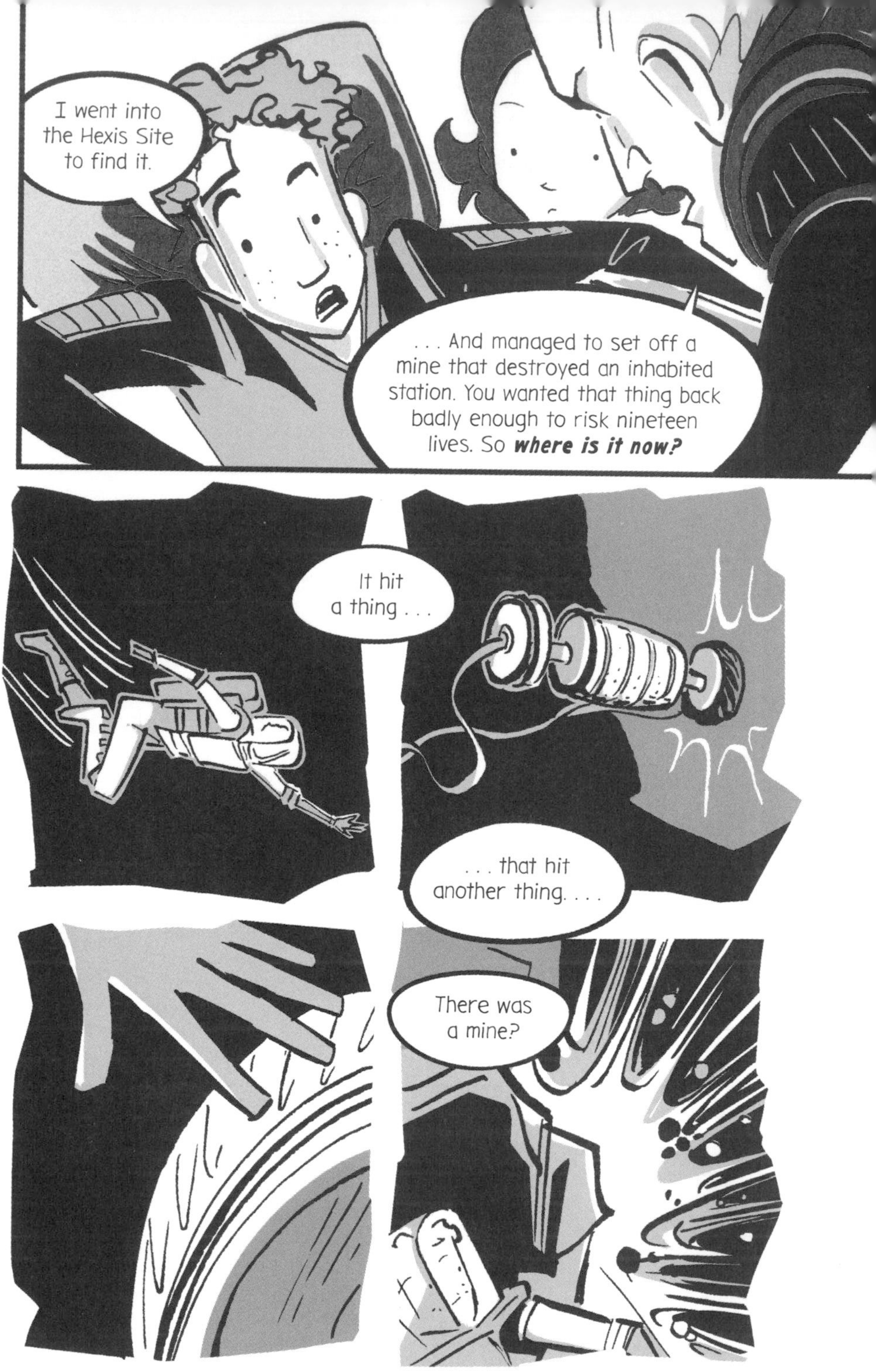
I went into the Hexis Site to find it.
. . . And managed to set off a mine that destroyed an inhabited station. You wanted that thing back badly enough to risk nineteen lives. So **where is it now?**
It hit a thing . . .
. . . that hit another thing. . . .
There was a mine?

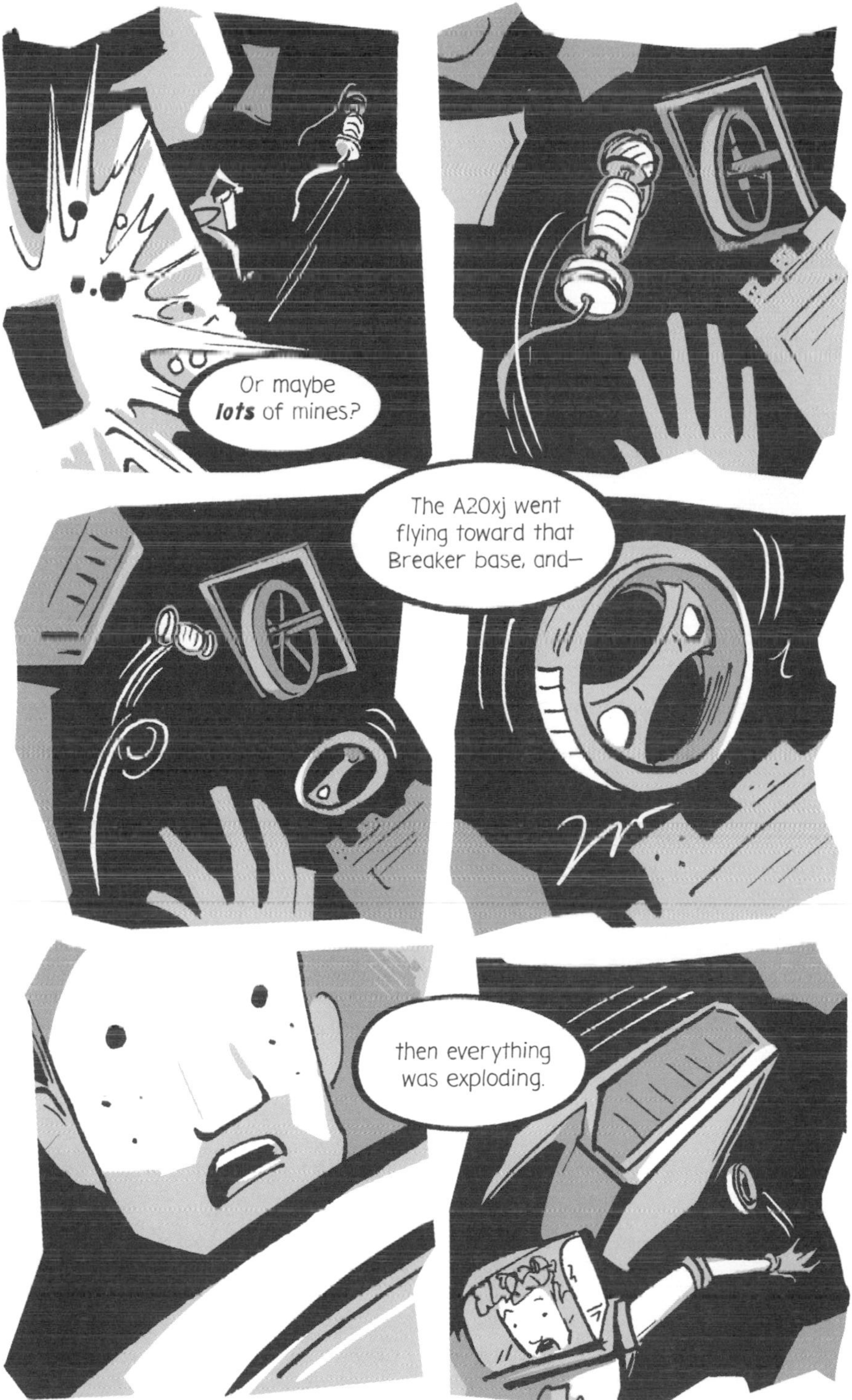
Or maybe
lots of mines?
The A20xj went flying toward that Breaker base, and—
then everything was exploding.

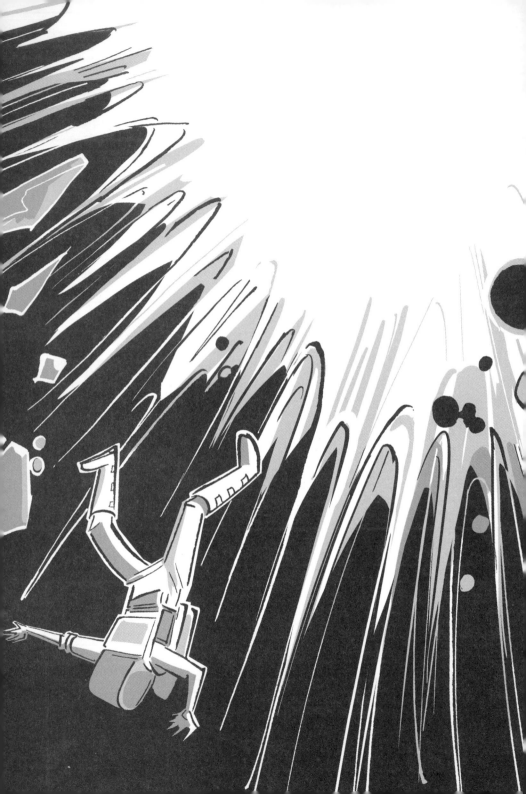

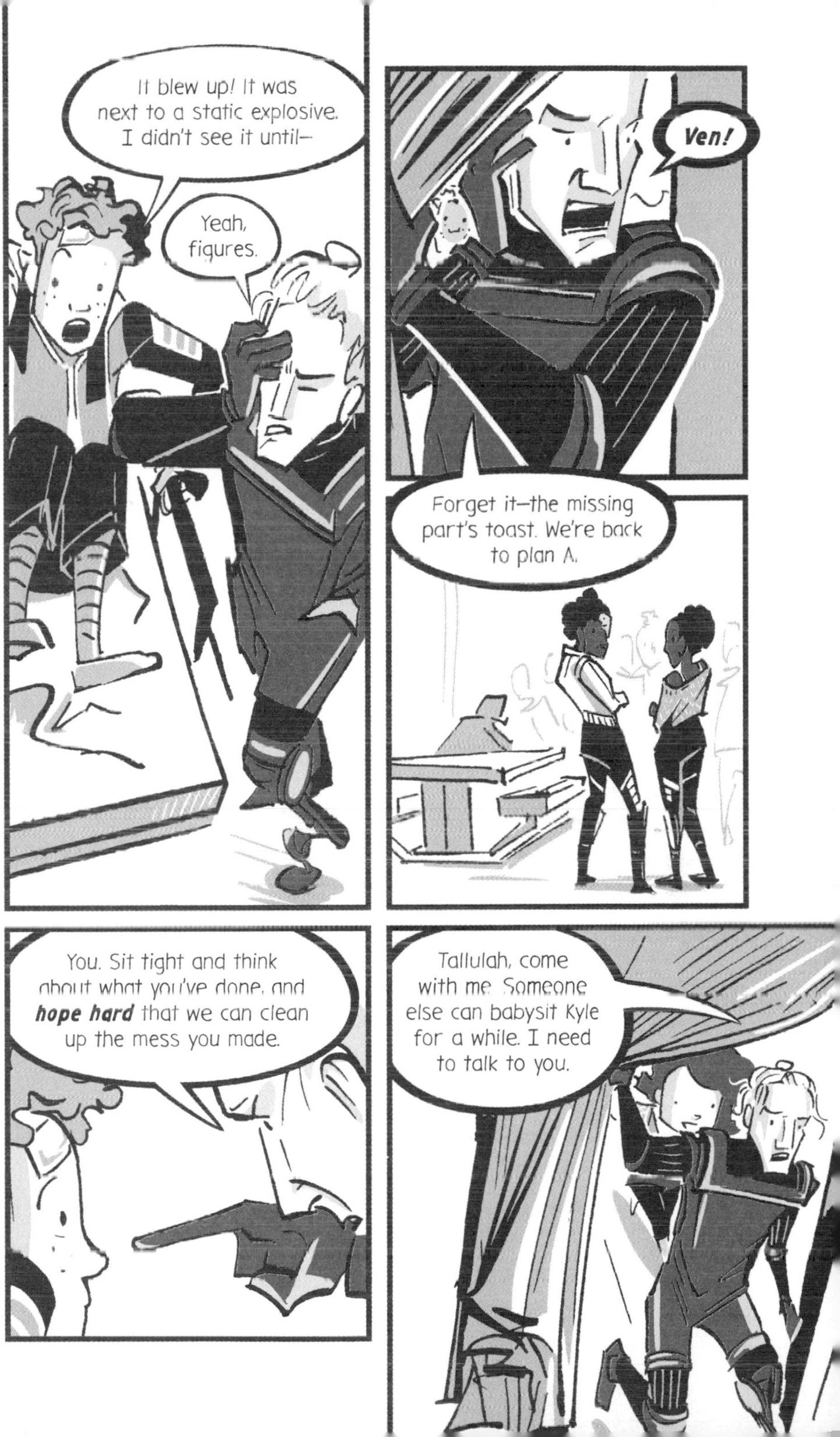
It blew up! It was next to a static explosive. I didn't see it until—
Yeah, figures.
Ven!
Forget it—the missing part's toast. We're back to plan A.
You. Sit tight and think about what you've done, and **hope hard** that we can clean up the mess you made.
Tallulah, come with me. Someone else can babysit Kyle for a while. I need to talk to you.

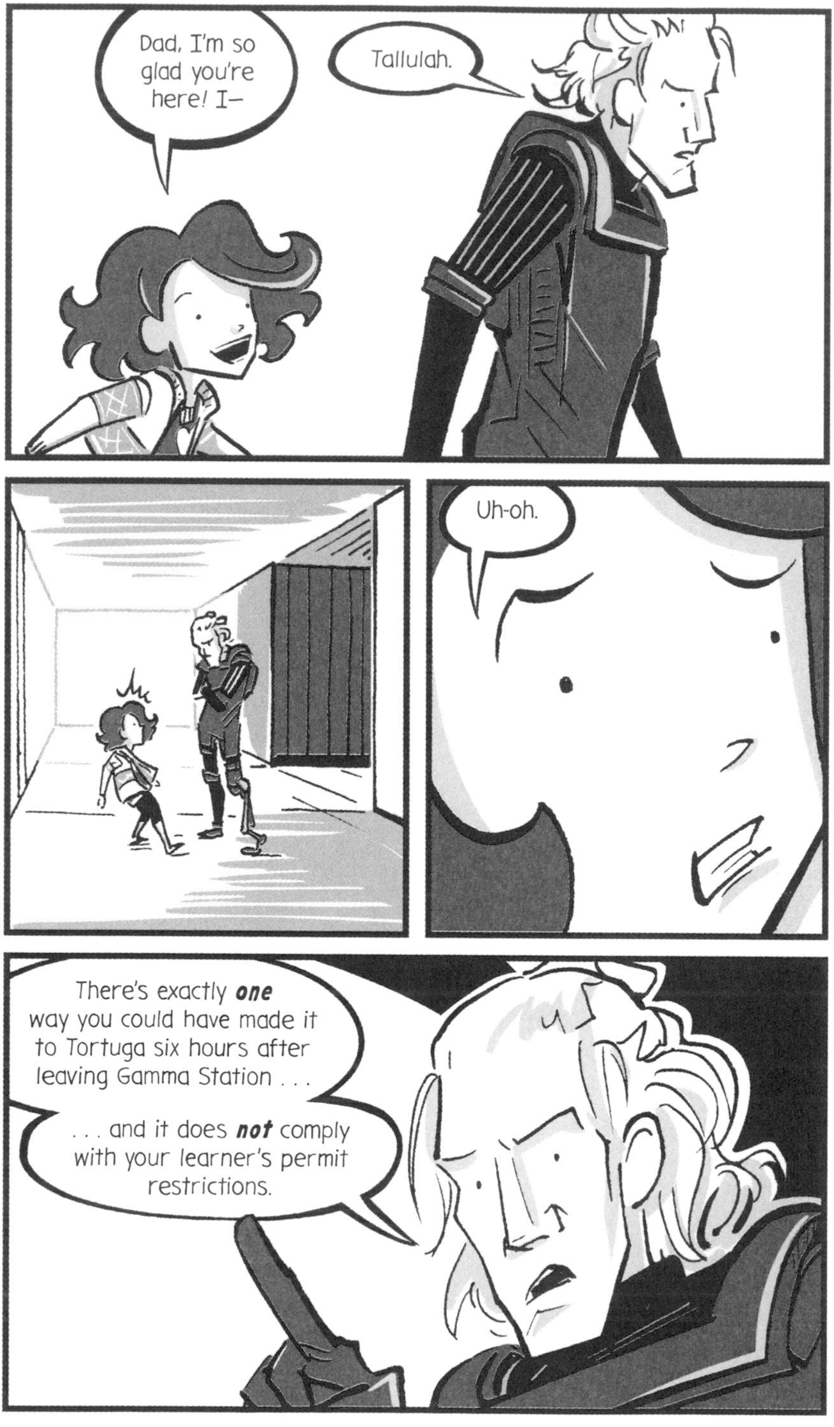

Dad, I'm so glad you're here! I—
Tallulah.
Uh-oh.
There's exactly **one** way you could have made it to Tortuga six hours after leaving Gamma Station . . .
. . . and it does **not** comply with your learner's permit restrictions.

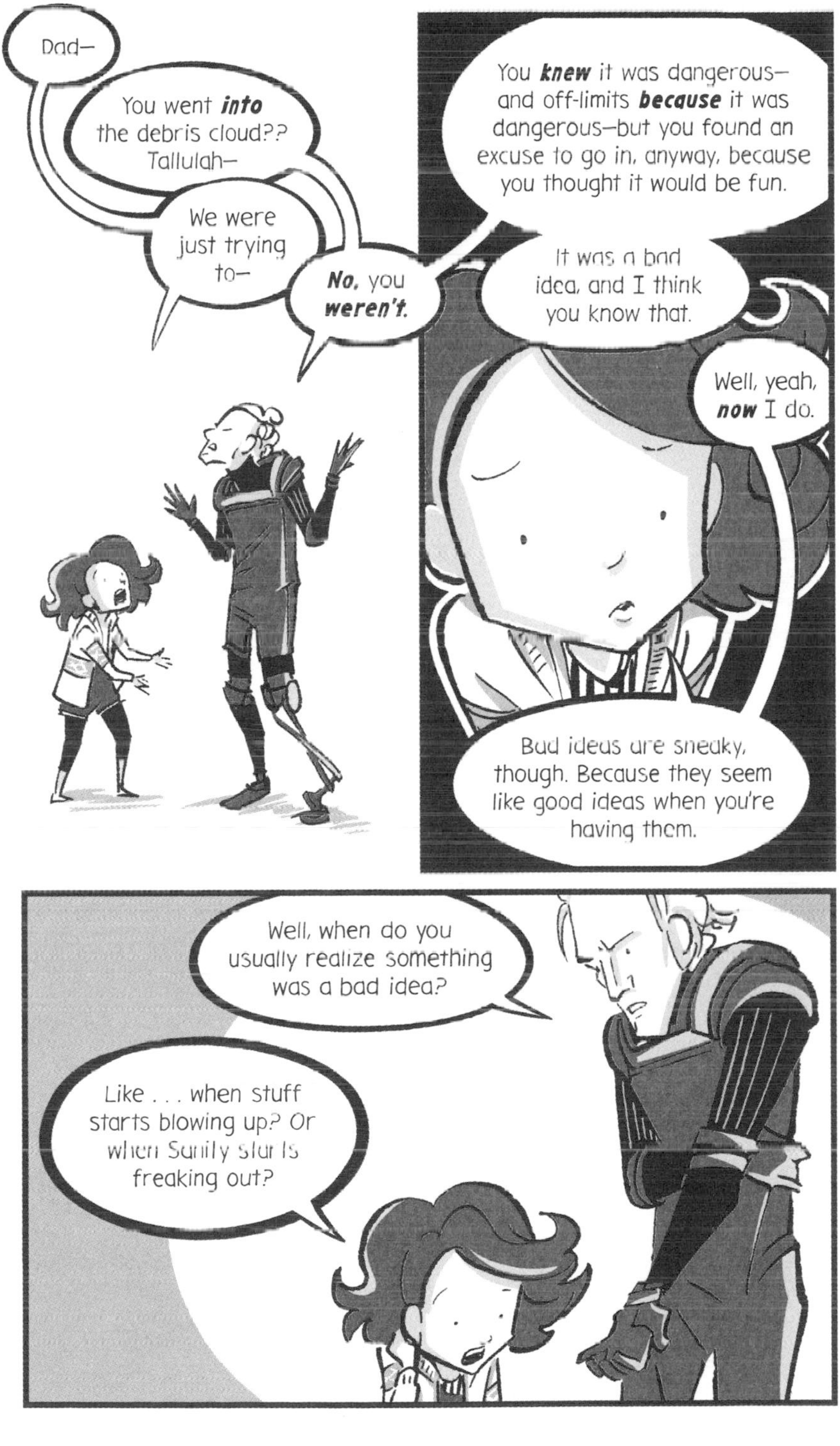
Dad—
You went **into** the debris cloud?? Tallulah—
We were just trying to—
No, you **weren't.**
You **knew** it was dangerous—and off-limits **because** it was dangerous—but you found an excuse to go in, anyway, because you thought it would be fun.
It was a bad idea, and I think you know that.
Well, yeah, **now** I do.
Bad ideas are sneaky, though. Because they seem like good ideas when you're having them.
Well, when do you usually realize something was a bad idea?
Like . . . when stuff starts blowing up? Or when Sanity starts freaking out?

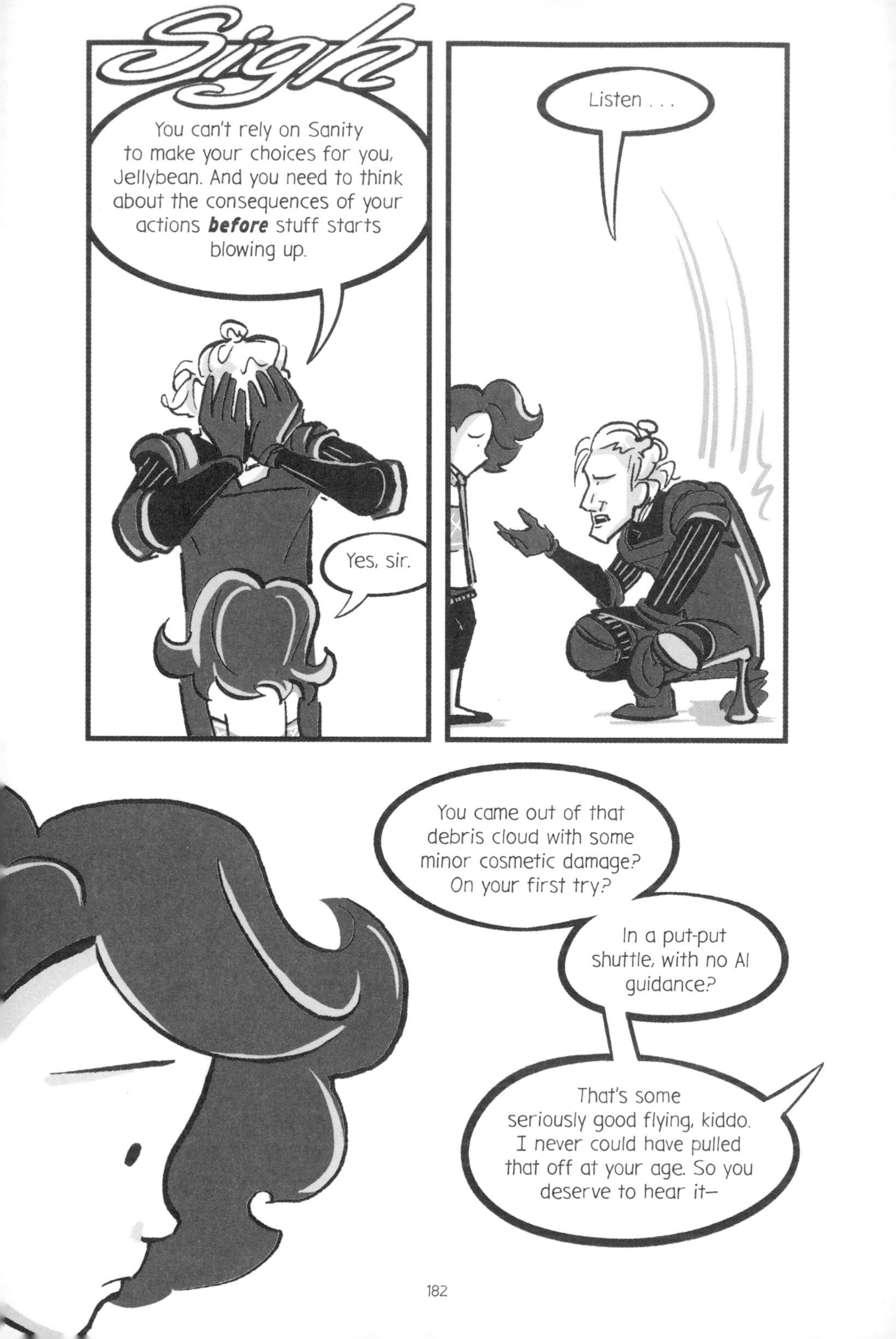
Sigh
You can't rely on Sanity to make your choices for you, Jellybean. And you need to think about the consequences of your actions **before** stuff starts blowing up.
Yes, sir.
Listen . . .
You came out of that debris cloud with some minor cosmetic damage? On your first try?
In a put-put shuttle, with no AI guidance?
That's some seriously good flying, kiddo. I never could have pulled that off at your age. So you deserve to hear it—

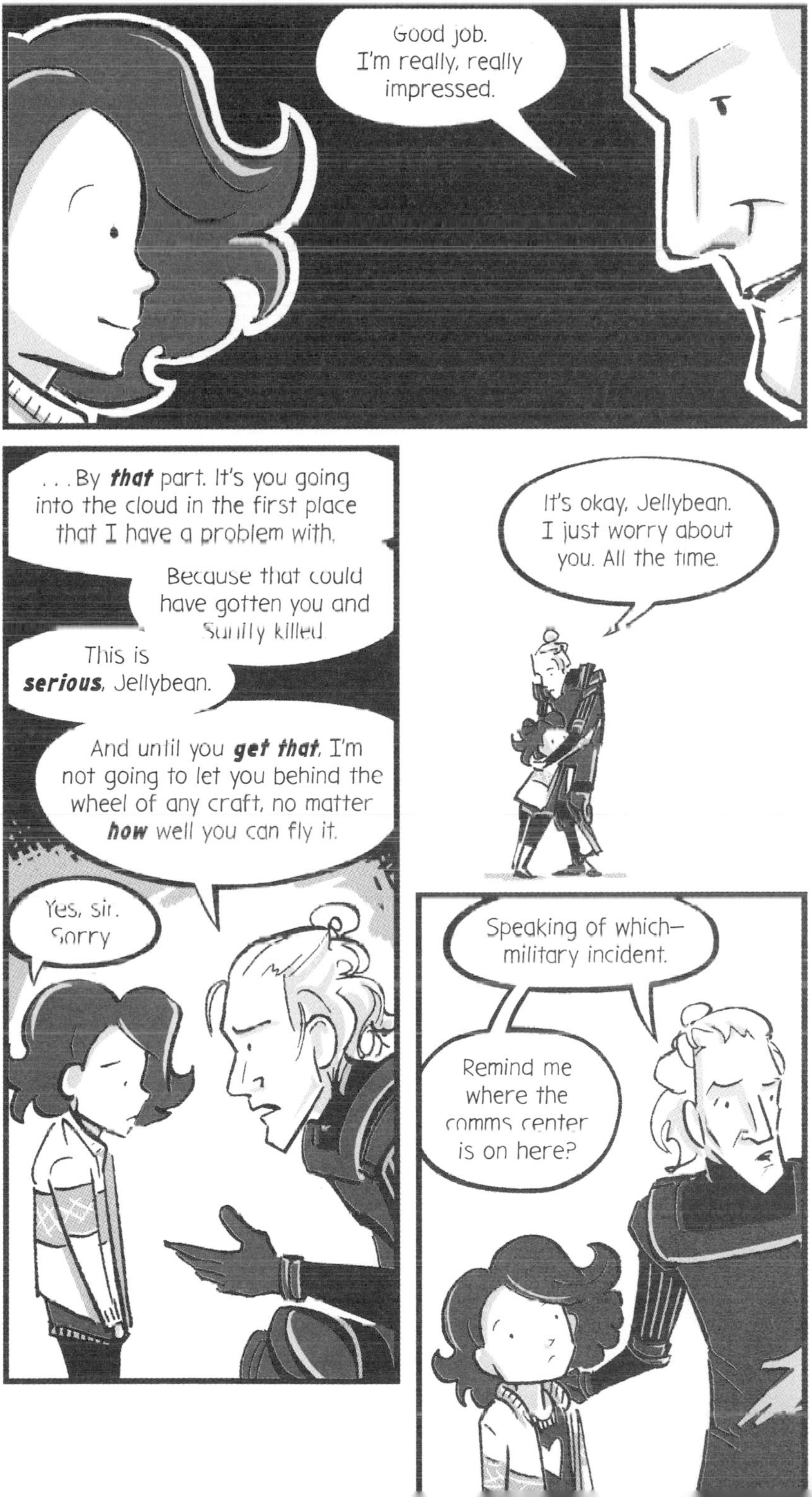
Good job. I'm really, really impressed.
. . . By **that** part. It's you going into the cloud in the first place that I have a problem with.
Because that could have gotten you and Sunny killed.
This is **serious**, Jellybean.
And until you **get that**, I'm not going to let you behind the wheel of any craft, no matter **how** well you can fly it.
Yes, sir. Sorry
It's okay, Jellybean. I just worry about you. All the time.
Speaking of which— military incident.
Remind me where the comms center is on here?

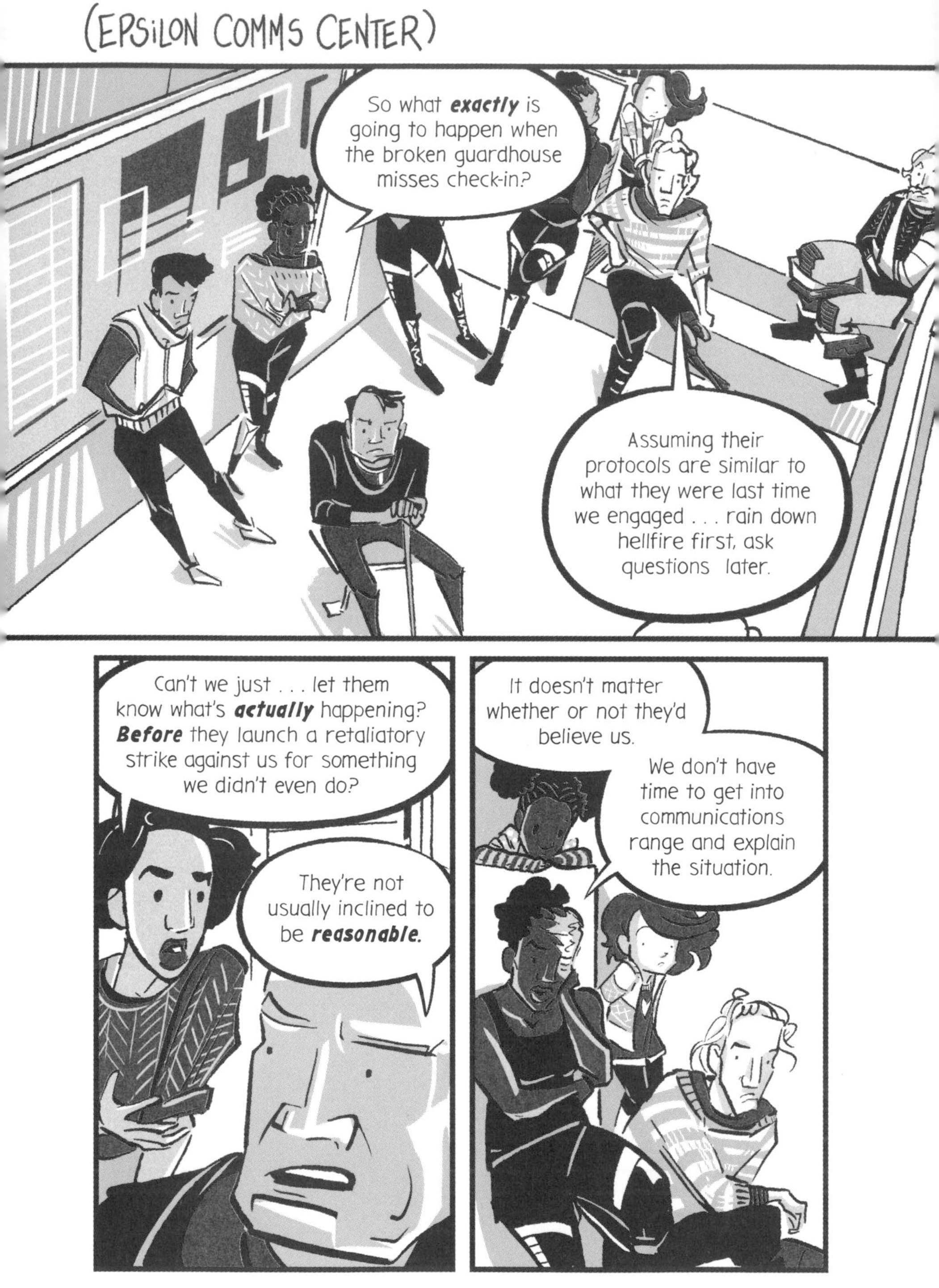
(EPSILON COMMS CENTER)
So what **exactly** is going to happen when the broken guardhouse misses check-in?
Assuming their protocols are similar to what they were last time we engaged . . . rain down hellfire first, ask questions later.
Can't we just . . . let them know what's **actually** happening? **Before** they launch a retaliatory strike against us for something we didn't even do?
They're not usually inclined to be **reasonable**.
It doesn't matter whether or not they'd believe us.
We don't have time to get into communications range and explain the situation.

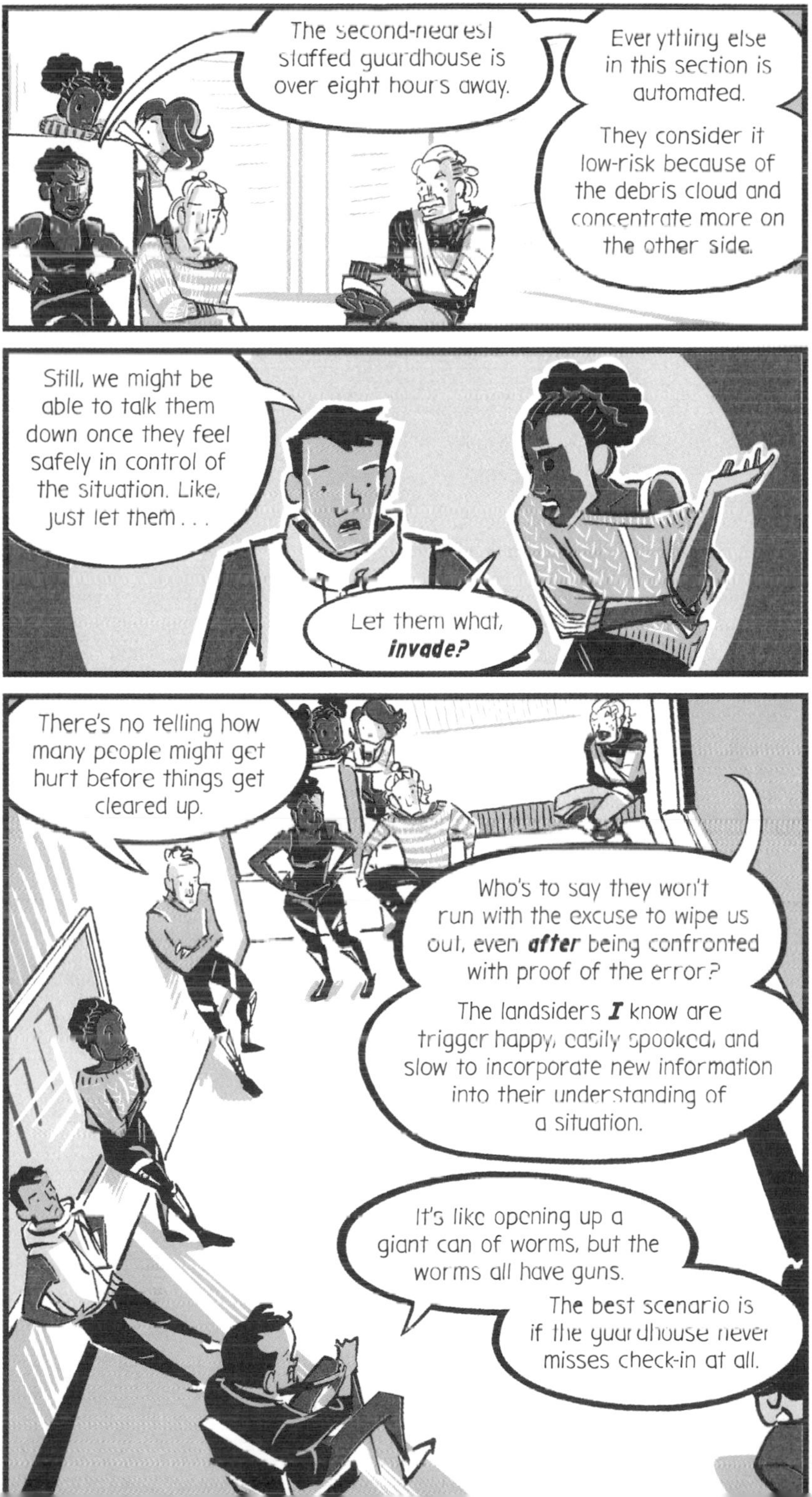
The second-nearest staffed guardhouse is over eight hours away.
Everything else in this section is automated.
They consider it low-risk because of the debris cloud and concentrate more on the other side.
Still, we might be able to talk them down once they feel safely in control of the situation. Like, just let them . . .
Let them what, ***invade?***
There's no telling how many people might get hurt before things get cleared up.
Who's to say they won't run with the excuse to wipe us out, even ***after*** being confronted with proof of the error?
The landsiders ***I*** know are trigger happy, easily spooked, and slow to incorporate new information into their understanding of a situation.
It's like opening up a giant can of worms, but the worms all have guns.
The best scenario is if the guardhouse never misses check-in at all.

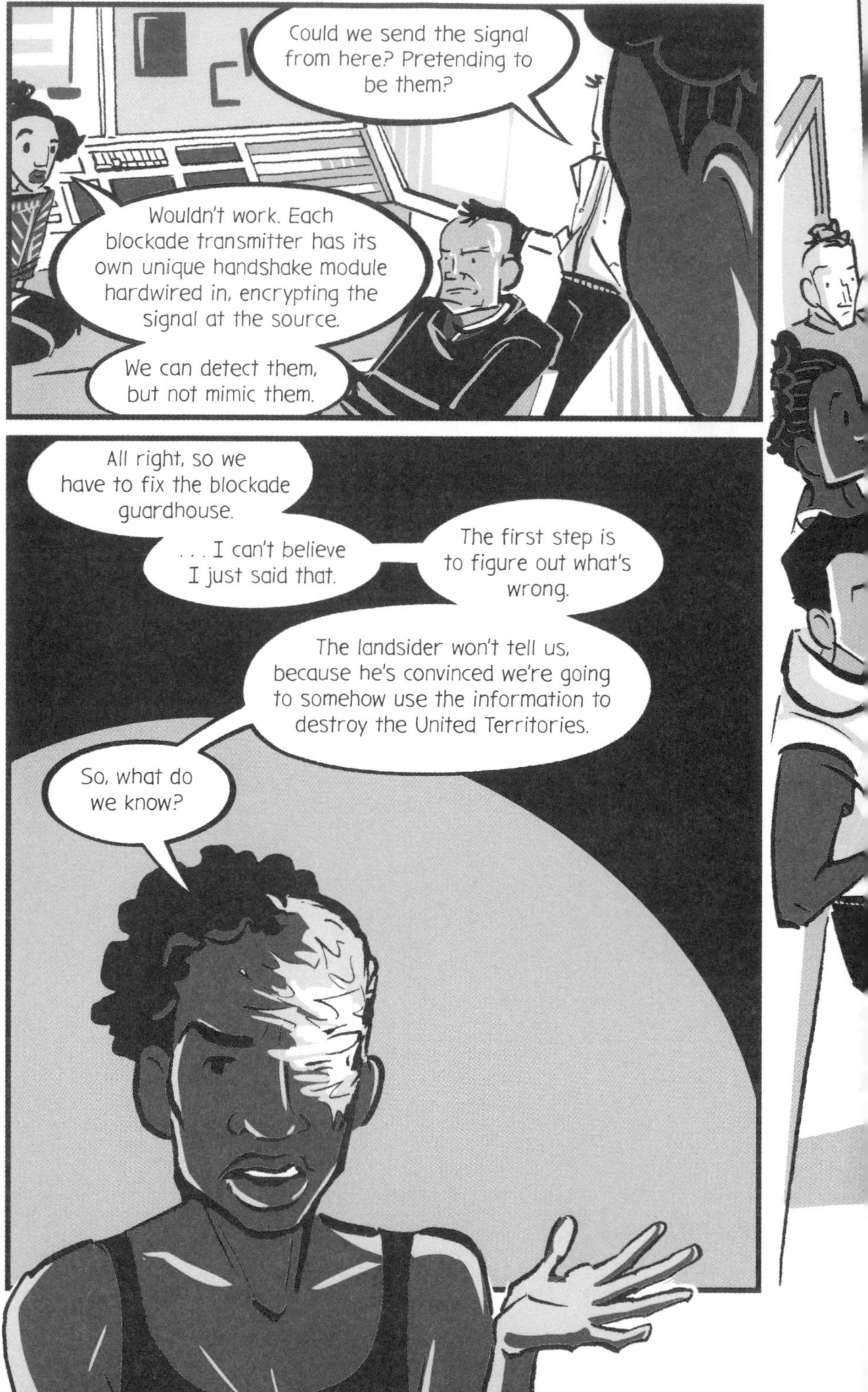
Could we send the signal from here? Pretending to be them?
Wouldn't work. Each blockade transmitter has its own unique handshake module hardwired in, encrypting the signal at the source.
We can detect them, but not mimic them.
All right, so we have to fix the blockade guardhouse.
. . . I can't believe I just said that.
The first step is to figure out what's wrong.
The landsider won't tell us, because he's convinced we're going to somehow use the information to destroy the United Territories.
So, what do we know?

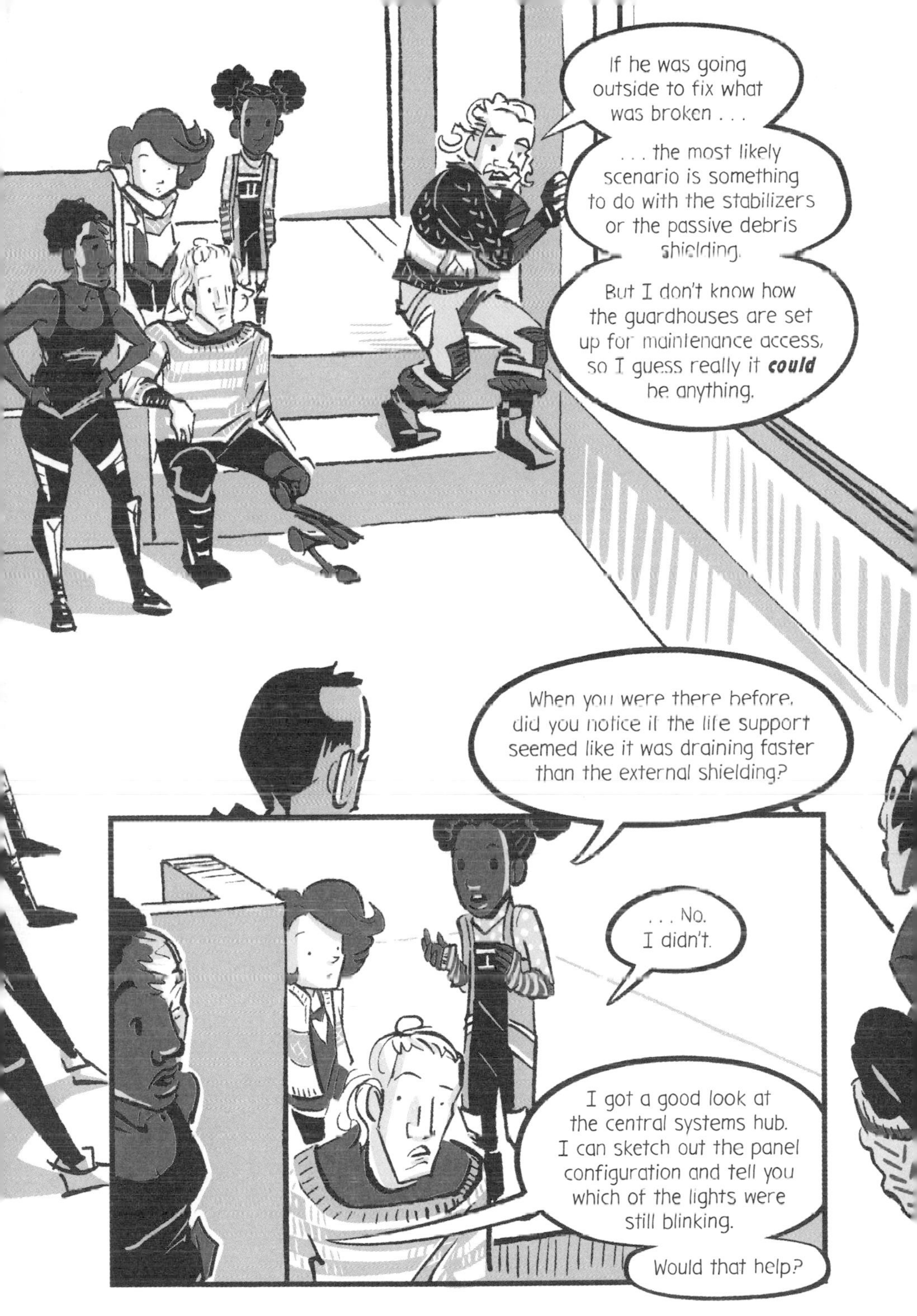
If he was going outside to fix what was broken . . .
. . . the most likely scenario is something to do with the stabilizers or the passive debris shielding.
But I don't know how the guardhouses are set up for maintenance access, so I guess really it ***could*** be anything.
When you were there before, did you notice if the life support seemed like it was draining faster than the external shielding?
. . . No. I didn't.
I got a good look at the central systems hub. I can sketch out the panel configuration and tell you which of the lights were still blinking.
Would that help?

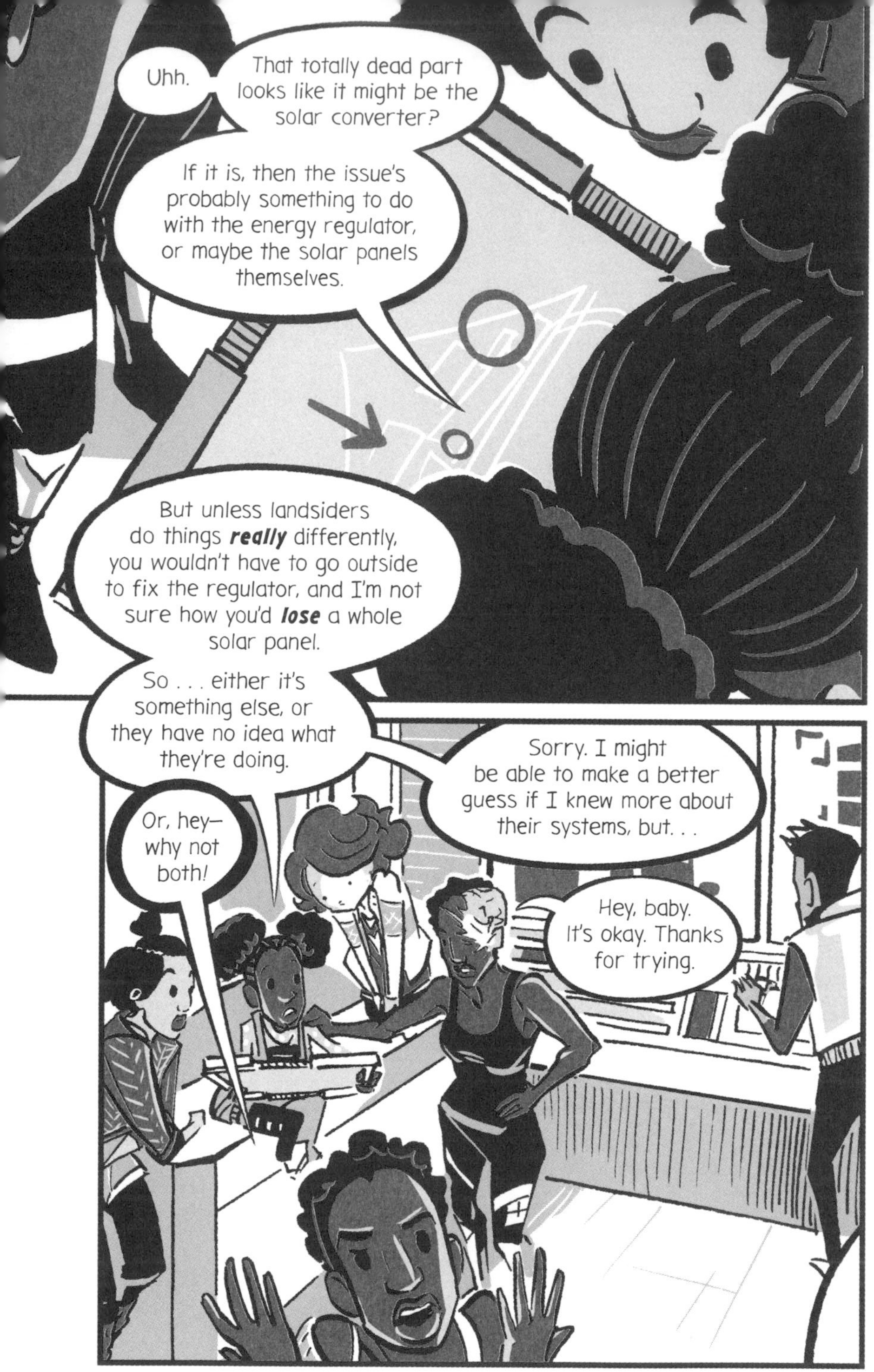
Uhh.
That totally dead part looks like it might be the solar converter?
If it is, then the issue's probably something to do with the energy regulator, or maybe the solar panels themselves.
But unless landsiders do things **really** differently, you wouldn't have to go outside to fix the regulator, and I'm not sure how you'd **lose** a whole solar panel.
So . . . either it's something else, or they have no idea what they're doing.
Or, hey—why not both!
Sorry. I might be able to make a better guess if I knew more about their systems, but. . .
Hey, baby. It's okay. Thanks for trying.

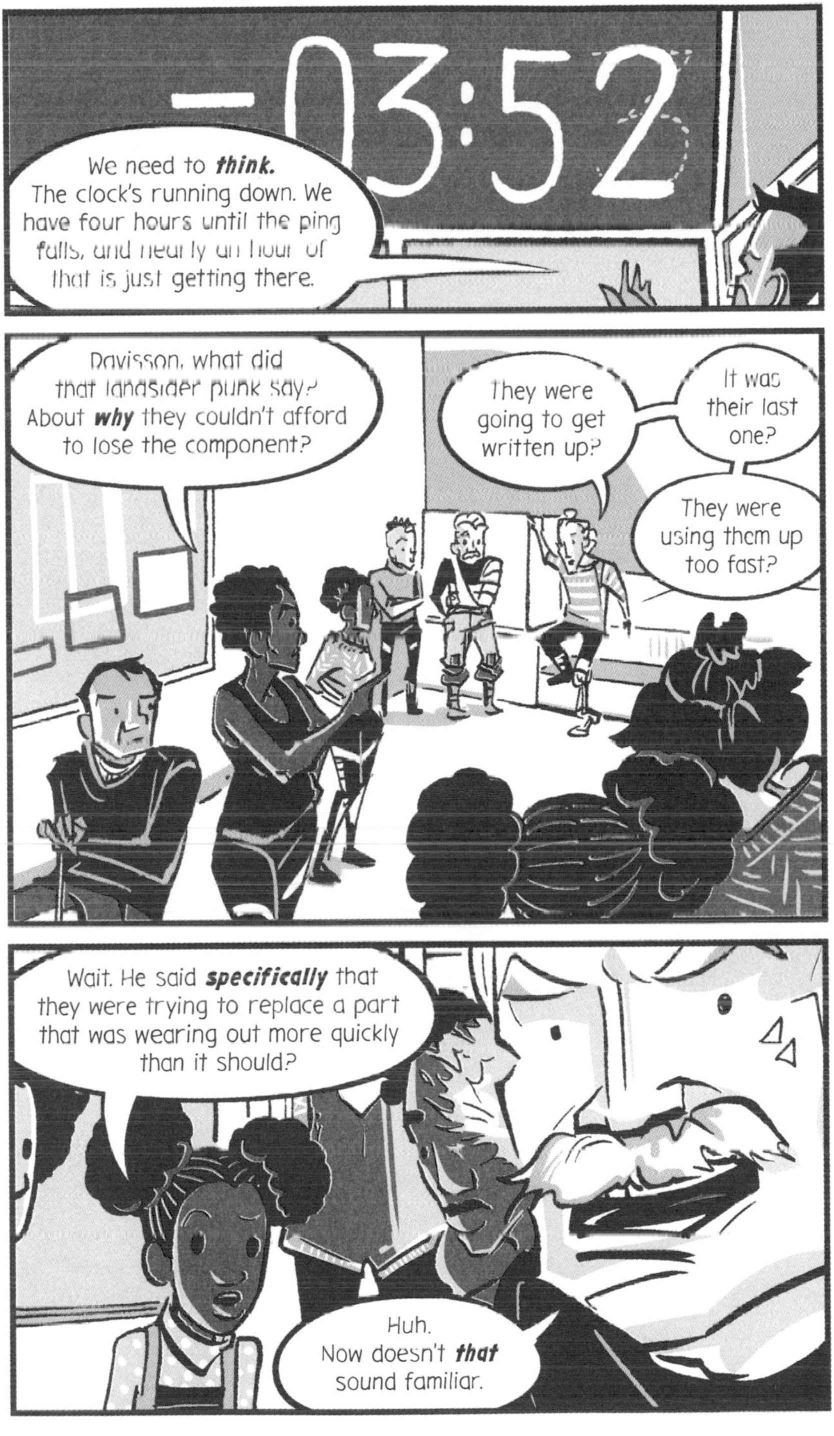
-03:52
We need to think. The clock's running down. We have four hours until the ping falls, and nearly an hour of that is just getting there.
Davisson, what did that landsider punk say? About why they couldn't afford to lose the component?
They were going to get written up?
It was their last one?
They were using them up too fast?
Wait. He said specifically that they were trying to replace a part that was wearing out more quickly than it should?
Huh. Now doesn't that sound familiar.

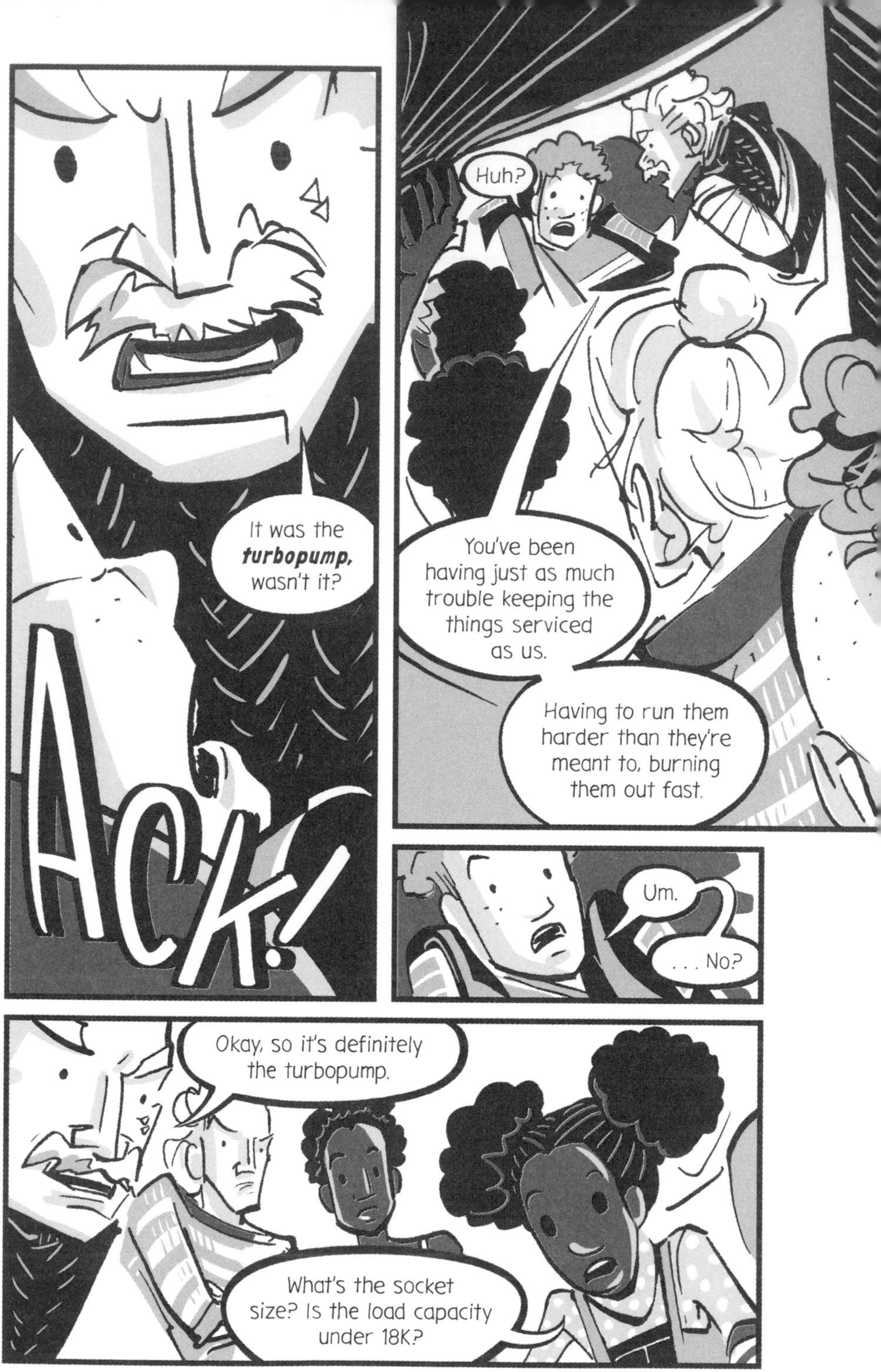
It was the ***turbopump,*** wasn't it?
ACK!
Huh?
You've been having just as much trouble keeping the things serviced as us.
Having to run them harder than they're meant to, burning them out fast.
Um.
. . . No?
Okay, so it's definitely the turbopump.
What's the socket size? Is the load capacity under 18K?

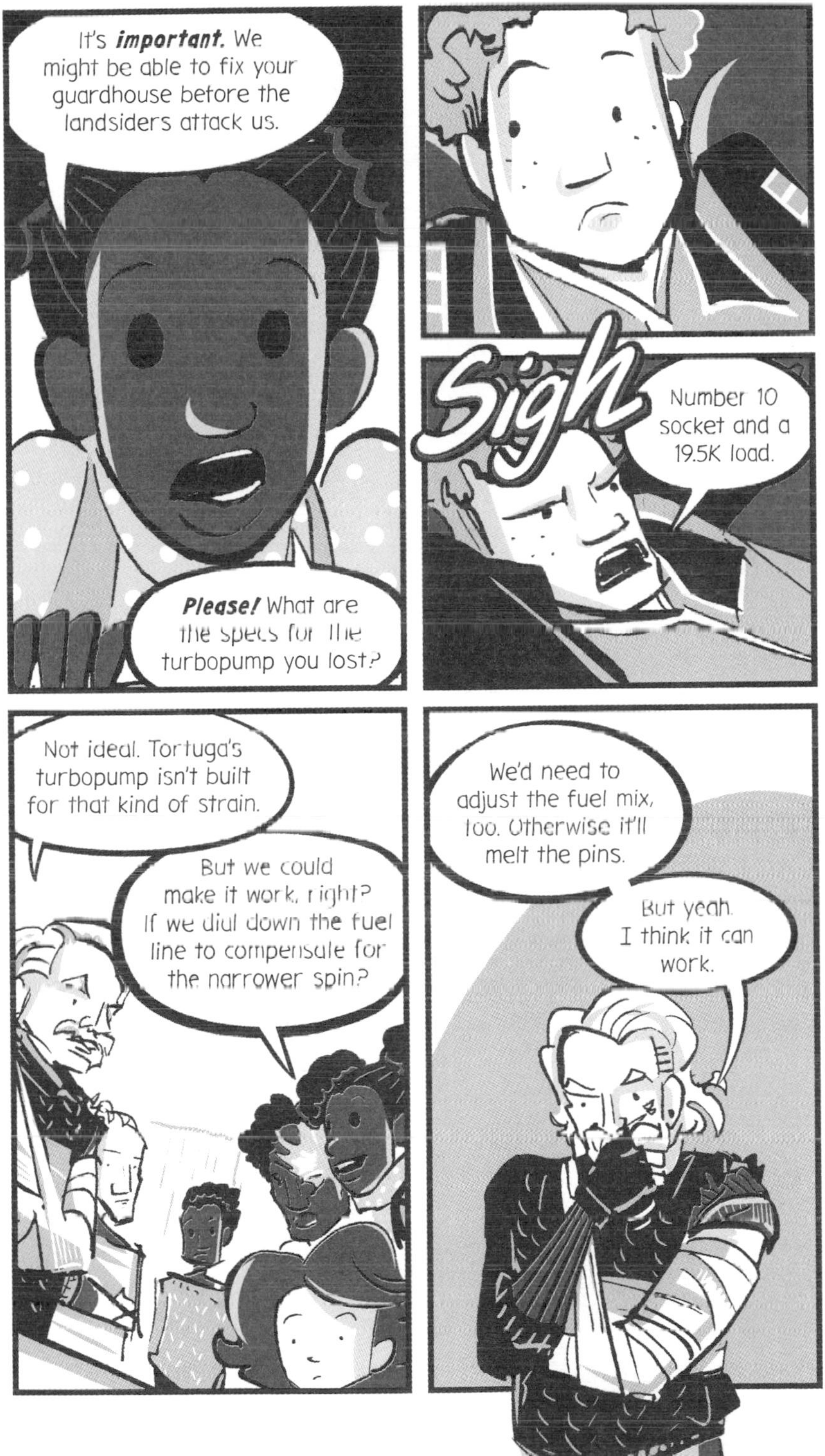
It's ***important.*** We might be able to fix your guardhouse before the landsiders attack us.
Please! What are the specs for the turbopump you lost?
Sigh
Number 10 socket and a 19.5K load.
Not ideal. Tortuga's turbopump isn't built for that kind of strain.
But we could make it work, right? If we dial down the fuel line to compensate for the narrower spin?
We'd need to adjust the fuel mix, too. Otherwise it'll melt the pins.
But yeah. I think it can work.

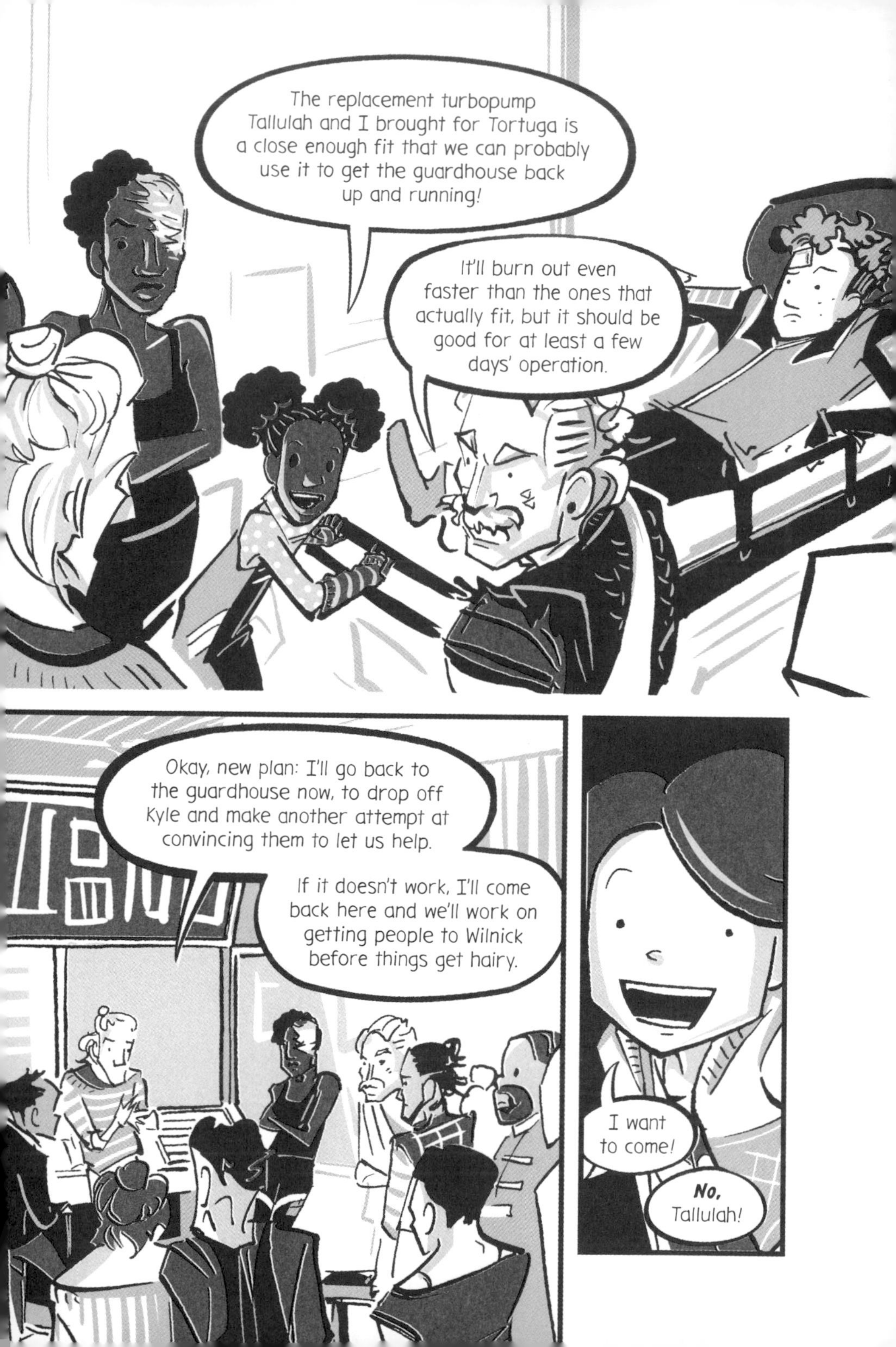
The replacement turbopump Tallulah and I brought for Tortuga is a close enough fit that we can probably use it to get the guardhouse back up and running!
It'll burn out even faster than the ones that actually fit, but it should be good for at least a few days' operation.
Okay, new plan: I'll go back to the guardhouse now, to drop off Kyle and make another attempt at convincing them to let us help.
If it doesn't work, I'll come back here and we'll work on getting people to Wilnick before things get hairy.
I want to come!
No, Tallulah!

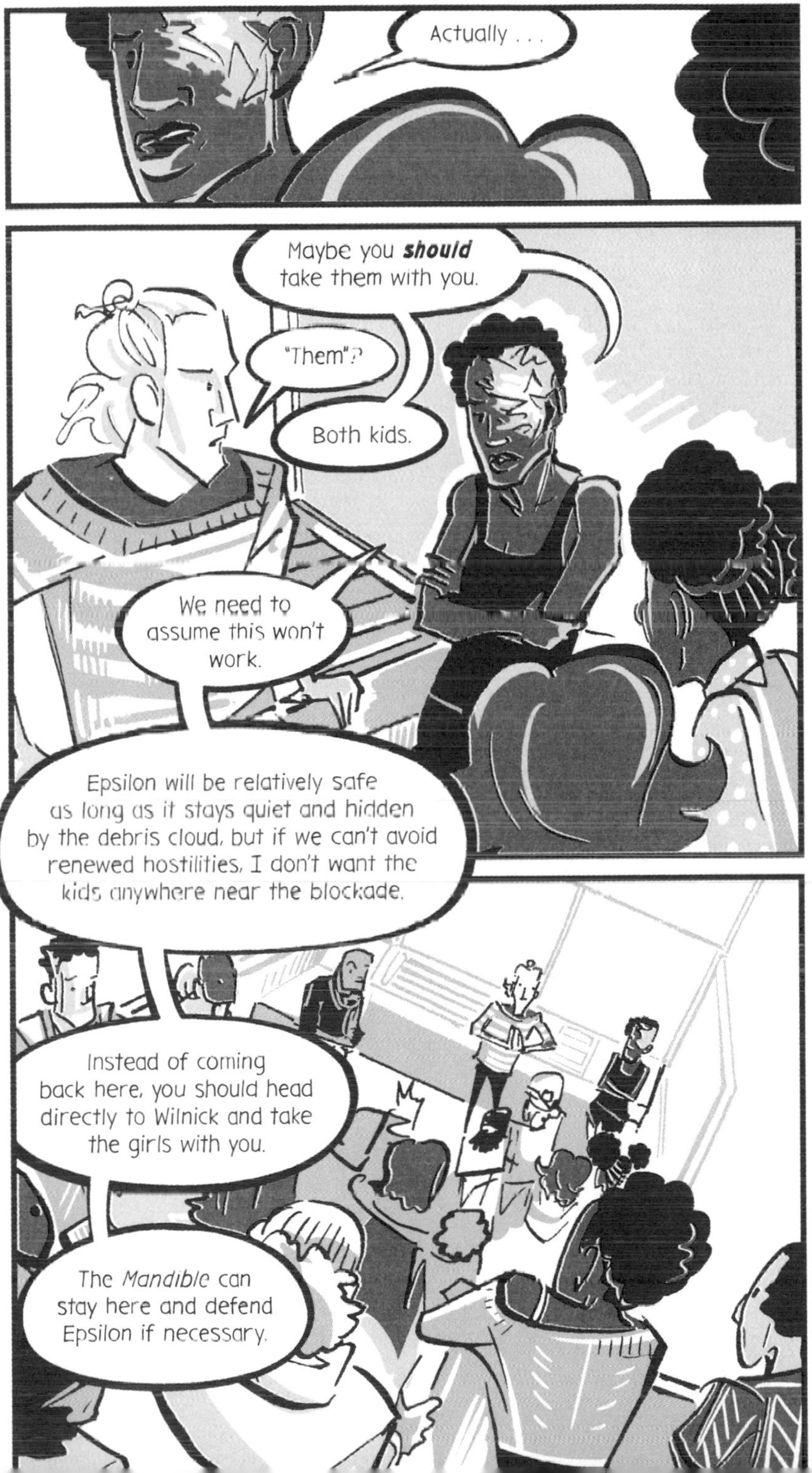
Actually . . .
Maybe you *should* take them with you.
"Them"?
Both kids.
We need to assume this won't work.
Epsilon will be relatively safe as long as it stays quiet and hidden by the debris cloud, but if we can't avoid renewed hostilities, I don't want the kids anywhere near the blockade.
Instead of coming back here, you should head directly to Wilnick and take the girls with you.
The *Mandible* can stay here and defend Epsilon if necessary.

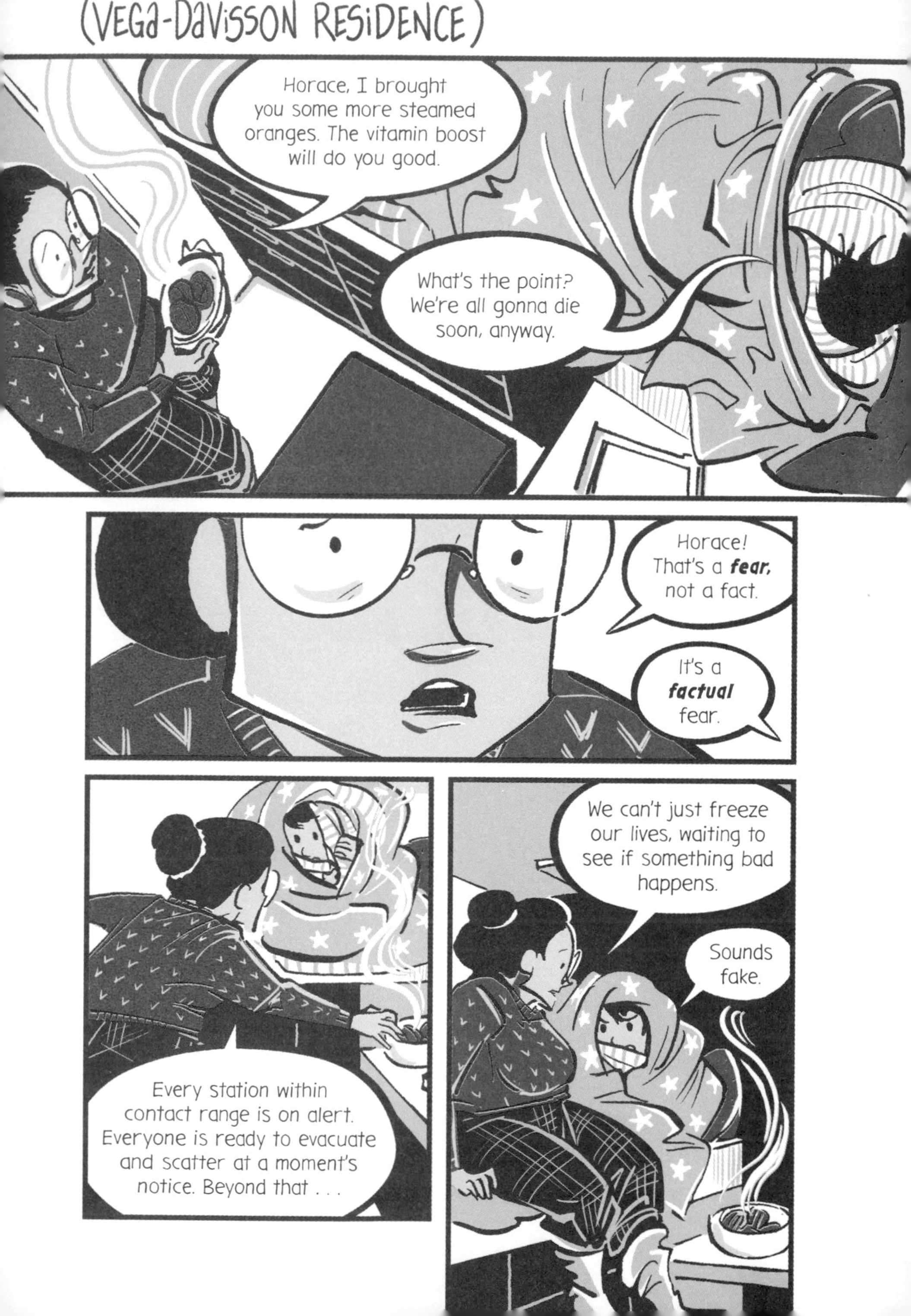
(VEGA-DAVISSON RESIDENCE)
Horace, I brought you some more steamed oranges. The vitamin boost will do you good.
What's the point? We're all gonna die soon, anyway.
Horace! That's a ***fear,*** not a fact.
It's a ***factual*** fear.
Every station within contact range is on alert. Everyone is ready to evacuate and scatter at a moment's notice. Beyond that . . .
We can't just freeze our lives, waiting to see if something bad happens.
Sounds fake.

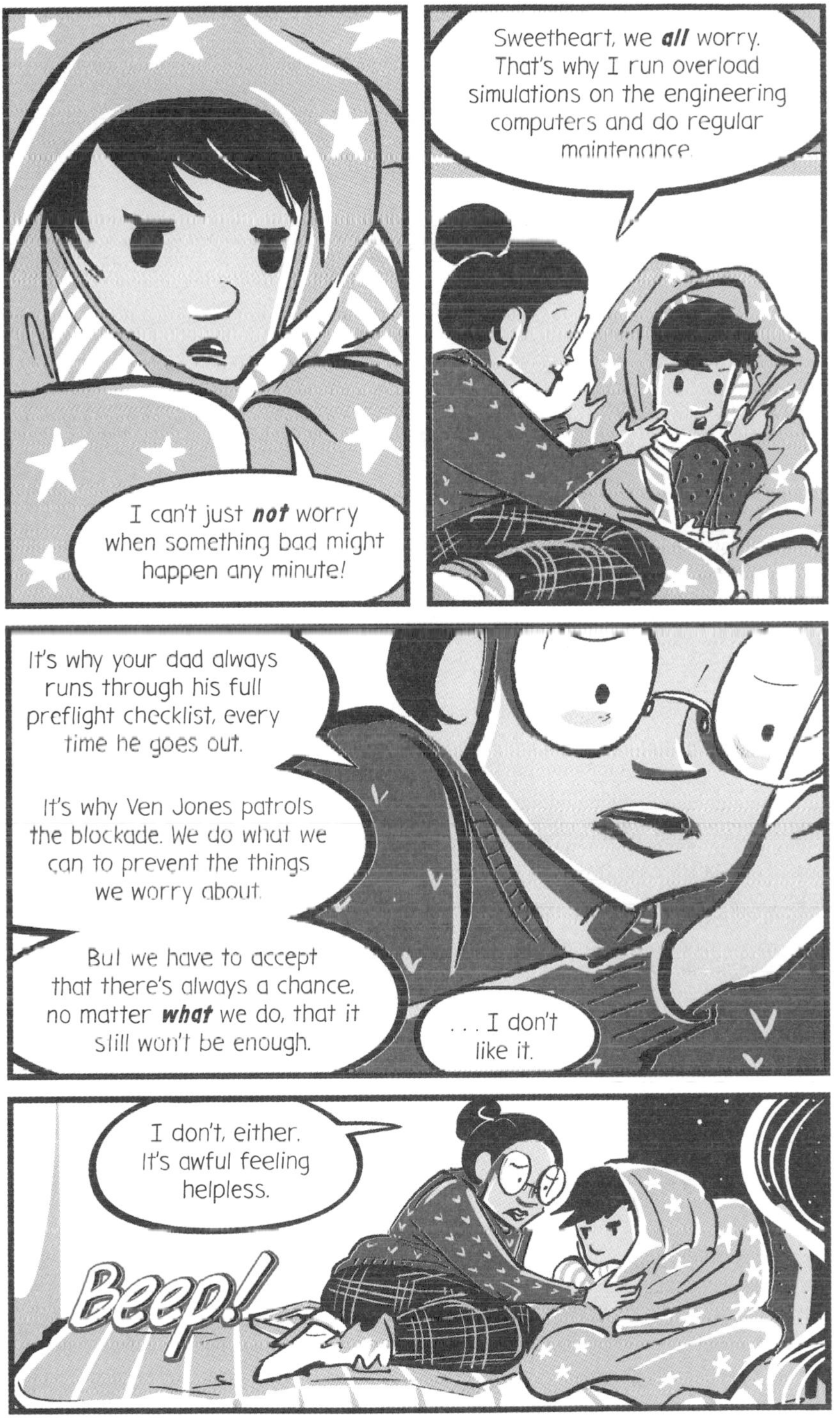
I can't just **not** worry when something bad might happen any minute!
Sweetheart, we **all** worry. That's why I run overload simulations on the engineering computers and do regular maintenance.
It's why your dad always runs through his full preflight checklist, every time he goes out.
It's why Ven Jones patrols the blockade. We do what we can to prevent the things we worry about.
But we have to accept that there's always a chance, no matter **what** we do, that it still won't be enough.
. . . I don't like it.
I don't, either. It's awful feeling helpless.
Beep!

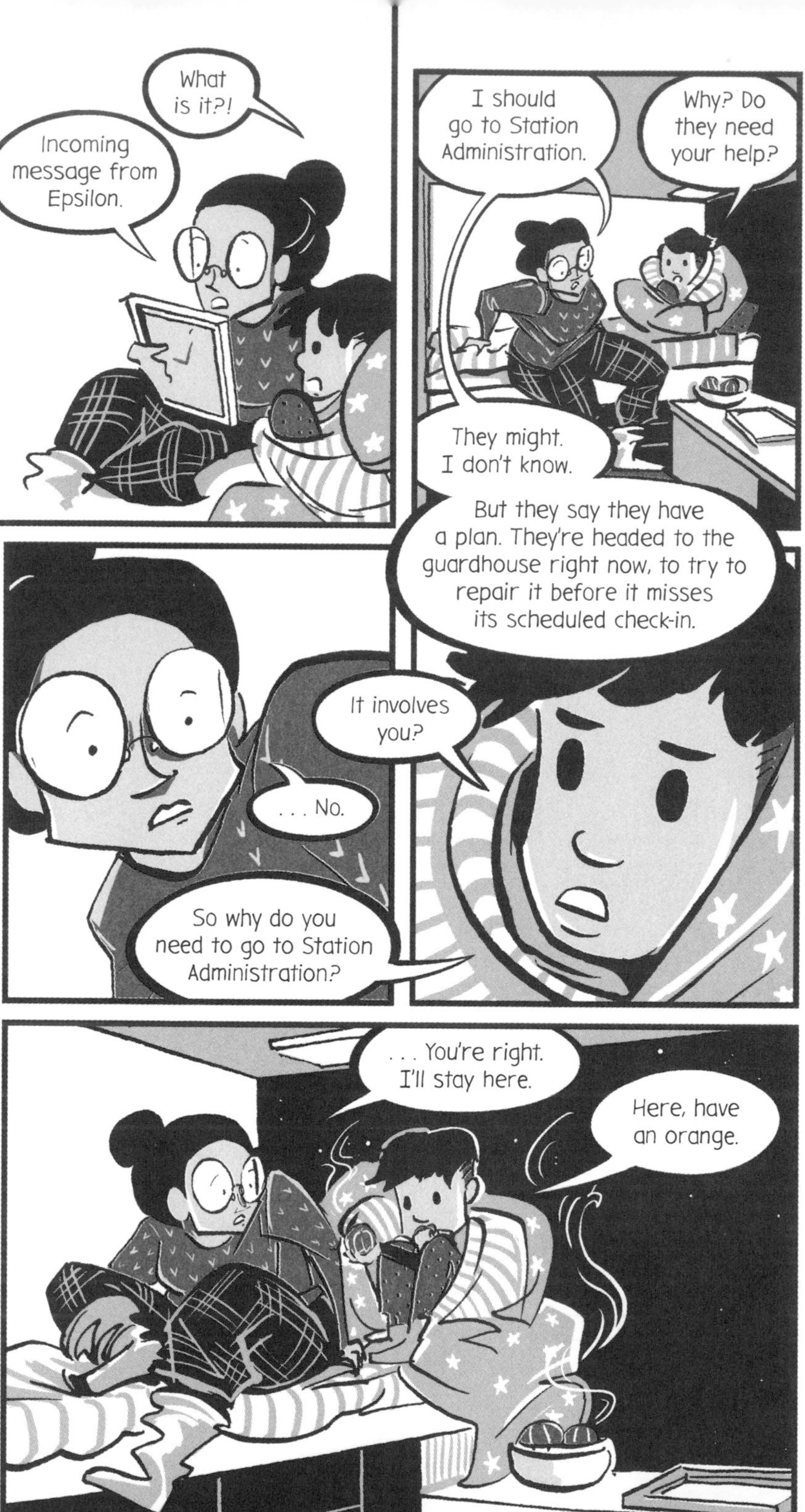
Incoming message from Epsilon.
What is it?!
I should go to Station Administration.
Why? Do they need your help?
They might. I don't know.
But they say they have a plan. They're headed to the guardhouse right now, to try to repair it before it misses its scheduled check-in.
It involves you?
. . . No.
So why do you need to go to Station Administration?
. . . You're right. I'll stay here.
Here, have an orange.

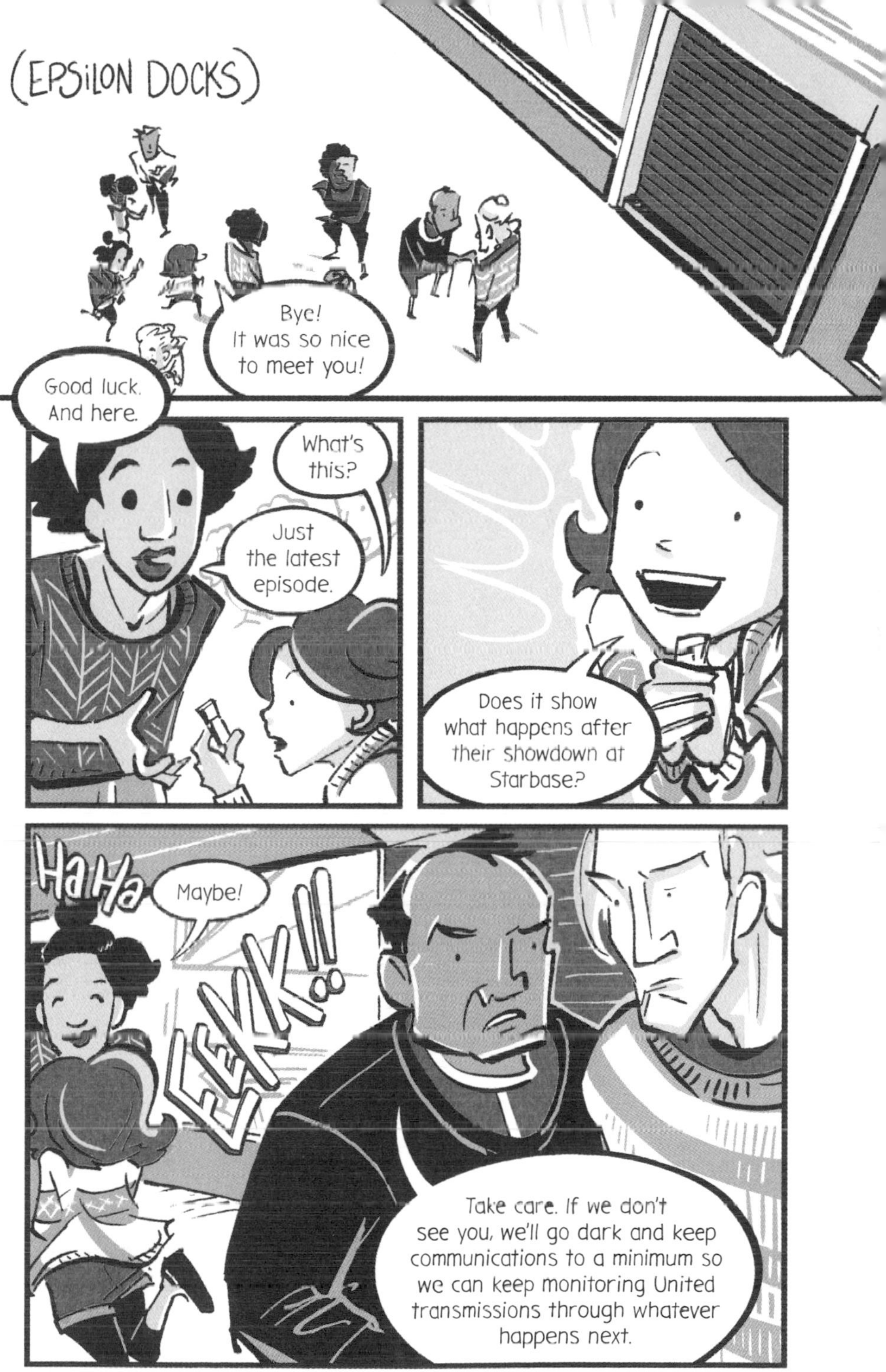
(EPSiLON DOCKS)
Bye! It was so nice to meet you!
Good luck. And here.
What's this?
Just the latest episode.
Does it show what happens after their showdown at Starbase?
HaHa
Maybe!
EEKK!!
Take care. If we don't see you, we'll go dark and keep communications to a minimum so we can keep monitoring United transmissions through whatever happens next.

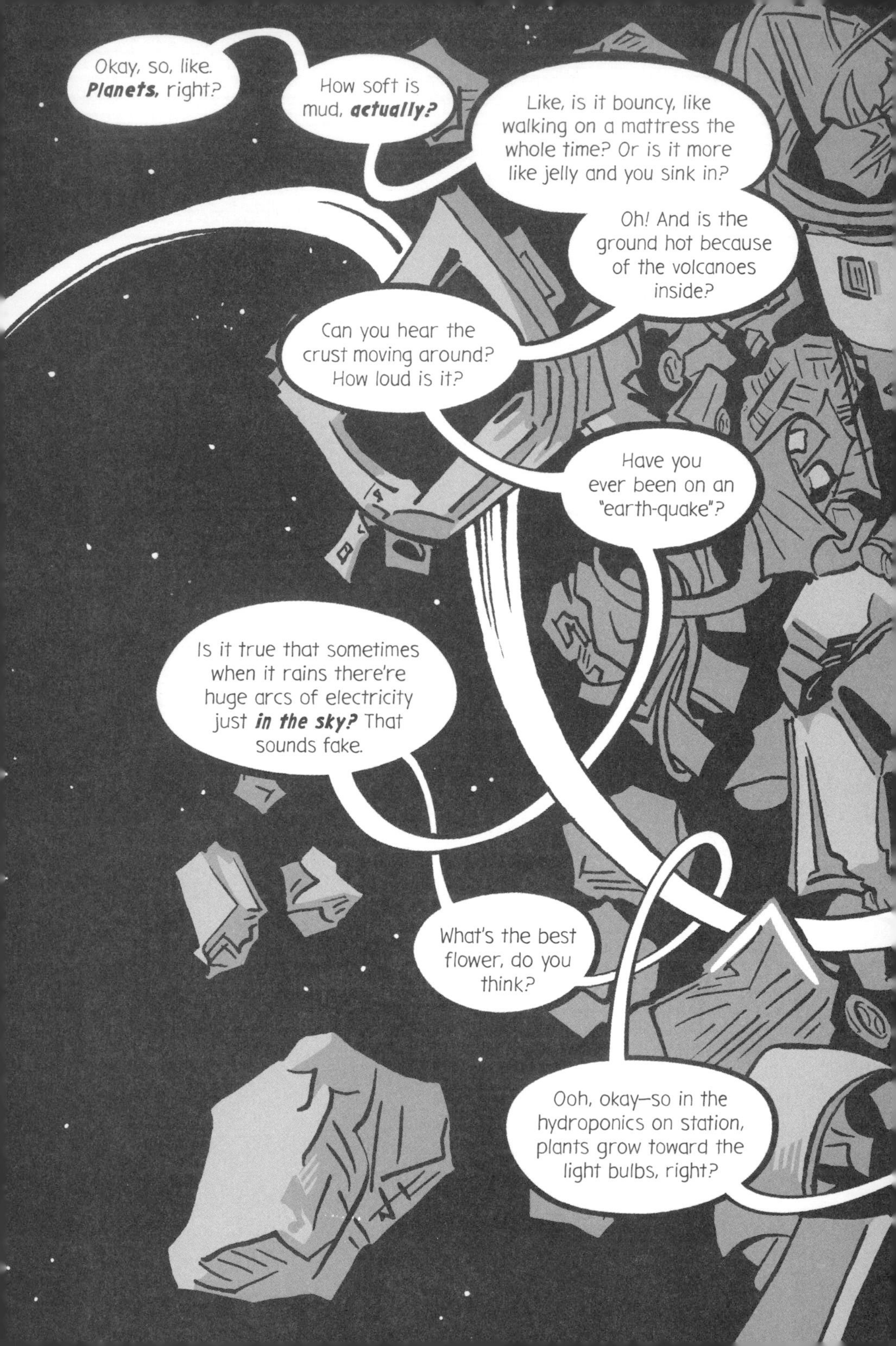
Okay, so, like. **Planets,** right?
How soft is mud, ***actually?***
Like, is it bouncy, like walking on a mattress the whole time? Or is it more like jelly and you sink in?
Oh! And is the ground hot because of the volcanoes inside?
Can you hear the crust moving around? How loud is it?
Have you ever been on an "earth-quake"?
Is it true that sometimes when it rains there're huge arcs of electricity just ***in the sky?*** That sounds fake.
What's the best flower, do you think?
Ooh, okay—so in the hydroponics on station, plants grow toward the light bulbs, right?

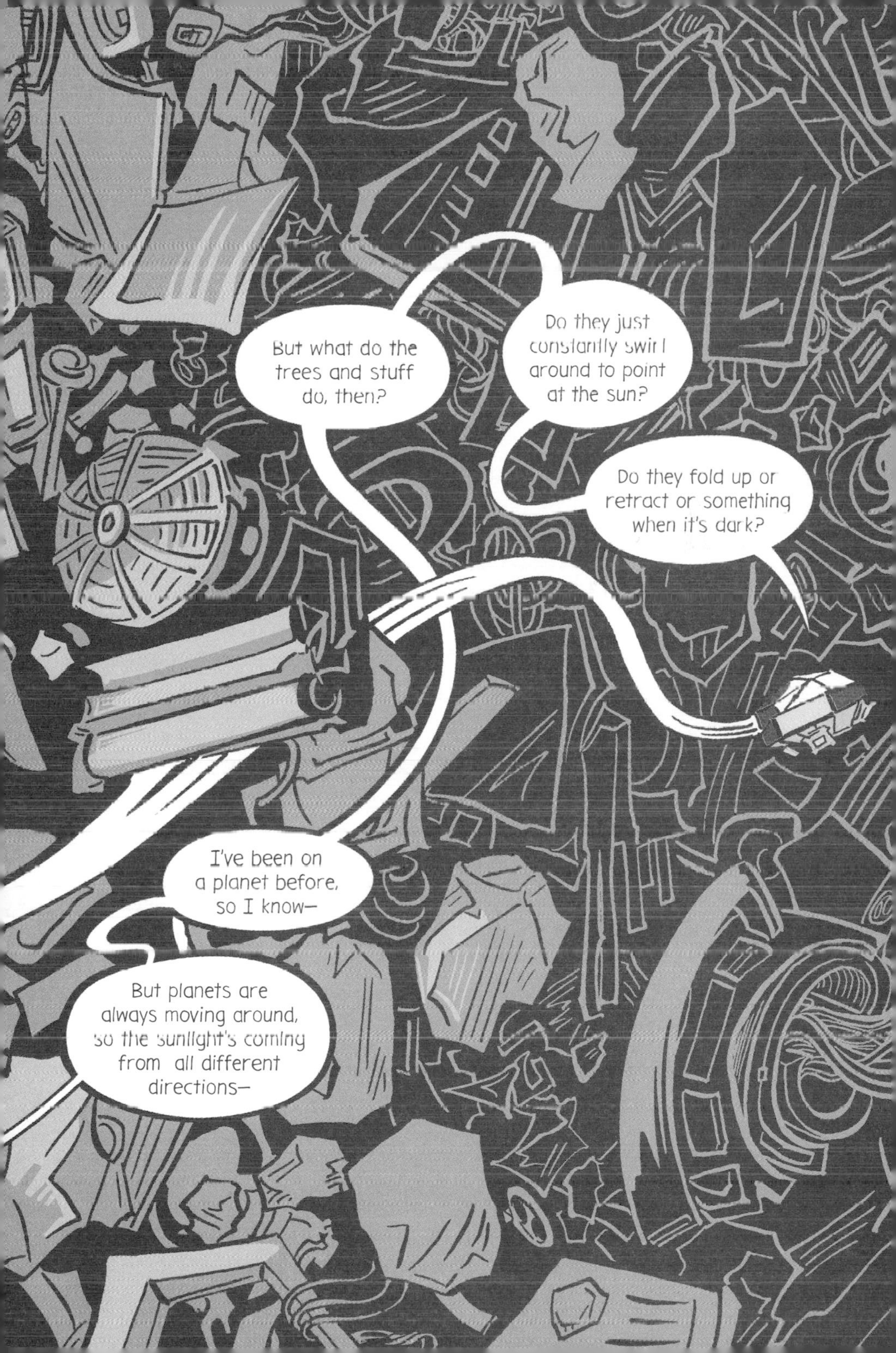
But what do the trees and stuff do, then?
Do they just constantly swirl around to point at the sun?
Do they fold up or retract or something when it's dark?
I've been on a planet before, so I know—
But planets are always moving around, so the sunlight's coming from all different directions—

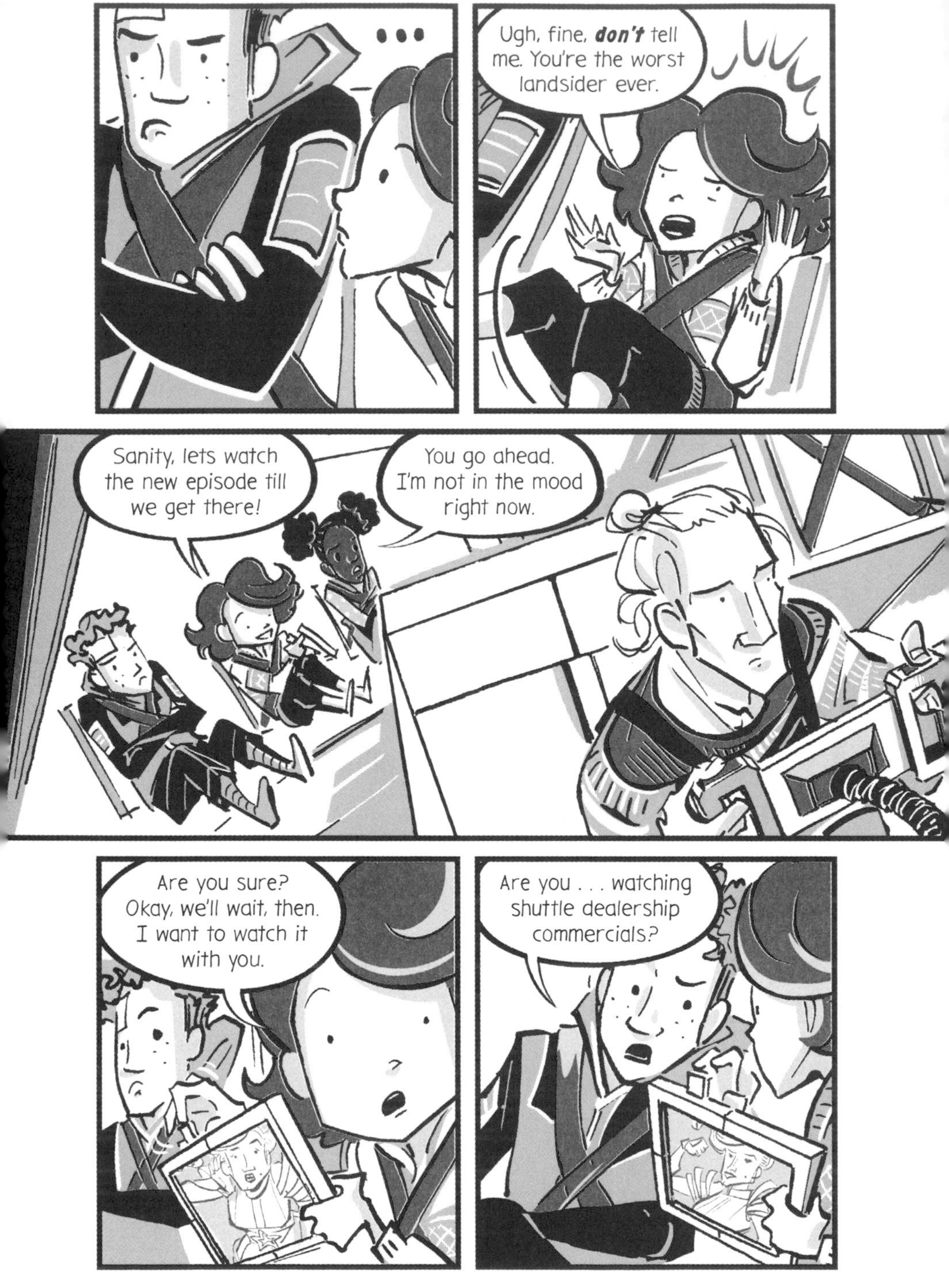

...
Ugh, fine, **don't** tell me. You're the worst landsider ever.
Sanity, lets watch the new episode till we get there!
You go ahead. I'm not in the mood right now.
Are you sure? Okay, we'll wait, then. I want to watch it with you.
Are you . . . watching shuttle dealership commercials?

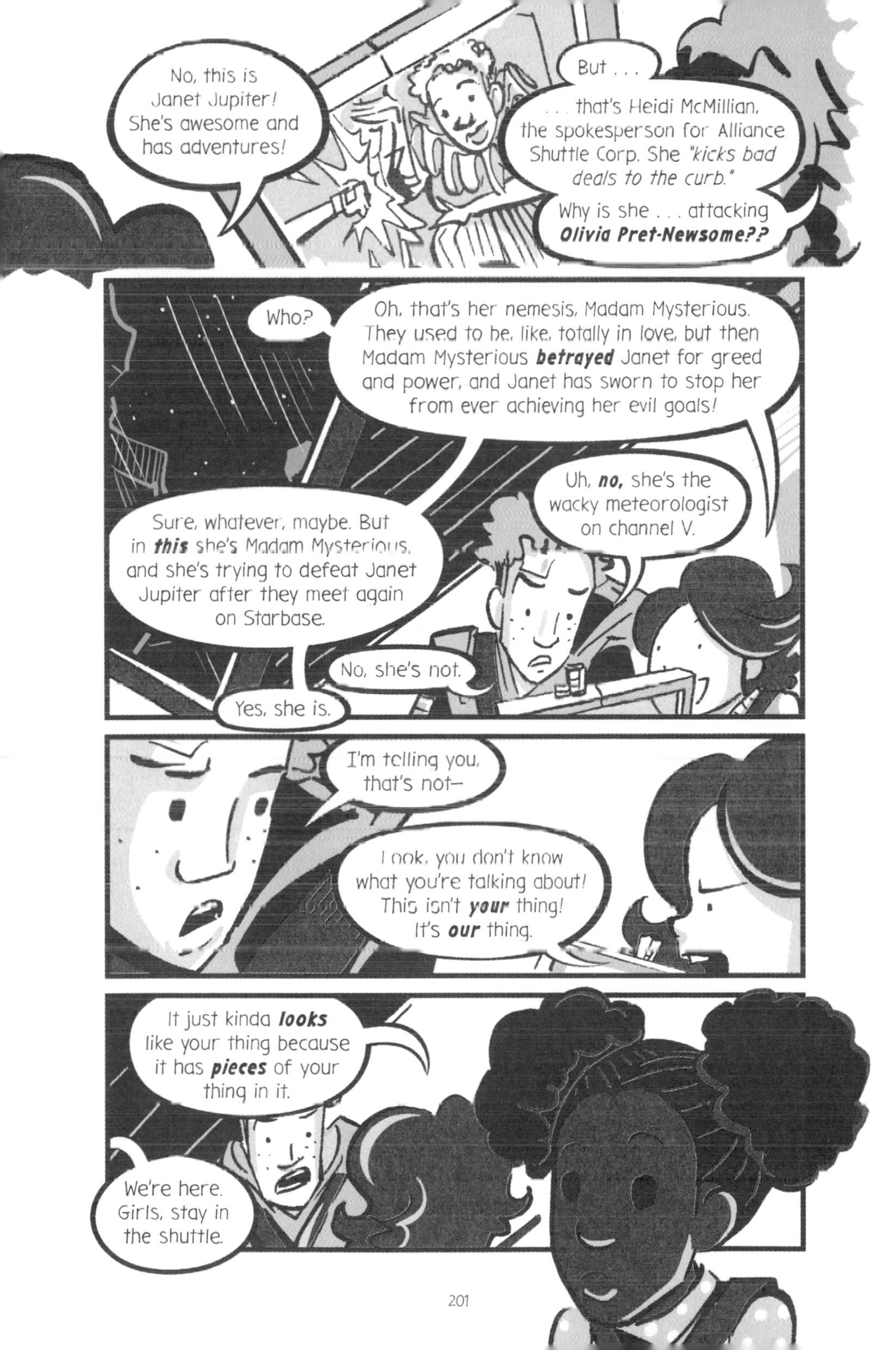
No, this is Janet Jupiter! She's awesome and has adventures!
But . . .
. . . that's Heidi McMillian, the spokesperson for Alliance Shuttle Corp. She *"kicks bad deals to the curb."*
Why is she . . . attacking ***Olivia Pret-Newsome??***
Who?
Oh, that's her nemesis, Madam Mysterious. They used to be, like, totally in love, but then Madam Mysterious ***betrayed*** Janet for greed and power, and Janet has sworn to stop her from ever achieving her evil goals!
Uh, ***no,*** she's the wacky meteorologist on channel V.
Sure, whatever, maybe. But in ***this*** she's Madam Mysterious, and she's trying to defeat Janet Jupiter after they meet again on Starbase.
No, she's not.
Yes, she is.
I'm telling you, that's not–
Look, you don't know what you're talking about! This isn't ***your*** thing! It's ***our*** thing.
It just kinda ***looks*** like your thing because it has ***pieces*** of your thing in it.
We're here. Girls, stay in the shuttle.

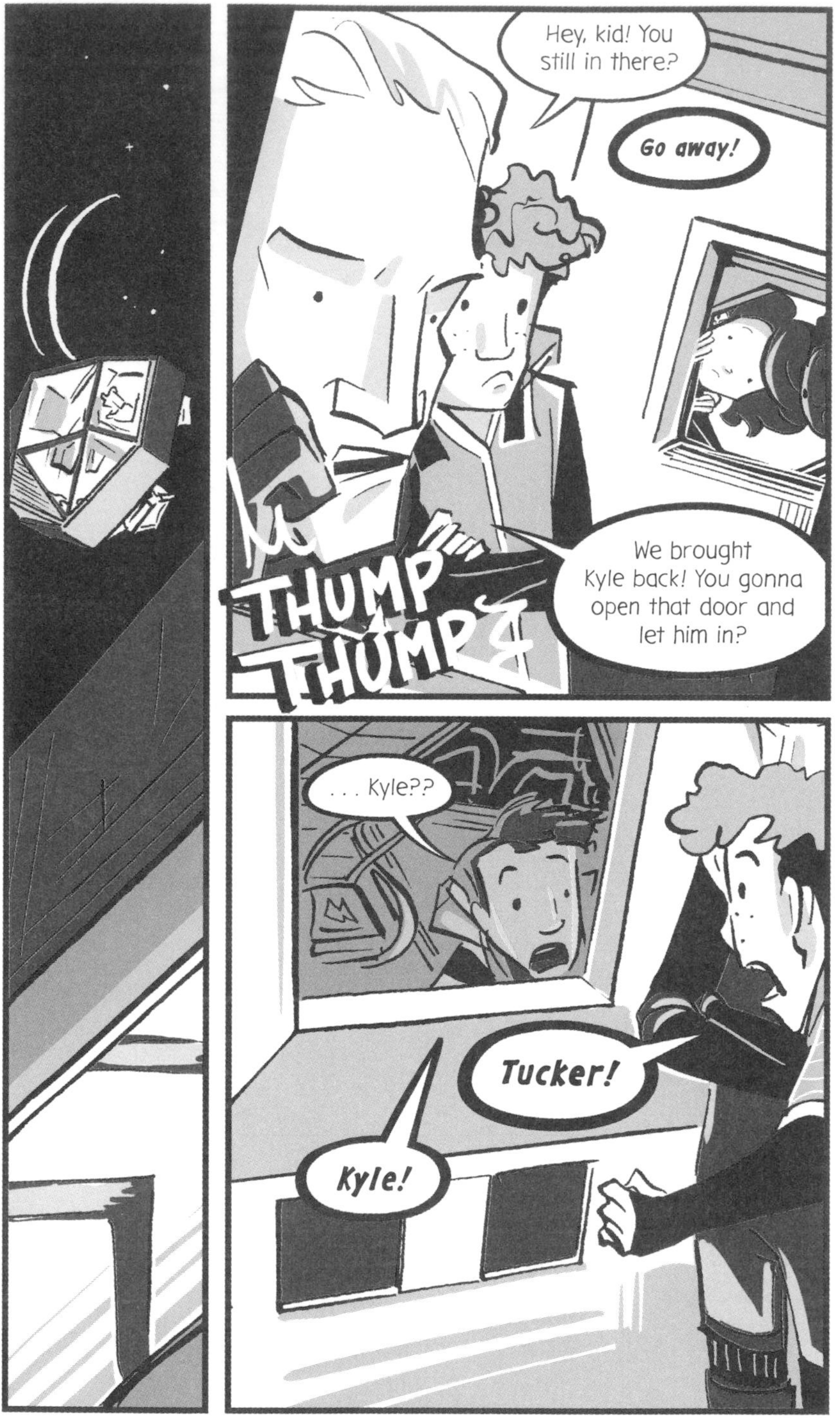
Hey, kid! You still in there?
Go away!
THUMP THUMP
We brought Kyle back! You gonna open that door and let him in?
. . . Kyle??
Tucker!
Kyle!

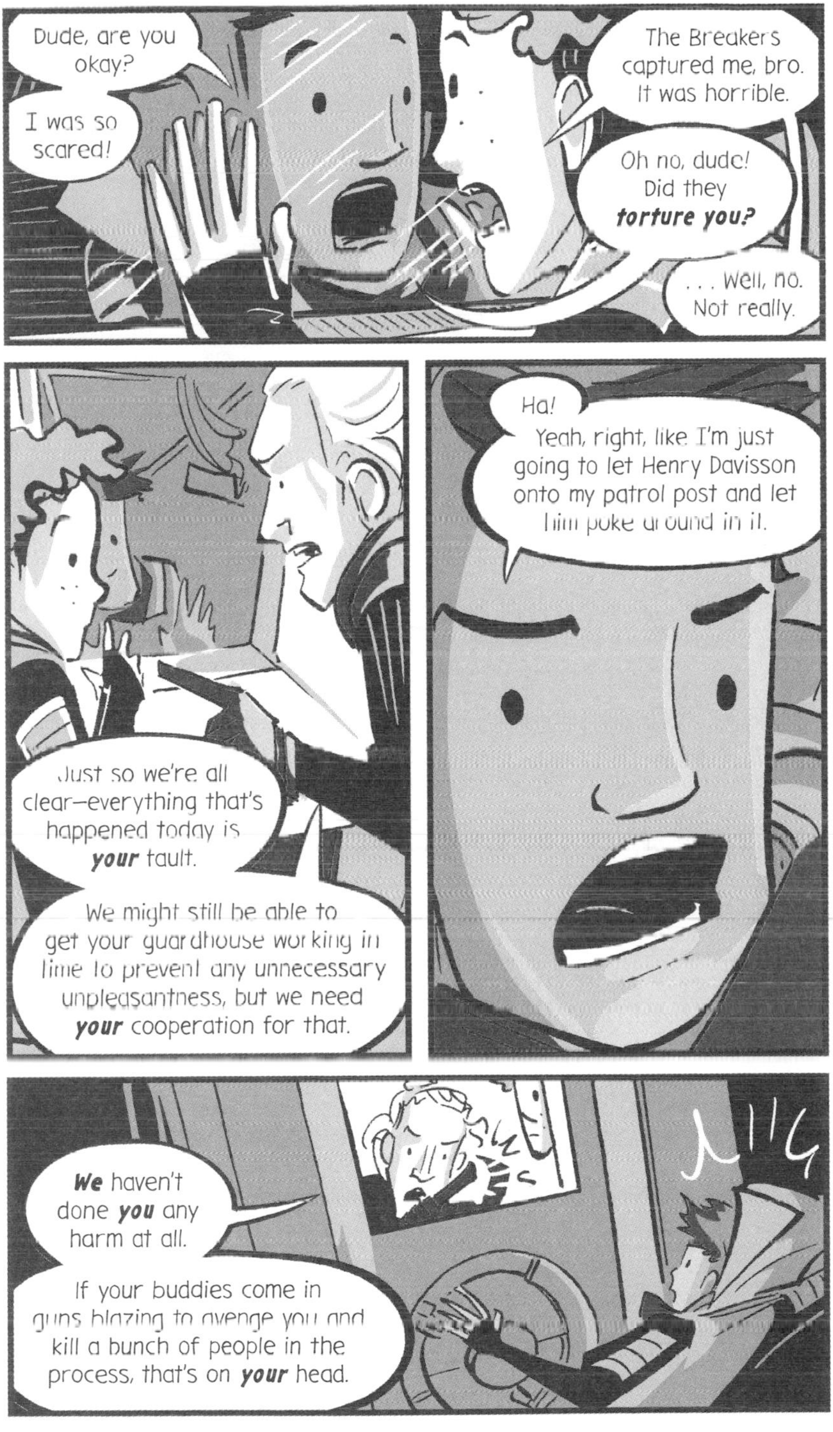
Dude, are you okay?
I was so scared!
The Breakers captured me, bro. It was horrible.
Oh no, dude! Did they **torture you?**
. . . Well, no. Not really.
Just so we're all clear—everything that's happened today is **your** fault.
We might still be able to get your guardhouse working in time to prevent any unnecessary unpleasantness, but we need **your** cooperation for that.
Ha! Yeah, right, like I'm just going to let Henry Davisson onto my patrol post and let him poke around in it.
We haven't done **you** any harm at all.
If your buddies come in guns blazing to avenge you and kill a bunch of people in the process, that's on **your** head.

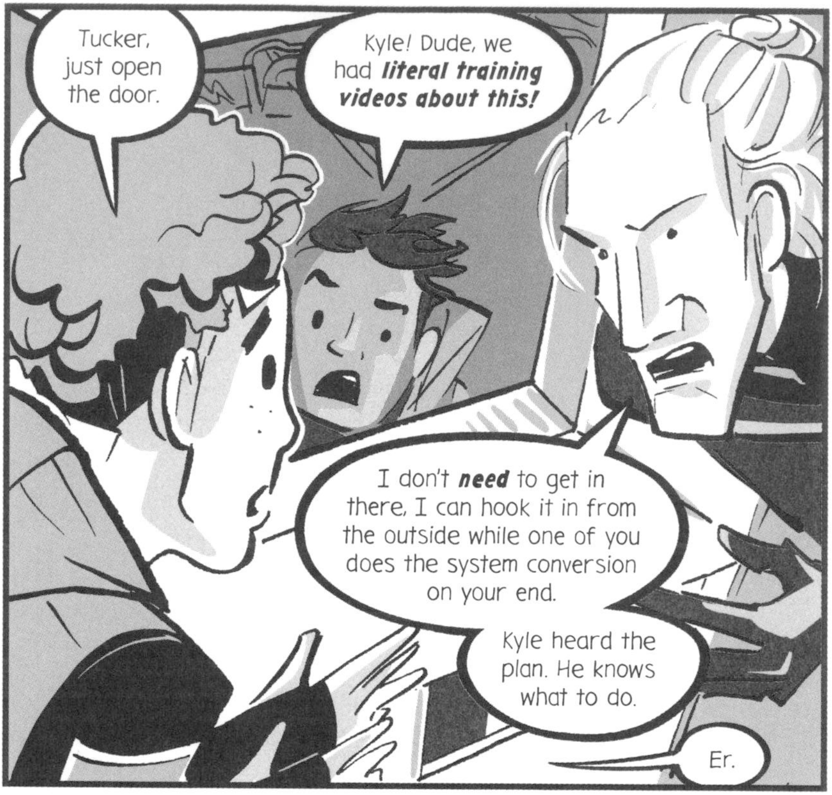
Tucker, just open the door.
Kyle! Dude, we had ***literal training videos about this!***
I don't ***need*** to get in there, I can hook it in from the outside while one of you does the system conversion on your end.
Kyle heard the plan. He knows what to do.
Er.

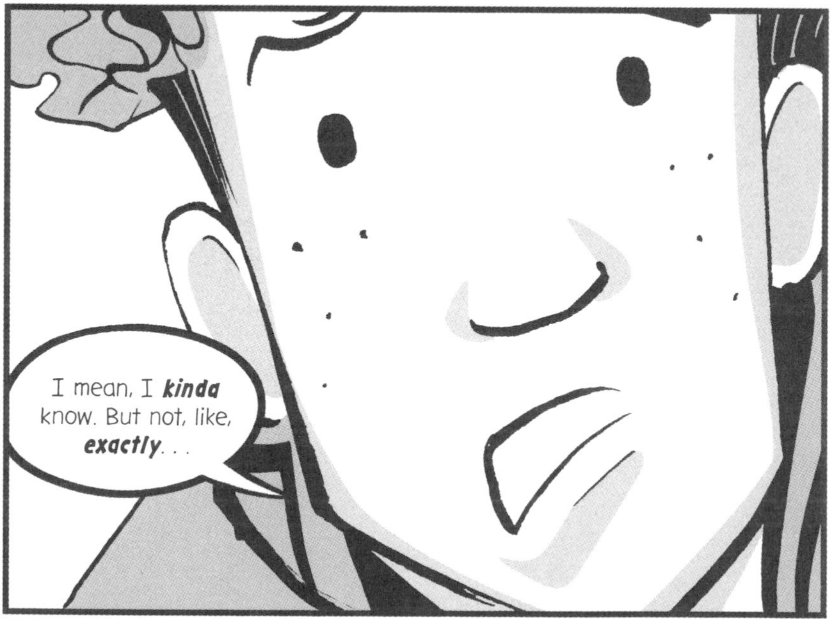
I mean, I ***kinda*** know. But not, like, ***exactly***. . .

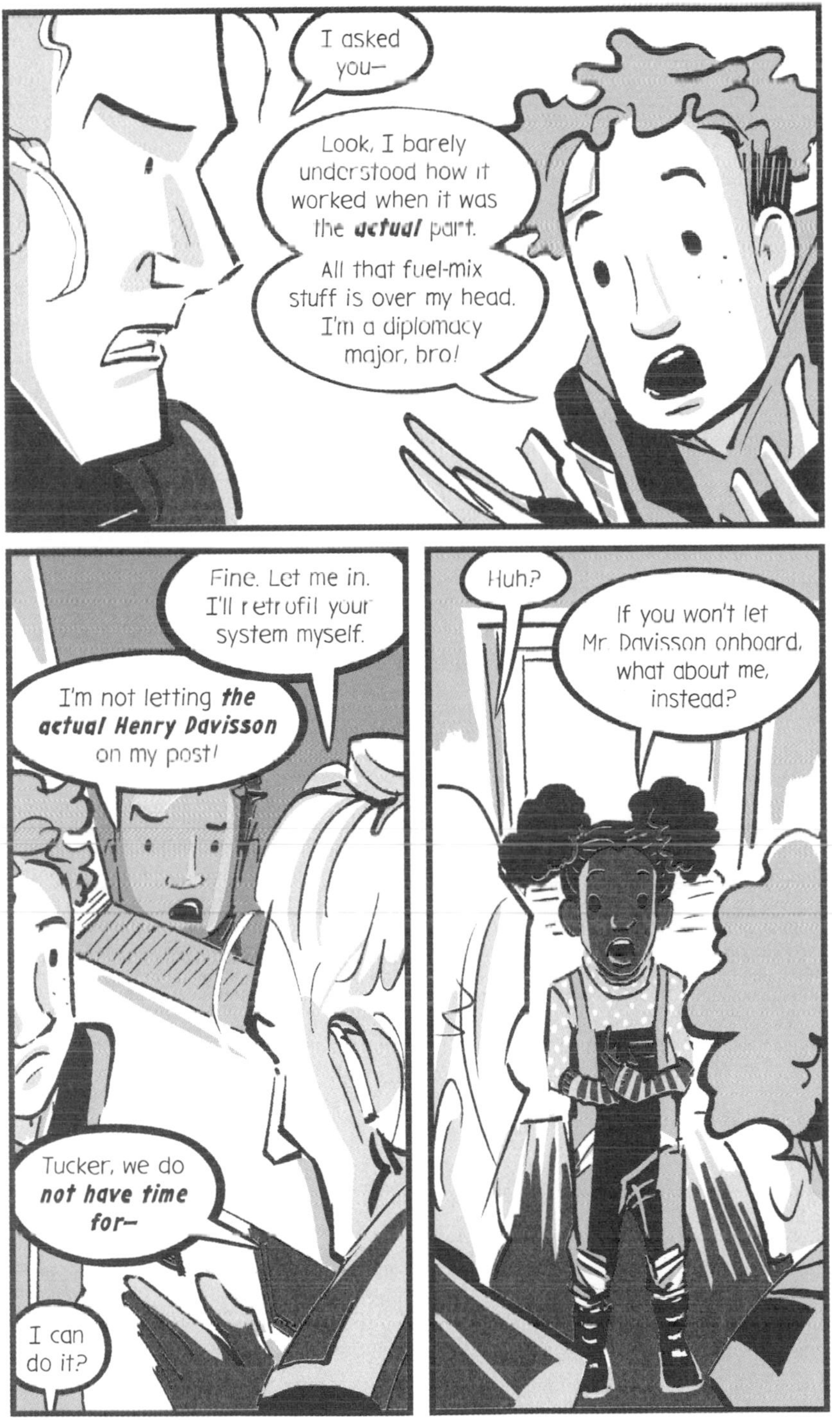
I asked you–
Look, I barely understood how it worked when it was the *actual* part.
All that fuel-mix stuff is over my head. I'm a diplomacy major, bro!
Fine. Let me in. I'll retrofit your system myself.
I'm not letting **the actual Henry Davisson** on my post!
Tucker, we do **not have time for–**
I can do it?
Huh?
If you won't let Mr. Davisson onboard, what about me, instead?

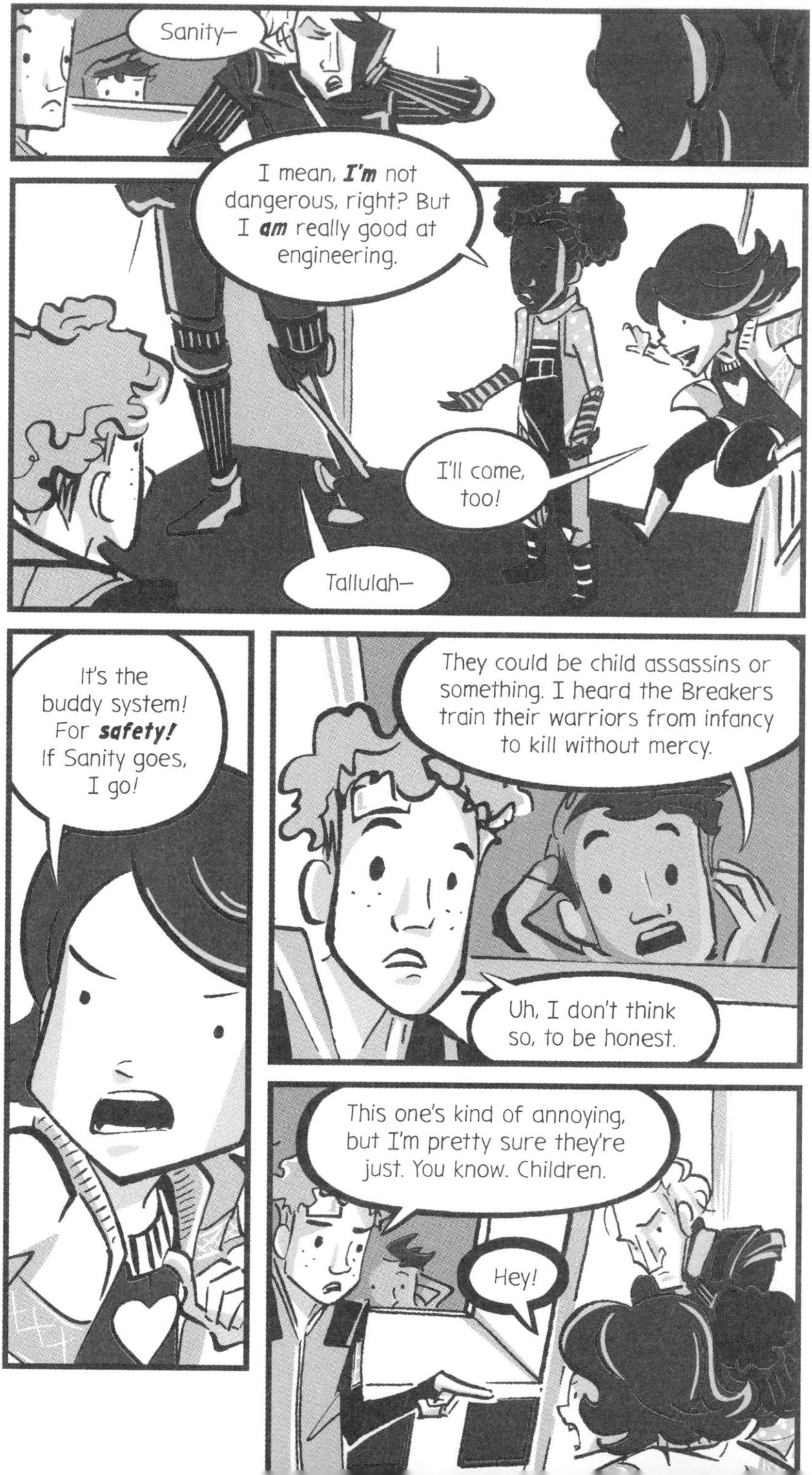
Sanity—
I mean, *I'm* not dangerous, right? But I *am* really good at engineering.
I'll come, too!
Tallulah—
It's the buddy system! For *safety!* If Sanity goes, I go!
They could be child assassins or something. I heard the Breakers train their warriors from infancy to kill without mercy.
Uh, I don't think so, to be honest.
This one's kind of annoying, but I'm pretty sure they're just. You know. Children.
Hey!

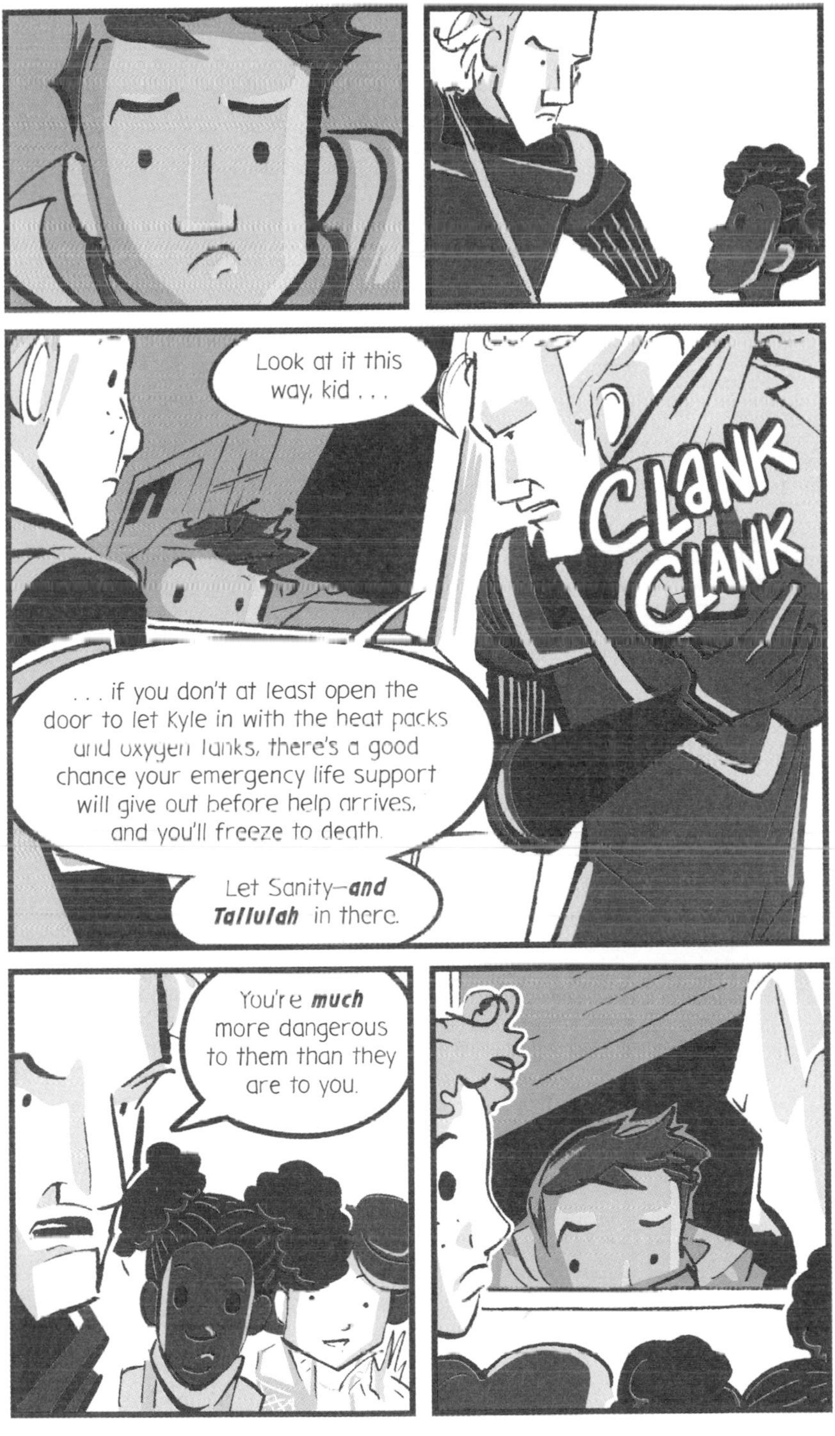
Look at it this way, kid . . .
CLANK CLANK
. . . if you don't at least open the door to let Kyle in with the heat packs and oxygen tanks, there's a good chance your emergency life support will give out before help arrives, and you'll freeze to death.
Let Sanity—**and Tallulah** in there.
You're **much** more dangerous to them than they are to you.

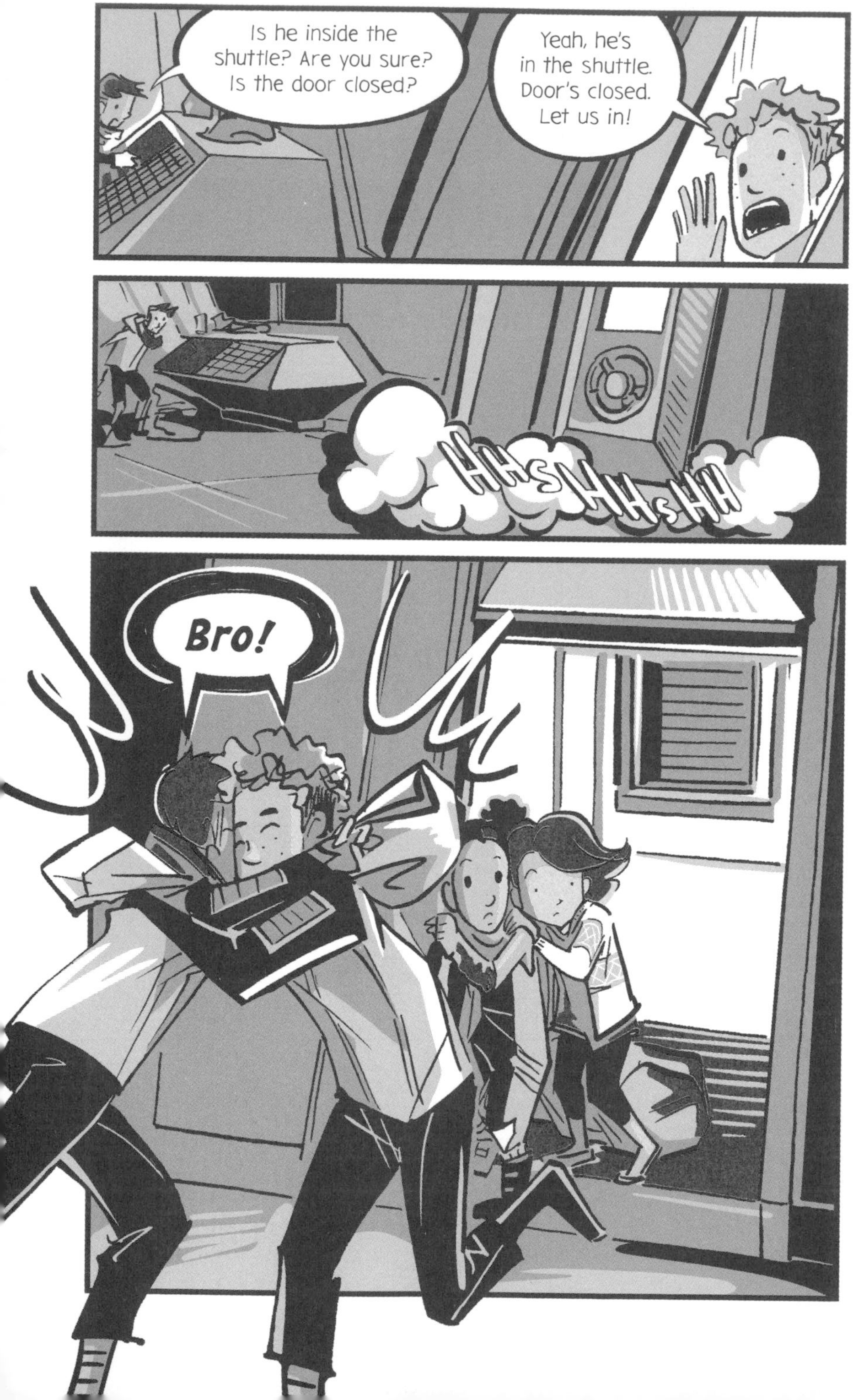
Is he inside the shuttle? Are you sure? Is the door closed?
Yeah, he's in the shuttle. Door's closed. Let us in!
HHSHHsHH
Bro!

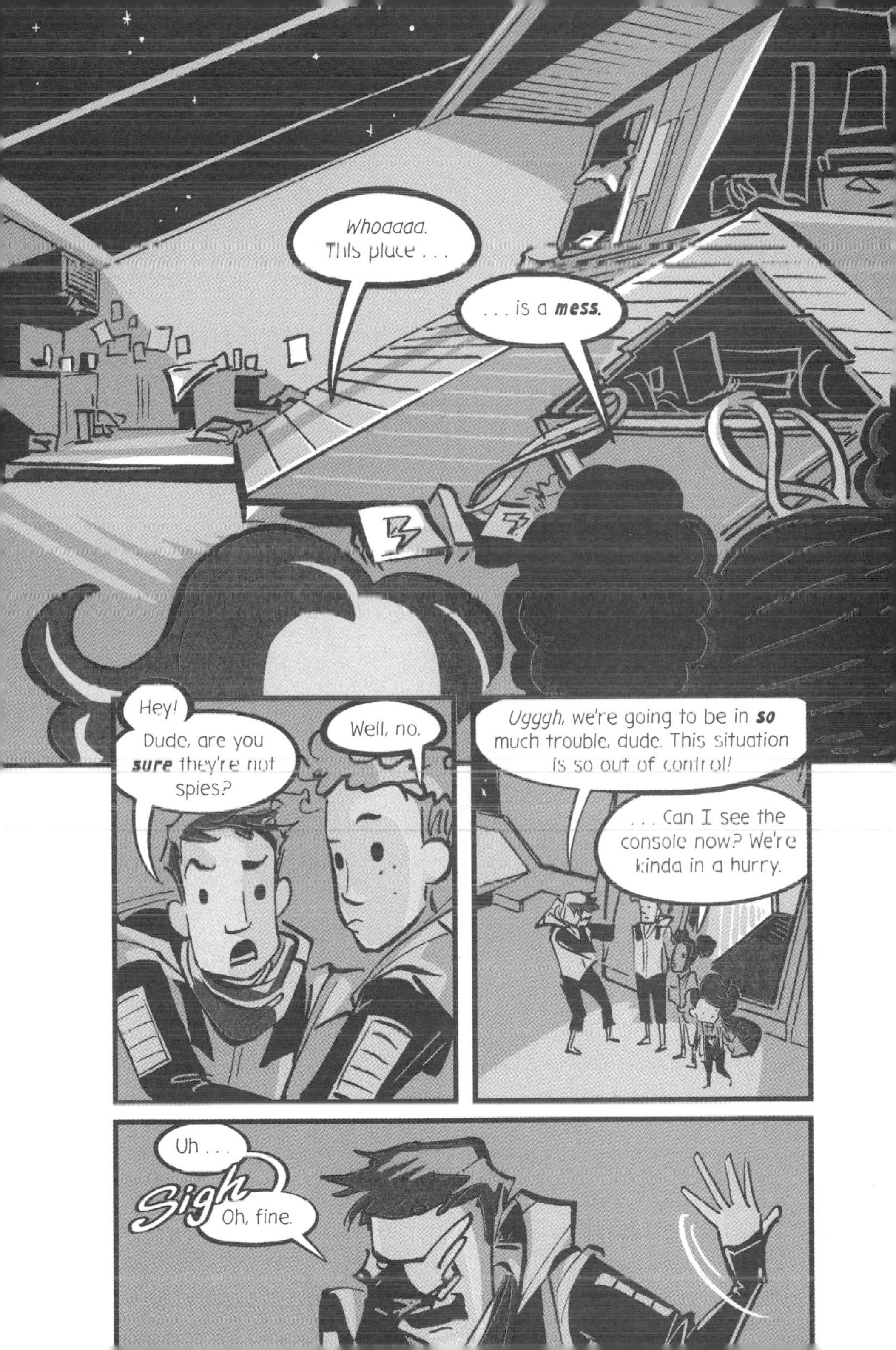
Whoaaaa. This place . . .
. . . is a mess.
Hey! Dude, are you sure they're not spies?
Well, no.
Ugggh, we're going to be in so much trouble, dude. This situation is so out of control!
. . . Can I see the console now? We're kinda in a hurry.
Uh . . .
Sigh
Oh, fine.

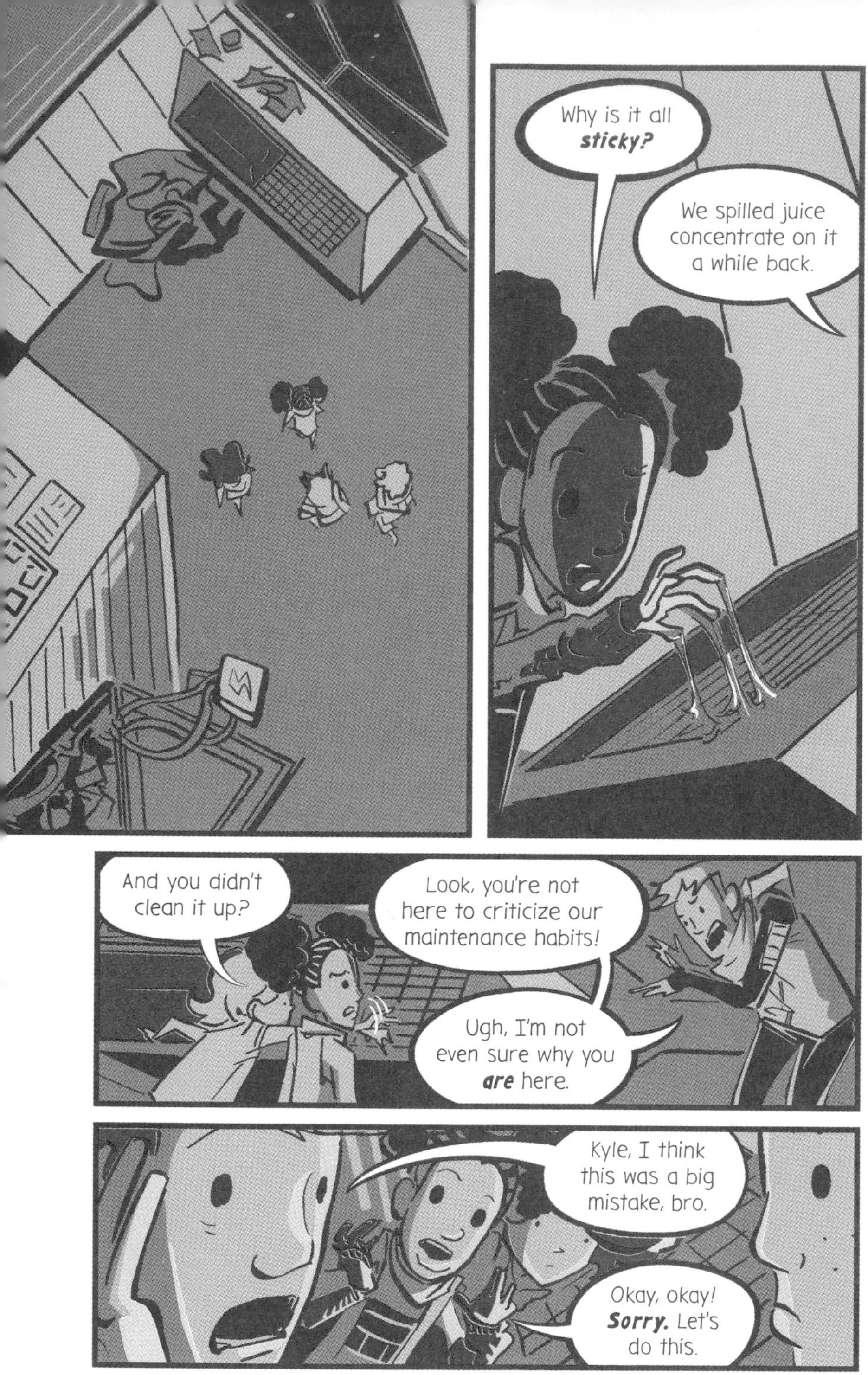
Why is it all **sticky?**
We spilled juice concentrate on it a while back.
And you didn't clean it up?
Look, you're not here to criticize our maintenance habits!
Ugh, I'm not even sure why you **are** here.
Kyle, I think this was a big mistake, bro.
Okay, okay! **Sorry.** Let's do this.

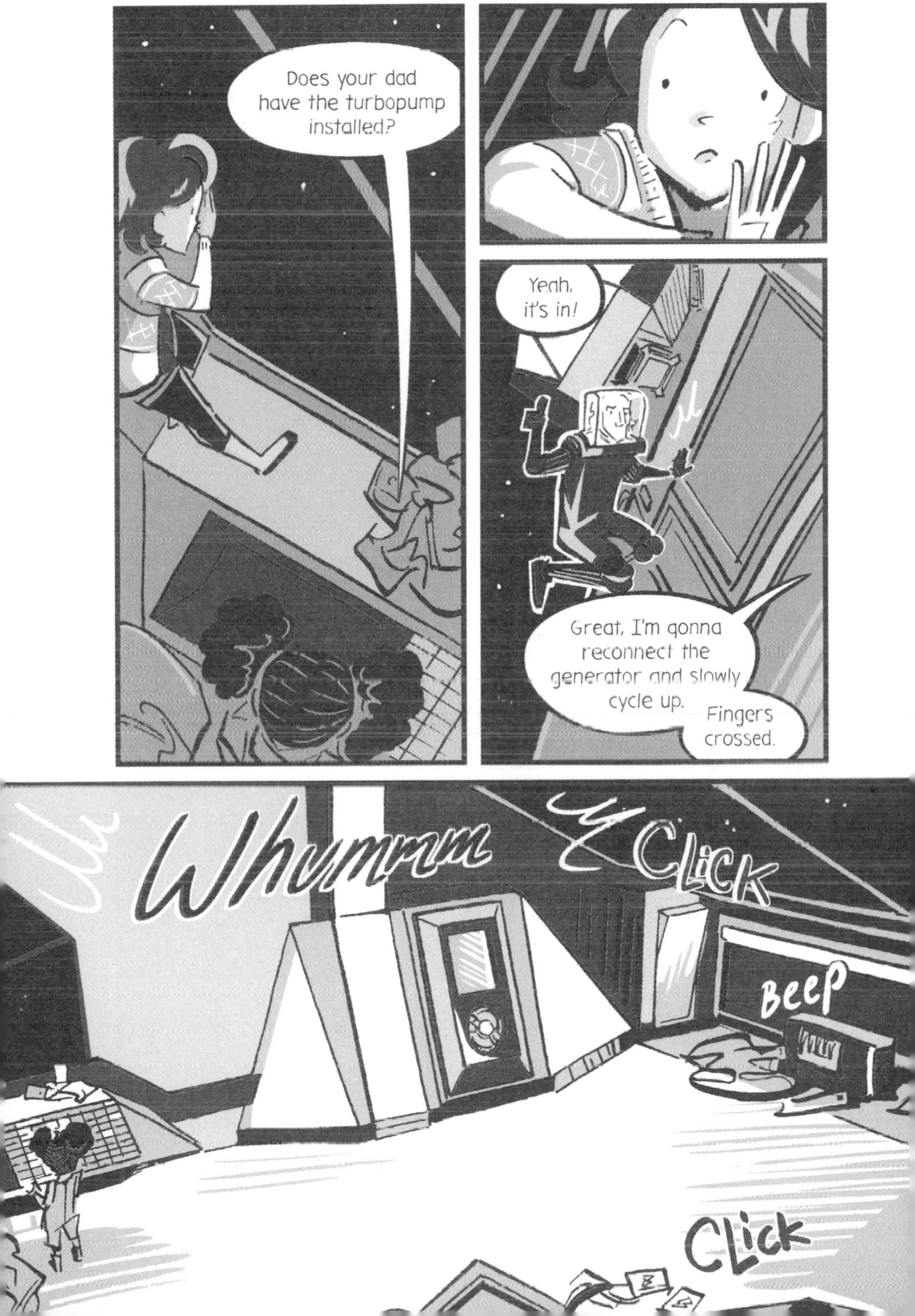
Does your dad have the turbopump installed?
Yeah, it's in!
Great, I'm gonna reconnect the generator and slowly cycle up.
Fingers crossed.
Whhmmm
Click
Beep
Click

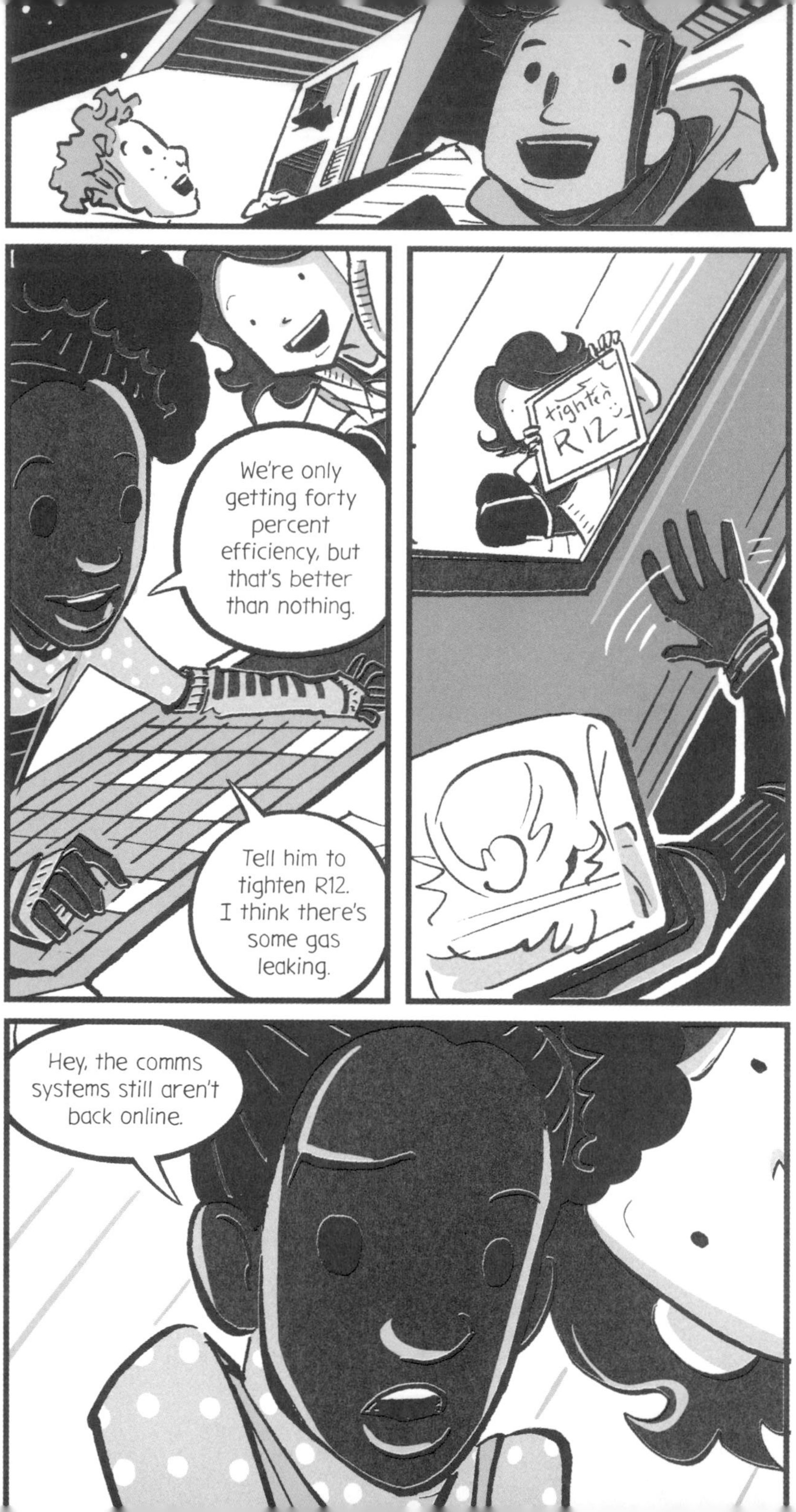
We're only getting forty percent efficiency, but that's better than nothing.
Tell him to tighten R12. I think there's some gas leaking.
tighten R12
Hey, the comms systems still aren't back online.

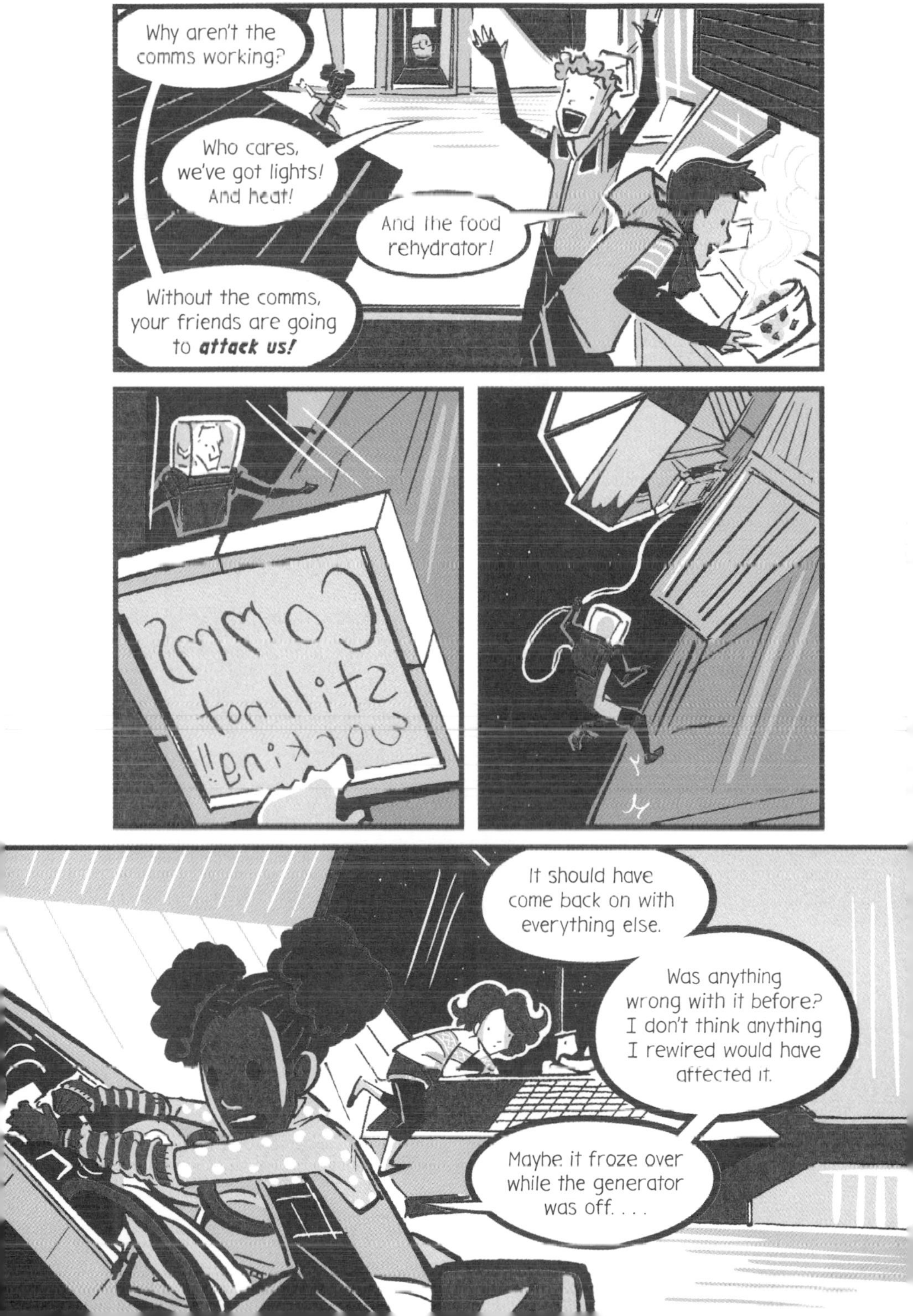
Why aren't the comms working?
Who cares, we've got lights! And heat!
And the food rehydrator!
Without the comms, your friends are going to ***attack us!***
Comms still not working!!
It should have come back on with everything else.
Was anything wrong with it before? I don't think anything I rewired would have affected it.
Maybe it froze over while the generator was off. . . .

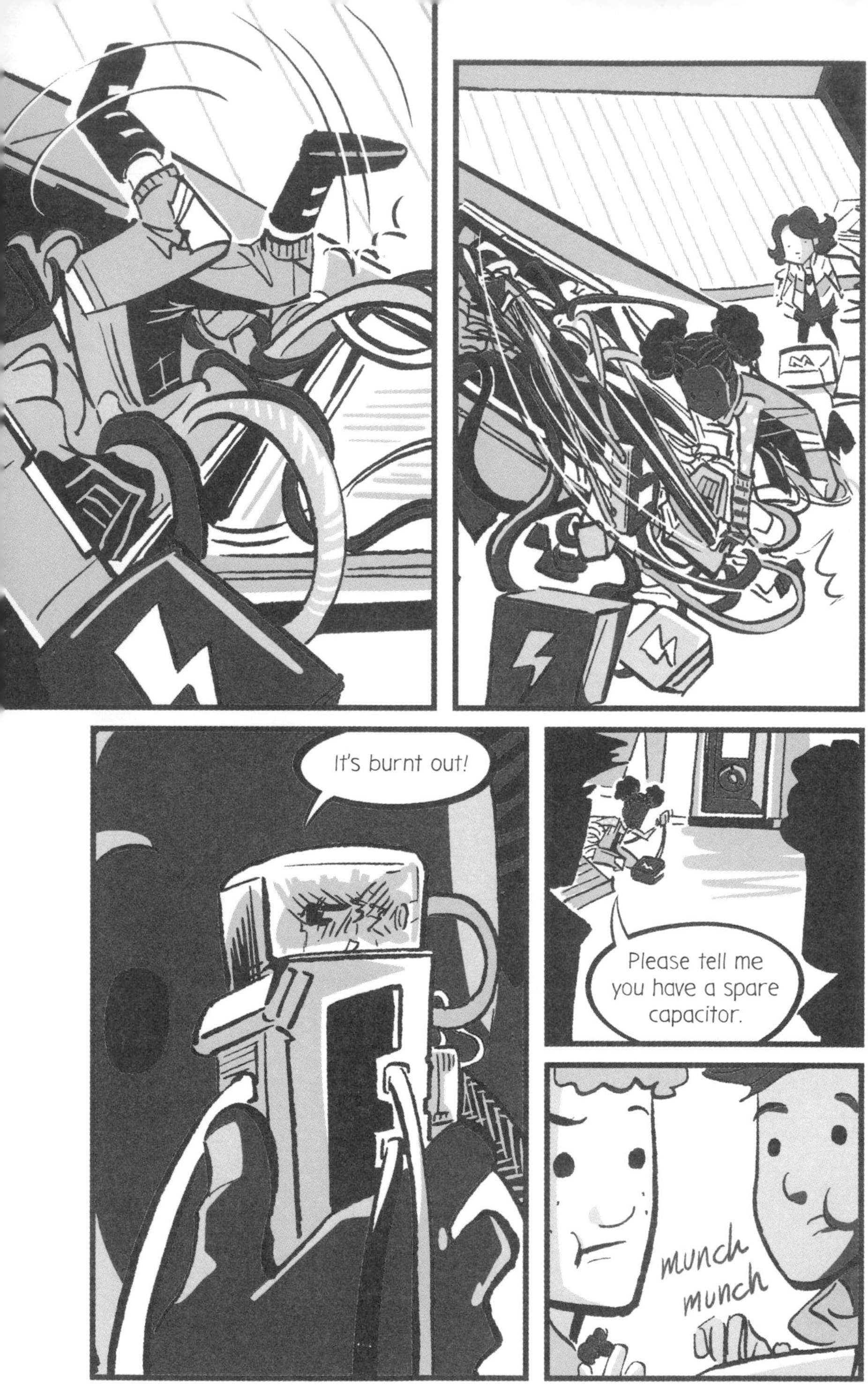
It's burnt out!
Please tell me you have a spare capacitor.
munch munch

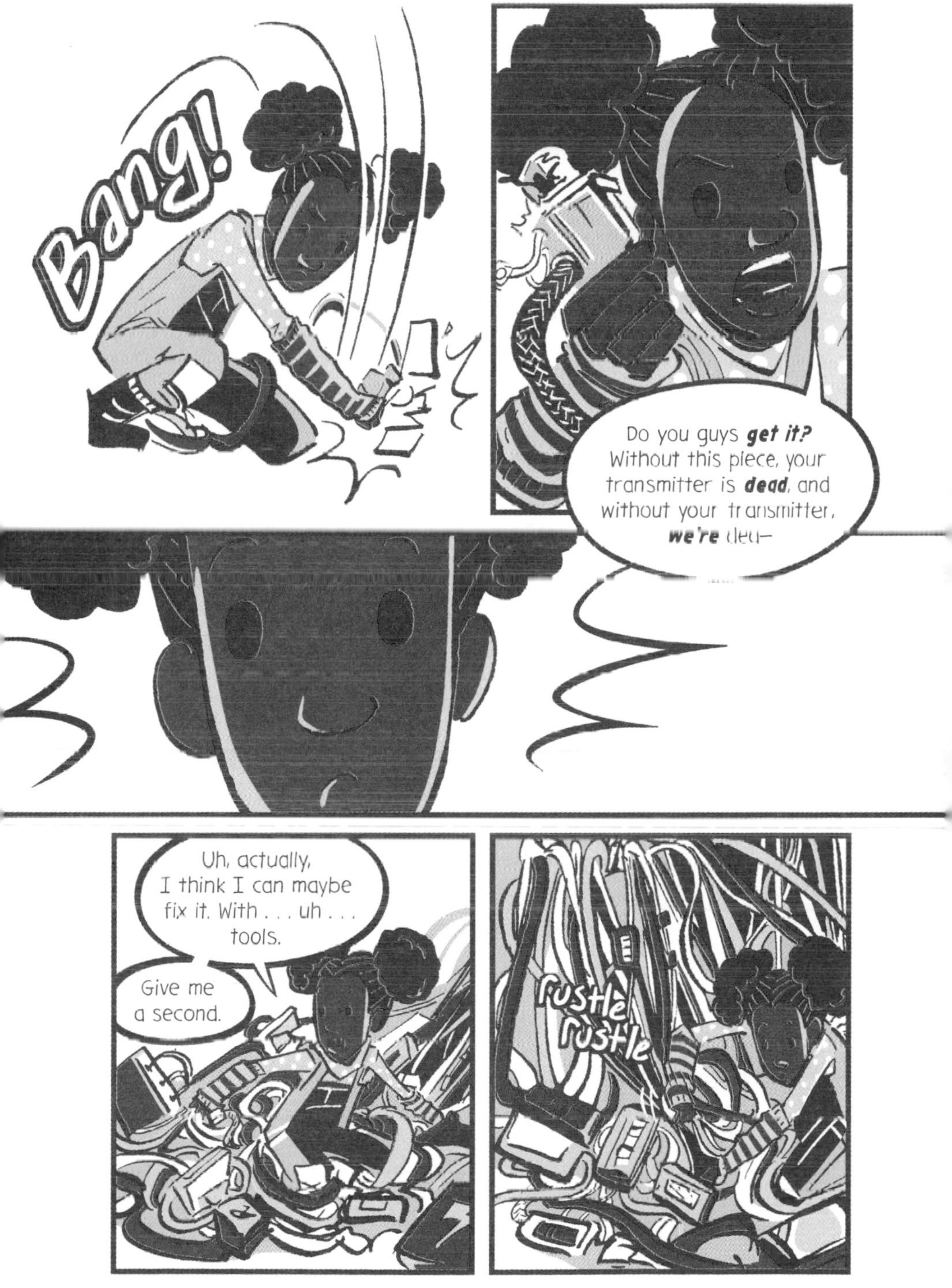
Bang!
Do you guys get it? Without this piece, your transmitter is dead, and without your transmitter, we're dea—
Uh, actually, I think I can maybe fix it. With . . . uh . . . tools.
Give me a second.
rustle rustle

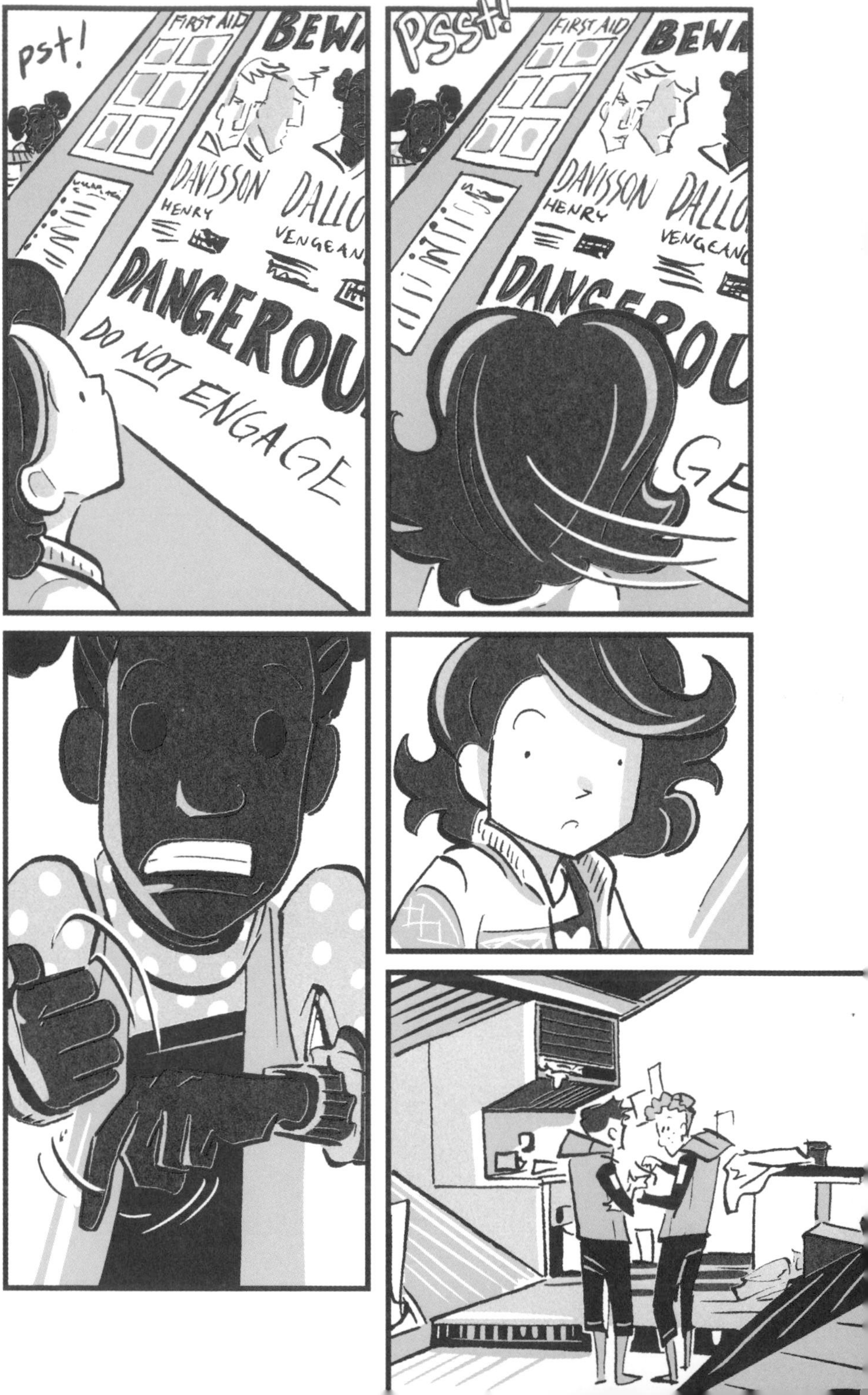
pst!
FIRST AID
BEWA
DAVISSON
HENRY
DALLO
VENGEAN
DANGEROU
DO NOT ENGAGE
PSST!

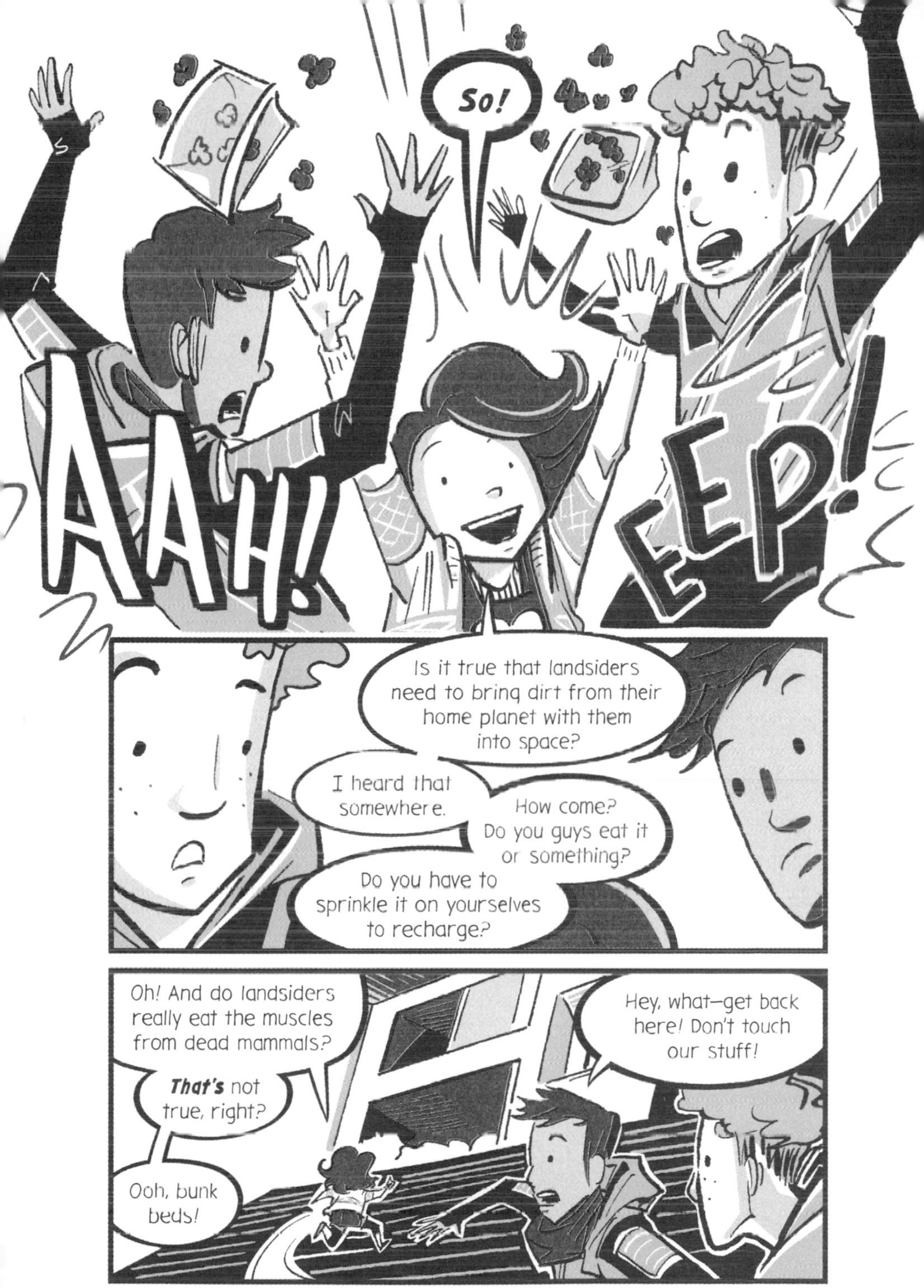
So!
AAH!
EEP!
Is it true that landsiders need to bring dirt from their home planet with them into space?
I heard that somewhere.
How come? Do you guys eat it or something?
Do you have to sprinkle it on yourselves to recharge?
Oh! And do landsiders really eat the muscles from dead mammals?
That's not true, right?
Ooh, bunk beds!
Hey, what—get back here! Don't touch our stuff!

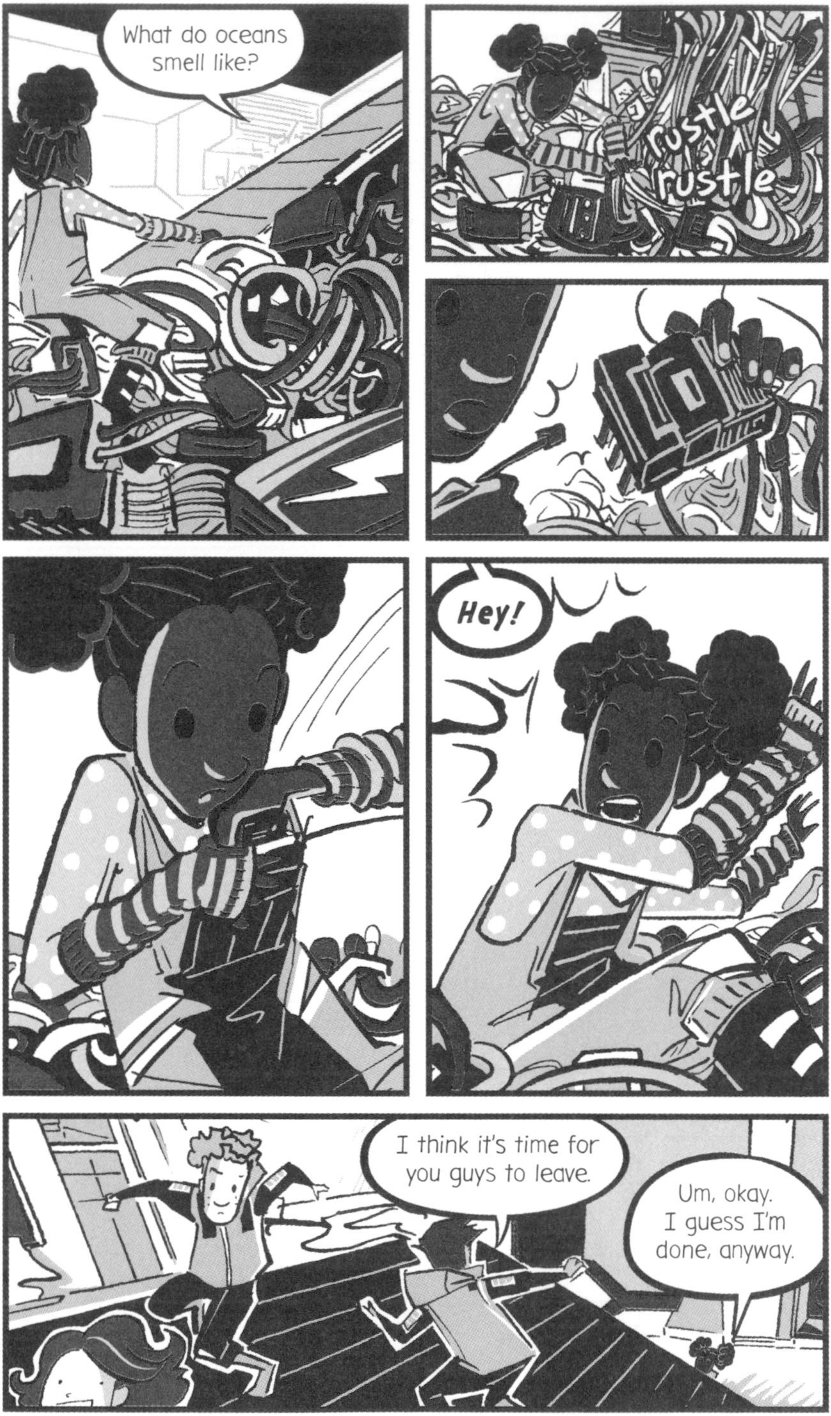
What do oceans smell like?
rustle rustle
Hey!
I think it's time for you guys to leave.
Um, okay. I guess I'm done, anyway.

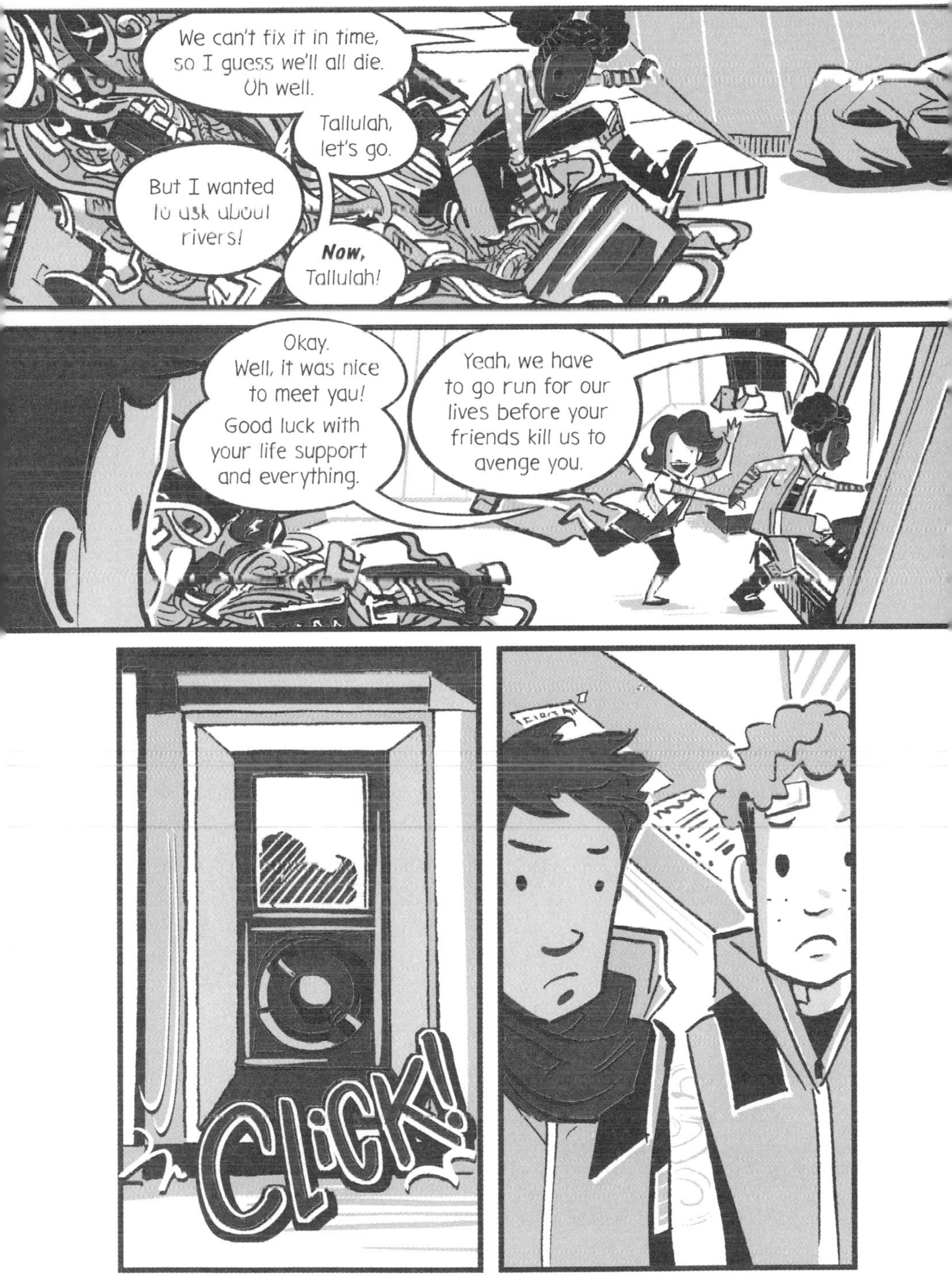
We can't fix it in time, so I guess we'll all die. Oh well.
Tallulah, let's go.
But I wanted to ask about rivers!
Now, Tallulah!
Okay. Well, it was nice to meet you! Good luck with your life support and everything.
Yeah, we have to go run for our lives before your friends kill us to avenge you.
CLICK!

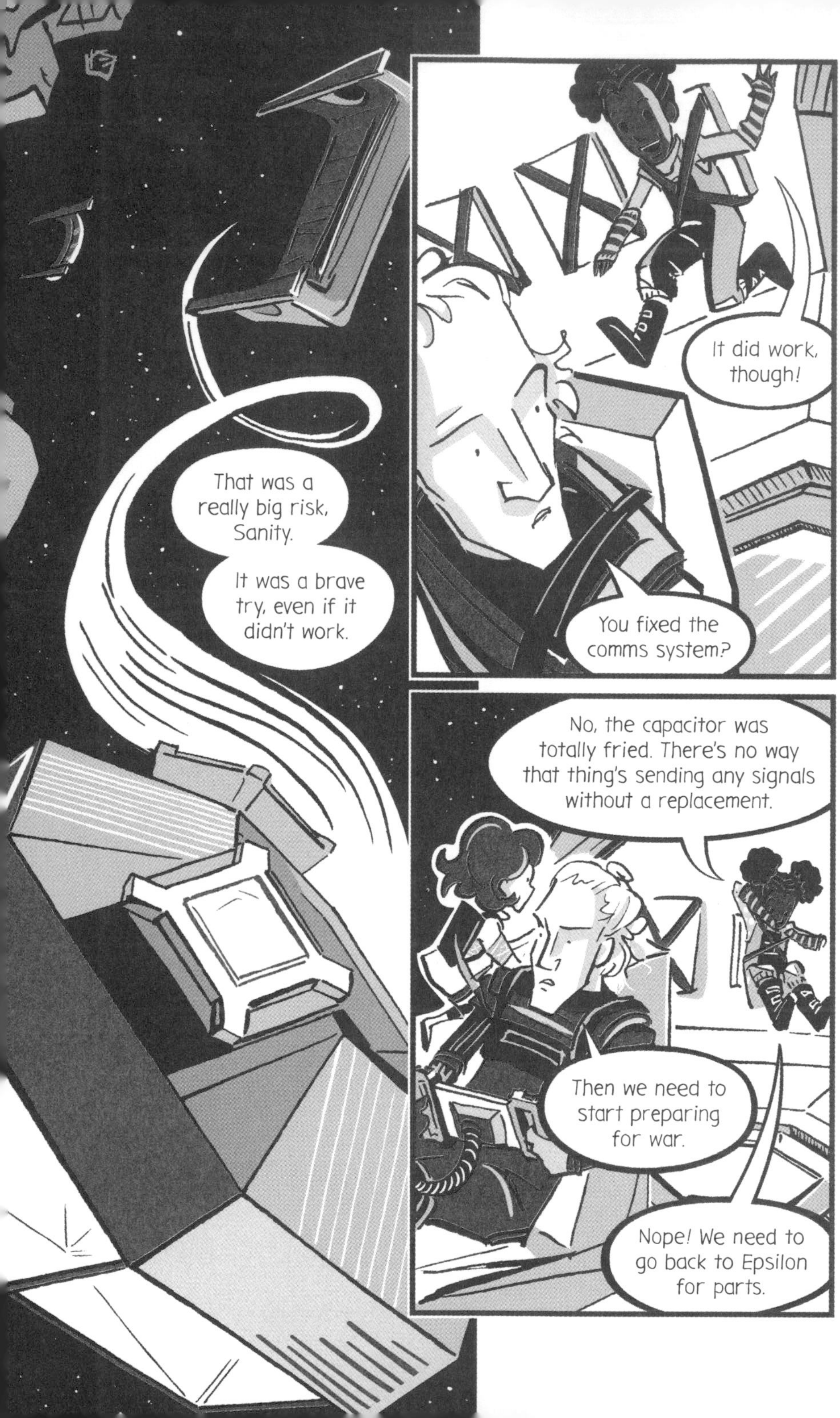
That was a really big risk, Sanity.
It was a brave try, even if it didn't work.
It did work, though!
You fixed the comms system?
No, the capacitor was totally fried. There's no way that thing's sending any signals without a replacement.
Then we need to start preparing for war.
Nope! We need to go back to Epsilon for parts.

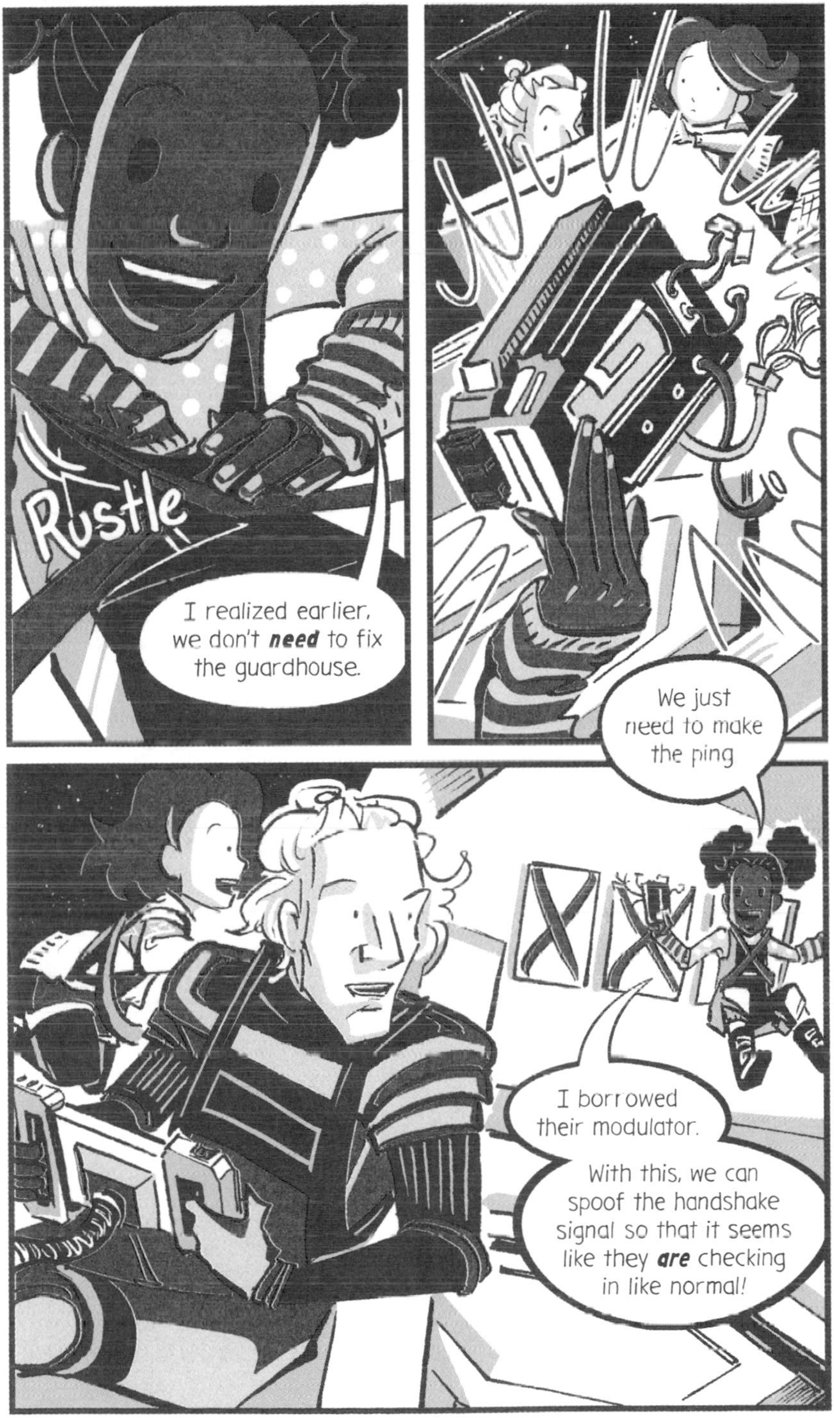
Rustle
I realized earlier, we don't **need** to fix the guardhouse.
We just need to make the ping
I borrowed their modulator.
With this, we can spoof the handshake signal so that it seems like they **are** checking in like normal!

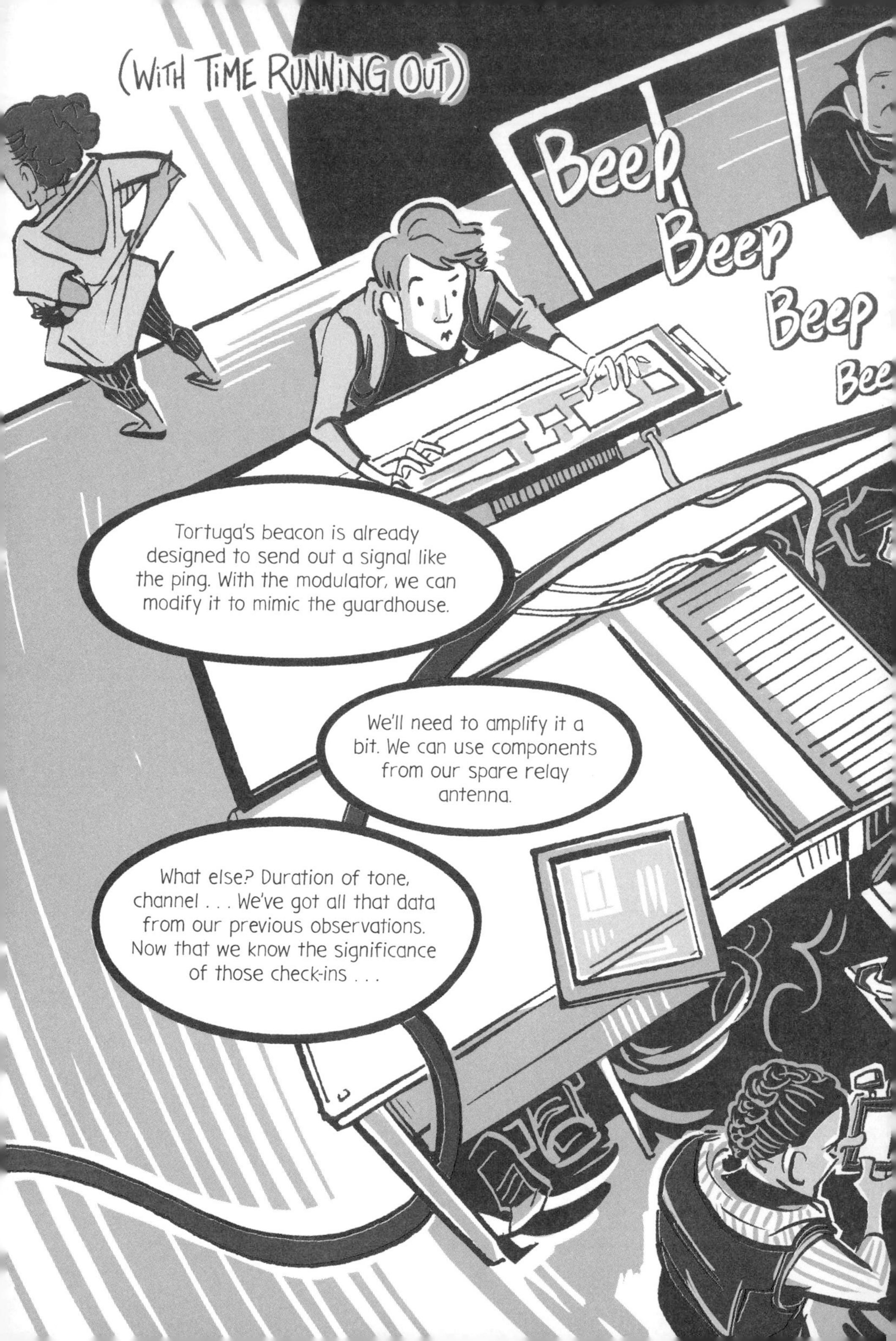
(WITH TIME RUNNING OUT)
Beep
Beep
Beep
Bee
Tortuga's beacon is already designed to send out a signal like the ping. With the modulator, we can modify it to mimic the guardhouse.
We'll need to amplify it a bit. We can use components from our spare relay antenna.
What else? Duration of tone, channel . . . We've got all that data from our previous observations. Now that we know the significance of those check-ins . . .

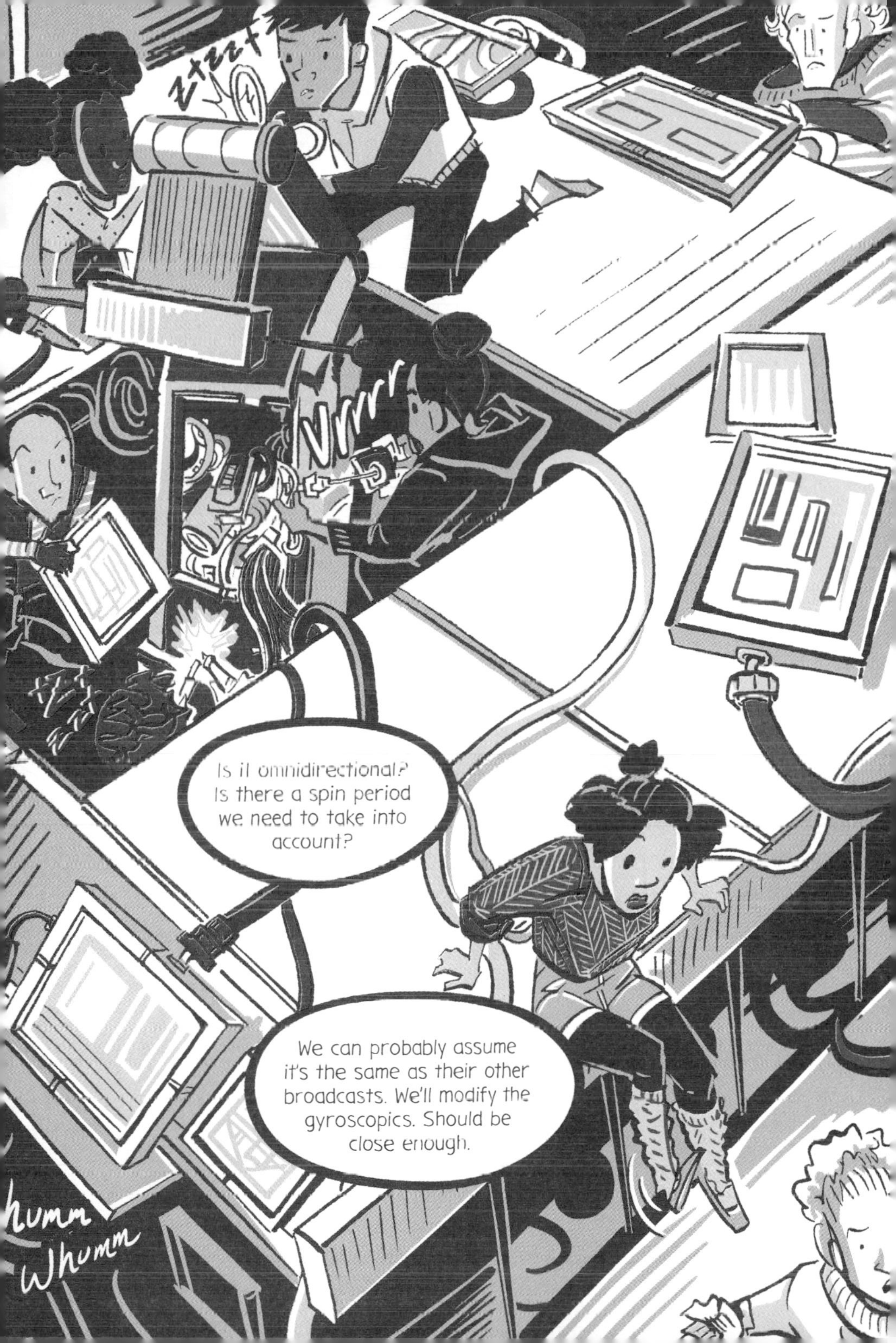
Zzzzz
Vrrrrr
Is it omnidirectional? Is there a spin period we need to take into account?
We can probably assume it's the same as their other broadcasts. We'll modify the gyroscopics. Should be close enough.
humm
Whumm

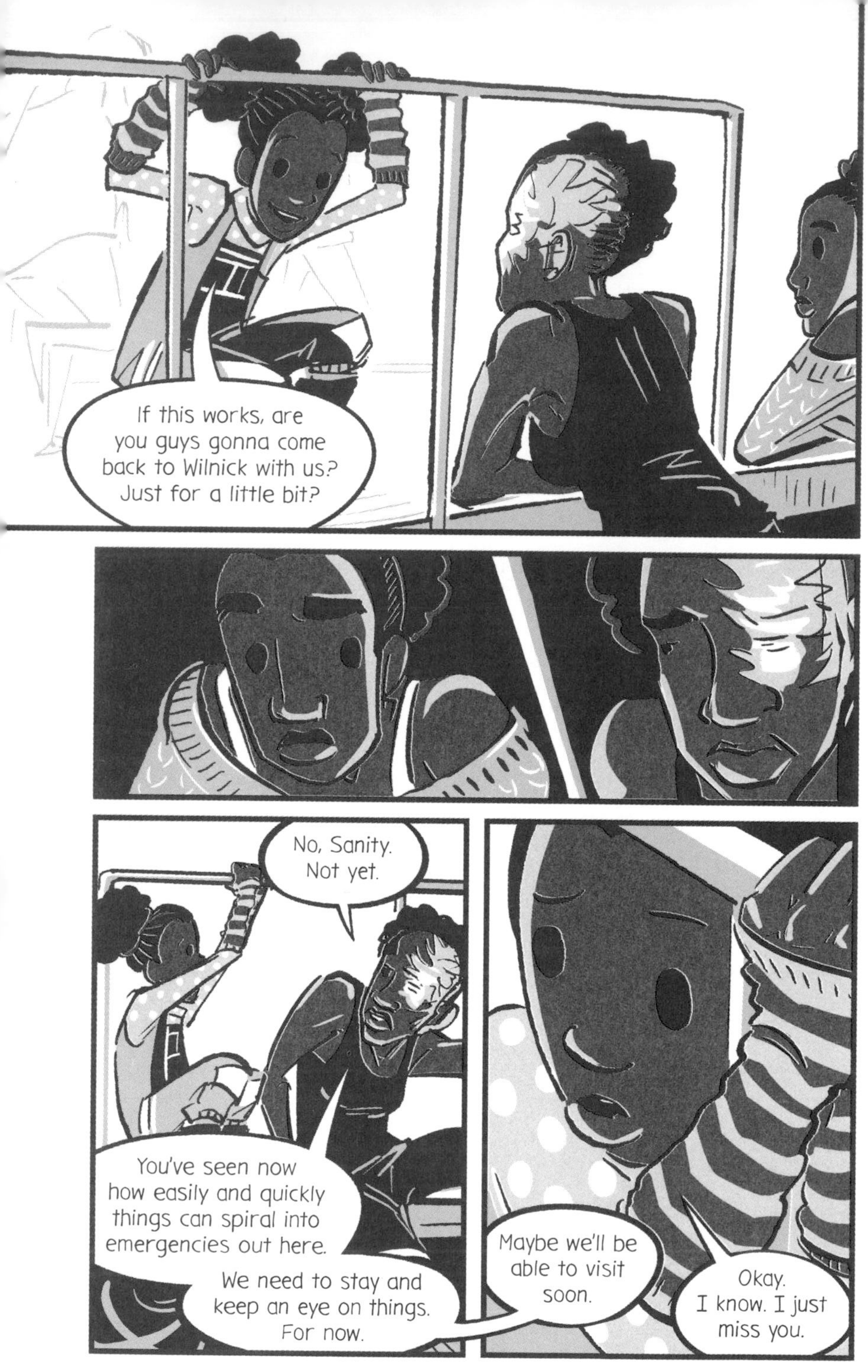
If this works, are you guys gonna come back to Wilnick with us? Just for a little bit?
No, Sanity. Not yet.
You've seen now how easily and quickly things can spiral into emergencies out here.
We need to stay and keep an eye on things. For now.
Maybe we'll be able to visit soon.
Okay. I know. I just miss you.

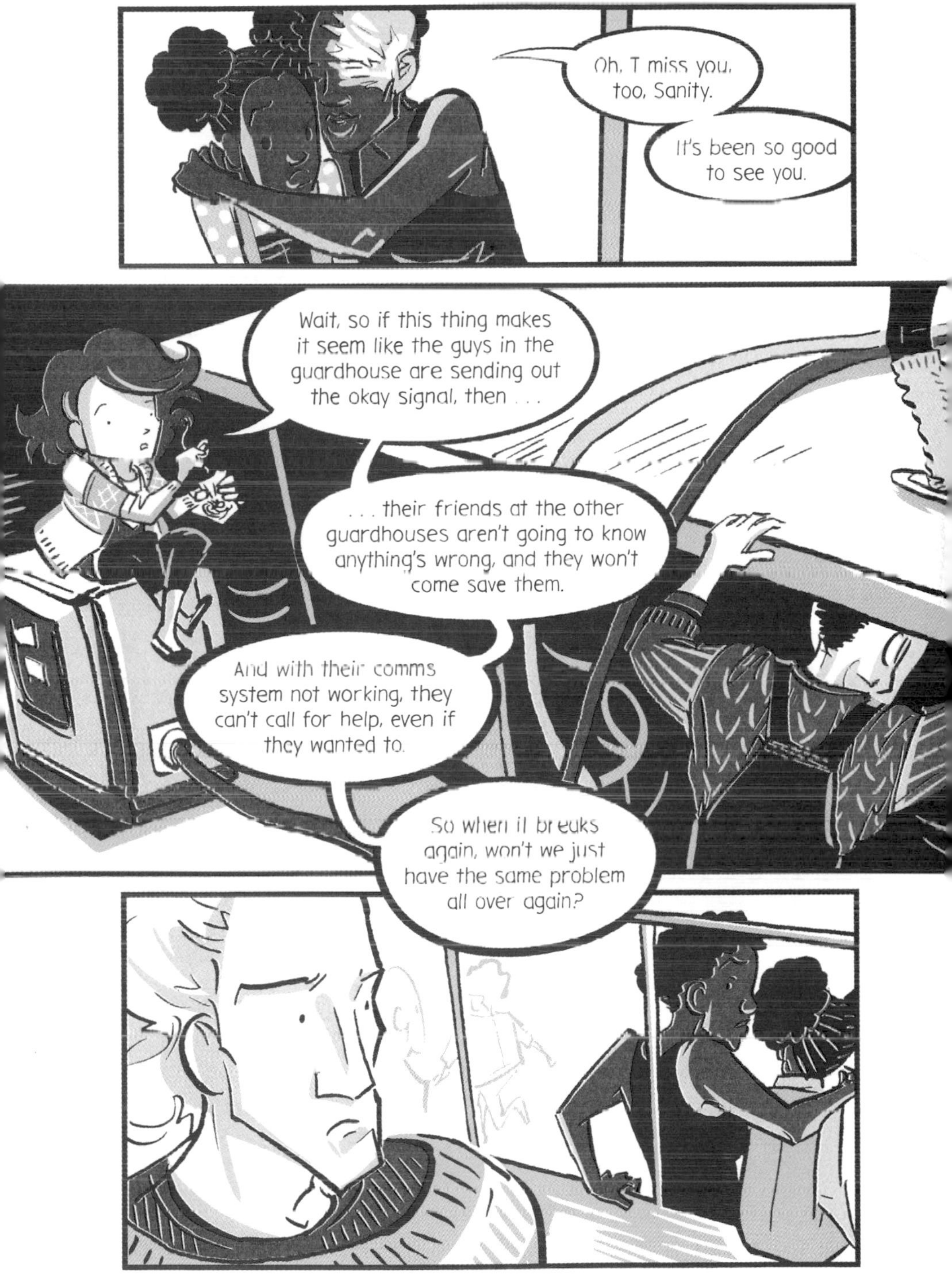

Oh, I miss you, too, Sanity.
It's been so good to see you.
Wait, so if this thing makes it seem like the guys in the guardhouse are sending out the okay signal, then . . .
. . . their friends at the other guardhouses aren't going to know anything's wrong, and they won't come save them.
And with their comms system not working, they can't call for help, even if they wanted to.
So when it breaks again, won't we just have the same problem all over again?

(UNITED TERRITORIES BLOCKADE POST)

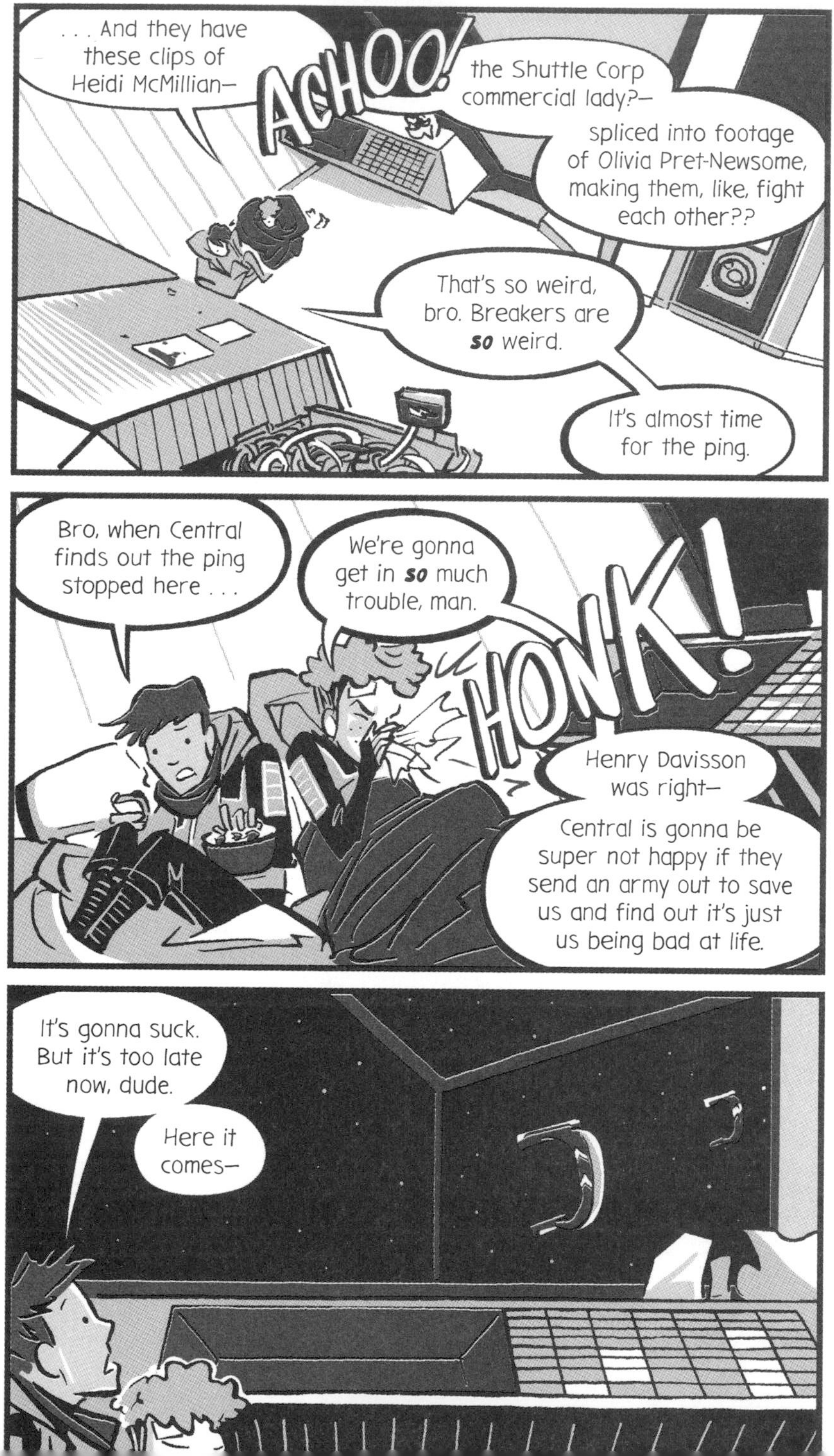
. . . And they have these clips of Heidi McMillian—
ACHOO!
the Shuttle Corp commercial lady?—
spliced into footage of Olivia Pret-Newsome, making them, like, fight each other??
That's so weird, bro. Breakers are **so** weird.
It's almost time for the ping.
Bro, when Central finds out the ping stopped here . . .
We're gonna get in **so** much trouble, man.
HONK!
Henry Davisson was right—
Central is gonna be super not happy if they send an army out to save us and find out it's just us being bad at life.
It's gonna suck. But it's too late now, dude.
Here it comes—

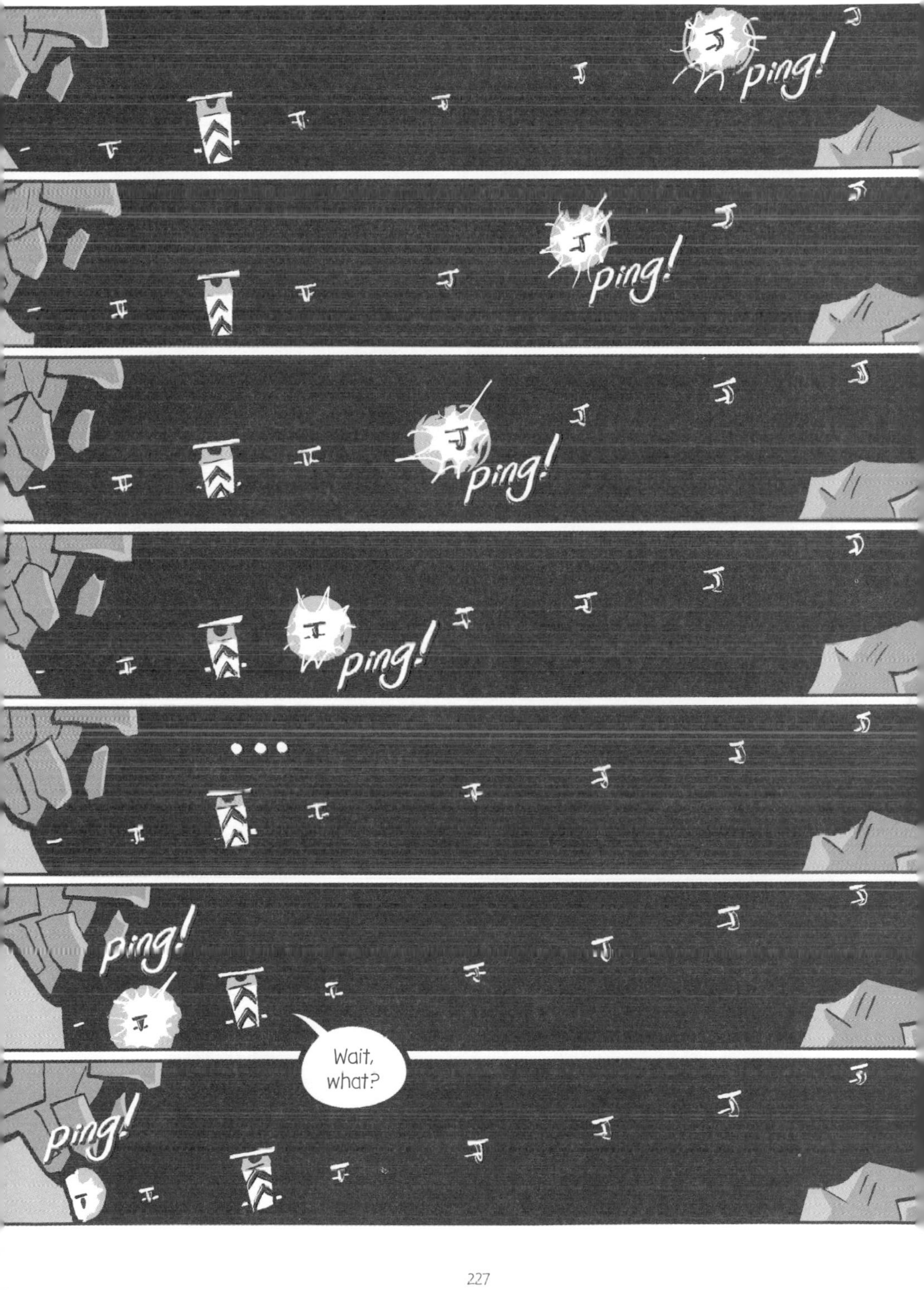
ping!
ping!
ping!
ping!
• • •
ping!
Wait, what?
ping!

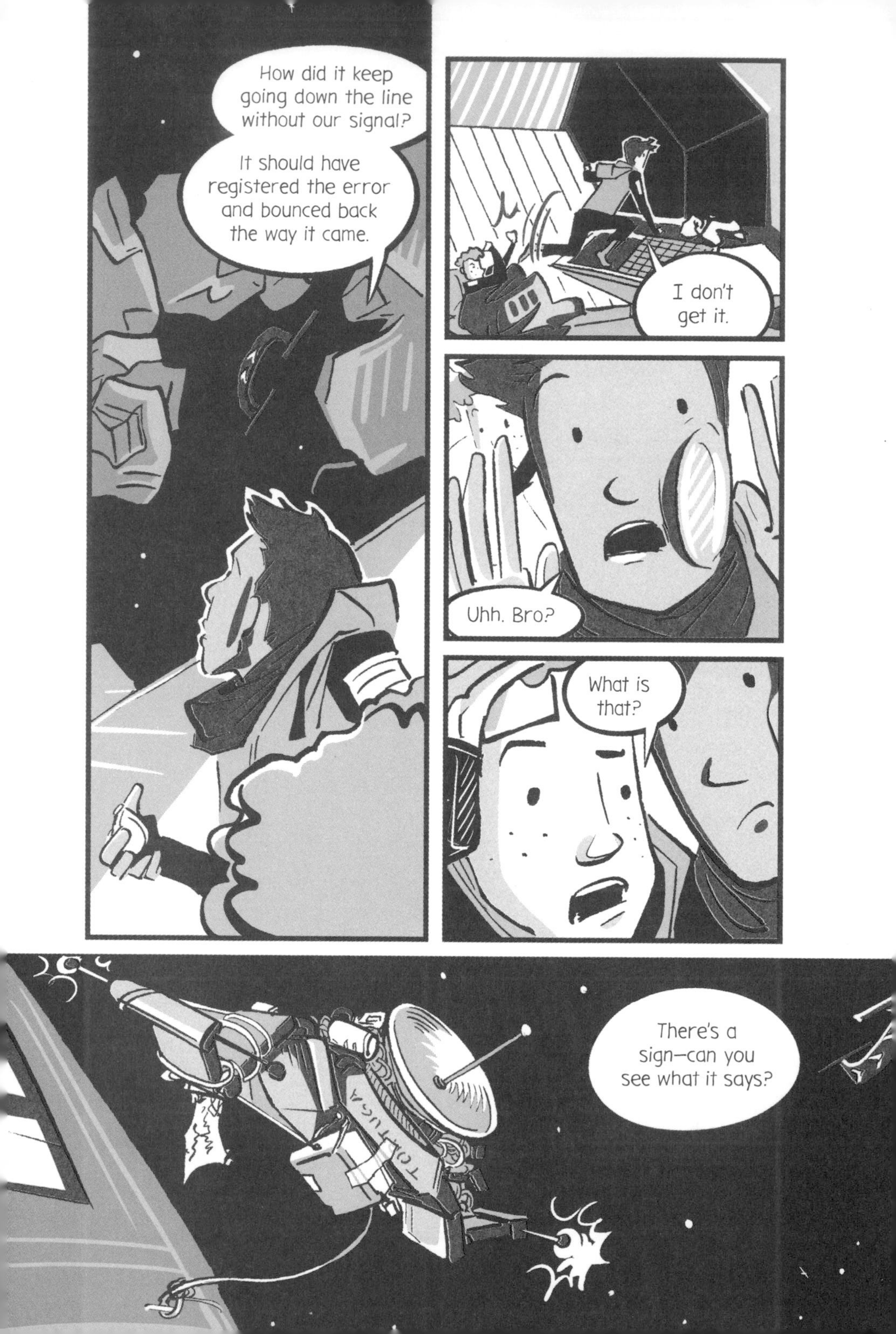
How did it keep going down the line without our signal?
It should have registered the error and bounced back the way it came.
I don't get it.
Uhh. Bro?
What is that?
There's a sign—can you see what it says?

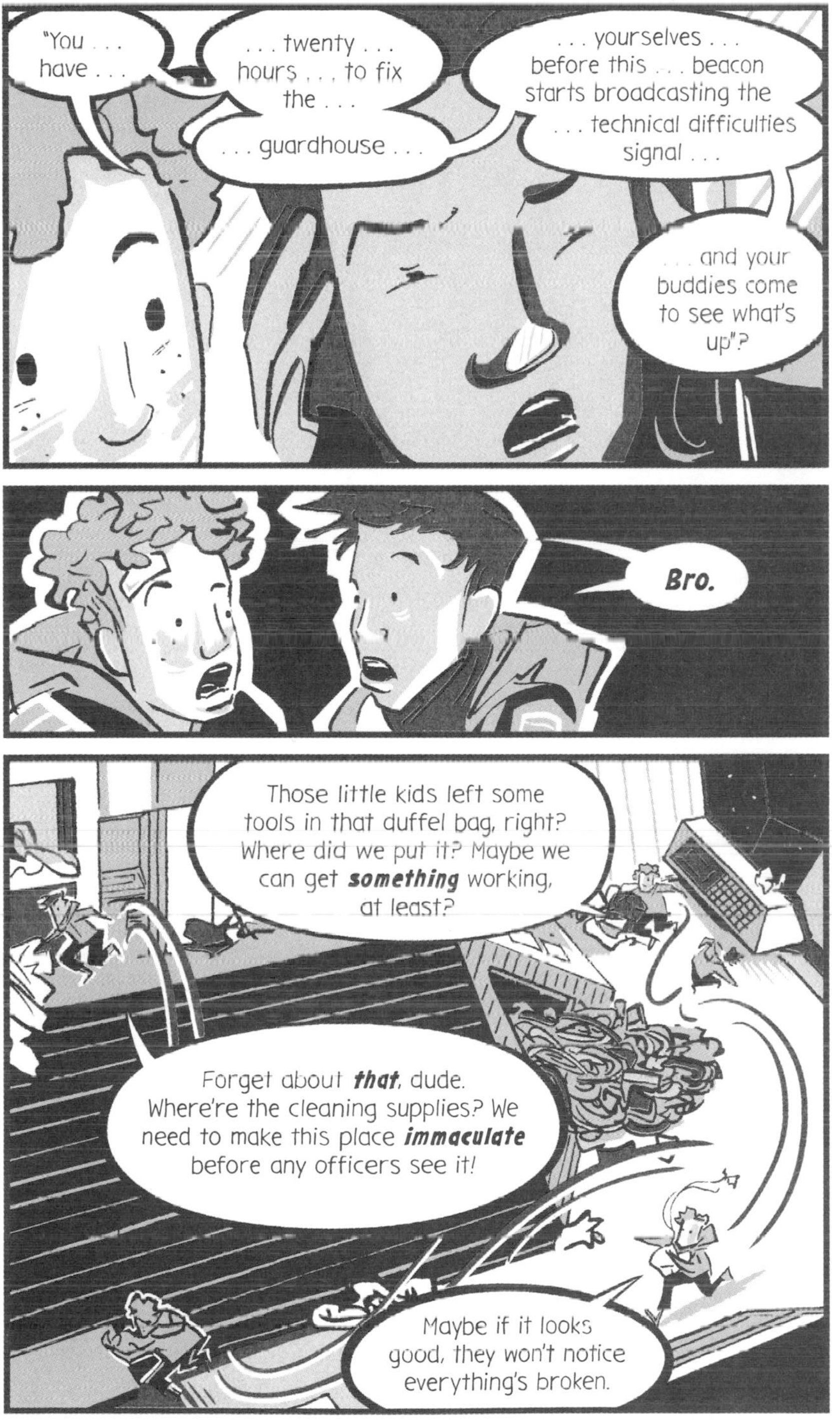
"You . . . have . . .
. . . twenty . . . hours . . . to fix the . . .
. . . guardhouse . . .
. . . yourselves . . . before this . . . beacon starts broadcasting the
. . . technical difficulties signal . . .
. . . and your buddies come to see what's up"?
Bro.
Those little kids left some tools in that duffel bag, right? Where did we put it? Maybe we can get **something** working, at least?
Forget about **that**, dude. Where're the cleaning supplies? We need to make this place **immaculate** before any officers see it!
Maybe if it looks good, they won't notice everything's broken.

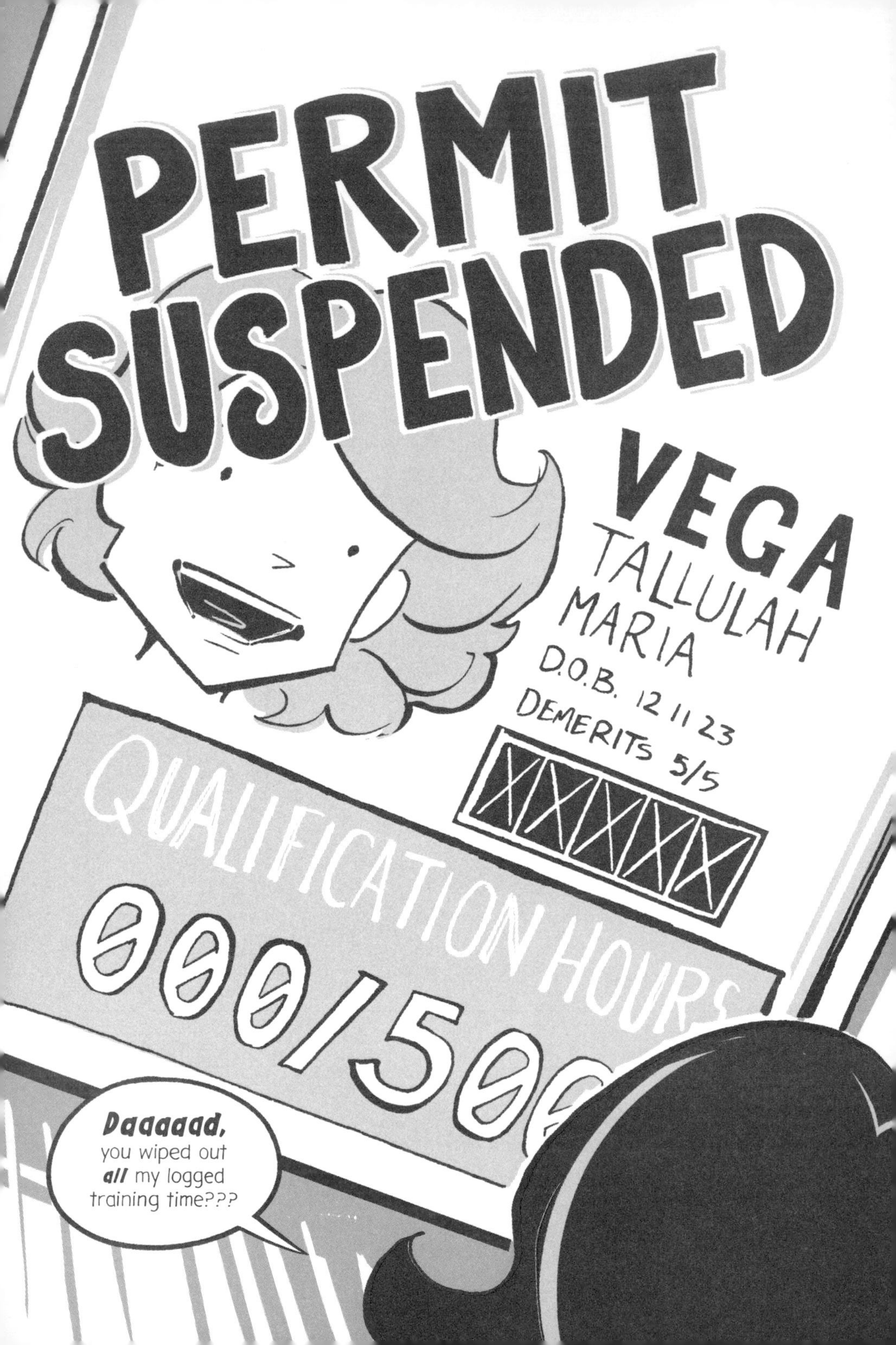

PERMIT SUSPENDED
VEGA
TALLULAH
MARIA
D.O.B. 12 11 23
DEMERITS 5/5
QUALIFICATION HOURS
000/500
Daaaaad, you wiped out ***all*** my logged training time???

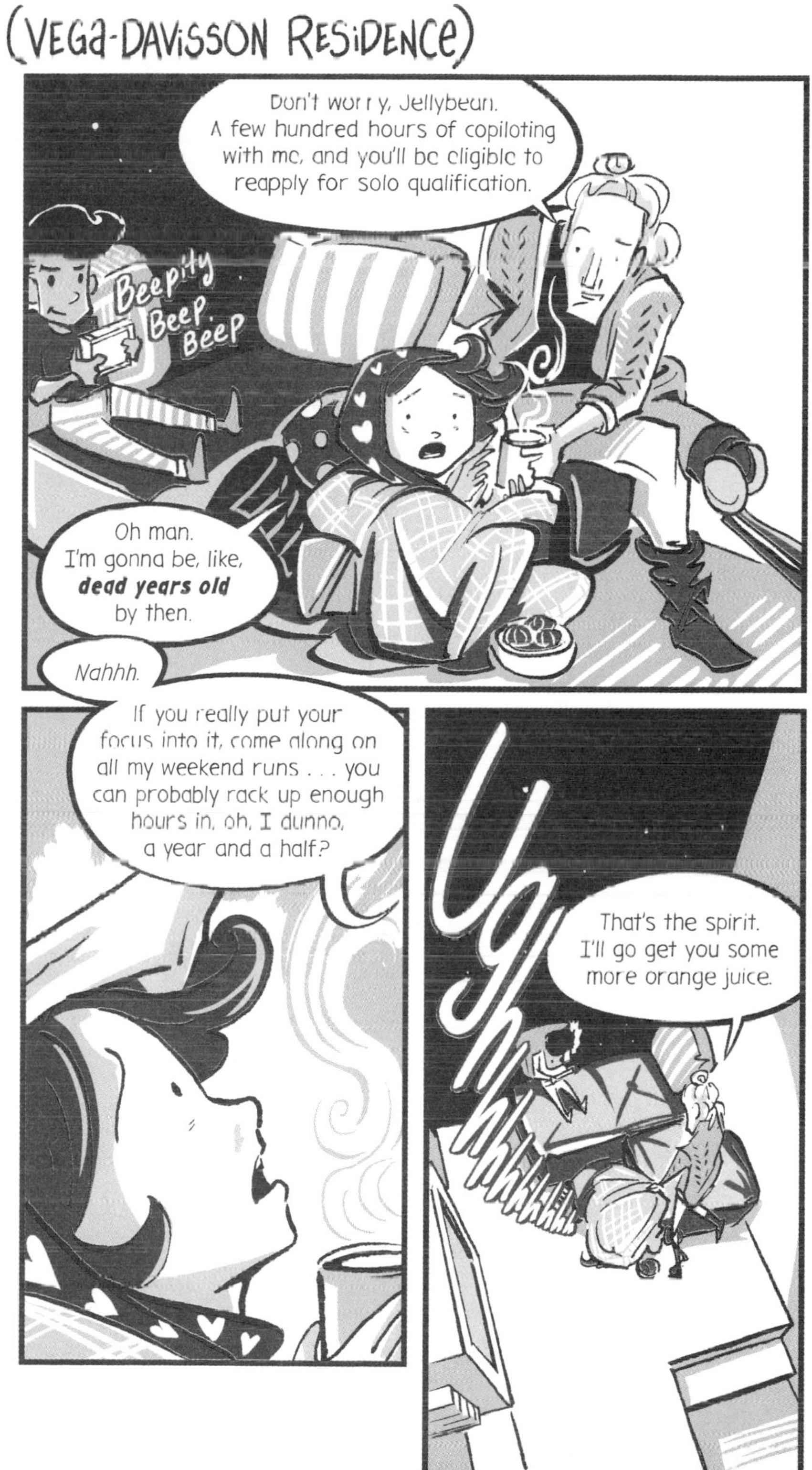
(VEGA-DAVISSON RESIDENCE)
Don't worry, Jellybean. A few hundred hours of copiloting with me, and you'll be eligible to reapply for solo qualification.
Beepity Beep. Beep
Oh man. I'm gonna be, like, **dead years old** by then.
Nahhh.
If you really put your focus into it, come along on all my weekend runs . . . you can probably rack up enough hours in, oh, I dunno, a year and a half?
That's the spirit. I'll go get you some more orange juice.

(JONES RESIDENCE)

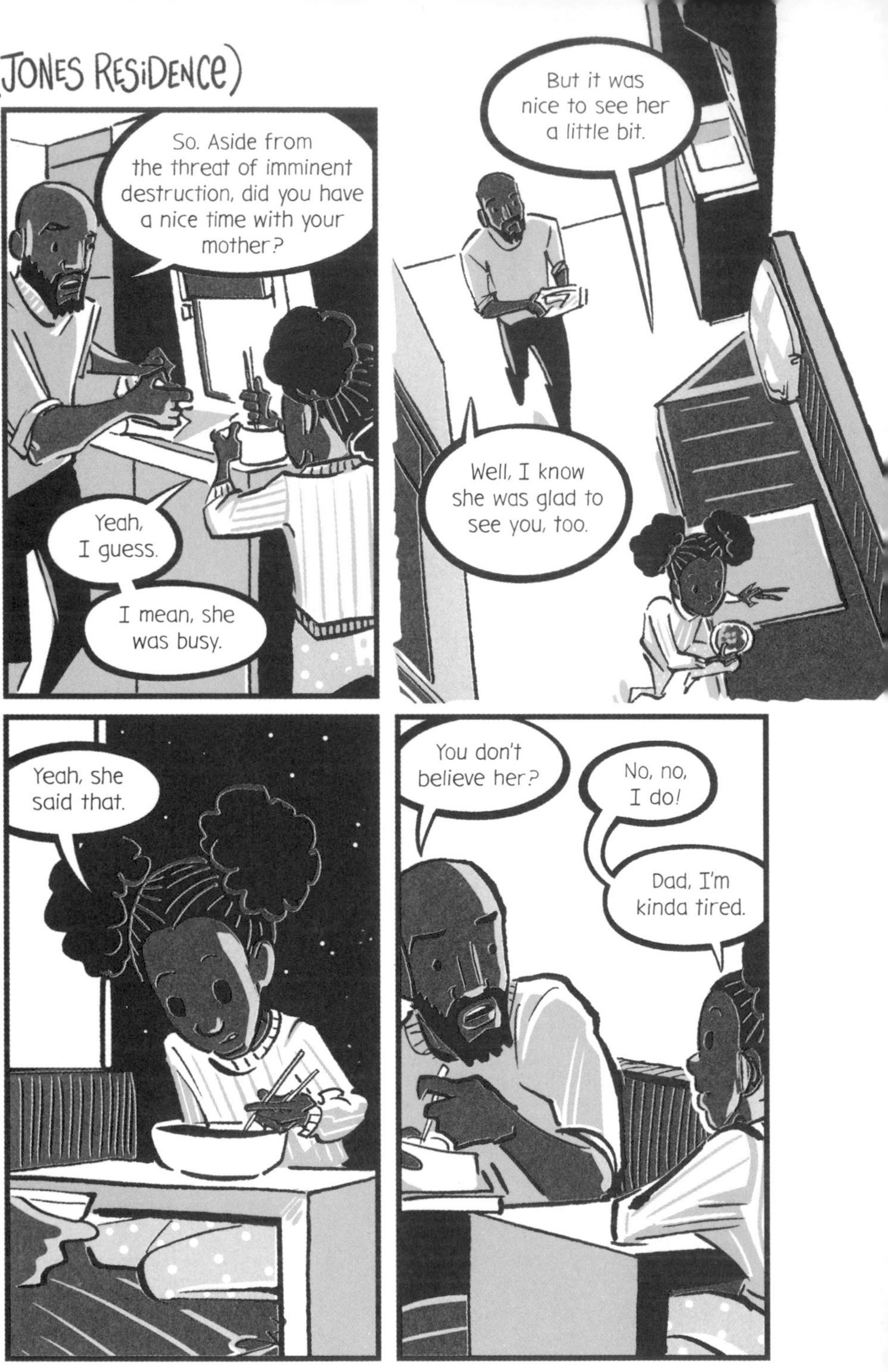
So. Aside from the threat of imminent destruction, did you have a nice time with your mother?
Yeah, I guess.
I mean, she was busy.
But it was nice to see her a little bit.
Well, I know she was glad to see you, too.
Yeah, she said that.
You don't believe her?
No, no, I do!
Dad, I'm kinda tired.

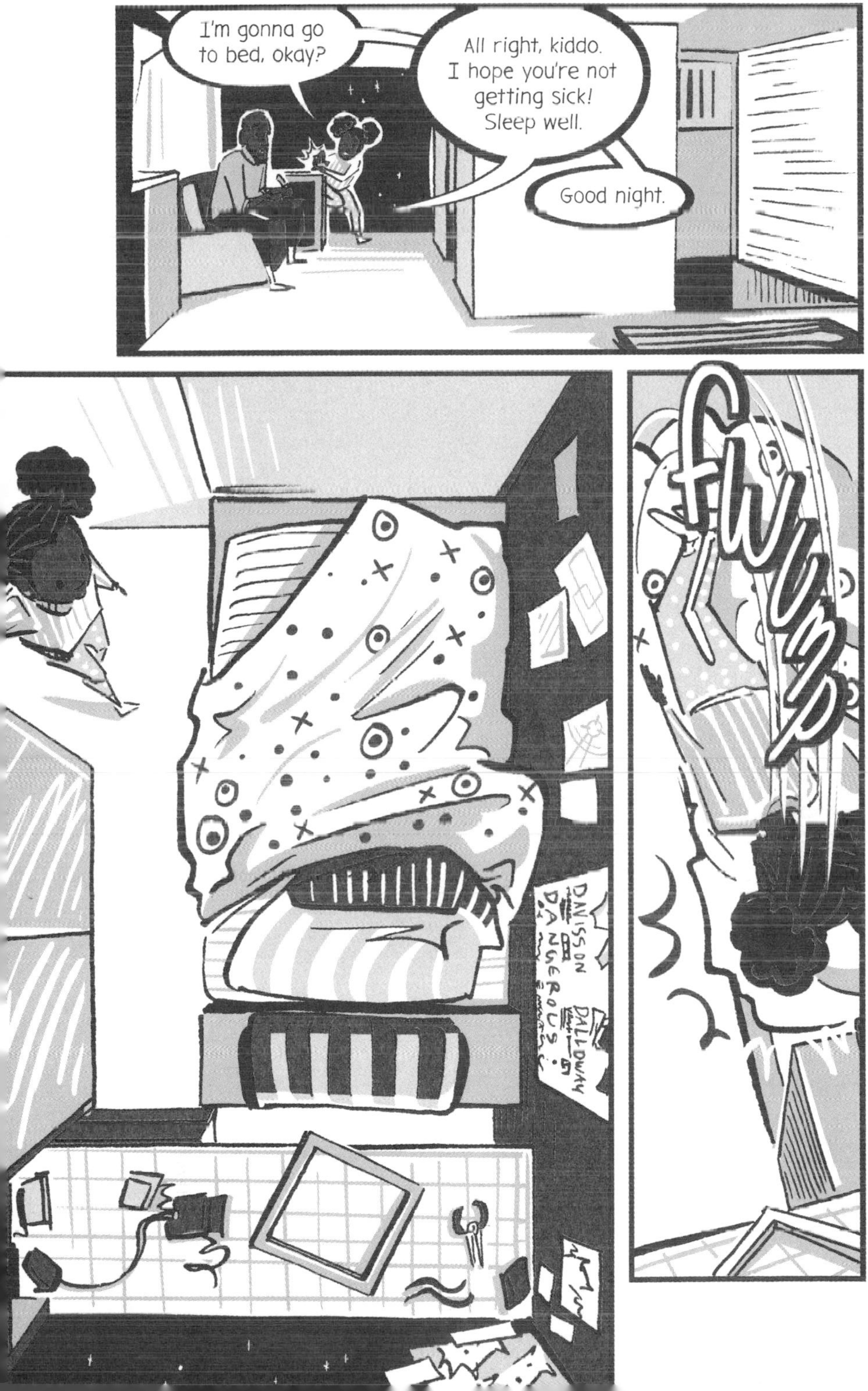
I'm gonna go to bed, okay?
All right, kiddo. I hope you're not getting sick! Sleep well.
Good night.
DAVISSON DALLOWAY
DANGEROUS
FWUMP

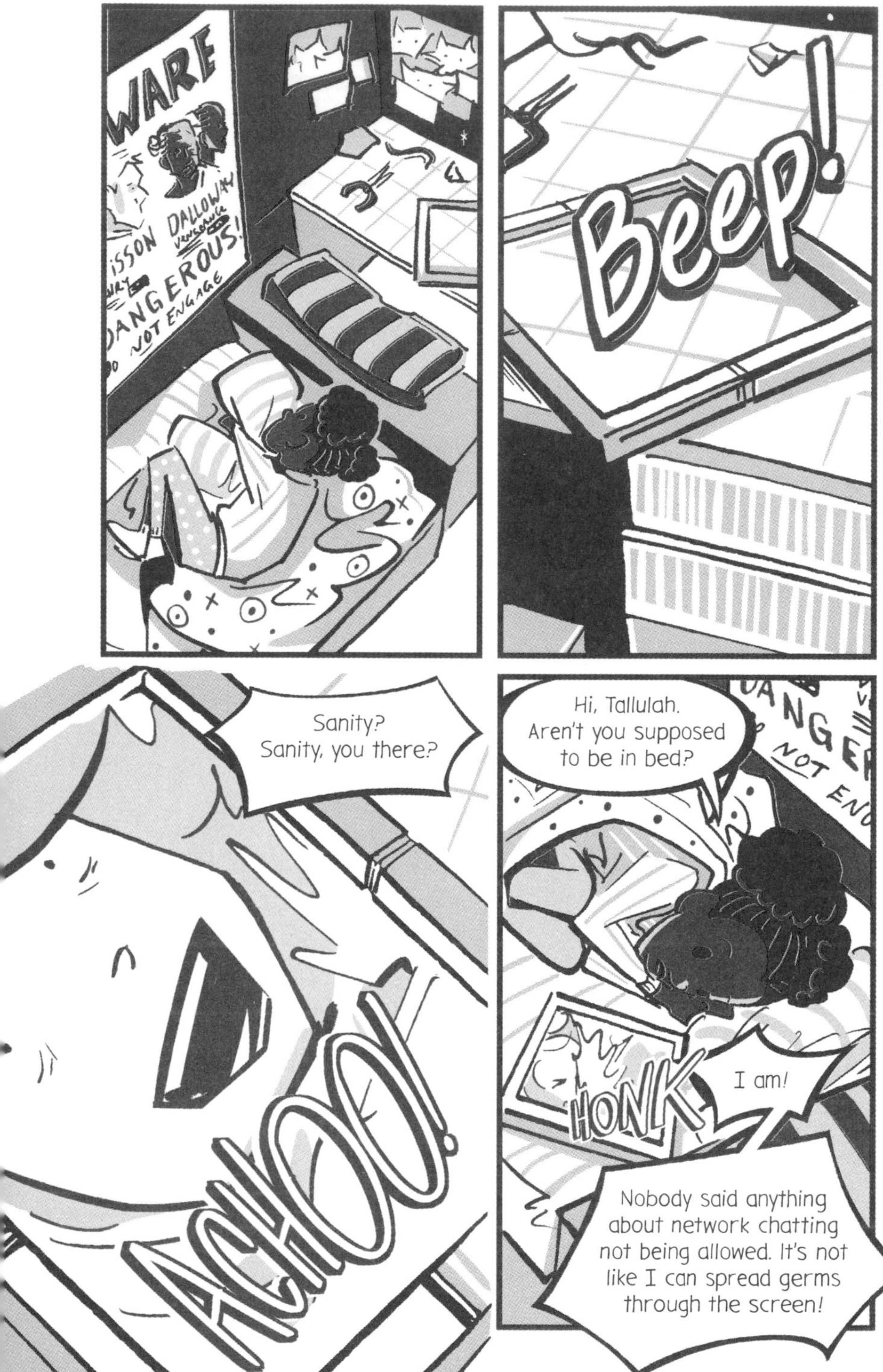

WARE
ISSON DALLOWAY
VENGEANCE
DANGEROUS!
DO NOT ENGAGE
Beep!
Sanity?
Sanity, you there?
ACHOO!
Hi, Tallulah.
Aren't you supposed
to be in bed?
HONK
I am!
Nobody said anything
about network chatting
not being allowed. It's not
like I can spread germs
through the screen!

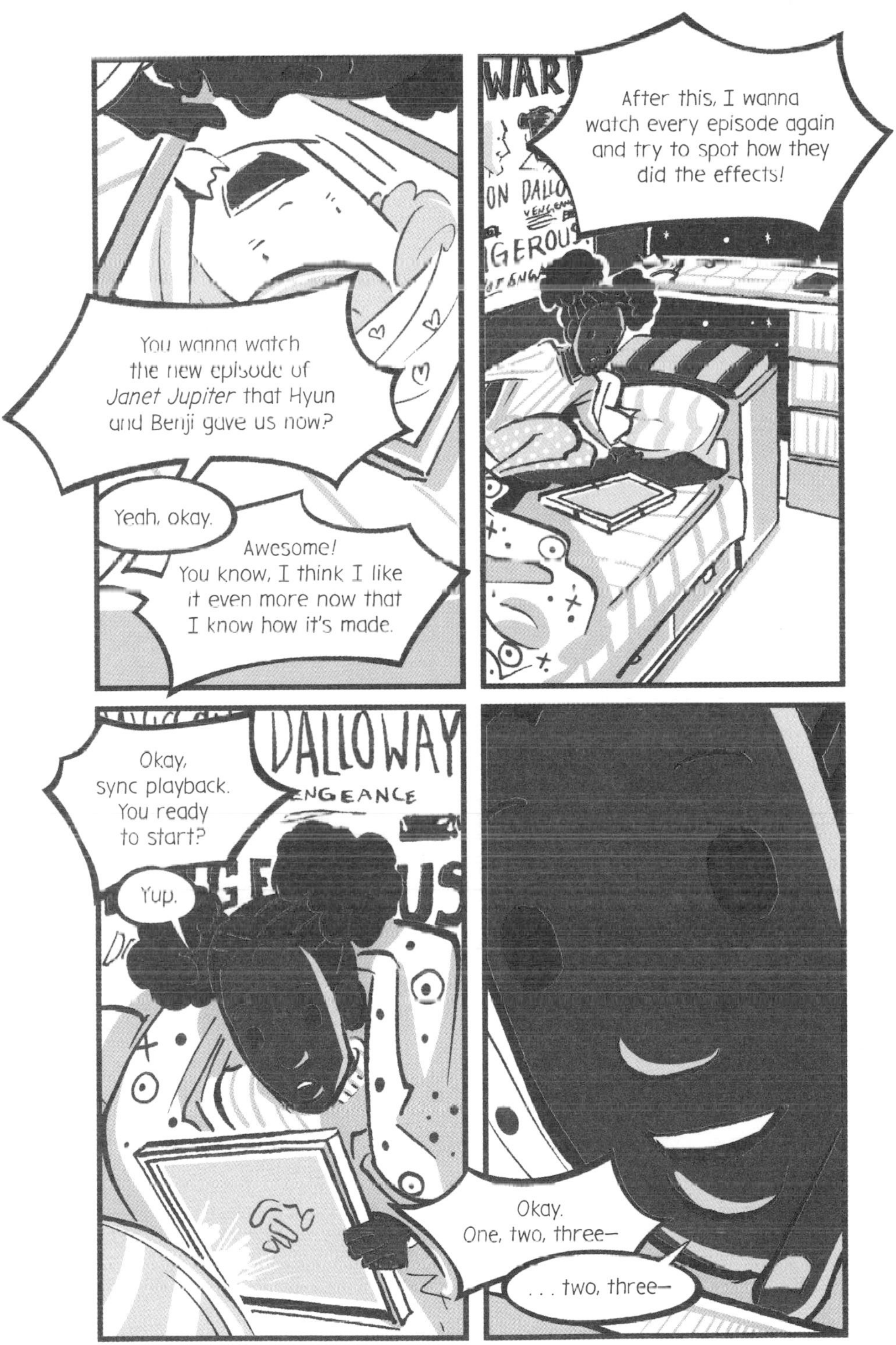
You wanna watch
the new episode of
Janet Jupiter that Hyun
and Benji gave us now?
Yeah, okay.
Awesome!
You know, I think I like
it even more now that
I know how it's made.
After this, I wanna
watch every episode again
and try to spot how they
did the effects!
Okay,
sync playback.
You ready
to start?
Yup.
DALLOWAY
VENGEANCE
Okay.
One, two, three—
. . . two, three—

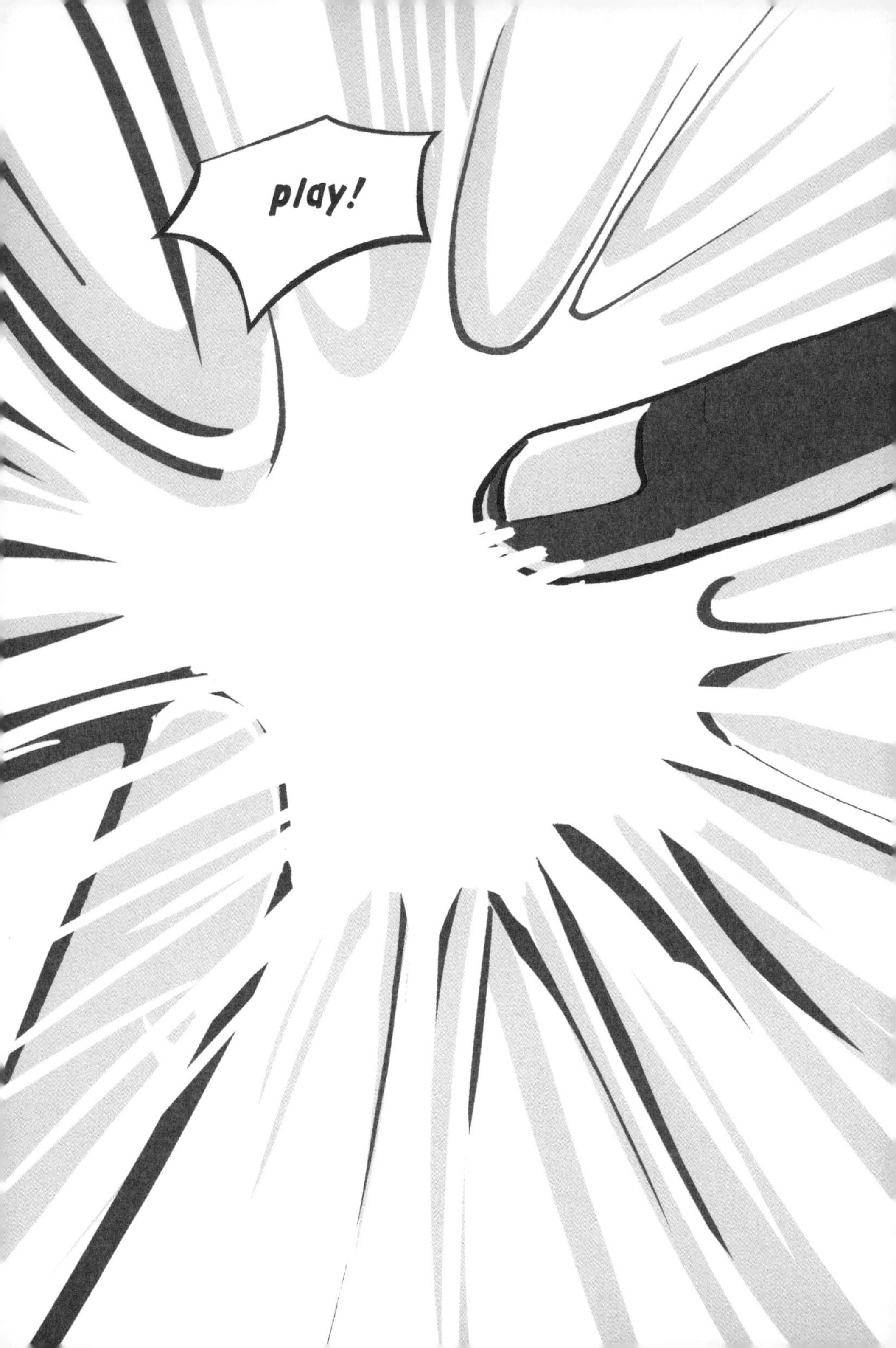
play!

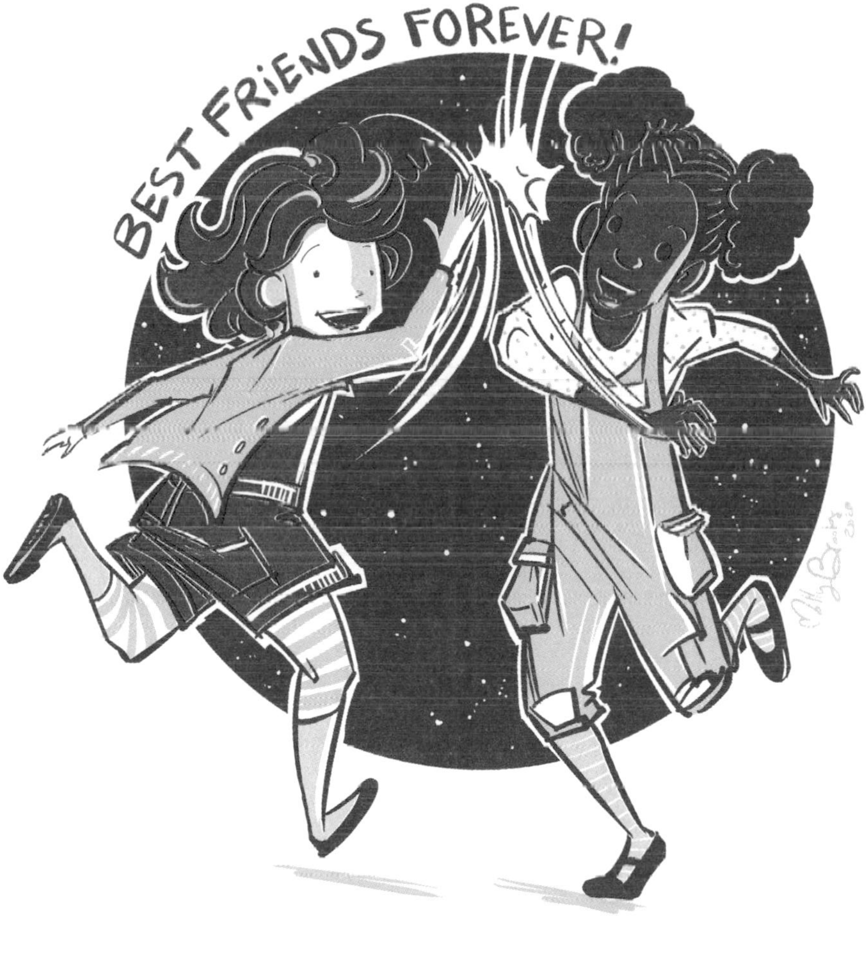
BEST FRIENDS FOREVER!

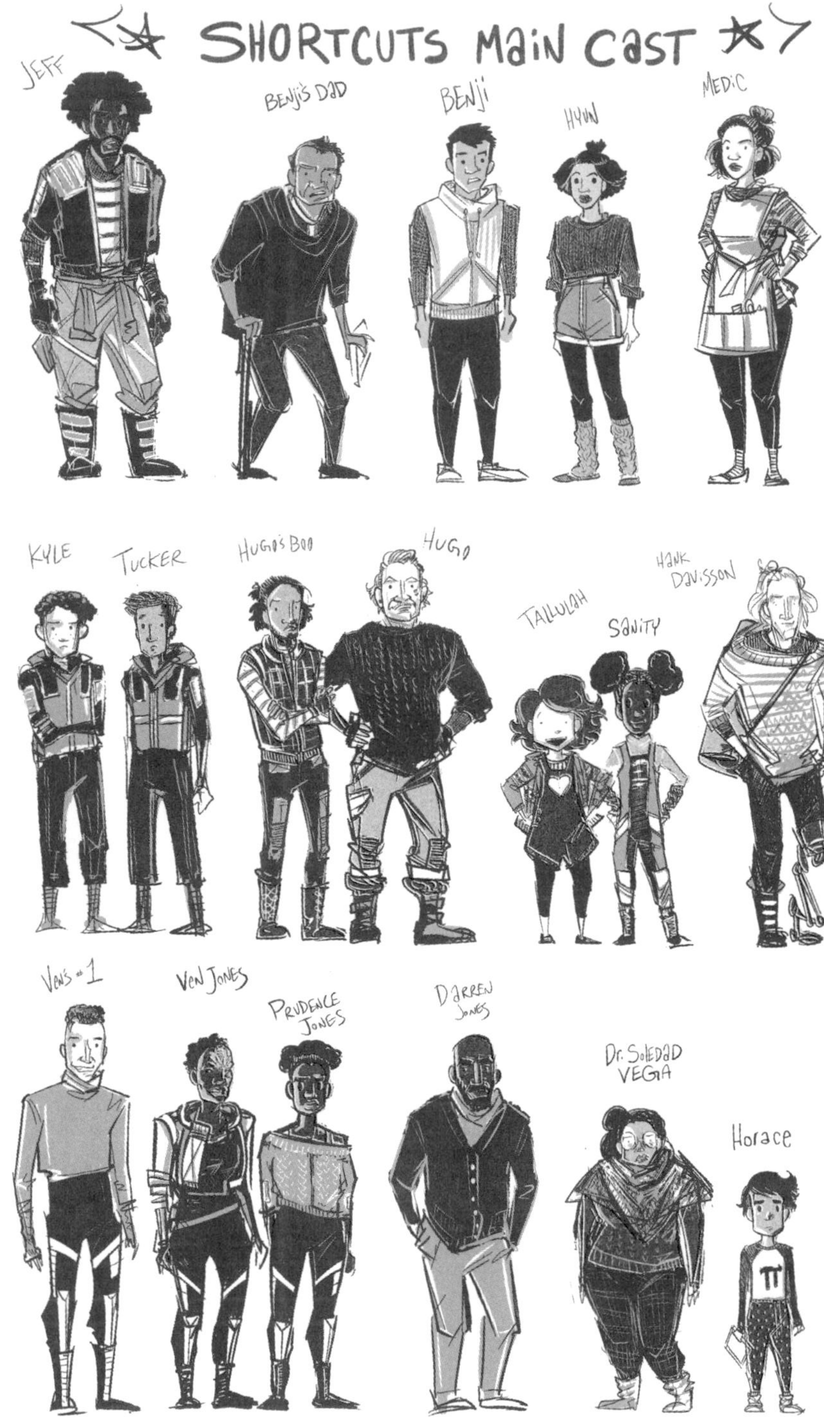
SHORTCUTS MAIN CAST
JEFF
BENJI'S DAD
BENJI
HYUN
MEDIC
KYLE
TUCKER
HUGO'S BOO
HUGO
HANK DAVISSON
TALLULAH
SANITY
Ven's #1
Ven Jones
PRUDENCE JONES
DARREN JONES
Dr. SOLEDAD VEGA
Horace

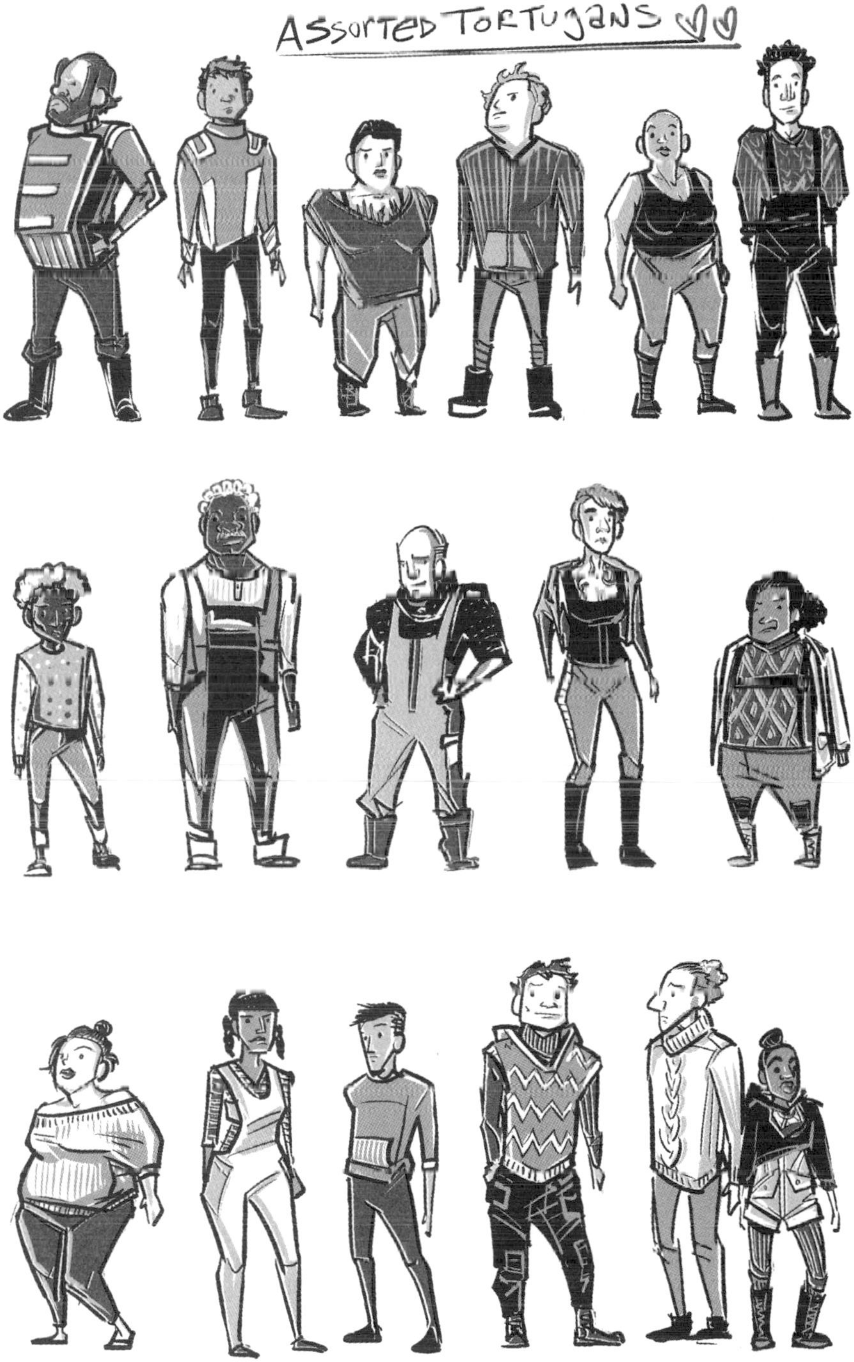
ASSORTED TORTUGANS

Sanity & Tallulah Main Cast

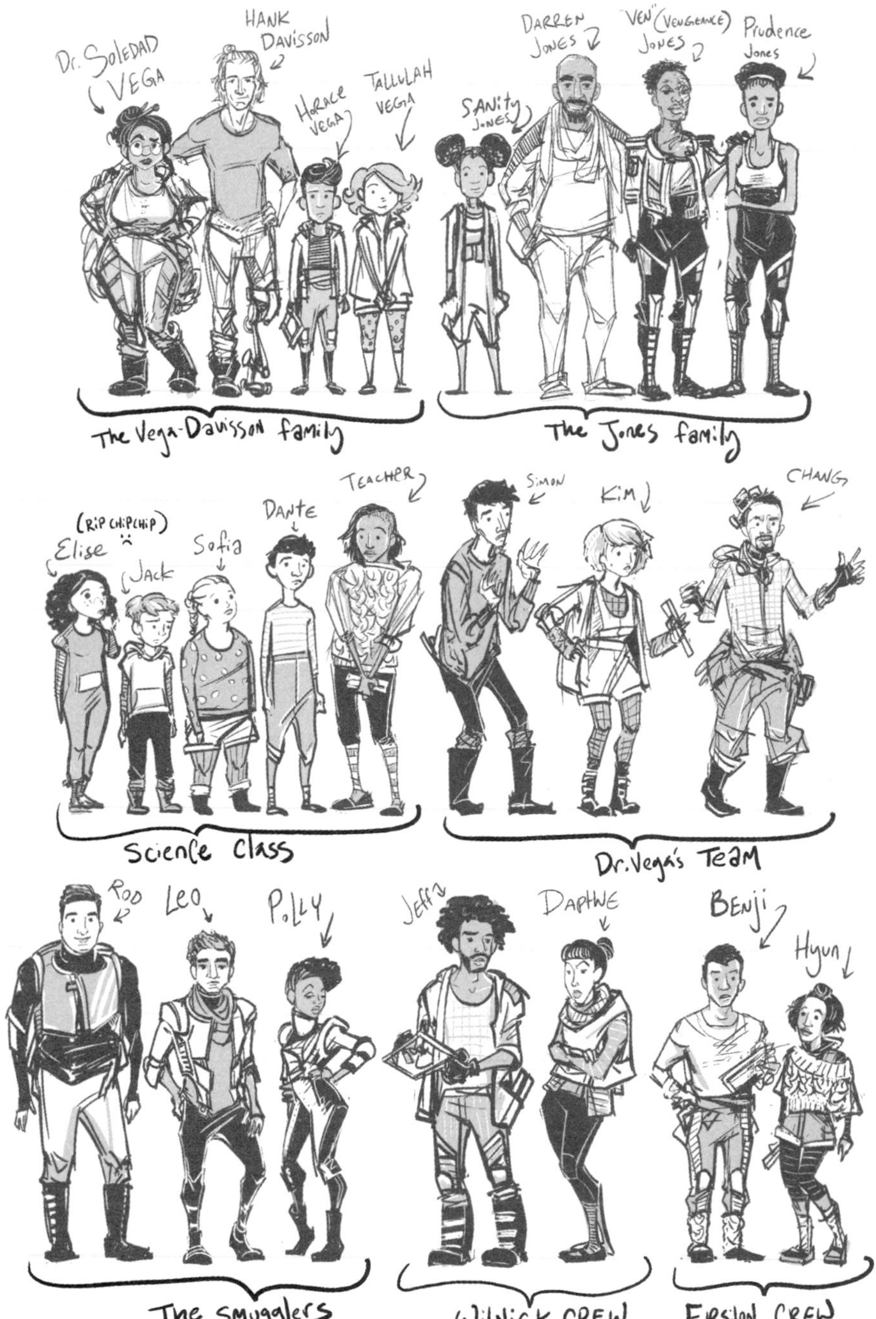
Dr. Soledad Vega
Hank Davisson
Horace Vega
Tallulah Vega
Sanity Jones
Darren Jones
"Ven" (Vengeance) Jones
Prudence Jones
The Vega-Davisson family
The Jones family
(RIP Chipchip)
Elise
Jack
Sofia
Dante
Teacher
Simon
Kim
Chang
Science Class
Dr. Vega's Team
Rod
Leo
Polly
Jeff
Daphne
Benji
Hyun
The smugglers
Wilnick Crew
Epsilon Crew

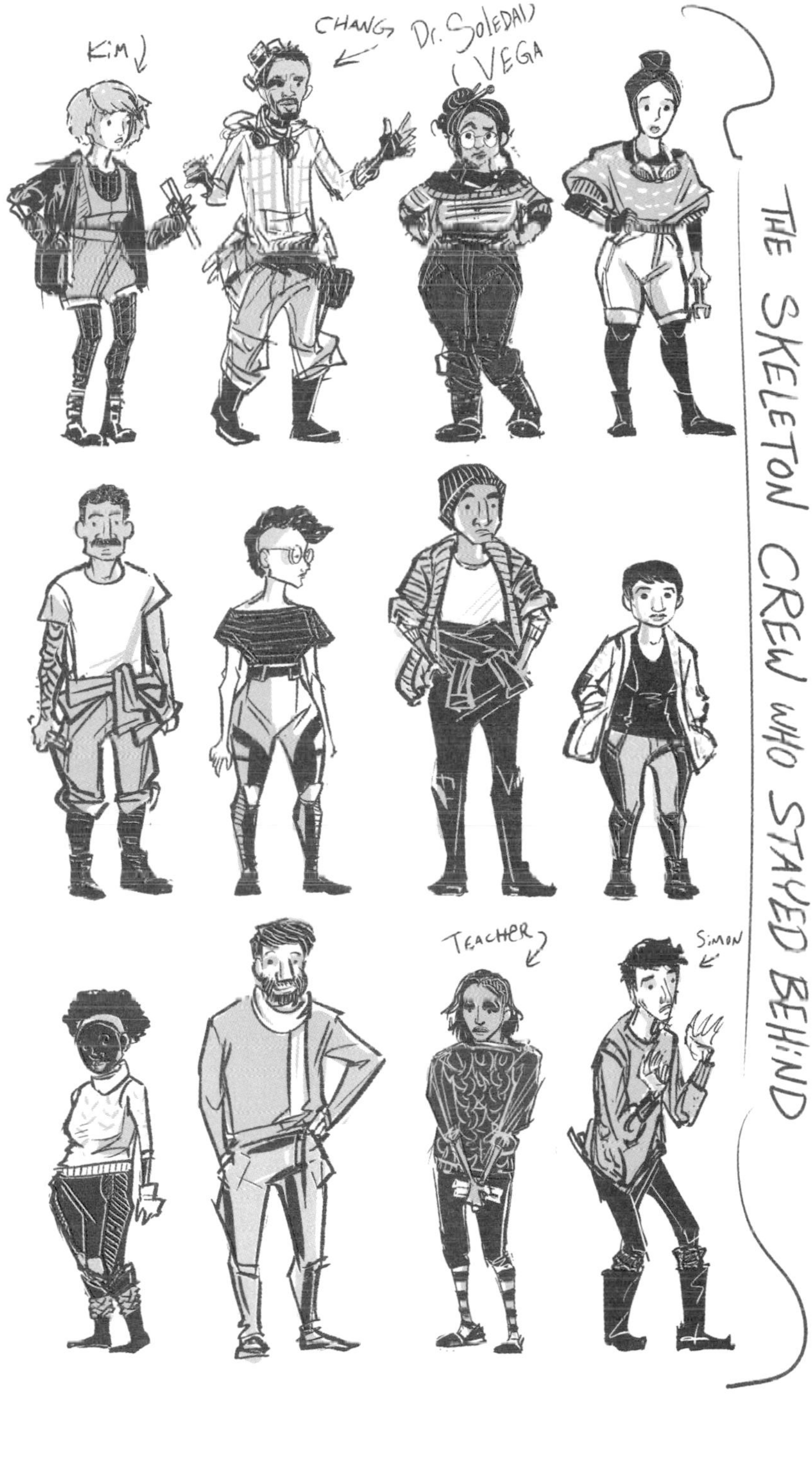
THE SKELETON CREW WHO STAYED BEHIND
KiM
CHANG
Dr. Soledad
Vega
TEACHER
SiMON

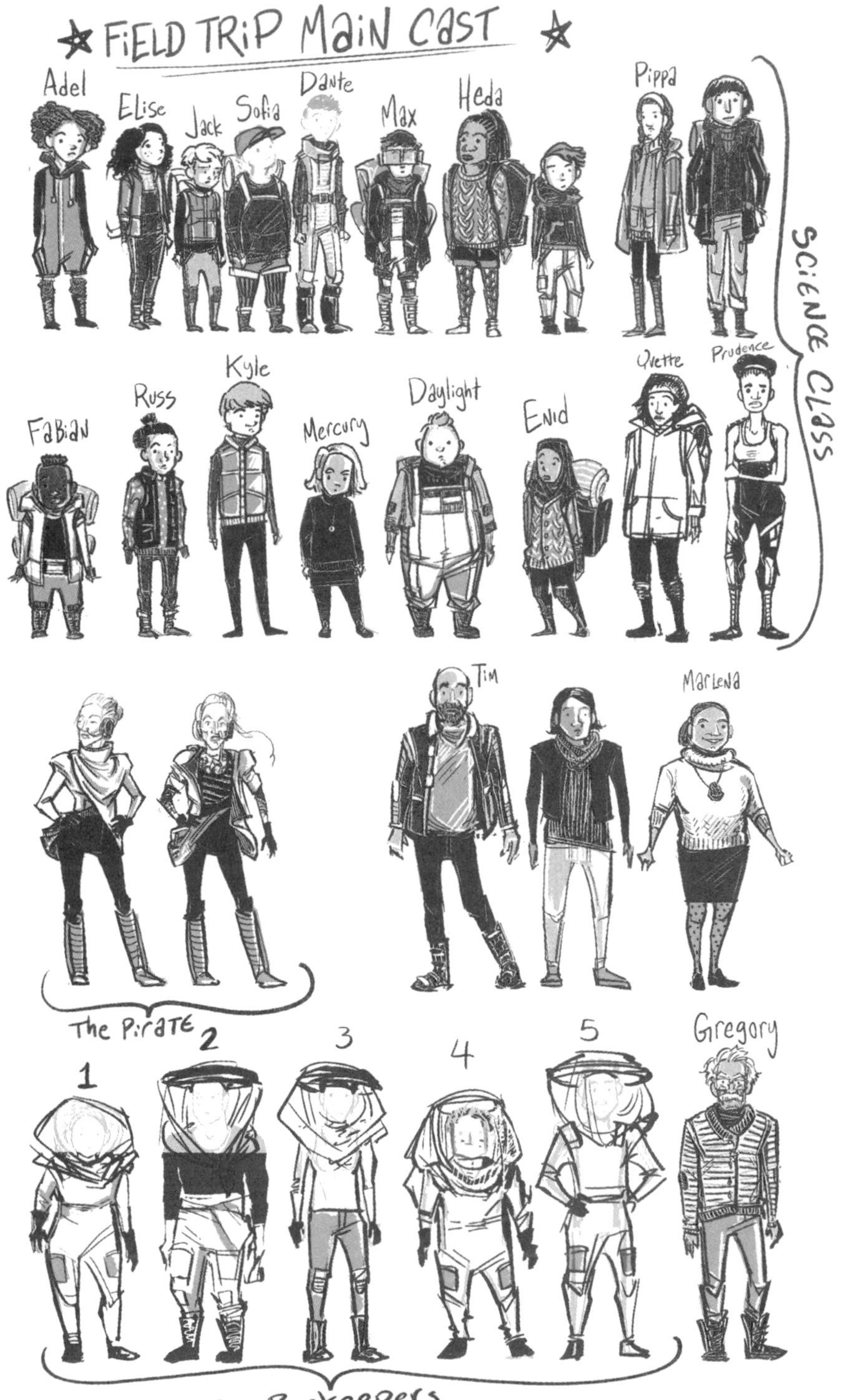
FIELD TRIP MAIN CAST
Adel
Elise
Jack
Sofia
Dante
Max
Heda
Pippa
SCIENCE CLASS
Fabian
Russ
Kyle
Mercury
Daylight
Enid
Yvette
Prudence
Tim
Marlena
The Pirate
1
2
3
4
5
Gregory
The Beekeepers

★ outfit reference ★

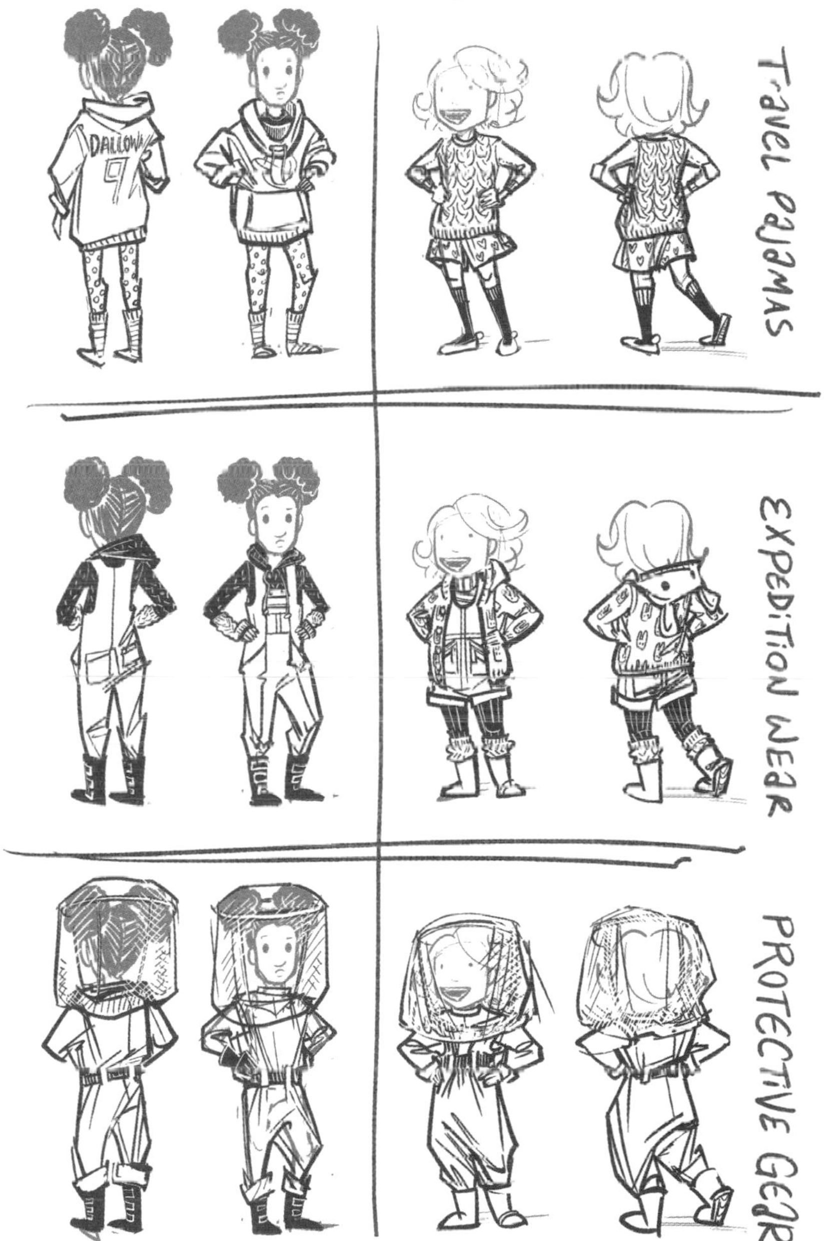
Travel Pajamas
EXPEDITION WEAR
PROTECTIVE GEAR

Molly Brooks

MOLLY BROOKS is the illustrator

of *Growing Pangs* by Kathryn Ormsbee, out in 2022,
and *Flying Machines: How the Wright Brothers Soared*
by Alison Wilgus. Her work has appeared in the *Guardian*,
the *Boston Globe*, *Nashville Scene*, *BUST* magazine, *Gravy*,
Kazoo magazine, ESPN social, *Sports Illustrated* online,
and others. You can find more of her art, including
numerous short comics, at mollybrooks.com.

Molly lives and works in Brooklyn, where she spends
her spare time watching vintage buddy-cop shows and
documenting her cats.